ISLAM and the Search for African-American Nationhood

ISLAM
and the Search for African-American Nationhood

Elijah Muhammad, Louis Farrakhan and the Nation of Islam

by

Dennis Walker

CLARITY PRESS, INC.

ISBN: 0-932863-44-2

In-house editor: Diana G. Collier

Library of Congress Cataloging-in-Publication Data

Walker, Dennis.
Islam and the search for African American nationhood : Elijah Muhammad, Louis Farrakhan, and the Nation Of Islam / by Dennis Walker.
p. cm.
ISBN 0-932863-44-2 (alk. paper)
1. African American Muslims—History. 2. African Americans —Religion—History. 3. United States—Race relations—History. 4. Elijah Muhammad, 1897- . 5. Farrakhan, Louis. 6. Nation of Islam (Chicago, Ill.) I. Title.
BP221.W28 2005
297.8'7'09—dc22

2005022975

To contact Dennis Walker:
donxaw@yahoo.com

CLARITY PRESS, INC.
Ste. 469, 3277 Roswell Rd. NE
Atlanta, GA. 30305

http://www.claritypress.com

In the memory of my mother
Grace Annie Walker
overlocker

and of my father
Patrick Joseph Walker
an Irish-Australian laborer

Table of Contents

CHAPTER 3:
THE DIFFICULT REBIRTH OF ISLAM AMONG AFRICAN-AMERICANS, 1900-1950 / 207

CHAPTER 4:
THE HEYDAY OF ELIJAH: HIS ARTICULATION OF IDEOLOGY IN THE 1960S AND 1970S / 296

INTRODUCTION

Introductory Remarks: Some Issues and Terms of this Study

This study tries to convey the sweep of the whole history of the growth of Islam and Arab influences into a sector in the personality of African-Americans. Its time-frame is from around 1600, when America was still only a chain of British colonies, to mid-2005. Its coverage could not be even at all points: I necessarily focus on some specific periods, personalities and movements within that frame. For the pre-20th century period, I mainly present an interpretation of the roles and scope of Islam within the institution of slavery practised in the Southern states of the independent United States up to its Civil War of 1861-65. For the periods after 1900, I give most attention to images of Islam, Africa and Arabs in the writings of the first African-American official historians, notably Carter Woodson and W.E.B. DuBois; to the Noble Drew 'Ali and the Moorish popular movement that he launched in 1913; to Elijah Muhammad as a religious thinker and leader of his Nation of Islam sect from 1930-1975; and to concepts of Islam, identity and the nature of the American system developed from 1975 over three decades in the successor-sects to the NOI headed by Warith ud-Din/Wallace Mohammed and Louis Farrakhan Muhammad. Space forced me to omit many Muslim thinkers and leaders of some quality both before and after 1975, such as Silis Muhammad, and also some figures closer than most figures we examine to the Sunni Islam of the Arab world. However, I have reviewed a fair bit of the interactions of the NOI and its successors with the black bourgeoisie and the secular protest movements among African-Americans. That interaction will heavily determine the final impact of Islam and the Arab world upon African-Americans.

The bulk of this book is about the (cultural) history of African-Americans up to 1975: yet I locate those aspects and motifs in that bygone history that most centrally influence the development of African-American Islam in our post-modern era. All African-American history is treated as a continuum with little distinction between past and present in this work.

The cumulative growth of Islam-derived elements as one rallying-point for African-Americans in an unfriendly country, tests how much diversity the American system can recognize and harbor. How much of an open-invitation society could America ever become for all humans? The study of the Islamic aspect of African-American self-assertion bears in many ways on how much space a range of non-Anglo groups will be able to wrest in America and what the outcomes will be for them, also, as they strive to survive as cultural communities, including in the central U.S. system's politics.

The twentieth-century development of African-Americans into a cultural and political quasi-nation that gropes for an unclear self-determination in some relation to the U.S. system may turn out to be the history of Everyman within that system, and perhaps throughout the post-modern world. The conditions and the discourses of blacks in modern America catch in a particularly severe form the inherent absurdity that any minority has to live out. No ethnic or religious minority can ever hope that their personality, lives and careers could ever bloom and grow with the almost unconscious spontaneity of those nationalities whom state power nourishes. Yet as globalization reduces even the most powerful states and populations to minorities in an integrating world where no one fully controls their own destiny, a wider and wider range of people—one day even Anglo-Americans themselves—will feel at least some of the dilemmas and frustrations African-Americans have faced and face in their unsure and ambiguous struggle for some sort of self-determination or self-realization in America. Everyone is now a (vulnerable) minority after the globe became one.

An opening explanation of some main inquiries, assumptions and terms of this study will help orientate readers before they plunge into the forests of my individual chapters.

Cultural Inquiry of the Book

To some extent, I wrote this work as a behavioral study. My data on the internal behavior of members of African-American Muslim movements and organizations, and their interactions with African-Americans beyond their belief-community, should aid wider analysis of quasi-elites in other movements in America, and to a lesser extent in the Muslim world, that have tried to make religions and political nationhood reinforce each other. But the elites or cliques that have dominated black Muslim movements in America have not had undivided oneness with either the members under them, nor with the total African-American population they claim a right to lead. They have pursued their own interests and class-formation as well as those of the "Nation" as a whole. Islamic movements among African-Americans thus have parallels to Third World charismatic religious-political movements that led masses in ways that increased the power and resources of cliques claiming sacred authority, and also fostered the growth of new nationalist bourgeoisies. Gramsci's theories of elite and class hegemonies, and the parallel Marxist paradigm that the young Wilfred Cantwell-Smith applied to bourgeois and feudalist hegemony over the movement for an independent Islamic state of Pakistan, somewhat fit the gradual growth of these "Black" sects in American life.

Above all, though, this book means to offer a cultural study of African-American Muslims. My book differs from most other analyses of African-American Muslims in the extent of its quotations not just from leaders but from a broader range of contributors in these movements. Even when I am not directly quoting from black American figures, the prose of my analysis takes care to follow closely the idioms and syntax of their arguments that I am examining. I have tried to show several elements flowing in to blend and form a new ethnic culture that could become adopted by African-Americans in general, but which is more likely in coming years to demarcate a separate Islamic sub-nation or rather a minority-nation. The strong distinct identity and repertoire of cultural practices of such a Muslim black "micronation" would not be framed and nourished by any homeland at all beyond stings of tiny (but numerous) enclaves. In following closely the aesthetic texture of what African-Americans influenced by Islam have actually said and written, I have in effect made them, or perhaps the African-American people, co-authors of my work. This will give my readers good protection from any proclivities in analysis that I otherwise might have tried to impose as a Caucasian writing from the Australian chain of communities far outside the American experience. I have placed within square brackets what I personally make of given passages by African-Americans, as a means to separate those spokesmen and myself even more clearly.

I have used the term "Black Muslims" (with capitalized "b") sparingly. It was a term invented by African-American scholar Eric Lincoln and taken up by America's sensationalist "white" media. It was the name under which Elijah's Nation of Islam became known to Americans in general. Many in the NOI tradition have rejected this term of outsiders that the sect did not originate, but I believe that it did catch the central racial focus of their preachings, and Elijah Muhammad did use it at points at press conferences and in interviews, to whites. As those in the Nation of Islam and its successors interacted more with a variety of Muslim peoples in the Third World, they came to see the title "Black Muslims" as clashing with the drive of Islam to bring human races together in one prayer-community. It is like Lenin's dislike of the title "Bolshevik" with which others tagged his followers and which stuck, until those in his movement came to use it with pride. In my usage, "Black Muslim" with the capital always refers to the members of Elijah Muhammad's sect and its direct successors led by such figures as Farrakhan, Warith ud-Din Mohammed, Silis Muhammad and others. I sometimes also use "black Muslim" without capitalizing the "b." Uncapitalized "black" indicates that it is shorthand for the jaw-breaker African-American, which conceives of the group in an ethnic way that may be more accurate than seeing it in terms of race.

The main charge laid by "black" and Euro-American critics of the Black Muslim movements has been that they mainly just talked, that they were unable to deliver results or institutions well-organized enough to change the conditions of most African-Americans or the course of history, or that the endless religious-national talk of the leaders and publicists of those groups was a con to extract money from African-Americans or make them do work with little or no pay, on the promise that God would decree better times to come—pie-in-the-sky. My own perspective will be that the discourse built up over almost a century by the various neo-Muslim movements among African-Americans has had diverse value in itself. Drawing from a rich variety of Middle Eastern and American cultural sources, black Islamic ideologies have equipped less fortunate African-Americans to understand America and world affairs more sharply and more plurally, thereby helping them to adapt realistically to others even when they did not join and thus neither made any contributions to those sects nor derived material benefits from them. The pre-1975 and the new NOI's rational identification of broad-gauge and long-term options and possibilities within the American system, but also in the global context, for diverse African-Americans did help that new wider African-American nation guide itself, regardless of whether specific NOI projects blossomed or foundered.

The sharpening of ability to apprehend the USA's social and political history aside, Black quasi-Islamic sects and their adherents also have aesthetic and intellectual quality that compels the respect of most who scan their communications, regardless of races. My stance throughout has been one of respect for the intelligence of the black Muslim politicians and journalists and ordinary adherents I cite—a regard stemming from the vitality and originality with which they appropriate, atomize, shred, adapt and transform the slivers of Anglo-English and Arabic, and of Anglo-American, Jewish and Islamic concepts and thought patterns that come to them from America and the Islamic countries. For a separated non-American Caucasian and non-Anglo writing from distant Australia, the Black Muslims' transformation of American and Arab materials has produced a protean new language and culture that must have some aesthetic richness for any English-speaker. It has stood up well on its own terms of catering for vital needs and long-term self-interest of successive categories of U.S. Blacks. Hence, my subject in this book has been the general cultural and thought-community for Blacks that has gathered around black Islamic sects, as much as a handful of their specific leaders, such as Elijah Muhammad, Farrakhan and Warith al-Din Muhammad, and their major colleagues.

I also put this study together over a decade out of conviction that features of the development of black Islamic movements in America have importance for understanding the evolution of a massive if flawed country whose English is my own native speech. Despite severe racial conflicts there, the Muslims are to some degree representative of American ethnic groups and culture in general.

The Community of Americans as the Context

I have written this study to seek continuities in the development of the Islamic sector of the African-American people, over the whole course of its development since the system of slavery took form in the British colonial period. My book is intent to avoid facile binary oppositions in that (a) it disregards many discontinuities and contrasts that American and other scholars have argued between periods of American and African-American history, and between periods in "Black Muslim" thought, and (b) it refuses to accept the binary oppositions that various Muslim discourses and sects have drawn between themselves and their ethnos, and white Americans and their system. Thus, our approach is wary of periodization of African-American Muslim history, and refuses to take at simple face value most Muslim denunciations and highly verbalistic rejections of the U.S. system. The system of and segregation that Anglo-Americans developed against "Negroes" in North America had a special ferocity, but the tension between (a) Anglo and Anglomorph ruling elements of successive elites and (b) other *ethne* (ethnic groups) they are resolved to contain and control, recurs throughout American history. This book will always seek to draw parallels between (a) the experiences or aims of African-Americans in a given period with (b) those of non-Anglo Euro-American groups, Celtic, Jewish, Slavic, Latin and other. We will trace interactions between African-Americans, including those in the Islamic tradition, and several non-Anglo "white" groups.

If ethnic tension and conflict, and the possibility that the country could develop multiple ethnic power centers, has been a constant in the development of the USA, processes of cultural bonding and integration, and constructive deals between the quasi-national groups, have also never ceased. This study, while tracing the roots of conflict between African-American and some other, Euro-American, ethnic groups in America (Anglos, and some Jewish Americans etc), also aims to trace beneath the purportedly binary discourse of the Black Muslims, elements taken from the USA's central Angloid culture. Deep if veiled—or frank—acceptance of America's more creative aspects and values in the protest Islam sector do direct the followers towards that mainstream, and, at least in its logic, perhaps to ultimate incorporation into it.

This work seeks to analyze Elijah Muhammad to some extent, and Farrakhan more, as in multiple ways quasi-normal American ethnic leaders—as against much Angloid and Jewish-American yellow journalism and micro-nationalist writings that have attempted to demonize a figure like Farrakhan as abnormal, an alien to America devoid of any rational or justifiable motives or aims, who has to be excluded from American life and with whom no rational negotiation could ever be possible. It is not so far from such hate-discourse to the repeated and concerted campaigns to starve, deconstruct, forestall and destroy the Islam-influenced Black ethnic group that these movements have been constructing in Afro-America since the early twentieth century. White Americans have too often projected their own guilt-hatred and fears out onto Black Muslim leaders whom the mainstream media have made larger-than-life figures: Elijah Muhammad, al-Hajj Malcolm X and Minister Louis Farrakhan are all examples. My aim in this and a hoped-for successor-volume is, by eliminating both demonization and idealization, to contract Islamic Afro-American leaders down to their natural human proportions. This may make it easier to make out their often modest but positive aims and projects that could provide a starting-point for inter-ethnic negotiations in which "the whites"—from their position of strength—could draw the Muslim sector of Black America into a constructive relationship with the system, if that system would only reform.

The writers and media of Europe and the English-speaking countries were discreetly pleased at the apparent readiness of African-American Muslim leaders before 1975 to take on a power-system few outside America truly liked. One out of four in my generation of university-educated Australians did not warm to the America that deafened everyone, and brandished as a symbol. Some in the West took the Nation of Islam and the various Black Power movements too much at their word in that context. In reality most confrontationist Muslim stances against "white devils" and Christianity were a smokescreen for their never-ending campaign to destroy African-American popular sub-culture, and Westernize uneducated blacks into fair copies of the white middle-Americans they lambasted. Post-modern African-American authors have lately voiced the need to get beyond what Eric Dyson (1995) termed the "Manichaean mind-set that distinguished between 'us' and 'them'"—the facile binary oppositions between evil, worthless devil-whites and (but only potentially) god-like Blacks, between Islam and Christianity or Jews—so strident in the rhetoric of Elijah Muhammad, Malcolm X and (sometimes) Louis Farrakhan.[1] As a sort of faraway convert to areas of promise in the American system, I try to modify dichotomizations that looked solid in the 20th century: the Civil Rights movement and the Black Christians I present were much more radical and Third Worldist than Muslim denunciations allowed, and the denouncing Muslims much more coexistent with the racist system than most people could see in the 20th century. This book sets out the good Anglo-Saxon-like qualities and drives that have kept Muslim activists at a remove from the Middle East, and tries to assess how much more constructive the Black Muslims can become, and will be allowed to become, by the system under which they must seek their sacred prosperity.

I grew up in a country, Australia, founded and run by a separate group of Anglos, at a time when they still practised some of their old bigotry and racism in employment against Celts. For the last 40 years I have also read more printed Arabic words than English ones. Thus, when, for example, I view Angloid and "Zionist" groups in America and Black forces led by Farrakhan locked in what looks like a deadly struggle, the accidents of my cultural background make me identify more with the black Muslim side — except that I have some cultural linkages to American Anglos and Jews as well. From here in distant Australia we can, if we want, see in the U.S. patterns of borrowings and affinities between ethnic groups, and ways out of conflict to American community, that are lost on most of the combatants themselves.

Our study, then, within its limitations, may work to deflate fears between U.S. ethnic groups through a surgical and frank review of things that have set them in conflict.

No attitude of respect can exempt a group—and particularly not the leaders of any micro-"Nation" or new sect—from critical analysis. Treating Minister Louis Farrakhan as representative of the whole class of white and non-white U.S. ethnic politicians, I have not accepted all statements by him about his motives or his achievements. A valid analysis has to hold Black political leaders—even ones who claim to represent God, which most micronationalist leaders, gentile or Jew, do in the USA now—to the same standards as "white" American politicians and intellectuals. And such a blended positive-critical approach can even bring in a deepened appreciation, and more human empathy, for such Islamic leaders as it deconstructs iconic discourses that make them reflections of the divine. In arguing that Farrakhan's concerns, concepts and aims (or Elijah's) have been more diverse than his formal ideology, and more modest, will debunk him at some points—but perhaps more often make him and his colleagues and peers richer, more open-ended, and thus more hopeful for the needs of America's future, given the peerless potential the huge country retains if racism and extreme micronationalism can only be brought within bounds.

If my personal Arabic-Anglo formal culture has long drawn me to the African-American Muslim movements that synthesized both, the affinity is with the ordinary followers of Elijah, or Farrakhan, or Warith as much as with those leaders. I have not relied on the speeches of the leaders alone, but rather tried to sample an overall cultural system to bring out the diverse hopes and aims, and the religious experiences, that led varied categories of African-Americans to make these movements develop.

Karl Marx took the side of the workers: he sought to investigate economic and social reality from the perspective of their interest, and also nominated them for a leadership role they could not sustain. This book tries to stand with the strivings, hopes and vital interests of the African-American masses who followed Muslim leaders as the path to achieve them. It will try to view the situation somewhat with the eyes of Elijah or Farrakhan or Warith, and their actions through what they were trying to accomplish. Psychically, the earlier Elijah of the 1930s, 1940s and earlier 1950s would have been very close to the ethos and to the interests of his people, which he was resolved to achieve through a new orientation and instruments. A gifted leader's guidance can send the development of a people off in directions that it wouldn't have taken by itself. But, like Marx, we will stand more with the hopes and needs of the mass of Muslim adherents than with even crucial leaders.

The analytical frame of this study is Americanist pluralist integrationism. I am a convert from devotion to anti-Western nationalisms to pluralism in its full and dangerous sense. Real pluralism always has an edge of risk, especially where the past relations between ethnic groups (*ethne*) or between nations in a state have been bad, as is the case in America. Plurality and freedom can let out long pent-up rage and thus destroy states. Or frankness can start negotiations where the groups already have in common things they want to preserve and tighten. In the end there is either freedom of association, cultures and speech for all groups in a wide state, or for none, or for only one. From its beginnings, there was more to America than Christianity. Conceding freedom and equal rights to Islamic blacks is not easy for Anglo-Americans to grant, particularly of late. But if they did let "the Black Muslims" flourish, even when they do sound off, it is very unlikely they could ever lapse back into the anti-Semitism with which they once marginalized Jews. The flourishing of African-American Muslims and Jews in the very Christian United States are intertwined (this applies to Hindu-Americans and Buddhist-Americans also). The survival of prospering Muslim societies in the USA will offer the way forward for all of America, and a cultural and human link to the Third World that may help both those worlds in the long term.

Middle Eastern Islam as Scripture and Civilization

While the "Black Muslims" have always been profoundly American, and are potential citizens should the U.S. system fully open up one day, Islam was among the ideologies entering into America — Communism was another — that enabled African-Americans to put space for maneuver and choices between themselves and the Euro-Americans.

The term "classical Arabs" in this book means individuals whose native speech or main speech was Arabic and who identified with the Arabs in history, up until the Mongols sacked Baghdad and murdered the last "Arab" 'Abbasid Caliph al-Musta'sim in 1258. By "classical Islam" or classical "Arab" Islam we mean Islam as conceptualized, led and implemented by Muslims whose literary language was Arabic up to the fall of Baghdad. However, Arab leadership and creativity continued past the fall of Baghdad in the far West of the Arabo-Muslim World in Muslim Spain—close to Africa, and thus a source of historical images for the popular "Moorish" movements and also for professional historians among the African-Americans from the early 20th century. The Catholic Castilians were finally to enter into Granada in January 1492 and later collectively expel its Muslims (and Jews).

The prescribed status of leaders in Sunni Islam has sometimes not amounted to much more than the secular functions of holders of temporary high office in the political systems of Western liberal democracies. The limited, strictly human, status of Arab Caliphs in the non-Shi'ite tradition was particularly evident during the period of the four "Rashidi" (Rightly-Guided) Caliphs (r. 632-660) who succeeded the Prophet Muhammad, and then that of the more monarchical Umayyad Caliphs who governed from Syria (661-750). Sunni Islam had egalitarianism at the assumption of the second Caliph 'Umar Ibn al-Khattab: when 'Umar asked an audience in a mosque to correct any deviation by him, one of those present interjected that if they saw any crookedness in him they would set it straight with the edge of their swords. (True, in the 'Abbasid Empire, influenced by Shi'ism and Persians, the Caliph was to be awarded the status of "the shadow of God on earth," a claim that prefigured the position some in the post-1930 Nation of Islam were to assert for the Hajj Elijah Muhammad). The Rashidi Caliphs were seen by Sunnism as fallible humans, who nonetheless did a generally good job for the Muslims because they implemented the injunctions of the Qur'an and the Prophet Muhammad as best as they knew how. Intention and lack of personal corruption, and control from the community of the believers in general, counted strongly here. It is true that the Caliphs and Sultans who are classified within the Sunni tradition were expected to implement laws of Islam in a more serious way than American presidents were Christianity, until the present born-again incumbent. Thus, claims after 1975 by Warith ud-Din Mohammed and his followers that Islam fits naturally into the U.S. system of the Constitution and electoral government (parliamentarism) only extend real elements already there in classical Sunni Islam.

The Uneven Adoption of Elements from Standard Islam and Arabic in Afro-America

There is no doubt that the United States in the early twentieth century was far-removed indeed from the Muslim countries from which wide oceans separated African-Americans. Islam, highly portable, can install itself quickly in new environments very unlike its original site in peninsular Arabia. But the lines of communication between early modern America and the mainly colonized old Muslim countries were uneven and often tenuous. Those strands from standard Islam that got through were often mere fragments. This work will also often refer to "atomized motifs" and "atoms" of Arabic that neo-Muslim black cults in America seize and install in their own protest discourses and the new religious life that they structure, so that it achieves their reformation and economic rebirth against the heavy odds. I believe that such "atomization" of borrowings being adopted from the writings of the Islam of the Middle East and South Asia has been a key feature of African-American neo-Islam in America. It was inevitable that an environment as different as America and its special needs would for a time shred some borrowings from standard Islam that already were not very intact when they arrived, after that long journey.

It is true that some narratives of classical Islam are more intact, after a fashion, in the complex theological discourses of African-American Muslim cults. Some episodes and incidents from the life of the Prophet Muhammad in Arabia are repeated. But these black protest neo-Muslims often did not quite submit reverently to that [Last Prophet's] career, or to the patterns of meaning in the Qur'an, in the sense that they often viewed those as prototypes that prefigure their decisive fulfillment in the careers and lives of the leaders and believers of the American black Islamic sect. Until the 1970s, there was a lack of a sense in Afro-America like that of the Sunni Muslims of the Middle East that the order established by Muhammad, the son of 'Abdallah in Arabia, was a unique implementation of God's will from which decline followed, and thus an order that can at best be duplicated by any Muslims who come after. The "Black Muslims" in America did not have that attitude of submission: they believed they could not just equal but surpass that first implementation of Islam in Arabia. Still, at least we have here patterns, even if Wali Fard Muhammad and Elijah Muhammad are seen as their culminating fulfillment. But often what is taken are not refracted patterns or fragments from standard Islam but only atoms of Arabic that have no pre-America structure of belief or tenets left.

The detaching of elements or just atoms from classical or standard Islam, and their installation in new American tenets and patterns of meaning, has drawn varied reactions from Muslims in or from the East. Some orthodox Sunni Muslims long vocally condemned attitudes of some in the old Nation of Islam before 1975 that the sect had a Messenger of its own who equaled or who might come to surpass the role of Muhammad of Arabia, his precursor. Such Sunni critics of the Nation could not take a long-term view of the accumulating diffusion of things from standard Islam and the Middle East that was taking place among all groups of Muslim blacks in America. Other Muslim thinkers in or from the Third World implied much more reflective attitudes to the problem. In muted, indirect language, they put the blame for the disparate tenets or "heresies" of the Moorish and NOI movements on the religious 'ulama' or scholars of the Middle East: the Muslim world's institutions had failed to build enough instruments to convey "real Islam" (al-Islam al-sahih) to peoples in the West, an argument that al-Hajj Malcolm X also got across to Middle Eastern Arabs after he split from Elijah. Ch. 3 shows how the liberal Islamist Zafar Ishaq Ansari, of Pakistan's Islamic Research Institute and a translator of the seminal neo-salafi Pakistani thinker Abul-'Ala' al-Mawdudi, felt the pain of African-American history enough to see that it was the racist environment of America that provoked and patterned responding tenets of the Nation of Islam, for which African-Americans are not to be blamed by Muslims in the Islamic Third World.

Other Muslims of Third World birth or descent who interacted in depth with the sects in the NOI tradition found, and are finding, new religious Islamist meanings in distinctive tenets that flowered in the black Muslim sects. If the stranger of these tenets were *shirk* (polytheism) or *bid'ah* (heretical innovations) as charged, then why did Allah decree them and allow them to spread in America? International Islamists who ask such questions took on board that if they are to actualize a truly universal, proselytizing Islam (*da'wah*) in their lives and preaching for all humanity, then they must at least be able to apprehend discourses in other populations on their own terms as a preliminary to making the facets of Islam that they propound at least understood. Some *du'at* (Muslim evangelizers) go further. They see strenuous engagement and dialogues with African-Americans, the process of "translating" Islam from its Arabic exposition "revealed" from outside human history (*munazzal*) into the compound discursive, cultural and historic terms of reference of that other people and world, as a process that distinguishes for Arabs, too, the things of true substance in Third World Islam, as it eliminates Middle Eastern elements that are incidental or distortions or accretions. For the liberal Muslim missionaries born outside America such as the Palestinian, Jamil Diyab, the engagement with African-Americans enabled them to understand some truths and aspects in Islam that would not have become evident had they stayed in the Arab heartlands of its first revelation. Some in the new generation of Arab-American, Pakistani-American or other ethnic Muslims born in America are coming to speculate that the evolution of Muslim black cults in America that had in them man-innovated heresies, or *bida',* may have been further willed by God or Allah in order that, amid the dross, those cults could themselves articulate understandings of latent aspects of the Qur'an and Islam that otherwise could not have been accessed by Arabs or some other Muslim nationalities abroad, given the limitations to understanding due to their ethnic cultures or histories. The African-American Muslims can teach truths in Islam back to their Arab and Eastern teachers.

The Problem of the Leaders and the Led

The leaders of African-American Muslims movements won great achievements against very heavy odds. To preserve those gains, leaders of any new cult or sect or any micro-"Nation" that is being constructed, and their inner circles of colleagues, require scrutiny because the lesser development of the sect's institutions and their adoration by the followers provide openings for them to manipulate, exploit and embezzle. Given the God-imposed charismatic nature of the appeal and authority they build, they are less subject to the scrutiny and safeguards with which the mainstream's institutions could check and control leaders of any type, but on which the dirt-poor black converts turned their back because that mainstream had not wanted them. While African-American leaders like Wali Fard Muhammad, Elijah Muhammad or Minister Louis Farrakhan clearly are religious leaders, this study also traces some affinities they had to the class of white and non-white U.S. ethnic politicians in the USA. Accordingly, I have not always accepted all statements by a given figure about his motives or his achievements.

I hope that this book will have suggested something of the protean depths and quicksilver changeability, the multitude of streams and diverse individuals in it at any given time, of the Nation of Islam and its offshoots.

I have tried not to write a study narrowly focused upon or confined to a limited number of thc top leaders in Muslim black movements in the United States. While this book is based most on the printed page, I have not just analyzed important ideological texts of Supreme Leaders, but sought out articles, speeches and newspaper letters by people in the second or third rank in these movements. That wider range of communications shows the back-and-forth exchange of concepts between leaders and members in the upper tiers of such movements, and those who have microphones and the printed page reacting to, and trying to meet, expectations of the range of ordinary members, rather than simply to control them. My wider sampling from such Muslim African-American tabloids as Elijah's *Muhammad Speaks,* Farrakhan's *Final Call* and Warith Deen Muhammad's *Muslim Journal,* and interviews I made with some American and Middle Eastern participants, offer a much sharper and broader sense of a whole community in formation and evolving. I would have preferred to use oral history more to ascertain the motives and the pay-offs of ordinary people who converted, and their gripes and dissatisfactions with some of the things they got in Elijah's Nation of Islam and elsewhere. Yet we can trace from the printed page, and now the internet, the evolution of an overall cultural system—the innumerable ways in which a wide range of individuals and families constructed or bent their Islams, whether heterodox or Sunni, to make them fulfil their ethnic and material needs.

While seeking always the economic and social reality of African-Americans in the perspective of their interest, I will try to assess the lives of the Noble Drew 'Ali, Elijah Muhammad, Louis Farrakhan and Warith (Wallace) Muhammad, from the point of view of the aims their visions set, and how far each achieved them. Those leaders' serious aims, the things to which they paid meticulous attention, often ran against the grain of those works in the social sciences, and more in ethnicity-inflamed mass media, that dismissed them facilely on the strength of their rhetoric as no more than hate-preachers. The leadership elites that led these Muslim cults directed their own and the mainstream media too much to their own persons: but a leader such as Elijah did skillfully tap the interests and the ethos of his people, which he was resolved to dislocate and reinvent to both their and his profit. A gifted leader's guidance can send the development of a people off in directions that it might not have taken by itself, or to goals which it by itself would not have had the clarity to achieve.

Again, though, even very charismatic and inventive leaders who start up a religio-national movement to some extent may only act as mirrors that draw in and decisively concentrate concepts and hopes that the people around them had long been thinking. This volume examines a classic case—that of Wali Fard Muhammad, credited by historiography to have "founded" the Black Muslim sect in Detroit in 1930. Who was Fard or Farrad or "Ford" and how important was he really? Clearly, he was some sort of trigger who got some sort of change or turnabout going in African-American history. Black Muslim history presents him as an Hijazi Arab who could pass as either black or white and credits him with having restored the lost nation of the so-called Negroes in North America to a knowledge of their own and the homeland in "the East" across the seas from which the white slavers had separated them. It is clear that Fard tried to lead African-Americans to some motifs and elements from both spoken and scriptural Arabic. Yet Detroit had the highest proportion of Arabic-speaking immigrant Muslims and Druze of any city or town in the USA. It is thus certain that at least some of the poverty-stricken poor blacks in Detroit's Paradise Valley slum of 1930 had been seeing printed Arabic pages and hearing spoken Arabic and the words Allah" and "Muhammad" years before Fard came promising to relink them to the very "people in the East" whom they had already long glimpsed in the flesh day after day. Fard's new religion looks like a reinvention of elements for an Islamic identity that his audience had to some extent already assembled. Thus, his Detroit audiences may have invented and constructed "Professor Ford" or "Fard" as much as he invented that neo-Muslim audience-nation.

My following work is alert to divergences as well as coincidence of the self-interests and the concerns of the leaders/elites as against the lay-memberships of masses or Nation of Muslim movements in North America. Even when an aura of the divine hung around Elijah Muhammad, we will see ordinary members maneuvering around him and his isolationist aspect to make sure the sect they had joined really did deliver the friendship with Third World Muslims that it had promised them. On one level, Elijah's son W.D. Mohammed, in leading the Nation of Islam into Arabic practises and the international community of Muslims, mirrored and carried through a general will that most members had been developing for several years before Elijah died.

Terminology: the Concept of "Micronationalism."

It is hard to settle on terms that are valid tools with which to analyze Islamic and nationalist movements among African-Americans. It has become ingrained in America, and among analysts of it who imbibe its culture and social norms, to depict the tensions as between Blacks and Whites or Black Americans and White Americans, and to validate "Black Nationalism" etc. This dichotomy has some input from the long-standing U.S. penchant to define social units from skin pigmentation. "White Americans" as a dichotomization against "the Blacks" is a clear construct, one almost designed to screen and sap the deep ethnic divisions among Euro-Americans, political expressions of which this book takes care to note. A difficulty for winning some freedom from the black-white dichotomy is that many African-American protest sects and movements have defined their own identity around it—we argue in our chapters, often as a device to evade cultural differentiation or relinking to Africa of a degree that would separate them from Euro-Americans more than they want.

The often-traumatized ethnic nation we discuss never reached consensus on what to call itself or its history. In the past some of its writers (eg. Carter Woodson and W.E.B. Dubois, whom we review) used the term "Negro" with pride, but many, including Elijah's Muslims, came to object to it from the late 1950s. It is true that "Negro" was an imprecise racial term that did not sufficiently state either the nation's linkages to Africa, or what its national culture might be, if anything. Many U.S. "black" spokespersons substituted "Afro-American" or "African-American." I am not entirely happy with this term either, although I use it most. In my own judgement, the U.S. "blacks" had not kept as many intact links to the places they came from as various "white" nationalities did. Many "Black Muslim" ideologues and writers throughout the twentieth century sabotaged so close a linking of their national identity with Africa below the Sahara. "Black Nation" or "Black Americans" would be closer to Elijah's thought, as would "Black Muslims", but they are mirror images of white racism's two macro-categories. Thus, I have tried to alternate and mix various terms for the U.S. nation that "Black Muslim" groups attempted to lead for most of the twentieth century, treating all of those terms as provisional or partisan constructs. Recent African-American micronationalist theoreticians have characterized their people as an ethnic group defined by distinct cultural traits rather than a race-group.

Since the late 1970s, the term "micronationalism" has gained currency in international political science. African-American Muslim sects have had limited numbers of long-term members, and the Islamic cultural tradition they assert has sometimes been interrupted and weak in America. These sects sometimes have had a penchant for public parade and self-display beyond what their resources justify, and with real costs to their success and development. But the systematic ideologies they have evolved have achieved results that place them well beyond those micronationalist outfits in which "a number of groups of adults play-act imaginary nations as a hobby" (Peter Ravn Rasmussen 2005—which does at the current time apply to some unorganized, decultured, ethnic groups in America, for instance to some varieties of Scottish-Americans). Some at the top became cynical and skimmed, but most activists and journalistic intellectuals, and indeed most of the leaders, of movements in the Moorish and NOI traditions have been serious and systematic in their programs and rituals to create a "nation of Islam" in the USA. Of course, the sense in which the Nation of Islam and other Muslim cults have pioneered forms of micronationalism in the USA differs from some other, small or peripheral, dominated groups in the USA and the Third World because tens of millions of Black people (and perhaps one day millions of Latinos and Arabs) in the USA are potential citizens of the Nation. Although there are problems of continuous intactness of Islam among African-Americans since their forefathers were transported to the continent from Africa, more than a recent "imagined community" (Benedict Anderson) is at play: our book will document that a durable culture-tradition blending Islam, Africa and Blackness into nationality was unremittingly built up over the whole length of the twentieth century. The black Islamic enclave-nation or micronation has proved durable as one option for all African-Americans and has built some of the institutional instruments of some of the major nations that have independence or which are contenders for it.

My use of the terms "enclave nation" and/or "micronation" to characterize some Muslim African-American groups, and the aim or outcome of one expanding, nationalistic sector of African-Americans as a whole, has to be considered carefully. I apply both "enclave nation" and "micronation" or "micronationalism" as functional terms to categorize both actual entities, and the short- or middle-term aims of movements from a range of U.S. ethnic groups that have crystallized since the mid-1960s in North America. The term "micro-nation" in particular may seem to some adherents of Minister Louis Farrakhan to shrink or miniaturize his achievement in drawing one million African-American males to a rather constructive, if ambiguous, protest at Capitol Hill, Washington, DC, on October 16,1995. Yet neither "micro-nation" nor "enclave-nation" need have much to do with the size, the smallness or largeness, of the *memberships* of given neo-Muslim or black nationalist movements in America. My logic with these two terms is different—they have to do with the size of continuous territory, of space or (in this case, the shredded and scattered) homeland of the "nation", not how many people it has. The two terms are my attempt, following other social scientists and analysts, notably Garry Trompf, who have conducted Australia-based research on such religion-tinged stateless nationalisms, to conceptualize the types of spatiality within which nationalist movements among non-Anglos have had to unfold in North America. Shifts of populations, demographic change, have played their part in shaping enclave-nations and micronationalisms in the USA—but also choices that those writers and movements made because Anglo-Saxon culture and ways pervade them, limiting their protests or revolts.

At the turn of the twentieth century, most African-Americans lived in the so-called "black belt" in the South, where they formed a majority in some areas. Black nationalists had some impulses to carve out an autonomous or independent homeland or state for African-Americans there that Stalin's apparatchiks took up and publicized around the globe in their turn. But the operation of the USA's dynamic economy destroyed the homeland prerequisite for any such nationalist independence of a classic pattern by drawing millions of Black migrants from Dixie to the great cities of the U.S. industrial North. What emerged there were urban enclaves of limited extent, such as Harlem. The restructuring of relations between WASPs and African-Americans in the "civil rights" era gave the enclaves more political meaning when electoral zones were drawn by the changing U.S. system on ethnic lines so as to get more Black parliamentarians into the USA's central core.

I hope to discuss the issues of the constantly-evolving Black enclave-nationalisms in detail in a companion volume where I set out in more detail the use made by ex-establishment Black politicians in the 1990s of Farrakhan's institutions and media to define, and muster support for, "secession" by Black and Hispanic suburbs from City-government zones. This more historical first volume, though, will describe how Celtic and Irish Americans through Tammany Hall built up non-Anglo enclave-nations within U.S. parliamentarism that have bequeathed some patterns and some space for the new Celtic and other micronationalisms among Euro-Americans that have been crystallizing in post-modern America. Most micronationalisms are ambiguous in their long-term aims, and this may be because they are, while they assert difference, procedures of self-organization to get America's ethnic groups into its mainstream. This high ambiguity or duality was there in the protest-Islam sect that Minister Louis Farrakhan constructed from 1978 in coordination with black bourgeois elements determined to move deeper into America and win more jobs in it, not to blow it up.

My two studies see the growth of African-American secular and Muslim protest movements, even when they proclaim a nominal "withdrawal" from the U.S. mainstream, as much more normal in terms of the way America in general has operated than the special racism they faced might lead us to expect. My term "micro-nationalism" has two applications. On one plane, I use it to characterize tendencies of Muslim protest groups because of their absorption of Arabic words and ideas to solidify into a distinctive micronation within—and apart from—the mainly Christian African-American enclave-nation within which they form and evolve. But another application by me of "micronationalist" refers to further loss of continuous spatiality or homeland that the African-American enclave-nation experienced in the late-modern and post-modern eras. There is, in the twenty-first century, no intact extensive homeland where African-Americans are or could become a majority, and hence a unit within America's representative polity system (its variant of parliamentarism). One taunt of Jewish micronationalists centered in their New York enclave since the Million Man March of 1995 has been that Farrakhan assembles marchers and crowds in such power centers as Washington rather than leading them to areas of heavy black concentration in the southern USA where there had been past impulses to establish an independent black homeland of a classical nationalist type. The taunt does not show much self-knowledge given the scattering of the U.S. Jews whom activists nonetheless continue to strive to make a "people," "the Jewish people in America." It evaded the ambiguity of all micronationalisms in recent America, given that a homeland for political secession is an outdated notion in the face of new technologies that give any sizeable dispersed group resources for cultural self-expression greater than those some major governments were ever able to muster in the bygone modern era.

The successes and upward-out mobility stemming from Civil Rights and the opportunities of the modern economy that all that widened, drew many sons and daughters of the disliked Blacks, Hispanics and Jews out from the old enclaves into upper American institutions. Now they must share such offices and universities cheek-by-jowl with each other and with Anglos and other established U.S. ethnic groups on a day-to-day basis. The point is that the new ambiguous integration that has been occurring scatters the neo-bourgeois, younger section of erstwhile enclave-nations far from old ghettos of concentration and mixes them all up together. Some have analyzed the "rage of the privileged class" of the black new bourgeoisie at the dislike they continue to meet in corporate America and government from Euro colleagues.[2] But if the Anglos, Blacks, Jews, Celts, Hispanics, ex-Slavs and Latins scowl at each other today in shared corridors and from adjoining desks, and identify and act every day with new technologies as all members of disparate wider nations, none of those individuals have any homeland under their feet that they can close off from other *ethne*.

Spatiality became less and less important for individuals in linking up with co-nationals in America, the more the twentieth century progressed. By post-modernity, the desk at which individuals sat, the ground under one's feet, a PC, an apartment and a bedroom were equally as functional as nationalist spaces as the thinning old ghetto- or enclave-homelands had been, because the homelands now are sectors in cyber-space, where, with scanners and the miniaturization of knowledge, a national could every day read from a U.S. micro-nationalist paper or site of choice and from a dizzying array of newspapers and journals in the old race-homelands of ancestry across the seas. Small vanguard groups can now communicate a vast array of data—in their own new languages of discourse—to large numbers over the internet with little more, or less, labor or expense than had been exacted under modernity even to launch and distribute a nationalist small magazine. With the contraction of government, and the substitution of the marketplace for it in recent U.S. mainstream ideologies, the micro-nationalist groups provide the sense of community and belonging that many post-modern individuals seize. Mainly a term about sizes of the continuous stretches of territoriality, "micro-nation" thus may not refer to the size of a political or ethnic group. And even the actual territoriality of a populous micronation is not small: it is large like the population concerned, but severely fragmented into scattered, non-connected segments or micro-patches.

As against the drive of certain major, middle-rank and tiny nations to achieve statehood, Muslim black movements in America have generally postponed its realization to some point at which God Almighty, Allah, will come to deliver the dominated nation. Nonetheless, a national culture and historical discourse of some breadth and vitality has evolved, as well as independent circuits of economic activity conducted in the name of the religious nation on the margins of the U.S. mainstream economy. Since 1913, black American Muslims have developed many attributes of a major nation, except for the size of the homeland, which at best amounts to enclaves, and for an increasing number of members or quasi-citizens is just dots of micro-homelands all connected by the web. The modern African-American historians and writers who saw Islam and the Arab world as one element in national identity, and the Islamic "cults" that arose in the ranks of the poorest African-Americans, have pioneered serious forms of enclave-nationalism, and of the nationalism of micro-territoriality, that make this tradition among African-Americans distinguished and special beyond all other non-Anglo groups that have been attempting anything similar. The exception may, perhaps, be Zionist and Jewish-American micronationalist movements that showed great creative innovation of their own since WWII, in the building of specialized nationalist institutions and lobbies far outstripping U.S. blacks.[3]

If I were writing this book again, I would perhaps lessen and vary my use of the term "micronationalism." One could attempt to refer to "minimalized internal nationalisms" or "deterritorialized internal nationalisms," or "homelands-devoid nationalisms in America." It is not easy, though, to find a fully valid substitute for "micronations" and "micronationalism," unsatisfactory as they also are. "Micronation" need not entail smallness of membership, but does hint at the cultural thinness in that form of nationality. Except for the Puerto Ricans, micronationalists do not seem to be at all eager to seriously work to secede from America. To this there is some pragmatic calculation: they know that the might of the mainstream American state makes secession impractical short of a general crisis of the U.S. system. In material interest, micronationalisms in the USA have often been designed to provide jobs and chances to become middle class to the sub-nationalities: not all micronationalists really want revolution or God to blow up an America in which many of them are winning livelihoods and wealth. But this issue of material interests that bind the *ethne* (ethnic groups) and even the micronational movements in them to the U.S. system overlaps into that of all the values, knowledge and shared culture they have derived from Anglo-Americans. The process of building micronations in itself makes them more Anglicized in certain respects. Thus, all that may happen in the end could be incorporation into the U.S. mainstream system as long-term micronation units. Yet although the African-American people are not overly demarcated in culture from Anglo-Americans, they do have Africa-derived original culture, such as in music and dance, and to some extent in idiom, cuisine and religion, that do define it as one more ethnic group, rather than a "Negro" caste-group wholly determined by racism.

The term used in this book for an ethnic cultural group in America is "ethnos," the plural of which is *ethne*, following the pattern of the Greek original. An ethnos is a proto-micronation before it is properly organized. Not all *ethne* have the high consciousness, purpose and compound aims bestowed by a vanguard that are needed to make them micronations. If to be micronational requires consciousness, then this study presents two vanguard or elite groups that have supplied intense awareness in Black America. One is the atomized jobless lumpens who are made a purposeful vanguard by the sharp consciousness of history and society that a millenarian religion or cult imparts. The second is a bourgeoisie in the ethnos whose growing attention to history and social structure is fueled by discrimination, marginalization and disadvantage. This book shows how popular Muslim cults and the disgruntled bourgeoisie developed parallel ideologies of national protest: by the post-modern period, both groups and their respective nationalisms had run together and fused.

Terminology: "neo-Muslim"; "lumpen-proletariat"; "Americanist"; "Zionoid"

I have in this study sometimes used the term "neo-Muslim." Not all African-American Muslims may be at ease with this term, which I myself, though, apply only to one category among them. On one level, neo-Muslim merely means a new Muslim, that is to say, someone who has converted to Islam, which is the sense in which I could apply it to a figure like Elijah Muhammad. The scholarly literature sometimes termed the Austrian Jewish convert, Leopold Weiss, who made himself Muhammad Asad, a neo-Muslim, despite the deep familiarity with Islam's Qur'an scripture and classical Muslim scholarship that he built up over a life-time, until his books helped many born Muslim intellectuals understand their Islam much better. A convert could construct a literate Islam not very different from that of some sect of born Muslims in the Islamic Third World: but being a convert comes in special settings that can affect ideology—and does provoke originality in constructing and developing it. In this book's usage, "neo-Muslim" identifies that it is often black converts to Islam who are being analyzed, and that theirs was a special modality of Islam. The work seldom applies neo-Muslim to these sects as a whole, and certainly not to their second or third generations—in the main, just to converted individuals. Thus, in contrast to his father, we do not view Elijah's son Warith ud-Din Muhammad as a "neo-Muslim" (although he did construct a "neo-Sunni" reinvention of his father's religion because influences from the Muslim world had been expanding so much among NOI members). Left Americans who switched to a pro-Reagan Republicanism were termed "neo-Republicans" or "neo-conservatives" by the literature, and it is important to distinguish them in that way because their antithetical starting-points as radicals or liberals structured much of their later "neo-conservatism." Jewish-American neo-cons, much severer in their application of the ideology they embraced, have real differences from the ordinary body of WASP Republicans who have been so from father to son. We have to focus particularities of structuring or of concerns in the special Islams that have been constructed by new Muslims in Afro-America. Because they were born as Christians, neo-Muslims among the African-Americans have rejected Christianity with special vehemence and inventiveness, and with some special grounds, compared to calmer Third World Muslims. Interestingly, the second and third generation of African-American Muslims, who are not neo-Muslim, are now showing more flexibility and surface courtesies towards a Christianity they never practised.

A useful aspect of the prefix "neo-" for me was its implication that the convert systematically constructs an Islamic ideology or life within a geographical and social setting completely separate from Islam. As a new construct, black neo-Islam radically selects from, and restructures, elements coming from Islam to make them address some new U.S. concerns or issues in distinction from the original ideology in the Middle East. That originality in structuring Islam is certainly true of all the Nations of Islam from 1930 onwards, even of Warith's sect that opened itself more than most to influxes of materials and culture from Arab Sunni Islam. The "neo-Platonism" constructed from Egypt and other Hellenistic centers had some innovated differences from the thought of the original Plato and his school back in Greece.

This book does not want its readers to differentiate African-American Muslims too much from Muslims formed in the Third World. A minority of the enslaved Africans carried from the Third World were Muslims with a good knowledge of Sunni Muslim theological and legal literature in Arabic. Residues and Arabic fragments from that heritage survived in African-American folklore into the period in which the Moorish and Nation of Islam sects were founded in the earlier 20th century. Nonetheless, this was a culture that the U.S. system had denied facilities and recognition, and starved. The odds those who converted to black new Islams faced in America to formulate an Islamic ideology were much tougher than were those borne by youth in Arab countries who made themselves Islamists who rejected the "neo-paganism" (al-jahiliyyah al-jadidah) of some 20th century Arab societies. Those societies *had* imbibed some Western influences and patterns, but Islam in its original language would have been lapping around those Arabs or Iranians in childhood and adolescence, whatever their parents' stances, and they would have formalistically taken part in a few Muslim rites—they do not pass through the sudden complete change and the extent of the new learning that African-American convert neo-Muslims have faced in the U.S. It is true, though, that motifs from Islam have increasingly tinged general African-American rap culture with which new generations of non-Muslim teenagers are growing up—setting up a context for later conversion that entails much less discontinuity than for the Noble Drew 'Ali or Elijah Muhammad and their followers before WWII.

The Prophet Muhammad of Arabia stated that every child is born a Muslim because that is the religion of nature, and that it was non-Muslim parents who made him or her something else. "Converts" to Islam are thus rather called "reverts" in Islamist usage. In the case of some African-Americans who converted into Moors or members of Elijah's Nation of Islam, they were also reverting, as well, to the suppressed Islam that their grandparents or forefathers had maintained during in North America.

A term that this book uses for many of the early black converts to Islam in America's urban north is lumpen-proletarians or lumpens. In our usage, it is a neutral social category. "Lumpen-proletariat" was a term early used by Marx to describe people in urban centers who could have become members of their industrial proletariats, but who did not because of various circumstances. Marx, who sometimes vented a racist distaste against Third World civilizations, looked down upon the lumpens as the lowest and most degraded section of the proletariat. They were defined by orthodox Marxist literature as the down-and-outs who make no contribution to the workers' cause, the outcast, submerged elements that made up a section of the populations of industrial centers, such as beggars, prostitutes, gangsters, petty criminals and the chronic unemployed. Given that we do not equate human worth with regular labor in factories and economic organizations, this book far from shares the classical Marxists' disdain for urban lumpens, which prefigured the horror at the black lumpens' lifestyle articulated from America's neo-Muslim movements, determined to make them factory-workers or bourgeois since the Noble Drew 'Ali in 1913. Some black lumpen language-forms or music, and their connection to the old Africa-influenced Gullah form of English, are more interesting than the flat Angloid print-English to which all Muslim sects in Afro-America have inclined—and spread among blacks.

Still, one sees how great was the need of the black lumpens for the Islamic movements to come to organize them and make them cohere. The black lumpens in the industrial cities of the U.S. North were not brought together in a far-extending community stretching beyond the neighborhood in the way that wage-labor, s, workers' libraries and union newspapers, and the modernizing direct relationship with industrial capitalists did factory-workers of all races in America. The black lumpens, to a great extent socially atomized and hostile to each other, met mainly in small groups in an immediate neighborhood, and received information mainly in such oral exchange rather than from newspapers so that their knowledge of wider societies and history was a deformed folklore that changes data in the mouth of each individual who takes up a theme. Their lack of fixed income gave some lumpen individuals a temptation to rob or defraud or use his or her neighbor. Islamic movements in black America, and in Egypt and Iran for instance in the Muslim world, morally cleanse lumpens, instill an attitude of community so that they want to help rather than harm their co-nationals, make them literate by obliging them to listen to taped orations in the standard language and read the Qur'an scripture and the glamorously oppositionist sect-newspaper, and give them a very detailed portrayal of imaged governing enemy-classes depicted to oppress, exploit and exclude them. While focused by a vivid enemy, especially at first, the Islamic movements, which all span classes, bring out qualities of goodwill, mutual love and hopefulness long latent in the lumpens, but suppressed by conditions and their status.

This book occasionally uses the term "Americanist." This term always entails some acceptance by blacks of the American system, but has two levels, although it always has some ideological approval of the American system in it. The most common sense of "Americanist" is tacit or frank acceptance that the course to be followed is for the micronation to seek to prosper in America, because it has enough creativity and wealth for that to be possible. Even in Elijah's lifetime there was admiration for the technological and economic skills of their "oppressors" (and *some* awareness of the sect's linkages of worldview and culture with Anglos) without, for the most part, swallowing the ruling "devil" WASPs' Americanist patriotism. That latter acceptance of the need of blacks to formally integrate a political and social community with whites within their mainstream system came under his son, Warith, from 1975. Warith did proclaim that America's political system and ideology were superior to atheistic Communism, and that America had become a state that African-Americans should uphold and enter—a fully Americanist stance. It may be better in any further volume to sometimes substitute "America-oriented" or "America-tinged" for "Americanist."

In this volume, and perhaps in two companion volumes concentrating on Farrakhan and Imam W.D. Mohammed that are to come, I had no alternative but to use a few special terms in order to focus properly my analysis of American societies and religions—sometimes at the risk that they could annoy or confuse some readers. For instance, I use the suffix ...oid, meaning that a phenomenon has some elements that point towards or come from another phenomenon, but not enough to as yet have become part of or an adjunct to it, given that the structuring given, and the elements from other phenomena, make it too different to "pass." An instance is my term, Zionoid. This carries no pejorative coloring or intent. I did not mean to say there that those American Jews who have adhered to post-1967 Jewish micronationalist movements were machine-like. Rather, my perspective has been to insist that special movements unfolded in American Jewry after the Six Day War in the Middle East that are different from classical Zionism, and sometimes even from a core pro-Israel political lobby in the USA itself. They cannot be termed Zionists because Israel and the atoms from Hebrew often just provide emblems that basically mark out the U.S. micronation they build or construct, as against the other evolving micro-nations or enclave-nations in America—that similarly, in their turn, have other mother-homelands of the mind overseas that likewise demarcate them from the others for American functions.

True, special groups took shape in the USA from 1967 which invented new religious Zionisms that have impelled American Jews to go to live in the West Bank. But overall, American Jews have always been eager to do anything for Israel other than to go to live there. Thus, it may not be too skeptical to wonder if any genuine Zionism ever did crystallize in America after 1880! Identification with Israel, with "Zion," with those Jews who settled in Palestine, has played a catalytic or focusing role in the intensely nationalist Jewish community that is being integrated, but this is a community that believes that America was the best thing that happened to the Jewish people in its long history, and is determined to remain there and flourish within its system alongside the other micronations. Hence my suffixed term, "Zionoid."

ACKNOWLEDGEMENTS

I derived my vocation to become an historian and write upon American society and Anglo-Saxon cultures in adolescence from the Austro-Hungarian philosopher Baron John Radvansky.

I could not have brought this thorough work through to conclusion without African-American friends and contacts who generously and constantly provided me with further primary materials, private data, and their views. The Gambian-American Howard University academic, Dr Sulayman Nyang, *Hijrah* editor Labib 'Uqdah of Los Angeles, John Trimble, Dr Jacob Holland of Washington, Harold Barnes of New York and Idris Michael Tobin, the Nation of Islam's Minister James Muhammad, and the Interlibrary loans section of the Australian National Library, all supplied me with issues and microfilms of Black Muslim and African-American magazines. Dr Yusuf Na'im Kly, at that time lecturer and assistant professor in International Law at the University of Regina, Canada, helped convey copies of his books and articles to me, and provided comments on my drafts. Mrs Shirley Muhammad, then head of Chicago's Clara Muhammad Foundation, supplied texts of post-1975 speeches and interviews of Imam Warith ud-Din Muhammad, Elijah's Arabic-influenced son. Ernest Muhammad of Minister Farrakhan's *Final Call* tabloid directed me to an internet site carrying old pre-1976 *Muhammad Speak* articles. Huseyin Elmas of Melbourne, Australia, and the Department of Religious Studies at Sydney University, Australia, provided stenographic backup at crucial early points in my project. Palestinian-American activist, Layla Diyab, provided me with Arabic-language and English primary materials from the Arab-American side of the international relations of Black Americans. Her cousin, Dr Jamil Diyab, an important player in the immigrant Muslim and Black Islam sectors of Chicago life over two decades from the late 1940s, generously, despite his years, answered at length my numerous questions over international telephone. Overall, my debt, and that of all my readers, to Michael-Idris Tobin of Florida is very great. He had patient and unshakable faith in my project and its importance, and over the years up to the time that this book went to print, kept up the unbroken stream of the Muslim African-American newspapers that he was ever ready to airmail to me. It is due to Idris that this book is so up to date with the latest developments as it goes to press.

In regard to guidance, Lawrence Moten of Melbourne provided Christian African-American perspectives on various aspects of Islam and its followers among his people of origin. Dr Garry Trompf, Head of the Department of Religious Studies and then the Center for Millenarian Studies at Sydney University, provided intellectual guidance when I took part in two projects that he conducted, one on the Cargo and millenarian cults, the other on enclave, micronationalist and littoral political movements and cults. Diana Collier of Clarity Press offered important macro-historical perspective on the history of the African-American people, and repeatedly repressed skepticism that the many delays by me warranted, as to whether this protracted project would, after all, ever make it to the printing press. I could not have finished this history of Muslims in Afro-America without the aid of all these activists, writers and scholars.

To all of the above I owe a great debt: but my analysis is wholly my own.

ENDNOTES

1 M. Eric Dyson, *Making Malcolm: the Myth and Meaning of Malcolm X* (NY: OUP 1995) p. xii.

2 See Ellis Cose, *The Rage of a Privileged Class* (New York: Harper Collins 1993).

3 I follow here some of the discussion and terms articulated by Peter Ravn Rasmussen in his "An Essay on Micronationalism, covering the full breadth of the phenomenon," available world-wide web 27 July 2005.

GLOSSARY
of Middle Eastern and other Technical Terms Relevant to Understanding African-American Muslims

Ahmadi/Qadiyani movement: this awarded its India-born founder Mirza Ghulam Ahmad (d. 1908) the function of a further prophet of Allah after Muhammad Ibn 'Abdallah of Arabia and also showed signs of linking him to Krishna and other Hindu incarnations. Its emissaries were active in poor black areas of the cities of the northern USA from the early twentieth century, and their translation, by Muhammad 'Ali, was often the text of the meanings of the Qur'an to which recourse was had by the African-Americans who organized the Nation of Islam from 1930.

Al-Fatihah: the opening surah of the Qur'an that leads the Muslims to pray to God for guidance so that they will avoid the fate of those who went astray or incurred His wrath on the Day of Judgement. This surah (chapter) is often recited in the Arabic ritual prayers of Muslims.

'Ali Ibn Abi Talib: cousin of the Prophet Muhammad, who married his daughter Fatimah: accepted by Sunnis as the fourth Caliph (khalifah) or political successor after the Prophet Muhammad, and considered their first Imam by all Shi'is, including the Isma'ilis and the Druze on the outer margin of Islam.

Amir: a military commander, prince, or local ruler who had built de facto independence or autonomy from wider Arabo-Muslim states that legitimized their authority and claims to rule from the wide universalist impulses in Islam.

Amir al-Muminin: "Commander of the Faithful." This title was used for the fourth Rightly Guided Caliph, 'Ali Ibn Abi Talib, regarded by the Shi'ites as their founder. But it was particularly used for the Caliphs of the third major imperial dynasty after Muhammad, the 'Abbasids, who ruled an Arab-led empire from Baghdad until it was sacked by the Mongols in 1258, and is chiefly a Sunni term. The title of Amir al-Mu'minin was again assumed in the twentieth century by Sufi Abdul Hamid, a black activist in Chicago and New York who organized pickets and boycotts against white-owned stores and businesses that refused to employ blacks.

Angloid: means a group or culture that has adopted, or by now inherently has the high literary language and many of the main traits of Anglo-Saxons. The suffix "oid" indicates some life-form or body of culture that has the appearance and some characteristics of another.

Anglomorph: something now in its central aspects essentially Anglo-Saxon. The suffix "morph" means one of various forms of an organism or species although, as it also carries a sense of things having been transformed, this can be at the end of a process of acculturation and comprehensive assimilation, which is what happened to the educated segments of most non-Anglo *ethne* in America.

Atoms of Arabic or Islam: "atomization" is the best way to describe an important modality under which Islam was born or reborn in America. Quite often, no sort of structure or clusters of elements from original Islam were transmitted: instead, one has this or that atom—a single Arabic word, a single motif, a single attenuated half-memory of a tenet from the Qur'an—that focus local concerns, African-American vital interests, situations outside anything ever conceived in the Middle East. The atoms were easy for African-Americans to install within new ideological tenets and new procedures that have unique made-in-America structuring. But as the atoms from Islam and the Arabs accumulate beyond a certain critical mass, they "suddenly" cohere to impose a changed structure of meaning much more like the tenets and societies of the Muslim Third World, although that model stays highly modified still, even in those most neo-Sunni in bent. From Elijah, we move to the Sunni-fying Warith, from the early proudly particularist Farrakhan who hinted a New Book might be coming to him from God we suddenly find activists in his sect who are heading towards deep engagement with and affiliation to the much more developed "immigrant" Muslim communities and the Muslim Third World from which they came.

Awliya': see wali.

al-Azhar: the major mosque and institution of higher learning founded in Cairo by the Shi'ite esotericist Fatimid Imam-Caliph al-Mu'izz (d. 975). A bastion of Sunni Muslim orthodoxy from the period of the rule of Salah al-Din al-Ayyubi ("Saladin"), al-Azhar was host to a fair number of members of the Moorish movements and Nation of Islam sects who studied Arabic and Islam there.

Basmalah: ie. the formula Bismillah il-Rahman il-Rahim, derived from the Qur'an, and meaning "In the Name of Allah, the Compassionate, the Merciful," with which Muslims precede action. It is often used in both Warith al-Din Muhammad's Sunnism-influenced African-American Muslim sect, and by Louis Farrakhan's revived Nation of Islam, often with display of the original Arabic calligraphy in the printed materials of both.

Batin: the inner or esoteric meaning of a Qur'anic text, or an Islamic religious duty or teaching. Shi'ite—and in particular Isma'ili and Druze—interpreters of the Qur'an sought inner or esoteric ("batini") meanings in its passages behind their external (zahiri) meanings which could be turned into metaphors or symbols. The method was sometimes applied in classical

Islam to other scriptures, as well as to rituals and natural phenomena. Somewhat similar symbolic metaphorization of NOI teachings and predictions, and of statements in the Qur'an and the Bible, has often been carried out by Farrakhan and Warith ud-Din Mohammed. Such practices in the NOI tradition favor some partial Shi'ite/Isma'ili/Druze origin, or influence, in the formation of the Nation of Islam in 1930. The Imam is the decisive authoritative source for the esoteric interpretation of scriptures and religious prescriptions. The elites around Imams, or who took them up as emblems, tended to consider that the inner or deeper batini interpretation should not be disclosed to the masses, who might misunderstand.

Bin: see Ibn.

Bismillah il-Rahman il-Rahim: see "Basmalah."

Caliphate (Ar.: Khilafah and Khilafat): the Muslim political institution or state headed by the "caliph" or successor of the Prophet Muhammad of Arabia. The Caliphate in the Sunni world came to its end when the Turkish leader, Kemal Ataturk, abolished the Caliphate in 1924 as an anachronism that could not be allowed to linger on from the collapsed Ottoman Empire.

Devils: see Shaytan.

Da'wah (lit. "the Call"): a term used by Sunni Muslim revivalist organizations in the Third World from around 1970 for the duty of Muslims to propagate Islam among non-believers. Warith's sect has active da'wah programs, for which it uses the Arabic term, among African-Americans—and also targeted to Hispanics, for whom it uses Spanish Qur'ans supplied by Sa'udi da'wah institutions.

Din: a religion. al-din: "the religion [of Islam]," often used in proper names.

Fatihah: see al-Fatihah.

Fatimids: Muslim dynasty of Isma'ili caliphs in North Africa who later ruled Egypt from 973-1171: they claimed descent from the Prophet Muhammad through 'Ali, who married the Prophet's daughter Fatimah.

Fida'i (plural fida'iyyun and fedayin): a volunteer who sacrifices his life for the national and/or Islamic cause. From the 11th to the 13th centuries, fida'is were sent out from Isma'ili fortresses in Iran and Syria to assassinate hostile Sunni leaders and office-bearers. African-American Muslims have been familiar with Palestinian fedayin guerrillas ready to sacrifice their lives against Zionists since Israel's territorial expansion in 1967. There is a layer in the psyche of the most ill-treated and alienated African-Americans that to an extent feels with this modality of struggle among Third World Muslims. The neo-salafi Wahhabism-influenced jihadists who hit technological, commercial America on September 11, 2001 had some discreet glamour among a limited number in groups that have succeeded the old NOI since 1975.

Fiqh: the science of Islamic jurisprudence. See "shari'ah."

Hadd (pl. hudud): "edge," "boundary," "limit": a technical term in Islamic law for the "limits" of various grave crimes mentioned in the Qur'an, and their punishments. They are implemented in Sa'udi Arabia, whose sometimes fairly severe legal system Louis Farrakhan is known to admire.

Hadith: a narrated statement attributed to the Prophet Muhammad. Plural ahadith.

Hajj: pilgrimage to Mecca or Makkat al-Mukarramah in Arabia, where the Qur'an was first revealed. With lengthened vowel, the word means "one who has made the pilgrimage to Mecca."

Halakhic: relating to the halakha, the legal, as opposed to the non-legal aggadic, aspect of Judaism. The halakha, like the shari'ah in Islam, is meant to regulate personal, social, national and international matters in detail, and to define in a binding way for the orthodox all practices imposed by Judaism. Orthodox Jewish halakha makes it very hard for non-Jews to convert to Judaism and marry Jews.

Halal: food that is permitted for Muslims to eat, such as the meat of animals that have been slaughtered in the name of Allah. See "Haram."

Haqa'iq (truths): in Isma 'ili and Druze thought, the external features (zahir) of religious obligations change with every prophet: under them lie the haqa'iq which are immutable and eternal truths of the realm of the batin (the hidden), known to the Imam and accessible only to the initiated elite. This concept is close to ideas among the Moorish movements in Afro-America that since 1913 have stressed the right of the Noble Drew 'Ali to substitute new rituals of worship in America that sometimes differ from those imposed by the Prophet Muhammad in far-removed Arabia, while the new movement maintains and spreads the valid truth of the latter. Like the Druze and Isma'ilis before them, many Moors believed and believe that Drew 'Ali publicly stated or explained only a portion of his divine truths, which will be made clear in some subsequent era.

Haram: foods, notably the meat of the polluting swine, that are forbidden for Muslims to eat; consumption of alcohol is also haram. Any act forbidden by God, the Qur'an and Islamic law. See "Halal" above.

Hijab: a headscarf of modest Islamic women that covers their ears and hair. This requirement of Islamic modesty is a flash-point for ill-feeling by non-Muslims.

Hijrah: the migration of the Prophet Muhammad from his native Mecca, where the city's rich were persecuting his movement, to Yathrib which was then renamed Madinah al-Nabi, the Town of the Prophet (="Medina"). The idea of withdrawal from an oppressive or irredeemably pagan society to a new center based on Islam recurs in the programs of the sect of Warith ud-Din Mohammed since 1975.

Hikmah: a term in the Qur'an meaning "wisdom", which later acquired various technical meanings referring to religious, gnostic or esoteric philosophy.

Iblis: see Shaytan.

Ibn: son, or son of.

'Id (sometimes spelt Eid in America): one of the major festival days in Islam. 'Id al-Fitr: the festival day of the breaking of the fasting month of Ramadan.

Imam: in Sunni usage, a leader of collective prayers who manages a mosque, a religious leader. The term has been used in Warith ud-Din

Muhammad's sect for his leadership following this restricted Sunni sense. All black Islamic movements in the USA since the late 1970s have been aware of the use of the term "Imam" to denote Ayatollah Khomeini's leadership of the militant clerical-Islamic revivalism that overthrew the Shah in Iran. This politicized Shi'ite radical conservatism in Iran had long been influenced by the neo-salafist (qv.) Sunni revivalist thought of the Muslim Brotherhood in Egypt, especially its theoretician, Sayyid Qutb, which defined imams in the modest Sunnite way. Yet those Imams of classical Shi'isms who were hereditary spiritual leaders in special relationship to God, who grants them sweeping powers to interpret religious texts, seem to prefigure many claims made in the NOI for Wali Fard Muhammad, Elijah Muhammad and perhaps one day, Farrakhan. The last of the maximal Imams of Shi'ite groups does not die but is occulted to God and will return to judge and destroy the evil world—claims also made by Farrakhan for Wali Fard Muhammad and Elijah Muhammad.

Intifadah: the spontaneous, low-level, diffuse "uprising" by Palestinians in the West Bank and the Gaza strip against occupation by Israel from 1988.

Isma'ilis: a branch of Shi'ite Islam that considers Isma'il, the eldest son of the Shi'i Imam Ja'far al-Sadiq (d. 765), as his successor.

Ithna'ashariyyah, i.e. Ithna'asharis, literally "Twelvers": the most numerous branch of Shi'ite Islam: Muslims who acknowledge twelve Imams in lineal succession from 'Ali b. Abi Talib, after the Prophet Muhammad.

Jahiliyah ("condition of ignorance"): refers to the life and thinking of the Arabs of the Arabian peninsula before the career of the prophet Muhammad and their subsequent expansion. This pre-Islamic Arabia with its pagan gods and its tribal feuds was the setting of the late 1920's play *Antar of Araby* by African-American elite scholar Maude Cuney-Hare, and was also mentioned by seminal African-American historians Carter Woodson and W.E.B. DuBois.

Jihad: This term was long mostly used in Arabic writings in the Middle East and in sub-Saharan Africa to denote "holy wars" against non-believers. However, since 1880, Muslim writers in relationship with the West or with American society have interpreted "jihad" in its root sense of "exertion," or an inner struggle for purification. The Prophet Muhammad of Arabia had indeed told some followers about the jihad or contest with their own souls that they would have, to master their own negative inclinations, after this or that military jihad (effort or fight) was over. Many Muslim migrants and their offspring who want to get into an unwelcoming America want to change the translation of "jihad" from Holy War to "struggle against wrongdoing" lest it obscure what for them in their position has to be its true meaning from the non-Muslim world. This is to ignore that "jihad" had sometimes meant violent resistance or counter-violence or attacking back in West Africa for Muslim Africans who had been deported to slavery in North America. They had been brought from societies in which severe Sunni movements were waging armed jihad attacks against animist neighbors, and against Muslim neighbors they denounced as wishy-washy or in cahoots with polytheism. The main meaning jihad would have had for those early Muslims in North America would have been violent counter-attack or war against Christians—although all but a few of them sidestepped that hopeless a course.

Jum'ah: Friday. Salat al-Jum'ah is the Friday noon prayer, the most important congregational prayer in the mosques in Islam.

Khilafah and Khilafat: see "Caliphate."

Lumpen-proletariat: a Marxist term to describe people in urban centers who could have become members of their industrial proletariats, but who did not because of various circumstances. They include the long-term unemployed, outcasts, beggars, prostitutes and petty criminals in great industrial cities. Lumpen proletarians were the main target for recruitment by the early neo-Muslim movements of the Noble Drew 'Ali (1913) and Wali Fard Muhammad and Elijah Muhammad (1930). They remain today a group heavily proselytized by Islamic sects that have become mainly bourgeois in membership.

Madhhab: Arabic word with a range of meanings including 'doctrine', 'movement' and 'creed'; a system or school of religious law in Islam.

Maghrib ("the place of sunset"): in mediaeval Muslim geography it referred to the western part of North Africa (present-day Morocco, Algeria and Tunisia, and also Muslim Spain.

Mahdi: "rightly guided one," a name applied in Muslim eschatology to the restorer of true religion and justice expected at the end of time.

Masjid: mosque (lit. "place of prostration"). Warith's sect from 1975 has used not just the Arabic singular but the Arabic broken plural form as well to denote mosques.

Mawla: 'Lord' or 'master,' often used in the Iranian and South Asian honorary epithet "Mawlana," a title that one Pakistani who courted Elijah's Black Muslims tried to bestow on Elijah. Mawla also came to mean, in some of the Muslim states of the classical Arabs, an originally non-Arab "client" affiliated to a powerful Arab or to an Arab tribe.

Millenarianism: belief-systems holding that the world is dominated by evil beings who exercise political power, that the believers have to withdraw from that corrupt and unjust mainstream for the time, and that God may soon destroy that world and the evil, ushering in a new permanent world of happiness and plenty for those elect ones who had rejected it.

Mujaddid: a renewer or reformer of Islam who purges it of corruptions. This term of Third World Muslims was applied from the 1980s to Warith by his adherents as a title to stress the break he worked with old Nation of Islam "heresies" (*bida'*) promoted by his father.

Mullah (pl. mullahs): derived from the Arabic mawla, denoting a Muslim religious cleric.

Mu'tazilah, Mu'taziliyyah: a term referring to diverse scholars in early Islam under the 'Abbasid dynasty who belonged to a rationalistic Islamic school of thought that stressed Divine Unity and Justice, and human free will. In its exploration since 1990 of the classical Muslim past, the sect of

Warith ud-Din (Wallace) Mohammed has focused on ideas in it, such as those of the Mu'tazilah and classical Muslim philosopher and scientists, that fit into quasi-secular modernity in American life.

Nur: 'light,' a term used for God, defined as light in the Qur'an in the "verse of light" Q 24:35: "God is the light of the heavens and the earth..." Shi'is have seen the term "nur" as meaning a light that perceivedly emanated through Adam, and via Muhammad into the family of 'Ali and his successors, the imams. The term "Light", sometimes with its Arabic original "al-Nur", recurred in the neo-Elijahian preachings of Louis Farrakhan after 1978.

Palmach: elite strike force established in 1941 in Palestine by the Haganah (army) of the mainstream Zionist movement, as distinct from the Revisionist fringe that was to produce the "terrorist" Irgun Tsvai Le'umi (National Military Organization) of later Israeli prime ministers Menachem Begin and Yitzhak Shamir.

Qadi: a Muslim judge in the Third World (pl. qudat).

Qalam: reed-pen. Q 96:4 states that God taught man 'by the pen'. According to some traditions of the Prophet Muhammad, the qalam was the first thing created by God. This concept identifies Islam as the religion of literacy and the printed page for African-American Muslims, many of whom convert in a condition of poverty.

Qiblah: the direction of Muslim prayer towards the Ka'bah, indicated in a mosque by a niche called mihrab.

Qiyamah: the Arabic term for the Last Day, the Day of Resurrection and Judgement of all individual humans who died throughout history. The concept appears often in the Qur'an. Belief in the Last Day has been considered a key pillar of the faith of Islam among Sunni and Shi'ite Muslims in the Middle East and "black Africa." It was denied by the hajj Elijah Muhammad, and Farrakhan's revived post-1978 Nation of Islam has been ambiguous on the issue.

Qutb: lit. 'pole' or 'pivot.' In classical Islam's mystical Sufi literature, such as the writings of Ibn al-'Arabi (d. 1240), it refers to the most perfect human being (al-insan al-kamil) who is thought to be the universal leader of all saints, to mediate between the divine and the human, and whose presence is deemed necessary for the existence of the world. For some Shi'i authors, the Qutb was the Shi'i Imam. The Noble Drew 'Ali, Wali Fard Muhammad and Elijah Muhammad had most of the functions of the Qutb in classical Arabo-Muslim thought.

Rasul: "messenger," applied by the Qur'an to the apostles of God, including the Prophet Muhammad who is called Rasul Allah, the Messenger of Allah. The classical Nation of Islam to 1975 did apply the term "the Messenger of Allah" to Elijah Muhammad, but not "Prophet" (in Arabic, "nabi").

Reincarnation: see Tanasukh al-arwah.

Sajdah: see sujud.

Salaf: the model ancestors or precursors of the early (Arab-led) centuries of Islam. The salafite movements begun by the likes of Jamal al-Din al-Afghani (1838/1839-1897) were a Protestant-like reformation of Islam:

the Ummah or global Muslim nation must purge the religion of post-classical accretions by returning to the codes and ways of the first (Arab or Arab-led) generations of the pious *salaf* (early forefathers). That return and purging of late-traditional Islam were the precondition for the colonized group to build political power and independence. The model for Islam imaged to have been bequeathed by those *salaf* was claimed by the Arab World's neo-salafi revivalist Jihadists as their justification to strike at established governments and at their American patrons. Such talks fascinate some African-Americans. Warith's sect is also reading writings by the Egyptian liberal Arabist, Muhammad Husayn Haykal (1888-1956) that depicted the first generations of the (mainly Arab) Muslims or salaf in ways that would fit an orientation to them into a liberal modernity coming from the West.

Salam: A term derived from the same root as that of the term "Islam." It conveys several meanings such as peace, safety and salvation, and figures in the standard form of salutation between Muslims.

As-Salamu 'Alaykum: "May peace be upon you." The standard greeting of Muslims throughout the world when they encounter each other. This greeting was first put into U.S. public space by the black mass movement of Elijah Muhammad, not by immigrant Arabs or Muslims.

Salat (pl. salawat): the Arabic-language formal prayers of Islam, in particular its five daily ritual prayers. Salat al-Jum'ah is the Friday noon prayer in mosques.

Shahinshah or "king of kings": one of the royal titles in Persia and Mughal India. Both secular Arab nationalists and pro-Khomeiniite Islamists have vented egalitarian rejection of the attempts of the two Pahlavi Shahs to establish hereditary monarchy in Iran, to the media of African-American Muslim sects. Positions towards Khomeini's "Islamic revolution" in Iran have been among the things that helped distinguish African-American Muslim factions from each other from 1978.

Shari'ah, lit. 'the path to be followed': the Sunni Muslim law, determined during classical Islam, which is supposed to regulate an all-encompassing Islamic way of life. From 1980, interest grew among African-American Muslims, including those headed by Farrakhan and Warith, in radical salafite groups in the Middle East that claim they will implement shari'ah as a comprehensive code of life and social order after they defeat repressive secular or established regimes. In past decades, the detail of Islamic shari'ah laws had been remote from African-Americans. Farrakhan's group has been aware of the stress on shari'ah in such Arab states as Sa'udi Arabia, but has also criticized legalistic rigidity there. From the late 1990s, some youth in Warith's sect have been going to Cairo and Damascus to study the Islamic shari'ah in Arabic in Islamic universities and institutes. Following an enterprise of some Muslims in civil society in the Third World, and some of their governments, the movement of Warith ud-Din Mohammed has been experimenting with "shari'ah banking."

Shaykh: Arabic term for old man, elder or tribal chief. It is also used in the Arab World as an honorific title for any religious dignitary, whether a Sufi spiritual guide, or of a certain rank in the Sunni Islamic 'ulama'.

Shaytan: Iblis is the name given in the Qur'an to the Devil, such as when he refused to bow down before Adam (Q. 2:34), but Shaytan or Satan is also used. The old Nation of Islam of Elijah Muhammad pluralized the Devil: all whites were a race of inherently evil, artificially-bred devils. The Druze, an offshoot of Isma'ilism, had applied the Arabic broken plural *shayatin* to Sunni Muslims who were trying to crush them. Writers in the somewhat Sunnified and accommodationist sect of Imam W. Mohammed (from 1975) have sometimes used the term "Shaytanic" to describe evil for the most part worked by whites.

Shi'ah, Shi'is, Shi'ites: followers of Shi'ism, the second largest denomination of Islam, after Sunnism. As well as following the sunnah of the Prophet Muhammad, all Shi'is believe in the Imamat of 'Ali Ibn Abi Talib and his descendants through Fatimah. The three main Shi'i sects are the Twelvers (Ithna'asharis), the Isma'ilis and the Zaydis in Yemen.

Sind: a province in Pakistan around the Indus Valley. In 958 AD, a Fatimid Isma'ili principality was founded with its capital at Multan, one of the cities of Sindh. Some have speculated that the founder of the Nation of Islam in 1930, Wali Fard Muhammad, was an Isma'ili who either came to America from Sindh or was the son of an Isma'ili who had migrated from there to some Anglo-Saxon country.

Sufi: a Muslim mystic who seeks direct communion with God, usually on behalf of the general body of Muslims who cannot themselves achieve it.

Sujud: a ritual posture of prostration in Muslim Arabic prayers with the forehead touching the ground.

Sunnah: a custom or practice of the Prophet Muhammad of Arabia that Muslims are obliged to follow even today.

Sunnah, Sunnis: members of the majority branch of Islam, from the term Sunni, which means a follower of the sunnah of the Prophet Muhammad.

Surah: a chapter of the Qur'an.

Ta'wil: the elucidation of the inner or esoteric meaning, batin, from the literal wording or apparent meaning of a text, ritual or religious prescription.

Takbir: praise or glorification of God (as in Q 74:3, etc.). It denotes the articulation of the formula Allahu Akbar ("God is Most Great" or "It is Allah who is the Greatest"). This phrase is used in the Arabic ritual prayer and also as a rallying-call of defiance by Muslims against non-believers who have superior strength. Deformed remnants of the Islamic ritual prayer kept some memory of "Allahu Akbar" alive among rural African-American poor in the South of the USA into the 1940s. The slogan "Allahu Akbar" was used by members of Marcus Garvey's Africa-directed nationalist movement and by the movements of Elijah Muhammad, Warith and Farrakhan to focus rejection of ill-treatment by whites, and of social disintegration of blacks.

Tanasukh al-arwah: the doctrine of metempsychosis, that is to say reincarnation or transmigration of the soul to new bodies after deaths: this doctrine of the Middle East's Isma'ilis and Druze (as well as of the Hindus and America's theosophists) was taken up by the Moorish Science Temple of America that the Noble Drew 'Ali launched in 1913, but not, though, by the Nation of Islam of Wali Fard Muhammad and Elijah Muhammad, founded in 1930.

Taqiyyah: precautionary dissimulation of one's religious beliefs, especially in time of persecution or danger, a practice especially adopted by the Shi'i Muslims. There are many examples of double-speak, layers of meaning and manipulation from African-American Muslim movements when they address non-Muslim blacks, and whites who have power.

Taqwa: piety, the quality of being God-fearing.

Tariqah: "way or path"—the path followed by mystical schools of interpretation in Islam, one of their orders. Since the death of Elijah Muhammad in 1975, members of the movements of both Warith ud-Din Muhammad and Louis Farrakhan have interacted with Sufi tariqahs (orders) of both West Africa and the Arab World.

Tassawwuf: Arabic term for Sufism, i.e. Islamic mysticism.

Shahadah, the formal declaration of the Muslim faith, normally recited during the ritual prayers.

Tashbih: anthropomorphism. A term used by classical theologians against those who took literally Qur'anic expressions such as 'the hand of God' (Q 57:29, etc.), God's sitting on the throne (Q 10:3) etc. Anthropomorphic conceptualizations of God for a time recurred in the NOI tradition in America.

Tawhid: tenet of the Oneness of God or belief in Divine Unity, one of the fundamental tenets of Islam.

Twelvers: see Ithna'asharis.

Ulama': plural of 'alim, meaning a religious scholar or learned man.

Umayyads: first major ruling Muslim dynasty that was based in Damascus (661-750).

Ummah (or in South Asia, Iran and Central Asia ummat): the community of followers of a specific religion or prophet, in particular the Muslims. It can mean community or nation. Applied by followers of Warith to distinguish their members as a community from non-Muslim African-Americans or within U.S. society as a whole. Sometimes the term is also used to denote an undivided global Muslim community that has some features of integration in which it matches or transcends local nations defined by homelands, races or languages.

Wali: saint, friend of God, or human friend, patron or protector. In a political context, the terms can also mean administrator or ruler (pl. awliya'). The name is common among West African Muslims and did exist among enslaved African Muslims in North America prior to the Civil War. The Qur'an warns the believers in Islam not to take Jews or Christians as their awliya', which some classical Arab exegesists interpreted as meaning "friends", and some, protectors. Probably the verse only forbids Muslims not to put themselves into positions of becoming so dependent on non-Muslims that they can in part determine how the Muslims act and how they interpret their Islam. Both Warith's and Farrakhan's groups have maintained the latter meaning, but say they can be friends with Christian blacks outside the mosques, including in their churches. Whether this is a friendship fed by a belief that the interactions are enabling the Muslims to coax such Christians towards Islam is hard to tell.

Zahir: the outer, literal, exoteric meaning of a passage in the Qur'an, and of Islam's rituals and religious prescriptions. From this literal layer of meaning, Twelver Shi'ite, and in particular Isma'ili and Druze writers claim to pass through to a perceived esoteric or inner plane of meaning of the sacred text. This batin or inner meaning may be expounded to a select circle by an infallible leader thought to have some special relation with God.

Zakat: obligatory alms for Muslims.

Chapter One

The Nation of Islam and Its Successors After 1975: From Millenarian Protest to Transcontinental Relationships

1:TO ELIJAH MUHAMMAD'S DEATH IN 1975

Elijah Muhammad led the Black Muslim protest movement in the USA from the Nation of Islam's first emergence in 1930 to his death on 25 February 1975. Under Elijah's leadership, elements from authentic Islam and from the Arabic language focused the ghettoed poor blacks' rejection of racial discrimination and inequality in American society. Elijah Muhammad's very special development of Islamic elements, however, carried serious deviations from comprehensive orthodox Islam. He made whimsical—or, his Sunnifying, Arab-orientated successor argued, tactical—changes to some of the Islamic precepts he did keep: the Ramadan fast, for instance, conveniently became a December fast, corresponding to the Christians' festive season in the USA—although this timing may also have been designed to break the grip of "pagan" Christmas on the adherents. More problematically, Elijah and his followers also asserted that he was the "Messenger of Allah" in the last days, a claim at variance with the Arabian Prophet Muhammad's ascribed status as God's final prophet. The Nation of Islam under Elijah certainly did creditable work in restoring pride and self-respect to poverty-stricken, ill-educated blacks who had been spiritually pounded and atomized on the margins of society by white racism. But Elijah's confrontationist stance against the whites went so far that it broke with the universalism of Islam: Elijah used to teach that whites are "devils" who *by nature* could not be Muslims, and that God, "Allah", would soon judge and incinerate them for their crimes against black humanity.

Following Elijah Muhammad's death on 25 February 1975, his son Wallace (later Warith ud-Deen Muhammad, and then finally "Mohammed," so that overzealous followers would not mistakenly ascribe the status and functions of Islam's last Prophet, Muhammad of Arabia, to him) became Chief Imam of the movement. Warith had a better knowledge of Arabic and of orthodox Islam than his father. In a tactful but firm and final way, he swept away all the mythologies with U.S. functions that, under Elijah, had dogged the black Muslims' actualization of Islam as preached in its homelands in the East. Warith declared that Muhammad of Arabia was God's last and culminating prophet to humanity. Warith also ended the retaliatory racial rejection of whites by his father. Whites were no longer to be viewed as inherently devils and any of them converting to Islam would be admitted to membership in his sect's mosques. "There will be no such category as a white Muslim or a black Muslim", Warith declared in June 1975, "All will be Muslims. All children of God".[1] Nonetheless, those African-American Muslims led by Warith were to continue to protest perceived aggressions and oppression by racist whites in North America and Africa, and by Zionist Israelis in the Middle East against both fellow blacks and co-religionists overseas, even into the 21st century.

In the twenty-nine years of his leadership, Warith ud-Deen Muhammad has synthesized at least part of the range of functions that a viable black Islamic movement must discharge in North America: successful missionary propagation of Islam among urban blacks, both the educated and those in prisons, but with a simultaneous deflation of those tensions with Negro Christianity built up by his father's hard-hitting approach. Warith also restructured Elijah's drive to establish a black collectivist private enterprise able to give African-Americans autonomy from Euro-Americans, privatizing many of the businesses and emphasizing individualist private enterprise. Yet his followers have always kept up a discreet drive to build and expand a separate economic circuit that maintains some blacks as a quasi-nationality or micronation, even when he does not outrightly term them a people. Warith has striven to construct good relations between his black Islamic sect and white Americans, including—especially in the later 1990s—Jews. He has encouraged adherents to see themselves as American citizens and seize every opportunity that the white-dominated American system offers to them. But some of the earlier millennial thrust of the Nation of Islam began to be reactivated from the early eighties in the new "Nation of Islam" led by Louis Farrakhan, although this too may prove in the end to be a road into the Euro-managed central U.S. system—the veiled integrationism that is at least latent in all so-called "Black Muslim" sects in America.

The Black Muslims' Original Millenarianism

Until 1975, following the teachings of the Honorable Elijah Muhammad, most black Muslims conceived America's blacks to have descended from the black tribe of Shabazz in the Holy City of Mecca, Hijaz, Arabia. They believed this to be the original homeland of all the world's blacks. About 6,800 years ago, according to this mythology, one Yacub, a dissident genius in the hitherto harmonious black community in Mecca, initiated the greatest of evils. By the time he was eight, precocious Yacub had graduated from all existing colleges and universities. His boasting and divisive talk irritated the Meccan authorities so much that they exiled him and 59,999 of his followers to the island of Patmos in the Aegean Sea. There, Yacub plotted revenge. A scientist skilled in genetics, he started breeding and cross-breeding humans. This genetic grafting, carried on by successive generations of his followers for centuries after his death, culminated in the creation of the artificial white devils. Almighty God Himself, Allah, had decreed this creation of the inherently evil white devils in order to test the blacks through sufferings and tribulations. The white devils, at first walking on all fours, living in caves and trees and coupling with the beasts, stayed on Patmos for 600 years before they escaped to the mainland of Asia. Within six months of their arrival in Arabia, the white devils' trickery ignited factional fighting among the "original" blacks. Upon realizing the whites were engineering their problems, however, the blacks mounted camels and drove them from Mecca on their bare feet in chains across the burning sands of Arabia to the caves of Europe. There the white cavemen developed the Western civilization that has since conquered the world, and slaughtered and enslaved black humanity. Allah gave the white cavemen 6,000 years to perpetuate their follies and evils. By 1914 their time was up, but he gave them an unspecified period of reprieve in which to reform and atone for their crimes against the blacks. Predictably, they recklessly persisted in their devilry.[2]

Since the moment during the Great Depression when Almighty God is narrated to have appeared incarnate in the person of the "revealer", Wali Fard Muhammad, to the hungry blacks of Paradise Valley, Detroit, Michigan in 1930, divine intervention to judge, destroy, crush and incinerate the evil white world, America first, has been a daily possibility. A headline of a 1965 issue of the sect's *Muhammad Speaks* newspaper ran "Falling, Falling the Old World!" featuring this warning by Messenger Elijah Muhammad:

> Though in appearance America seems steadfast, she is moving towards the ultimate end. Salvation must come to the so-called Negro. The time of the ending of this world is now... The end is predicted and hinted in many places. Daniel (in the Bible), however, gives you a better knowledge of it than in any other place. And, the Qur'an's prophecy is exact. Do not expect ten years. The fall will be within a few days.[3]

While this was an extreme and urgent millenarian twinge, until Elijah's death in 1975 the bulk of his followers did think of him as "the Messenger of Allah" in the Last Days. From the mid-fifties to the mid-seventies, members of the Nation of Islam took seriously reports of flying saucers, which were predicted to figure in the Final Judgement. When, by AD 2000 at the latest, Allah was to annihilate all white Americans, and all Negroes who chose to live with them in their modern Babylon, huge tidal waves, storms, hurricanes and epidemics would be but a prelude to a more decisive event from the heavens. A huge half-mile-long Mother space ship would drift across the sky, releasing fifteen "baby planes", whose pilots had been brought up to destroy the world and who had never smiled. They would pour down an unbroken stream of incendiary bombs and poisonous gases onto the North American continent, igniting violent fires that would burn for 310 years, perhaps destroying all save those blacks who believed in NOI doctrine. To these elect, the baby-planes would drop leaflets in Arabic and English, directing them to routes by which to avoid the flames. After Allah had executed all whites in this Last Judgement, He would give the righteous blacks authority over the whole globe, ushering in "the New Islam", the final Age of eternal peace and happiness that bore considerable resemblance to the rather physical Paradise on Earth for which the Jehovah's Witnesses hoped after their parallel Judgment.[4]

Elijah's protest eschatology hardly lacked its paradoxes and concealed ambivalences. While the prophecies anticipated the destruction of white America, they themselves were more a home-grown mutation of Protestant apocalypticism than a transplanting of Islamic conceptions out of the Arab world. In revolt against the popular black Protestant fundamentalism in which he had been steeped from childhood, Elijah's 1965 outburst derived more from the Book of Daniel than the Qur'an. His vision of the Final Judgement gave recognition to, but thereby drained away, the underlying racial fury against the white enemy, pent up as corrosive self-hatred in most blacks. But it was left unclear whether the blacks themselves would hit back at the white Satans in a preliminary Armageddon, or whether Allah the Executioner would do all the fighting necessary. This eschatology, paradoxically, heightened black expectations to flashpoint yet simultaneously dampened down and controlled all the rage of the black lumpen psyche, then channeled it away into the arduous endeavor needed to become economic competitors of whites through collective enterprises.

A number of scholars and African-American observers have wondered if the founder of the Nation of Islam, Wali Fard Muhammad, was of an Isma'ili or Druze origin. Isma'ilism (active in the Middle East in the 9th to 13th centuries) was an outgrowth of the Shi'ite Islam that was influenced by Greek philosophy. Hierarchical in outlook, Isma'ilism held that discourse has successive levels of meaning that are known only to correspondingly graded levels in the religion's adherents and leaderships. This may have been duplicated in the black Muslims' layered language and ambiguity when mobilizing the black masses in a protest "secessionism" that culminates only in putting the followers near—or even in—the U.S. system in a modest prosperity, while making the sect's elite rich. Or Fard could have been descended from, or he and/or his followers could have listened to the Middle East's Arabic-speaking Druze, an offshoot of Isma'ilism. Judgement Day is always close for lay Druze, as for the Nation of Islam. The Druze employ Isma'ilism's gradated levels of discourse and understanding in a hierarchical leadership. Similarly eclectic, they see worth not only in the Qur'an but in a number of scriptures, including the works of philosophy of the ancient Greeks, exalted as precursors by secular America.

The Drive for a New Economy and a New Language under Elijah Muhammad

Although Elijah prophesied doom for the white devils, he saw no contradiction in calling for the building of a self-contained communal capitalist economy as an expression of a separate black nationhood. He proclaimed "hard work, thrift, and the accumulation of wealth" as religio-national obligations, and during the late 1950s and early 1960s publicized success stories of entrepreneurial initiative, the most vivid among them being a converted "mechanic on the street" who then as a member of the Nation of Islam came to own a five-storey garage and five towing trucks.[5] Millenarist predictions of the impending incineration of the whites were thus meant to give ghetto blacks confidence to compete with whites economically. The predictions fueled and cloaked a grueling process of self-Westernization in which converted blacks would replicate many of the very patterns of organization and enterprise lived by those whom Elijah denounced as doomed white devils.

However, Elijah's "Economic Blue Print for the Black Man" invoked "communalism" rather than private gain at the expense of their brothers: true Muslims should never boycott the businesses of their Muslim or black brothers; a bowl of soup should be shared by half between two black brothers; the blacks should work as hard "in a collective manner" as the white devils did for their own private advantage; members of "Black Muslim" temples would be required to give one tenth of their weekly or yearly earnings to the new Nation which was working for the collective welfare. The supportive, if authoritarian, ethos created under the Nation won the assent of the rather underpaid, unions-rejecting employees in BM grocery, clothing, dressmaking, dry-cleaning and other firms, because they felt they were working in their "own businesses" or were involved in "black ownership".[6]

The NOI's religion and puritanism were perfectly crafted to maximize the chances that the new collective business—and the mom-and-pop Muslim little corner stores—might make it through the early harsh odds to attain profitability. During Elijah's "Three-Year Economic Program for the Black Nation in America" of the early 1960s, African-Americans were to live frugally. No one was to waste money on luxuries such as expensive suits, extravagant foods or fine automobiles, cigarettes, whisky, etc. Once the program accumulated a million dollars in savings, the Nation would make it the basis for a separate nationalist banking system to service the financial needs of African-Americans, many of whom had faced degrading and exclusionist practices from the mainstream banking system.[7]

The Muslims' drive to become businessmen was aided by the breakup of the Christian-led Civil Rights movement, and the destruction that urban riots by blacks wreaked on white businesses in the ghettos of the North. After the 1967 riots in Newark, "a four to five block strip on South Orange Avenue [became] replete with Muslim restaurants, cleaning establishments and small shops," replacing those of the departed whites.[8]

By the mid-'seventies, the Muslim endeavor to construct a black cooperative capitalist economy had been sufficiently successful to win them respectability among middle class blacks and intellectuals, who had long been disdainful of the hitherto lumpen movement. By 1974, for instance, Charles 67X, as editor of *Muhammad Speaks,* issued a confident rebuke to "the educated blacks", with their "stench of marijuana", wife-swapping, bebop dancing, expensive habits, and their intellectualizing presumption that "only ghetto dwellers need to live by a decent moral code, as though they need no moral reform." But this challenge in itself showed that the Nation of Islam was now intermeshing with the black bourgeoisie and intelligentsia. In this very same context, it was announced that the Educational Seminar for the Muhammad University of Islam, College Division (in Chicago) had brought together hundreds of followers of Elijah who had certificates and degrees:

> The fact that Muslim physicians, dentists, attorneys, pharmacists, mathematicians, educators, social scientists, and every other type of professional dignitary imaginable, now follow Messenger Muhammad should be cause for open-minded consideration on the part of every black 'thinker'.

While Charles 67X may have been resentfully aware here that some members of "the bourgeoisie ... [still] don't want the rest of us around", he was increasingly viewing them as future recruits, nonetheless.[9]

Along with these drives toward a new economy, and a widening class appeal, came the steady infiltration of the Arabic language and Arab practices into the movement. Under Elijah, Black Muslim belief, terminology and practice were still often strikingly American rather than Middle Eastern. Even up to the time of Elijah's death, and despite his own requests for change after his 1959-60 pilgrimage to Muslim countries, NOI places of worship were called "temples" more often than mosques.[10] This practice was abhorrent to Muslims from the Third World who visited the NOI's centers. The Egyptian, Mahmud Yusuf al-Shawaribi, a visiting lecturer of soil science at two U.S. universities, in the 1950s objected to the NOI that they had to change the term for their houses of worship to "mosques".[11]

Although it was his son Wallace (thenceforth Warith) who secured the decisive transition to the acceptance of a comprehensive Islam, detached atoms of Arabic vocabulary did nonetheless enter and cumulatively permeate the sect's life under Elijah, often serving as foci for its parochial anti-white and millenarian sentiments. The sect early applied Arabic etymology to give the name of the incarnate man-god, Fard, political meaning, interpreting it as "independent" (among Arabic-speakers it usually conveys "individual" or "separate") to make his July 1930 arrival in Paradise Valley point to a future black state: this also equated the advent of Fard with the functions of the 4th of July of American statal nationalism. This blending of Arab and American cultures thus structured new meanings for community. Elijah also extolled Arabic as "the mother language of all the languages... the first and the last," as well as the unique beauty of Arabic characters.[12] Some time before

1965, Elijah Muhammad extolled the Qur'an as from a Black God through a Black prophet so that the devils tried to keep it from the Blacks. Its teachings would wake up the Blacks, but "to get a real Qur'an one should know the Arabic language in which it is written".[13] All this transformed U.S. Negro attitudes toward language. Accepting the Arabic greeting "As-Salaam Alaikum" employed by Elijah or Malcolm X helped restore a robbed identity, breaking the sense monolingual ghetto blacks had had that any non-English speakers they overheard, e.g. Chinese, were "talking gibberish". This transformation of attitudes by Elijah's Muslims of the 1950s and 1960s towards outside languages set African-Americans free to learn in the 1970s as a connection to the Mother Continent, Africa, and to develop relations with the Chinese and Vietnamese.

Before 1975, Arabic and Islamic motifs in the Nation of Islam addressed local torments and needs not intelligible to Muslims born outside the unique American context. Yet, their intimately American functions implanted these vocabulary-items at the very emotional heart of African-American experience at the street level. In April 1962, for instance, members of the Nation of Islam banded together to resist the pistol-whipping of two of their number by the Los Angeles police. In collectively shouting "Allahu Akbar!" (It is God who is the Greater!) they unnerved the police, which might have helped trigger violence by the latter: one Muslim was martyred and another six received bullet-wounds.[14] While "Allahu Akbar" might become a war-cry in a race war one day, in this 1962 incident, it signalled a refusal by the Muslims to let the police provoke them into counter-violence so that they could kill them. The police entered the mosque, lined the Muslims against the wall and slit their trousers off, taunting them that "we shot your brother outside: aren't you going to do anything about it?"[15] We see here how Arabic formulas and Islamic tenets coming from the Middle East distanced constriction and murderous hatred in America from the psyches of NOI members so that they maintain mental autonomy and steel-like self-control and discipline. And the East recognized its separated relatives: from the faraway Mother Continent, Presidents Nasser of Egypt and Nkrumah of Ghana issued statements criticizing the Los Angeles violence, as did the most prominent civil rights leaders in America.

The pre-1975 Muslims were as ambiguous in matters of languages as on most other things. Psychologically, the daily use of "as-Salaam 'Alaykum" as the greeting of a restored national identity could nourish cultural independence in poor ghetto blacks from the tongue of the white Anglo-Saxon overlords and open the way to learning Arabic or sub-Saharan African languages. But the Arabic shibboleths were also differentiating converts to Elijah's Islam from their black neighbors in the ghettos, whom some came to despise as self-penalizing losers. Yet the NOI's ridicule that poor Negroes "mess up" the alien English language cut out any scope for forms of spoken English evolved by Africans living in the U.S., such as the Creole language, Gullah, as one possible basis for a distinct nationalist print-English. As they hold up a formalistic or symbolic Arabic, these sects popularize by their protest discourses the literary print language of the Anglos from whom the adherents were supposed to be separating in some sense or another.

Semi-Sunni Islamic tenets and rituals were to come in the following decade. Already under Elijah, though, some slivers from Arabic functioned as emblems for a collective nationalist identity—and of a collectivist private enterprise also—with which to face not just Christian white America but also its Christian Negroes. Malcolm X brought the Arabic alphabet along when he came visiting to argue and fence with such Christian black clergy as his ideological opponent/friend Rev. Wyatt T. Walker of the "non-violent" Southern Christian Leadership Conference.[16] In naming his third daughter Ilyasah, the feminine form for the Arabic name for "Elijah", Malcolm was further applying Arabic grammar as well as vocabulary-atoms to the formation of a new Islamic black nationhood in North America.[17] Transcriptions of the Arabic terms for the functions of given Muslim stores or enterprises were sometimes included in their signs under Elijah: thus, the holy language of the Middle Eastern heartlands of the faith were also becoming insignia of the sect's secular neo-capitalist enterprise, too, in the USA. Use of Arabic by NOI private enterprises could have followed naturally from widening use of a range of atomized vocabulary from it in an emerging Muslim spoken English. Yet by using a word from Arabic, the businessman stressed to adherents and others that this was a Muslim-owned shop, offering honesty and religion-related products such as halal [religiously permissible] foods, and differentiating its nationality from that of whites through its linguistic manifestations. Or it could have been a religio-political attempt from above to use public signs to implant Arabic terms for everyday objects vividly in the minds of the adherents and the general Afro-American public patronizing such shops [as "Zionist" businessmen have done to propose or confirm Hebrew or Yiddish vocabulary among U.S. Jews] in order to create a visible cultural presence, [18] much as Quebecois nationalists in French-speaking Canada tried to legally enforce the writing of all public signs, including those of businesses, in French to help preserve ethnic identity.

By the time Elijah lay on his death-bed, Arabization was widening in NOI ceremonial life. Ultra-nationalistic Arabs had been brought into the central rituals. "By holy contract under Islamic law", in 1975, "two of Minister Louis Farrakhan's daughters" were married "to a grandson and nephew respectively of the Honorable Elijah Muhammad", with the men of the wedding party wearing fezzes and with hoods religiously veiling the hair of the women. The elegant suits and dresses approximated to mainstream American stylishness, as did the giving of rings and the cutting of the cake. But there were definite attempts to meet Islamic-world religious requirements: America-resident Palestinian professor and political activist, 'Ali Baghdadi, "masterfully performed the ceremony in Arabic and English to give the wedding... a new meaning".[19] The funeral rites that the sect gave to Elijah's wife, Clara, and to Elijah himself in 1975, had the believers facing East; they were conducted in English and Arabic, although drawing on the Old Testament, reflecting an ongoing duality, or blending, of cultures.[20] In 1974, a Missouri African-

American who had joined the NOI around 1960, made the first of his five pilgrimages to Mecca. The future Imam Shakir A. Mahmoud, who received a mainstream M.Sc., was to travel widely in the Middle East and Africa, and under Warith was to establish and teach Arabic and Islamic Studies in the sect's private school system. Carrying forward Elijah's drive to convert blacks in the prisons, Mahmoud served as one of Warith's (government-salaried?) Muslim Chaplains in that system.[21]

Tensions were smoldering beneath the surface before 1975, caused by the conflict between some tenets in Elijah's teachings and some motifs from the Qur'an or from Arab-led classical Islam. Ken Farid Hasan, his mother and siblings would race to back porches or fields, or the whole Muslim community would drive to a hilltop, to watch "the light from the Mother Plane" trail across the heavens between two and five in the mornings. While under Elijah, "we used to tick off on our fingers the many sciences the early Muslims excelled at," among them astronomy: "the West improved and expanded what the Muslims established." Hasan came to feel that the followers were not viewing that real space to be studied with physics and astronomy, but "mythological space where only the Mother Plane could go. We failed to continue the [classical] Muslim tradition" [–which, it might be contended, leads to the science of modern America].[22]

Some enthusiasts studied Arabic under 'Ali Baghdadi in the pre-1975 Nation of Islam. But the demands of hawking the sect's newspapers and fish while holding down conventional full-time jobs left only limited time. It was after Warith "lifted the burden off us" in 1975 that specialists could develop who taught Arabic in the sect and published books for that purpose. One, by Imam Abdul Hakim, a veteran from the pre-1975 NOI, was used in Northeastern University and in the 1990s brought him good royalties from the large proportion of adherents now intent on studying the language of the Qur'an.[23]

Within the U.S. context, the increased use of Arabic words to 1975 did spread the feeling that a new national culture was being constructed ("recovered"). This set the sect-members free to excise/select from Afro-American culture as much as, or more than, from Anglo culture. The Arabic terms focused [a dual] a distancing and a constructive stance towards both "Caucasian" and "Black" Americans: the "nationalist" business enterprises at least were not insurgence and might come to more and more resemble—or one day even join?—America's mainstream economy. Nevertheless, overall, the shifts towards Arab vocabulary-items and classical Islamic motifs under Elijah were still doctrinally superficial or atomistic, for the time: the Islam of Afro-Asia was not being adopted wholesale as a system. For all Malcolm X's urgent drive to fuse the sect with global Islam, most black Muslims to 1975 remained cultural Americans who were only romantically attracted to Arab culture,[24] of which they had limited knowledge and from which they selected practices and beliefs tailored to their own American needs. Millenarian visions and particularistic neighborhood enterprises still outweighed acculturative factors, but the seeds of what was to come under Elijah's son and successor, Wallace/Warith, had been sown, nonetheless.

Theological Adjustments up to 1975: The Emergence of Warith ud-Deen Mohammed

The sweeping changes Warith introduced in the black Muslim movement seemed revolutionary to the wider American and black public at the time. In reality, the transformation of 1975 and onwards resolved pre-existing tendencies to mutate the sect's Protestant-looking millenarianism into a conventional, low-key, humdrum, standard Islam as practised in Arab countries. As followers prospered and the class configuration of adherents altered, both the blatant racism (or counter-racism) and projection of an eschatological incineration of the white devils became less acceptable. Accordingly, a variety of highly-placed leaders in the sect patiently emptied Elijah's more worrying concepts of their content, though without repudiating them outright during his declining years. Wallace (later Warith) was not the only son of Elijah who phased out his father's demonization of the whites while the beloved founder-figurehead was still alive. Herbert (later Jabeer) refined it with even defter sophistry. Some years before formally converting to Islam upon his defeat of Sonny Liston in 1966, Cassius Clay (thenceforth Muhammad Ali) discussed the concept of white devilishness with Herbert, who was then one of his father's powerful deputies. For Herbert by the 1960s, "a devil" was watered down to

> one who truly leads people from Allah... a mental attitude born out of false pride and self-exalting lies... one who goes against the natural order of creation... The Holy Quran teaches us: 'No Associate has He.'

Thus, even a black who denied that God was "the Greatest" could become a devil. This was a new view of whites as people who committed crimes against the blacks because the Devil exercised possession of their minds rather than because they themselves were inherently devils by nature. When Herbert stated to Cassius Clay that "God has the power to destroy the devil without destroying the people", he had already dropped Elijah's talk of a final incineration by God-dispatched space-ships. The Nation of Islam was no "hate sect", and "Muslims in America do not hate anybody". The White Establishment, Herbert maintained, might have taught blacks to hate themselves, but the struggle of the Muslims was now directed against the inferior "conditions" imposed on blacks.

> The history of oppressed people shows that they must learn to appreciate themselves, to love themselves... My father teaches that we must have pride and respect for ourselves... Whites who treat us with respect are not looked upon as devils, not by my father.[25]

Herbert Muhammad at least paid lip-service to his father's ideology, but his brother Wallace/Warith was well known for his open, public rejections of Elijah's deviations from "Islamic orthodoxy", even prior to his father's death in 1975. At several points, Warith's rebelliousness even landed him outside the sect. His drive to change the Nation of Islam movement initially derived from Jamil Diyab, a Palestinian immigrant who was finally expelled from the movement and who then denounced Elijah as a heretic. Doing very well at Arabic as a young student in the NOI secondary school, Wallace was discreetly directed by Diyab to "look for new meanings" in the Holy Book which were not consonant with the protest millenarianism of Fard and Elijah.[26] Once appointed to be the Minister of the Nation of Islam's Philadelphia Temple from 1958, Wallace-Warith already strove for the formation of a broad-based front with such mainstream black civil rights movements as the NAACP—the exact opposite of his father's policy of boycotting the secular or Christian organizations of other blacks. By 1964, Wallace had temporarily broken with his father and the Nation of Islam leadership, and was encouraging Malcolm X—suspended from the movement in the same year—to carry through his conjunction with the normative Arabian Islam of Mecca. The Nation of Islam's "only possible salvation", he told Malcolm, lay in "accepting and projecting a better understanding of orthodox Islam".[27]

When Warith returned to the fold he was reappointed as a prominent Minister. In the last years of his father's life, he preached soothing messages of a gentle, disembodied, cherishing God, unconnected with the perceived incarnation of Wali Fard Muhammad, and eschewed all talk of white devils. His was a bland, still rather contentless, and de-politicized, version of Islam, extolling "the beneficence of Allah in the creation" and natural phenomena such as evaporation and rain. For the two years before Elijah's death in February 1975, his was nevertheless regarded as an oppositionist theology, with Wallace's name rarely appearing in the Nation's official organ, *Muhammad Speaks*. Wallace's cheerful, non-confrontationist religion, though, spoke to the growing sector of the sect which had achieved material prosperity, become middle class, and had been tinctured with Arabic and standard Islamic texts from the Qur'an and the Arab Prophet Muhammad's sayings *(hadiths)*. It was this strengthening neo-bourgeois grouping, in fact, which made sure that Wallace was chosen as his father's successor in February 1975, with an implied mandate to take the movement in a different direction.[28]

Arab World Attitudes to Black Muslims to 1975

Their anti-Americanism made the conservative scholars of Sunni and Shi'ite Islam in the Middle East flexible towards the Nation of Islam in the late 1960s and early 1970s. In a seminar at Cairo's al-Azhar University in the early 1960s, the firebrand *shaykh* (religious scholar) Muhammad al-Ghazzali, no stranger to insurgent Arab Islamists, brushed aside doubts that some NOI tenets might exclude it from Islam: the [Arab] Muslims had to welcome this group that had accepted Islam as a path to their liberation. The Middle

East Muslims should rectify misunderstandings in NOI beliefs through institutions for the international propagation of Islam—which al-Ghazzali shrewdly doubted the Muslim heartland states had adequately developed as yet. Furthermore, some Middle Eastern Muslims themselves had their own myths that deformed their Islam, the salafist al-Ghazzali tartly observed. Dr 'Abd al-'Aziz 'Amir and the aged Azharite scholar Muhammad Abu Zuhrah both wanted Arab preachers to go and live among the Black Muslims. 'Abd al-Rahman Fudah cautioned that rumors about wrong tenets among them could well have been fabricated by neo-Crusader and Zionist enemies of Islam.[29]

Monitoring from the Iran of the Shah and the Americans, the Shi'ite cleric Hadi Khosrow-Shahi agreed with the constructive approach to the NOI of the Arab Sunnis he was observing in the 1970s. Following the Islamic Revolution in Iran, successive Islamist administrations there welcomed Farrakhan, despite the fact that at the time they did so, Farrakhan's successor NOI had revived some of Elijah's old distinctive beliefs. Now, immigrant Shi'ite activists in the USA, sometimes starting in the prisons, drew a fair number of African-Americans into the collective prayers at their multiplying mosques across America.

After Elijah Muhammad's death in 1975, Warith and Farrakhan had to develop their sects in America in a context of constant communications about what constitutes Islam, coming from overseas Muslim institutions and regimes, and from the Muslim immigrants pouring into America as globalization got under way.

2: THE POST-1975 "BLACK MUSLIM" MOVEMENTS

Relations with Other Faiths, especially Christianity, under Warith's Leadership

Under Warith ud-Deen Mohammed's leadership, the successor-sect won a constant stream of converts from black Protestant Christianity to Islam. U.S. prisons provided one main recruiting ground. His personnel were performing valuable services to American society: after they converted blacks to Islam in prisons, they then took charge of their rehabilitation after release. In general, urban American blacks almost completely lack the ill-feeling towards Islam which has long been widespread among U.S. Euro-Christians and Jews. Black Christians appreciate this success of Warith's and Farrakhan's followers in rehabilitating African-American prisoners and drug addicts, in establishing an alternative network of black Islamic schools and in establishing black businesses to lift blacks out of poverty. White anti-Islamic Christian organizations tried to involve black American Christian clergy in projects to counter Warith Mohammed's and then Farrakhan's propagation of Islam. But few have consented to take part, despite some buried resentments among the clergy at "Black Muslim" (Nation of Islam) vilification during the 1960s of Christianity as a slave religion concocted by whites, and of black clerics as fawning lackeys of those devils. From 1983 onwards, as he built a role in U.S. politics for his new NOI that revived some ideas of Elijah, Farrakhan skillfully wooed and cajoled the black Christian clergies into a united front with his movement against "Zionists", neo-conservative administrations, and for cleansing and development of the Afro-American minority.

The widespread respect and acceptance which black Muslim sects command from Christian or non-religious Afro-Americans was very important for their security as a vulnerable religious minority in the difficult decades that followed Elijah's death in 1975. The Muslim sects have a self-confident attitude towards both black and white Christians—and take the initiative to arrange occasions that bring their followers together with other faiths. Such social meetings, usually termed "Interfaith Assemblies" by Warith's American Muslim Mission, defused tensions between Muslim and Christian by providing pleasant social contact—music as well as speakers. At the same time, Warith's successor-sect and then Farrakhan's splinter-movement skillfully made black converts to Islam through such interaction. The greater openness to Christians and Jews of Warith's successor-sect, which had its origin in 1975, eased its integration into general American society (in which most whites follow variants of Christianity and Judaism). The use of Biblical motifs by Warith's rival, Farrakhan, from the 1980s helped him tighten a poly-sectarian political front out of disparate Black groups in U.S. electoral politics, while at the same time working to convert some of the Christian African-Americans whom he involved.

Imam Warith's and then Minister Farrakhan's less abrasive, apparently more accepting, attitude towards Christian African-Americans seemed to forge a united black community, in stark contrast to the stance taken by Elijah Muhammad. While he lived, Elijah had talked of a proud, self-sufficient black community, but done little to weld it in co-operation with Christian black leaders. Elijah's vitriolic and contemptuous denunciations of Christianity as the religion of slavery and a tool of white domination made it psychologically difficult for black Christian clergymen to cooperate with him. For Elijah, the whites gave the Black the "poisoned book" of the Bible that required him to join the "slave religion", which taught him to love his oppressor and to pray for them who persecute him. It even taught him that it was God's will that he be the white man's slave. For Elijah Muhammad, the Bible was "the graveyard of my poor people", enjoining them to love their enemies and bless those who curse them (cf. Matt. 5:34-4, 39-40) Throughout nature, God has made provision for every creature to protect itself against its enemies; but the black preacher has taught his people to stand still and turn the other cheek. He urged them to fight on foreign battlefields to save the white man from his enemies; but once home again, they must no longer be men. Instead, they must patiently present themselves to be murdered by those they have saved. Thus the black preacher is the greatest hindrance to the blacks' progress and equality.[30]

As an ideological emblem, Christianity had a key function in the Civil Rights strategy of such leaders as Martin Luther King during the 1950s and

1960s. The obligations entailed by a Christianity shared between America's whites and blacks was a crucial psychological weapon with which the civil rights leaders morally pressured whites to release blacks from subordination and marginalization. But Elijah Muhammad and his Muslims had derided the specific aims of the Civil Rights movement. For them, the desegregation of white eating facilities, stores, places of entertainment etc. was meaningless or even harmful to the blacks, since it contributed to the diffusion of their purchasing power. Whereas the long-oppressed blacks should have been developing their own separate business and economy, desegregation would have them spending more money than ever before in the businesses of the white devils. American blacks would be transferring an even greater portion of their $20 billion dollars annual income to their white exploiters. Elijah denounced the Civil Rights movement's tactics of blended Christian-Gandhian non-violence as an open invitation to whites to violently repress blacks with impunity. The Christian black puppet "leaders" were disarming blacks and drugging them with cosmetic civil rights gains that obscured the real needs of the black poor.

The Muslim newspaper, *Muhammad Speaks*, continued to snipe at Christianity as an instrument of the satanic white oppressors right up to the death of Elijah Muhammad on 25 February 1975. The paper carried savage caricatures and cartoons that depicted black clergymen as fawning, bought lackies of white bloodsucking merchants. After Elijah died, however, Warith and his editors quickly toned down such broadsides. He moderated the critique of Christianity in the context of American society, and courted the good will of the American white majority instead of denouncing them as devils. His new moderate stance toward Christianity was widely welcomed in the ghettos and suburbs alike as an essential step towards welding the USA's blacks into a coherent political nation.

In 1977, in a speech given when consolidating his leadership and transforming Elijah's quasi-Islamic cult into a Sunni Muslim movement, Warith moved towards friendlier relations with the Christians, white as well as black. On one hand, he stated the uncompromising orthodox Sunni Muslim position that he had developed from the Qur'an: "the truth of Prophet Muhammad, which is that the truth of the Holy Qur'an, shall prevail over all the falsehoods of the world, though the enemies (the idolatrists and the polytheists) may be adverse". While he urged his followers to make the truth of Qur'anic revelation "recognized" in America, he was careful to suggest that pious Christians and Jews would not be among the "enemies" who would oppose this, for:

> whether we call ourselves Jews, Muslims or Christians or other names, we all belong to one family if we believe in one God and if we accept the revealed scriptures that came to prophets of God... It is no need for us to be working against each other when there are so many evil doers, real devils, in the world.

Satan now was a force for evil who could put on various racial and ideological identities at will, a choice, rather than all members of only one race. Warith also defined the message of Muhammad of Arabia as for all places and times: "it is not a truth for yesterday or a truth that predicts of another truth to come"—thereby refuting the claims of Elijah to be the culmination of all previous prophets.[31]

Warith's overtures towards the Christians have had real impact (a) in integrating America's now multi-sectarian black community, and (b) in America's nation-building. In regard to the black community, the stress by Warith and Farrakhan on the affinities (rather than differences) of Christianity and Islam has served as a good formula for much interfaith contact between black Muslim Imams and adherents, and black Christian clergy and congregations. With the past divisive antagonism defused, churches and mosques (masajid) have worked well together in relief activities in the depressed areas. Many black civil rights leaders in the 1950s and 1960s were Christian clergymen. Although still registering the religious difference, African-American Muslims under Warith and then Farrakhan and his followers could now join company with Christian fellow-blacks in ceremonies and functions honoring eg. the Reverend Martin Luther King's birthday. For Imam Ibrahim Pasha, King's 1984 birthday in Chattanooga showed that the "struggle for justice... [by the Bilalians: his then Arabic term for Afro-Americans] is not being limited by religion, economics or class differences".[32]

Not that Warith from 1975 ceased the Black Islamic critique of Christianity his sect had been developing since 1930: rather, he had contracted it and made it more subtle. A barrage of propaganda was still kept up to stress how intertwined white racism against blacks and Christianity in its Western versions have been. And while public critiques of Christianity's core theological tenets of the incarnate man-god (Jesus) and divine Trinity have been moderated, these successors to the old Nation of Islam tradition continue to characterize churches as places whose religious art saps the self-respect of blacks and like heroin paralyzes their will to resist racism. Warith time and again in the 1980s argued that "as long as 'white' (Caucasian) people think that their physical image is in the world as the image of God, and as long as non-Caucasians and Caucasians worship a Caucasian symbolic image of God on the cross", there will be trouble. "If we don't want dope in our communities, how much more should we be against a Caucasian image of God that makes Bilalians think inferior and act inferior" and fosters an "artificial" superiority complex in whites?"

Along these lines, Warith launched the Committee for the Removal of All Images that Attempt to Portray the Divine (C.R.A.I.D.) in June 1977. His apparent concentration of the attack upon the images of Christianity rather than its central doctrines served his neo-Sunni Muslims well. Various traditional black Christian churches still contained statues of human-god Jesus and of the apostles of Christianity, representing them as white. With the C.R.A.I.D. campaigns, Imam Warith threw the black churches in the ghettos on the defensive without conspicuously putting African-American Muslims in the confrontationist, divisive position of attacking the central tenet of Christianity per se. Warith was able to legitimize the C.R.A.I.D. campaign within mainstream U.S. institutions by support from activities that some, mostly non-Muslim, Afro-American mental health professionals had initiated to warn how white religious images can damage blacks psychologically.[33]

As a result of C.R.A.I.D. conventions, leaders in Warith's sect were let in to reach many black congregations within Christian structures. For the Dallas-Fort Worth area, Imam Qasim Ahmad was able to claim "good support from many reverends, preachers and pastors", because they all were "working [together] on common goals"—helping lift the ghetto masses out of poverty and immorality, marching together against wrong images in religion. Christian African-Americans were moved in church services by the black Muslim ensemble led by song-writer Wali Ali, and joined in its refrain which questioned "why we pray to a Caucasian man". It was while giving a 1982 talk in a Methodist Church and in the context of a C.R.A.I.D. convention in Dallas, that Warith made his coalitionist approach an ideology as well as a tactic. Global Islam was now woven into local relationships between U.S. groups. To validate his call for "Muslim-Christian unity in the effort to make life better for the [African-American] people", he cited the creative coexistence that Muslims and Christians once achieved in Arab Spain, although this ended in mass expulsion in 1492—to the regret of ordinary Christians there, Warith hastened to add.[34] The problem of the Christian-Muslim divide among Blacks, and Warith's recourse to classical Muslim macro-history to narrow it, persisted. A full two decades later, in 2004, W.D. Mohammed gave a speech in a Harlem Baptist church in which he presented himself on a national footing as having come "to address the condition of his people, the African-American people." He was explicitly trying to lead his own adherents "away from the spirit that we should separate from our Christian... African-American brothers and sisters." To reverse this, Warith affiliated himself to the classical Arab-led Muslims in a selective, critical way. He let slip that the anti-Christians among his followers were classicist Islamists themselves in that they followed those Muslim leaders who "after the passing of the Prophet [Muhammad] lost the true idea of faith and its purpose and have become afraid of Christianity and imagine that it has power over the Qur'an and the Muslim life"[—which may itself have implied a strategy on his part to use contact with them to sap the tenets of Christian blacks?]. The classical Islamic model that Warith held up was from the earliest point: those followers of Muhammad who fleeing the persecution by the pagans in Mecca were granted asylum in the Christian kingdom of Abyssinia/Ethiopia. That ancient welcome from the Christian society of Ethiopia obliged contemporary Muslims to be the allies of Christians (and all good people) who do good works, imaged Warith.[35]

Under Elijah Muhammad, the NOI theme that images of Christianity's prophets and god-human as "Caucasian" were crucial for white "mental control" of blacks had focused rage already seething in African-American teenagers, converting them.[36] Was Warith after 1975 genuinely narrowing or even ending his tradition's war against Christianity, or did he regard its past association of whiteness with godhood as just one, visible, side-effect of its inbuilt blasphemy of deifying a human? Was Christianity still his real target, giving what he had to believe as now an orthodox Muslim?

By the 21st century, leaders of Wallace/Warith's sect had been taking part in multi-racial meetings and conferences of the religions attended by whites, including American Jews. Warith Mohammed had evolved what looked like cordial relations with Euro-American and Hispanic Catholic clerics. The August 2, 2002 issue of *Muslim Journal* announced that W. Deen Mohammed's sect was selling a book by Imam Mustafa El-Amin titled *Christianity and Islam: Highlighting Their Similarities: The Road to Peace.*[37] Another August 2002 article in Muslim Journal recorded that some Catholic leaders in inter-religious relations urged the 63 million Catholics in the U.S. to be tolerant of Muslim compatriots after September 11, which ignited all the American mass-culture stereotypes and images of Muslims as terrorists out to murder women and children. That was a stand for which Warith and his colleagues were understandably grateful.[38]

Euro-Christian churches could not be taken over from within, and Imam Warith Mohammed had to court their favor. The sect may have entered and advised black churches, though, as a tactic to sap and erase their Christianity over the long term. Warith and his imams suggested that they were devoid of animus against Christianity's central tenet, and were merely coming into the churches to help direct their Christian brothers and sisters away from certain malfunctions. But it was long much harder for black Christians to get into his mosques to advise! In 1985, Warith had warned his followers not to take Jews or Christians as "protectors" (awliya') [Qur'an 5:51]: inter-faith meetings did not mean that "Muslims should invite non-Muslims to come in and help Muslims work out their direction." Nor were his Muslims as yet "established" enough, either, to employ Christians or whites [a tightening-up from his father who had employed some in NOI businesses]. A full ten years after becoming leader, Imam W.D. Mohammed was still ruling out inviting non-Muslims to his conferences even to imply a different viewpoint. Jews and Christians had their own concerns at heart: "once I start looking to them to protect [and direct] my Islamic life, I am in serious trouble".[39] Were the black churches who let him enter and pass through them?

Coalitionism: The Farrakhan Group's Attitudes to Christianity

From its outset in the late 1970s, Farrakhan's revival of the NOI, like Warith's group, broke with Elijah's old vilification to evoke closeness to Christianity as the living religion of the largest single section of African-Americans. These over-emphatic gestures to Christianity sometimes had a propagandistic and Machiavellian texture—one often suspects that both Farrakhan and Warith and their adherents want to get closer to pious black Christians in order to wean them away to Islam over the long term. Compared with Warith's group, Farrakhan and his followers gestured to Christianity more in the context of their tireless campaigns to construct a broad political united front with all non-Muslim African-Americans. While Warith wanted his sect, with its never-ending changes of names and forms, to build reasonable relations with all willing Christian groups, black or white, Farrakhan was in the opposite position of already enjoying a huge—nominally Christian—African-American following that dwarfed his 50,000 to 100,00-strong sect, much smaller than Warith's, which had a range of schools and other institutions that Farrakhan was never able to build.

Farrakhan manipulated Muslim and Christian terminologies to slide around the disparities between the two religions, addressing his Black Christian audiences with metaphors and rhetoric that would be received naturally by them as Christians, towards a joint politico-racial protest in the setting of which they might, many years down the track, convert to his Islam en masse. A central meaning of "Islam" in Arabic is "submission to the will of Allah". In Alabama in August 1996, a large Black audience erupted in applause to hear Farrakhan mention Jesus Christ. A "Muslim" is one who submits his or her will to do that of God. "Christ," he said in the style of the Third World's Orthodox Sunni Islam, "submitted his will to do God's will: therefore, to be a true Christian or a true Muslim is one and the same". Because it served the profound need that African-Americans feel for a unification of their now multi-sectarian people, at least some of the Christian Blacks present clearly failed to grasp that Farrakhan's semantics had in fact replaced the Christian deification of Jesus with the Islamic conception of the Prophet Jesus ('Isa) as only a distinguished human following in the tradition of the chain of prophets who had served God and liberated their peoples in the Middle East—his Christian audience were just relieved to learn that the Muslims too believed in Jesus, as well as united black self-help in the here and now.[40] During his 1986 lectures to university students in Ghana, Farrakhan shrank Jesus—"a man born of a woman"—down to the same human dimensions as the prophet Muhammad in Arabia, to an educated audience that was mainly nominally Christian. The "serious leadership" of Jesus and Muhammad in reviving, civilizing and uniting their bygone peoples, Farrakhan and perhaps Ghanaian President Jerry Rawlings and certainly the Rev Jesse Jackson were now duplicating for blacks in the late 20th century.[41]

By legerdemain, then, Farrakhan had ended Christ's status as One of Three Persons of God that is the basis of Christianity, making ordinary African-Americans complicit in this shift in general mass African-American religion towards Islam that had been underway since 1913 but especially after 1960. In their millenarian spasms, Farrakhan and his adherents may covertly detest stubbornly Christianist Blacks as irrevocably tainted by whites and thus themselves marked as among those whom God may soon annihilate. Yet the transition from millenarianism to an ameliorist drive to change social and political marginalization by organizing a united front of "darker"—or even in the end just "poor"?—Americans can gradually erode this dichotomization of Muslim and Christian groups within the "united" African-American community if it achieves enough results.

It was a moot point at the close of the twentieth century if either Farrakhan or Warith's groups have ever truly changed the sect's old virulent antipathy to certain aspects of Christianity. As Farrakhan and his ministers directed compliments at least to black Christianity and those of its clerics who had also sought to improve the socio-economic well being of African-Americans, his paper in the 1980s and 1990s continued to print the old blanket indictments by Elijah Muhammad. In one, Elijah derided Black "lovers and followers of white Christians" who could not love and unite with each other in their churches. This flowed naturally from the fact that "the basic aim and purposes of the religion, Christianity, was to deceive other races, namely, the black, brown, yellow and red, to make an easy prey for the white race".[42]

3: RESPONSES TO THE POST-1973 SOCIAL CRISIS

The Muslims' Struggle Against Ghetto Decay, Crime and Black Lumpen Sub-Culture

During Elijah Muhammad's leadership, as we saw, the Nation of Islam sustained the most uninhibited, never-ending torrent of denunciations of whites. However, various scholars viewed much of this tirade as a verbal screen behind which the black Muslims installed a far-reaching critique of the ethos, sub-culture and life-style of the black ghettos' lumpen-proletariat poor. The real target of their attacks has thus been black popular culture, which they wanted to eliminate as a barrier to the achievement of focused enterprise and material prosperity in the mainstream of America's society and economy. In this sense, most or all Islam-influenced movements among African-Americans have always, in trying to make poor African-Americans more Islamic, concomitantly also made them more, not less, like the white Americans they denounced in business enterprise and techniques. A melancholy possibility is that Elijah and some adherents, in denouncing the cynical tricks and manipulations of discourse with which some Euro-Americans exercised power against blacks and non-whites, may have imbibed some of those techniques.

Under Chief Imam Warith's leadership from early 1975, the "Black Muslims" continued their pursuit of this prosperity, but it was a goal they saw more and more clearly would take much longer and be much harder to achieve in America than they had conceived under Elijah. The rejection of black urban lumpen life-styles, formerly implicit under Elijah, became frankly, explicitly and systematically analyzed under Warith. In 1984, the *American Muslim Journal* publicized Dr Thomas Sowell's book, *The Economics and Politics of Race*. In this work, so the journal told its Afro-American readers, Sowell had shown that Asians and Jews succeeded economically despite the handicap of racial dislike they faced from white Christian Americans. In contrast, Bilalians (Blacks), Puerto Ricans and Mexicans had a "cultural flaw" that prevented them from succeeding materially and in careers in the USA—and which, Imam Warith stressed, consigned them to poverty, unlike immigrant blacks from the West Indies or Africa, Asians and Cubans.[43] Warith's contention, however, was that the ghettos' long-standing under-development and criminality could be overcome, that individual blacks could flourish in small-scale businesses, and that his Muslim adherents could integrate themselves into the mainstream of American society rather than withdraw from it.

Warith made many friendly gestures to the U.S. system but that system's authorities were slow to smile back at the African-American Muslim community. In 1984, the Graham Correctional Center in Hillsboro, Illinois, denied converted prisoners their religious right to carry out "Jum'ah [Friday collective] prayer". The "Muslim ummat" (congregation/"nation": Iranian and South Asian version of Arabic "ummah") in the prison therefore filed suit against the institution to win their right to practise the rituals of Islam in full. But under Warith's non-confrontationist leadership, his sect's chaplains preferred to build working relations with prison authorities in which they worked to constructively register protests and secure benefits for incarcerated blacks, amid the accelerating spread of Islam. For some black critics, the frequent use of Arabic phrases by Warith's followers (and Farrakhan's to a lesser extent) smacked of middle class intellectuals, but it could also function as one point of attraction for the category among lumpen blacks incarcerated in U.S. prisons that is most alienated from American society. A symbolic or emblemic withdrawal from the English language through study of Arabic and the injection of splinters of it into daily speech can be therapeutic for the blacks who have been most wounded by America and have most injured each other. The limited Arabic distances and relativizes the unfriendly Anglomorph America for an interim—also the function of Hebrew and Judaism for Jews in their entry of America. The assertion of Divine space through a sacred—yet very political—language does not entail any armed confrontation against the system that would be much more dangerous to the blacks than for the whites.[44]

Although the types of hostility to America that both Warith's and Farrakhan's sects focus vary, as a presence each has also worked to make the prison sector of the U.S. system work more constructively. The prison component of the U.S. elite understands and responds to that. Farrakhan's sect, too, has reformed, as it converts, a fair number of African-American prisoners, so that some hard-pressed prisons allowed his ministers, as they had Warith's chaplains, free entry. In mid-2005, California's oldest prison, San Quentin Penitentiary, even let Farrakhan himself in to address the staff and those under detention. Farrakhan stressed that nearly seven out of 10 inmates who are released return within two years because they have not been properly rehabilitated in prison and they are not offered lawful employment when they leave. In the vein of the earlier more militant black Muslim movement, Farrakhan hinted that some unnamed whites "at the top" wanted to keep blacks in the prisons. Yet the atmosphere was relaxed: he complimented the veteran woman warden for bringing the civilizing touch of a female, an aspect of God, to bear. He also reflected that the aim of Islam was not to cause hatred and division but to teach Blacks to respect themselves, and as a consequence the others (=whites!). All prisoners listening could be redeemed. An official of Governor Arnold Schwarzenegger came, perhaps in recognition of Farrakhan's work to stop black and other gangs killing each other in California.[45]

Elijah Muhammad was adept at putting the Nation of Islam on parade in Negro neighborhoods. This was to ensure that Islam, its practices and his group were woven inextricably into the daily life and needs of urban Afro-Americans in general, not just the lives of the believers and converts. The Warithite Muslims' observance of the holy fasting month of Ramadan in the city of Camden, New Jersey, in 1984 carried forward that pattern. At the end of a Zuhr (Noon) prayer, Resident Imam Fareed Munir reminded those in the masjid (mosque) that "we are obliged to not just read our Qur'ans but also to live the Qur'an physically". Comprehensive Islam, he asserted, required "the believers ... as citizens of the city ... to demonstrate their concerns regarding the mental and physical decay taking place in the city". He thereupon led 80 members of the Camden masjid on a "Moral Walk" through the streets of Camden. Under the "benign neglect" that black ghettos have all-too-often experienced in the USA, the block-long Kaighns Strip "is proliferated with trash of all types—paper, liquor bottles, drug paraphernalia and people of the same persuasion. Over the past few years a number of people have been killed on the strip". After Imam Munir formed a circle of the believers, "the believers recited Al-Fatihah [opening surah of the Qur'an] and immediately afterwards began cleaning the entire block". The masjid security team stood by throughout the cleaning to safeguard the Imam and particularly Muslim sisters from neighborhood thugs.

During their parade through the black areas of Camden, the black Muslims held up placards: "Imam W.D. Muhammad is Our Moral Leader", "Save Our Children: No More Dope", "No More Prostitution". Over an amplifier, Imam Munir denounced deviant features of lumpen-proletariat black ghetto life-style and bid for the support of the non-Muslim bystanders. "The good people of the City of Camden are not the criminals—the pimps, prostitutes, junkies and freaks are the criminals". Showing their support, numerous non-Muslim black passersby joined the march and helped the Muslims clean up the block.

The Ramadan march in Camden showed the credibility and respect that African-American Muslims had won among the urban black poor in the USA. They were presenting an Islam that held out the promise that a viable black community could be brought together even in ghettos blasted by severe urban blight and social ills. Their Arabic formulae and rituals have served as emblems that focused their hostility and resistance towards existing less desirable black lumpen behavioral patterns and culture, more than against the Angloid-American system that was the ostensible target. Having cleaned up the Negro slum in Camden, the Muslim men, women and children "with tools and signs in hand ... proceeded back to the masjid, reciting in unison "Allahu Akbar, Allahu Akbar" (God is the Greatest) and "La Ilaha illallah" (There is no God but Allah). Such Arabic statements of Islamic belief , as slogans mirrored the continuing creative tension between the black Muslims after 1975 and the milieu in which their sect crystallized, their simultaneous sense of belonging in—but determination to transform—the black ghettos. There is potential for violence in such militant denunciation of other existing sub-cultures, resented by some of the ghetto non-Muslim lumpens they are determined to reclaim. Before leaving the cleaned strip, Imam Munir warned the local residents that the Muslims "would be monitoring" it and had "another strategy" if the "riff-raff" dirtied it again.[46]

The drive of Wallace/Warith's Muslims to eliminate crime from black communities in America could cost martyrs at any minute. Activist Richard Walker Karriem preached Islam's reformatory truths to the pimps, prostitutes, drug pushers and homosexuals in the notorious Farish Street area of Jackson, Mississippi. On 7 January 1984, the criminal element murdered Karriem. After burying him, Imam 'Ali Shamsid-Deen of the Jackson mosque led the attending Muslims in a protest march down Farish Street. The marchers' slogans against pimps, prostitutes, drugs and homosexuals drew support from some onlookers and also hostile shouts from others. The black Muslims' pressure and militancy greatly impressed Jackson Mayor Dale Danks: an at least "temporary and cosmetic" intensification of police patrolling in Farish Street followed. In other cities, such as Brooklyn, New York, members of local pro-Wallace/Warith congregations attempted to facilitate police raids on drug trafficking in black ghettos and even set up armed guards to ensure drug dealers did not return to the old haunts from which the Muslims had driven them. But the poor police response made the Muslims suspicious that the drug peddling involved elements in the police force itself.[47]

While Warith probably built up a stable audience (as against members) of over two million over his thirty years of leadership, it was Farrakhan with his name-recognition for masses who would be listened to by the most alienated, most atomized, black youth completely outside the system. Unlike Warith, Farrakhan also was seen as not just about Islam but a representative of the African-American ethnos as a whole, and thus a potential mass-leader with the standing to negotiate on its behalf with contiguous *ethne*. Farrakhan over 25 years, aided by his mass-media, accordingly strove to wean black youth off drugs, helped negotiate truces between black gangs, and tried to stop Blacks and Latinos from drifting into conflict with each other. In a mid-2005 address at a California college, he tried to sensitize gang leaders to the pain mothers felt when their sons were killed in "senseless violence in our communities," and the inherent value of life. Offering to give his life if the gang-members would only stop fighting, Farrakhan lamented that after fifty years of his activism "I am tired of looking like some entertainer that you have come to hear, then take yourself back to doing what you are doing." The new NOI—as always—delivers its sharp pan-Islamic focus on international relations in addressing young alienated local groups on the USA's domestic crisis. In this "Stop the Killing Rally," Farrakhan contended that "America is the chief gangbanger for her pervasive history of killing for power": when the Taliban rejected America's demand to lay an oil pipeline through Afghanistan, its negotiators had warned "you either get a carpet of gold or a carpet of bombs." After the Berlin Wall fell, the CIA reassigned some of its agents in Europe to set black gangs fighting, he imaged.[48]

These Muslim sects' juxtaposing of local social pain with fragments of the foreign language Arabic, and with international conflicts of America with Third World people, could one day focus some truly radical rejection of the system by masses they admonish. But Farrakhan, like Warith's imams, has been well aware that many or most ordinary blacks are not taking the social exhortations to heart. Farrakhan, like the Warithites, has often been trying to help keep America from falling apart. In the twenty-first century, such constructive roles in holding together America's fragile social fabric predominated over his residue of the old NOI's sense that God might destroy the world, however much the USA's problems and issues of power could foster that level of despair.

Addressing Chicago African-Americans in early 2005, Farrakhan again said that he would offer up his own life for an end to "the killing of one another in our communities." His was a great and by nature righteous people, but one that had been made evil, perhaps only temporarily, by "circumstances" [=whites and social structure] and by lack of knowledge. The Qur'anic surah "al-'Asr", the Age or Time in which all are in loss "except those who enjoin one another to truth and enjoin one another to patience" (Q 103) evoked some crisis. This 2005 response of Farrakhan to social disorder could make that surah's wording, and the American social situation he described, cover any of four solutions for African-Americans: (a) God might destroy most humans, (b) U.S. society could disintegrate, (c) African-Americans might somehow exit from that society in some kind of self-determination or (d) the dominant Euro-Americans might reach a settlement with their black fellow-Americans. In regard to wholesale extermination by God, Farrakhan referred his audience back to old teaching of Elijah Muhammad that "we are living in the time of the Judgement," already showing itself in unusual blizzards and earthquakes that will become more and more the cold violent winds with which God destroyed the wicked in ancient times. But regret at unraveling and disintegration in U.S. society was stronger in this communication from Farrakan. As well as the hierarchy of the whites over the blacks, there are internal class and generational divides splitting the ranks of the African-Americans, also.

Because he wanted to win some of the most alienated youth, and because he truly felt some of their pain, Farrakhan in 2005 saw class dimensions or adjuncts to national oppression. The Roman authorities had built their power on the backs of the poor, and thus feared Jesus because he was a revolutionary. Farrakhan implied that the indigenous rich, too, disliked Jesus' message. He rebuked closed churches and mosques that the poor and youth refused to hear because they had no concern for their interests or to reach them. Here Farrakhan may have harbored some introspection and self-criticism of his second Nation of Islam. His sense that he and his followers were developing a financial and class status that could set them aprt from the poor masses they claimed to lead may have been focused for him by an incident in classical Islam that he mentioned. The Prophet Muhammad Ibn 'Abdallah, attentive to a powerful figure he was courting, once turned away from a poor blind man who wanted to question him: Allah rebuked him in surah 80 'Abasa, "he Frowned," of the Qur'an. As regarded possibility (c), i.e. some partial separation/exit or complete independence from "the Caucasians," Farrakhan referred to God's prediction to Abraham that his seed would serve as strangers in a land that is not theirs, then come out of it with great substance. Thus, the special Time in which the walls of racism and injustice are coming down in America could end in independence.

But now, for Farrakhan, class divisions separating blacks from each other were more in play than before. About possibility (d), that blacks and the white power structure might come to terms if he could again muster above one million people before Congress in Washington as pressure, Farrakhan was ambiguous as usual. Elijah Muhammad had said that the unity of "Black people" would be more powerful than a hydrogen bomb [=it could explode America into violence, although a second March on Washington at its outset would still only be pressure or a form of lobbying of a representative body]. Farrakhan spoke of reparations from the whites as "serious work that needs to be done." This may be the ameliorist solution for which he secretly hoped. But he was, realistically, not very hopeful. He preferred to at least place a demand note that would never be considered so as to free his people of their illusion that there could be a benevolent White man in the White House. Would it be revolution then? Finally, Farrakhan quoted the Qur'an that Allah will never change the condition of a people until they change within themselves" (Q 13:11). "You have the power to make a change in yourself" he told restless youth—all these stormy, socially angry, apocalyptic discourses of the Muslim sects could once more boil down to self-improvement and reunification of a humane black society under guidance from a Leader and the Bible and the Qur'an. In regard to choice of language and its aestheticism, this speech by Farrakhan was going towards Warith's group because most of it was covered with a patina of citations from the Qur'an and an episode in the life of Muhammad of Arabia, and applied simple Arabic grammar to analyzing a black crisis and solutions to it, although he did still quote the Bible somewhat.[49]

From Elijah's Rhetorical Secessionism to Frank Integration

Preceding data on the milder Wallace/Warith movement underscored that intractable problems in the ghettos could make any "Black Muslim" movement resolved to set them straight set off the violence that is always pent up and latent. Yet the attempts, not very hopeful, by Warith's followers to make U.S. institutions work were not opposed to the main thrust of the development of these related sects over decades. Despite the Black Nationalist rhetoric against the white devils from 1930, these sects' real enterprise was reformation and transformation of the American Negroes that would fit them into many of the main patterns of productive American society—changes that would not require any real secession. In the economic sphere, all leaderships in the NOI tradition tried to inculcate in converts something that was very like the white Anglo-Saxon Protestant work ethic, the American entrepreneurial, go-getter spirit, and material acquisitiveness. Under Elijah Muhammad, in particular, the drive to achieve prosperity had a collectivist nationalist twist, with a real sense of responsibility for the well being of the other members. Elijah Muhammad's Nation of Islam founded a $95 million empire of interlocking black Muslim small businesses and farms. It was a black co-operative capitalism with Islamic emblems. The Qur'an's concerns to construct families and to regulate, not end, commercial activity also fed the sense in the various NOIs that male members of families are responsible for providing for wives and children through entrepreneurship or other employment, however hard that may be to find or devise in economically depressed segregated ghettoes.

Upon Warith's succession in February 1975, the push to enter the mainstream of American life became more patent. He now abolished the NOI national flag of a white crescent on red background that Elijah had propagated: adherents now had to salute America's national flag, the stars and stripes. The collectivist NOI enterprises were extensively privatized, but the believers were given the priority as purchasers, and the sect continued to coordinate the drive to succeed in business as a collective enterprise of the sect, with Islam now invoked as a motivation more than the frank nationalism of Elijah. When Warith was lifted on the shoulders of 20,000 Muslims shouting "Allahu Akbar" (God is the Greatest), and thus proclaimed Chief Imam, the American economy was still performing strongly, which made prospects for taking his movement into the economic mainstream look bright. Warith's integrationism and American patriotism looked to be an appropriate strategy for black Americans. The rise of oil prices from 1973 onwards, however, gradually sank the U.S. into economic depression; and the effects on urban lower-class blacks were severe.

By mid-1982, Reaganomics was in full swing and it had become very hard for many African-American Muslims to believe that the white mainstream of American society could ever take the well-being of under-privileged blacks to heart. The operation of the untrammeled free-market forces under the Reagan administration devastated the black Muslims' property holdings, businesses and living conditions. The tone of Chief Imam Warith Deen Muhammad's speeches and statements became markedly somber, in keeping with the grim conditions facing lower-class urban American blacks, still an important constituency and recruiting-ground. Warith chose "The Dignity of Work" as the theme for the 1982 Annual New World Patriotism Day Parade. This speech expressed (a) the black Muslims' tenacious determination to challenge the U.S. system positively, or to make it yield returns to Afro-Americans; and (b) the harsh reality that employment opportunities continued to elude many U.S. blacks.

Warith stressed a theme which had been central in Nation of Islam communications under his father, Elijah, prior to 1975—that uneducated, poverty-stricken American blacks have to take at least some responsibility for their own fate, and try to lift themselves up by their own exertions. For younger blacks faced with poverty, Imam Muhammad counseled a resolute, earnest, unflagging initiative. As Muslims, their drive to meaningfully relate to American society had to be focused on the well-being of their families, despite the very unfavorable conditions amid which blacks were trying to reconstruct families. Imam Muhammad recalled his own period of poverty when he had left the Nation of Islam in protest at the tenets and policies of his father, Elijah. Warith, with his wife and children, had been on his own then: unable to get anything else, he had washed windows to keep the respect of his family.[50]

Imam Warith here reiterated a core theme that the sect had always maintained since their emergence in 1930. Labor, lawful work that does not harm others and is socially recognized, is essential for all male black Americans. Throughout all the permutations of their attitudes to white mainstream society, the black Muslims have always maintained their drive to construct patriarchal families and win jobs for their male members. Indeed, in all the periods of their movement, they have invested work, jobs—and resultant final economic affluence or independence—with religious significance. [Islam is a holistic religion: its holy book, the Quran, discusses the full range of dimensions of the believers' needs: physical, socio-economic, political and spiritual]. For Muslims, to be dependent and on welfare is death—which was the rhetoric of Farrakhan's movement also.[51]

When he was leader, Elijah Muhammad had prepared his followers to expect little from the U.S. system. In altering this policy, and somehow hoping that the U.S. system could still be remade to meet the blacks' vital needs, his son, Warith, exhorted his followers to try out more participatory solutions. By 1982, however, his hopes had in large part dribbled away: the American capitalist system was not eliminating the ghettos and their attendant problems. True, in his talk on work at his sect's annual Patriotism Day Parade he was still groping for new expedients to extend the capitalist system to make it function for, and incorporate, blacks. He had already discussed with followers the use of "I love America" pageantry and publicity of those Patriotism parades to "reach out to ... the big companies". He toyed with a strategy in which "some of those foundations established by the big companies that have done so much already to help human beings live a better life, would come out and identify with this grass-roots cry to society for help". He believed that it was in the enlightened self-interest of the great capitalist American companies to respond to the black Muslims' constructive challenge to the system. Most "people without money, people without jobs, people without a high culture base" "just start screaming and tearing the place down." Not that he was after financial contributions to his sect from the American capitalist big companies: what he wanted was for the companies to "fund programs" that would increase jobs for African-Americans and draw the existing black American private enterprise into the mainstream American economy. The alternative to some such partnership, Warith hinted, would be a property-destroying, violent Black Nationalist protest movement.

Imam Warith, admittedly, could hardly overlook the suspicion and hostility of the powers-that-be towards attempts at innovation to or modification of the system, yet he pressed on to suggest that "the establishment or the government" should subsidize the part-time employment by blacks of the lonely black elderly who needed modest auxiliary roles, which they could get within his sect. "Every time you suggest an idea like this", he recognized, "people think you are Socialist, people think you are Communist. But I think that's intentionally done to frighten us away from insisting that society be sensitive to social change". Warith was only too well aware of pressures to insist that America conform to Friedmanite paradigms, and thus to free market forces, regardless of the consequences to blacks.[52]

Despite the setbacks inflicted by recession and Reaganomics upon the drive of Warith's Muslims to build up black private enterprise, acquire property and achieve prosperity, the sect doggedly persevered with its quest. The black Muslims' campaigns of collective buying and selling of essential commodities, mainly food, crudely foreshadowed by Elijah's NOI, into the 1980s and early 1990s significantly lowered the followers' expenditure on food, cushioning them against inflation. By 1984, after nearly a decade had passed since the death of Elijah, Warith's Muslims still remained interested in small privately-owned businesses as a road to break out of the cycle of poverty. However, they were also alert to new openings in the professions within white corporate capitalism and in government—such as legal assistants and in computer law.[53] It was the American way: up, over and out. By the 21st Century, Imam Mohammed's sect had a stratum of rising businessmen, police officers, officials in local government, and skilled personnel in the pharmaceutical and other industries. Members had been equipped to succeed in the professions by their drive to win degrees in mainstream universities.[54] The projects and patterns of collective uplift by W.D. Mohammed's sect have diversified or changed since 1975. Nonetheless, in mid-2005 the sect was celebrating the Collective Purchasing Conference with an annual Memorial Day. Warith's group may be using such rituals, ratified by city-level governments in the U.S., to draw in Christian small business persons among African-Americans, and from other groups (probably Hispanics and immigrant Muslims) into its drive for "Economic Dignity" through small enterprises.[55]

Overall, the class status and incomes of a large part of Warith's adherents gradually rose over the years, despite difficulties in some intervening periods. His political positions shifted to further the membership's changing interests. While Warith/Wallace started his leadership as something like a left-Democrat, who put into the minds of his followers that they should vote for Jimmy Carter, he sometimes veered later in the 1990s towards giving support for the Republican Party, for some contexts at least.

Unlike Warith and his sect, Farrakhan and his revived new Nation of Islam from 1979 were slow to drop for good the millenarian hope that Allah might incinerate the whites who calmly viewed the torments and disintegration of the masses of blacks. Yet the two had the same elements, albeit in differing proportions. In denouncing its effects upon Arab and Muslim populations across the oceans, Warith's followers could vent their anger against the internal U.S. system. Lacking the coherence of Elijah's discourse as ideology (he had dropped key outdated features and myths that had held that together), Farrakhan swung between quasi-secession, incineration by God, and seeking affiliation with or functioning within, the U.S. system as economy and government, as all now possibilities. In the latter course, system-engagement, the new NOI has considered both (a) Republican-like self-help, the Black poor redeeming and raising themselves through collectivist ethnicity and private enterprise, and (b) Democratic Party-like statal ameliorism in which government gives some timely aid. Approaches (a) and (b) have likewise been tested by Wallace/Warith's group.

Farrakhan's tenseness and dividedness vis-à-vis America's mainstream capitalism and government won him a hearing from the established black bourgeoisie. In 1997 he addressed the Blacks in Government's ("BIG") convention in Washington. His separation-affiliation duality there served as their warning to the system for which they worked, to give them greater respect and more roles. In his secessionist mode, Farrakhan argued that neither during nor after Emancipation "have we been even asked whether we wanted to be a part of this government that had enslaved us." In the other direction, he now saw the U.S. Constitution [which Imam Warith put beside the Qur'an] as inspired from the teachings of Jesus because the wise, skilled Founding Fathers had loved the Bible, although not enough to apply it to blacks. Ah, if only the U.S. system could be extended to apply that Constitution's provisions to African-Americans as well! Jesus had required his adherents to feed, clothe, shelter and treat "the least of my brethren" as much as him. Both the teachings of Christ, and the pursuit of happiness specifically protected under the U.S. constitution, thus demanded that the U.S. government actually govern in the ghettos to end the hunger, the homelessness of ex-soldiers in cardboard boxes, lack of health insurance and medical treatment, and lack of good schools there [=a second New Deal?]. But instead of making itself thus "rooted in God," the government was violating these human rights of "the American people" [*sic*] of whom only thirty percent had voted for Bush Jr.

Farrakhan had a fair bit of Warith's commitment to make the U.S. central system work. But if it could not be, then he was ready to consider more options than was Warith. If government remained way off base, then the U.S. constitution provided for "the Right of the People to alter or abolish it." Yet to what might that boil down, for him too—mobilizing the black vote to get someone other than Bush elected? Pulling Farrakhan to such a moderate, constitutional, integrationist solution was his dawning religious sense that the groups in the quilt of "the American people" all equally reflected the God who created America—a touch of the recurring Christian and old NOI sense of the believers as the collective body of God. But that also might make him feel the anger among poorer Euro-Americans at domestic and foreign policies of the government that wronged them too. He understood why many more Timothy McVeighs might be coming, although he was well aware that blacks might suffer from that.[56]

Farrakhan was playing on the insecurity of bourgeois African-Americans oppressed in hostile workplaces in order to affiliate and recruit them. Their ameliorist wish to improve the uncordial U.S. system that at least offered them livelihoods, and the second NOI's own drive for businesses, wealth and status, made revolts and divine incinerations less desired.

4: POST-1975 ATTITUDES TO OVERSEAS MUSLIMS AND AFRICANS

Black Muslim Attitudes to Israel and Middle Eastern Affairs

Verbalistic support over decades for the Palestinians in their struggle against Israel has been the main trans-continental pan-Islamic endeavor of the black Muslim sects of Elijah Muhammad, Warith ud-Din Muhammad, and Louis Farrakhan Muhammad. Any serious conjunction of African-Americans with Arab correligionists in the Middle East had to entail some engagement with Palestinian nationalism, given that the creation of Israel broke the geographical continuity of the Muslim world, created dispossessed Palestinian populations, sparked wars that killed many Muslims, and that some important shrines of Islam were in the territories conquered by the Jewish state in 1967.

On the whole, the more bourgeois followers and media of Warith after 1975 criticized faraway Jews in Israel while down-playing ethnic tensions with American ones: they tacitly carried forward the construction of the Americanist community for which Warith/Wallace called. The sect's orientation to distant Arabs thus did not harm their internal U.S. integrationism. In contrast, Farrakhan's media sniped at U.S. Jews more than Israeli ones, while carrying substantial coverage of the Middle East, and analyses by Palestinian nationalists.

African-American solidarity with the faraway Arab world was also fed by the progressive deterioration of Black-Jewish relations in the United States from the 1950s. However, a sometimes superficial conjoining of the Palestinians' plight and that of the American lumpen blacks made attitudes peculiarly bitter during the 1980s.[57] Warith's columnists deduced that the United States' bankrolling of an Israel that looked expansionist in their ideology, siphoned away funds from America's own poverty-stricken blacks. "This year [1984]", wrote columnist Munir 'Umrani in Warith's paper, "Israel, which is actually Occupied Palestine, is supposed to pay you, the U.S. tax-payer, U.S. $945 million you probably didn't know you were owed", but "the U.S. won't get a penny back." 'Umrani, whose black Muslim terminology thus deliberately denied the right of a Zionist state of Israel ("Occupied Palestine") to exist, angrily observed that the U.S. Congress would vote Israel all the additional funds it needed in 1985 whether it complied with the economic austerity program President Reagan supported or not:

> Timid politicians wouldn't dare risk the wrath of the Jewish community in the U.S. during this election year (1984). If Israel really wanted to clean up the economic mess it is in ... [it] could save money by ending its brutal occupation of Southern Lebanon. The Israelis are reportedly spending more than U.S. $1 million a day to stay in Lebanon. But why should they care? U.S. citizens will silently foot the bill.[58]

'Umrani was unrepresentative of Warith's sect not just in the detail of the accounts he projected of Middle East movements and nationalisms, but also in his (very occasional) fusion of them with parochial conflicts between African-American politicians/African-American interests and local Zionist lobbyists. Thus, backing came from *American Muslim Journal* for Jesse Jackson's 1984 run for the U.S. presidency, for which he received a modest Libyan donation that enraged local Zionists, despite the indifference to Jackson's candidacy fostered by Warith himself in his sect. Such support from the paper in effect also by implication legitimated Jackson's campaign-deputy Farrakhan, Imam Warith's rival,[59] now entering into the larger American mainstream. Jackson needed Farrakhan to help him carry the African-American masses: despite micronationalist Jewish criticism, Jackson was slow to abandon him during the campaign.

Munir 'Umrani's ultra-political journalism in the 1980s on current events in the Middle East and the Third World was uniquely sharply-focused and copious given some Americanist stances promoted by Warith for the sect. In 1984, a reporter questioned him if he were a Communist, so similar did his criticisms of "U.S. meddling" in Central America sound to those by Nicaraguan leader Daniel Ortega at the UN. 'Umrani replied that he was "a Muslim who doesn't have a rabid fear of communism"—he feared Allah only.[60] 'Umrani reads to have started his political life in or near the Communist Party of the USA, in which he may have interacted daily with Jewish-Americans: this socialization gave his attacks on Israel some documented, intimate detail. As Warith's sect took more and more from the Middle East, 'Umrani jumped over from his Left internationalism to the Islamist internationalism of Khomeini's revolution of the Shi'ite clerics in Iran, like Warith not always friendly to nationalisms. 'Umrani repudiated the Arab nationalism that the old NOI's members had liked, as a creation of imperialists to divide and rule, and took "Islamic" Iran's side in its war with Saddam's Arab nationalist, secular 'Iraq. But his reconstructed pro-Khomeini pan-Islam remained centered around the PLO and its heroic fight when the Israelis invaded Lebanon in 1982: the Arab states should have aided the Palestinians, not Saddam.[61]

'Umrani's militant support for the [ambiguous] PLO and [ambiguous] Khomeiniite Iran did not fit with Warith's gestures to U.S. Jewry or with

Anglo-America. Now individualistic chaos marked discourse about the Muslim World under Imam W. Deen. 'Umrani had made a distinctive contribution to exploration of Middle East politics among Warith's followers.

As adoption of culture and concepts from Middle Eastern Muslims speeded up under Warith after 1975, his "Black Muslims" extensively took part in anti-Israel, pro-Palestine gatherings and occasions organized by Arab-Americans. Their attendance at such political functions of Arab-Americans not only deepened the "Black" or "Bilalian" Muslims' anti-Israeli stance, but also modestly tinctured them with the Arab or Palestinian national culture (such as folk-music) that included Arab experiences only tenuously related to Islam as such.[62]

It was long undecided how far the Americanist drive of Warith's sect to integrate with Jewish as well as Anglo fellow-citizens, and political shifts and attempts at negotiations in the Middle East itself, would limit the long-standing relationship of African-Americans of the NOI tradition with Palestinians. After he succeeded Elijah in 1975, Warith Mohammed brought back the Palestinian, Dr Jamil Diyab, who had befriended Elijah Muhammad in the early 1950s, and been Warith's Arabic teacher, though later expelled by the Messenger for subtly teaching Sunni Islam to the kids. (In the early 21st century, Diyab, at eighty, was still teaching Arabic to the children of Warith's followers in Arizona!) Diyab's dynamic female cousin, Layla Diyab, set up an invitation from President Yasir 'Arafat to Imam W.D. Mohammed and his editor, Ayesha Mustafaa, to tour the Holy Land in "top protocol" in 1996. Their journey's title "A Prayer for Peace In Jerusalem" was Arabophilia compatible with Americanism, friendship with some U.S. Jews and with the ecumenical efforts of U.S. Christians and Muslims to push Israel towards efforts for peace and a two-states settlement.[63] Warith's responses in Jerusalem were heartfelt but still somewhat dualistic. The strong presence of the Israeli military in Palestinian areas reminded him of the omnipresence of policemen in Chicago's black neighborhoods in his childhood: "I thank God for the resolve of my people not to be crushed". Yet he also thanked God "for the good people in the American society—Whites and Jews—who came to the aid of Blacks".[64] Perhaps he hoped that there were liberal Jews in Israel who would come to the aid of the Palestinians whom, his article charged, Israel was squeezing out.

African-American scholar Yusuf Nuruddin (2000) has researched some tensions or failures to connect between African-American Muslims and some immigrant professionals. Here, ethnic disparities were exacerbated by class gaps: "Pakistani medical doctors, engineers, accountants, pharmacists, etc. have little in common with, say, the significant numbers of African-American Muslims who have converted to Islam while serving prison terms".[65] Elijah Muhammad in 1956 had already reproached immigrant Muslim Arab grocers for selling pork and liquors: too many Muslim diplomats in Washington and at the UN downed alcohol. Under Warith, some black Muslims again objected at Arab-run convenience stores in ghettos that sold religiously prohibited wine and pork. Yet, friendly cajoling was also used by Imam Warith's followers, to which some Arab shopkeepers responded: the idea of an American group taking up Islam—suggesting that a practised Islam might survive in America—reactivated the Islamic faith in such Arabs in Atlanta in 2002.[66]

In contrast to Warith's publications that focused on Israeli "aggressions" in the Middle East, Farrakhan's media long sniped more at American Jews. However, contributors on Middle Eastern conflicts to the second NOI's *Final Call* sometimes fused Israel's "misdeeds" with the domestic sufferings of U.S. blacks. Veteran Palestinian-American activist, 'Ali Baghdadi, did that in 1990. When both the U.S. government of George Bush, Sr. and Congress claimed to be waging a war to combat drugs, a cause that had the support of most U.S. citizens, Baghdadi, following Farrakhan's speeches, charged that that was Bush's cover to invade Panama in violation of international law and the UN Charter, causing the death of 2,000 Panamanians. In Baghdadi's coverage, though, NOI discussion of this issue again circled around to include Israel, which, driven by its desire to make a fast "buck," was not only providing terrorist training and arms to the drug cartels in Latin America, but also directly taking part in the drug trafficking that was "destroying millions of Americans". Baghdadi was citing this alleged role to incite the African-American leaders to pressure the U.S. government into ending the $4 billion it transferred each year to Israel. Those taxes otherwise might have helped feed America's hungry and provided shelter for its homeless.

Some sentences of Baghdadi in this *Final Call* piece had some sense of the U.S. as not fully in control of its own policies. The U.S. government and U.S. Congress, that both claimed to be waging a war against drugs, were fully aware of the Israeli role in poisoning and drugging their citizens: the awareness had gone beyond intelligence sources and seeped into U.S. radio and TV stations and mainstream press that Baghdadi listed. At this point, Baghdadi exaggerated the Zionist lobby's strength in U.S. domestic politics by stating that taking drastic measures against Israel "terrifies" the American government. At other points, however, Baghdadi was not making Israel or parochial Jews the scapegoat: he blasted the earlier Reagan administration as "itself deeply involved in cocaine trafficking to raise funds for its secret and illegal resupply of the contras" insurgency in Nicaragua.

Many items contributed to *Final Call* have not truly fitted into the classical bi-polar dichotomizations set up by Fard and Elijah—both its writers on overseas issues and the readership that can refuse to buy the paper are now too sophisticated for that. Farrakhan tended to depict Manuel Norriega as a non-white victim of U.S. imperialism, but Baghdadi suddenly blurred him into drugs and Israel when he imaged that Mike Harari, a high ranking Mossad (Israeli intelligence) officer, had served as Manuel Noriega's close advisor, and that the U.S. let him flee to Israel when attacking.[67]

Communications on international affairs that look militant on first reading but have no genuine heroes multiplied in *Final Call* as African-Americans headed to the new 21st century. The all-round corruption they imaged ended the NOI's old triumphalism about the freedom struggles and new independent states of the Third World. While Baghdadi's image that "Israel's selfish interests, unfortunately, determine U.S. domestic and foreign policy" might encourage African-Americans and Arab-Americans to put together a counter-lobby to correct the U.S. system from the mainstream, his own generation of immigrants may have been too embittered by the toxic anti-Arab racism that had awaited them from Anglo-America to work seriously to organize such a constructive entry into that system.

The increased solidarity that post-1975 black Muslim sects felt with Afro-Asian Muslim peoples has occasionally caused tensions with the white America to which Warith wanted to openly affiliate his sect. The political stances of sect leaders like Warith or his then-nemesis, Farrakhan, are not always straightforward. During the Iranian-American crisis following the overthrow of the Shah, for example, Warith's adherents adopted an ambivalent, if sometimes critical, stance towards American policies. In November 1978, Muhammad 'Ali said that he was on his way to help mediate in the crisis caused by the holding of American hostages in Teheran. In this case, 'Ali was voicing the sense U.S. black Muslims have had of standing between two worlds, in which they yearn to make themselves go-betweens to reconcile America and the Muslim countries, seen by them in this mood as locked into conflicts by mere misunderstandings. But then, in the interview, 'Ali openly urged the USA to send the Shah back to Iran (as Khomeini demanded) on grounds that the country was "harboring a thief" who had stolen $U.S. 17 billion dollars from the Iranian people.[68]

A similar duality was to appear in the other, more Elijahist wing of the black Muslim movements. In the 1990s, Louis Farrakhan Muhammad was to project his small sect out as the imaged vanguard spurring and perhaps directing a mass movement that brought together all sectors of the African-American people. In the wake of the historic march on Washington by one million African-Americans that he organized in August 1995, Farrakhan went on World Friendship Tours in which he reached out to Muslim regimes in the Third World in a highly dualistic, qualified way. With his health in decline, Farrakhan now had to tighten his links to overseas Muslim governments in an effort to convince the white U.S. establishment that it would have to pay a prohibitive diplomatic price if they ever moved to crush the NOI at the Zionoids' urging. Iran was one of the Muslim states he visited in 1996. There, like Muhammad 'Ali, he was trying to balance the Iran of his religion against the U.S. regime under which he and his followers had to live, and whose English they spoke. In a more synthesizing, Americanist mode, Farrakhan groped for some constructive way to connect the two states in the interest of both, as well as of his sect. At a Tehran rally commemorating the 17th anniversary of Iran's revolution against the Shah, he hinted at playing a role as an emissary for Washington. As an intermediary between a Muslim state and an Anglo-Christian power locked in severe conflict, he could, he argued, serve as the most trusted ambassador because "I can go places where most ambassadors cannot be trusted" (=including Tehran).[69]

As was the case with Elijah's *Muhammad Speaks* tabloid, *Final Call*'s coverage of the Middle East and Africa has been considerably to the left of the sect's caution about political and social change within America at least. Support for Arab nationalism, al-Qadhafi's Libya, Palestinian nationalism and the Iran of the Ayatollahs led it to transmit highly political critiques of the U.S. system as imperialist, and to consider human political action and insurgency—not solely intervention from outside history by God—as possible roads to sovereignty and happiness.

The New NOI Starts to Empathize with Powerless Whites in America

Yet, as with Imam W.D. Muhammad's sect, the political responsiveness of Farrakhan's new Nation of Islam to the Arab and Muslim Worlds also could link up with ordinary white Americans, now seen as almost as victimized by the system and the Zionists as were the blacks. The Irangate scandal of 1986-1989 revealed that Reagan's administration had been selling weapons to a faction of the Iranian ayatollahs under the urging of Israeli intelligence figures: the proceeds went to the Contras in Nicaragua. In millenarian mode now, *Final Call* excerpted the Qur'an's narrative (23: 45-48) that when God sent Moses and his brother Aaron (Harun) to Pharaoh and his chiefs, the latter arrogantly cried lies, and thus made themselves among those whom God had to destroy. The archaic pattern of Middle Eastern religion is portrayed as perhaps about to recur between the white American establishment and the likewise recently enslaved blacks for whom Farrakhan speaks. Yet now not all whites are the same: some are co-victims. Lies and deceit in the name of freedom and democracy had always been the modus operandi of U.S. governments. "But now this web of falsehood and trickery spun by President Reagan and his chiefs threatens to choke the life out of the American government, to the detriment of the American people, hapless victims of this latest treachery."

Here, NOI analysis was swinging between (a) a yearning for retribution and Incineration of the evildoers by God, to (b) political resistance by Arab and Muslim states and movements against America and (c) a cloaked sense that, in the degree of freedom of speech allowed in the USA, some liberal whites might help blacks not just to expose but thereby hopefully correct malfunctions in the American system. In criticizing U.S. institutions together, white radicals and black Muslims already were starting to act as objective collaborators and potential co-citizens in a single endeavor to reform them through ameliorism. Abdul Wali excerpted *Under Cover: Thirty-Five Years of CIA Deception* (1985) in *Final Call*: in its introduction, Tom Gervasi had assailed covert action violence by the "intelligence establishment" abroad as "not in our national interest but against it: in the long run it is self-defeating". [Would Farrakhan's Muslims and the Euro-American liberals/leftists soon join up to manage a common U.S. "national interest" and restructured system together?].

The NOI and Overseas Islamists

Abdul Wali Muhammad seized on Reagan's behind-the-scenes dealings with "the nation he [in public] called the chief terrorist, Islamic Iran". The secret bargains refuted the U.S. government's cynical "misinformation campaign" that al-Qadhafi's Libya was the center of "international terrorism" and that Reagan had been right to bomb it in place of Iran. *Final Call* was "pointing out the unseen involvement of the Zionists" while "defending Col. Qadhafi"—Farrakhan's financial backer and friend—"from unfounded charges".[70]

While Abdul Wali Muhammad here did not project the cultures in the Muslim states that white America hated, "Islamist" Iran's official ethos of struggle sometimes was conveyed integrally to Farrakhan's followers. In 1992, *Final Call* carried the full text of an address by Iranian President 'Ali Husayn Khamenei condemning the arrogance of Bush Sr's America, its delusions that its power and wealth entitled it to intervene in Third World countries under the pretext of human rights and bringing elections. A *Final Call* editorial titled "Pride goeth before destruction" attached (a) Khamenei's denunciations of America to (b) millenarian warnings that God might soon destroy America that drew from Qur'anic verses and the Bible, to (c) exodus with Farrakhan, again the Moses of African-Americans, to (e) a sense that there are some more realistic or better whites, in this instance French, Belgian and German journalists with their muted alienation from American power.[71]

The new NOI gestured to Arab World Muslim revivalists. In a February 1992 interview to *Final Call*, Farrakhan condemned, a tad simplistically, the perceived nullification by Algeria's military of a "democraticaily-elected Islamic government". "A certain [Westernized, governing] class of Algerian people" had not wished to live under the Islamic state and Islamic law that "a popular Muslim government would bring in". This had made them block by force the will of the majority of the people. Farrakhan cited the warning of the Qur'an (61:9) that God would make His true religion overcome all other religions "although the polytheists may be averse." Elijah and his ministers had depicted the vague governments of the Arab, Muslim and African worlds as uniformly good and harmonious. Now Farrakhan depicted some of them as polarized against their peoples, and against the Islamists who confronted them in response. He did guide his followers to identify with the Ikhwanite-salafist faction in Algeria, which he (superficially) termed an emanation of the same Islam as his own movement. Farrakhan's rather formalistic solidarity was fueled by his view of the Algerian establishment class as part of a global power structure centered in the USA—which now was indeed providing some military and financial support to help that government to stay in power. The Bush administration connived at the deprivation of the rights of the people of Algeria to a duly elected government because it feared the global rise of Islam: "the Western governments will unite to crush Islam". But Elijah—decades before the rise of militant Islam—had told him that Islam would "in the 21st century [become] the major power in the world," following the collapse of communism.[72]

The cumulative flow of the Arabic vocabulary and system of grammar into the minds of the adherents and audience of Farrakhan's revived NOI never stopped throughout the 1980s and 1990s. The Arab or other immigrant Muslims in that process propagated scraps of Arabic among African-American Muslims as focii for political meanings in conflicts between groups. As an instance, Palestinian-American activist, 'Ali Baghdadi (1996), wrote: "despite the unbearable pressure exerted by the United States and its agents among the generals and politicians in Turkey, Najmuddin Erbakan, the new Prime Minister of Turkey, has lived up to his name which means the 'star of the religion'". By seeking economic cooperation with Iran, "he has kept his pledges he made to the Turkish people at home and to 1,300 million Muslims worldwide".[73]

Warith's group after 1975 developed a more aesthetic or reflective and religious engagement with Arabic as attractive in itself (it is the language of the Qur'an). Yet in the 1980s, like such African-American journalists of Warith's tabloid as Munir 'Umrani as well, Arabic words and some details of Arabic grammar often took on a politicized vividness in the context of attacks or subjugation by "Caucasian" Christians and Jews in the Middle East/the U.S. against U.S. Blacks/Middle Eastern Muslims. 'Umrani applied the Arabic broken plural masajid to convey the mosques he imaged that invading Israelis and a Christian militia were destroying in Lebanon in the 1980s. Such jihadic, ultra-politicized application of Arabic, though, ran against Warith's policy of accommodation with Christian and Jewish fellow-Americans.

The two groups—the U.S.-orientated Nation of Islam protest tradition and the highly-educated Arab or Muslim immigrant-professionals whose views Baghdadi communicated—were very different in some of their concerns. Still, both the black Muslims and the Nasserite and then neo-Khomeiniite immigrants had been hostile to the West as a bloc, and had yearned for an answering bloc of Muslim countries in the Third World to build counter-power for the powerless whom America was seen to be exploiting. The industrial, modern terms in which such a pan-Islamism defined the sovereignty to be wrested back somewhat spoke to the economic, collectivist-capitalist, thrust of black Muslim nationalist self-assertion and self-development in America in the face of the same mighty Western system.

The engagement with Arabic grammar and vocabulary by Farrakhan and his adherents after 1980, and by a few radicals in Warith's sect, was further energized within struggles for power between whites and the African-American and Third World people of color.

Cargoism

Peoples and countries that have no real sovereignty and poor resources often in desperation hope that some outside state will deliver wealth and resources to them. Indeed, they consider that the entitlement of their peoples. Warith toured the Gulf countries and other Arab states in late 1976 to declare his sect's union with Sunni Islam in an era of buoyant petrol revenues—a good portion of these states were donating to Islamic populations and propagation everywhere around the world. Warith and his Muslims—and from the 1980s, Farrakhan's group, also—continued to search for some economic dimension for their widening, now much tighter, relations with Muslim countries around the globe. Both Warith's followers and Farrakhan have groped for some long-term financial, economic and political interaction in which some successor-sect of the NOI acts as those Islamic states' intermediary or processor of a transfer of resources or economic exchange with African-Americans in general. Malaysia's launching of the Proton, the first car to be exported to the West by Muslim countries, brought out this economic drive within African-American pan-Islamic identity. Warith's Los Angeles magazine, *Hijrah*, proposed that Proton conclude dealerships with black Muslim business people who would retail the car to African-Americans and the general American population.

It was not exactly that hopes of economic profit structured the community identifications and tenets: rather, the tenets and their definitions of race and religion-defined community were focusing the ways in which Warith's Arabizing followers were perceiving economics. "Islamic Malaysia will enjoy great success with this venture if a dual marketing strategy aimed at the general population, especially on the west coast, and a strong pitch for the Muslim dollar, is pursued." The item inflated Muslims among the African-American populations to 8 million, but the requirement to turn a profit would require dealers to pitch the car to immigrant Muslims also. That these groups would be more likely to consider a car from a Muslim country, especially if sold by Muslims, might swing the awarding of dealerships to African-American Muslims, which American (and Japanese) companies' racist reflexes had made them reluctant to award. Thus the Islamic connection might provide a point of entry for the USA's blacks into its economic center. This 1988 attraction to Malaysia carried forward some old NOI blurring of the borders of the Black Nation out into the Arabs, Muslims, Asiatics and people who speak Spanish around the globe. It sought a united front of Black, Muslim, Latino and Asian businessmen to lobby dealerships from car companies, mustering pressure from Congress.[74] But can African-Americans and the Arab and Muslim states really shake off their histories of struggles for survival to focus solely on a de-politicized pursuit of economic well-being? This same issue of *Hijrah* with its passable articles constructively surveying Malaysia also carried an interview with Nur Misuari of the Moro National Liberation Front of the Philippines about his people's protracted insurgency.[75]

When, in the wake of his 1995 Million Man March on Congress, Farrakhan left on wide tours of the African and Muslim countries, he bore high hopes from many non-Muslim blacks in academia, politics and government, business and finance that he could win trade, finance and jobs from those states for African-Americans. As his popularity fell back to its previous level again, Farrakhan on his return claimed that Mu'ammar al-Qadhafi had promised to remit billions of dollars for the development of the depression-gripped African-Americans. The offer, though, may have been imagined or inflated by Farrakhan: it brought him valuable publicity when American officials dismissed him as a foreign agent. Colonel al-Qadhafi has a well-earned reputation in Africa for not delivering donations or loans he promises.

Black Muslim Attitudes to Africa Below the Sahara

The 1970s, 1980s and 1990s were decades in which African-Americans—culturally, politically, in personal interaction and as entrepreneurs—engaged with sub-Saharan Africans to unprecedented extents. What roles did Farrakhan and Warith's sects assume vis-à-vis this enterprise? Did they and their ideas help or hinder the reconnection with the Mother-Continent that increasing numbers of African-Americans wanted?

The reconnection was at first problematical, as most transcontinental relations are. Playwright Maya Angelou, a friend of the late Malcolm X, who interacted with Nasser's Egyptians as well after she married a black South African, in 1986 recalled U.S. Africanist "Revolutionary Returnees" who found that the Ghana of Nkrumah refused to know the repatriating relatives: "these Africans... are treating me like Charlie [whites] did down on the plantation". "Many of us had only begun to realize in Africa that the Stars and Stripes was our only flag... It lifted us up with its promise and broke our hearts with its denial".[76] Her affect toward Africa declining, Angelou in the end contributed to a Whitmanesque Angloid public poetry that, in inducting historically marginalized groups into the Americanist political mainstream, suppresses any last African-American or other ethnic rhythms or voice.[77]

In some ways, black American Muslims in the post-1975 era of the leadership of Farrakhan and Warith interacted and identified more with West Asian Arabs than with black Africans, as the cultural affinity that had been constructed showed itself stronger than race as a bond. This fulfils a pattern already prefigured under Elijah who valued the Arab world more than the West Africa from which most American blacks originated during the slave trade. However, because two thirds of speakers of Arabic reside in the Nile Valley and North Africa, the Arab World and Africa overlap. And yet, African-American Muslims have built up some religio-cultural and social "reconnection" to the Black African world and cultures from which the slave masters wrenched their forefathers. These interactions and contacts with "Black Africans" could lead to new economic pan-continental relationships, fostered by modern communications and global economic integration. However, the black Muslims' special identification with Muslim black African communities in the 1980s and 1990s also entailed low-level tensions in their contacts with non-Muslim "Christian" Africans, who were ascendant in those new African states, in part as a prolongation of previous millenarian concerns.

Genuine hospitality from the people of Gambia to tourists made the country a favorite of young African-Americans in search of ancestral identity in the late-modern and post-modern eras.[78] In his best-selling "faction" novel, *Roots* (1976), which subsequently led to two popular television series, Alex Haley romanticized West Africa, especially its Muslim areas. He stressed that black Americans' connection with the lands from which their enslaved forefathers were taken away in chains had never been broken.[79] The Muslims after Elijah developed Haley's themes with vigor. Early in 1984, Warith's press highlighted the adherent Barkary Taal's two vacations with his wife in

West Africa, during which they visited the Muslim village in Gambia to which Taal believed he had traced his family origin. "Ironically it was Alex Haley's ancestral Islamic village of Juffure in Gambia, West Africa." West Africans repeatedly identified Taal as a long-lost Mandinka on the basis of a nickname his grandmother had called him and because of his high cheekbones. In Juffure, an old female griot (or traditional reciter) identified Taal as "lost blood" descended from a villager kidnapped by white slavers, from a reading of Taal's palm, intuition and old genealogies. Taal knew that this data did not meet "Western man's understanding of life... fingerprints or photographs". At least one native of Juffure benefited from the reconnection—Taal's "21 year-old ancestral nephew" who went to America and lived with him while attending adult education classes.

While African-Americans have a deeply-felt need to revive a continuous racial and cultural community with some group in Africa, the cultural ethnocide of slavery, and the subsequent white American racism that was almost worse, had nearly snapped their links to that Mother-Continent. They lacked the unbroken trans-oceanic links or memories or even exchanges like those that most white ethnic groups in America kept up with their communities and areas of origin in Europe. Taal and his wife came to Africa fired by passionate hopes of refusion: on coming down from the plane, he shared Malcolm X's impulse to kiss the Mother Continent's soil. If this African-American Muslim was white-hot, his Gambian Muslim hosts may have coolly manipulated his psychological needs, evoked a blatantly fictitious joint origin, to keep the stream of African-American pilgrim-tourists coming to Juffure, along with the chances of development. Yet the black American Muslim tourists sought by the calculating villagers of Juffure would be much more compatible with the village's mores than would white non-Muslims, or Christian Afro-Americans. As well as the colorful clothes, ceremonies and hope that he could regain lost lineage there, a specific ideological affinity drew Taal to Juffure—that of Islam, itself. "Many [Afro-Americans] have visited Juffure, but no one has come back to speak of the Islamic spiritual feeling of Juffure—that's the key. The Mandinkas are a very spiritual people".[80]

Even more than grass-roots Gambian peasants, African officials in the USA are aware of the ever-growing need African-Americans have felt since the mid-1960's for the continent of origin, Africa. Like Juffure's villagers, the African officials fan it in order to draw black Americans into long-term semi-intimate relations intended to improve the economic and material prospects of black Africans and their states. African diplomats and officials in the USA are respectful of the African-American Muslims in this context as long-standing pioneers of black capitalism in North America, and thus as potential traders or investors. For their part, these Islamic sects' media publicize all overtures from African officials for new economic relations between black Americans and Africans. Along with Tanzanian and Ghanaian expressions of interest, for example, the Egyptian Counselor, Dr Husayn Hassuna, was quoted as saying that "the door is open for whoever wants to come and ... [Egypt] is ideal for Bilalian [Black American] businessmen because they can relate to the culture".[81] The Nigerians opened a Consulate in Atlanta in 1982, seeking ready access to the black business classes of a city where African-Americans had been recording many successes. Moses Ihonde, as Nigeria's Consul-General in Atlanta, was soon interviewed by *World Muslim News* about his strong bid for economic ventures by Muslim African-Americans. To make his country attractive to them, he stressed that "Nigeria is a country of predominantly Muslim population though there is a large number of Christians there also", with "no conflict between Muslims and Christians"—an optimism for the media that did not descry the future. He warned African-Americans, though, not to let "the advanced technology" to which U.S. blacks, in company with other Americans, had access, create "impatience" and the demand for "immediate return on your investment" that had made it hard for U.S. blacks, just like other U.S. investors, to stay on in Nigeria.[82]

Farrakhan and Ghana: 1986

On his 1986 visit to Ghana, Farrakhan experienced and responded to the realities of black Africa in a way not consonant with Elijah's idealized image of global black unity, "the East" and Mother Africa. He found latter-day Ghana was fragmented, run-down, underdeveloped and—a word he used time and time again to describe it—"poor"; and he soon became fully aware of the depth of the division and ill-feeling between African Muslims and the much better-educated, prosperous, and politically more powerful Christians in this and other sub-Saharan black societies. Farrakhan therefore muted the Nation of Islam's past vituperative antipathy to Christianity and the Bible, and insisted that Christianity and Islam were virtually just two labels for the same spirit, as all Africans united to liberate and develop their continent from Cairo to the Cape. At the same time, he quite misread Flight-Lieutenant Jerry Rawling's military-based regime as a sincere attempt at Islam-like egalitarian nationalist governance. Rawlings was attempting to renew the vision of Kwame Nkrumah, Farrakhan felt in 1989.[83]

Like the critical articles on Black African dictatorships in Warith's journals, Farrakhan's response to caste-divisions in India in the 1980s instanced growing "Black Muslim" awareness of oppression, ethnic divisions and poverty in those Asian and African societies once mythologized and idealized under Elijah. Disillusionment and the painful achievement of differentiating visions here mark a significant progression in the U.S. "Black Muslim" consciousness—from the original trans-continental protest mythology to actualized trans-continental relationships with Africans, Arabs, Asians.

Africa in the 1990s

The 1990s saw a progressive widening of interaction with West Africa by followers of both Farrakhan and Warith, and by bourgeois African-Americans in general. With travel to West and Arab North Africa now common for black American Muslims of even modest means, the formal representations of Africa from both Farrakhan and Warith's sects have a sharpening realistic focus on the gritty textures that some of those societies and states have.

A 1999 article titled "Islam in Senegal" by Basheer Alim portrayed an adherent of Imam W. Deen Mohammed at home in that state's capital, Dakar. Ninety per cent of the 9 million Senegalese were Muslims and Alim prayed the Friday (Jum'ah) prayer at the Grand Mosque, although Dakar had its share of "big city" social problems (thefts, etc) comparable to those of New York or Chicago. Alim evaded the desperate street-vendors by learning a few words of French and the local Wolof, and walking around in local robes. His article showed good attunedness to the complexities of the conjunction of old and new worlds, Islam and French language and cuisine, and of cyber cafes with masses of unemployed. All, together, made up that growing, unevenly modern city, Dakar. Alim in 1999 was carrying forward the drive of all these Black American Muslim sects to "carry" cultural reconnection to Africa and Asia on some newly devised economic relationship or vice versa. He had a good eye for Senegalese arts—fabrics, wood-carvings, leather goods, music—and had come "to make contact with Senegalese artisans to import their works to the USA for display and sale".[84]

By the end of the 20th century, African-Americans in the tradition of the first NOI were developing nuanced and rich responses to sub-Saharan societies. They were penning critical, compound political analyses, but also connecting aesthetically with those peoples from whom enslaved ancestors had been torn. Both Farrakhan's and Warith's sect towards the close of the 20th century were jockeying to position themselves as the retailers or tourism enablers—firms that would get paid money—between West Africa and the growing black American bourgeoisie that needed artifacts and encounters from it for the African-American nationalist culture it was constructing in America.

The response that Farrakhan won from both the Arab World and sub-Saharan Africa has been limited. In the major West African state, Nigeria, sympathy came from Muslim military rulers disliked by the civilian middle-classes, who were increasingly supported in their struggles to restore parliamentarism by their African-American peers—Rev Jesse Jackson at the fore. In hugging the Libya-aided General Sani Abatcha (ruled 1993-1998) and other Nigerian high military, Farrakhan won few new admirers among the black bourgeoisie back home.

The regime of smallish Ghana, which needed dollars, had become a long-term friend. Its president, Jerry Rawlings, structured his government's projections of national and African identity to draw the most African-Americans possible into Ghana's life. Rawlings was capitalizing on the roles of Ghana's old prisons and castles as one-time centers for the export of slaves to the Americas to draw African-American tourists for ritualized tours modeled on those of the U.S. Zionoids' Holocaust industry to Poland, etc., and to encourage African-Americans to invest and retire in Ghana.[85] The NOI wanted to become the agency that would be salaried to show the tourists around. Accordingly, Ghana hosted the Nation of Islam's convention in October, 1994. In 1997, Rawlings urged adherents and sympathizers of Farrakhan to tour Ghana's slave-export castles and the graves of U.S. pan-Africanists like W.E.B. DuBois, as well as Nkrumah's, and to invest and trade. An accompanying message to the Saviors' Day convention of Farrakhan's sect from al-Qadhafi voiced "support [for] your peaceful democratic struggle to register millions of Blacks in the elections registries, so that by the beginning of the 21st century you become a very influential force" in U.S. parliamentarism: at the time, a reasonable possibility, given how the 1995 Black Million Man March had reflected the community of Muslim and Christian blacks under Farrakhan's "superb leadership."[86]

But all the globe-trotting of Farrakhan since 1980 failed to win him many consolidated relations with Africans. The Ghana of Jerry Rawlings was one of the few states in a constructive relationship with the USA to acknowledge Farrakhan, while al-Qadhafi's support in the name of "Africa and the Muslim World" could lead Farrakhan's "revolutionary struggle" to the reverse of the promised "victory", given Anglo- and Jewish-American loathing of that Libya.

Still, Farrakhan's new Nation of Islam had inserted itself into crucial points of the African-American new bourgeoisie's stylized reconnection with Africa. This smallish sect's presence tugs the U.S. black bourgeoisie towards more Islamic sectors of sub-Saharan Africa, and its own culture motifs further deepen the Islamic dye of the new transcontinental micronationalism being constructed by Black America. When the "Roots Festival" patronized by the local government was being held in mid-1999 in the Gambia, the Nation of Islam hosted the grand opening of the Alex Haley Mosque in Juffure with Gambian President Yayah Jammeh. The new NOI had financed its construction after Farrakhan found out that previous funds had been wasted.[87]

Even in the media of Imam Warith Mohammed, Africa has the potential to spark conflict with the U.S. system as his sect tries to enter it. On one hand, the post-independence states beneath the Sahara are being demystified. Many Nigerians were poor in the world's sixth largest oil-producer because its leaders embezzled billions—but also because of the multinational corporations with which those leaders made agreements. This 2002 article called African-Americans to support the non-violent sit-ins by [as yet] "unarmed" women in Nigeria's South against California-based Chevron Texaco Oil. Those women were demanding that the company hire their sons and use some of the oil they extracted to provide electricity, roads, schools, clinics and water services.[88]

The followers of both Imam W. Deen Mohammed and Farrakhan have inclined towards those radical nationalist groups and governments beneath the Sahara that were open to Islam and Arabs: these help affiliate African-Americans to both those worlds, together. The Africanism selected was that which was sympathetic to those Arab and Muslim forces and regimes that have an image of standing up to America and Israel. Let's look at one item from Warith's tabloid. Voicing concepts of "black" and "white" blocs in the world like those in Elijah's old Nation of Islam, Nelson Mandela in 2002 assailed the U.S. and Britain as working to invade "black" 'Iraq on the pretext of Weapons of Mass Destruction it did not have, while ignoring "white" Israel's nuclear bombs. "Racism" made the U.S. and Britain go outside the UN once it had come to have "black secretary generals like [Egyptian] Butrus Butrus Ghali, like Kofi Annan".[89] Such items in Farrakhan and Warith's media frame sub-Saharan Africa and the Arabs together as one wide community, in pigmentation broadly conceived, and in other connections or affinities.

5: THE RISE OF FARRAKHAN: THE CHALLENGE FOR WARITH

1984: Farrakhan and the Jews

The figure of Farrakhan has meant many things to many groups at different times, to some extent even internationally, and various interpretations have been made of the motives of his actions in 1983-1985, vis-à-vis Jesse Jackson, Jews, and the U.S. presidential primaries. I am to analyze this turning-point in Farrakhan's career in a broad-gauge book about him, his thought, and the culture of his revived Nation of Islam. Thus, I offer here only some preliminary, tentative reflections to start to get to grips with the issues.

There was some sincerity to Farrakhan. He had a natural furious communal component in his personality which the dichotomies of Nation of Islam ideology had sharpened. The rise of these inter-ethnic tensions in the early 1980's also came in the wake of decades-old ill-treatment of blacks by Jewish-American, as much as Anglo-American, retailers, real-estate agents, officials and politicians, set out by us in Chapter 3. As a cleaning-lady, Farrakhan's own mother had been caught in this long unequal interaction between "the Jews and the Blacks" in America, although she may have exchanged some facets of Caribbean and Jewish culture with at least *one* more relaxed Jewish household. Farrakhan was also a religious man or professional cleric: like the young militants surrounding him, he read the Holy Qur'an revealed to the Prophet Muhammad who had had to face some Jews unwilling to give up social power in Yathrib, Arabia after he came.

Even more clearly, though, Farrakhan was a U.S. politician. He was now becoming one of the politician-leaders of the new religio-political micronationalisms that had gotten well and truly off the ground among the middle classes of diverse *ethne* of Americans by 1980. Playing on the past ill-treatment of ghetto blacks by a fair number of white American Jews, and also on the widespread disfavor among African-Americans towards U.S. Jewry's extraterritorial state in the Middle East—perceived, not always fairly, to occupy and exclude Palestinians—Farrakhan's "denunciations" of Judaism and Israel from 1983 spoke to pre-existing social experiences of lumpen, but also upwardly mobile African-Americans, most of whom remained Christian. The black bourgeoisie had been waiting for a leader who could voice their conflict with the established Jewish elite they saw as blocking their upwards progress in careers—preferably one who would have his own counter-connection to the Arab-Israeli conflict, to really strike back into the heart of that opponent's psyche. A Muslim African-American cleric here would be better than a Christian one! Farrakhan was sniffing all those winds gusting through the African-American psyche, but also through America's mainstream politics.

While his Nation had identifications and principles at stake, calculations about ways to achieve his ambitions may also have fuelled Farrakhan's broadsides. In the lifetime of the Honorable Elijah Muhammad, Farrakhan had gradually become a prominent nation-wide representative for the Nation of Islam, enjoying something like respectability in white American society and mainstream U.S. institutions, sometimes even being invited to address secondary school students.[90] It had been hard, after Elijah's death, to be reduced to just one of several deputies under Warith, and so Farrakhan broke with Warith's authority to become a leader again in his own right. True, he also had policy reasons to split from Warith: the Imam's effusive Americanism and his breakup and privatization of many NOI businesses that had been collective had grated NOI veterans around Farrakhan as harmful to the sect's nationalism. If Farrakhan had behind him only a secondary splinter group, with Warith still regarded during the early period of succession from Elijah as the leader of "Black Islam" in the USA by blacks, whites and the Arab states alike, at least he now had some independent power and maneuverability.

The left-Democrat Rev. Jesse Jackson, leader of People United to Save Humanity (PUSH), had been at the fore of a range of African-American politicians and opinion leaders who had engaged with the Arab-Israeli conflict, which Ziono-American politicians too, from their side, pursued in U.S. politics to head and control Jewish-Americans. After President Carter in 1979 dismissed Andrew Young, the USA's Black Ambassador to the UN who actually spoke with the PLO, Jackson flew to meet Yasir 'Arafat, to "mediate between the Palestinians and Israel." By taking up the symbolic issue of Israel/Palestine, Jesse Jackson put himself forward as a figure declaring independence of Afro-Americans from those strata of Jewish-Americans that had by now built up power in U.S. politics and society. His sincere outreach to Palestinians and Arabs, which was never to reap many resources out of them, made Jewish communities and educators, and Anglos on school boards and in state legislatures, withhold promised funding of Jackson's PUSH/Excel programs to improve the education of African-American pupils. Jackson had feared some such cost, but hoped his conjunction with the Arabs would teach African-American pupils to stand up for what they believed in, regardless of the political consequences.[91]

Jackson then started a political partnership with Farrakhan in which the latter, as a Muslim cleric, was a further link to Arabs. When Jackson went to to negotiate the release of downed U.S. airman Lt Robert Goodman, an African-American, Farrakhan impressed the Ba'th Party officials there with his ability to intone Arabic verses from the Qur'an. This cultural relatedness helped persuade Syrian strongman Hafiz al-Asad to release pilot Goodman in late 1983, despite the reluctance of his army, which was so vulnerable to such U.S. aerial bombing.[92] (Since the core of the Syrian Ba'th elite was from the 'Alawite minority, a sect related to the esotericist Druze and Isma'ilis by whom Fard or his converts could have been influenced, they were—like Farrakhan—far from Sunni Muslim literalism and practices: he and the Ba'th clicked.) Israeli and Zionist observers worried at the inclusion of n diplomatic personnel in black U.S. homecoming ceremonies for Goodman, even at one held in a church. The USA's more feral Zionoid micronationalists were now on the watch for any Arab or Islamic connection of Jackson that they could cite to destroy him in mainstream American public life.

In 1984, Farrakhan became a warm-up orator, and his followers workers, for Jackson's campaign for nomination as the Democratic Party's candidate for the U.S. presidency. Jackson's PUSH was reported to have received a $200,000 grant from [through?] the Arab League, and $10,000 from a Libyan diplomat. U.S. Zionists could not make that enough to deny Jackson government funding or a hearing in mainstream America: henceforth, Arab donors could be as acceptable in U.S. electoral politics—at least for black candidates—as the Ford Foundation or U.S. Jewish organizations. Jackson was truly changing U.S. parliamentarism in 1984 because he and Farrakhan together were becoming able to mobilize for electoral politics, simultaneously, from the poorest and most desperate and the best-educated strata of African-Americans. In the early 1980s, young black graduates trying to break into the professions faced social Darwinism from neo-Republicanizing Jews with seniority: indeed, exuberant, meticulously planned, onslaughts from Jewish nationalist organizations against affirmative action were making it harder for blacks from deprived backgrounds even to get into universities in the first place. By taking part with Jackson in the presidential primaries, Farrakhan secured a prominence in black ethnic politics that was now visible to outsiders. Then his denunciations of Jews and Israel and his triple entendres about Hitler—destructive of patron Jackson's campaign and potential new chances for U.S. blacks in American politics—made him stand out even more as a champion of black and Third World ethnicity, at a time when Warith, as did Jackson on the secular left in his way, was sticking to a dual policy of formal dialogue with American Jews while retaining recognition from the Arab states.

While Farrakhan was supposed to aid his millionaire friend Jackson's political campaign, from the beginning he may also have felt driven to catch publicity in the Euro-American media, in order to be elevated in the minds of the African-American community into the equal partner to Jackson, or perhaps to surpass him. After his heyday as Elijah Muhammad's National Representative ended in 1975, Farrakhan's audiences over America as a whole had been contracting, although he retained his populist touch in the ghettoes of a few cities. An aide of Jackson observed that Farrakhan was using the presidential primaries as a "step up for the Nation of Islam" more than mobilizing blacks to vote for Jesse.[93] So, were both men now running for the presidency of black America? True, internal NOI discourse at the time shows that Farrakhan was also pushed towards his denunciations of Jews by the expectations of militant followers. Among such younger members, the Qur'an's denunciations of some ancient Jews in Arabia who tried to block Prophet Muhammad in Medinah so long ago, were increasingly sharpening their sense that American Jewry's role in shaping the NAACP and other civil rights organizations had been designed to harm—not help—blacks.[94]

In regard to the range of blacks who listened to him in politics, Farrakhan in 1983-1985 achieved some of the requirements to become a mass leader, a "national figure" with strong reach across the whole United States. The following he was starting to win had a better range than Jackson's, since both the poorest, most desperate blacks and the better-educated youth, a proto-elite, were at least considering what he said. This dual following made it hard for the bourgeois Jackson to accede to the intense pressure from Jewish-American organizations to repudiate Farrakhan, even though the latter was harming him in the mainstream Euro-American community: as Jackson put it, "my purpose is to bring blacks into the system, not drive them away," and Farrakhan could deliver the ghetto poor better than he.[95] Farrakhan's *organized* following, though, was but a limited cult, as it remains in our new century. He as yet lacked the institutions, contacts and resources to communicate with the publics and governments of the Arab states that were available to Warith's much larger sect, and he was further handicapped in being less prepared to adjust his group's version of Islam towards Arab Islamic norms, even if his vocal "anti-Semitism" and controversies with American Jews compensated somewhat. Jackson's TV-tracked campaign, despite Jackson's own moderacy, gave Farrakhan the chance for the expanded exposure he needed. Some non-ethnicist African-Americans thought that Farrakhan now deliberately tried to grab screaming headlines around the world by projecting a tone of diffused, focusless rage against not just the state of Israel but Judaism in general, in order to detonate the desired hysteria from American Jewish organizations that duly made him the U.S. and international celebrity he craved to become. To some extent, Farrakhan had been pushed and cornered into making his stand against a group that not a few African-Americans regarded as their ethnic enemy, on a basis of the history. Some analysts have stressed that Meir Kahane and his Jewish Defence League (JDL), active in both Israel and the U.S., had made death threats against Jackson if he continued to run, given his arguments that the Palestinians also had to be offered something by U.S. Middle East policy. This school of analysis sees Farrakhan as having sincerely stumbled into over-emotional language about Jews in general when coming to the verbal defense of his friend. Both Kahane's Jewish Defence League and Farrakhan's weak new NOI were still somewhat marginal in the Jewish-American and African-American communities respectively (although widening), but both now used the Jackson campaign in the presidential primaries to exchange possibly sometimes feigned threats of physical violence so as to highlight themselves as the main defenders and champions in each of the two minorities.

For the long term, Farrakhan would need recognition and funding from the Arabs and other Muslim states. If Jewish attacks highlighted him as one of the most militant opponents of Israel in the USA, the Arabs would pay to bring him and his colleagues to their countries. He could then cheaply visit the black African countries and various black minorities around the world that he wanted to look over as he groped around for a clearer vision of some recovered black American identity. Indeed, al-Qadhafi's Libya, Saddam Hussain's 'Iraq, the Iran of the ayatullahs, and possibly some Sa'udi Arabian bodies and some powerful Muslims in the Nigerian military were believed by some in the new NOI to have proceeded in later years to secretly donate millions of dollars to the sect as a potential lobby in the USA.

The politician Farrakhan may have said very little specific in statements by him that Judaism was, for instance, "a dirty religion." He could not be certain that the Zionists and Zionoid micronationalists would rise to the contrived bait. Those organizations were concerned to track, and find something to help destroy, Jesse Jackson, the first black professional politician of any weight to have questioned some interests of Israel in mainstream U.S. politics. For a time they did not often bother to monitor Farrakhan's own speeches during the campaign, despite old published reports by them that had included pre-1975 criticisms by him of some Jews, under Elijah. An outburst against Jews by Farrakhan to an obscure radio station did finally get into the mainstream press, though. The Jewish nationalists duly took it up, first as a means to end Jackson's political career, but then as a long-term motif for Jewish-American folklore and print-discourses. "Farrakhan" now was being manufactured into a godsend for portly salaried officials of Jewish organizations faced with the problem of young Jews who were wondering if they faced any serious enemies in America, and, because they did not have enough Jewishness in them for it to mean much, were walking away from Jewish life in America. The bogey of "Farrakhan" and "Black anti-Semitism" might pull them back into the fold and assure the salaries of the institutions' officials.

Farrakhan had met Arabs, especially refugee Palestinians who had migrated to America, on and off over decades since becoming a Muslim. Despite such links, though, he hardly showed much detailed concern now for the priorities, interests and ethos of Palestinians and Arabs in his "outlandish" remarks about Israel to which African-Americans now found themselves reluctantly responding, while highly aware that he made them to draw attention. Once he came under hysterical and pretend-hysterical attacks from American Zionists, the African-Americans and the Arabs automatically rallied to Farrakhan, just as he may have expected.[96] Farrakhan had crafted his mock-furious "anti-Semitic attacks on Judaism" superbly, making its charges deliberately diffuse and contentless so that no Black or Arab bankroller could ever hold him to any specific action against any set of Jews, or against any individual feature of Israel or Zionism.

Becoming a counter-lobby was something he and the second NOI were to sidestep more than once.

For winning support from the black bourgeois constituency, though, Farrakhan and his media and colleagues were to continue to milk "anti-Semitism" and the notoriety it gave him for many years. Arguments from dictionaries by his journalists that his remarks during the campaign about Judaism had not been meant by him to offend had a pro forma, almost merry and in-your-face tinge. Most issues of *Final Call* to the end of the 1980s kept up criticisms against this American Jew or that for doing harm in some area of African-American experience.

In the political events of 1983-1985, Farrakhan was the beneficiary of shifts in U.S. society and religions that had to be formalized in its central discourse by some Afro-American, preferably a Muslim, at some point. If mainstream politics could not incorporate the emergence of large minorities of Arab-Americans and Islamizing Blacks on the social landscape, allow them input into U.S. Middle East policies alongside Anglos and Jews, and deal constructively with the Middle East's Muslims as well as Israel, then America could not function properly. Exclusion would risk driving those groups into formulating and pursuing political expression of their identities and interests outside and perhaps against, as opposed to within, that system over the long term. Although loud, Farrakhan's assaults on the screen of holiness around Israel and Jews had been perfunctory indeed. Sensing their harmless contrived dimension, many U.S. media-persons let his attacks pass because opening American Jewry and Israel to criticism was one of the necessary preludes to long-term integration of America on widened bases. The rising black bourgeoisie, and the immigrant Muslim lobbies now developing, had to be allowed to challenge Jewish compatriots and Israel just as Jews had become allowed to critique Anglos (sometimes paralleling them to Germans) after WWII, and in international affairs over Vietnam. In his final 1984 address to the other candidates and the Democratic Party, Jesse Jackson tried with skill and insight to get across to Euro-Americans this need to unify Americans by incorporating change and emerging groups as the population ratios altered:

> The white, the Hispanic, the black, the Arab, the Jew, the woman, the Native American, [Americans of all races in need of release from poverty], the small farmer, the businessperson, the environmentalist, the peace activist, the young, the old, the lesbian, the gay, and the disabled make up the American quilt. We are copartners in the Judeo-Christian traditions. Many blacks and Jews have a shared passion for social justice at home and peace abroad... We are *bound* by Moses and Jesus, but also *connected* with Islam and Muhammad.[97]

Farrakhan and the East's Orthodox Islam

During Elijah Muhammad's period of leadership from the 1950s to 1975, organizations of immigrant orthodox Muslims in the USA often denounced tenets he presented as not in accord with Islam. In part, the pitiable vulnerability of the small immigrant Muslim community pushed some among such despised spokesmen to cater to the prejudices of Anglo-Americans, for whom Muslims and Islam were unimportant, or potentially threatening. For the most part, Elijah defied such orthodox Muslim bodies in America, but his successor, Warith, was bent on Sunnification and that transformed NOI theological relationships with Third World Muslims. When Louis Farrakhan's splinter group revived some of Elijah's old teachings and practices, Warith tried to use that to delegitimize Farrakhan's claim to be an Islamic leader. Farrakhan, for one thing, had somewhat revived in 1978 the belief that Elijah Muhammad as well as the Muhammad of Arabia was a Messenger of God: his followers increasingly asserted that much in the Bible which was supposedly referring to Jesus was really about the true "Christ", Elijah, instead.[98]

A piquant reversal of roles occurred when Ted Koppel's TV program "Nightline" respectfully interviewed Farrakhan in 1984 as an important "Black Muslim" leader in America. In response, Warith wanted to bring representatives of immigrant Pakistani, Indian, Albanian and other orthodox Muslim groups onto Koppel's show to deny that Farrakhan really subscribed to the religion of al-Islam as given by the Prophet Muhammad in Arabia 1400 years ago.[99] But by the 1980s, the immigrant Muslim communities in the U.S. were much larger, self-confident, and sometimes more militant than in the 1950s and 1960s, and few immigrant Muslim leaders were ever to clearly repudiate Farrakhan as a non-Muslim to curry the favor of whites. Farrakhan was becoming a frequently televised national figure in the USA in the context of his involvement with Jesse Jackson and the resultant Black-Jewish conflict. It was natural that many immigrant Arab and other Muslims in the USA joined the blacks to rally behind Farrakhan when the Zionists targeted him; and this made it hard for Warith to delegitimize him Islamically during the ongoing polarization and cross-fire between the ethnic groups.

Symptomatic of Farrakhan's increasing legitimacy among immigrant Afro-Asian Muslims in the USA was a press conference organized at the end of 1984 by the immigrant-led Muslim Development Corporation at Howard Inn in Washington, DC. It was attended by journalists from all over the Muslim world. Farrakhan mouthed the blatantly tongue-in-cheek orthodox Islamic doctrinal noises and the denunciations of Israel that his audience wanted to hear. Playing down his resurrection of some particularistic cult tenets of Elijah, Farrakhan stressed his bid to carry his community into the mainstream of Islam. He said that the "Nation of Islam", as he had revived it, believed in the Holy Quran as the final word of Allah and in the Prophet Muhammad as the last Prophet. The new NOI did not look upon Elijah as the founder of a new religion, but only as the innovator of a methodology to bring the blacks gradually into mainstream Islam. Farrakhan also denied the media charge that he was a racist, and said Islam "does not countenance race, caste or color". "Unfortunately", he went on, "we live in a color-conscious society; and if we preach we should love our color, it is to express our love of Allah who created us like this".

Farrakhan blasted the American government for its policies in the Middle East that made Israel stronger. He argued that Muslim oil money deposited by Arabs in Jewish-owned banks in the USA was being used to destroy Arabs and build Israel, and he pleaded for this money to be withdrawn to "bail the blacks out of the depths of poverty and encourage them to move towards mainstream Islam." [This could simultaneously usher blacks into the USA's central economy.] However, in a return to the old time separatist slogans of the dead Elijah, Farrakhan elsewhere argued that American blacks have the right to a separate homeland of their own if they are continuously treated as second class citizens.[100]

In 1990, Farrakhan was permitted to address the Continental Muslim Council.[101] Some immigrant Muslims still termed Farrakhan and the NOI non-Muslim even after he organized a Chicago pan-Islamic conference with representatives from the Arab and Muslim Worlds attending, in July 1997. But representatives of the immigrant-founded Islamic Society of North America (ISNA), long critical, were to attend the NOI's 28 February 1999 Saviors' Day and its Friday Arabic collective prayers at which Farrakhan and quasi-SunniWarith finally reconciled.

Farrakhan never moved in tenets as close to the Sunni Islam of "the East" as Warith, who yet was politically cautious. Yet he was now striving to apply in current macro-history some of the transcontinental impulses in Elijah's bygone much more mythological discourse—the expectation that a trans-oceanic connection with the Islamic center of alternative power and wealth will suddenly bring prosperity and sovereignty "from the East" to poverty-stricken, abused blacks in America. In his "cult of the Cargo", he laid claim to some of the capital that their Arab co-religionists were transferring from across the seas to America, and he fused religion, economics, black ethnicity, and the parallel emancipation of both the Black American and Arab nations from the perceived global Jewish enemy, at the expense of the millenarian impulses remaining in his sect's world-view.

Economics: Sufficient as Self-determination?

If Elijah claimed it necessary that the blacks should secede economically and politically from the white-dominated core of America, an interview with the BBC in late 1985 drew from Farrakhan some nuanced projections that

> As long as we have to depend on the whites of this nation to feed, clothe, shelter and educate us, and also give us jobs, then we will never be able to earn their respect, nor become self-respecting.

He alluded to Elijah's old plan for a "three year economic savings", and proposed that since "Black folks in America spend nearly $400 million a year on toothpaste [and] nearly $700 to $800 million a year on mouthwash, soaps and other detergents", they should produce these commodities themselves and set up their own system of distribution. Starting small, but growing over time [—no Divine Incineration for a few years!], the blacks would thus be enabled to start farming and buy factories. But, inevitably, this meant coming to terms with the whites, rather than seceding. It meant becoming producers rather than remaining pariahs in the whole society. There was undeniable force in Farrakhan's claim that he was only trying to achieve for blacks the same combination of separate communal institutions, ethnic economic units and participation in the American mainstream that other American ethnic groups such as the Jews had built for themselves in American life.

When challenged in the same interview about the Jews, his alibi if he failed, Farrakhan alleged that they over-controlled retail distribution outlets, and had economically coerced at least one black capitalist partner into withdrawing from collaboration in his projects. The rich powerful Jews were trying to destroy his sect's constructive economic endeavors. He denied, however, that he was anti-Semitic, for the Arabs as well as the Jews were Semitic people, and thus he himself as a Muslim had a Semitic dimension. He was, rather, only "against Zionism", and stressed quite accurately that none of his speeches had ever incited any black audience to make a physical attack against any specific Jew, Jewish store or Jewish synagogue. He had just, as a potential friend of American Jews, been "pointing out a fault that has to be corrected, otherwise these things fester and grow up into an ugly thing that could become violent down the road".[102]

Vibert L. White, a defector from the NOI, was to charge in a 2001 retrospective that Farrakhan and his colleagues in the 1980s mismanaged and wasted on consumption and properties for himself and his family the $5 million al-Qadhafi lent for the NOI's economic development. Thus, the organizations that the new NOI set up to produce and market toiletries, detergents and fish and other foods repeatedly broke down under heavy debts and back-taxes, this assessment ran. White also argued that in the 1990s a same pattern of lack of seriousness about the productive enterprises, and incompetence, undid attempts by the NOI to buy and develop agricultural lands in the South, and even the NOI's security teams that at first won multi-million dollar contracts from Republican politicians and agencies to cleanse crime from housing estates that had Black residents.[103] It is clear, nonetheless, that such attacks from the mainstream U.S. press or institutions on the new NOI's economic record did not take fair account of constriction by Jewish micronationalist organizations of opportunities for the sect's businesses in American life at its crucial point of self-institutionalization.

Farrakhan's sect kept up its calls and efforts for an autonomous Black Nationalist economy for over a quarter of a century. In mid-2003, *Final Call* rapped African-Americans for remaining "the largest consumer nation in the world" that was wasting $631 billion per annum purchasing from non-black shops and companies so that all that money flowed away out of the "Black Nation". U.S. corporations that marketed meats or textiles often had farms to produce the raw materials. The few remaining black farms had to be kept in business as the new NOI, reviving Elijah's pre-1975 project, strove to build a self-contained national economic circuit, including farms.[104] The NOI tried to galvanize blacks into building a Black Nationalist economy by evoking the bygone annihilation of Greenwood District. That old black business center in Tulsa, Oklahoma had built prosperity to an extent that prompted white mobs, high city officials and a plane to level it on 1 June 1921.[105]

Overall, Farrakhan and his supporters, and other Islam-influenced African-American sects of their type, have been ambivalent to Christian and Jewish whites whom they rhetorically assailed. They admire the ethnic self-organization, institutions and economic dynamism of the opposed Euro-American ethnos, and strive to duplicate it: with a different configuration of the factors, they may one day achieve constructive relations with Anglo- and Jewish-Americans of mutual benefit. While Farrakhan in 1985 at various points swung to the incinerations of Judgement Day or economic separation from America, he covertly also held open the possibility that his cult's nationalist-collectivist economics and political participation would lead blacks into America's mainstream.

Ongoing Millenarianism

The interactions of Farrakhan and his sect with Amerindian groups, such as the Hopi, reinforced that aspect of NOI ideology that was decidedly less realistic, and which was basically an Elijah-inspired neo-millenarianism. In September 1985, Farrakhan's journal, *Final Call*, reported that he had been "beamed up on board a space craft" to hear the voice of Elijah Muhammad expose a military plot by President Reagan; and there were claims that God's "angelic hosts" were working to support Farrakhan "in conjunction with an Intergalactic Federation of Star Brothers" as the modern Babylon's "final days" approached. Common UFO sightings were reckoned to be nothing other than glimpses of squadrons of babyships swarming over the earth in cyclic rhythm with Farrakhan's speaking tours.[106] There is great pressure from the lumpen and jailed converts who, given the sharp pain that drives them to consider Islam, are a source of pressure upon NOI leaders not to drop the Judgement and its incineration. In 1999, Raymond Scott and his cellmate in California were preparing for the final destruction of America of which "the Honorable Elijah Muhammad has warned us in his book *The Fall of America"* back in 1973. This African-American prisoner hoped that the "millenium computer bug" that some Euro-Americans feared would devastate America's spacecrafts, aviation, national security and surveillance in the year 2000 [which was never to actualize] would be the beginning. "May peace be upon The Nation of Islam and *The Final Call* as we approach the destruction of this evil nation," hoped these blacks behind bars.[107]

While, then, in his realistic or constructive modes, Farrakhan played down or jettisoned Elijah's projection of a Judgment Day that would come to destroy the whites, perhaps to start with an Armageddon world war, he could not completely repress the millenarian impetus in the ranks of the sectlet amid the desperation of many in the ghettos.

The Farrakhan-Warith Contest to 1990

Both Warith and Farrakhan were clearly the ideological progeny of Elijah and the old NOI. Warith presented the 30 million African-American people as "a race of consumers" possessing no normal, productive economic role in America, as against other ethnic groups in America. "We are a constrained colony of consumptive spenders who are too burdened to come to grips with our habits which enrich our [white] beneficiaries". Warith's demand for blacks to become productive was very like the Farrakhan group's suspicion of Welfare. But unlike Farrakhan's apparent preference for withdrawal from, and verbal confrontation with, mainstream U.S. society, Warith urged his followers and those blacks who have not embraced Islam to pursue a sort of street-wise "patriotism". Warith has strongly argued that American society is only sectionally oppressive or evil, that black suffering is tragic precisely because it negates the very real potential for a humane society that America has. "We see in the U.S. Constitution something that is compatible with the concept of man in our Holy Book Qur'an". "American democracy" and its idea that "every man is created equal" is a political ideology that the Qur'an itself motivates Warith and his followers to actualize now in American society, after so many false starts.

The weakness in Warith's position was that he stressed an individualist religion, while Farrakhan, helpfully branded a "black Hitler" by his unsalaried Jewish micronationalist PR workers, always called strongly for the building of a national movement. For all Warith's de-ethnicization of the movement as he strove to affiliate to global Islam, Farrakhan won burgeoning orthodox Muslim support which included immigrant Pakistanis and Arabs. His denunciations of Israel and Jews had electrified: such Muslims linked to the Third World accepted Farrakhan's drive for the development of a specific African-American ethnos in America, turning a blind eye to distinctive tenets in his sect. A consistent stream of Muslim visitors from Third World countries were soon passing through Farrakhan's Chicago headquarters. Among them was the 69-year-old Indian South African "Imam", Ahmad Deedat, a triumphalist denouncer of all Christianity, who in 1987 endorsed Elijah Muhammad's "use of gradualism in bringing black people to Islam" and tried to coax the immigrant Muslim community in America to reach out to blacks as their brothers, not seek community with whites. The NOI paper hailed Deedat as Islam's foremost Bible scholar.[108] The second NOI's primary and secondary school in Chicago in the late 1990s served as venue for the annual fund-raising dinner of the Nigerian Islamic Association of USA (NIA), held at the end of the fasting month of Ramadan. Here, Farrakhan and his movement really were bringing his followers into interaction with the Muslims of the West Africa whose ancestors they shared, and exposing at least some to the speeches of Nigerian Muslim academics.[109] Such contacts with Third World Muslims are injecting more Arabic vocabulary into NOI spoken and print English, and certainly work to fy Chicago's NOI core-membership over the long term.

Warith's branch of the movement came to be seen by many ordinary blacks as lacking the sting of the flamboyant, gripping, verbally confrontationist leadership that Farrakhan brought to the fore. Although many of his fellow-blacks called him and his sect "traitors" for not standing with Jackson and Farrakhan, Warith held fast to his milder message of "sobering up, principles and practical direction, clear-headedness"—negotiation and compromise with their white fellow citizens with whom African-Americans would always have to share one single country, in the hope that both black and white would progress together. Imam Warith applied his God-revealed Qur'an to judge what he termed the masses' drunken "Black fixation," at the cost of the race-popularity among blacks that confrontationism against whites brought Farrakhan.[110] With Warith there was no strident evocation of the Devil, whether as white or Jew, and little of the cargoistic, millenarian and retributive rhetoric emanating from the Farrakhan circle. Yet neither faction's positions—not Warith's pragmatism, new patriotism and frequent words from Arabic, nor Farrakhan's special neo-millenarianism—were to prove able to change conditions enough to make most U.S. blacks cease rejecting both as unrealistic dreams of "heaven on earth".

6: MATURE WARITHITE ISLAM

W. Deen Mohammed's successor-sect to the NOI maintained the drive to build wealth in America that its prototype had pursued from the 1930s. This determination to make it economically in mainstream middle-American terms seems to be the most serious project of these sects. The privatization of many of the old NOI's businesses and the greater scope thenceforth offered to individuals to exercise their initiative and reap the benefits from that, over the long term made Wallace's neo-Sunni sect a rewarding base for the energetic among them. (Yet, the old NOI's collectivism had been able to motivate many of its members to also work long creative hours without expecting much personal reward.) While self-enrichment by individuals through their hard work—something more like the social atomism of U.S. small private enterprise—now predominates and most property is private, Warith's group recognizes that some collectivism is still needed, especially to start out. Investing by members still is guided by "the immediate community members centered around the Collective Purchasing Conference." The CPCs, inter alia, bring members together to identify and pool resources to buy merchandise and products that will sell well in the local black communities, so as to "keep the monies [circulating] within our own community".[111]

Individuals are offered precise advice on how to discipline their families' spendings in order to build up a starting capital. From the CPC, members, or families in the sect, then branch out into investments of their own in real estate, technologies, stocks and bonds. Individuals in the sect must teach business and financial principles to their families. The final economic units are the patriarchal families these sects reconstruct for blacks: the aim declared for economic labor is to pass the returns on to future generations in such families, which are not yet quite on the Middle American nuclear families model.[112]

The sect's religious ideology and culture as well as its structures continue to spur and facilitate the drive of individuals to make themselves wealthy. As Lonnie Abdul Saboor, Chairman of the National Muslim Business Association, put it (with a Qur'anic quotation): "as we attempt to develop our businesses, it is important to realize that Allah [remains] the Chairman of the Board". Saboor wrote for "the [Muslim] business owner who is growing," or would grow if he kept improving his management skills as he increased staff, to become "a company". Counsel taken from classical Arabic Islam helps motivate and guide that drive: the advice of the Prophet Muhammad to "seek knowledge from the cradle to the grave" requires the Muslim businessman to keep attending business courses and conferences and to network. Without such "personal growth", the businessman will repeat the same mistakes and his enterprise will collapse, warned Abdul Saboor.[113] Islamic religious rituals and a light ethnic nationalism were apparent in a 2004 "New Africa Market" organized by Warith's sect in Chicago. "Come shop and spend with your own self and kind with sense. Buy with God in mind." The Market would close for Sunni noon salat (ritual prayer in Arabic: the tabloid used the Arabic term on its own). Yet, simultaneously, the Bible too here still helps lead the followers of W.D. Mohammed to see business as an expression of religion. Economic growth is one of the four rivers that, insofar as he recalled the text, the Bible states "went out from the Garden" of Eden [Cf. Genesis 2:10-14].[114]

A stance of both Warith and Farrakhan's sects, then, has been that a drive to get rich is not enough to make black individuals succeed in business. To make it, they need further motivation from an Islamic-religious and ethnic or national discourse, also crucial to their drawing enough of a clientèle. The success won by Warith's group over thirty years from 1975-2005 to establish an Islamic sub-economy has been substantial but far from complete. David K. Hasan in 2004 wanted "our Muslim families and others [=black Christian clients] to be able to get rid of meat from big food chains as soon as possible and put halal [=God-consecrated food slaughtered by Muslims] in their place." At that point, small masajid [=mosques: note the Arabic broken plural] scattered over the country were placing limited orders for the Islam-prescribed meat directly with Warith's Chicago HQ. If the meat, etc., was distributed from hubs in regions, they would cut transport costs and time and set prices based on the regional marketplaces. Hasan thus wanted to make his sect like America's large retailers, making jobs for the young brothers and sisters, including students who had to cover their expenses. Hasan was unabashed that he was talking economic nationalism, rather than an ordinary private enterprise for self-contained individuals or narrow families. He saw his project for Islamic regional hubs to distribute diverse products to *all* sect members as resuming a mechanism under the first leadership of the Honorable Elijah Muhammad: but with his successor sect's much greater experience and depth of leadership, "why shouldn't we be able to do 10 times as much today?" But would Hasan, too, pay (perhaps have to pay) some workers and volunteers with chickenfeed wages and hopes?[115]

In some ways, then, Warith's sect that has favored individualism in economics and culture may be returning to aspects of the collectivist Islamic non-territorial Nation of Elijah: however, Arabic and Qur'anic ideas now differentiate the Nation more than race. But several projects and institutions of Warith have collapsed over the last three decades, and the odds are against his micronation building a full autonomous Islamic economy that could last. In April 2005, Warith conceded that his sect was "struggling financially to make our business vision, for our community and most of all our investors, successful." An investment business is not a loan company, and W.D. Mohammed warned investors to stop pulling their money out because then "we have nothing to develop the businesses. That is what has happened." Yet their "love" (ideology) was making some leave their investments in the sect enterprises.[116]

Although stress is still given to unit-enterprises that can yet still link together in a micronationalist cluster, and upon the private enterprise of Muslim individuals as the road to prosperity, some middle class adherents of W. D. Mohammed pass over into America's central mega-institutions, governmental or private. Indeed, such mainstream bodies that employ professionals recognize Warith's sect as one constituency and catchment reservoir. When the 5-campus University of Medicine and Dentistry of New Jersey in 2000 awarded 1,200 professional degrees and certificates to the largest class in its history, some adherents originally educated in the sect's schools were among the recipients: Warith and many of his Imams were in attendance. In a side-ceremony, adherent Wayne Malik Smith, now Mayor of Irvington, N.J., offered to expose the students of the sect's schools to city government by having them work as interns in his office. Warith urged his followers present to make themselves mainstream professionals and public servants.[117] The institutions of Warith's sect are improving and winning outside recognition: they can be stepping-stones to careers in key mainstream institutions. Clyde El-Amin, a former principal at one of the sect's schools, in 2005 was chosen as President of the multi-campus Kennedy-King College in Chicago, where he would be able to apply his past skills to helping disadvantaged students get a quality education against the odds.[118]

Although Warith's "Black Muslim" sect is more individualistic and ideologically less standardized in comparison to his father's, it thus still has more than a touch of some of the old collectivist features—inevitably so, because they were more and more reading the Qur'an that weaves together the interests of individuals and their collective community. The blending of collective Islamic rituals such as Arabic group-prayers with economic endeavors continues. While now the property of individuals more often than of the sect, these African-American Muslim businesses continue to interlock into an economic circuit that rotates the monies to keep them "within the community". What, though, is their "community?" Warithite organizations that identify target markets wager on some extra, a nationalist bonus sympathy, from Christian Black, as well as Muslim, customers, that might tip the balance of whether the Muslim businesses make enough sales to last, or collapse. The ongoing Black Nationalist aura around Warith's bland "Muslim American Association" won it some free advice and training from non-Muslim African-American businesspersons. But at the final level that counts, the adherents may be loyal only to their own Arabic-emblemed collective self, a much smaller African-American Muslim micro-"Nation" that they no longer often call such.

From 1975 over decades, Warith's followers kept up their drive to buy farmlands and build self-contained Muslim communities throughout the USA, with an iron will. In 2002, a group of followers purchased 25 acres of choice multi-purpose land in Baltimore County, Maryland. Twenty-two years before, during an earlier attempt to purchase, leaders in the area had tried to run the believers out. Now the group planned to develop the estate's agriculture but also to build commercial establishments, a bank and multi-unit dwellings—a Muslim mini-economy—as well as offering social security through housing for the old NOI's pioneers, and single-family homes. Arabic words from the evolving Muslim English further defined this micro-community. Mentoring camping programs at the estate to give manhood training to sect male teenagers were dubbed "Rijal Retreats" (Rijal, the broken Arabic plural for "adult males"). The mosque's name, "al-Inshirah" [="the expansion" or "relief"], was to evoke Qur'an 94:5-6 that hard, punishing work finally wins release, and is a way for humans to direct themselves to God. But the hospitality of the estate members was termed "our African tradition" by a visiting Warith. Its leaders were aware of Baltimore's siting in the old "Underground Railway" route by which blacks once escaped slavery in the South.[119] By 2002, after twenty years of effort, the sect's community at New Medinah outside Hattiesburg, Mississippi, was replacing trailers with the new homes of a long-term town for Muslims. This "complete [self-contained] community" offered meat slaughtered according to the Islamic ritual, and in economics was trying to develop Islamic banking systems in accord with Shari'ah (Islamic jurisprudence), which prohibited the charging of interest.[120] This sect's building of little self-contained rural communities could, in aggregate, bring about a sort of non-continuous homeland under Arabic mottoes and Islamic emblems for an African-American Muslim micronation.

Islamic ideology and Arabic shibboleths, then, have more socio-economic functions than ever in that sector of the NOI tradition that has continued under Warith. Both continue to distance and analytically objectify America in the minds of the hard-driving bourgeois adherents, cushioning their feelings from rejection or failure in it, which makes them resilient. This special Islam's inculcation of a more and more well-informed sense of a wide, millennia-old Islamic macro-history centered in the Middle East trains members to see broad developments in modern U.S. history in perspective as well. The dual consciousness thus fosters hypothetical thinking and alertness to U.S. economic details and patterns: such skills equip them to identify shifts in technologies and in markets that their companies can seize or avoid.

Despite occasional efforts by Warith to contract Islam or select from it so as to fit it into the U.S. system, strong tensions continued between the adopted Sunni Islamic and Arab ideas and the requirements of America. Global Islam imposes some prescriptions in dress, diet and conduct that grate against various streams of American mores, whether mainstream or African-American. As long as the sect cannot expand its own system of Islamic schools enough to educate all its children within its own ethos, some have to attend government schools. There, such symbols as the head-scarf (hijab) required of female Muslims can activate U.S. media denunciations of Muslims as alien terrorists and oppressive of women.

In one instance occurring in 1999, Jannah, a sect teenager, would take off her hijab as soon as she was delivered to her school: when found out, she told her mother that her reason was that she "didn't want to be singled out as different". After counsel by her mother, father and sister, Jannah then did wear the hijab in school as her first demonstration that the "world" would not sap her obedience to Allah in her life. But her father was also aware that some "majority blacks" had high expectations of the Muslims who might well refrain from drinking or wearing mini-skirts—some non-Muslim classmates would encourage Jannah to hold to her principles. It works for their trans-generational survival that the sects of Islam have implanted into the minds of even African-Americans of a pagan, permissive ethos that Muslims have title to diverge, in customs that win half-approval from some of those very people whose lifestyles Islam challenges. Further, the parents of Jannah egged on their daughters to achieve as highly as their sons in school —in that, they were very middle-American, although also rekindling principles in the Qur'an and the sayings and model practice of the Prophet Muhammad that likewise prescribe equality in education for women.[121]

The American mainstream and its cultures do now evince some flexibility vis-à-vis such once-strange minority religions as Islam. America does not have the anti-Arab obdurate "laicism" of the racist French state that has not allowed Muslim females to wear hijabs to its schools—sparking attacks from Farrakhan's faraway tabloid in Chicago. But after September 11 many adolescent Muslims are being made to feel by some African-American peers—not just by authority-figures—that the ethos their parents inculcate is not welcome as a tradition that would perpetuate itself down generations. The issue is whether Warith's Islam and the American patterns will prove mutually flexible enough to enable his followers to implant their sub-culture and patterns within American normality and culture. This in turn may well decide if the parents can keep their children within the sect and within Islam.

In this final period of the permutations of his sect in the 1990s and after, Warith and his media only occasionally mentioned "African-Americans" as the prescriptive ethnic identity to be built. Some tantalizing loose ends, though, showed that a final closure of meaning on this issue of nationality in America had not been achieved. Warith came by his orthodoxy through the instruction of Arabs who gained entry into the old post-WWII Nation of Islam because they were needed to teach the Arabic that Elijah wanted, despite his misgivings that they might unsettle his youth. Some of those Arabs of the 1950s and 1960s were already extraterritorial nationalists, and their successors and offspring around Warith's and Farrakhan's sects of course became micronationalistic in the fashion of most other American groups after 1965—and continued to unsettle Warith's followers in the 1990s. In 1999, Warith's adherent, Daniel 'Abdullah, mounted an Americanist argument that the American civil war *was* to abolish slavery (pace Elijah). But recalling an article by Layla Diyab asking how she could fit her Palestinian identity with her identities as a Muslim and as an American citizen, suddenly 'Abdullah reflected that

> it is no different for us... With the rich and growing ethnic divisions America has experienced, particularly in the last 2 or 3 decades [=micronationalization], it is no longer wise for African-Americans to ignore their own rich ethnic identity.[122]

While Warith's sect has been wary of formalized nationalist self-identification since 1975, nonetheless, its media's projection of diverse Middle Eastern, African and U.S. histories, bygone and current, can justify and aid diverse identity choices and plural national groups in America.

Classical Muslims and the Modern West

W. Deen Mohammed's media came to offer adherents pathways into the complete history and cultural patterns of the classical wide Islamic populations that shared high Arabic. True, that usually was a phantom culture taken from semi-scholarly books in English that fit well into America's rational high WASP thought. Warith's newspaper directed followers to a 2002 book *Intellectual Achievements of Muslims* on that classical greatness, authored by Western-educated South Asian Muslims. The reviewer, as W. Deen Mohammed does, argued that Islam—e.g. the Qur'an's order to humans to seek God's activity in the heavenly bodies and seasons—first motivated the classical Muslims to create their new science. This originated the experimental method, upon which the West then built its modern science. The item gave succinct—or sparse?—data about the contributions of classical Muslims like Ibn al-Haytham (965AD-1039) to optics, and to universal mathematics by other classical Muslims, such as al-Khawarizmi (d. 850) whose algorithms still carry his name in the West. Those classical Arabs and Muslims favored by W. Deen Mohammed's sect justified exchanges between Islamic and other cultures and America's civilization: at the outset, the 'Abbasid Caliph al-Mansur (r. 754-775) had set up an institute to translate the needed Greek and Indian books, and Ibn al-Haytham and other Muslim scientists had anticipated the theory of Evolution.[123] The pro-Warith reviewer passed on a swipe by one of the authors against the later Sunni religious scholars ('*ulama*') and later madrasahs (Sunni religious schools) as a "priestly" elite that toadied to the courts of tyrants and discouraged philosophy and critical research, thus contributing to the fading of science, and to loss of originality in Islamic law.[124]

U.S. values and needs influence what writers of Wallace's sect select from classical Islam. *Muslim Journal* advised the adherents to read a 2002 study of "Muslim Spain" (700-1492) by Maria Menocal (Cuban-American) which stressed adjustment to each other of its ruling Muslims and its Christians and Jews by which they together created vibrant culture and thought such as no one group could have built up on its own. The Qur'an motivated successive Caliphs to allow Jews and Christians to practise their faiths, stated the African-American Muslim reviewer. The reviewer was frankly seizing these classical motifs of a cooperative, pluralist Muslim Spain to forestall both the Euro-American writers and the Third World Jihadist Muslims who each hoped for violence between Muslims, Christians and Jews as inherent for the 21st century. Warith had sought in Muslim Spain a prototype for dialogue between Muslim and Christian blacks in 1982. Now, in 2002, that Spain was providing the pattern for a realistic acceptance of diverse America as it is, and a readiness to play by its formal rules, for the payoffs those promise to all.

Here at least, Warith and his adherents did not hope to convert most African-Americans—let alone Euro-Americans—to Islam in the foreseeable future. The classical Arabs who conquered and ruled Spain gave Jews much more tolerance and upwards social mobility than they had enjoyed previously, including some top posts as advisers. Such a model could both accept local American Jews and at the same hold out hope that Muslims might be rewarded with the same opportunities and admission by Christian Euro-America. But the classical materials had their own life and dualities. Thus, the Warithite reviewer had to allow that the Christian church was hostile from the outset to any Muslim presence in Europe, and that "Christianity under the leadership of Pope Urban II [was waging] the Crusades against the Muslims to recapture the Holy Land during the same period" that Church scholars were tapping the vast libraries in Cordova. In the end, in 1492 the "Spanish Catholics expelled Jews and Muslims from Spain".[125]

Elite South Asian Muslims and immigrant elite Muslim professionals in the U.S. made Islam's scriptural phraseologies coat the West's modern sciences. African-American Muslims were seeking both community with those immigrants and to themselves gain entry into mainstream America by pointing out Islamic similarities—indeed, precedents—to valued aspects of western culture. Warith was further aware that at international "peace" meetings with Jews, their leaders mentioned that the relations of Jews with "the Muslim scientists" in Spain had been one source of their "revival." Imam

W. Deen saw the sciences as "missing in the Message of Islam today," although, like Hindus and the Chinese, Muslims were trying to become creative in science once more. Warith's ideology of the sciences as ever-expanding knowledge passed on from peoples to peoples and from one religion to another ruled out yellow or black or white as categories: there was only one, universal, world, and a single America, both of which his followers had to enter.[126]

Still, the materials that W. Deen's sect offered were two-edged on most matters. Diverse faith-groups could and should work together. Muslims, Christians and Jews had built science and philosophy and high culture together in Spain. Then, though, genocidal expulsion ended that [New York-like?] plural liberal community. Materials and data from the Arabo-Islamic world were all grounding the Imam's younger followers to contribute to central and apex America. African-Americans being pointed to business endeavors, learning the integral Arabic Qur'an from recitations CDs by sect imams, being sent to Damascus to study Islamic law, and the adherents' familiarity with Arab politics—all this group's expanding skills could help the American system negotiate and manage constructive deals and settlements with Middle Easterners as globalization drew everyone together. So would America give them such jobs and roles? Was it a system that could ever be constructive to any Muslims and Arabs, given its drive to seize and corner resources? Would Warith's new people have better luck in America than their coreligionists had in Spain? [The U.S. system, too, had not, in its past, been any stranger to the transportation and confinement of nationalities.]

By the 1990s, the media of Warith's movement was projecting a final synthesis of calm rationality in which all social passion had been spent and in which most Americans came together in multiple integrative structures as a matter of course.

Jews' and Arabs' Ongoing Input into African-American Identity

As in 1975 when he invited whites to join the sect, Warith now in the 1990s challenged, almost with relish, one of the key shibboleths of African-American ethnicity: he reached out not just to Jewish fellow-Americans but to some of their organizations that had worked with least double-mindedness to make the U.S. serve Israel's interests. This drew fire from a range of other Islamizing and nationalist groups in Afro-America. The (pro-Farrakhan) tabloid, *New Trend*, a coalition of immigrant and African-American Sunni Muslims that had once supported Khomeini and which denounced the U.S. system in season and out, assailed a mid-1995 address by Imam Warith to the Executive Committee of the B'nai B'rith Anti-Defamation League (ADL) in which he praised the Jews as "a people who have believed in God and promote justice on this earth". "In me you have not only a person who respects you highly, and believes in what you are, but who wants to see you more successful". In this broadside against Warith as a possibly apostate Zionist hireling, *New Trend* identified the ADL in America as an espionage organization that had cooperated with the FBI's surveillance of black, Islamic, Arab, Left, Amerindian and other activist groups in America.[127] Yet Warith's half-dead ingratiating English before the ADL may have only thinly cloaked his own ongoing fury against the group to whose power in U.S. life he was now adapting his sect for its own good.

Now Warith's final Americanism, for the time at least, drew his followers into inclusive institutions in which they could be addressed by Ashkenazi Jews. At one function, holocaust survivor Gilbert Metz compared his experience in Germany to Milosevic's killing of Kosovo's Albanian Muslims, and challenged the Jews, Christians and Muslims present to go back and raise money from their communities for its people. With Muslims, Christians and Jews coming to each other's rescue, Imam Harisuddin endorsed the Jews' slogan "Never Again" as also meant by them to apply for all other victimized humans.[128]

In the end, the layers of Wallace's Americanist conjunction with the Jews who shared the country could be as ambiguous in both outcomes and motive as much other black Muslim discourse. Although U.S. Jewry had shifted somewhat since the 1980s from "Zionism" to a particularistic America-framed Jewish micronationalism, and many of its individuals were entering radical, final assimilation to Anglo-America, major sectors remain highly oriented to Israel. The audibility of other incompatible groups through developing technologies, the unremitting inflow of data from and about them (and their overseas descent-homelands), is among the main stimuli in the defining and consolidating of micronations in the era of globalization and the post-modern. Even as they engage with Jews, Warithite African-Americans are reading more and more print-products of their organizations: this could help educate a new generation of African-American Muslims into a much tighter solidarity-community with Palestinian and Arab movements in the Middle East. The collapse of the peace process, amid Sharon's incursions to incrementally reconquer the West Bank and the Gaza Strip, rallied Warith Deen Mohammed's followers to the Palestinian side amid the three years of violence of the Palestinians' second ("al-Aqsa") intifadah.

It was mostly the Islamic groups in the occupied territories who were hitting back hard at all Israelis, not 'Arafat and the secularists: but suicide bombers did not fit into the post-1975 American Muslim Mission's hankering for good relations between Americans and compromise solutions to conflicts. But now, in 2002, the violence in Israel-Palestine under Ariel Sharon again pushed the sect towards becoming a sort of lobby for the Palestinians among African-Americans as a whole. Addressing the entire African-American community from a 107 years-old black newspaper in 2002, Imam Mikal Saahir still rapped the suicide bombings by "the Palestinians" as "un-religious". Israel's "security as a state is a must", but "justice for the Palestinian people" by ending its occupation was the way to win that "homeland security" for the Israelis. Imam Saahir secularized the collectivity and struggle of the Palestinians, referring to the fact that they include many who are Christian and Druze "(an off-shoot of Islam)", and that "the Palestinian-

Israeli conflict is not an Islam versus Judaism problem but one of occupation and statehood". But some verses of the Qur'an and sayings of the Prophet Muhammad that he cited to criticize the suicider bombers were two-edged, and could mitigate them as counter-attacking against the occupation and the squalor and violence imposed by the Israeli system under Ariel Sharon.[129]

The in-depth engagement of African-American Muslims with Palestine from 1967-2005 built up sharp, diverse and sometimes intimate and disturbing data about both the Palestinians and their Israeli enemy. The final realistic picture had to have some patches of gloom. In mid-2002, from the pages of Warith's paper, the secularized Christian Palestinian-American, Edward Sa'id, assailed "brutality, autocracy and unimaginable corruption" by Yasir 'Arafat and his Palestinian authority, and the "absence of a strategic plan". The self-serving, weak 'Arafat had never really reined in the Islamists, Sa'id contended: the bombings had convinced many around the world that "we are indeed terrorists and an immoral movement".[130] It was one more of many diverse items offered for the grandchildren of Elijah to sift in a new century. They had come far from the gripping flat dichotomizations of heroic al-Fatah/PLO and evil Israel of *Muhammad Speaks* in the wake of 1967.

Edward Sa'id was not wrong that relations between Israel and Palestine were a domestic political issue in the USA! Violence between faraway Israelis and Palestinians was fueling a renewal of "Black-Jewish" tensions in U.S. high politics and society. In mid-2002, a debate on which side not just the African-American masses but their political representatives should take on Palestine yet again brought into the open the decades-long inequality of these two American "peoples" in institutional mainstream politics. Five members of the Congressional Black Caucus (CBC) voted against a May 2002 resolution in Congress that supported Israel in its "war against terrorism" and interpreted Yasir 'Arafat and his secularist Palestinian Authority as the coordinator of the terrorist attacks. When Congressman Earl Hilliard from Alabama then lost his seat to a political newcomer, he and some CBC colleagues charged that it was because "the Jews of the United States" [really U.S. Jewry's c. twenty percent Zionist minority] had put $1 million into that challenger's campaign. But as well as protesting his interactions with Palestinians and Libyans that angered the AIPAC, parochial Jewish magnates in Alabama had also griped that Hilliard had not done enough for "business" (=them) in his five terms. Now, Hilliard argued that most black members of Congress were again at pains to appease such Zionist organizations as the American-Israel Public Affairs Committee (AIPAC): if they questioned Israel taking Palestinian land, then they could be "taken out at any time during our election". The defeated Hilliard demanded that African-Americans in general, too often uninvolved as yet, should now start building up "war chests" to back their political representatives in elections.[131] [If it were to happen, that would make the blacks much more like U.S. Jewry!]

Secular and Christian black activists contribute to the stock of unfavorable images of Israel in the psyche of Warith's followers. These wider African-American groups both could be led by the Muslim sects in a serious counter-lobby, and at the same time are a source of political pressures on sects such as Warith's and Farrakhan's to join in some anti-Israel project. Anti-Israeli and pro-Palestinian reflexes among African-Americans, and perhaps even in the sub-consciousness of some in the Muslim sects, are still fed by old Christian culture, despite secularization and all the advance of Islam. In early 2004, Warith's tabloid published an article with these emotions by Bernice Powell Jackson, a high-ranking Christian who was Executive Director of the Racial Justice Commission of the United Church of Christ. Her anger at Ariel Sharon's all-out offensive to crush the second Palestinian intifadah focused around holy places of the New Testament vivid in carols and other mass religious culture of Christian blacks. Bernice Jackson had visited the West Bank and gave a solid, vivid account of the 400 mile-long Wall of concrete, razor wire and gun-towers that Ariel Sharon was building through the West Bank to pen in its starved Arabs and separate some of them from their farms. A 25 foot high concrete and barbed wire fence might soon surround Bethlehem, "the town where the Prince of Peace was born," and Beit Sahour "where the shepherds were said to have received the news of the birth of the baby Jesus." Understandably for her position, Powell's interactions had mainly been with the Christian communities among the Palestinians. The article was crafted to draw black American Christians into the strategies and instruments of the Palestinian Christians to survive in their country. "Israeli defense forces" had bulldozed and bombed away the olive trees near Beit Sahour. Citizens of several European nations, directed by the YMCA, had planted several thousand olive trees to replace them, but now the Wall would tear those down as well. Powell directed African-Americans how to contact Arab East Jerusalem's YMCA and pay for an olive seedling. And to write to (=lobby) President Bush, Jr.[132]

As a group that has been penned into ghettoes in America, African-Americans, Christian and secular as well as Muslim, had to react sharply to Israel's "separation wall" designed to break up the Palestinians into "prison camps." Within America, Bernice Jackson was seeking joint action with Muslims against drug culture, youth gangs and fire-arms in a 2005 article in Farrakhan's newspaper, in which she assailed Bush, Jr.'s high expenditures on the armed forces, and his tax cuts for the wealthiest Americans, which cut off dollars needed for schools and mainstream activities for at-risk black children.[133]

Only time will tell if Muslim sects will ever have the clarity or the priority to systematically mobilize such Christian emotions as Jackson's for a united front of Muslim and Christian blacks and Arab-Americans to counter the Israel lobby in the U.S.

African-American Congresswoman Cynthia McKinney was close to Warith, Farrakhan, and to Arab-Americans and Arab and Muslim embassies. Warith's sect was striding towards becoming a counter-lobby when Imam Najee 'Ali came to Atlanta in August 2002 to support McKinney's re-election campaign as the pro-Israel lobby closed in on her with dollars for opponents.[134] But all her brothers and her Arab friends could not save her.

The Middle East was central even in the engineering of her subsequent ballot-box downfall: the enemies spread it about through the Georgia media that she was a dangerous "loony" who had argued that President Bush knew in advance of the September 11 attacks but let them go ahead so as to tighten the grip of his administration on power. Cynthia McKinney had never said any such thing—she had simply asked why, given the enormity of the calamity, the government had not hurried up with an investigation into the events of September 11th—but the concoction ended her, electorally, for the time being.[135]

After years of painful building of trust with American Jews, in 2002 W.D. Mohammed's sect even looked like it was being inevitably sucked into the vortex of a united African-American front against Israel and U.S. Zionists similar to that which Jesse Jackson and Farrakhan, and the Zionoids' need for a bogey, had focused in 1983-1985. Jesse Jackson invited Imam Warith Deen Mohammed to a September 2002 forum of his People United to Save Humanity (PUSH) as a representative of the Muslim component of the African-American nation: the key-note speaker was 'Amr Musa, Secretary-General of the League of Arab States, who was flanked by top African-American clergymen. Both Jackson and that Egyptian were ambiguous at the PUSH forum about Palestinian suicide bombings. Jackson told Israel to only go after HAMAS, not the whole Palestinian people. 'Amr noted that "all foreign military forces have been resisted" in history, although the Arab League stood with America against "terrorism" internationally. Muslim and Christian African-Americans, Egyptians and the Yasir 'Arafat whom Israel blatantly indicated it might kill at any time, were all briefly fusing together into one imagined "family reunion" across continents. Although no doubt aware of their caution about politics, Jackson asked Warith's sect to help recruit 10,000 new members to PUSH. Jackson warned Bush, Jr. not to attack 'Iraq, and Egyptian 'Amr told his potential African-American counter-lobby that he was an African: he voiced the Arab World's liking for African-Americans and their music and songs.[136] Still, although now swinging back to the Arab camp after a truce with Zionism, both the Reverend Jackson and the Imam—like that Arab League SG present—still strove for a two-states solution, as the U.S. government, too, claimed to be doing.

In 2002, Imam W.D. Mohammed still wanted African-Americans to build constructive relations with their Jewish compatriots, and promote (like Jackson), a two-states settlement in the Middle East. But a flashpoint would come for his group if some Jewish lobby too openly broke professional black politicians who questioned why so many billions should be siphoned off in aid to Israel and away from the USA's black poor. Yet many U.S. Jews, although now very rich, continued to aid the Democratic Party that still furthered some class interests of non-affluent blacks: would any political showdown between these two ethnic groups ever actually ignite?

Since 1995—earlier than Farrakhan—Warith had grasped the reality that his country's Jewish nationalists had the institutions to deny sustenance, prosperity and entrance into the American mainstream to any African-American group that took them on. Veiled send-up and vaudeville acquiescence are a serious device with which African-Americans have long confused and contained opposed groups that have power to harm them in America. Yet the American theosophist tolerance and the accommodation to nearby Jews that Warith chose buckle when Islam as a universal community-ideology, some links from Arabic, conflict between the social and developmental interests of local "Blacks and Jews", and some social relations with Palestinian-Americans are all ignited together by extreme violence in the Middle East. Then the cultural make-up of the Afro-American Muslim micro-people may suspend, in regard to some Jews, the Americanist community that is a natural impulse of all groups in America.

ENDNOTES

1 *New York Times* 17 June 1975 cited in Daniel Pipes *In the Path of God: Islam and Political Power* (New York: Basic Books 1983) p. 275.

2 Cf. A. Bontemps and J. Conroy *Any Place But Here* (New York: Hill and Wang 1969 edn) pp. 226-9; Malcolm X *Autobiography of Malcolm X* (Harmondsworth: 1968 Penguin edn) pp. 258-62.

3 *Muhammad Speaks* 26 February 1965 p. 1, quoted Bontemps and Conroy, *Anyplace But Here* pp. 226-229.

4 See Ken Farid Hassan, "Remembering the Motherplane: reflections on the Nation of Islam", in *Hijrah* (Los Angeles), Fall 1988 pp. 14-15. Both the Jehovah's Witnesses and the NOI that came afterwards, saw the year 1914 as ushering in the destruction of the gentile nations of Satan and the establishment of a new order under God Himself on earth. Both groups believed that only an elect numbering 144,000 would enjoy paradise after the Judgment: Claude A. Clegg, *An Original Man: The Life and Times of Elijah Muhammad* (NY: Saint Martin's Press 1997) p. 72.

5 E.U. Essien-Udom, *Black Nationalism: A Search for an Identity in America* (Chicago: University of Chicago Press 1962) pp. 194, 164.

6 Ibid., pp. 164-5, 169; also Clegg op cit p. 158 for Elijah's economic programs and their functions in making him a serious contender against Martin Luther King and the other integrationists.

7 Clegg op cit p. 158.

8 Michael Nash, "'The Son of Thunder,' Who Was Minister James 3X Shabazz? Nation of Islam History in Newark, N.J. — 3", *Muslim Journal* 8 November 2002 p. 11.

9 Charles 67X, "Meeting of the Minds", in *Muhammad Speaks* 10 December 1974 p. 2.

10 Malcolm X *Aut* pp. 368-9; see advertisement "Visit Muhammad's Temples of Islam", in *Muhammad Speaks* 20 December 1974 p. 23.

11 al-Shawaribi, *al-Islam fi Amrika* (Cairo: c.1960) p. 130.

12 Essien-Udom pp. 125, 219-220.

13 See Most Honorable Elijah Muhammad, "The Glorious Holy Qur'an Sharrieff," *Final Call* 7 June 2005 p. 19. In the accompanying photo of him as a fairly young man, Elijah was holding Yusuf 'Ali's English translation with facing Arabic text: he recommended both that and the Ahmadiyyah translation.

14 See Peter Goldman, *The Death and Life of Malcolm X* (London: Gollancz 1974) p. 97; Benjamin Goodman, *The End of White World Supremacy: Four Speeches by Malcolm X* (New York: Merlin House 1971) p. 8; Malcolm X *Autobiography* p. 334.

15 Kofi Natambu, *The Life and Work of Malcolm X* (Indianapolis: Alpha 2002) pp. 252-253. The injured among the arrested Muslims were not treated for two days.

16 Goldman, *The Death and Life of Malcolm X* p. 95.

17 *Autobiography* p. 334.

18 A picture in *Muhammad Speaks* of 7 February 1975 p. 14 showed the sign "Makbaz Bakery and Sandwich". The transcription "Makbaz" for "Bakery" favors it coming from below from daily use in a spoken variety of English in the sect: the correct transcription would be "Makhbaz," and that Arabic fricative *kh* was sometimes carried in BM print-prose, however pronounced by readers and even orators.

19 Mary Eloise X, "Two Great Families Unite!" in *Muhammad Speaks* 14 February 1975 p. S4. The Arabic christian names of Elijah's nephew and grandson contrasted to the Western ones of Farrakhan's daughters.

20 Clegg pp. 264, 276.

21 "Remembering a Very Special Imam: Imam Shakir Abd-Allah Mahmoud April 16, 1936-Oct. 15, 2004," Muslim Journal 5 November 2004 p. 9

22 Ken Farid Hassan, "Remembering the Motherplane" loc cit p. 14.

23 See Nathaniel Omar, "Meeting the Challenge to Teach and Learn Arabic", *Muslim Journal* 19 July 2002 p. 11. Abdul Hakim's computer-processed book was titled *Arabic Phonics and Grammar.* Essien-Udom in 1962 already noted one adherent Kwrmenr X (Crowley) who was studying both Arabic and Russian, and for a college degree: p. 249.

24 Essien-Udom op cit p. 291.

25 Muhammad 'Ali with Robert Durham, *The Greatest: My Own Story* (London: Mayflower 1977) pp. 248-9.

26 See Zafar Ishaq Ansari, "W.D. Muhammad: The Making of a 'Black Muslim' Leader" (1933-1961)", *American Journal of Islamic Social Sciences* pp. 255-6. An Egyptian teacher in the sect rated Wallace's grasp of Arabic as "well above the average": Essien-Udom p. 82.

27 Ansari, "W.D. Muhammad..." p. 260; Malcolm X, *Aut* p. 453.

28 See Alverda X, "Purification is Divine", in *Muhammad Speaks* 14 February 1975 p. 3; for the widening appeal of Wallace's cheerful proto-Sunni message to some in the sect; Ansari, loc. cit. p. 247.

29 Sayyid Hadi Khosrow-Shahi, *Nabard-i-Islam dar Amrika* (Tehran: c. 1974 pp. 12-14). I am grateful to Mrs M. Kouhi, Director of International Communications at the Tehran International Studies and Research Institute, for sending me a xerox of this book in 2002.

30 Most of the anti-Christian positions taken here can be found in C. Eric Lincoln, *The Black Muslims in America* (Boston: Beacon Press 1961) pp. 76-80; *Muhammad Speaks* esp. 13/8 (1973) -14/25 (1975); cf also Malcolm X, *Aut* pp. 257-8, 298, 320-1.

31 W.D. Muhammad, "The Mercy of Allah", in *Radiance* (New Delhi) 3 July 1977 p. 4.

32 K. Raheem, "Muslims Help Observe MLK's Birthday", in *American Muslim Journal* 6 January 1984 p. 19.

33 "Muslims Take Efforts to Remove Racial Images to Kansas City H.R. [Human Rights] Commission", in *American Muslim Journal* 16 July 1982 p. 7.

34 Wali Akbar Muhammad, "CRAID Walk in Dallas Climbs to Success", in *American Muslim Journal* 27 August 1982 pp. 5, 9; Samuel Ayyub Bilal, "Dallas Hears Three Powerful Talks by Imam Muhammad" in ibid. 10 September 1982 p. 4. Imam Qasim Ahmad said that "over the past two years we have spoken in about 500 churches in the Dallas-Ft Worth Area"(!): Ayyub Bilal, "Dallas Hears..."

35 Hakim Sabree, " 'For My People,': the African-American Born Out of Slavery," *Muslim Journal* 5 November 2004 p. 8.

36 Idris Michael Tobin, growing up in California, had been incensed by "hypocrisy", the failure of his parents' church's clerics and congregation to practise what they preached, but it was the issue of white religious images that converted him to the NOI at the age of 12: telephone conversation 24 June 2003.

37 *Muslim Journal* 2 August 2002 p. 31.

38 Nathaniel Omar and Ayesha K. Mustafa, "Muslims, Catholics and other Christians Reaffirm Ties", *Muslim Journal* 23 August 2002 pp. 19, 29. Both the African-American Muslims and the Catholic clerics who were dialoguing here well knew that charges of pedophilia hung over the credibility of that church in America.

39 *Imam W. Deen Muhammad Speaks from Harlem N.Y.: Challenges that Face Man Today* (Chicago: W.D. Muhammad Publications 1985) pp. 114-116. pp. 84-87.

40 Dionne Muhammad, "A torchlight for the South: Minister Farrakhan brings inspiration to Alabama", *Final Call* 27 August 1996 p. 7.

41 Farrakhan, "Ghana University Address 19 February 1986" (audio-cassette of Nation of Islam).

42 Elijah Muhammad, "How Can We Unite?", *Final Call* 1 March 1987 p. 19.

43 "Economist sees Cultural Flaw among Bilalians," in *AMJ* 13 January 1984; cf. Mrs. Sanjio Muhammad, "So You Want to Start Your Own Small Business" in ibid. p. 11. Sowell's book was published in New York in 1983. Imam W.D. Mohammed mocked in 1985 that Haitians "Black, too, like we are" came with nothing to the USA but [at] once in, quietly labored to acquire: unlike African-Americans they established no Haitian Movement and wasted no time working to get a "friend in the White House" and taking their problems to other people: *Imam W. Deen Muhammad Speaks from Harlem* pp. 114-116.

44 For the restrictions see *AMJ* 31 August 1984 p. 3. Yet Sunni-like orthodoxy in prisons could get out of hand. Imam W.D. Muhammad urged his converts in prison not to turn militant over issues of diet and foods that were really secondary. Imam W.D. Muhammad, *Religion on the Line: al-Islam, Judaism, Catholicism, Protestantism* (Chicago: W.D. Muhammad Publications 1983) pp. 12-15.

45 Minister David Muhammad, "Minister Farrakhan Exhorts Prison and Inmates to Reform," *Final Call* 5 July 2005 pp. 20; the gangs pp. 21-23.

46 For coverage of the demonstration, see Khalil Saleem, "Reflections on Camden Muslims' March against Prostitution", in *AMJ* 20 January 1984 p.10; cf Harold Abdullah, "Ramadan Fuels American Muslims" in ibid 6 July 1984 pp. 3, 19.

47 Donna Sharif Ali, "Murder of Muslim Ignites Protest" in *AMJ* 6 April 1984 p. 3 (on the martyrdom); Robert Dannin, "Muslims Wage Holy War on Crack" in *Hijrah* Fall, 1988 pp. 7-10 (on Brooklyn).

48 " In the Name of Allah, the Beneficent, the Merciful: Minister Farrakhan delivers an admonition to the dutiful," *Final Call* l5 July 2005 pp. 3, 22. For a 2002 effort by Farrakhan to get his message of reconciliation, healing and peace across to the gangs in Watts, Farrakhan's Message to the 'Gang'Leaders", *Final Call* 19 March 2002 pp. 20-21

49 Farrakhan, "By the Time: Surely Man is in Loss," *Final Call* 21 June 2005 pp. 20-22.

50 Imam W.D. Mohammed, "The Dignity of Work: Human Dignity Demands Lawful Employment" in *American Muslim Journal* 23 July 1982 pp. l, 5.

51 For the suspicion of governmental welfare in Farrakhan's successor-sect see Mattias Gardell, *In the Name of Elijah Muhammad: Louis Farrakhan and the Nation of Islam* (Carolina: Duke University Press and London: Hurst 1996) p. 319.

52 Imam W.D. Mohammed, "Dignity of Work," ibid 30 July 1982 pp. S3, S7. Cf Milton Friedman, *Capitalism and Freedom* (Chicago: University of Chicago Press 1962) pp. l33-6.

53 See Gladys Zarif, "Careers in Law" *American Muslim Journal* 6 January 1984 p. 6; Mrs. Sanjio Muhammad, "So You Want to Start Your Own Small Business" in ibid. p. 11.

54 "Masjidullah Honors Community Achievers for Academic Excellence", *Muslim Journal* 9 August 2002 pp. 13, 23.

55 *Muslim Journal* 17 June 2005 p. 1.

56 Farrakhan, "The True Role of GOVERNMENT", address to the BIG convention in Washington D.C. on 23 August 1997, *Final Call* 1 July 2003 pp. 20-21.

57 For the background of the parochial Black-Jewish relationship see esp. R.G. Weisbord and A. Stein, "Negro Perceptions of Jews between the World Wars", in *Judaism* 18 (1969), pp. 428-47; Arnold Forster and Benjamin R. Epstein, *The New Anti-Semitism* (New York: 1974) pp. 207ff, and Lincoln op cit pp. 165-9.

58 Munir 'Umrani, "Israel to Get More U.S. Aid", in *American Muslim Journal* 7 September 1984 p. 4. 'Umrani was more royal than the king, since the terminology used by Sa'udi Arabian diplomats at the time made clear the Kingdom's

preparedness to recognize a Zionist state in part of Palestine: Wali Muhammad Uqdah, "Saudi's New Ambassador", in ibid 6 January 1984 p. 4.

59 Imam W. Deen Mohammed dismissed Jackson's campaign to become U.S. President as "more symbolic than real." But *AMJ* under 'Umrani's editorship applauded Jackson's judiciously-phrased criticisms of Israeli and U.S. actions in the Middle East and rallied support for him against the U.S. neighborhood Zionists. See "Jackson Critical of Lebanon Shelling" (condemning Reagan) *AMJ* 24 February 1984 p. 21 and "Reveren Abernathy Predicts Jesse Jackson Win" ibid. Dr Ralph Davi Abernathy was Dr Martin Luther King's successor as president of the Southern Christian Leadership Conference. Warith was well aware in 1985 that most African-Americans disliked him for not saying on television that Rev. Jesse Jackson should be President: see *Imam W. Deen Muhammad Speaks from Harlem* p. 146.

60 The questioner was Jim Mencarelli of the *Grand Rapids Press*: 'Umrani, "Why We Should Resist Zionist pressure", *AMJ* 16 March 1984 p. WNE 4; cf. 'Umrani, "A Message to Young Journalists" *AMJ* 3 February 1984 p. WNE4.

61 'Umrani, "U.S. Should Stay Out of Iran-Iraq War", *AMJ* 2 March 1984 p. WNE4.

62 *The American Muslim Journal* of 10 August 1984 p. 10, for example, advertised panel discussions and lectures on the "Second Annual Commemoration for the Victims of Sabra-Shatila Massacre and Untold Story of Ansar Prison Camp", an occasion organized by the Palestine Human Rights campaign in Chicago in that month. Prominent Arab speakers from the U.S. and overseas addressed the Banquet Dinner and the Palestinian folk singer, George Kirmiz, performed.

63 Email from Layla Diyab 2 March 2001. Cf Layla Diyab and Ayesha K. Mustafaa, "How Long Will We Pray? For As Long As It Takes... A Prayer For Peace (Still) in the Middle East", *Muslim Journal* 27 October 2000 pp. 1, 6, 20.

64 Ayesha K. Mustafaa, " 'A Rose by any other name...' (Shakespeare)", *Muslim Journal* 21 February 1997 p. 6.

65 Yvonne Haddad and John L. Esposito, *Muslims on the Americanization Path?* (OUP 2000) p. 246. Iraqi-American political scientist Dr Ibrahim al-Sa'id (11 January 2003) also characterized to me some parallel Arab-American professionals as feeling remote from poor African-Americans and as seeking to integrate into the USA's Euro elite.

66 After Friday prayers, Warith's followers in Atlanta urged "our immigrant Muslim brothers and sisters who operate gas and convenience stores" to stop selling alcohol, swine and lottery tickets for "the good of their souls in this life and the Hereafter." They proved "relieved that someone has finally come calling them back to the faith": "Muslims who Sell the Forbidden" *Muslim Journal* 16 August 2002 p. 7. Elijah's classical 1956 criticism was carried by the Pakistani Abdul-Basit Naeem's *Moslem World and the USA* which was directed to both immigrant and Afro-American Muslims: Essien-Udom p. 185. Future historians might try to trace from oral sources and ethnic Arabic publications in the States channels of communication and the exchanges between these two American groups over the decades.

67 Ali Baghdadi, "U.S. blind to Israeli drug traffic", *Final Call* 23 July 1990 p. 17.

68 "Muhammad 'Ali Steps In", in *Malay Mail* 28 November 1979 p. 2.

69 *The Militant* 11 March 1996 p. 2.

70 Abdul Wali Muhammad, "Plague of confusion descends on U.S. government: Pharaoh Reagan and his chiefs spin web of lies and deceit", *Final Call* 15 January 1987 p. 2, 14, 31. Abdul Wali was citing Darrell Garwood, *Under Cover: Thirty-Five Years of CIA Deception* (New York: Grove Press 1985).

71 (Edit.) "Pride goeth before destruction", *Final Call* 24 February 1992 p. 16; "Iran critical of America", *Final Call* 24 February 1992 pp. 13, 15.

72 Interview of Farrakhan, *Final Call* 24 February 1992 p. 20. Whether more Americanist or not, Warith's tabloid used similar motifs to condemn silence by the U.S. and other Western states on the Algerian military's suppression of the FIS in the wake of the aborted electoral process: Misbahu Rufai, "Challenging the Democratic Paradox", *Muslim Journal* 21 February 1992 pp. 6, 21. Misbahu

condemned the USA's invasion of Panama and charged destruction of black areas there in a manner very much like Farrakhan.

73 Ali Baghdadi, "Erbakan of Turkey dares to say 'NO' to America", *Final Call* 27 August 1996 p 13. Baghdadi's transcription of Erbakan's given name ("Najmuddin") was Arab, as is the name, but varying from its form and pronunciation in Latin-script Turkish ("Necmettin").

74 "An Automobile for Consumers and Dealerships: Malaysia's Proton Saga", *Hijrah* Fall 1988 p. 25.

75 Robert Dannin, "Interview: Bangsa Moro! Muslim Rebellion in the Philippines", *Hijrah* Fall 1988 pp. 26-27.

76 Sandi Russell, *Render Me My Song: African-American Women Writers from Slavery to the Present* (New York: St Martin's Press 1990) pp. 140-141.

77 Angelou's public political poetry seeking integration peaked in her poem "On the Pulse of Morning" that she read at the inauguration of President Bill Clinton: Lilamani de Silva, "The Poetry of African-American Women: Making Cultural Difference Meaningful", *The Sri Lanka Journal of the Humanities* 21:1-2 p. 113. De Silva compared this poem of Angelou to "The Gift Outright" that Robert Frost recited at the inauguration of [the equally tawdry] JFK.

78 C. Asha Blake, "AMC Student Takes A Trip to the Motherland: Part II", *Newscope* (student publication of Atlanta Metropolitan College), February 1992 p. 2.

79 "Faction" was a term devised in the 1970s for a book that blends a skeleton of a historical truth or narrative and imaginative reconstruction of the past that borders on fiction. *Time* et al applied "faction" to Alex Haley and *Roots*.

80 Hilda el-Amin, "Visit Africa, See its Richness!" in *American Muslim Journal* 27 January 1984 pp. l, 4, 18-l9.

81 "African Diplomats Feted: CACC Opens Regional Office", in *World Muslim News* 15 January 1982 p. 15.

82 Sabir Kasib Muhammad, "Nigeria Encourages Business with Bilalians", *World Muslim News* March 1982 p. 4.

83 Farrakhan was maneuvering within the sectarian tensions of Ghanaian society. He was largely the guest of the smallish group of Muslim Ghanaian academics at the University of Ghana. There must have been signals from them for Farrakhan to deflate at least evangelical fundamentalist Christianity, but if so, he side-stepped it, in an effort to help integrate a cohesive African political community that would span the sects. Nkrumah had been popular among American Black Muslims in the 1960s and had become posthumously popular among educated Ghanaians in the late 1970s and 1980s. Clearly, though, by 1986 Rawlings had become a collaborator with the IMF, dealing out tough economic medicine to an increasingly resentful population: see W. Keeling, "Ghana's Strongman Haunted by a Can of Worms", in London *Observer* (London), 28 May 1989 p. 28.

84 Basheer Alim, "Basheer in the Senegal: Islam in Senegal", *Muslim Journal* 30 July 1999.

85 "Ghana goes for the Afro Tourists", *New African* April 1997. While registering that nationalist organizations in the U.S., the Zionists, Zionoids, and the Nation of Islam etc, all try to structure commemoration of death and pain in the homelands of ancestry to sustain themselves, we sharply feel the historical reality of the mass sufferings and genocides that took place in Europe and Africa.

86 "World leaders speak at Saviours' Day '97", *Final Call* 11 March 1997.

87 Eric Ture Muhammad, "Nation of Islam names mosque in Gambia after Alex Haley", *Final Call* 23 March 1999 p. 6.

88 Bernice Powell Jackson, "Women Power in Nigeria: Give Jobs to Our Sons" *Muslim Journal* 9 August 2002 p. 23.

89 George E. Curry, "Mandela sees an 'element' of racism in the U.S. Plan to Attack Iraq", *Muslim Journal* 4 October 2002 pp. 6, 14.

90 Goldman, op.cit. pp. 393-4. In 1975, Farrakhan took part with Berkeley Mayor Warren Widener (African-American) in the occasion of the proclamation of Honorable Elijah Muhammad Day by his city government: Lawrence C. X and J. Smith, "Farrakhan Warns Blacks 'Stay Vigilant'", in *Muhammad Speaks* 14 February

1975 p. 7.

91 Ernest R. House, *Jesse Jackson and the Politics of Charisma: The Rise and Fall of the PUSH/Excel Program* (Boulder and London: Westview Press 1988) pp. 48-49. The PUSH/Excel programs had elements in them to encourage voter registration by blacks.

92 Marshall Frady, *Jesse: the Life and Pilgrimage of Jesse Jackson* (New York: Random House 1996) pp. 336-339]

93 Aide Eric Easter quoted Frady op cit p. 351.

94 See private conversation with Khalid Abdul Muhammad at the time, in Vibert L. White's *Inside the Nation of Islam: A Historical and Personal Testimony by a Black Muslim* (University of Florida Press: 2001) p. 104.

95 Frady, *Jesse* p. 353. Jackson's personal investment in Inner City Broadcasting, a private company, reached $1 million by 1988—it was very hard for him to convince the ghetto unemployed that he was one of them.

96 E.O. Colton, *The Jackson Phenomenon: the man, the power, the message* (New York: Doubleday 1989) pp. 83-6, 203-25; Charles E. Silberman, *A Certain People: Jews and their Lives Today* (New York: Summit Books 1985) pp. 339-43; and Frady, op cit pp. 343-356. See also James Muhammad, "More Blacks Accept Farrakhan as Leader", in *Final Call* 27 January 1986 pp. 1, 8.

97 House, *Jesse Jackson and the Politics of Charisma* pp. 180-181.

98 Jabril Muhammad, "Farrakhan the Traveler: Understanding Jesus: the Farrakhan, Muhammad Link" in *Final Call* 30 September 1986 p. 27.

99 "Muslims Combat Misconceptions of Al-Islam", in *American Muslim Journal* 7 April 1984 pp. 5, 23; Tariq H. El-Amin, "Nightline Keeps Viewers in the Dark" in ibid 4 May 1984 p. 21.

100 "Farrakhan's Advice to the Arabs", in *The Muslim World* (Karachi) 8 December 1984 p. 5. This need to withdraw Arab oil-money from American banks was from the 1960s a widespread theme of Arab World Islamists such as the armed Egyptian jihadist, 'Umar 'Abd al-Rahman: see "Liqa' ma' al-Duktur 'Uma 'Abd al-Rahman: al-Khudu' li-Amrika aw al-Khawf min Quwwatiha Shirkun billah" (A Meeting with Dr 'Uma 'Abd al-Rahman: Submission to America and Fear of its Power is to Ascribe Partners to God—Polytheism), *Risalat al-Jihad* (Libya) February 1987 p. 61. Yet Farrakhan had given his own twist to the Arab impulse to make it nourish his own people.

101 Lincoln, *The Black Muslims in America* (3rd ed, Michigan: Eerdmons and NY: Africa Word Press 1994) pp. 268-9.

102 "Farrakhan Speaks on London Television", in *Final Call* 27 January 1986 pp. 17, 23.

103 White, *Inside the Nation of Islam* pp. 172–180, 90-93.

104 "A message that can't be denied" (editorial), *Final Call* 15 July 2003 p. 16.

105 Cinque Muhammad, "Consumer nation! Black America squanders potential power through spending habits", *Final Call* 15 July 2003 pp. 7, 34. For Greenwood see Tim Madigan *The Burning: Massacre, Destruction, and the Tulsa Race Riot of 1921* (N.Y.: Thomas Dunne Books 2001). An Oklahoma Commission to Study the 1921 Tulsa race riots published a report that in April 2001 led to the formation of the Tulsa Reparations Coalition sponsored by Center for Racial Justice Inc.

106 See esp. Tynetta Muhammad, "The Comer by Night" in *Final Call* 15 February 1987 p. 36; cf Jabril Muhammad, "The Warners of God" *Final Call* 15 January 1987 p. 25; Guy Muhammad, "UFO on Display in Arizona", in ibid 14 February 1987; and "More UFO Sightings in the Midwest" in ibid. For stimulation from Amerindian millenarianists, see Wauneta Lone Wolf, "The Mothership on Big Mountain: Presence of Sacred Wheel Indicates 'The Eagle Wants to Land'", in *Final Call* 30 September 1986 p. 30.

107 Raymond Scott (letter), "Will we accept our role in prophecy?" *Final Call* 2 March 1999 p. 17.

108 "Taylor, Deedat Visit Palace", in *Final Call* 15 January 1987, pp. 12, 24.

109 "Nigerian Muslims share Eid feast at MUI," *Final Call* 2 March 1999. However, this item carried no details of actual conversations between NOI and Nigerian Muslims.

"Eid" is "Id al-Fitr", the festival that ends the fasting month.

110 Imam W.D. Muhammad, *Religion on the Line* pp. 136 and 128-9, and *Imam W. Deen Muhammad Speaks from Harlem* pp. 146-147.

111 Aziz Munir, "Planning Growth and Development Together Through Investing in Our Community and World Markets", *Muslim Journal* 2 August 2002 p. 7.

112 Aziz Munir, *Muslim Journal* 4 October 2002 p. 7.

113 Lonnie Abdul Saboor, "Achieving Business Growth", *Muslim Journal* 26 July 2002 pp. 7, 22. Saboor was active in the sect's first "Southern Sectional Business Conference," interspersed by Arabic ritual prayers, held in Georgia in mid-2002: *Muslim Journal* 26 July 2002 pp. 7, 8.

114 Mohammed Idris, "First Sundays Vendors' Space Available at $10 Each," *Muslim Journal* 5 November 2004 p. 9. King James Genesis actually evoked four heads of a river, of which the fourth was the river Euphrates.

115 "Business in Our Lives: Hub Distribution Concept Ready for Implementation," *Muslim Journal* 16 January 2004 p. 7.

116 "An Interview with Imam W. Deen Mohammed on Graceline and Businesses Aims—Part II," *Muslim Journal* 27 May 2005 p. 17.

117 Tony Al-Amin, M.D., "Many Muslims become Professionals", *Muslim Journal* 2 August 2002 p. 3; cf Atique Mahmood's account of adherent Tariq Malhance, Chicago City Comptroller, in *Muslim Journal* 11 October 2002 pp. 1, 26.

118 Interview by Nathaniel Omar with El-Amin in *Muslim Journal* 24 June 2005 pp. 1, 5.

119 Asia Ali, "Masjid al-Inshirah Purchases 25 Acres of Land", *Muslim Journal* 9 August 2002 pp. 9, 29. Rijal is the Arabic broken plural of *rajul*, an adult male.

120 Dr Rashad N. Ali, "New Medinah: an Inspired Vision", *Muslim Journal* 11 October 2002 pp. 13, 19; Imam Rausan T. Tamir, "The ILM Institute of Chicago's Visit to New Medinah", *Muslim Journal* 11 October 2002 pp. 13, 22, 26.

121 Capacine Abdul Aziz (Clinton, Maryland), "A personal account: Hijab in public school", *Muslim Journal* 27 August 1999 pp. 27, 11.

122 Daniel 'Abdullah, "New Africa-America Heritage Day: A Pillar of New Africa", *Muslim Journal* 6 August 1999 pp. 3, 27. The article by Layla Diyab was "A Question of Identity: A Story behind a Story" published in *Muslim Journal* in January 1999.

123 Review of the book *Intellectual Achievements of Muslims* by Ibrahim B. Syed, Dr Ayub K. Ommayya and Dr Shawkat 'Ali (New Delhi: Star Publications 2002), *Muslim Journal* 9 August 2002 pp. 11, 22.

124 Part II of review, *Muslim Journal* 16 August 2002 p. 22.

125 Khalil Abdel Alim, "The Glory of Muslim Spain," *Muslim Journal* 26 July 2002 p. 23—review of Maria Rose Menocal's *The Ornament of the World: How Muslims, Jews and Christians Created a Culture of Tolerance in Medieval Spain* (Boston: Little & Brown 2002).

126 Warith, "MAS Chicago Annual Islamic Convention 2002 Jumuah Khutbah".

127 "Imam W. Deen Mohammed Reveals Links with ADL: Rabid Zionist Group Admires Him and he Admires Them", *New Trend* September 1995 17:7.

128 Imam M. Harisuddin, "Never Again: Holocaust Survivor called for aid to Kosovo", *Muslim Journal* 23 July 1999 p. 3.

129 Imam Mikal Saahir, "Israel's Security vs. Palestinian Justice", *Muslim Journal* 2 August 2002 pp. 6, 26, 29.

130 Edward Sa'id, "Palestinian Elections Now", *Muslim Journal* 26 July 2002 pp. 6, 26.

131 Hazel Trice Edney, "Middle East Conflict Spills over into Black Politics", *Muslim Journal* 23 August 2002 pp. 6, 23, 29.

132 Bernice Powell Jackson, "O Little Town of Jerusalem," *Muslim Journal* 9 January 2004 p. 28.

133 Bernice Powell Jackson, "A real crisis: Our children are dying," *Final Call* 21 June 2005 p. 24.

134 "Aid to Congresswoman McKinney", *Muslim Journal* 23 August 2002 p. 23.

135 Greg Palast, "The Screwing of Cynthia McKinney," www.alternet.org 1 December

2003.

136 Ayesha K. Mustafaa, "Human Dignity is not Negotiable" *Muslim Journal* 11 October 2002 pp. 1, 9, 12, 22. When, before his address, Jackson spoke over the telephone to Yasir 'Arafat, he had heard Israeli "bullets from American guns" pounding on his compound in Ramallah. Omar Shareef, President of the African-American Minority Contractors and an adherent of Warith, now was on the Operation PUSH board.

Chapter Two

African Islam in the Evolution of the African-American Nation: Formation and Development of America's Multi-Ethnic Society

"The past is never dead. It is not even past"
William Faulkner, *Intruder in the Dust*

This Chapter examines the pre-modern past—and images about it that various ideological categories of African-Americans have evolved since WWI. It reviews the course of African-American history from enslavement to the creation of a majority quasi-nation, the English-defined "white people," in America. The Chapter will also measure the crystallization of Anglophone ethnic sub-nations in the leadup to the emergence in 1930 among African Americans of a group self-designated as the Nation of Islam. Chapter 3 will assess the emergence of neo-Muslim sects among African-Americans in the 20th century as an instrumental technology of the mind, a politico-religious ideology crafted to address the dislocations and crises that cumulatively faced African-Americans in the first three decades of the twentieth century. While this Chapter does seek some exact facts and bygone patterns in the pre-emancipation past of African-Americans, we are exploring a living history whose motifs direct, and are seized and adapted by, U.S. nationalist and religious groups and races to define self and relationships with other groups.

Even the earlier NOI's concepts and culture in the 1930s drew upon preceding African American intellectual currents and protest movements in North America. This chapter traces how the Africa of origin, the trauma and oppression of African-Americans under the slavery system evolved in America, and the formation of ethnic "nations" in it, were seen by two groups. The first group is earlier African-American professional historians. The second category is Afro-American movements that have built up related cultural-nationalist frameworks of analysis since 1945: they include secularist nationalists as well as Islam-influenced or neo-Muslim blacks. In every generation since 1900, there has been a cluster of African American groups with culture-orientated ways of viewing history to which protest Islam makes some sense as one option in restoring stripped identity and for spiritual as well as politico-economic development of the black nation. This and Chapter 3 will focus Islamic aspects of the Afro-American past and of the pre-1975 Nation of Islam's heritage which could still continue to resonate amid the new crisis that faced blacks and American society as a whole in the post-modern climate that followed Reagan's "conservative revolution."

The growth of "Black Islam" in the 1980s and in particular the 1990s into the widest mass protest movement ever mounted by African-Americans crowned a long process of evolution. The post-1977 sector of the black Muslim movement shaped by the leadership of Louis Farrakhan Muhammad was only one heir of the original Nation of Islam founded by Wali Fard Muhammad and Elijah Muhammad in 1930, which had itself succeeded earlier Islamic movements in the United States (chapter 3 reviews Noble Drew 'Ali's Moorish Science Temple of North America).

In class perspective, the history of black American Muslims can be divided into three phases:

First period, 1930-c. 1955: During this initial period, the Nation of Islam was a vocal social protest movement conducted by, and directed at, the black lumpen proletariat of the great cities of the USA's industrial North. Although rejected by the African-American middle classes, the movement in this period did selectively appropriate and recycle some motifs that its preachers took from elite Black Nationalist historians and academics.

Second period, 1955-1975: The sect continues to primarily recruit from the North's lumpens: but as it raises them to neo-bourgeois status, they win more acceptance and even converts from the black bourgeoisie which was becoming nationalist.

Third period, 1975-2000: On succeeding his father Elijah, Wallace-Warith Mohammed further directs the adherents to the achievement of bourgeois prosperity and individualist incorporation into America's professional mainstream and liberal parliamentarism, which—unfortunately for him and that effort—then started to contract under Reagan's radical-right ("conservative") revolution. Simultaneously with trying to integrate into America, Wallace/Warith directs the attention of his followers to Sunni Islamic religious patterns and Arab causes—two enterprises not always easy to synthesize. The secession of Louis Farrakhan Muhammad from Warith's following occurred in 1977. The new, smaller organization Farrakhan constructed to carry forward Elijah's protest ideology has been viewed as the vehicle of the more impoverished adherents hit hardest by the Republican Party's neo-conservative revolution. However, Farrakhan's revival of the parochialist Nation of Islam social protest "cult" from its outset drew support from petit-bourgeois blacks hit by such policies as the rollback of affirmative action, as well as from the impoverished masses suffering in the ghettos.

This chapter reviews images of the Muslims and Arabs of Africa and the Middle East projected by the earlier historians and intellectuals of the USA's evolving Negro elite. While the USA's black Muslims have often been insular and discreetly strove to duplicate the standard patterns of American life, their affirmation of the name of Islam had to link them in the minds of American blacks to a faraway world that hinged Africa and Asia. We will locate the Islamophile and Arabophile themes in that Negro elite's long-standing intellectual discourses that would make educated blacks more open-minded to a sect asserting Islam as an option, even when that sect in its social make-up was mobilizing lumpen blacks who might socially challenge that black bourgeoisie's interests. And however severe the bouts of inter-class hostility could get before 1975, from which Warith Mohammed sought reconciliation, the originally lumpen adherents themselves often detected and seized literate pro-Islamic themes current in that bourgeoisie. Thus, "Black Islam" in the USA was early able to represent very poor African-Americans with diverse motifs of protest that could be made to transcend a narrow class base. As the century went forward, this increasingly enabled it to incorporate a range of divergent classes into a new national protest movement that carries forward ambiguities derived from America's earliest history.

While a given national "history" is constantly being reinvented within ethnic or class groups, any identify thesis has to be able to draw from historical facts and materials that already exist (although some of them may have become little known) in order to be able to last. The claim to lead of any prospective elite is weakened if it cannot find any or much precedent for its enterprises in the pasts of the set of people on which it wants to clamp down its leadership. Attempts by Anglo elites and some more altruistic liberal groups to evoke a single integrative "melting-pot" American nation were bedeviled by harsh memories of past conflicts between the *ethne* that resisted the re-structured, selective past that those with power diffuse down from above through tendentious mass-media and by parading token ethnics they coopt. Efforts by the USSR's elite to integrate a Russian-speaking humane "Soviet people" whom it portrayed in the late 1950s to be "drawing together" also foundered on the same problem of oral memories of massive past violence by Russians under the Tsars and Stalin, and of the Islam those tyrants tried to finish.

But the issue of precedents has also been a problematic for the drives of the Moorish Science Temple and the Nation of Islam and its offshoots to portray their messiahs and counter-elites as the natural leadership of African-Americans. This chapter reviews early—African—Islam in North America in the run-up to the formation of the current U.S. ethnic groups. We have to provisionally assess the extent of the Muslim minority among the Africans transported to North America, how much vitality its culture had, and how much of Islam—or even just a memory—was transmitted down to the generations of African-Americans who in the 20th century were to accept the claims of neo-Muslim cults that they really were offering the restored original, "natural", religion of the Black Man.

1: ISLAM IN AMERICAN SLAVERY

The Nation of Islam sect took initial form in the mid-1930s among unemployed poor African-Americans reeling from the Great Depression in the slum of Paradise Valley, Detroit, Michigan, USA. Its preachers denounced whites as inherently evil devils bred by genetic grafting who might shortly be collectively incinerated by God for their acts of oppression against black humanity. Thus, the new sect's millenarianism was in large part a response to a local situation of pervasive oppression by white officials and social workers in Detroit. Slivers from the religious discourses of Detroit's large Arab minority of that era helped provide a religious, anti-Christian rallying-point to fight hopelessness. From the vantage point of the Arab countries, the nascent NOI's Islam long looked deformed, changed out of recognition by the American Christian concepts that dogged its structure even as the sect rejected them. Yet the new "Black Islams" of the earlier 20th century had roots, stronger for some cases than others, in previous Afro-American attempts to practise the religion in America.

British treatment of Africans who were brought to the West Indies, many of them for slave-breaking prior to transfer to mainland North America, had in it a calculated cruelty—approved back in the metropolis by many, even in the intellectual elite. Sir Hans Sloane, the President of the Royal Society of Britain, in 1707 set out punishments that the whites of Jamaica imposed on their slaves, "a very perverse Generation" as he defined them. He endorsed nailing enslaved Africans who had revolted to the ground and slowly roasting them to death with flames gradually moving up from their feet to their heads, castrating those who committed more minor offences, and for escapees, fastening heavy manacles around their ankles or piercing their mouths with spurs. Oversights by slaves called for whipping until blood would flow: some slave owners used to follow up the latter punishment by rubbing pepper and salt into the wounds.[1]

Islam was among the African religions the chained Africans brought with them to North America. Islam had its decisive impact on West Africa from the 15th to the 19th centuries, the years of the transatlantic slave trade. Nearly half the Africans brought to America came from communities that Islam was at least influencing.[2] The Muslim faith of a fair portion—fifteen to twenty percent—of the Africans brought to North America in the asphyxiating holds of the slave-ships meant that Islam was present in those areas that became the United States of America from their very beginnings as British settlements. Pagan-led coastal statelets of West Africa had wars with inland areas of Senegambia and the hinterland savanna kingdoms that were much more Islamized: they sold Muslim blacks they captured off into slavery in the New World. These recently enslaved people were Sunni Muslims, many of them highly literate in Arabic. The white slavers, however, acted to snap the Africans' link with Arabic as a literary language as soon as they got them aboard their ships. The British explorer, Mungo Park, with his unrivalled knowledge of West Africa, estimated that one seventh of Africans shipped to the West Indies for "slave breaking" for North America read and wrote Arabic. The early Islamophile Africanist nationalist, Edward W. Blyden, in 1887 imaged that the slave master of one ship cast the Arabic books of the slaves overboard because reading them in New World captivity would "make them sick of heart".[3]

Although the slavers found it more lucrative to bring children and teenagers from Africa because more of them could be packed into the slave-ships, enough Muslim teenagers had memorized the Qur'an to enable them to write it out again in America. Thus, manuscripts of the Arabic Qur'an continued to circulate among the enslaved in the USA. After 1960, Islam-influenced Black Nationalists in the U.S. were to project somewhat diverging visions of the interaction between enslaved Africans and the quickly developing settler society. Late 20th century African-American professional historians extrapolated from data on such early British settlements as Virginia (founded in1607 and which became the center of tobacco plantations), that the initial slavery "negroes" experienced in North America was almost like the temporary indentured servitude suffered by deported Gaels or transported poor Anglos: manumitted blacks of exceptional energy and intelligence could go on to acquire landed property for themselves. The colonies then gradually moved from slavery as a *condition* only to be inflicted on non-Christians to the form it was later given as the *hereditary* status for African-Americans.[4] Y.N. Kly, a civil rights veteran, but then later a Canadian chairman of Malcolm X's Organization for Afro-American Unity (OAAU), and whose father was a Muslim, strove to develop bases for African-American national autonomy in America from human rights and international law. His reconstructions of early African-American history stressed the unremitting determination Anglo-Americans demonstrated to terminate any traces of Islam among their black slaves, or any resistance from such Muslims.

Some Muslim African-American authors, though, have noted that not all enslaved Muslims were to remain on the segregated margins of American society after they arrived in the New World. Clyde-Ahmad Winters (1978) assessed that American society in its formative period was "flexible and was still developing as it tried to absorb various European and African social elements". Yarrow Mamout (=Mahmud), an African Muslim who was set free in 1807 and lived to be over a hundred, made himself one of the first shareholders in America's second chartered bank, the Columbia Bank: his somewhat Semitic-featured or Hamitic-featured portrait now hangs at the Georgetown Public Library in Washington: was he a Fulani?[5]

Anglo-Saxon society in North America had a margin of liberalism more accommodating of African Muslims, albeit such liberalism reveals enough tawdry shadings under the ray of scrutiny. When Ayyub Bin Sulayman Ibrahim Diallo refused to drink wine in 1731, his Anglo "master" recognized his Islam, offering him a place to pray and other conveniences "in order to make the slavery as easy as possible".[6] A certain respect for Islam as another literate form of scriptural religion with some relation to Christianity, and some open curiosity towards West African cultures, underlay the notices that the ethnologist Theodore Dwight Jr published on enslaved Africans and their languages in the 1830s.[7] Dwight even attacked the notion of the inferiority or incapacity of the Negroes, insisting on the high level of both Islamic and pagan civilizations in Africa. Dwight wrote of Muslim Africans whom he had met, lamenting that among the victims of the slave trade in North America were "men of learning and pure and exalted characters, who have been treated like beasts of the field by those who claimed a purer religion".[8]

A pioneer of Black Nationalism in the Americas, Edward Blyden was one link between (a) the old transplanted African Islam that lingered in the U.S. countryside and (b) the later modern African-American national thought articulated in English books and journalism coming out of urban centers and written by Christian blacks born in the Americas. Blyden's youthful interest in global Islam had been fed by some Arabic manuscripts of the enslaved Muslim, 'Umar Ibn Sa'id, which Dwight in 1865 had sent on to Daniel Bliss, president of the missionary Syrian Protestant College, for purposes of propagating Christianity in Black Africa.[9] One founder of Negro-American historiography, Carter G. Woodson, was in 1935 gratified by the quasi-equality implied in the attempts by Euro-American scholars in the 19th century to deepen their knowledge of Arabic and Islam by recourse to local Muslim "slaves" who were "the learned and most aristocratic of the tribes".[10] Dwight and his colleagues' old 19th century publicization of Muslim slaves in musty volumes of *The Methodist Quarterly Review* was in the 1960s injected into the discourse of the Civil Rights and Black Nationalist mass movements by Jewish-American Charles Silberman in his 1964 best-seller *Crisis in Black and White*: Silberman was specifically legitimizing, by reference to Muslims among the enslaved Africans, the title of Elijah's neo-Muslim movement to be among the groups competing to lead black Americans. In 1999, Warith Deen Mohammed's newspaper directed its African-American readers back to (post-Christian?) Blyden's old nineteenth-century works extolling the self-sufficient West African Islam of that age.[11]

Power and Dialogue

One slave owner procured a Qur'an in English and had it read out to the enslaved 'Umar Ibn Sa'id,[12]—but that might only have been to open him up for his subsequent seeming conversion to Christianity. While Anglo-American and British officials and scholars ultimately returned the Fulani "Job Ben Solomon" to his home-area of Africa, this was with designs of using him to propagate Christianity among its Muslims and secure trade with the Gambia. "Job the Son of Solomon" (Ayyub Bin Sulayman) had been born in 1701, the son of an Islamic scholar who acted as mayor of a town in the kingdom of Futa Toro near the Gambia river. On his way to the coast to sell two boy slaves to an English ship, he was waylaid by the Mandingos, at that time enemies of the Fulani, and sold to the English skipper with whom he had meant to cut the deal. Ayyub ended up being sold to a tobacco plantation in the British colony of Maryland. When, following an attempt to escape, it became clear he was a Muslim, would have been an *amir* in Africa's interior, and was literate in Arabic, he was taken to Britain where he met—that proto-liberal scholar of the academy, Sir Hans Sloane, as well as Britain's Royal Family.

After U.S. independence, a later enslaved Fulani, 'Abd al-Rahman, was to feign conversion to Christianity so that he could buy the freedom of his family and then, under the auspices of the American Colonization Society, be taken back to evangelize Africa—where he duly threw off the mask. These Anglo-Saxons, before and after America's independence, had the same power to determine if the African "slave" ever got back to Africa or not. There certainly was a high disparity of power between the masters and the Africans whom they owned under Anglo law as though they were stock-animals or goods. Could any Anglo-Saxons ever allow an African to exist as a non-Christian equal in their societies? Can there ever be real religious dialogue between whites with power and people of African descent whom they control? Ayyub's English interlocutors had wanted to turn him into an instrument to Christianize Africa, but he won their respect both for himself and for his Islam through that dialectical lucidity they often had cause to rue. "Job" carefully read their Arabic translation of the New Testament, searching for verses that would bear out the doctrine of Trinity, but reached the conclusion that none were to be found there. The cleric, Thomas Bluett, replied that the English, too, believed in only one God, although he opted not to "puzzle" the African by expounding the Trinity.[13]

The crude religious dialogue already opening here in the eighteenth century between the elite of the Motherland of the WASPs and an enslaved Muslim from Africa, though, had ambiguities that cut in more than one direction. Before Bin Sulayman finally boarded ship for Africa—loaded down with Arabic translations of books of the Bible from the Society for the Propagation of Christian Knowledge—he was to sit for a portrait. Given traditional Muslim reservations about art with verisimilitude in it, Ayyub made sure in advance that the portrait would only be to remember him by, and that the English scholars would not worship it as he had seen the French worship images on the walls of the chapel in one of their neighboring forts back in Africa. When his face was completed, Ayyub asked the young artist to depict him wearing his national dress. When that Christian queried how he could portray a form of dress he had never seen, Ayyub triumphantly asked how, then, European artists could dare draw images of a God "whom no one ever saw?" Ayyub was finally depicted in a turban and tunic with a Qur'an hanging from his neck.[14] After the death of Elijah Muhammad in 1975, his successor and son, Wallace/Warith Muhammad, would wage campaigns charging that images in churches purporting to depict god Jesus, the Madonna and saints as white psychologically harmed blacks who had stayed on in Christianity. Warith's Islamist rejection of any images of the divine was to offer, leaving the issue of Palestine aside, common ground with spokespersons for Judaism vis-a-vis Christians in interreligious dialogues.[15]

The attempts of Africans to maintain their Islam in North America in the era of slavery, and even to articulate it as an option for everybody, were mounted in the face of the refusal of many WASPs to allow freedom of belief and livelihoods to "Negroes." This ingrained loathing of religious independence for blacks was to recur in the twentieth century in FBI strategies and campaigns to end the Nation of Islam and the Moorish movements, and in prohibition of the practice and study of Islam and Arabic in U.S. prisons, schools and other facilities.

A sense of Africans, animist or Muslim, as solely innocent victims of Western slavers is qualified by the interaction with intruding Europeans of such an elite Muslim as Ayyub Bin Sulayman, prior to his abduction from Africa while en route to sell other Africans into slavery. African Muslims or animists were not always the moral opposite of America's nascent WASP system of the 17th, 18th and 19th centuries. The Qur'an listed setting free a slave among the "sheer height[s]" (*al-'aqabah*) of moral ascent that the selfish rich refused to scale,[16]—it has, though, no clear verse ending all enslavement. It is clear that in West Africa some black-complexioned Muslims sold animists they defeated, and even Muslims of other linguistic or ideological groups, to Anglo-Saxon and other Western slave ships, just as pagan Africans sold Muslim Africans whom they raided or defeated. To exile anybody from their country is to maim them, although some who sold fellow-Africans may not have understood that the enslavement abroad to which they consigned their captives was becoming harsher than slavery in West Africa with the passage of time. Yet some Africans who sold neighbors who had fought them or thought or spoke different, may have relished the harm it did them: the remuneration was not the only inducement for that category. In twentieth century America, both the Islam-tinged black nationalist sects and their Jewish-American micronationalist enemies have addressed the linkages between divisions among West Africans and slavery in the Americas.

On the eve of the independence of Ghana and other British and French African colonies, visiting author Richard Wright felt a stab of dislike towards West Africans because some of their forebears could have sold his into American slavery.[17] This image from the past did not nourish the possibilities for restoration and tightening of historical relationship between African-Americans and Africans that decolonization opened up from the 1950s. Malcolm X in the 1960s conceded when facing his own African-American constituency that African groups had taken part in the sale of Africans into New World slavery: the slavers applied the white divide-and-conquer tactic, selling guns to one side so that it could easily defeat the other, with those captured becoming the prize of war. "I doubt if any of them over there really knew what they were sending us into" but "we sold each other": Africans thus felt a portion of the guilt that whites or Arabs should feel.[18]

The use of enslavement and slave-trafficking by African entities in conflicts with other African groups was to be cited by some white American writers in the 1990s in order to dilute or relativize the roles of Jewish strata in the international slave trade that black Muslim writers were underscoring. Historian Winthrop D. Jordan in 1995 argued that the new Nation of Islam's historiography of slavery, which highlighted Jewish merchants, in effect depicted Africans as mere objects of trade without any capacity to deal with or make decisions about their own lives and their history, which "included the activities of powerful men who traded other Africans to Europeans". Black Muslim history thus "ignores diversities in Africa".[19] This motif has become a staple of Jewish micronationalist polemics against their African-American opponents in the USA. The sometimes relatively liberal Allan Dershowitz (who lunched in youth with Malcolm X), in 1997, in assailing Farrakhan's stress on Jewish merchants in the slave-trade, wondered how an organization of Muslim Black Nationalists could overlook "the vital role of African chiefs" in capturing and providing slaves for the trans-Atlantic trade, as well as "pioneering work" of Muslims of all complexions in the export of slaves from sub-Saharan Africa.[20] Among African-Americans, professor of linguistics John McWhorter—who writes against the Black Muslim tradition—lamented in 2000 that he had found it hard to get his classes of African-Americans students at Berkely to accept that most slaves had been sold to Europeans by other Africans, more than captured directly by Europeans with lassos (as depicted in the films *Roots* and *Amistad*).[21]

African American Muslims are ever more nuanced and pluralizing, however, than their Jewish and other Euro-American opponents would ever give them credit. In the late twentieth-century, Farrakhan and some of his NOI's writers did voice some awareness that some categories of West Africans once took part in the enslavement of the forefathers of African-Americans: this perception helped nourish the recurring ambivalence of this discreetly Americanist sect to 20th and 21st century West Africans. Gardell cites a 1993 statement by Farrakhan that some West African populations shared in the responsibility for selling the blacks into New World slavery, and should compensate African-Americans by donating a territory in which the latter could make a fresh start. Farrakhan also urged the U.S. government to help the African-Americans found a state in Africa with the inducement that it would offer America "a strong foothold on that strategic continent".[22] Here, in his later thought as his sect engaged more with the U.S. system, Farrakhan might be viewed by African nationalists and officials as proposing a synthesis of African-Americans' and the U.S. state's interests without much regard to—or even at the expense of?—those of West African blacks. This motif of Farrakhan again instances the ambivalences and sharp swings, strains, inner division and alternations of communities that "Black Muslims" often show when they have to deal with a variety of international entities and cultures simultaneously, with both the self-interest of these sects and emotions at play. The 1980s and 1990s saw a quick, fluid, adaptable movement in the media of Farrakhan's as well as Warith's sect from mythologies about the pre-slavery African and Arab worlds to serious, nuanced, realistic views of at least 20th century African history that do rate as non-triumphalist and modern, and do not scapegoat "whites" for those problems in Africa which they did not cause. (We shall have to wait to see if the NOI's bitter polemics about Jews in slavery in their final outcome bring the sect to some kind of realistic and even constructive new engagement with the Jewish-American ethnic "enemy").

The reconstruction of the Muslim community among enslaved Africans in North America by recent historical scholarship will highlight Islam to African-Americans in the 21st century as an international civilization that often maintained the personal interests and collective autonomy of blacks. The wide world of Islam had other entities in it, notably the Arabs, whose aid the first African-Americans courted to balance and weaken the might of the American whites who encompassed them. This use of Arabic to muster a countering power-center prefigured the crude letters by Malcolm X from his first prison conversion to muster Arab diplomats for his own and for the African-Americans' interests. The Fulani (Fulbe) 'Abd al-Rahman Ibrahima had written an Arabic document in 1827 claiming he was related to the royal family of Morocco, to whom it was then duly passed on by the American consul. The Moroccan Sultan in his turn requested Ibrahima's liberty, in return for which he would release some Americans he held. The U.S. Secretary of State then interceded, and Ibrahima's master manumitted him.[23] It was an early international political application of Arabic from America's black minority.

Brent Turner's ideological Africanist study (1997) repeatedly disconnected Arab and African Muslims more than the history of their maintenance of exchanges and loose community warrants. He tended to view Ibrahima as manipulating the white Christian Americans' orientalist conflation of black African Muslims and Maghribi Arabs as both "Moors"—but was the community this freedom-deprived man evoked with the Moroccans simply an illusion or trick? After all, Ibrahima had won significant concurrence from faraway North Africa that he did have a connection of blood as well as of literate Islamic knowledge with them. The legists and merchants (not just the troops of 1591-3) that moved from Morocco (and also Algeria) into sub-Saharan Africa generated some real blood-connections and two-way movement of cultures and people. The African Muslims enslaved in North America retained memory of the fairer-skinned Berbers and Arabs who migrated to West Africa, and later African-American historians such as DuBois registered the presence of a few Arab and Berber North Africans among the enslaved who contributed to the genetic pool of the African-American nation that was to evolve. Such enslaved African Muslims as Ibrahima may sometimes have thought of the populations that wrote Arabic above as well as below the Sahara as their broader Islamic community from which they had been kidnapped.[24] After his manumission, Ibrahima was dressed by the missionary American Colonization Society in robes and a fez and sent on a tour of the New England States to give credibility to the Society. Yet his repeated affirmations that Islam was the best religion made some blacks who attended recall Islamic backgrounds and Arabic names, and impressed early black masonic lodges that perhaps rejected Christianity as well as slavery. Ibrahima did not last very long on the Protestant religious speaking circuit.[25]

An issue of some relevance today, though, is how many of these African Muslims in North America developed much sense of community with the animist or Christianized slaves or ex-slaves there. Some animist and Muslim Africans in America remained sharply aware of all the harm the others' groups had done to theirs in the brutal wars in Africa that had landed many of them into their New World slavery in the first place. Salih Bilali of St Simon's Island off Georgia had been highly educated in Islamic jurisprudence back in West Africa, and in America duly observed Ramadan, never drank liquors and read his Arabic Qur'an: "he holds in great contempt the African belief in fetishes and evil spirits".[26] During the second American war with Britain in 1813, Bilali, an enslaved Muslim of nearby Sepalo island, offered his master to muster in its defense "every Negro of the true faith, but not the Christian dogs you own"—a phrase that to some extent also disrespected the religious dimension of the white who in Anglo law "owned" him.[27] Thus, differences of religious belief remained crucial in community formation for Muslims who were struggling to maintain their Islam in so inhospitable an environment as North America.

Yet some statements of America's Muslim Africans that have survived had in them some elements boding well for a multi-sectarian African and thus African-American identity. Muhammad 'Ali Bin Sa'id of Bornu was only moderately religious: he was drinking when originally enslaved and sent to Libya, and thereafter adroitly had himself placed with a succession of rich masters in Europe and the New World with whom he made himself literate in six languages. After being manumitted by the Russian Prince Nicholas Trubetskoy in 1860, he published an English-language memoir in which he lamented "the condition of Africa my native country" and wondered how "her nationalities [could be] united" to beat off "the superior weapons" of the Europeans.[28] Bin Sa'id's remarks in part followed from a bookish multi-lingual acculturation to the total West, cosmopolitan travels and socialization with all sorts of white nationalities, including Slavs. While these highlighted a total Africa in response, they were not typical of the much more parochial contact with a narrow range of whites of most enslaved Africans in America.

Allison (1999), though, tried to argue that the Muslim Africans' cosmopolitan interaction with North Africans and Arabs and their culture before enslavement, and their ability to transcend sub-Saharan ethnic categories in Africa, helped them in North America to develop bonds of community with other Africans there more easily than could enslaved animists who were still more bound within the narrow ethnic cultures in which they had lived back home.[29] Enslaved Hausa Muslims in Brazil did convert Yoruba and Igbo animists for armed confrontation against Portuguese slave-owners in the 19th century, but there is not much documentation of such inter-ethnic propagation of Islam for mainland North America in this period.

Jihad? Integration?

Some Islamophile or neo-Muslim African-Americans in the later 20th century tried to present enslaved Muslim Africans as culturally and ideologically able to launch or spark a "revolution." The idea of fighting the enemies of Islam with jihad—interpreted here as meaning armed rather than spiritual Holy War—had been increasingly applied by Muslims of West Africa against animist neighbors, and some enslaved Muslims undoubtedly had impulses to wage Holy War against their white tormentors in North America. In the 1850s, the runaway Osman ('Uthman), a huge bearded figure who had been a chief in Africa, hid out with firearms in a Virginia swamp from which he terrorized the countryside, being hunted by posses.[30] Attempts have been made to argue that enlistment in the Union Army during the Civil War by blacks from Georgia's Sea Islands and their cooperation after that war in the Union army's hunting down of white confederate soldiers may have been fueled by Islamic influences in those islands.[31] Yet few of the transported Muslims seem to have identified enough with their non-Muslim fellow-slaves to apply their alternative international writing system to the secret organization of any concerted revolt by blacks in several areas simultaneously, which Arabic letters could have made much easier. African-American academic Samory Rashid (2003), building on Yussuf Naim Kly (1999), has argued that during the period of British control and afterward in early U.S. history, Africans, many of them Muslim, did conduct wars for self-determination in South Carolina, Georgia and Florida. Directed by the Islamic idea of *hijrah* (withdrawal from oppression), enslaved Africans escaped to areas subject to Spain, from which they then took part in, e.g., the wars of the Seminole (runaway Africans and Creeks) Indians to beat back U.S. military expansion (1816-1858). Recent Muslim African American nationalists note that Osceola's wife was African.[32] Yet that "liberated area" would be well past the USA's then margins.

Another category of Africans, especially Muslims, brought social qualities and agricultural skills with them from Africa that enabled them to achieve position and a modest prosperity, in a few cases becoming something almost akin to junior partners of the white slave-masters in the South. Such a position was achieved for a time by Salih Bilali, who from 1816 to 1846 as an overseer for a white slave-owner in Georgia's Sea Islands, directed 500 workers on plantations rotating crops similar to those grown in West Africa as well as olive trees and date palms similar to those in North Africa.[33] The skills in brick-working and carpentry, livestock and in agricultural and human management that such Muslims already had in Africa gave them bargaining power that sometimes could limit the capacity of their slave-masters to culturally regiment and Christianize them. Salih Bilali's "master" stopped one of his (Muslim?) slaves from building an Africa-style palm-frond hut: he did not stop Salih passing on his name, Bilali, to his son.[34] Some slave-owners allowed enslaved Africans with valuable skills to maintain patriarchal families that lasted, and may have turned a blind eye to Islamic marriage ceremonies and itinerant Muslim preachers in the Sea Islands.

Muslim and other enslaved Africans often fled and sometimes resisted, but they also contributed not just their sweat but their crucial skills to the foundation of America and its system. Such Muslim Africanist nationalists as Malcolm X (1963) turn out to have long been right when they depicted that European agriculture had been limited and that it was their African-Asian crops and agricultural system, and their skills in metalworking and other trades—not "sweat"—that made the enslaved Africans so "profitable" for America.[35] In the 1960s, Malcolm would try to galvanize the debilitated unemployed or tipsy of Harlem by hailing them as descended from black kings and queens.[36] Late 20th century scholars were to document that North America had indeed bought a good number of individuals from West Africa's Islamic governing families and Arabic-literate educated classes—the elites most at risk of capture in wars against other Africans.[37] Such Africans were an asset to the progress of an America where most of the whites had not gone to school: some of them could have kept written records and accounts in Arabic for white "owners" who had to reciproate for these services. The aid given to the young U.S. system during its second war with Britain in 1813 by Bilali in the face of blandishments by the British that they would set the slaves free, shows some enslaved Muslims already calculating that certain interests, not just geopolitical calculations, now linked them to the North American system, whatever their dislike of white as well as black Christians.

Syncretism or Dissimulation?

African Islam in America developed finely-honed skills of ambiguity, dissimulation and charade-accommodation, although these features later fostered syncretism and Christianization over the long term. If the Euro-American amateur ethnologists were monitoring the enslaved Muslims, the Muslims may also have been monitoring the WASPs who ruled them. Trying to work out what made the WASPs the kind of humans they were, a Mandingo of Georgia, removed to Florida in the 1850s, wrote down in Arabic characters bits of the King James translation of the Gospel of John.[38] While many Muslims in Africa were practising religion-justified violence against animists or quasi-Muslims at the time that the Anglo-American polity was emerging and developed, others, before they were enslaved, had had cooperative relations with pagan polities as traders, advisors or Arabic scribes.

The enslaved Muslim, 'Umar Ibn Sa'id, of North Carolina, an Arabic teacher from Futa Toro, may have been an advisor to a non-Muslim court, although he also took part in jihads—victorious animists may have sold him into his American slavery. His acculturation to animist Africans would have provided a prototype for his subsequent accommodation to America's Christian Anglo system, although that could have had in it Muslim precautionary dissimulation, finessing, manipulation and frozen-down discreet spiritual resistance. In later attending church from 1821 and getting baptized, 'Umar may have been outwardly accommodating himself to assure that Anglomorph Americans would continue to allow him a leisurely life in which he could maintain his Arabic literacy. His religious accommodation was balanced or negated by his apparent failure, so unlikely in a scholar who had been multi-lingual back in Africa, to master English, which limited the capacity of his white controllers to monitor him or communicate to him. His connecting with Christianity got him one of the Protestant Bibles in fractured Arabic, but he regularly wrote out from it for curious whites only two passages he felt were compatible with the Qur'an.[39] Ibn Sa'id may have felt that getting *something* to read in his religious language was better than being allowed nothing.

For a fair proportion of Muslim Africans enslaved in North America, dislike of paganism fostered a lack of empathy for non-Muslim Africans: moreover, both groups knew that revolt even by the two together could only be suicidal. More Muslims instead applied Islam and Arabic to build themselves discreet cultural space from the whites' slave system without taking up arms against it. This was to be the pattern of the neo-Muslim movements of the 20th century, too. The 20th century sects—including Elijah Muhammad and both Warith and Farrakhan—would long spasmodically voice indifference to or dislike for pagan Africa like that of America's first Muslim African slaves so long before. Some attitudes orally transmitted from slavery times to the 20th century African-Americans who embraced (or re-embraced) Islam may have contributed to this alienation from animist Africa, in tandem with the racist contempt for it that Anglo-Americans have never stopped voicing.

From the earliest encounters, practitioners of the old African Islam—even before those individuals were enslaved in Africa—were sharply aware of the Christian tenets and cultures of Western peoples, and very swift in evading, challenging and escaping conquest of their psyches by Christianity. This acute and subtle cognizance of Christianity, white and black, and the capacity to improvise critiques of it, and to deflect Christian opponents amid a dire lack of Islamic culture resources, would also mark the history of the Moorish movements from 1913 and of the Nation of Islam and of all its successor-sects from 1930 onward.

Arabic literacy was an instrument and a weapon that kidnapped African Muslims used to communicate with each other in an America whose Euro-Americans had a low literacy rate. As well as making them a coherent American ethnic group, the Arabic language was also applied by some individuals to link their interests into international relations and overseas Muslim power centers alternative to the America that encompassed them. Following the Million Man March of 1995, Farrakhan was to conduct a "World Friendship Tour." In it, he was to try to muster a common practice of Islam to forge connections with Muslim-led states around the globe in order to raise the price white America would have to pay if it moved to crush his sect.

The tenacity with which a section of Africans in America held fast to their literate Islam in Anglo-Saxon America—foredoomed by their lack of the printing press and English Qur'ans for the new generations—must resonate for any African-American or Arab or Celt today. Yet there seems something not quite heroic or political or grand about some of these tantalizing enslaved Muslims. Most of them seem to have been unmotivated by any vision of themselves as striving for Africans in general either in the Mother Continent or in America. Cultural minorities have sometimes been empowered to better roles by colonial rulers because difference makes them slower to align with the ruled majority. Enslaved Muslims in America may have been placed in compromising situations, due both to their skills, and to their Arabic education that made them culturally different from the others. Cornelia Bailey of Sapelo Island, discussing her grandfather, a descendant of the enslaved Bilali Mehomet, an enslaved Fullani Muslim who had been highly educated in Islamic jurisprudence in Africa, recalled that:

> A lot of old people would say, "We held ourselves... in a certain way." So, we was a little bit different and so and so, they really didn't like us for that. Grandmama say, they never really like us... Plus Grandpa was a... was the overseer. And a overseer, whether you black or white, you gotta be kinda tough. So, you could imagine... he wasn't very well liked. Also, here he was, this man with a different language, can speak a different tongue, and also the white boss at the time appointed him over all the rest of 'em... so, you could see... he wasn't very liked.[40]

Yet the African-American nation was still in formation. Christian, racist America was a doubly harsh environment for Muslim blacks that narrowed thinking down to personal survival, the cultural and spiritual autonomy that Arabic and Islam offered individuals, and the informal community of close kin.

Atoms from Islam Transmitted Down New Generations

In the "ring shout," American Negro Christian worshippers, even up to the 1950s, clapped while shuffling counter-clockwise in a circle. The African-American scholar Lorenzo Dow Turner (1942, 1949) and Sylviane Diouf (1998) ascribed that "shout" to a single circumambulation of the Ka'bah stone by Muslim pilgrims to Mecca, termed *shawt* in Arabic.[41] Such pilgrims keep the Ka'bah on their left as they circle it anti-clockwise. There is documentation of Africans in North America who had made that pilgrimage to Arabia before enslavement (some of them would have gone on to Jerusalem's al-Aqsa mosque, later a flash-point of Zionist-Palestinian conflict).[42] However, Michael Gomez (1996) and Robert Allison (1999) explicated the ring shout as meant to weld together Igbo and other pagan religions and African ethnic groups into a new "pan-African" community in America. As regards the ring, Gomez, Allison and Stuckey only see autochthonous African and Anglo-Christian elements getting syncretized: we hold that Islam was at least added in a triple blend. Gomez sees the ring dance as adapting in North America Africa's honoring of the ancestors. At African-American funerals, it helped the souls of the deceased fly "home" to the mother-continent from which the

African-American people under formation would now always be separated.[43] But the anti-clockwise *shawt* movement by the ring of Muslim pilgrims around the Ka'bah connects those circumambulating to their dead parents and ancestors because they pray Allah to forgive them and lodge them in Paradise: God then conveys the prayers on to the souls of the departed which retain high awareness in the graves pending His Resurrection and Last Judgement of all humans. The circambulation of the *hajj* is also intended to pull far-separated peoples together into one belief-community around the Ka'bah, as the likewise anti-clockwise shout brought together those from diverse regions of Africa.[44]

The Euro-American, Thomas Wentworth Higginson, in 1862 noted a palm-leaf African hut in a shout prayer meeting on the South Carolina coast, but also that the participants "keep steadily circling like dervishes" (heterodox sufi mystics of the Middle East).[45] Divergences from Islamic Sunni sobriety in the ring shout could accord with sufi rites in Africa and the Middle East as well as exuberance from African paganisms.

Islamic, African and Euro-Christian elements all coalesced in a triple synthesis during the first formation of the African-American culture and nation. The early South's African-American harvest festival again had a counter-clockwise ring ritual. It combined West and Central African pagan yam festivals with white robes and with bowing towards the dawning sun that looked a bit like the first of Islam's five daily prayers. Islam's first prayer (fajr: dawn) is designed not to be confused with pagan worship of nature: however, as later generations of blacks lost memory of the essential tenets of Islam they came to view aged Muslim kin whom they had seen pray as bowing to and worshipping the sun. Diouf argues that the shared festival of the harvest brought into association three black communities that it kept distinct for a time: Christians, followers of traditional African religions, and Muslims, each of which gave their own twist to the rituals.[46]

Christian white societies in the eighteenth and nineteenth century were hostile to Islam, yet individual enslaved Muslim Africans practised their religion in the bleakly alien North American society and sometimes transmitted it to their children. Katie Brown of Sapelo Island, Georgia, also a descendant of Bilali Mehomet, recalled that Bilali and his wife Phoebe prayed with beads: "They wuz bery puhticulah bout duh time they pray and they bery reglah bout duh hour. When duh sun come on up, wen it straight obuh head an wen it set, dat duh time they pray. Day bow to duh sun an hav a lill mat to kneel on. Belali he pull a bead an say 'Belali, Hakabara, Mahamadu', Phoebe she say 'Ameen, Ameen'."[47] Bilali instances a modality of literate African Islam that did keep up the regular Arabic prayers in America that impressed the faith on a second generation. But the Muslims in North America seem not to have established equivalents of the underground Arabic schools in Brazil that were able to transmit the practice of Islam to much more than two generations. The neo-Muslim Clyde-Ahmad Winters, not of the Nation of Islam tradition, argued in 1978 that the incapacity of enslaved Muslims to institutionalize and thereby transmit Islam was caused by the separation of black families by the 1790-1860 interstate slave trade that relocated over two million slaves across America in order to provide the labor required by the westward expansion of cotton production. Such sales of humans often separated children from their mothers: "this destruction of black families made it impossible to teach religious values to direct descendents of slaves from Africa", in contrast to the Arabic schools in Brazil and the Caribbean.[48] The continuity of families among African-Americans in some U.S. islands that did pose Islam as an option to new generations was not typical of mainland North America.

That the worship rites were in a foreign language, Arabic, made them incomprehensible—amusing, rather than to be taken seriously, yet still tantalizing—for the third generation growing up in America. Thus, Rosa Grant of Georgia reminisced that her grandmother came from Africa and "ebry mawnin at sun-up she... bow obuh and tech uh head tuh duh flo tree time. Den she say a prayuh. I doh'n membuh jis wut she say, but wun wud she say use tuh make us chillun laugh. I membuh it wuz 'ashanegad'. Wen she finish prayin she say 'ameen, ameen, ameen.'[49] ("Ashanegad" seems Rosa's garbled memory of the Islamic prayer-formula "Ashhadu anna Muhammadar..." ie. "I bear witness that Muhammad [is the prophet of God]"; "Belali Hakabara" is "Allahu Akbar", Allah is Greatest, which was to be revived into a polarizing motto to collectively distinguish American blacks from the devil whites under Elijah and Farrakhan.

As late as the 1940s, then, some old African-Americans would narrate their memories of enslaved or freed Muslims and their offspring, including distorted fragments of Arabic vocabulary from their prayers. Still, only muddled memories of ritual manifestations of Islam, not a living faith or any notion of its tenets, remained among U.S. Blacks in the 1930s, the point at which the neo-Muslim movement of Elijah Muhammad took shape. The fragmentary folk-memory of a scriptural non-Christian religion from Africa, though, lent some legitimacy to the claim of the new neo-Muslim preachers from 1913 onwards that they were restoring the original religion of the Black Man in calling for the repudiation of Christianity with a new holy book. In 1989, Yussuf Naim Kly, a Sunni Muslim who has formulated strategies to foster the development of a black, Africa-linked nation unit in North America, stressed that Noble Drew 'Ali and Elijah Muhammad were natives of the Georgia and South Carolina coastal region where old people voiced a smattering of garbled Arabic and Islamic prayer formulas for two decades after Drew left it for Newark (then Chicago) to found his Islam-emblemed cult in 1913: Elijah Muhammad, too, grew up in that Gullah-speaking region of the South before he left to Detroit where he helped found the Nation of Islam in 1930. From the late 1980s, Kly thus held a view like the 1965 explanation of the Jewish-American scholar, Morroe Berger in a journal read by the black bourgeoisie—that the birth of the black Muslim sects from the 1920s was a resurfacing of a long-suppressed weak folk-tradition of remnants of Islam handed down from slavery times by oral transmission.[50] Farrakhan's Jewish-American biographer, Magida, in 1996 speculated that the first name of Elijah Muhammad's father, Wally, was really *Wali*, a Muslim saint able to work miracles in West African sufism, and that Elijah may have been exposed to some Arabic words and rudiments of Islam in childhood.[51]

Specific continuities traced by Kly would indicate shredded remnants that survive and mutate in atomized form down the generations without Islam surviving as a coherent thought-system on American soil. Kly focused on sugared rice-balls distributed in African American families at sunset after a day of fasting in Georgia and the Carolinas: a vestige, he argues, of the breaking of Islam's Ramadan fast. [The African word for that confectionery that he cites, *sarika* (*saraka* is given by some authors), may be from the Arabic *sukkar* (sugar, candy)]. Kly also stressed that such rice-candy or rock-candy was traditionally handed around at funerals among Southern African Americans tinged with folk-remnants of Islam to symbolize "the sweetness and joy of returning to God" similar to the practice that Elijah Muhammad taught his followers.[52] There could indeed be a continuity of a (displaced) motif of Islamic religious practice and life-style here but it is not a continuity of doctrine since rites and varied customs around funerals among Third World Muslim peoples are to underscore that the soul returning to God will, after Judgment, have an individual eternal life. In contrast, the sweet melting in the mouth at Elijah's funerals—and those of Farrakhan after 1977?—symbolizes that the loved individual is now in final dissolution: the consoling immortality held out is vicarious, that of the Black Nation carried forward in its surviving, reproducing, members [—which parts of the Hebrew Bible may have conceived for the Chosen People?]

At the time that Noble Drew 'Ali and Fard Muhammad and Elijah launched their respective Islam-tinged cults, then, some memories of shards of Islam may still have been getting transmitted to disgruntled young blacks of the rural South who then migrated to the great cities of the North and accepted that neo-Islamic preachers there *did* speak for "that old-time religion." Some barest essentials had been maintained in folk-memory: the alternative religion brought from Africa had been literate with a holy book shorter than the Bible, and its original seat had been far to the East of the West Africa from which the enslaved precursors had been brought [i.e. in the Middle East].

Many decades after that, Malcolm X's daughter, Attallah Shabazz, thought "my grandparents were from two different religions": her clergyman (if Garveyite) grandfather came from a Christian family, while "my grandmother was exposed to Islam in a non-rigid way because of the culture around her" in the West Indies.[53] After the death of her husband, Malcolm X's mother—despite the dire need of her family for food—turned down a gift of pork from a neighbor on the ground that hog's meat was unclean. Malcolm charged this to have been among the grounds on which white social workers classified her as insane and incarcerated her in an asylum.[54] It is tantalizing that the black Muslims were able to whip up a veritable psychosis against pork among African-Americans after 1930. While Louise Little was a Seventh Day Adventist at that time, the affinity of such early neo-Muslims as Elijah Muhammad for sections of the Old Testament (or Judeophile variants of Christianity) prohibiting pork really could have been an overlay upon one of the fragments from a defunct African Islam transmitted in African-American folk-tradition.

Vague and fragmentary memories and motifs of an old African Islam, transmitted orally in a weak or atomized, quasi-secret, tradition, then, made a minority of American blacks likelier to accept the claim of the neo-Muslim "Moors" and the black Muslims that the new religions they offered would reconnect them to a national past and identity that had been stripped from them.

The Islam of a portion of the African slaves also was further developed as a motif by the neo-Muslim preachers themselves. Thus, Eric Lincoln, in a landmark 1961 study of the Muslims widely read in the black bourgeois stratum, wrote that one of the NOI's preachers replied to doubts raised from an audience by quoting from white historical sources: these included data that a certain slave-holder in North Carolina "owned" a Muslim African literate in Arabic and unusually gifted in mathematics. Lincoln observed that the preacher built upon this one case the *non sequitur* that all the enslaved Africans brought to America were Muslims able to speak Arabic and highly educated scholars of mathematics.[55] But this is to miss some sober realism in the NOI's vision of history.

Malcolm X, a new convert, undertook wide readings in Norfolk prison colony's library from 1948 to 1951, and tried to present to the convicts Elijah Muhammad's teachings about the glorious pre-slavery history of the Blacks and an Islam that was "the natural religion of the black man." The white man obliterated the past of the enslaved, so that no Negro in America is able to ascertain his correct family name or even the tribe from which he descended. "I told them that some slaves brought from Africa spoke Arabic, and were Islamic in their religion": many of the "Negro" convicts he targeted were not prepared to believe it until he showed them selected passages in books by white scholars.[56] Here yet again, the qualified thesis of a limited Muslim African provenance argued here by Malcolm, and his early tendency to list diverse "tribes" (proto-nations) in the West Africa of provenance, looks more sober, judicious and pluralizing than many white American scholars and even some African-American ones like Lincoln have ordinarily allowed for NOI discourses. It is not always true that either black Muslim ideologue-orators or writers "ignore diversities in Africa" (Winthrop Jordan 1995).

Still, doubt that the group could have had any past positive relationship with Islam in history, in the late 1950s and early 1960s held back some African-Americans otherwise drawn to the Nation's project of collective business activity.[57] The Sunni Muslim, Clyde-Ahmad Winters, noted similar objections from African-Americans in 1976 that their group never had had any pre-Christian creed other than pagan African religions (an Anglo-Christian stereotype).[58] In 1976, *Roots*, the "faction" work of Alex Haley, asserted that he had traced the ancestry of his African-American family back to the village of Juffure in Gambia. This best-selling book and the series of TV films based on it projected to millions of black Americans rather watery images of a West Africa that had been Muslim when their ancestors had been kidnapped from it. Elijah's son and successor Wallace/Warith in 1977 depicted the TV series' portrayal that some of those enslaved from Africa had been Muslim as "divine" historical recognition and legitimization for his African American Muslim movement to millions of viewers.[59]

But some African-Americans open to Arabic and Islam protested that the TV films were not giving *enough* recognition to either as core components in African identity. As the first episodes of the initial *Roots* series were screened, Janice L. Cooke objected that "once again the black experience has been pimped": Haley had to explain to "the black community" why he had let Hollywood shift the focus of his original book, of which about one third had explored the culture and lifestyle of the Mandinka people in Africa. "*Roots* (the novel) reveals that our ancestral tribes were an extremely religious and spiritual people even before the introduction of Christianity into Africa... able to both read and write Arabic." The TV version had "robbed" black Americans of this "rich heritage" of an Africa "mother-country" in which the blacks were still "victims" in "South Africa and Rhodesia".[60] Warith's sect publicized the study of Allan D. Austin, *African Muslims in Antebellum America* (New York: Garland Publishing 1984) which copiously excerpted forgotten historical North American texts documenting Sunni Islam in the history of America's African slaves. One pro-Warith magazine carried a fascimile of the first surah of the Qur'an as written out in Arabic by Prince 'Abd al-Rahman during his enslavement along with a sketch of the old man (and a photo of Islamophile Blyden)—one of many instances it mustered to illustrate "The Islamic Presence in North America" down history.[61] Farrakhan's newspaper, *Final Call*, though, did not in the 1980s and 1990s much project the Islam of enslaved Africans in North America or the Islamic learning of the areas of West Africa from which they derived. Such an exploration would present tenets of Sunni Africans at variance with some doctrines that the Nation of Islam had developed in North America, and *Final Call* preferred to carry articles about, in some cases, mythical earlier history set in Africa derived from "Afrocentric" materials.

The latter part of the 1960s saw the crystallization among African-Americans of organized groups that claimed to be missionaries for international orthodox Islam. The great hopes for the Third World's new states and anti-Western and leftist movements in the era of the 1960s and 1970s encouraged a portion of African-Americans to identify not just with an America-framed Black Nationalism but, by extension, with Black Africa and the Arab nationalist forces fighting Israel. They wanted to synthesize a dual U.S.-framed national identity that would have enough links to Africans and overseas Third World cultural heritages and causes to achieve autonomy from Anglo-American culture. An instance was the Masjid ul-Ummah ("The Community Mosque": later "Islamic Party of North America") founded in July 1969 mainly by Afro-Americans in Washington, a city whose population was seventy percent African American at the time. Masjid ul-Ummah came into existence to propagate an Arab- and Pakistan-patterned Islam amongst all races living in the city. Yet the fact that it was trying, for the most part, to convert black Christians living in the city obliged the organization to use the logic of Black Nationalism to some extent. Its first Sunday lectures included such subjects as "Islam and Africa" and "Islam and Slavery": these early lectures concentrated on the Islamic background of a portion of the West Africans who were made slaves in America—the forefathers of the Afro-Americans the movement was trying to recruit. These neo-Sunni preachers consciously cited historical documents to convince the listeners that the religion of Islam was not foreign or new in America, or to them, because a certain number of Muslims had been living in the U.S. for hundreds of years. Members of the movement gave such lectures in the predominantly black Howard University and in black secondary schools.[62] As well as Muslim slaves in the North American areas that came to form the United States, writers of this movement were also interested in Muslim insurgencies among enslaved Africans in Brazil in the earlier 1800s.

Neo-Islamic currents and movements among African-Americans in the 20th century had a problematic import for the drive by new educated strata to recover elements of original African culture. However bitter they were about past use by white groups of Christianity as one more psychological weapon with which to dominate blacks, African-American Muslim writers shrank from the more self-contained animist African cultures from which most of the first enslaved Africans had been torn. When Ken Farid Hasan in 1985 felt around the wreckage of enslavement history for the first African cultures that it shredded, he was drawn to such aesthetic creativity as "drum making, iron working, wood carving (utilitarian and religious), basket weaving and cloth weaving [that] were killed off by the limitations of plantation life." Residual conditioning by Christianity as well as Islam, though, made it hard for Hasan to embrace whole such bygone cultural systems being taken away from the transplanted West Africans where their religious component was "celebration of gods" without any link to any Abrahamic ("Semitic") religion. Citing in support the poet and playwright LeRoi Jones, another convert to Islam, Hasan sought continuity with Africa in the music and dance that successive generations of African-Americans evolved amid slavery and later forms of racial exploitation. He perhaps felt relieved that "the dance of the slaves, after just one or two generations, had lost all" the polytheist, animist religious meanings that it had had back in Africa. His highly selective approach to animist African cultures seemed almost to welcome the destruction of African animisms by New World slavery. The existence of Muslims among the first enslaved pointed to a sector of West African life that could be fitted more easily into the Christian assumptions pervading America, his country. Farid Hasan hastily cited works by Dr Abdul-Hakim Muhammad and Allan D. Austin documenting that "many of the [original] slaves were Muslim": indeed, "most of West Africa was familiar with Muslims and Al-Islam if not under their direct influence". That background had made it easy for "our people" to completely accept Christianity in America.

When Hasan was viewing Christianity together with Islam vis-à-vis animist areas of Africa, he saw both as "faith in a singular God." He voiced a loathing of "fetishist versions" of Christianity to be found among blacks in Haiti, Puerto Rico and Brazil, where wider ranges of African cultures and concepts had indeed survived.[63] Hasan's 1985 resort to the Muslim sector of West African slaves and West African history carried forward occasional coldness of Elijah Muhammad and his adherents in the 1960s and 1970s to non-Muslim, non-Christian populations in sub-Saharan Africa, long stereotyped by conservative WASPs as "primitive" (see chapters 4 and 5).

Most of the above communications from African-Americans were in search of literate African cultures or "civilization" able to match—and at the same time offer autonomy from—the ultra-articulated Western civilization that will always flow around the USA's blacks. Anglo-Western civilization in that modern period of American history still favored monotheism and a scripture as well as written historiographies as repositories of the continuity of a nation and/or of a cluster of nations, even as they construct a new universal industrial and technological civilization. Modern Americans have tended to think in terms of wide blocs or camps in international relations (e.g. "Free World/ Communist bloc"). All these tendencies in the mainstream favored global Islam in the features of Africa that U.S. blacks would opt to recover, over old local paganisms in the "Mother Continent." These preferences of the modern West and the need to match and hold them at bay on their own terms gave the drives by African-American cultural nationalists to recover African identities a structural bias favoring those sectors of Africa's past and societies in which Islam, the Qur'an, and Arabic, or at least the Arabic script, had roles. Many African languages such as Hausa, Wolof, Bambara, Mandinka, Fulani and Swahili had been written in Arabic characters before colonialism, and in the 20th century retain many Arabic words and clear Islamic influences. Islamophiles and Arabophiles like Blyden, DuBois and Carter Woodson, new Muslim African-Americans, and thirdly, U.S. Africanist nationalists—all exchanged data about sectors of African life that African-Americans should recover, in which Islam and Arabic had been active.

Post-1960 Reactions to Slavery and Forced Assimilation

Beyond conversion or "reversion" to Islam, the oral folk-memory of ordinary blacks up to the 1940s offered motifs that could be heightened by ideologues into a drive to install Arabic or some West African tongues as auxiliary languages in African-American nationalism. In the 1950s and early 1960s, Malcolm X was tightening Elijah's mythologized images of transcontinental relationships into a resolute drive to truly connect the sect into "the East"—the Asian as well as African state entities that were now actualizing their independence. Malcolm received friendly hospitality and guided tours in Nasser's Egypt in 1959. Once, one of his hosts asked how he was a Muslim while unable to speak Arabic. Malcolm answered the Arab that this was because he had been kidnapped for 400 years and as a result he had been robbed of his true language and religion.[64] While Nasser's elite was aware that in the global reach of Islam, vast numbers of Muslims did not speak Arabic, it was sending off bale-loads of Arabic publications and teachers to change that.

After he left Elijah Muhammad, Malcolm further developed motifs that could be tightened to lead to a kind of linguistic nationalism—or at least into a Black Nationalism to be further differentiated from the English-speaking U.S. environment by splinters or shibboleths from some language from Africa that the enslaved forefathers had known when taken to North America. There were two foci in Malcolm's attempts to retrace an African language or languages robbed by slave-breaking and deculturization in North America: mother tongue, and some ritual religious language (or languages). Malcolm depicted the slave-makers as determined to stamp out the mother tongue "scientifically" through separation or execution of both mothers and children when the latter showed signs of learning the parents' language. To reduce people to true slaves, the slave-makers had to make them dumb: once the language is taken, "you are a dummy": "you can't communicate with people who are your relatives, you never have access to information from your family" about your heritage or the land and people that the mother came from.

But Malcolm also saw religions as a key front of the race-war between the blacks and the Euro-Americans determined to break them, in North America. Brilliantly reinventing the meanings of the Christian Negro spirituals, Malcolm argued that some enslaved African mothers would pray in their own way and language, and the child in another field would make it out and imitate: "in learning how to pray he'd pick up some of the language." "The white man will let you call on that Jesus all day long... Your calling on somebody else in that other language—that causes him a bit of fear, a bit of fright".[65] Once the names, language, and identity of the Africans were destroyed, Malcolm analyzed, "we became like a stump, something dead ...over here in the Western Hemisphere": "everybody could step on or burn us"[66]—which was to underestimate autonomy and subtle resistance within the new Anglophone culture and Christianity that "Negroes" constructed in America under and immediately after slavery.

Slavery and the psychological architecture of America's racist system, as his Islam focused them, thus pushed Malcolm to rally to a language from Africa that would have religious functions. This was most likely to turn out to be Arabic for him, given his NOI formation, and that his thought often subsumed Africa under "the East," although few West African mothers indeed ever spoke with any child in it. Malcolm called on his religiously mixed African-American followers to become "multi-lingual": his Organization of Afro-American Unity had already set up a class in Arabic and was to follow it with one to teach Swahili.[67] He had felt loss, and like a child, when, in sub-Saharan Africa, he heard "original mother-tongues such as Hausa and Swahili being spoken" and had had to wait for what had been said to be translated.[68]

When Sa'udi Arabia's King Faysal provided him with 25 fully paid-up scholarships for study at Egypt's al-Azhar mosque-university, Malcolm X hoped that his young followers would seize this "first link back to the African continent". Hakim Abdul-Jamal at least was more drawn to the histrionics of a local "Mau Mau" movement unfolding in North America;[69] however, Malcolm's disciple, Khalid Ahmad Tawfiq, whose father had been with the Moors, took one of the scholarships to al-Azhar, where he founded the American Muslim Students Association. Tawfiq took part in Muslim Brotherhood (*Ikhwan*) demonstrations at al-Azhar in the leadup to Nasser's disastrous defeat by Israel in 1967, and was deported. Back in Harlem, Tawfiq founded the Mosque of the Islamic Brotherhood in 1967 which melded Sunni Islam and Arabic into the urgent needs of African-Americans and with Africanist nationhood: they placed Arabic script about Allah onto Garvey's old red, black and green Africanist flag for a new composite synthesis.[70]

Although populist Black Nationalism in the USA was conceptually much cruder in Malcolm's lifetime than later, Malcolm was fairly careful in his choice of words about Africa: he left no doubt that the enslaved brought to North America had had diverse languages and creeds.

The Evolving Critique of Christianity

In the mid-1960s, one Harlem convert to Elijah's Nation of Islam lashed Christianity as "the worst thing that ever happened to Negroes". Without its passivity-inculcating prayers, there would have been "thousands" of insurgent Nat Turners and Denmark Veseys in the era of enslavement.[71] But since 1950, attacks against Christianity as a psychological tool that white racists tailored to train African-Americans for slavery have not come from black Muslim preachers alone. *The Nkrumaist*, a paper of secular Africanist nationalism friendly to Stokely Carmichael's Pan-African Revolutionary Socialist Party, in 1991 tried to document such a function of Christianity from the era of slavery in North America. Drawing on a long-standing tradition of unease about Christianity among black leaders, *The Nkrumaist* charged that white missionaries in the 19th century routinely taught the African slaves catechisms designed to instill fear and self-contempt as well as the belief that European slave owners ruled by the will of God Almighty. The Africanist tabloid excerpted such missionary lessons as those sardonically republished by Frederick Douglass' paper *Southern Episcopalian*, in Charleston, long before in April 1854:

> Q: Who gave you a master and a mistress? A: God gave them to me. Q: Who says that you must obey them? A: God says that I must. Q: What book tells you these things? A: The Bible. Q: What makes you lazy? A: My wicked heart [and the Devil].[72]

Looking back in 1991 at slavery and the struggle for emancipation, this relatively secular, communism-influenced Black Nationalist writer thus kept up the unnuanced indictment by pre-1975 black Muslim ideologues of the deployment of Christianity as an instrument of psychological warfare by white slavers against blacks. But such anti-Christian communications must set the post-1950 black Muslims and secular Africanist Black Nationalists in their context as successors in a long chain from early 19th century Negro protest discourses. The Qur'an prohibits alcohol. In 1845, Frederick Douglass had denounced that the white slave-owners set up the Christmas and New Year holidays in order to sink their slaves into a whisky delirium as "the most effective means [for] keeping down the spirit of insurrection".[73]

While the apparently devout clergyman Douglass could hardly have been a crypto-Muslim (well, could he?), Gomez (1996) wondered from linguistic and geographical contexts if he had Muslim African forebears: certainly, cultural remnants from Islam long tinged the black populations along the South Carolina-Georgia-Maryland coast, Douglass' matrix.[74] Douglass was Americanist in that he denounced projects by the Negro elite proposing to send literate African-Americans to civilize and Christianize Africa: they instead had to stay in their "true home" to abolish slavery and achieve the equal integration that was possible in their country, America. This particular article by Douglass was ambiguous towards Christianity: it was already being propagated in West Africa by "the labors of faithful missionaries", which could either be a pan-Christian tribute by him to those mainly white propagators or some swipe that missionary Christianity—maybe that religion itself?—would be a waste of the African-Americans' precious time and energy.[75] Douglass was ahead of his era on women's rights.[76] Yet a crypto-Muslim might have welcomed a missionary link that would give access to Muslims in West Africa.

Still, in calling for escape by the U.S. slaves to freedom in the North. the "Reverend" Douglass evoked the exodus of Moses' Hebrews out of enslavement in Egypt to power in Palestine. Here, these pre-bellum resistant black preachers were justifying escape by citing Old Testament verses compatible with a Qur'anic narrative of Moses and Pharaoh. Moreover, Douglass and others' call for flight to the North by slaves could also have drawn on oral residues of the theme of Hijrah—the migration of the Prophet Muhammad and his followers from persecution in Mecca to political power in Medinah. At the more personal level, two white Methodist class leaders he knew had led the mob that stormed and destroyed Douglass' Sabbath School for African-Americans in 1833.[77]

The "Black Muslims" who in the 1960s and 1970s denounced Christmas as yet another means employed by Christian and Jewish white traders to separate the blacks from their money, and then, also, Maulana Karenga's invention of the Kwanzaa festival (with its Arabic-strewn Swahili maxims) as a substitute for Christmas—both carried forward Douglass' distaste for Christmas from the slavery era. The cultural survivals from Islam under slavery and its splinters being introduced from foreign sources in the 20th century suddenly get new meaning within a 20th century politico-social order in which religions function as ideological weapons of the warring races. When he became a Muslim convert behind bars, Eldridge Cleaver's forming anti-white worldview was further focused by an 1852 oration of Douglass on the occasion of July 4. In it, that clergyman to be sure denounced those political celebrations as a sham given slavery, and the Euro-Americans' fondness for opposing tyrants back in their mother-continent Europe as "brass-fronted impudence"—but in two tantalizing sentences, he also condemned their "religious parade and solemnity... your pure Christianity" as "impiety and hypocrisy" to cover their crimes against the Africans.[78]

Original Languages and 20th-Century Nationality

The literary Arabic language, defined long before by the Qur'an that came from God, was politicized in the 1950s and 1960s era of pan-Arabism into a threatened national essence that was the stake firing, for example, the struggle for independence of the Algerians against French colonial rule. In reimagining the era of slavery, Malcolm felt impulses to apply a linguisto-religious nationalism that young radicals who came after him would find hard to make real, given the diversity of African languages, cultures and religions. Later Africanist nationalists among the African-Americans also were to show direct influences from Arab linguistic nationalism in their reconstruction of slavery in North America.

The Marxism-influenced and Africanist Black Nationalists were to develop Malcolm's sense of the functions of languages during slavery well into the 1990s. The Chicago *Nkrumaist* in 1991, although calling for the unification of Africa under a "scientific socialism" system as the only path to the liberation of "Africans" around the world, still painted precolonial Africa in idyllic terms, as Malcolm had done before—as a homeland for the mind where "education progressed naturally and the human personality was fostered and nurtured to help meet the needs of the society in a productive and humanistic way." Critical class analysis was not a strong point here![79] In contrast, *The Nkrumaist* reconstructed, the calculated depersonalization of Africans during the Atlantic Slave Trade debilitated the African psyche, causing Africans to be not only victims, but also facilitators of their own miseducation, creating what Nkrumah called "the crisis of the African Personality". During the long march to the sea, the kidnapped Africans were thoroughly and roughly examined, branded, forced to carry bales and rocks so that they would be too exhausted to escape, then sold at trading posts at the end of the journey. Often only one third survived to be placed aboard the slave ships. This traumatizing process had been designed to sever nearly every prior oral connection to the societies from which the slaves had been ripped—family and kinship arrangements, language, the tribal religion, the taboos, the name a given slave had once borne.[80]

In America, the use of traditional African languages could draw physical punishments. *The Nkrumaist* cited Franz Fanon, a diaspora-born black whose ideology formed on the margin of the Algerian revolution, that "language is a powerful weapon: a man who has a language consequently possesses the world expressed and implied by that language"—an Arab-like view of life. The pan-Africanist American paper incorporated the analysis of the Algeria-resident, FLN-aligned Fanon that when the African was forced into the position of learning the oppressors' language, he or she lost self-command. The psychologically debilitating effects of constantly being stereotyped as inferior, savage, heathenistic and chattel property were also a part of the informal slave education. The practice of forcing Africans to adopt new identities through name changes was an extremely effective tactic used to assimilate and subordinate them.[81] The non-Muslim Africanism of the 1990s thus retained the black Muslims' therapeutic concern since the 1930s to reverse cultural depersonalization imposed under slavery, and their drive for a largely symbolic restoration of "original names"—coupled in the case of the Muslims at least with the imposition in practice of standard U.S. Anglo-English upon the poverty-stricken converts as the sole medium of the NOI press that they would now read in a new nationalist literacy.

Malcolm X and the NOI, Franz Fanon, Arab linguistic nationalism in Algeria, and the writers of Negritude have all contributed to the U.S. "pan-African" activists' sense that whites inflicted "depersonalization" and "linguistic dualism" on colonized Africans and on the diaspora in North America. Eliminating "the people's sense of being" inflicts "a cultural catastrophe" and "confusion" in each new generation. However, the U.S. "pan-Africanists" tended to regard the Africans' pre-colonial "metaphysics and gods" as well as languages as a precious lost authenticity, which they set against the "lobotomized" deculturization of those Westernized Africans who received high Westernizing education or became "Negro Europeans" in the great Western cities.[82]

Generally speaking, it has to be allowed that the practical attempts to reconnect linguistically with the Mother Continent by African-Americans open to Islam and Arabs have had but sectionalized results to date. Pressure from the black linguistic nationalists did get Swahili put on the New York governmental high school system in the 1970s: the nationalists also produced at least one tasteful and well-conceived Swahili counting book for African-American children—one that also orientated them to the fact that many of the East Africans they might one day meet would be Muslims who prayed in mosques.[83] But the main or serious impact since 1950 from Arabic and from sub-Saharan languages has been in the sphere of personal names.

To a mass African-American reading public, anthropologist Sheila Walker in 1977 voiced a secular bourgeoisized version of the value the black Muslims had put on the recovery of the robbed "original" names. In renaming Africans whom they took away as slaves, the white masters were symbolically cutting them off from their African identity and heritage, and from their sense of nationhood. She endorsed Malcolm X as "a hero" whose repudiation of his Anglo-American family name and final shift in identity to the orthodox Islamic name of el-Hajj Malik el-Shabazz sought "a more internationalist world view and political perspective." Speaking for her black neo-bourgeois class, which she imaged had turned in the late 1960s from "assimilationism to cultural nationalism and separatism", Walker rejoiced at the new "aggressive pride in the African heritage" that replaced Anglicizing "slave names" with names from Africa. These were "usually Swahili names with meanings pertinent to the struggle" although "African leaders past and present like Shaka, Kwame

Nkrumah and Sekou Toure began to provide the heroic, strong, inspirational names." Sheila Walker noted, though—and categorized within the legitimate return by African-Americans to "their genetic and cultural roots" across the sea—an ongoing sector of African-Americans, "influenced by, but not adhering to, the beliefs of the Black Muslims", that in the later 1970s was carrying forward the conferring of Arabo-Islamic names that sect had pioneered. The TV series *Roots* that depicted pre-colonial Africa and early slavery was the source of many of the African personal names African-Americans were now conferring upon their children.[84]

The reassertion of non-Western names from Africa and the Middle East after 1950 reflected a significant change in stances toward America by African-Americans. But there was some ambiguity as to whether it was truly "secessionist", or rather some assertion of proudly equal ethnicity like the sharpening cultural particularism by American Jews and other U.S. ethne after 1967, that might instead be a preliminary to dignified entry into the U.S. system. Opportunities for Blacks as well as Jews and all non-Anglos were growing with the more and more flexible attitudes among Anglo-Americans toward non-whites and non-Christians in the wake of the African-Americans' struggles in both the South and the North.

In any case, a certain lack of coherence had to dog the renaming process so long as the signals coming from Africa itself were so diverse. The mass-circulation *Ebony* noted in mid-1977 that when Nigerian playwright and poet Wole Soyinka proposed [a de-Arabized] Swahili as the common language to bridge Africa's 700-plus languages, "he was vigorously opposed" at a colloquium associated with the pan-African festival, Festac, just held in Nigeria. African-Americans were taking notice of that particular Festac: not only were Nigeria's top politicians and governing military orating on Africa and the decolonization of identity there, but America's Stevie Wonder sang, Farrakhan represented Warith's Sunnifying Nation of Islam, and a bevy of African-American activist academics at the colloquium repudiated U.S. policies in Africa and America's capitalist and racist system. *Ebony* wanted the "fusion of culture and politics" (armed revolutionaries from South Africa had come) to help the globe's black peoples construct a united front against the common enemy. But Nigerian officials and politicians did not expect U.S. blacks to radically withdraw from their Western culture.[85]

Elijah Muhammad had dismissed black speech in America as "messed-up" English: the authenticity he and his media imaged that blacks could recover through learning Arabic, and more seriously in nationalist collective businesses, masked the imposition of Anglo-English upon his followers, and on hundreds of thousands who read *Muhammad Speaks*. But then the young Stokely Carmichael in 1968 characterized spoken Black English as not an uncivilized failure to achieve real English, but commendable national resistance by African-Americans. Cats who came from Italy, Poland, Germany or France could speak English perfectly after two generations. But African-Americans never did "because our people consciously resisted a language that did not belong to us."[86] Carmichael, though, does not seem to have conceptualized any program to reinvent any variety of spoken African-American English into a nationalist literary print-language, although major Negro poets had long written some of their verse in "dialect".

Enclave-nationalist academic in international law Yussuf Naim Kly, familiar with Algeria and various types of overseas nationalisms, in the 1990s wrote in favor of the restoration and expansion of Gullah creole English, still spoken by 500,000 in the USA, as "the African-American language." While Kly recognized that domination over the process of extending Gullah into a literary language had in 1989 been taken by a team of Bible translators, he had witnessed that many Gullah speakers, although Christianized, remained "not closed to Islam." Still, Kly wanted research to be done "to determine if [Gullah] also carries traces of Islamic or Arabic influences," as well as those from the 25 West African languages or dialects and from English that had more basically contributed to its structure and vocabulary.[87] The context of the partly Muslim Southern African American history and culture evoked by Kly and neo-Muslims such as Clyde-Ahmad Winters, which led them to favor varieties of Africa-structured "Black English", might as easily encourage exploration by a wider range of African-American ideological groups of literary Arabic as an instrument to help them reconstruct the history of specific areas of West Africa from which the African-Americans originated. Whether the now-precarious Gullah can be made an auxiliary literary language on the ground among Gullah-Geechee people, and thereby a component of some greater African-American nationalism remains to be seen: attempts to construct a motivating historical view and public musical rituals for some such enterprise were mounted in the late 1990s by Marquetta L. Goodwine of the Afrikan Cultural Arts Network (AKAN).[88] In response to such political pressure, the U.S. House of Representatives in March 2005 passed a bill promising federal assistance to maintain and preserve the culture of areas of southeastern America stretching from North Carolina to Florida as a historic homeland of the Gullah-Geechee people. (Still, the post-modern communications revolution and new economy that is connecting once-isolated islands and rural black communities with huge bridges into mainstream America, and scattering Gullah-speakers, could finally end that language). The extension of Gullah or varieties of street-level Black English into a literary language of an African-American enclave-nation within modernity would run against the paradoxical drilling by Muslim and Africanist nationalist media over many decades of something close to standard English into vast numbers of ordinary African-Americans.

Our above review of the earlier history of blacks in America showed that enough slivers of culture or links from Africa did survive slavery for serious efforts of reconnection to be mounted by nationalists in the 1920s and again from 1950. While deformed and severed at places by slavery, and then by ongoing systemic oppression, that all made transmission through the generations difficult in America, Islam was one of the elements Blacks brought with them from sub-Saharan Africa. The ambiguous and qualified attempts by neo-Muslim sects in the 20th century to relink African-Americans to Muslim populations in the Middle East and "Black Africa" are thus not the mythological concoction that Angloid and Jewish and also some hyper-Africanist writers in America have imaged. Various black protest sects and movements acted as conduits for a new influx of Arabic, Swahili or such tough West African tongues as Yoruba, Ewe, Ibo or Hausa, or ancient Egyptian, into America, but seem not yet to have established new stable elites or strata literate in those languages. These movements' contribution to the evolution of quasi-linguistic or cultural-ethnic nationalism among African-Americans has to date been mainly the popularization of a limited repertoire of Arabic and Swahili or Pharaonic greetings and phrases among the middle class and lumpen masses to distinguish the black nation from the white groups.

2: JEWISH PARTICIPATION IN SLAVERY AND SEGREGATION

Counter-power is always needed to give the grievances of any group the threatening weight that forces opposed groups in power to hear or read them in the first place. The participation of Farrakhan in the 1984 presidential primaries and his vast 1995 Million Man March conferred enough potential clout to force diverse Jewish spokespersons to address a new black Muslim historical discourse.

Jews were not the only often disliked white group that had been drawn into slavery at the side of its Anglos. John Mitchell, one of the insurgent Free Irishmen, fought with the Confederacy after deportation from Ireland. The novel and film *Gone With the* Wind pictured some Irish-Americans at home among the magnolias, in grand white mansions such as Tara, with slaves galore who were happy to make their lives easy before the Civil War broke out in 1861.[89]

"Jewish" trading, ownership and exploitation of enslaved Africans prior to the American civil war was conducted initially from Amsterdam in Europe, and then from a smallish Jewish minority in America that was but a prototype of the powerful community to be established by the great waves of Yiddish-speaking Ashkenazi immigrants who were to come from Central and Eastern Europe after 1880. During the tensions of the 1960s, many Jewish-Americans denied that their enclave-people in America should assume any share in restitution and reparations to its blacks on the grounds that the bulk of their Jewish forebears had arrived in America well after the Anglos evolved and then abolished slavery as one of the bases of the system—since they had been in "Lithuania" at the time, "Jews have not been historically partners to the Negro enslavement and oppression in the United States".[90]

But two decades on, the issue of Jewish-Americans having to take a share of the rectification of the historic enslavement and oppression of Blacks [in American history] became central to the conflict between Jewish and Black micronationalisms when the Nation of Islam's Historical Research Department published "the first volume" of *The Secret Relationship Between Blacks and Jews* in 1991. Mattias Gardell, a non-American albeit "white" Scandinavian scholar sometimes sympathetic to Farrakhan and the NOI, still credited in 1996 that Harold Brackman's 1994 Zionoid micronationalist apologia for Jewish treatment of blacks in America had "easily refuted the [NOI's] main [historical] arguments" about a disproportionate Jewish role in the enslavement of Blacks in the Americas, showing the Black Muslim-promoted work to have been "poor scholarship".[91]

Brackman's work had evinced a closed nationalist ideological system in its refusal to concede that Jewish-Americans had anything at all to atone for in the treatment of blacks by white people in American history—granite that went with the hegemony of the hardline micronationalists over American Jewry in the 1990s. But a residual liberal fringe on the margin of American Jewry voiced considerable unease at the facile self-righteousness of Brackman's polemic against Muslims, pre-modern and contemporary—not just against those in America in the 1980s and 1990s but against Arabs in Asia and Africa also. In reply, Ralph A. Austen, a Jewish-American scholar of African-American history, thought Brackman's branding of "the Arabs" as "the true villains of the African slave trade" rather like the scapegoating of Jews for New World slavery that the Zionoids charged against Farrakhan's Nation of Islam: "in fact", Austen rebutted, "the Muslim or Oriental slave trade out of Africa involved mainly Berber, Swahili and other Black African raiders and merchants rather than Arabs" (a point we shall see to have been argued by African-American historian W.E.B. DuBois almost fifty years before).

While not always devoid himself of Brackman's drive to minimize the statistics of Jewish involvement in slavery in the Americas, Austen still exemplified painfully slow but real progress by some more self-reflective American Jews in the 1990s towards facing the mixed record their ethnos has vis-à-vis African-Americans. A range of scholarly articles by Jewish professional historians on the Jewish role in slavery had lain scattered in specialized journals: but it had been left to Farrakhan's sect to make the first popularizing synthesis that confronted blacks and Jews in general with their common past, Austen allowed. "The fact that our forefathers were generally, and at times quite significantly, on the side of the slavers in the cruel world of the Atlantic economy may also help call in question the whole image of Diaspora Jews as 'victims' in medieval-to-modern world history". Thus, the more diverse and thus nuanced view of his ethnos that the Black Muslims have made possible in American public discourse struck Austen as almost a liberation from the far-from-"benign" myth of Jews as the best friend and allies of African Americans—a pre-1980 mythology of denial that would only set up a new generation of American blacks and Jews for political polarization and ethnic conflict. "The most uncomfortable elements of our common past" have to be faced "not to apportion or remove guilt but rather to learn who we are through what we were and to incorporate this knowledge into the struggle to become something better".[92]

In contrast to a few liberal, critically-minded individuals, ordinary micronationalist Jewish-Americans after 1980 manipulated historical data and community-categories with a functionality that made it impossible to ever hold the globally diffused Jewish race-collectivity they imagined to any account for anything, let alone restitution. On one hand, internet Jewish nationalist sites such as <soc.culture.jewish> in the 1990s had special sections defining Marranos—originally-Jewish forced converts to Christianity—in Spanish- and Portuguese-speaking societies as detached components of the Jewish nation whose descendants are rightly now being reincorporated through outreach. Yet when black groups raised the issue of their participation in the enslavement of blacks in Africa and the Americas by early lightly-Christianized Jews or crypto-Jews, their membership in the Jewish nation was denied by Jewish-Americans wary of restitution or even having to concede any scrutiny of any Jews to any other group.

In 1991, Seth Rosenthal lashed out over the internet at African-Americans James Strong and Leonard Jeffries who had charged that "Jews helped run the slave-trade" [which is the historical truth stated by Jewish nationalist historians who minimize the role]. Instead of listing "a few [early slave-] ships that have supposedly been traced to Jewish owners," Black Nationalists like Jeffries and Strong should concentrate on Arabs who had owned non-American black slaves into the 1960s. In any case, the racial Sephardic Jews in question, based in Barcelona and Lisbon, were not real Jews: "we are at least 50 years past 1492, and for Mr Jeffries' information there are no longer any Jews in Spain or Portugal, only Marranos and Catholics." Rosenthal's surging race-solidarity, though, then subverted his efforts to place the Spanish- and Portuguese-speakers at issue outside a Jewish people determined by religion. "[Jeffries] blames ethnic Jews who are forced converts under fear of death by burning at the stake, who still experience riots at the hands of local Spanish and Portuguese, and who are constantly at risk of having all their possessions appropriated by the civil authorities... for the African slave trade. Getting to the New World was the only chance for freedom for most of the crypto-Jews, and many of them took the chance, perhaps by enlisting on merchant ships used for the slave trade".[93]

Professional historian David Brion Davis (1997) allowed that "small numbers of Sephardic Jews and Marranos did play a crucial role in refining and marketing sugar [in the Americas] and then in shifting trans-Atlantic commerce, including the slave trade, from Portugal to northern Europe". However, "most Marranos or New Christians were Jews only in the Nazi racist sense of the concept".[94] Yet the Rabbinate was able by the 17th century to reincorporate into formal Judaism the bulk of the *conversos* who came to Amsterdam from the Iberian peninsula and who had not been allowed to practise Judaism openly for 100 years: some took circumcision at an advanced age.[95] Rosenthal did condemn Spaniards and Portuguese—Christian ones—for exterminating Amerindians and enslaving Africans in the New World. This whole Jewish-nationalist thought-frame blocked out the oppression some Africans simultaneously faced at the hands of some Jewish as well as Christian Portuguese-, Spanish- and Dutch-speaking whites. For this current, exploitative patterns of interaction cannot be registered when Jews take part, and no possibility of empathy can arise for any non-Jew subjected to abuse by any Jew.

In fact, ethnic self-criticism or introspection vis-a-vis African-Americans has been rare in most groups in America's Jewish communities, apart from a few radical liberal intellectuals who were often not Jewish nationalists of any kind. The controversies that swirled around *Secret Relationship*, though, underscored points of spiritual involvement by the 20th century's great Ashkenazi Jewish community, not just its small slavery-era precursor, in American slavery and racism. While critiquing in 1995 *The Secret Relationship*'s thesis that Jews held slaves disproportionately to other Euro-Americans, Winthrop D. Jordan nonetheless discreetly nudged his Jewish readers towards a realization of how widely America's mature 20th century Jewish minority had imbibed the general white American indifference to past victimization of blacks. In shadow-boxing with the NOI, Jordan blasted the 1991 book's reliance on secondary and rather dated early 20th century Jewish-American sources, rather than consulting primary sources of the slavery era or post-1980 analytical studies that are more up-to-date academically. Yet the NOI's sampling of Jewish-American actions and communications—precisely because it was skewed in that way—itself brought out the spiritual assent of a sector of the mid-20th century Jewish intelligentsia to the long-vanished chattel slavery at the point at which Jews were making it in America.

The Nation of Islam's Historical Research Department had drawn much of its data from a 1961 paper titled "Jews and Negro Slavery in the Old South, 1789-1865" that Rabbi Bertram W. Korn read as president of the American Jewish Historical Society. Whatever the methodological objections Jordan raised as an historian of slavery to the NOI's use of such a now-old, and non-primary, source in the 1990s, the Korn paper illustrated the connivance towards slavery-era racism among American Jews overall by the 1960s. Whereas the NOI researchers suggested that Jews in the South were the group of whites most liable to hold slaves, Jordan insisted that Korn had documented that they had [only] the same proclivities as their Christian compatriots of the same skin-pigmentation. Still, Jordan was troubled by the absence of a moral landscape or any human empathy in many 20th century (Ashkenazi) Jewish-American historians when they traced slavery's degradation of black fellow-Americans: "Korn's 1961 article today seems downright blind to the suffering of the victims of the slave trade and their descendants." Jordan reconstructed that such studies as Korn's manifested the drive of Yiddish-speaking Jews newly arrived from Europe in the early 20th century to "establish themselves as full participants in their new country." They—and especially their offspring—understood that slavery was a key aspect of the American experience they wanted: hence Korn's matter-of-fact attitude in 1961 that the few Jews in the antebellum South "treated their slaves no better and no worse than other slaveholders, and without exception endorsed slavery" exactly like the other whites there.[96]

The Nation of Islam's new historiography forced some Jewish communalist intellectuals (after a fashion) to face in America's mainstream intellectual media the full gamut of the behavior of Jews towards black fellow-Americans. In January 1996, Martin S. Goldman, Director of the Center for the Study of Jewish-Christian Relations at Merrimack College, Massachusetts, lost his cool because *The Secret Relationship* charged that local Jews "helped to suppress the violent slave revolt led by Nat Turner in Southhampton County, Virginia, in 1831." That a few Jewish-sounding names appeared in the master-lists of the hundreds of Virginia state militiamen who turned out to crush those African-American insurgents, Goldman assured *The Atlantic Monthly*'s ethnically diverse readers, "is of about as much historical importance as the fact that some of the militiamen were left-handed or that some were married". These words did not even try to deny the oneness of Jewish with Christian Southerners in their joint socio-political system that tormented African-Americans into hopeless revolts: both then gunned them down together when they finally did rise.[97] Jason Silverman (1997) recorded that Jewish immigrants in the Old South took part in the apprehension, prosecution and jailing of escaped slaves as constables, turnkeys, sheriffs, marshals and detectives.[98]

The wealth of pre-Civil War Charleston depended far more than that of any other Southern city upon slavery. A Sephardi Jewish community active in trade built up there in the 18th century. The city had the oldest synagogue in constant use in North America: and, in 1836, meeting an influx of Ashkenazi Jews migrating from Europe, it became the first "Reform" Temple in America, although that self-Westernizing reinvention of Judaism had started back in mother continent Europe only a short while before. Thus, the Charleston Jews' attitudes to those enslaved humans became DNA inbuilt into the future greater Jewish-American community that huge immigrations of Ashkenazim from Central and East Europe were later to construct around Reform Judaism as a means to get into, and succeed in, America. Charleston was a center for the import and then sale of Africans because the economy of its region was based on the growing and processing of corn, rice, cotton, indigo and sugar, all labor-intensive: thus, inescapably, the affluence of the city's merchants and traders was built on the sweat of slaves. Many of the notices in Southern newspapers about escaping African "slaves" with Arabic names came from the areas around this preeminent city of Southern slavery.

In 1850, Isaac Meyer Wise, who was to become the leader of Reform Judaism for all the United States, visited Charleston to consider a position as rabbi there. He was impressed with the sophistication of its Sephardic Jewish community and the status and acceptance it had won from the city's "refined" Anglo-Americans: for the first time in his life, he was "the guest of American aristocrats". In "cultured" Charleston, he was "domiciled in splendid rooms" with a Negro at his "disposal".[99] From the British period, an unceasing flow of ships had left Charleston to the triangular international slave trade. The polarization of blacks and whites in Southern history would henceforth lead most of its Anglos to offer semi-equal business and jobs opportunities to Jews as loyal comrade-whites, while still keeping it hard for them to get into some of the top social clubs.

The same cultural and social conjunctions that worked to bring the South's Anglos, Celts and blacks together into one American nation also drew its Jews and blacks towards each other under slavery, but perhaps less strongly. Friendlier, promising interactions between the Jewish minority and African Americans in the old South that worked for a new humane composite community could not stand against all the factors shaping the divided caste-society that evolved. Salzman and West's 1997 collection *Struggles in the Promised Land* averred that some cross-racial unions between Jewish males and black women in ante-bellum Charleston "assumed the quality of a marriage, long, respectful and emotionally and materially satisfying"—somewhat different from the sexual abuse Christian white males with power more often committed against enslaved black women. This book—still tinted throughout with residues of the Jewish-American left-ameliorist ethos and its drive to assemble elements for a renewed (now more realistic) Jewish-black alliance— referred to acts of kindness by early Southern Jews to their interracial offspring. One of its writers argued that Isaac Cardozo paid the bills for the education of his three biracial sons in Charleston schools for free blacks. Yet these boys may in fact have had to pay their own fees: one was apprenticed in carpentry when he was twelve. (It runs against the 1997 book's image of Isaac Cardozo as a quasi-husband and his offspring as family that, after he died in 1855, son Francis had to work for five years in his trade to fund a Christian theological education in England and Scotland: thus, his father may have bequeathed little or no monies for his sons' needs.)

Contributor Earl Lewis allowed that multiple social attitudes in the South's early synagogues made it hard for out-of-wedlock children that some of the South's Jews fathered from enslaved African-American women to have been admitted and raised in those worship-communities as ethnic Jews—although a few were admitted. Isaac's brother, Jacob Cardozo, was a prominent editor and political economist who "contributed to the formation and dissemination of the pro-slavery" ideology that sustained the white South (Jason H. Silverman 1997): "the reason the Almighty made the colored black" reflected Jacob "is to prove their inferiority"—a perfect blending of his Americanism and his Judaism.[100]

The attitudes to blacks could vary somewhat between individual Jews even within a single family that derived livelihoods from the enslaved. The Sephardi husband of Rachel Salom D'Azevedo was an auctioneer who would have dealt in blacks as a matter of course, along with the other commodities in Charleston. Yet when she died in 1843, her will had bequeathed the four enslaved females she "owned" to her daughter on the understanding that upon her daughter's death they would have quasi-free status. Manumission might take a long wait! Yet Rachel had come from a Britain that had abolished slavery in 1807. If she was compassionate, she had to maneuver around a Charleston law of 1800 that made the manumission of slaves illegal.[101]

Jewish left-integrationist Jason Silverman (1997) argued that there was a duality of feelings in the Jewish Southerner planter, Judah P. Benjamin, who warned that the slave "boils with revenge": he was a human being whose feelings should be considered more, although "his mind is comparatively weak".[102] We can allow that Benjamin had an iota of empathy for ill-treated slaves—as well as the plantation aristocracy's pragmatist fears that slavery might be overthrown. Still, it is hard to see how any person with much pity for humans in general could have organized the diplomatic, military and economic war-effort of the confederate states in defense of slavery, which is what Benjamin did as the Confederacy's secretary of war and secretary of state—the role for which he would be remembered by such African-American nationalists of the 1980s and 1990s as Playthell Benjamin (who had an ancestor Judah owned—hence the joint name).[103]

In a 1999 Zionoid micronationalist work—penned to minimize roles of Jews in slavery that Farrakhan's NOI was highlighting—Saul S. Friedman tried to distance "the Jewish people in Louisiana" from Judah Benjamin. He characterized the eminent Confederate statesman as "alienated from Judaism", citing his church marriage to a Catholic woman, and speculated that "this man so often identified with the defense of slavery" converted to Catholicism on his deathbed. It is clear from Friedman that Benjamin was regarded and accepted as a Jew by his apex colleagues in the confederate government, if sometimes sourly.[104] Judah Benjamin was fully representative of the interweave or quasi-fusion of Louisiana and other Southern Jewries with Anglo and Latin Christian compatriots into a new "white people" defined by its united struggle to keep blacks under control.

The data in *The Secret Relationship*, as Muslim and secular African-American activists of various affiliations snatch it up and diffuse it out through a wider and wider range of nationalistic publications, has of course not obliterated the kinder acts or programs of some distinguished Jews towards blacks struggling for civil rights, which in their turn, are now history. The data has, though, blown up for good the innocence of the myth of a special friendship or alliance of Jews as a collective with blacks against German-like Anglosaxons. Dr Kawkab Siddiqi, a lecturer at an African American college who had been with the Jama'at-i-Islami back in his native Pakistan, from the 1980s mustered his gadfly tabloid, *New Trend*, to bring together anti-Zionist African American Muslims however heterodox they be, Arab *salafi* anti-American fundamentalists, Ba'thist 'Iraqis, Palestinian strugglers secular and religious, Irish nationalists—and then German-American micronationalists of a vintage national self-reassertion, all in support of Palestine.[105] From *New Trend*, the more or less neo-Sunni Dr Alauddin Shabazz, a contributor to both Farrakhan's and Warith's tabloids, took up and developed some data and themes of *The Secret Relationship*. With routine functions by Sephardi Jewish merchants of the East Coast and the Caribbean, ships left Newport in New England with rum to be traded along the coasts of West Africa for enslaved humans who were then shipped on to the West Indies to be traded for slave-labor sugar [some were sent on for auction by Jews and Anglos in Charleston] that those ships then carried back to Newport for the production of rum, which then again was shipped to... By the mid-18th century, one "triangle trade" ship reached or left Newport every day of the year. The trade provided diverse openings for Jews to achieve wealth and respect in Anglo-America.[106]

Iberian Jews who migrated to Brazil had helped found the first major New World sugar plantations worked by the slaves whom they also had often retailed: they later helped disseminate that system around the Dutch and then the British-colonized islands of the Caribbean.[107] In a 1993 mass-circulation article carried by the *Washington Post,* David Mills (African-American) tried to focus the kind of historical scrutiny that the Zionoids were denouncing onto the roles of Jews as planters, as auctioneers and retailers of captured Africans, and as insurance underwriters for slave ships not in North America only, but also in South America and the Caribbean islands.[108] While the NOI work, *The Secret Relationship*, did not see that the share of Jews in the trans-Atlantic slave-trade fell after the 17th century, Winthrop Jordan allowed that it had shown that the "flourishing community of Jewish merchants" of Newport City, Rhode Island, was active in the 18th century trade in rum and African slaves. Jordan did take issue with the NOI study's contention that "*all* the stills in Newport were owned by the Jews": he mustered at least one ex-Quaker WASP who had one there on the eve of the American Revolution.[109]

From *New Trend*, Dr Alauddin Shabazz (African-American) excerpted the chilling correspondence of Newport Jewish slave-merchants with the personnel of their ships as well as other merchants: he took this "demonic" discourse from the Carnegie Institute's *Documents Illustrative of the History of the Slave Trade in America.* We are made to hear the voices of a nightmare group for whom the survival or health of their cargoes of terrified victims—in the case of the females, often much-raped and thus suicidal—mattered only for the bearing it could have on profits. Yet Alauddin's article failed to document, any more than had *The Secret Relationship*, that the Jewish share in the slave-trade from Newport was "a monopoly" as he imaged.[110] Data with a mass circulation provided in Mills' 1993 *Washington Post* article showed the artificiality of placing Marranos who traded or oppressed Africans outside a global Jewish People once the existence of the latter is argued. That super-rich shipper of slaves, Aaron Lopez, had been a Marrano in Portugal but in Newport came out as the pious Jew who in that flourishing city in 1759 laid the cornerstone of the first synagogue of the USA.[111]

Saul Friedman, a Jewish micronationalist historian, in 1999 fused Farrakhan, Saddam Hussein, Mu'ammar al-Qadhafi, Lyndon LaRouche, and Tom Metzger of the White Aryan Resistance with "the devil" manifested in Hitler, at least as the Devil's "imitators" and "lackies".[112] Very much one product of the ideologized hatreds between U.S. "nationalities" in the 1980s and 1990s, this apologia collaged data, figures, estimates and graphs to clear "the Jewish people" in America of as much "wrongdoing" during slavery as it could. The book, though, found it hard to mitigate the activities of Lopez much. Friedman allowed that Lopez "was on fairly intimate terms with the more notorious slaving captains of New England", and had intricate knowledge of the leaders in West Africa from whom he purchased the humans, and of the problems liable to affect the profits in his transportation and sales of those he enslaved. He instructed his captains to secure the Africans being transported with irons because they were "less than human." Lopez was regarded by his WASP fellow-Americans as fitting well into their values. A

Christian clergyman eulogized him on his death as "the most universally beloved man I ever knew," and the inhabitants of Leicester collectively mourned him for his "integrity" with a philo-Judaic cliché. During the American war for independence, Aaron Lopez had chosen the side of George Washington.[113] Generally, Friedman's estimates put participation by Jews in North American slavery as at least at the level of their ratios in the total white populations of specific areas. In regard to the shares of Jews in the Guianas and Surinam, Friedman denied that "the purchase of one quarter of slave imports [by Jews would] constitute domination of the trade".[114]

While the historical data does not sustain a disproportionate Jewish role in slavery of the extent that the USA's new Islamophile and neo-Muslim African American intelligentsia was to charge in the 1990s, the pre-20th century precursor-Jewries had certainly been no friend of African-Americans. Even on the eve of the civil rights movement, a good section of their huge Ashkenazi successor-minority was still pursuing a similar Americanism designed for all whites that was far from intent on inducting African Americans. After 1980, Jewish micronationalist publicists dismissed the Black Nationalists' demands that American Jews contribute to the reparations white Americans owed. But their denials of any responsibility by Jewish Americans might disintegrate in the face of the structural links between Jews in the South and those in the North, and between the precursor-Jewry and the success of the Ashkenazi Jews who migrated to the North after the abolition of slavery. Even in the North, many Jews had founded much of their wealth and their institutions upon the traffic and exploitation of Africans.[115] Farrakhan's NOI published long lists of top late-20th century Jewish families in the North which had started out on that basis of slavery-wealth.

On the whole, few elite Jewish American publicists and intellectuals could respond constructively to the new opening up to discussion in the 1990s of Jewish roles in slavery. Most of them were averse to even looking at the data. A.M. Rosenthal, an unwearying vilifier of Arabs in the *New York Times*, in 1993 dubbed accusations from Black Nationalists that Jews had financed the slave trade as "not quite the equivalent of [the charge of] Christ-killer, but coming close".[116] Such comparisons of U.S. Black Nationalists to anti-Semites who had massacred Jews in Europe ruled out any conversation or negotiations, and could excuse violence against at least some African-Americans at some future time.

In the 20th century, lynchings of blacks in the faraway South had been denounced by some Yiddish poetry in the great populations of immigrant Ashkenazi Jews in the cities of the U.S. North. The sympathy was fostered by these Jews' own lesser hardships in getting into America. Although autodidacts who could be crude in their poetic techniques, the Yiddish "sweatshop" poets of New York could weave aesthetic sensitivity into their vivid accounts of extreme Anglo exploitation in textile and other factories, that made it hard for the often barely literate Jewish male immigrants to hold together the families and offspring they saw so little. Morris Rosenfeld (1862-1922) wrote: "look for me not where myrtles green!/Not there my darling shall

I be./Where lives are lost at the machine,/That's the only place for me." Amid these tight conditions of newly-arrived Jews, Yehoash (1872-1927) in his poem, "Lynching", denounced the Anglos who bullied both enclave-peoples: "you dig you/Dig nails into his [a lynched African-American's] ribs/Knives into his heart/Spitting on his agony/You left him dangling/On the tree".[117] But how many Yiddish poems applied introspective scrutiny to the racism and slavery-like practices that some Yiddish-speaking Ashkenazi Jews were more and more inflicting on their black neighbors in New York? Some radical Yiddish papers did sometimes rap those Jewish merchants who assaulted or fleeced blacks, and Jews who took part in "White" societies directed to stopping blacks from moving into suburbs.[118] To be sure, Yehoash's poem eerily evoked the presence of Yahweh around the asphyxiated Negro.

How much of this genre is sincere sympathy for blacks? And how much just using suffering of African-Americans as one more stick with which to hit the moral title to lead of the Christian Anglo-Americans who had not always welcomed Jews? After all, most Jews in the South—but also some Northern Jews—assented to or aided its white supremacism and segregation. When President Roosevelt sent a petition to the Tsar in 1903 protesting a pogrom against Jews in Kishineff, African-American leaders objected that it carried the names of senators from Mississippi who justified lynching. The Philadelphia B'nai B'rith leader, Solomon Cohen, retorted that most lynched blacks had committed the crimes charged, in contrast to the moral—and intellectually so much more advanced—Jews in Europe who were true innocent victims.[119] In 1937, a Jewish resident of Birmingham invited visiting relatives from the "civilized" North to go out with him to a local Saturday night lynching: some of the visitors were "willing", some "appalled".[120] Although it was to aid the black civil rights movement later, the B'nai B'rith Anti-Defamation League in the 1940s still held aloof from actions by African American groups to pressure more rights and opportunities, as "subversive" of America and its war-effort.[121] In the Civil Rights era, Jewish activists came down from the North. However, "long before there was any talk of Negro anti-Semitism, Jewish laymen in the South were demanding that their rabbis 'stick to religion and leave civil rights alone', precisely the same instructions the Methodist, Presbyterian and Baptist laymen gave their clergy".[122]

The initial crude effort by members and sympathizers of the Nation of Islam in the 1980s and 1990s to re-apprehend the era of slavery, with a specific focus on Jews as a component in the white American nation that was forming, did recycle some hoary defamations by Euro-American anti-Semite, Henry Ford. The long-term effects, though, of this reconsideration of that relationship may one day provide an impetus to better communication between Jews, African Americans and Anglos that may make it possible to at last integrate a humane multi-ethnic Americanist community on a basis of reciprocal honesty, and better self-exploration and self-reflection on the part of all ethnic groups. A chain of historical coincidences that included (a) the Holocaust, (b) the greater resultant awareness of WASP Americans of their own anti-Semitism and where it could lead, and (c) the rise from the end of the Second World War of Jewish groups that built wealth and institutionalized power in the USA's two key cities, all together had long made any print-scrutiny of American Jewry by other ethnic groups a key taboo in modernist American life. The Islam-tinted intelligentsia forming around the Nation of Islam was now starting to focus on Jewish-Americans the sort of unremitting scrutiny that some Jewish-American intellectuals and media-persons directed against the ascendant WASPs after World War II (especially during America's misadventure in Vietnam). That overdue scrutiny had been crucial in the evolution of a more open society of later modern America, while the new Islam-tinted African-American intelligentsia's opening of some roles of the by then rich and powerful Jewish sector of America to discussion by other ethnic groups may now help carry the U.S. into the next stage of the much more radically decentralized and ethnically-devolved post-modern America. The integrative common ground would remain a resolve of all nationalities to make big money together in the capitalist private enterprise system within a renegotiated new U.S. federation of all residents that better suits all the possibilities of the post-modern age. Thus, Islam's function as a rallying-ground for self-assertion by African-Americans against Jewish compatriots already has not been viewed by all among the latter as all bad. Letting out pent-up steam and grievances can defuse potential violence and usher in overdue bargains and settlements. Certain home truths could help to set both groups free.

NOI discussion of Jews in slavery caught the interest of many varieties of nationalists among African-Americans in the post-modern era, but not in some other sectors of Islam. The theme was seen by many in Warith Deen Mohammed's sect as a ploy by Farrakhan to highlight himself in politics as the champion of African-Americans against a confirmed enemy micronation. Imam Alauddin Shabazz was an exceptional figure who long published in both Warith and Farrakhan's media. It has not been Warith's policy to legitimize his sect by evoking conflicts with American Jews as such, whom he has tried to mollify. As the new intellectuals in Warith's sect explore the twentieth century history of African Americans, it may highlight Jewish-Americans as a much more numerous opposed group than was the case for the slavery period. The Muslim convert Sufi Abdul Hamid (see Chapter 3) has drawn increased interest among the widening Islamic intelligentsia that gradually formed in and around Warith's Islamic sect following the death of his father in 1975. Yusuf Abdus-Salaam in 2004, in a perspective-article, "Islam's Roots in Harlem" (*Muslim Journal* of 19 March 2004) of Harlem as a continuous place of residence by African American Muslims since enslaved Islamic Africans were first brought there in the British period, reviewed Hamid's leadership before WWII of activism to force white employers to hire Blacks in both Chicago and then New York. Abdus-Salaam went over the bygone contest between Hamid and William Blumstein in Harlem, but without terming the latter Jewish or distinguishing Jewish from other white business persons in Harlem. That accorded with Imam Warith's line of avoiding conflict with U.S. Jews while critiquing the policies of the faraway Jewish state of Israel.

Overall, the data that by the end of the 20th century had been brought together about "Jews and Blacks" in the period of America's formation eerily transcends its own time. It is overwhelmingly likely that a fair number of Jews in the South, including urban ones in Charleston in particular, "owned" Muslim African slaves during that era of the formation. In what ways did both these two religio-ethnic groups already muster their respective scriptures—the Qur'an and the Torah—in the struggle of each against the other? It is unsettling that a prototype may have already been created by the early 1800s for inequality of power and the religions-focused conflict between these two U.S. micronations in the 20th century. That would make the tensions with Jewish-Americans that after 1983 highlighted Farrakhan as the Islamic leader for African-Americans, just one more installment in something older and ingrained that may recur in almost karmic cycles between these two groups in the USA until a decisive Americanist integration will come to break that sterile closed circuit.

3: THE ANGLO-AMERICANIZATION OF OTHER "WHITES" AND THE FORECLOSURE OF MICRONATIONALISMS IN THE EARLIER TWENTIETH CENTURY

The Formation of the Ethnic Groups

The evolution of ethnic communities in America has raised two types of identification. The first was an atmosphere of white-vs-colored polarization that gave Anglos title to Anglicize the other whites they would then admit into America's "white people" after a fashion, under the brutal bargain. The second tendency saw the evolution of enclave-nationalisms, and after 1980, of the micronationalisms less interested in territoriality, that could challenge the system or just band an ethnic group together so as to get it into parliamentarism, government and then the central private-sector economy. The second tendency, the articulation of micronationalisms in American life after 1980, was crucial for the rebirth of the Nation of Islam under Farrakhan. Under Elijah to 1975, the old NOI did not highlight ethnic plurality in whites—unlike some in Farrakhan's new NOI after 1977.

As a nationalist religion founded in Detroit by a possible scion of an immigrant [Druze?] Arab family, or of one headed by a South Asian Isma'ili Muslim in New Zealand (which Warith's impressions may favor), the Nation of Islam is a meeting of (a) the Afro-American tradition, which has many ultra-American Anglo-derived sectors, *with* (b) immigrant ethnic minorities that spoke languages other than English in earlier twentieth-century America. Non-Anglo immigrant and ethnic groups waving other languages as their banners became micronationalistic after 1970: from 1977 some of their heightened motifs would stimulate the discourses of Farrakhan's new Nation of Islam. We thus now consider the degree to which non-Anglo ethnic minorities could articulate political and religious separatism in the leadup to the birth of Wali Fard Muhammad's Nation of Islam in 1930.

Overall, the economic, social and ideological incentives offered by the USA long worked to counter the potential for micronationalisms among even those "Caucasian" ethnic groups that Anglo racism most enraged. The English writer, J.A. Spender, was struck in 1928 that a single American culture could quickly stamp and absorb immigrants from the most diverse countries. The United States had won a unique prosperity by keeping her doors wide open to mass immigration, he argued, in contrast to the restrictions on movements of populations practised by other colonial countries. Immigration had helped America raise her population from four million in 1790 to the 119 million it reached in 1927.[123] Some non-English-speaking parents clung to their old traditions, but many of their children had adopted Anglo-Saxon culture as their own. Spender thus found it misleading to infer the ethnic or political sympathies of an American from his name or ethnic origin. Against the Kaiser's hopes, many German-Americans had married English and Scottish-descended Americans, with the result that their children lost all identification with their German origin. Such Anglicized non-WASP professionals promoted the culture and educational patterns of England that came to them through literary English, and which would continue to define America.[124]

Spender predicted—only a half-truth over the long-term—that this Americanization dynamic would rule out the development of political micronationalisms in America that would define themselves against Anglo-Americans through commitment to the political interests of overseas states or countries of provenance. He reflected that large numbers of the Germans who emigrated to the United States in the nineteenth century did so to escape the military and despotic conditions there, and had thus been out of sympathy with modern imperial Germany.[125] Many Arab and Muslim immigrants in the later 20th century were to be similarly alienated from the authoritarian systems of government of the states from which they came, and for which they in consequence refused to lobby in America's mainstream, a pattern not lost on the intelligentsia that African American Muslim movements have been developing since 1970.

Spender in 1928 rated Anglo-Saxon culture and the "melting pot" homeland as having assimilated at least the Northern European, Celtic and "Nordic" elements to the composite American type. Latin and Slavic immigrants remained more problematical.

The micronationalisms with presence in mainstream representational politics and bodies (parliamentarism) that African-Americans and Jews pioneered from the 1960s, had by the end of the 20th century evolved into an unprecedented cluster of ideologies with supporters among most ethnic groups in America. The new ideologies elaborated a plethora of cultural instruments and institutions to diffuse these definitions of self in each given ethnos throughout the succeeding eras of new mass media and the information revolution. From the late 1960s, history and language courses relating to America's diverse nationalities would be implanted in America's topmost educational institutions where they were to seem to compete with Anglo-Saxon cultural forms. While the USA had never had non-Anglo enclave-nationalisms with that much articulation before 1960, the potential had been there for a century—an option that had not hitherto been realized because some key elements for nationality were missing.

The elements for internal ethnic nationalisms that had come together by the 1920s included some weaving of (a) homelands of provenance in combat with the homelands of devil enemies across the ocean into (b) parochial American electoral politics. Spender, a sharp observer, noted how Mayor W. H. Thompson of Chicago declared himself ready to "hit ["invading" visitor] King George on the snout". Here, that athlete mayor was courting the votes of the Irish, Latins and Slavs and other inferiorized stocks by delegitimizing the nativist Anglo-Americans as lieges who took their orders from a British government. Such use of British leaders was always meant to turn the tables on the "Nordic" American who charged that Catholics, Latins and Slavs would not integrate as loyal—decultured—Americans. Thompson had opposed U.S. entry into WWI to rescue a bleeding England.[126]

Where allowed to vote, African-Americans, like the other non-Anglo ethnic groups, tried to make electoral units and seats reflect and nourish their ethnos. Abraham Grenthal, a Republican Jewish assemblyman in New York, in 1924-1928 mixed well with the growing number of Negroes in his ward and fought for low-income housing legislation, rent control and other measures on their behalf. But modeling themselves on the white ethnics, budding black politicians organized an insurgent ticket that deposed him in 1929. As one active black put it: "there is an overwhelming sense among members of my group that one of their number should be a member of the Assembly [for] the 19th district"—"all [other] racial groups throughout the city, Italians, Jews, etc." were pursuing that means to win minority groups "elective representation".[127] It seems, though, that "Negro" figures in U.S. electoral politics, local or national, linked their ethnos much less to the interests of overseas homelands of origin than did Anglo and Celtic politicians of the era.

Overseas states such as Britain, Israel, the Palestinians, the Soviet Union, South Africa, etc., have long been evoked in political discourses in America at least as symbolic motifs in domestic issues related to the unequal distribution of power and wealth between the "races" or the *ethne* in America. Spender in 1928 already rated the internal conflicts that motifs about Britain focused as "a serious and anxious problem" for America's national integration: if her "politicians are going to... form racial blocs which will vote together and possibly draw gunmen into their feuds" then the melting-pot might become a volcano and the unity of the country be endangered.[128]

Since its foundation in 1930, the NOI has always projected a highly blurred and open-ended vision of the worldwide "Black nation" to which it in theory affiliated its converts. Its ambiguous definition of people of many diverse face-features and hues as "Black" proceeded from general American ideas and patterns at the time in which Wali Fard Muhammad and Elijah Muhammad founded the sect. There has been a good deal of variation over the decades as to which populations Anglomorph Americans place outside the bounds of whiteness. In the 1920s, the period in which Marcus Garvey's United Negro Improvement Association was articulating an Africanist nationalist ideology and Fard and Elijah's worldview was forming, Anglo-Americans were become more restrictive about whom they would admit as fellow-whites. Traditionally, most immigration had been "Nordic," from the United Kingdom and North Europe, but from 1880 America drew more from the Latin and Slavic populations of South and South-East Europe. When the 1920 census appeared, the native-born Anglo-Americans, the "hundred per centers," lamented that they had sunk to only 61 per cent of the white population and 55 per cent of the whole population.[129] Alarmed Anglo academics pressured U.S. administrations to pass legislation to limit the Latino influxes from countries to the South, even if such laws might harm relations with Latin America. There were both anti-Semites and Judeophiles among the USA's white Christians, but most Anglo ultras accepted Jews as white comrades of good standing when the context was the struggle to keep out or control Negroes and Orientals. Thus, in 1916 the leading anti-Japanese organization in San Francisco, the Native Sons of the Golden West, held a mass meeting to raise funds for persecuted European Jews.[130]

Thus, at the point of the Nation of Islam's birth, a new racist Anglo-white nationalism had taken form in America that placed Latinos, Italians, Arabs, and sometimes Jews outside the parameters of the cluster of truly white races from which a new Anglo-cultured and dominated American nation could be welded. The new racist theorists fused the Asiatic and Mediterranean peoples they rejected with the African-Americans as all to be excluded: no more Asiatics, whether Chinese, Japanese or Indian, were to be admitted into the U.S., and the Negroes, now numbering in the ten millions, had to be kept segregated. The central drive was to keep the narrowly-defined "white race" pure. Lothrop Stoddard popularized a global sense of the "rising tide of color" that exaggerated the capacity of Islam and Muslim populations in the Middle East and Africa to challenge the Western powers—thereby highlighting Islam and the Arabs to Garveyites and other African-Americans as a power-center alternative to the West.[131] Such highly literate and copious Anglo race ideologues had by 1930 ironically helped popularize among blacks notions of transcontinental reconnections and alliances with Japan—sympathy for which was to get Elijah Muhammad jailed during World War II—and with Arab nationalisms, with which most African-American movements were to toy to the close of the twentieth century.

The development of Black Muslim community ideology has always responded receptively to varied outgroups facing dislike from within the racial or neo-conservative discourses of Anglo-America. Religions often deepen racial categorizations in America. Fearing their group could get swamped, the Anglo and Anglicized race-writers and politicians of the 1920s denounced the influxes of Latin Americans as liable to increase the Catholic Church's power and thus threaten the Protestant ascendancy. From its beginnings in the 1950s, Black Muslim mass journalism, including both Farrakhan's and Warith's, has always popularized anti-U.S. movements in Latin America, and in the 1990s could even consider the Catholic church as a potential ally in its function as a vehicle for Hispanic people in the U.S. against White (or just WASP?) Power.

In the 1980s, the Black micronationalist theoretician Y.N. Kly, an academic in international law, tried to devise a legal framework of international minority rights to integrate minority nations as recognized units into the multinational states in which they reside around the world. In a 1989 historical retrospect, Kly depicted "America's ruling elites" as ultra-calculating and systematic in their assimilation of immigrants. America's successive WASP elites alternated diverse policies to maintain Anglo-Saxon racial dominance. Kly saw various types of community as having been possibilities in U.S. history. A community of unionized laboring people in tension with the WASP elite could have developed. But that elite brought in new waves of diverse "white" immigrants from Southern and Central Europe for use as strikebreakers and cheap unorganized labor, balancing against each other a large number of ethnic groups separated by languages. Kly quoted a statement from President Theodore Roosevelt in 1905 to argue that another aim of the elite in bringing in a much more diverse range of Europeans was to channel them to areas in the South where African-Americans might come to outnumber whites.

But dispersing the new diverse immigrants away from New York was also meant to culturally harm *them* as well: scattering and mixing them would ensure that those nationalities would not be able to preserve their languages and cultural and social identities. Kly acidly observed that their mixing Africans from different tribes and nations in building institutional slavery had taught the earlier settlers the art of Anglo-Americanizing populations brought from abroad. The elite evolved a white American nationalism under which all groups from Europe were to consent to be fused into a single new white nation: they would relinquish their ethnic cultures in return for the benefits of incorporation into America. The ruling Anglo elite from the 1850s mustered legislation and public funds to develop universal free public schools as the instrument to linguistically Anglicize Catholics, in particular, however much that cost.[132]

Kly's sharp sense of the diverse origins and loyalties of U.S. whites, of the constructed nature of the "white" American identity, and hence of alternate community possibilities in American history, would have counterparts among journalists of Farrakhan's new Nation of Islam in the 1990s. Some NOI writers in that same post-modern era were to share Kly's alertness to tensions between Catholic "whites" and WASPS, and his sense of Mexican-Americans and Amerindians—and poor whites?—as in one trench with the Blacks vis-a-vis the Anglicized white dominant group. When not yearning for Allah to incinerate America, Abdul Allah Muhammad in 1996 would welcome recent appointments to the Supreme Court that had made its Protestant members a minority for the first time in the 207 years since it was founded. Muhammad wanted U.S. law, deformed by Republican administrations, to again prescribe reparative opportunities for African Americans and to get them, Muslims and Latinos, all bound in alliance, into U.S. institutions. These had to cease to be instruments for patronage in the hands of the descendants of the WASP ethnic clique that had founded the United States and the Supreme Court, etc.[133]

By 1930 and the birth of the Nation of Islam, then, the United States had become more obsessed than ever with the balance and purity of the races. Yet the American system had already achieved much towards welding a new single Anglomorph nation across the very great differences of races, of climates, and the intense particularism of the federated states, over so vast an area.[134] The "Black Muslim" movements would henceforth strive to draw African-Americans into a duplication of the patterns of enterprise and social organization by which Anglo-Americans had built wealth and social control in America, but under an insignia of Islam.

Ethnic Entry into the American Parliamentarist Political System

Black Nationalists in the USA early followed efforts by non-Anglo white populations to solidify their communities into political micronations and enter, or relate to, the U.S. system as such, rather than individuals deethnicizing themselves and then entering. Alexander Crummell in an 1882 paper on "The Race Problem in America" argued that races and nations kept their essential characteristics through all recorded history. The Irish in America remained Irish, the Germans German and the Jews Jewish. Unlike assimilationist black progressives such as T. Thomas Fortune—who foresaw biological amalgamation with whites—Crummell saw no reason to expect "the future dissolution of this race" in America.[135]

The existence in the United States of ethnic groups with a potential to evolve into political nations of some sort was noted by analysts and politicians throughout the 20th century. German-Americans were like African-Americans before World War II—or like Arab-Americans from 1965 with their high ratio of students and academics—in having prolific academics and publicists who articulated in print various options vis-à-vis the U.S. and Anglo culture: (a) extraterritorial loyalty to the German state; (b) assimilation and integration into Anglo-America; or (c) some interweave and synthesis of the two high cultures and the two polities that could foster the growth of micronationalities within the U.S. system.[136] The German Emperor had boasted before World War I that he had twenty-five million subjects in the United States, and a handful of German-Americans did discreetly,in "accidents", blow up war materials the U.S. was shipping to Britain before it formally declared war on Germany (WWI). The Hitler regime helped some German-Americans maintain an ability to read German, whose ethnic societies and lobbyists duly joined with isolationists to again delay U.S. entry into a world conflict. Yet in neither world war did most German-Americans display dual loyalties of political significance once their State, the United States, declared war on Germany. Irish-Americans, too, had been reluctant for the U.S. to come to the aid of England in World War I, but once the government of Anglo-supremacist President Wilson declared war, they fought with complete loyalty.

In the later 19th and in the 20th centuries, Irish-Americans played an important role in international relations by sending Irish nationalists enough resources to enable them to fight on against the British Empire, and against the post-WWII British state (similar to African-American mobilization against South African apartheid in the 1970s and 1980s). Like African Americans, Irish refugees from the potato famine were segregated as a lumpen proletariat in northern urban slums, where they faced worse bigotry in America than they had from Protestants back in Ireland. For the length of the 18th through the early 19th centuries, it remained doubtful if Anglo-Americans would ever accept the title of the Irish to be classified as "white" with the entitlements that would bring.[137] But the Irish used gaining the control of police and fire departments of the North's great cities as the springboard to wrest political clout and positions from the WASPs who wanted to bar them. Soon, St Patrick's Day parades—a contrived form of ethnic self-display invented in America—came to influence electoral politics in Boston, New York and Chicago. The Tammany Hall pattern enabled the political machines the Irish built up to command real power in city-level politics and in the Democratic Party to the mid-1950s.

Back-to-Africa nationalists were closely observing Irish-American movements in the 1920s. Speaking in 1922 in New York, Marcus Garvey held up as one model for African Americans the movement for the independence of Ireland that had been led by Eamon de Valera, "who gained millions of Irish adherents in this country".[138] As well as its important aid to anti-English nationalists in the overseas homeland, Irish Catholic movements had mobilized the ethnos within America to force resources and chances out of that system. But, beyond ethnic patronage, some Catholic politicians oversaw the institution of government-based facilities that offered growth and opportunities to all Americans. Al Smith, inaugurated as governor of New York in 1919, expanded badly needed social services. Yet his nomination for the U.S. presidency—as daring as Jesse Jackson's runs decades later—was smashed by unremitting anti-Catholic venom fired at him from all corners of Anglo-America. Still, the clout the Irish had assembled in city politics compelled respect from the anti-Celts. That extent of penetration of the American mainstream, though, posed the question of whether the ethnic group would keep its identity. When John Fitzgerald Kennedy became president, the Irish had won recognition of their right to participate in mainstream American politics at every level, yet the ethnic appeals by politicians to Irish-Americans as such did not slacken. Mayor Richard J. Daley colored the rivers of Chicago green in his relentless rituals to move into the public domain what attenuated Celtic culture Irish-Americans still had. As Farrakhan was to strive to shake the hands of visiting Nelson Mandela or Chairman 'Arafat' before the TV cameras, so Daley brought leaders from the homeland of provenance into his mass public ethnicist rituals, such as the mayor of Gaelic-speaking Galway, western Ireland. Signs bore shamrocks and "Chicago GO Bragh"—a tiny opening back into the Gaelic-speaking rural Ireland from which the forefathers had once come.[139] Farrakhan, also, would make the multitudes of "Blacks" he drew to his open-air collective nationalist rituals in the 1990s chant Arabic phrases with him, although that, unlike Daley, was to define ethnicity in terms of the language of a world religion that had originated outside the homelands of origin and the local languages spouses and their children spoke with each other in West Africa.

Success can destroy minority nationhood. The rewarding integration into the U.S. political system, governance and professions that the Irish political machine bosses had wrested was making their people more like their old WASP enemy, now colleagues in mainstream politics, diluting away what shrinking or fossilized affinities they still had to the Celtic world after so long in America. The potential for Irish-American micronationhood looked set to peter away into formalistic emblems and intermarriage. Yet, in the 1960s, a stratum of Irish-American creative writers, intellectuals and future academics was forming who in the 1980s and 1990s would confront their ethnos with the full luxuriance of the culture, old language and causes of that Motherland across the seas.

Masco Young, editor of Elijah's magazine, *Salaam*, in 1960 equated the NOI movement with the Jews, Italians, Irish and Catholics who proudly strove to perpetuate their cultural heritages in America.[140] More convinced than his boss, Elijah, that the vote might prove a form of power in America, Malcolm X also saw the ethnic units through which it had long incorporated non-Anglo populations into the American system. Through Tammany Hall, "New York City's first Irish Catholic Mayor was elected in 1880, and by 1960 America had its first Irish Catholic President": "America's black man, voting as a bloc, could wield an even more powerful force".[141]

The diverse forces in and around Farrakhan's Islamic national movement in the 1980s and 1990s more and more sharply focused, through his mass media, a vision of African Americans as a victimized enclave-ethnos or quasi-nation throughout American political and social history; a narrative, though, that can have in it some pluralization of whites also. Farrakhanist micronationalism in America, which can draw on Middle Eastern pan-Arab and Arab-American thoughts, more and more accurately visualized other Arab, Latino and Jewish political ethnicities and quasi-nationalisms in the USA. If it could in turn visualize U.S. Celtic political and cultural groups in a nuanced way, that breakthrough in focusing the deepening pluralism of white Americans might multiply the Nation of Islam's survival strategies in North America.

While some Farrakhanist communications after 1980 (eg. Nate Clay) still indicted whites in an undifferentiating way, others (we analyze Conrad Worrill) had come to pluralize Euro-Americans much more, and glimpsed the past pain and the particularities of white ethnic groups that had known exclusion but ended it by power they wrested and built up by means of quasi-nationalist self-organization in America.

Nate Clay, editor of the *Chicago Metro News* as well as a contributing editor of *Final Call*, and one of the veterans of the civil rights struggle who turned micronationalist, in 1987 still had a non-pluralizing fixation on Chicago's late political machine boss, Richard Daley (1902-1976) who ruled the city as mayor for 22 years (1955-1976). During that long reign, Chicago had been hailed across the country as "the city that works", and America's seekers and wielders of power had ritualistically journeyed to the Windy City to beseech the blessings of that last of the "big city machine bosses", the man who could make or break U.S. presidents. Still, Clay voiced no idea how hard Daley had had to work—and through how much initial WASP race hate he had had to stride as a Celt—before he built that power.

As a Black Nationalist, Clay opposed his own ethnic counter-narrative to praise of Daley by white academics and journalists:

> Black people, who started pouring into Chicago from the cotton fields of Mississippi in the early '50s, were boxed in, segregated in tawdry little kitchenette apartments run by Jewish landlords, jumped on by hate-filled cops for the slightest real or imagined transgression: they were herded into a few wards where they were ruthlessly exploited by Daley's oppressive political machine. ...Conmen Uncle Tom Black politicians and preachers were sent to those overcrowded hovels to strawboss the field niggers and deliver them over to the massa at election time. Daley was elected mayor in 1955 on the strength of the Black vote delivered by Congressman Bill Dawson.

If the "great builder" Daley could be given credit for the glittering high rises and the palaces of commerce where the city's bagmen and businessmen operated in the shadow of City Hall, he merited blame for the Robert Taylor Homes (the largest high-rise public housing complex in the country) and the ruthlessness with which he ran expressways through Black neighborhoods while redeveloping Chicago. He had ordered his policemen to "shoot to kill" blacks who rioted following the April 4, 1968 slaying of Dr. Martin Luther King, Jr.[142]

Richard Daley had got his clique and a fair number of his people into the prosperity of America's mainstream economy that *Final Call*, too, covertly sought for African Americans. Clay, though, showed that it was not easy for some pro-Islamic Black Nationalists preoccupied with the pigmentation divide to see the plural ethnic gauntlet Daley's group had faced, and the conflict techniques they had devised to thrust their way into the system. Some lessons and techniques that could work for African-Americans too were missed by Clay, in contrast to Malcolm X's sharp eye.

Yet both mega-"Mayor" Richard Daley and sect-leader Elijah Muhammad after a time sensed that they both led parallel enterprises. Daley's political machine and thus the Chicago Police Department came to terms with the Nation by the 1960s: thereafter there were seldom the raids, police brutality and denials of permits for assembly that dogged the sect's mosques and congregations in other U.S. cities. While no question of personal liking arises with such hard leaders, Daley respected the fact that Elijah could, if he wanted, have ordered his disciplined followers to mobilize a strong protest vote by African Americans that might help unseat his administration in Chicago. Mayor Daley, tied to the Democratic Party, proclaimed March 26, 1974 as Chicago's "Honorable Elijah Muhammad Day", in a political context in which the NOI and the Republican Party were looking each other over as Elijah hinted that for the first time he might allow his followers to vote.[143] Some African-American scholars and activists have wondered if Elijah had for years not been greasing the palms of Daley's party machine to win the immunity from harassment that the NOI enjoyed in Daley's Chicago. Shortly before his death, Elijah told the FBI that he had come to respect America, and—somewhat as Warith shortly would do, with his own dualism and ambiguity—urged his followers to respect the flag of the white man while it still flew over them. He told them to stop calling whites devils because some negative blacks [among them those who blocked Elijah] were devils, too.[144]

After Farrakhan recreated the old millenarian-heretical Nation of Islam in 1977-1978, at least some in his camp developed a more pluralizing vision than Clay of the unflagging quasi-nationalist drive that propelled disliked white groups into core America. The new post-1980 black micronationalism in the USA itself developed cultural links to Africa demanded by preceding extraterritorialist, Africanist nationalists of the likes of Stokely Carmichael. But the micronationalist successors shifted this globally unitary Black Nationalism by assimilating it to the nature America has always had for all groups trying to install themselves into it. Contributing to this advance of perception in post-modern black nationalism, Dr. Conrad Worrill from *Final Call* in early 1989 warned "the African-American community in the United States" that developing "our fight for self-determination and dignity" would require a deeper exploration of the pluralist nature of the American dynamic. The European-American dynamic had always divided whites into groups, each of which fought for its own distinct "nationalism in America without calling it that"—[=ambiguous internal ethnic nationalisms/micronationalisms that might equally challenge the U.S. system or get the adherents into it if they could muster the strength and pressure to achieve that].

The critiques of the post-1970 rise of identity politics from Angloid and some Jewish Americans are dismissed by African-American micronationalists like Worrill as a transparent ploy to deny blacks the means by which white groups had already acquired wealth and power. When African-American people talked about nationalism, they were often charged with being racists or anti-white. However, replied Worrill, the historical record demonstrated clearly that "[micro-]nationalism has been the primary method by which every national/ethnic group has achieved and maintains power" in the USA, although groups that had made it now mute their formal national terminologies when their interests dictate.

The African American micronationalism being developed in the later twentieth century acknowledged its debt to the founder—and now patriarch—

of anti-Israel[145] Black Nationalism, Harold Cruse. Worrill praised Cruse's 1967 book, *The Crisis of the Negro Intellectual* as the "most profound analysis of our movement," [although Cruse could not at that time-point, the 1960s, have the internal nationalist terminologies and international minority rights framework that Yussuf Naim Kly, Worrill and other African-American theoreticians would develop from 1980]. Only on the face of it had America, from its foundation, idealized the rights of the individual above everything else. In reality, argued Cruse and his disciple Worrill, America was "a nation dominated by the social power of groups, classes, in-groups and cliques—both ethnic and religious". Individuals in America could actualize few rights not backed up by the political, economic and social power of one group or another. For African-American ethnic nationalists Cruse and Worrill, "the individual Black person has, proportionately, very few rights because his ethnic group (whether or not he actually identifies with it) has very little political, economic or social power (beyond moral grounds) to wield".[146] Worrill urged African-Americans to review the techniques of past construction of various forms of power and cultural strength that had enabled Greek-Americans, Irish-Americans, Italian-Americans, Polish-Americans, German-Americans, Jewish-Americans, and newer American national groups of Third World provenance, to achieve their vital interests in America.

Until the late 1950s, Anglo-Americans amounted to a self-segregating dominant nationality in American life, although they could blur their particularistic demands into a purported general white American nationalism when that helped preserve their hegemony. Since World War II, large sections of American Jewry have been mobilized by the Zionists to muster financial aid and lobby resources out of successive U.S. administrations, that built Israel into a state with the strength to expand against its neighbors. Polish-Americans and other groups of East European provenance lobbied all U.S. administrations after WWII to strike a hard line towards the Communist regimes of the countries from which their forefathers came.

Anglo racist exclusion and violence against African-Americans had, in American history, gone far beyond that directed against any quasi-"white" ethnic minorities. Hence, the Nation of Islam up to 1975 voiced an eschatological radicalism—extermination by God—that vented a black counter-hate of a frankness that few white ethnicists came near to in their public discourses at least. Over the long term, though, the Nation could have the same function for Blacks as had some white movements that built local strength and social services for despised ethnic groups at the local level, and then joined the Democratic or Republican Party or the left movements as points of entry from which to claw their way into America's mainstream politics alongside the other groups. President Nixon had been struck by the Nation's regard for private enterprise, and may have been preparing to enter into negotiations with Elijah when Watergate engulfed him and the Messenger died. After his 1995 Million Man March, Farrakhan and his followers moved still further away from cursing U.S. society, and in the direction of a constructive engagement with the Euro-American political system. In return, the second

NOI's leaders were coming to be viewed as possible partners by a fair range of white politicians in parliamentarism. The American system of pluralist entry for groups that have the collectivist resolve now fosters the growth of Irish-American, African-American, Polish-American and Hispanic-American activist new bourgeoisies that are highly dualistic, or swinging, about where their main commitment goes. In the post-modern era, globalization, the development of international communications and contacts, and the contraction of the U.S. central government that used to promote Americanist nationalism, all in tandem have diffentiated the evolving micronations more than anything seen before.

Still, even from its launching in 1930, the Nation of Islam of Wali Fard Muhammad, Elijah Muhammad, Malcolm and Farrakhan always had some potential to figure in a Zionist-like extraterritorial enclave-nationalism that could mobilize the masses of American blacks. It came at the tail-end of an Africanist mass movement conducted by the mildly pro-Arab Marcus Eurelius Garvey (1887-1940—deported from the U.S. in 1927) who had let his institutions and forums in the U.S. give a hearing to Islam. In regard to literate high cultures, early neo-Muslim movements in the USA from Drew 'Ali onwards unfolded near an intellectual context of the publication from academia of Africanist historical works by Carter G. Woodson and W.E.B. DuBois, et al. Their books were often pro-Arab and pro-Islamic, sometimes outspokenly so.

4: EARLY ELITE BLACK HISTORIOGRAPHY VIS-À-VIS ISLAM

The Asia-highlighting narratives about the past, origins and enslavement of "the so-called American Negro" propounded by the Nation of Islam from 1930 have often been rejected by African-American as well as Euro-American observers as non-historical mythologies. In focusing on Arabia, the NOI's protest mythologies were charged to have covertly voiced low esteem for sub-Saharan Africa and the Muslims' blackness, even as they offered a rallying-point for protest, in apparent counter-hatred against whites. The Jewish-American reporter, Peter Goldman, in 1974 cited the theme of an "Asiatic" nationality and the "Asiatic Black Man" whom white devils had kidnapped from a wider "East" as instancing how the Muslims in the early 1950s, in common with U.S. Negroes in general in that era, "shrank from their blackness in sad little ways."[147] For three decades, the preferences of many of the blacks whom the NOI was striving to recruit pointed its preachers to a general "East" away from Africa on its own. The Nigerian Essien-Udom claimed in 1962 that one of Elijah's ministers told him that extolling Africa would not attract most U.S. blacks because they viewed it as a "vast jungle": the term "Asiatic blacks" was more "neutral".[148]

Yet the Nation of Islam's 1930 macro-history that bracketed Asia and Africa, and Arabs and sub-Saharan Africans, could fit into, and was early confirmed and nourished by, themes in the literate historiography of Africa and African-Americans that was being gradually built up by the mainstream-educated black elite. Both NOI mythologies of an emergence in Asia, and Easternist and Arabophile themes from the intellectual elite could have drawn upon vague folk-tradition among some poor African-Americans that their ancestors had had real connections to the Islamic "East". Still, related impulses to investigate and restore linkages with the Arabian peninsula and Arab peoples have long run through a wide range of culturally different classes in the African-American nation, and have perhaps connected them.

We now review motifs of Africa and its place in macro-history propagated by black elite scholars that over many decades have given educated African-Americans favorable images of Islam, and of the Egyptians and the Arabs as cognate people of color. We have scanned the seminal works of Carter G. Woodson and W.E.B. DuBois who, between them, founded the academic historiography of the African-American people. Their often to some extent Islamophile works were having their impact upon those African-Americans in quest of a historiography just as the first neo-Muslim movements took their early shape and ideological structure in North America.

Carter G. Woodson (1875-1950) gained his PhD from Harvard University in 1912. In 1915, he founded the Association for the Study of Negro Life and History. In 1916, Woodson edited the first number of *The Journal of Negro History*, which under his direction for the next 30 years established the serious study of African-Americans and their past, long dismissed by Euro-American academics, in the institutions of U.S. higher learning. While Carter penned an impressive range of works on African-American history during his career as an academic at Howard and other U.S. universities, he also transformed African-American consciousness by the long-term institutional mechanisms and conduits he devised to diffuse his and his collaborators' data out among Americans at large over decades. To circumvent the indifference of Anglo-cultured publishers to titles on "Negro" history, Woodson set up Associated Publishers with himself as president. The Black History Week he founded, still observed in the twenty-first century, utilized the schools as outlets for the new national historiography.

W.E.B. DuBois (1868-1963) was one of the founders of the National Association for the Advancement of Colored People (NAACP) in 1909 and from 1910-1934 edited its magazine, *The Crisis*, the main forum for a new black elite that, as it tried to thrust itself into the professions, had lost patience with the accommodationism of Booker T. Washington. DuBois had received a PhD from Harvard University in 1896 for a thesis on the North American slave trade: his subsequent writings included specialized monographs on aspects of the social experience and on specific communities of African-Americans, as well as more popularizing books that attempted to survey—not always in even depth—the whole extent of the "Negro" experience in Africa as well as the New World. DuBois was an architect of four international Pan-African congresses held between 1919 and 1927: he died in exile in Ghana in 1963. He fostered the rebirth of Islam among African-Americans through his popularization of Arabic and the Arabic-speaking world as among the forces that had formed sub-Saharan Africa and its thought. Like the proto-Islamic sects, DuBois urged African-Americans to develop a separate "group economy" based on enclave-nationalist cooperatives as a means to counter the poverty inflicted by the Great Depression and the exclusion blacks with bourgeois aspirations faced in the mainstream economy.

Christianity Marginalized

A fair number of cultural-nationalist historians in Afro-America early developed a unitary vision of the history of Africa and Asia. They held not just that Islam as a macro-historical phenomenon had in general served more than harmed the interests of the black Africans, but that ties of loose community bracketed sub-Saharan Africans and the Arab world. Islamophilia, and in a few cases Arabophilia that extended identification out into West Asia, grew among earlier African-American intellectuals in a context of secularizing community enterprises, such as pan-Africanism and pan-Easternism, that could foster coldness towards Christianity as a creed. Increasingly, Christianity was seen by African-American historians and opinion leaders to have been tailored for centuries as a psychological auxiliary of European and American power over people of color. At least as theory, the writings of Woodson called African-Americans to a pan-Negro community with Africans who had diverse beliefs but had been made a broad human group by a range of geographic, racial, cultural and other factors that were all non-religious. The American Negroes could not stipulate Christianity as a precondition for building community with Africans among whom there were more and more Muslims, and still hope to integrate that association spanning two continents, such secularized or post-Christian African-American scholars sensed. Engagement with Africans thus worked to further dechristianize the black American elite's view of the world and create real openness to Muslims. DuBois' books often juxtaposed Christianity with capitalism, racism and imperialist expansion in Africa and Asia.

The ultra-literate indictments of Christianity by DuBois in particular shared many motifs with the denunciations by Nation of Islam preachers at street level after 1930. In a 1947 synthesis-work he brought together in old age, DuBois stressed the Christian ethos with which that hero of Elizabethan England, Sir John Hawkins, validated the part he and his crews played in the slave trade. Like the NOI preachers, DuBois seized upon the symbolism of the name of the ship— *Jesus*—that Queen Elizabeth I had allotted him, and also on Captain Hawkins' stress on such Christian precepts as "serve God daily" and "love one another" in the rules for behavior he had drawn up to make his slave-trading crews more cooperative and purposeful in their tasks as traffickers of humans.[149] In his seminal 1922 history of the African-American people prior to the birth of the Nation of Islam, Carter Woodson had already ascribed Hawkins the slaver to a more "primitive" phase of history in which "right was restricted to [Christian] blood kin: ...there was no moral law restraining one from abusing the subjects of non-Christian nations".[150] From the inception of his preaching in 1930, the founder of "the Black Muslims"

(NOI), Wali Fard Muhammad, had highlighted the figure of Hawkins and his good ship, Jesus, as an embodiment of the malevolent evil of the white enslavers and their imposition of their resistance-sapping Christianity on their black victims.

Following Elijah Muhammad in his *The Supreme Wisdom*, Malcolm X in 1963 was to tell Afro-Americans that John Hawkins "used Jesus to bring you here—and they've been using him to keep you here, too." "The man took all this world and gave you Jesus and that's all you've got is Jesus". Even towards the end of the 20th century, Farrakhan and his successor-sect would further adapt, modify and recycle Hawkins and his "Good Ship Jesus".[151]

In the 1980s, Warith gave "Hawkins" a critical twist: that captain reassured the Muslim West Africans with Arabic phrases and his ship's bearing a Muslim prophet's name, offering to take them to a new rich land—all to trick them into slavery. Warith was so Sunnified by then, though, that he painted the Fard who told that story as another con man who was following the same procedures—he tricked his converts away from their general community with promises of protection and money, and when he had them alone with him, he exploited them.[152]

The Hawkins figure is one interesting—long-lived— instance where historical motifs brought to light by elite Black Nationalist intellectuals and publicists are seized and retailored by quasi-Muslim blacks at street level to be woven into millenarian protest mega-narratives of history that they then direct to ill-educated urban masses.

The attitudes of earlier 20th century Black Nationalist intellectuals towards Christianity varied with the macro-historical contexts and depending on whether the Christians being discussed were "of color" or white Westerners. When the context was one that had Westerners as well as Africans and Arabs/Muslims in it, DuBois manifested a drive to bracket his "race" (=all Africans in the world) with Arabs against a given Western group. He reported that the Christian Copts of "African Egypt from 630 welcomed the Arab invaders as their deliverers from the yoke of the Byzantines" [who were Westerners, although their brethren religiously]. But in situations in which no Europeans figured, DuBois could sympathize with Africans who shared blackness and Christianity with him in conflicts they had with Muslim Arabs. In that different context, DuBois referred to some Christian states in pre-colonial Africa with a touch of pride, including the Nubian kingdom in the Sudan which he depicted as briefly invading Arab-occupied Egypt "in 722 under the leadership of King Cyriacus in defense of its Copts."[153] Usually, intellectual Africanism in the U.S. has awarded primacy to (a) a wide, inclusive but broadly non-white, entity of Africa and Asia in conflict with the West over (b) religious or sectarian considerations that would constrict imagined relationship to only those Africans who were already Christian or could be made so.

From the outset, U.S. Africanist thinkers had been quite ready to internalize some Arab and Islamic culture as one of the preconditions entailed for an inclusive relationship with Africans, given that Islam had been among the basic elements that had formed Africa. Thus, in the first chapter, "The Negro in Africa", of his 1922 history of African-Americans, Carter G. Woodson paid considerable attention to the interaction of Islamic culture as it penetrated sub-Saharan Africa with the indigenous cultures of the populations that awaited it there, especially in West Africa, from which the ancestors of most Afro-Americans had been brought. Woodson depicted most of the interaction as between two equal parties, during which the black African side maintained its political sovereignty—preserving its continuity as it absorbed new elements that were Arab in origin. From 1000 onwards, he characterized, "the Mohammedans" came mainly as merchants stimulating commercial exchange between the blacks without transforming local civilization, although they deeply influenced the life and history of the people.[154] Woodson's book offered somewhat generalized descriptions of some of those sub-Saharan African states that adopted the religion of Islam and some elements of its civilization. Songhay, whose history extended from 700-1335, was a wide organized empire that for a time resisted "the Mohammedans" until its 16th monarch adopted their religion around 1000.[155] Among its monarchs was Soni [Sunni?] 'Ali, a brilliant soldier. But the greatest of all Songhay's leaders for Woodson was al-Hajj Muhammad Askia [usurped and ruled 1493-1529] "who brought [his] country into contact with Egypt and the world in general" and established colleges, stimulating [Arabic-medium] studies of law, literature, the natural sciences and medicine.[156]

Woodson appreciated the importance of establishing wider commercial and scholarly links with other peoples for any nation to progress towards prosperity and civilization. As DuBois was to do in 1947, Woodson identified isolation as the most serious danger threatening the peoples of Africa across their history in view of the continent's "frequent elevations of terrain" and its shortage of usable coastline and harbors. For Woodson, the closing off of North Africa by Christendom, and the inaccessibility of the West African interior from the rocky coast, "sealed the fate of the greatest Negro empires in history—empires whose culture was equal to, and in some respects farther advanced than, that of West Europe at the time".[157] Christian Europe at this point for Woodson holds the ambiguity such an energizing threatening Other often has in many cultural nationalisms. Wariness about harm from interaction establishes borders (much less against Arabs than Europeans); yet a simultaneous need is implied to keep up more equalized, looser exchanges with that western or Muslim Other after the Africans, like the Arabs, actualize their borders. The Nation is not really self-contained in Woodson's thought, which often suddenly becomes coldly realistic and sober.

The archeological study of West Africa was not well-developed when Woodson and DuBois wrote. Carter Woodson had already been as acutely aware in 1922 as DuBois would never cease to be that Arabic sources written by visitors from the Arab world from around the year 1000, or by Muslim black writers living in sub-Saharan Africa itself, were the main written source for West Africa's history for the pre-colonial period.[158] This was liable to make African-American culture-aware nationalists receptive to Islam or Arabic as two crucial elements that had early been installed among the very West African states and populations to which they worked to relink African-Americans. The lack of existence of Christianity in the areas of provenance of Negro Americans in West Africa before the arrival of the West—in contrast to long-standing Coptic Christianity in Ethiopia in Africa's East—further worked to purge African-American cultural nationalists of the old sectarian evangelizing tendency that had dogged the earlier back-to-Africa enterprise (albeit only in a pro forma way for such Islamophiles as tongue-in-cheek mock-missionary, Blyden).

Arabic Writings of Africans Recycled

Real voices of Muslims translated from Arabic were heard in both Woodson and DuBois' works. In its West African setting, Arabic offered a high literary tradition predating and absolutely independent of the Westerners both historians hated—a tradition that recorded sub-Saharan events and societies, while judging them from the viewpoints of Arabs or, when Muslim blacks wrote, of Islamic ideology. Thus, DuBois excerpted first-hand reactions by the Arab traveler, Ibn Battutah, in 1352 to the society and customs of the West African townspeople of Melle. The Moroccan was open-minded, and positive overall: he was nonplussed at their matrilineal system of inheritance, but approved their penchant for Islamic legal scholarship, their textiles and clothing, and the appearance of their women.[159]

As early as 1922, Woodson offered African-Americans a genuinely Islamic religious interpretation from within Islamo-African experience and thought, of an event that one or two 20th century writers in America (e.g. John Henrik Clarke in 1976) would view also as a quasi-national clash between invading North African Muslims and Black Africans. In 1591-3, the invading Sultan of Morocco, al-Mansur, defeated the main Songhay army and established a loose control over the core territories of that empire. Woodson in his general history of African-Americans excerpted the Arabic chronicle *Ta'rikh al-Sudan* by the Timbuktu writer 'Abd al-Rahman al-Sa'di, who characterized the Moroccan invasion that overthrew the Songhay dynasty as God's punishment because some of its men had drunk wine and inclined to Unbelief.[160] Here we have the flowing-in of an Islamo-African religious explication of history—the rise and fall of power elites and states in this case—not just historical facts from Arabic sources that African-American historians might detach and install into their own West-derived analytical frames. Songhay's African Muslims themselves originally had taken some motifs for this view of history from the early great Arab Islamist discourse, not the Qur'an only, as mediated by North African scholars coaxing them into an integral, practised Islam.[161] True, al-Sa'di's puritanism could also fit into the Bible's critical stance to blasphemous and corrupt courts and statelets of ancient Hebrews that non-Jews overcame as the sword of God: that Old Testament was already in the African-American psyche when Woodson, DuBois and other early African-American historians first picked up texts about pre-colonial Muslim West Africa.

The infusion of Islamic and Arabic elements into the forming African-American elite through this category of pioneer Negro historians could easily have become much more massive and integral than was to be the case. The diverse tasks and the limited linguistic capacities and resources of these overstretched nationalist scholars—not any lack of interest or will—constricted how much Arabic materials got through. Woodson had a copy of al-Sa'di's *Ta'rikh al-Sudan* in Arabic and in its French translation. For Woodson and his aide, Lorenzo J. Greene, the book was heartening rebuttal of "those skeptics who believe that the Negro has never created, nor ever will create, anything of importance in either the political, economic, social or military realms." The "gloating" Greene proposed that the French version of that work on "the great black civilization of the African Blacks" be translated into English. Woodson replied, and with some shrewdness, that too many biases, errors, misinterpretations and omissions would inhere in translating from a translation. "I am waiting to have a Negro who knows Arabic translate it from the original Arabic."[162]

The ethos and grain of al-Sa'di's originally Arabic, Muslim, work was projected in a multi-cultured way by contributors to Woodson's *Journal of Negro History*. As early as that journal's second volume, A.O. Stafford hailed it as "a great historical work embracing all the countries of the Niger." Some West-formed and Islamic frames were coming together: Stafford compared the work in its sweep and coverage of human nature to Homer, although he conceded that it lacked the stylistic excellence of those two ancient Greek epics. Like Woodson, Stafford was attracted to al-Sa'di's Islamic reflection on mortality, crime, and the evanescence of power, which could fit into the Greek tragedy with which Afro-American intellectuals were familiar, and also into some Old Testament religious critiques of ancient Hebrew governing cliques. Al-Sa'di's chronicle nourished in Stafford an ambivalent or dualistic attitude to Muslim Africans who had exercised great political power. Stafford balanced (a) the literate piety that the *hajj* (Pilgrim), Askia Muhammad, displayed in seeking out Arab theologians and the 'Abbasid shadow-caliph in Cairo *against* (b) his rather free use of his sword to conquer his neighbors back home. From the *Ta'rikh al-Sudan*, Stafford exposed the murders of family and relatives committed by various West African Muslims out to seize or maintain monarchical power, while still voicing deep respect for the scholarly, cultural and administrative achievements that black Africans attained in Muslim Timbuktu. The ethos being fostered for 1917 prefigures the later 20th century's critical or dualistic late-modern or post-modern engagement with historical states that define the writer, more than it is like the glorification and apologetic attitudes to their nations by the modernist-nationalist historiographies in that century's earlier decades. This cluster of African-American scholarship and media fostered a relaxed and open attitude to political and racial/ethnic boundaries in Africa's history. As against one or two much later Africanist writers, Stafford—like Woodson and DuBois—did not generalize from al-Mansur's conquest of the Songhay state that North African Arabs or Berbers were a historical enemy to black West Africans.

Without any critique, Stafford presented motifs of al-Sa'di's world-view that blurred West Africans into the Middle Easterners: e.g. the claim of the Songhay that they had originally come from Yemen—and that some of their ancestors were among the magicians whom Moses vanquished, an attempt by those Islamized Africans to fit their original animist paganism into the Qur'an's narrative of a macro-history that nonetheless centers on the Middle East.[163]

Woodson's reluctance to start a translation effort that would have to be flawed by the limitations of African-American academic resources in his period, delayed by decades the launching of an African-American tradition of Arabic studies that could have become independent of white Judeo-Christian orientalism in U.S. universities, and given African-Americans access to the past and identity of some groups in West Africa. Still, Woodson's movement or school popularized Arabic-derived materials from the Middle East as well as sub-Saharan Africa. In 1929, Greene told Woodson of a plan to prepare a book of African hero tales for Negro youth, to counter feelings of race-inferiority communicated to them from the dominant culture. Woodson advised that "in the sphere of the great emperors and conquerors I would mention Gonga Musa of the Mandingo empire; Soni 'Ali, one of the greatest kings of the Songhay Empire and a contemporary of Ferdinand and Isabella in Spain and Henry VII in England; Askia the Great, a contemporary with Charles of Spain and Henry VIII of England; scholars like al-Sa'di and Ibn Ahmed; poets like 'Antarah of [pre-Islamic] Arabia and Alexandr Pushkin; novelists like Alexandre Dumas père et fils" and some newer African-American writers, businessmen and inventors.[164]

It remains to be seen how long-term will be the patterning that gropings of early African-American academics for a pre-modern quasi-classical literature from Africa ran into apex African-American nationalism. The dynamic may yet bring about a more specialized and rigorous influx of Sunni Muslim intellectualism and high Arabic into the African-American nation. Yet the foundation historiography shows that future African-American Arabists will have their own Africanist foci and originality. They will take in the history and culture of the Middle East and the Arabs, with special reference to the roles of blacks there.

Qualified Identification with Wider Arabo-Islamic World

Both Carter Woodson and DuBois, alike, sought a general African continent of provenance that had to extend above the Sahara. Each placed empires of West Africa that were officially or formally Islamic or at any rate Islam-influenced within a more general context of nourishing economic and cultural interaction with the peoples of the Mediterranean basin, particularly its Arabs. Both historians, though, as nationalists took judicious note of the continuity of some African culture and the benefits that these sub-Saharan entities carried forward within their accelerating adoption of Arabic literacy and trade with Arabs.

Beyond West Africa or sub-Saharan Africa, both DuBois and Woodson were prepared to visualize blacks as one component among many making up a far wider community that Islam had assembled in macro-history. Woodson had already considered the Arab and Islamic civilization centered in North Africa and Asia as partially the products of blacks. He had written with pride not just of the black states of sub-Saharan Africa but also of the roles of blacks or mulattos over the full geographic extent of the Arab entity, for example as poets in Arab Spain, and in Morocco, in the south of which a Negro leader he did not name founded a city [Sijilmassah] in 757. [Sijilmasah was indeed founded as a departure-point for caravans between North Africa and the Western Sudan: it was a meeting-place between Arabs, Berbers and sub-Saharan Africans]. The Arabs had not imposed any color line but "blended readily with the Negroes." Woodson wrote that the process of the integration of the two races led to some Arabized blacks rising to prominence, such as 'Antarah Ibn Shaddad who became the national hero of the Arabian peninsula and one of the great poets of Islam.[165]

Beyond Africanism and special interest in those Middle Easterners who looked like them, Woodson and DuBois in such sentences were coming to identify, in a loose qualified way, with the wide Arabo-Islamic entity in history.

So long as at least partly Negroid people were among the combatants, Woodson felt some sympathy for the Islamic side in its clashes with white Christian Europeans, even in that continent itself. Thus, he portrayed Africa as having had a sort of stake in the survival of Muslim Spain. (True, some radically secular romantic historians among Westerners and white Americans had identified "the Moors" with progress and literacy in Spain, and the Christian forces that in the end expelled Muslims with repression of Free Thought). In 1939, Woodson got around to penning on his own account a volume on *African Heroes and Heroines*. Among those for emulation, he vividly recreated Yusuf Ibn Tashufin (d. 1106), the Berber leader of a puritanical Islamic sect in a desert on the margin of North Africa. Yusuf, at the pleas of the Muslims in Spain who were gradually being conquered by the Spanish-speaking Christians, entered the Iberian peninsula and at al-Zallaqah in 1086 dealt the resurgent Christians a crushing defeat that kept Andalusia (Ar.: al-Andalus) within Islam for centuries. Woodson felt that Ibn Tashufin and his forces were racial kin to a strong extent: "in this army were some thousands of blacks armed with Indian swords and short spears and shields covered with hippopotamus hide". It was all "an African conquest by an African dynasty" on camels, although Woodson had some ambivalence about the drives of the "Berber, Arab and Negro admixture" of North Africa and the Sahara to encroach on deeper "Negroland". Overall, Woodson interpreted Muslim rule in Spain in terms of "the long intercourse between Spain and Negroland". In holding Ibn Tashufin up for emulation by African-Americans, Woodson portrayed him as a "wise, shrewd man, neither too prompt in his determinations, nor too slow in carrying them into effect": he did not consider that Ibn Tashufin's drawn-out caution could have been the technique of a cold-hearted or even sadistic politician to finesse Spain's hard-pressed, fun-loving Muslims into accepting his absolute rule, and his Islamic puritanism, by the time that he finally did invade to save them.[166]

Even more so than Woodson, DuBois came to view Africa and Asia, and in consequence Arab/Islamic history and African history, as two intertwined extensions of the other. His mature work, *The World and Africa*, brought out this tendency in full. In the chapter devoted to the contributions of blacks to Asia and its civilizations, DuBois came close to denying that the human category "Blacks" had to be of African origin. Throughout history, he argued, the link between Asia and Africa had been very close: the two continents may have been connected in pre-history and the black race had appeared in both continents in the earliest records [for example in Sumeria/'Iraq], which for DuBois placed in doubt which of the two continents held the point of origin of the blacks.[167] The "Mohammedan civilization" originated in the deserts of the Arabian peninsula in Mecca, which had been in a part of the world that the ancient Greek writers had termed Ethiopia. The Arabian peninsula must have had an extensive population of "Negroids" from the most ancient periods: accordingly, DuBois argued the Negro blood of some companions of the prophet Muhammad, such as Bilal and of some of Islam's greatest conquerors, among them the conqueror of Spain, Tariq Ibn Ziyad [in reality a fair-skinned Berber?][168] With a certain amount of historical justification, DuBois—somewhat like Egypt's Arabo-Islamic nationalist 'Abdallah al-Nadim in 1893-4—argued the lack of any fixed, prescribed racial content for the category "Arabs", given that Islam in the course of its expansion fused a new expanded Arab nation out of many diverse races. The term Arab, DuBois stressed, is awarded in Africa to any Arabic-speaking person who professes Islam, whatever race or mixture of races he has: it is a cultural group.[169]

In DuBois' analysis, then, "the Arabs" were a cultural community that had been brought together around a common religion and language out of diverse previous races, one to which "Negroes" descended from pure or diluted African origins had contributed. Thus, not merely Muslim-led states in sub-Saharan Africa but the history of the Arabs as well could get appended to the identity that this variant of writers were constructing for African-Americans. As well as seeking "Negro" elements in the history of Muslim Spain, DuBois concentrated on Islamic Egypt, stressing the role of such black leaders there as Kafur (r. 946-968). He offered detailed accounts of black personalities in the courts of Egypt's heterodox Fatimid dynasty (governed 909-1171), including the wives of some of its Caliphs.[170] DuBois had drawn this data from a history of Egypt in the Middle Ages by the British orientalist, Stanley Lane-Poole, published in London in 1914. The writings of Lane-Poole (e.g. on Muslim Spain) and of Arabophile British orientalists of the 19th century were to be recommended to African-Americans by the media of the neo-Sunni Warith Muhammad after he succeeded his father in 1975.

In seeking data on Muslim-influenced eras and sectors of Black Africa, DuBois judiciously scanned such translations of Arabic primary works as were available to him, for example the geography of Leo Africanus (al-

Hasan Ibn Muhammad al-Wazzan 1485-1554: b. Grenada, died Rome: visited Gao, West Africa early in the 16th century).[171] DuBois was acculturated to a range of the languages, high cultures and intellectual traditions in the full West that perhaps no other Afro-American scholar of his era could match. His luxuriant multi-culturedness helped direct him to Arabs above the Sahara. His interest in the part-African 'Antarah Ibn Shaddad, a pagan warrior and poet of Arabia at the end of the 6th century AD, was fueled by "Rimski-Korsakov's symphony *Antar* with its wealth of barbaric color", as well as romantic English historians and the partial English translation Captain Terrick Hamilton had made early in the 19th century of sectors from the 32-volume collection of doggerel Arabic tales about 'Antarah.[172] (The latter popular epic, recited to the uneducated as the equivalent of a never-ending ill-scripted radio serial, was most improbably ascribed to the great classical philologist, al-Asma'i).

Along with the early historians, some more aesthetic African-American writers, too, were installing the roles of blacks in classical Arab life into a new African-American high literature on their own account. Lorenzo Greene, a collaborator of Woodson, noted in 1930 that Maude Cuney-Hare had penned a play, *Antar of Araby*.[173] Maude Cuney was the daughter of a prominent Texas politician, Norris Wright Cuney, who had got out the Negro vote for the Republican Party there after 1884. Her gold-bronze complexion and brilliant large eyes had turned the heads of many after she entered Boston's black elite, among them young graduate W.E.B. DuBois. Even after she married a member of the African-American elite of Boston, she remained close to DuBois until her death in 1936.[174] Did an artistic woman renowned for her racially ambiguous "Levantine beauty" (Levering Lewis) nourish DuBois' opulent Arabophilia that blurred African and West Asian "races" out into each other?

The constantly evolving narrative of 'Antarah defines crucial traits of Arab national identity throughout Arabic literature from its beginnings in c. 570 AD. Its original core has always remained constant. 'Antarah was born in Arabia before Islam, to a respected Arab in the tribe of 'Abs and an Abyssinian woman he captured in a tribal war. 'Antarah constantly pressed his father Shaddad to set him free from his subordinate caste status as a bastard in which he is supposed mainly to herd camels. His vacillating father always refused until yet another attack threatens to end the tribe: as 'Abs faces that peril, Shaddad has to manumit the only warrior who can beat it off, and the father of Abla has to allow 'Antarah to marry the woman who loves him. In Arab civilization, 'Antarah stands for the eloquence, martial prowess and reciprocated love for one woman that are ideals or prescribed aspects in the Arab national personality.

While the real 'Antarah faced some social prejudice because of his African features and his caste-status, his tribal Arabia was a milder place on issues of blood than the America of Maude Cuney-Hare late in the 1920s. In her play likewise, 'Antarah seeks equality in Arab society from a position of achievement that gives him bargaining power: he has won the respect of most in the tribe, including its "king" Zuhayr, as the foremost warrior defending the group, and as the poet who articulates its ethos. The king's son Malik has a brotherly attitude to him and wants to induct 'Antarah into the tribe's leadership. This from the outset has made 'Antarah a contender for entry into the 'Abs leadership, for free Arab status and for the hand in formal marriage of his non-African cousin Abla, which few African-Americans could have attempted with a high-society Euro-American woman, the equivalent of Abla, in Cuney-Hare's America of the late 1920s.

How well does Cuney-Hare's play read as literature eighty years later in the 21st century? Did she truly convey much from faraway America about the very different world of pre-Islamic desert Arabia? I believe that she did focus some features of ancient peninsular Arabia, from interest in that culture and past for itself. Her dialogues and characters do catch, from within, the claustrophobic intimacy of the individuals of the piccolo mondo of a small tribe that could be destroyed by raiding enemies at any moment, and all of whose members know what all the others are doing at most times. She did convey the resounding voices and the inputs females inevitably had in the rituals and politics of the society clamped together within so small a space (their shifting encampment) in the chain of the pagan tribes of Arabia before Islam. Cuney-Hare had read with some care the translations of the seven suspended poems or Mu'allaqat of pre-Islamic Mecca published to that time by, for instance, the British romantics, Lord Wilfred Scawen Blunt and Lady Blunt. She had read Captain Terrick Hamilton's hoary translation of sectors from the 32-volume folk-epic about 'Antarah. She had read E.W. Lane's old multi-volume translation of *The Thousand and One Nights.* Cuney-Hare plucked sentences and images out from those authentic Arab sources and transmuted them in a new sequence and structure into dialogues that do have in them some genuine syntax from Arabic that would still sound natural when declaimed on some stage. The dialogues have relaxed use of a small number of recurring Arabic words or phrases such as Aboolfawaris or "Father of the Mounted Warriors," a title that 'Antarah has long shared with "king" of 'Abs, Zuhayr. Cuney-Hare took care to find and use the real names of pre-Islamic Arabian idols for use in oaths by the characters. Her stage directions at the outset advised its actors to scan the fine old engravings from Arab life in Lane's *Arabian Nights* to learn real Arabian gestures of salutations and greetings. She did implant in African-American audiences, heavily consisting of school adolescents, some elements of the aesthetic and social texture of Arab life, which she liked.

While the styles, atmosphere and overall movement of this play do come off, and its literary high English is rich and wide, there is some fustian and too much hyperbole in the dialogues: this, and some over-opulent details about Arabia, were pollution from the popular epic composed in a different urban environment in the late 'Abbasid era or later. Cuney-Hare could perhaps have achieved a sharper representation of the original harsh peninsular Arabian environment, and a crisper, more solid language, had she favored Jahili (pre-Islamic) poetry more as a source. Two or three of her characters come across as nuanced believable humans who are more than a paradigm about inequality. Amarah is made the deadly enemy of 'Antarah by his rivalry for the same woman, and by his defect as a small-minded, toxic coxcomb, as well as his racial prejudice against 'Antarah whose 'black skin" he does insult at one point. The father of 'Antarah is a good study by Cuney-Hare. He is a vacillating, divided character. Shaddad has the urge of many fathers to keep a son down. A weak, conventional side of him stubbornly resists ending 'Antarah's caste marginality. Yet he does not seem to have any prejudice against his son's pigmentation. Abla's father Sulaymah has maneuvered 'Antarah into a hard or impossible venture in 'Iraq before he can marry Abla, but Shaddad is deeply traumatized by the report of his son's death. When 'Antarah returns in triumph loaded down with treasure and enslaved captives to the acclaim of the whole 'Abs society, Shaddad is exultant that "he is indeed my son and a part of my heart." There *are* two or three rounded characters with inner diversity in this play.

To some extent, Cuney meant her pagan ancient Arabia to clarify issues of the America within which she penned the play in the late 1920s. 'Antarah from the start is a contender for the hand of a bejeweled and richly-garbed woman, which few blacks could have been for marriage to an equivalent Euro society-woman in her USA of the late 1920s. In one passage, King Zuhayr advises Shaddad to make his son an equal freeman. When Shaddad asks "who is the Arab who ever did such a thing before me?" Prince Malik replies "let the Arabs follow thy example; good practices are to be admired even though they may be new." This passage had clear resonance to the optimism of the Negro intellectual and literary elite in the 1920s that prosperous America was liberalizing and would now admit them as they displayed brilliant, unprecedented gifts.

A troubling feature of Cuney-Hare's play is that its final movement sounds almost to endorse caste-stratification and the abduction and enslavement that could befall any Arabian in the age of the pre-Islamic tribal vendettas and lack of government. The disclosure at the play's end that 'Antarah's mother was an Abysinian princess, rather than an ordinary Abyssinian, is accepted to place him and her in some different category for which abduction or marginalization are more of an offence. The play takes in its stride that at the close 'Antarah brings to 'Abs Grecian and Abyssinian slave girls, and that he makes an Abyssinian one do a dance before his tribe in the hour of his triumph and marriage. The ancient Arabian and perhaps Cuney-Hare's indifference at points to caste and some slavery has affinities to Dubois' own over-flexible reactions to caste and slavery in African and Islamic societies. This was an elitist African-American cultured minority, with the clarity and pleasant ease of quasi-aristocrats, that thought it had more title to enter mainstream white society and win wealth and power there than did ordinary African-Americans.[175]

The slowly expanding black bourgeoisie and professional Negro creative writers were reading the history books of Woodson and DuBois and their colleagues. There was no question of the lumpen blacks who converted to the Nation of Islam in the 1930s and 1940s being directed to the Arabs and Islam by the superb range of Western works that by 1947 influenced the multi-lingual DuBois. Yet the later generation of much better-educated African-Americans who were to join and write for Warith ud-Din Muhammad's successor-sect after 1975 would read the 19th century Arabophile works from Britain.

DuBois became open to atheistic Communism, but his transcontinental outreach to the Arab world and Black Africa at one and the same time still had high ambiguities somewhat like those that still underlie drives by African American Muslims for community with Third World peoples in post-modernity. Understanding, and establishing relations with, Muslims and Africans across the seas starts from, or entails acculturation to, a very wide range of Westerners and Western writings. However anti-imperialist the initial motivation may be, reconnecting with lost brethren across the seas entails that the questers take up informational and analytic tools of the dominant Western nations. At some point they then may adopt wide sectors of those nations' scholarship and aesthetic culture as now valuable in themselves, not just usable sources to actualize new relationship with a "Mother Continent" or wider [Muslim] "East." The tasks of the reconnection with non-Westerners are apt to draw African-Americans into America and the West's best learning and cultural life and institutions, even as they form deep relations with Arabic and Arabs and Africans. Thus, Islam and outreach out to Arabs and Muslims overseas are not to be dichotomized against getting into America: in many ways they throw up new links to Anglo and Jewish fellow-Americans, against whom Islam symbolizes self-assertion or protest *in the short term.*

As well as sharing a certain identification with a wide Arab entity, both Woodson and DuBois glorified Pharaonic Egyptians on the basis that about one quarter or one third of them had some blood from initial Negro settlers who had later fused with incoming Mediterranean people to form Egypt's original population.[176]

Woodson and DuBois were mainly thinking of the past at their stage in the historical development of African-American nationalism, in which contacts with Arab and Muslim persons were fewer. But the two historians' images of participation by blacks in (a) Arab North Africa and West Asia as well as (b) Pharaonic Egypt, would from the 1950s help point African-Americans to political solidarity with Arab nationalist forces and states in their struggles against Western governments and Israel that followed World War II. This historiography's sense that Egypt and also North Africa and Muslim Spain had a range of connections to the populations below the Sahara helped condition African-Americans to stand with Egypt when Britain, France and Israel attacked it in unison in 1956. Stokely Carmichael urged African-Americans in the wake of the 1967 Six Day War to aid Nasser's Egypt against Israel because it had been part of the history and culture of Africa since Pharaonic times (see ch. 5). The elite historians' interest in Moorish Spain also may have helped feed the "Moorish" sects started by Noble Drew 'Ali in 1913, and black Muslim and black leftist solidarity with Spanish-speakers in or from Latin America after 1950, plus NOI drives to recruit Hispanics as "Blacks" under both Elijah and Farrakhan.

In enumerating the nationalities of the enslaved Africans at the time they were taken to America, Woodson described the Senegalese as among the most intelligent of the Africans: "with an infusion of Arab blood", they were valuable for the American economy by reason of their skills as mechanics and artisans.[177] DuBois consistently maintained throughout his works that African-Americans had been formed from the full range of racial types found across Africa including "distinct traces" of the blood of both Arabs and Berbers, although the coasts of West Africa had been the main area of origin.[178]

Muslim Slave-Trade Palliated?

This set of African-American writers even showed some impulses to downplay slave-trading by Arabs/Muslims in East Africa, or to place it within wider global contexts that condemned the West more. The extent to which they did this to prevent harm to the development of new relations with Arabs requires research. Woodson in 1922 depicted the "Mohammedan" slave-trade as having only recently ended and as "a disgrace to certain Eastern nations during the latter part of 19th century and even into the 20th century." But then he accepted the assertions of Islamophiles among romanticizing white Western Orientalists, and perhaps of Anglophone Muslims, that the religion of Islam did offer a universal brotherhood that its adherents had been actualizing to some extent. Accordingly, Woodson reasoned that enslavement was not an irreversible condition under Islam: all the slave was required to do was utter the confession of faith of Muhammad in order to then become a member in the religious community "enjoying equality with the richest and best".[179] Somewhat more nuanced and realistic about the prospects for enslaved Africans and their progeny in the Arabian peninsula, DuBois cited W.G. Palgrave (1866) who had observed there that Negroes could without difficulty marry their sons and daughters to the Arab lower and middle classes. It was only exceptional individuals of the consequent mixed race who acquired noble-like status, becoming richly-garbed amirs who were "sued" by Arabs of the purest Qahtanite and Ishmaelitish stock.[180] DuBois regarded such late Arab societies as offering more hopes in life for Negroes than did Anglo-Saxon systems, but he did not always depict instant equality for slaves. Overall, the practice of slavery by Arabs and Muslims did not make Woodson or DuBois criticize Islam as a religion, or see even the traditional late Muslim society in which slavery had recently been practised as completely lacking some redeeming openness and flexibility that enabled even enslaved individuals to achieve some upward social mobility.

DuBois did at one or two points condemn enslavement of animist Africans under the more destructive form it took in the 19th century as Arabic-speakers began to penetrate deep into the interior of East and Central Africa. In condemning, however, he still evoked affinities and overlap between the Muslim groups responsible and black Africans/African-Americans. This 1947 position of DuBois was influenced by the overriding hatred he felt by that time for the white West's expansionist power and for the capitalist system it furthered. In at least the 17th, 18th and early 19th century forms of enslavement by Muslims in East Africa, the Arabs had stayed mainly along the coast and the trade had not transferred many to the Arab world, Iran and India. The mild domestic slavery found among African tribes, Arabs and Persians had not—so DuBois argued in this mood—prevented the slave or his son from becoming a statesman or a poet: in any case, the position of servants to Muslim leisure classes, or soldiers, was milder than "serf" labor for a white profit-motivated commercial class that European capitalism inflicted on Africans.

DuBois analyzed the expansion of Arab slaving operations in hinterland East Africa in the 19th century as resulting from the demand of Western commercial markets—in particular those of the United States—for the ivory that those quasi-Arabs made the Africans they had just enslaved carry on their shoulders to the coast. After prices in America and London rose in the 1820s and 1830s, American and European traders set up establishments for buying ivory in Zanzibar, supplying arms to Arabs to shoot the elephants and coerce the natives. [This expansion of slavery was thus in part a function of Zanzibar's self-modernization on Western lines prior to the British conquest.] In a vitriolic passage, DuBois ironized that in America and the West "neither the society darling nor the great artist saw the blood on the piano keys," and characterized the growing clamor in Europe and America for the suppression of this slave-trade as quintessential Anglo-Saxon "philanthropy and 5 per cent"—a pious missionary veneer for the imposition of an imperial system for commercial profit and exploitation.[180]

But DuBois' analysis was even more unconventional and radical in its progression to nuanced understanding of the complex cultural and racial overlaps and fusions underlying such stereotypical Anglo-Saxon categories as "Arabs", "the Arab slave-trade", "Africans" and "Mohammedans" in pre-colonial East Africa. Further undermining the motifs and categories of Islamophobic Western discourse, DuBois questioned its term "Mohammedan Arab slave-traders": the East and Central Africa leader and slave-trader "Tippoo Tib" (Hamid Bin Muhammad: 1840-1905) was always called an "Arab" when his photographs clearly showed him to have been "what Americans would denominate a 'full-blooded' Negro".[182]

While assenting that Arabic-speakers—many of whom he defined as "Negroes"—were the main organizers on the ground of the expanded traffic in slaves in 19th century East Africa, DuBois did not lose sight of the roles of purer African elements in its conduct. He projected an adequate vision of the full racial complexity of the entity of the Swahili-speakers, composed of a spectrum of types ranging from bilingual white-complexioned Arabs, to mulattos and black Africans speaking Swahili as their mother tongue, to wider groups of inland Africans who in interacting and trading with the Swahilis and Arabs had adopted Swahili as a lingua franca for communication between far-flung areas, and were in the process of accepting their Islamic religion.

Anti-Western motives could sometimes distort their perceptions of the world. But DuBois and Woodson did help African-Americans progress to a more nuanced understanding of the complex cultural and racial overlaps of such categories as "Islam", "Muslims", "Arabs", and "Africans" in pre-colonial East Africa. This alertness of DuBois in 1947 and perhaps Woodson in 1922 to the fluidity and the internal diversity of any African Muslim community-category rates as a modern perspective, that stands up well before the simple, homogenizing, mythologizing usage of anti-NOI Jewish-American polemicists that was to raise so much dust in the last two decades of the 20th century.

The Long-Term Legacy for Scholarship

African-Americans were well served by such pioneer nationalist writers as DuBois and Carter Woodson who gave them a complex and many-layered vision not just of the African continent of origin but of the intertwined history of Asia as well. DuBois inoculated African-Americans against the anti-Arab Islamophobia—a form of anti-Semitism—that Anglo-Americans vented around him in his youth, and which was further spread on their own account by the USA's Zionist lobby after the birth of Israel, and from 1970 by America's new Jewish micronationalists. It is not true that Woodson and DuBois always ignored the suffering Arab-directed enslavement inflicted on hinterland animist Africans in the 19th century. They did, though, distinguish periods in Arab-African interaction on the Eastern side of Africa, and also direct African-Americans to view ethno-cultural communities in Africa as fluid and permutating entities.[183] The questioning, flexible attitudes that the founders of African-American national historiography inculcated would remain important after 1980 in a period in which U.S. Zionists and Jewish enclave-nationalists were to challenge neo-Muslim and Islamophile African-Americans to condemn various categories of Arabs as "villains" and enemies of black Africans. The foremost U.S. Protestant "aid" organization working to roll back Islamic belief around the world, World Vision, could not but award DuBois a resentful certificate for all he had done to prepare the way for that rival creed, Islam, in America as, for instance, editor of the crucial journal *The Crisis* with its 70,000 circulation among the forming African-American elite.[184]

The national historiography that Woodson and DuBois built at breakneck speed, rewove the continuity of the experience of their people from the African continent of origin, through slavery and Christianization in America, to the new possibilities that opened for African-Americans after World War I. This new coherent macro-consciousness of African-Americans was a prerequisite for the modern nationhood they then went on to build. Not all white liberal historians, though, rejoiced that Negro historians had emerged able to treat the experience of Africans and black people in the USA as at least their scholarly equals. DuBois' original and incisive revaluation of the 19th century expansion of Muslim enslavement in East Africa was dismissed out of hand as solely anti-white "color astigmatism" by Harold Isaacs in his 1963 study of the unfolding African-American rediscovery of Africa.[185] Comfortable with the unvarying, essentially anti-Semitic, stereotypes his Angloid-American academic setting retailed of Arabs and Muslims, Isaacs refused to register DuBois' careful distinctions between the different phases and types of Muslim slavery, and especially not his remarks on the roles of Western markets, demand, personnel and technology—e.g. old Sepoy guns supplied by British traders[186]—in finally pushing the Arabs and Muslims involved into Central Africa. This, though DuBois' tables of the leaping imports of [often slave-carried] ivory into London from 1788-1884[187] are so damning.

The anthropologist Melville Herskovits (1895-1963) reviewed Woodson's 1936 *The African Background Outlined* as a "book [that] bristled with undocumented accusations". Charging that the "bibliographies are incomplete and show a strong anti-White basis", he patronizingly advised Woodson to read recent scholarship on Haiti and Brazil. The 1993 perspective of Jacqueline Goggin was that Woodson, at the close of the twentieth century, still towered as an historian above such Euro-American competitors. The sweep of Woodson's studies—his multidisciplinary fusion of anthropology, archeology, sociology and history, unrivalled in academia when he penned his works—to our day simply catches the totality of the African-American experience better than the works of U.S. Angloid scholars, including even those Jewish-American liberals and leftists who, despite Herskovits' strictures against "anti-white" historiography, vented ethnic ill-feeling of their own against Anglo-Americans in their studies focusing around African-Americans. Goggin (1993) notes that the pioneer Woodson broke with his white counterparts in drawing on such previously ignored primary sources as letters, speeches, folklore and the autobiographies of both free and enslaved blacks, and in utilizing African folklore and oral testimony from Americans. It was only in the late twentieth century that some Euro-American historians began to apply to Black American studies the variety of approaches that such African-American academics as Woodson had pioneered long before, concluded Goggin.[188]

The school of research into culture elements of African origin among North American blacks that Herskovits launched was not to give much recognition to motifs from Islam. Herskovits in the 1940s did fieldwork in the islands of the British West Indies among the cult of the "Shouters" Spiritual Baptists: his write-up on the African survivals in that cult ignored the clearly Islamic origin of barefoot prayers and prayer-mats in those churches, circumambulation of special central altars, and the Islamic tinge of the handshakes of the adherents.[189] While Herskovits had some ethnic background in Hebrew that could have directed him, he did not look for Arabic or Islamic origins of any of the practices and folklore he dissected. Yet, Islamist African-Americans were to find it hard to move beyond his major contributions to the understanding of African continuities in the cultures of New World blacks. In 1985, Ken Farid Hasan (pro-Warith) was still citing Herskovits for the African grammatical foundations of African-American forms of English (Gullah) or creole French, while warning that he had to be read with caution.[190]

Euro-American academic scholarship has contributed to self-understanding by black Americans, but Woodson and DuBois offered a broader sweep of data about Africa and Muslims likelier to help them build a range of U.S. and transcontinental political communities. A few of the pioneer Negro historians such as Woodson had known what it was to labor with their hands to support their initial education. Yet as African-Americans who directed their scholarship to achieve the interests of their nation, DuBois and Woodson could often leap over undemanding, smaller identities and local U.S. phenomena to focus wider connections. These links outwards have been essential for (a) knitting the diverse classes of African-Americans together into nationhood, given the quasi-Muslim identifications already unfolding at street level and (b) to directing the African-American nation in general to check out the possibilities for religious or political communities with Arabs and Muslims on other continents. The elite historians equipped African-Americans to take part in the construction of pan-African unity and then of a wider Afro-Arab bloc, in part as instruments to win and maintain sovereignty or autonomy from imperial states.

New Historiography Unites Diverse Black Classes and Groups

There have been many instances, over many decades, of the class divide and tensions between the impoverished ghetto elements from which the Nation of Islam and its successors recruited and the black bourgeoisie. But the foundation masterpieces of Black Nationalist historiography have shown that the bourgeoisie during the early construction of Islam within the African American community was itself imbibing intellectualized views of the African lands of provenance that would henceforth make that bourgeoisie less likely to challenge myths of provenance articulated by Drew 'Ali's Moors and the Nation of Islam, etc. The Moors' and the early NOI's myth of the original "Asiatic" origin and nationality of the blacks brought as slaves from Africa—although mainly suggested by the Bible and the Qur'an—had some congruence with both Woodson and DuBois' drive to document historical links and community between Africa and Asia. Indeed, DuBois in the period even toyed with the idea that the continent of origin of blacks might—rather than Africa—be in Asia, of which he mentioned areas that literate Americans knew were Arabic-speaking in the 20th century.

Carter Woodson in 1922, early enough to be in the formative reading of the worker or lumpen figures who went on to found the black Muslim movement in 1930, speculated that the records of archeologists might indicate that the earliest African "was not necessarily Black, but of an Asiatic type of Negroid features," which was close to the way that the founder Fard and Elijah Muhammad from 1930 described the Asiatic Arabic-speaking Black Man before he migrated to the West Africa that curled his hair. Even when he was writing, the peoples of Africa "exhibit in their racial characteristics all of the divergences found among people of color in the United States." Thus, the USA's racial categorizations of light "mulattos" as belonging among the "Negroes" prodded Woodson to include or affiliate Africa's Berbers and Arabs into his wide community of provenance. Perhaps extending a reflex fostered in his people by their Holy Bible, Woodson, like the NOI, descried "a movement of peoples and of civilizations from Asia into Egypt, and from Egypt up the Nile into the interior of Africa, and again from Egypt westward to near the Gulf of Guinea".[191] Legends among some West African nationalities imaged migrations or influences from Arabia and Egypt as their original provenance. Western historians have debated cultural diffusion from Pharaonic Egypt.

During the earlier history of the Moorish and NOI sects, the pattern was one of (1) some confirming motifs from the bourgeois nationalist historians reaching the Muslim lumpen sect leaders who in turn (2) diffused them out into the not highly literate masses those sect leaders addressed and, in a fashion, educated. This movement of motifs from the bourgeois elite's highly rational and materialist historians to masses prone to state their protest through religions, built up over the decades. The works of Carter Woodson and DuBois were among the sources that Malcolm X read while in prison between 1948 and 1953 and then utilized for his later development of the Islam of Elijah Muhammad. Carter Woodson provided Malcolm with his basic images of the black empires in Africa before the blacks were brought as slaves to the United States, and of "the early Negro struggles for freedom" in North America[192]—themes Malcolm after his release proceeded to popularize among the African-American masses as the NOI's finest orator and TV star in the 1950s and 1960s. DuBois' comprehensive pan-Africanism when he had sought relationship with West Asia in history, Malcolm politicized in the 1960s when he denounced the white man who "maneuvered to divide the black African from the brown Arab" and the "Christian African" from the Muslim African on the continent of Africa.[193]

The united front media of the new Nation of Islam established by Louis Farrakhan in 1977-1978 was to direct African-Americans in general to Woodson and DuBois, and their Islamophile delimitations of an Africa-focused community. Dr Conrad Worrill, chairman of the USA's National Black United Front, from the pages of Farrakhan's newspaper projected a somewhat Africanist micronationalism peppered with [often Arabic-derived] Swahili and ancient Egyptian words. In 1999, Worrill exalted Carter Woodson, whose founding of "Negro History Week" in 1926 had started the African Centered Curriculum Movement that, having passed through the Black Studies courses at universities wrested by Black Power students in the 1960s, was flourishing at the close of the 20th century. The new post-1965 history courses in schools and universities (he did not mention cutbacks) had reconnected African-Americans to "our homeland Africa." They showed African-Americans "the interconnection of the African people throughout the world" in the face of American education's persistent stance that the Negro was a historical nonentity that deserved little coverage in curricula. (Yet mildly Africanist Worrill and Farrakhan's *Final Call* tabloid—following Woodson himself—had their latent Americanist-integrationist drive in their demand that new courses and research explore Black history's contribution and "impact on this country," as well as the world.)[194] For young black students and professionals in the early 1990s, African-American History Month (once, the less ethnicist, more race-based Black History Month, or, originally, the still more tame Negro History Week) motivated by showing that "we are not only the products of history but also its makers. We begin to organize our efforts collectively. We study hard and always do our best"—the modest, normal American competency and life into which so much Black Nationalist and black Muslim rhetoric pans out.[195] Like Worrill and Farrakhan's Nation of Islam, this set of youth at Atlanta Metropolitan College in 1992 was highlighting Woodson's *The Miseducation of the Negro* as the guide by which African-Americans could apply their tertiary education to ameliorate the problems of their people as a collective.[196]

As Farrakhan in the late twentieth century grappled with the problem that death could be striding towards him, data from the much earlier African-American historians who had founded literate collective identity, were still among the elements continuing to push the black Muslims to engage with those areas of black Africa that would entail relationship with the Arab world. In his 1947 glorification of the Mandingan kingdom of Melle, DuBois had discussed the 1324 pilgrimage of its greatest king, Mansa Musa, to Mecca. The long journey of his extensive caravan had impressed his kingdom's magnificence and wealth upon people across "the East." In December 1997, as Farrakhan started his World Friendship Tour from Bamako, Mali, he defined his tour as a modern successor to history's greatest Islamic pilgrimage by the ancient Mali Empire's Mansa Musa across the grueling Sahara Desert with gold-dust [to the Arab heartlands].[197] Thus, the recreation of Africa by the African-Americans' preeminent historians continues to fan the tendencies in populist Islam-influenced sects to a special Africanism that also reaches out to besieged Palestinians, 'Iraqis and Khomeiniite Iran.

Some Islam-influenced areas and eras of West Africa evoked by DuBois and Woodson recurred in a range of African-American discourses in the late modern and post-modern periods. Those materials were recycled in an Africanist, anti-Islam fashion by the historian John Henrik Clarke in a widely-read special issue on Africa of Ebony in 1976. True, a lot of the data he presented about the great leaders of West African history incidentally could not but illustrate the key roles of Arabic and Islam in the state structures, high cultures and educational institutions that they fostered. As had been the case with DuBois, Clarke went over the 14th century Emperor Mansa Musa's conjunction with the Middle East, and quoted characterizations of the empire of Ghana, Timbuktu, etc., by such Arab geographers as al-Idrisi and Leo Africanus (1485-1554). There was a great demand by Timbuktu's schools, judges, doctors and clerics for Arabic books imported from the Middle East. While Clarke's bent was to depict Arabs as from their early classical age interested in West Africa solely for the gold, slaves or anything else they could get out of it, such data ran against his insularist Africanist frame. After the death of Askia the Great, the Songhay empire gradually broke up, and was destroyed when the armies of the Sultan of Morocco, al-Mansur, captured Timbuktu and Gao in 1591. "The University of Sankore that had stood for over 500 years was destroyed and the faculty—including

Ahmad Baba, the greatest Sudanese scholar of the age—was exiled to Morocco," grieved Clarke. The invaders and subsequent Berber and Arab raiders from the North who "showed no mercy" thus destroyed West Africa's lost "Golden Age" [a key concept most nationalisms evoke, along with an enemy destroyer-nation]. The sweeping, long-term "wreck and ruin" wrought by the Moorish occupation so devastated most of West Africa as to give the impression to the Europeans when they came that "nothing of order and value had existed in these [African] countries"—fueling over 400 years of Western racist contempt for African and African-American history.[198]

Clarke's scapegoating ignored that black Islamic and animist cultures and states, including literate Arabic education and authorship, had been flourishing when the Westerners arrived in West Africa: Western scholars had been documenting Arabic manuscripts since WWII in particular. In the 1980s and 1990s, Clarke was consistently to further the campaigns by Afro-Centrist academics and writers against Islam and to argue against alliances by U.S. blacks with contemporary Arabs.[199]

Clearly, the old historiography of Carter G. Woodson—to be recycled among African-Americans in the 1980s and 1990s through a flood of readers and academic studies—gives a better sense than the later-modern Clarke of the range of relationships between (a) Arabs and Berbers and (b) black sub-Saharan Africans. Woodson had odd bursts of Clarke-like images. He once imaged "the Mohammedans" as bringing, from outside, a Koran that registered the same Divine Being in which the animist Africans had believed, while opposing their propitiation of good and evil spirits. But "thousands of Africans died rather than change their religious faith" as did thousands of Muslims in those "holy wars"—which, though, were mostly conducted by black African Muslims "more zealous in [Islam's] propagation than the foreign Mohammedans themselves".[200] For Woodson, the few Arab or Berber clerics who might have been present were not movers of the "jihads" that black African Muslim zealots waged for whatever reasons against Muslim or animist blacks [and which saw captured black Muslims sold by victors into slavery in America].

On the whole, Woodson caught sharply, and in a nuanced way, the back-and-forth nature of most interaction between North and sub-Saharan Africa, its modification of the genetic pool of the Berbers and Arabs to the North, the participation of blacks in the armies, courts and scholarship of Muslim North Africa and Spain, and the usual sovereignty of most West Africans as they chose what suited them from Arabic and Islam and Arab Muslims.

Woodson's data could lead African-Americans of diverse classes to stand with Arab-Berber struggles against Westerners in the era of decolonization in Northern Africa. But as a sort of Westerner, his feelings ran both ways. On one hand, he was interested in the tenacity with which Muslims resisted the imposition of French and British colonial rule: "it took generations of extermination to pacify the country sufficiently to justify the hope that European settlement, backed by European capital, would be a safe investment". In the other direction, a Western side to Woodson felt a strained affinity to the "order and exploitation along modern lines" towards which such as Admiral Lyautey of France led the populations they "crushed" (in Morocco, in this case). Here Woodson accepted the justification of the British and French that they were neutral arbiters in Africa as far as religious groups were concerned: the European nations had taken the side of correligionists among the Africans only as an excuse for initial conquest: as the Muslims realized that their resolute "new lords" would not disturb them in the exercise of their religion, they resisted the "economic imperialism" of Europe less and less.[201]

Here, Woodson vacillated between (a) dislike of Western imperialist conquest and (b) his cultural links as a resident of the West to European self-justifications from rational efficiency, and from economic profiteering that still might bring some development to native populations. But 1939 was well before the decisive Arab and African nationalist movements and post-WW2 decolonization.

The details of Woodson and DuBois' influence on the men who conducted the first Nation of Islam from 1930 remain to be traced, but the media of Imam Warith and his sect direct sympathisers to their works in this new century. In 2004, Imam A.A. Noah Seifullah traced Woodson's academic career in Warith's tabloid, noting as an integrationist motif that he chose the second week of February for Negro History Week because both Frederick Douglass and Abraham Lincoln had been born in it. The data that Woodson popularized still had extreme tension and duality for this African-American Muslim in 2004. Lincoln or no, it had been very hard for African-American people to wrest emancipation from slavery and achieve the opportunities America had. Following Woodson's bleak and ambiguous vision of the experience of his group, this Warithite Muslim in early 2004 stressed the horror of the conditions African Americans were placed in under slavery, and the crucial role of their own efforts in finally winning them a flawed freedom. Great numbers of them had never given up their aspirations to become free: it was this black flight that had imposed the Fugitive Slave Law of 1850 as a temporary compromise between the slave-holding and non-slave-holding states. In the tradition of Woodson, Seifullah painted U.S. institutions as slow to apply their functions and equity to black, as against other, Americans. When, under slavery, African-American Drew Scott petitioned the U.S. Supreme Court for liberation of the enslaved, it had only found that no Black in America could ever be a citizen, and that Scott thus had no right to present their case to the Supreme Court. Woodson in particular has thus bequeathed to Muslim thought among the African-American people a micronationalistic attitude that while the blacks have to get themselves into the U.S. system as full citizens, and although that system has liberal groups and institutions with some wish to help them in that, the blacks have to apply unremitting pressure and struggle to make those institutions work: that is because, in this frame of perception, hostile and liberal forces are always delicately balanced in white American society, and it is the thrust of African Americans that pulls the balance to equity and membership. Black people will get into

America and win equal chances there, but they always have to remain organized and determined as a quasi-people within that system to make it work for them. Woodson's analyses of the history of the American group justify Martin Luther King, Jr., as the resolute veiled radical who wins entry more than a full integration, in the thought of W.D. Mohammed's sect that has its own cloaked militancy and micronationalist tendencies.[202]

Clearly, such pioneer African-American professional historians as Carter G. Woodson and W.E.B. DuBois did get much of their data about the African past across to more popular Islamic movements among African-Americans. Popularizers as well as scholars, they had intended their works to help construct a new cultural nationality down to the level of the poorest black masses, in that way. They had with clarity pointed African Americans to tasks in restoring a continuous culture and history of the African-American people, such as learning Arabic and drawing on manuscripts about African history in it. The early historians, though, had not been equipped, or lacked the conditions, to themselves *as an elite* carry through such a task in their historical period. After the death of his father in 1975, W.D. Mohammed led a sect whose membership came to include more and more prosperous middle class people, and a new black Muslim intelligentsia, some of whom were linked to universities. Some of the new intellectuals succeeded in learning to read classical Arabic and became good teachers of it, in accordance with Warith's drive to connect his sect to the Arab World's Sunni Islam. Warith had to give precedence to building relations with Arabs and their literate Islam, but his sect and its improving intellectual resources did not, between 1975 and 2000, generate much research from Arabic works into the history and culture of Muslim West Africa. Despite its admiration for Carter Woodson, the sect over that long time-span did not actualize his call for translations from Arabic works to communicate pre-colonial West African history to Americans, nor did his main tabloid much convey specific Arabic works by West Africans to the African-American public.

In the 21st century, the adherents of Warith want to engage more deeply with the heritage of Arabic learning in West Africa, which they have had the language qualifications to do for many years. They now understand its fragility with a new sharp focus. Abd al-Malik Mohammed in 2004 valued the tradition of NOI popular protest-Islam insofar as it could construct a bridge back to that learned African Islam that his people originally had had. "As slaves, our religion publicly vanished under the harsh circumstances of chattel slavery," but then reemerged on July 4, 1930 when Wali Fard Muhammad came to Detroit to proclaim the Nation of Islam. Abd al-Malik tactfully termed that bygone new society of Muslims in the West "inexperienced," endorsing Fard's teachings on a functional plane only, as a temporary instrument "structured" to give "ethnic dignity" and moral "purification" to blacks who were facing "imposed social mistreatment." He tried to read Fard and Elijah as directing the adherents to "dig deep" into the scriptures for truths beyond these initial teachings (=to Sunni Islam), and stressed the old *Muhammad Speaks* diagram of a New World black and an Arab-garbed African one clasping hands across the globe. For Abd al-Malik, this symbolized a reuniting that now would restore to America's blacks "what has been lost in the journey of time." To further that reuniting, he urged the believers to attend the fundraiser of the Timbuktu Educational Foundation "to preserve several of these valuable manuscripts that will enhance efforts to reunite and reconcile our past and our beloved forefathers' and brothers' honor." Abd al-Malik was like Dubois in that he quoted directly a vivid passage from Leo Africanus /al-Hasan Ibn Muhammad al-Wazzan (1485-1554), who depicted the generous subsidies King Askia Muhammad kept up to support the research of men of learning in Timbuktu. The establishment of Qur'anic studies in the city, ran Abd al-Malik's Islamist analysis, had led to advances in medicine, astronomy, botony, optics, law and other "sciences"—"a truly enlightened past" [=a past fitting into the West's modernity?] that a group in Warith's sect wanted to restore to African-Americans.[203]

The speeches at the fundraiser itself brought together many Islam-restoring strands of the high intellectual and the popular-political traditions in modern African-American life. Sister Precious Muhammad, one of the followers of W.D. Mohammed, recalled the bygone Edmund Blyden who had gone to West Africa with Arabic Bibles to convert Muslims in the 19th century, but abandoned his mission because he was so impressed with the knowledge of the Muslim scholars, with whom he preferred to associate in Africa: he took an Arabic name and had a Muslim janazah (funeral): he was the founder of pan-Africanism among African-Americans. She mentioned the names of some Africans enslaved in America who had held fast to Islam. On the masses-contact side, Sister Precious mentioned the Noble Drew 'Ali, and that the Garvey Movement had a hymn "Allahu Akbar" (Allah is Greatest) among others "with Islamic themes." The presentation to the Conference by Dr Jose V. Pimienta-Bey, a visiting assistant professor of African-American studies and history at Ohio University, was in accord with the literate historiography of DuBois and Woodson, and with the Moorish nationalist ideas of the more popular tradition of the Noble Drew 'Ali—Pimienta went beyond the West Africa of the forefathers of African-Americans to North Africa and the impact of the Moors or Moroccan Muslims through Spain upon medieval Europe. In a Western country, America, Muslim African Americans are compelled by the surrounding culture they share to relate themselves in some way to the general civilization of the West from its Grecian beginnings. Thus, Dr Jose Pimienta-Bey stressed that it was the Moors in Andalusia from the 8th through the 14th Centuries who provided breakthroughs that led Europe into the Renaissance and interdisciplinary education. It was the Moors who in 1154 created a silver globe that suggested the world was round to Europeans who had conceived it to be flat; who introduced the idea that diseases are spread by germs; and who forebade people from wearing the clothes of those who had died of disease or from cooking from their pots. In a tint from the Africanist John Henrik Clarke of 1976, Pimienta-Bey did allow that a drawback of the expansion of Morocco was that it "hastened" (a judicious term) the fall of the Songhay Empire in Mali. Still, racially and in identification, Jose Pimienta-Bey blurred North African and sub-Saharan African Muslims into each other. Imam Musa Bala Balde of the Timbuktu Education Foundation set out the threats to the thousands of manuscripts in Timbuktu from termites, water damage and dry rot.[204]

Long-Term Patterns of Meaning

Our above data presented early, formative elements in African-American high historiography that perennially surface in much Black Nationalist thought in the USA and which append Arabs and Islam to the Africa with which the African-American nation now has to reconnect itself. At least from the early 1950s, the pattern of overlap is one in which motifs from black elite academia and intellectualism flow into the media of neo-Muslims of much poorer ghetto origins. The motifs ratify those converts' religion-prompted commitment to an Africa linked to the Arabs, but thereby over time granting them the detail of that world's *history*. We have reviewed images of Africa and Asia's history among elite historians that would encourage the black bourgeoisie to welcome any future relationship with the Arab and Muslim peoples into which black neo-Islam might open. "Negro" intellectual life by 1930 had long elaborated Islamophile elements that thenceforth would open a hearing for ragged-collared lumpen neo-Muslims in the apex elites. The two originally so disparate groups could thus ideologically and socially flow into each other with much more speed than some sociological analyses expected.

The pattern was long the flow of Arabophile or anti-Christian historical motifs down from the bourgeoisie's historians. But from the 1960s, the parallel once-lumpen ideology that drew on Islam was, through hostile publicity by whites and the studies published on it by African-Americans scholars establishing themselves into academia, in its turn flowing out into the black bourgeoisie. As that expanding bourgeoisie converted from integrationist Americanism to "Black Nationalism" in the 1970s, many of them—already somewhat preconditioned from the Arabophilia in their own class's high culture—could somehow swallow blatant mythologies in "the Nation's" ideology, and join the NOI. Thenceforth the high bourgeois and the lumpen neo-Muslim streams of U.S. Black Nationalism reciprocally influenced each other to their depths. Yet the two discursive traditions had always at least tended to buoy each other over many decades. Had the elite African-American intellectuals and academics felt more impulses to defend Christianity, the black churches would have had more historical, and respectable rational, arguments with which to limit the mass proselytization by the earlier lumpen neo-Muslims.

The earlier black American professional historians had implanted enough recognition of Islam as an aspect in the history of Africans and African-Americans for Islamist or Third Worldist activists to highlight within a reinvented nationalist identity later, from 1970. The writings of African American historians from academia, through mass-media that transmitted them, diffused awareness of Arabic and Islam among the West Africans of origin among the black middle classes in general. In 1976, a two-page colored sketch of Askia in the mass-circulation, *Ebony*, depicted him sitting on a throne with patterns like those of West African Kente cloth, but with some North African influences in his clothing and that of the host come to pay homage. The colorful, eye-catching item credited Askia with reducing the tax burdens on commoners. "A devout Muslim, he administered Songhay strictly according to Islamic law." The final aim of the advertisement, though, was to direct African-Americans to Budweiser Beers, which no devout U.S. Muslim would drink. Another issue carried a similar striking two-page sketch of the conquering Shaka, King of the Zulus.[205]

Both Woodson and DuBois had deep linkages to America and to the West in their national makeup, but neither softened the harsh enslavement, systemic exploitation and marginalization that Euro-Americans had inflicted upon blacks in their history that had elements for separate nationhood.The patterns of this past interaction have remained in the behavioral and thought DNA of all groups in America into the 21st century, and still make the national integration of an undivided American people very hard.

The new micronationalist arguments and controversies in America after 1980 confirmed that Jews can and have fulfilled all the options of behavior towards blacks that Anglo and Celtic Americans have patterned. Like WASP and Celtic Americans, some American Jewish individuals have exchanged songs, stories, friendship and love with African-American individuals. But the South underscores the other exploitative possibilities that Euro-Americans from all groups have committed against African-Americans. It was a glimmer of hope for a future Americanist community that, in the post-1980 era in which a new U.S. Jewish micronationalist cinema (eg. David Mamet) justified fighting blacks, some Jewish liberals took hesitant steps to face that past.

In the 21st century, the now Arabic-literate adherents of Warith, and also those of Farrakhan to some extent, have badly-needed cultural skills to place themselves at the fore of crucial projection of sub-Saharan African history and cultures to African-Americans in scholarly articles and books. The structural bias of their Islamic intellectual equipment will direct serious exploration of the past in the continent of origin more towards its Islamic aspects and links to Arabs at the expense of the more self-contained and local pagan cultures in West African history. The latter have been highlighted for decades by the Africanist faction that has had predominance in academia and literate discourse, but the make-up of African-American perception of their African foundations of nationhood could become more Islamic as Muslim blacks—some of them genuinely from Africa—establish themselves more in U.S. academia.

ENDNOTES

1 Douglas Grant, *The Fortunate Slave: An Illustration of African Slavery in the Early Eighteenth Century* (London: OUP 1968) pp. 77-81, 99. Sloane had lived in

Jamaica as a young doctor, where he married into the planter stratum.

2 Robert J. Allison, "The Origins of African-American Culture", *The Journal of Interdisciplinary History* 30:3 Winter 1999 p. 478.

3 British explorer Mungo Park cited by E. W. Blyden, *Christianity, Islam and the Negro Race* (Edinburgh: Aldine Publishers 1967) p. 227.

4 African-American professional historians Thomas J. Davis and Margaret Washington to "Africans in America: America's Journey through Slavery: the Terrible Transformation," SBS television Australia 2 January 2000.

5 Adam Lebor, *A Heart Turned East: Amongst the Muslims of Europe and America* (London: Little, Brown & Company 1997) pp. 249-250.

6 Clyde-Ahmad Winters, "Afro-American Muslims—from Slavery to Freedom", *Islamic Studies* (Pakistan) v. 17:4 (Winter 1978) p. 191.

7 Clyde-Ahmad Winters, "Roots and Islam in Slave America", *al-Ittihad* October-November 1976 p. 19.

8 Charles Silberman, *Crisis in Black and White* (New York: Random House 1964) p. 81.

9 Richard Brent Turner, *Islam in the African-American Experience* (Bloomington: Indiana University Press 1997) pp. 51, 40.

10 In a 1935 work, Woodson, in discussing "noble Africans captured", observed that "a slave of this type (it might have been 'Umar Ibn Sa'id himself) was taken to the University of North Carolina, sometime before the Civil War, to instruct one of its professors in the Arabic language and literature". In this passage, Woodson had a tone of religious neutrality between Islam and Christianity: 'Umar Ibn Sa'id faithfully read his Qur'an for a period but then started attending a church. Woodson, *Story of the Negro Retold* (Washington: Associated Publishers 1935) excerpted James L. Conyers Jr (ed) *Carter G. Woodson: a Historical Reader* (NY: Garland Publishing Inc 2000) p. 235.

11 Basheer Alim, "Islam in Senegal" (his reactions while touring), *Muslim Journal* 30 July 1999 pp. 6, 26.

12 Allan D. Austin, *African Muslims in Antebellum America: Trans-Atlantic Stories and Spiritual Struggles* (New York: Routledge 1997) p. 135.

13 Grant op cit p. 96. The great Scots scholar of Hebrew and Aramaic, John Bowman, like Ayyub before, could not find, in 1982, any genuine statement of trinitarian belief in the four gospels. He concluded that the trinity tenet was formulated only with the 4th century Council of Nicea, and that of Chalcedon in the 5th: Bowman speculated that it had derived from the ancient Pharaonic god-king Osiris slain by Seth whom his wife, Isis, then resurrects. See Bowman, "The Debt of Christianity to Ancient Egypt", University of Melbourne paper 1982.

14 Grant op cit p. 107.

15 See, e.g., Imam Warith's dialogue with Rev. John Knox from the United Methodist Church in La Mirada, California; Fr. Steven Blair and Rabbi Lawrence Goldmark on the Los Angeles KABC radio program "Religion on the Line" in Imam W.D. Muhammad, *Religion on the Line: al-Islam, Judaism, Catholicism, Protestantism* (Chicago: W.D. Muhammad Publications 1983) pp. 75-83. Rabbi Goldmark noted that—conflict over the Middle East apart—"there are so many similarities between the Muslim faith and the Jewish faith, especially in this area of [rejection of] imagery" in houses of worship: p. 82.

16 Qur'an 90:1-13 surah "al-Balad" (The City).

17 Harold R. Isaacs, *The New World of Negro Americans* (New York: John Day 1963) pp. 251-3.

18 *Malcolm X on Afro-American History* (New York: Pathfinder Press 1967-1990) p. 48.

19 Winthrop D. Jordan, "Slavery and the Jews", *The Atlantic Monthly* September 1995 p. 112.

20 Allan Dershowitz, *The Disappearing American Jew* (Boston: Little Brown 1997) pp. 122 and 361: Dershowitz here draws on C. Vann Woodward of Yale University, and on an ADL tract, *Jew Hatred as History.*

21 John H. McWhorter, *Losing the Race: Self-Sabotage in Black America* (New

York: The Free Press 2000) pp. 195, 68.

22 Mattius Gardell, *In the Name of Elijah Muhammad: Louis Farrakhan and the Nation of Islam* (Carolina: Duke University Press and London: Hurst 1996) pp. 309-310.

23 Turner pp. 30-31. Sylviane Diouf, in her *Servants of Allah: African Muslims Enslaved in the Americas* (NY: New York University Press 1998) p. 137, argues that a white friend of Ibrahima had in the first place made up the idea that he was related to the royal family of Morocco: the fact remains that Ibrahima had been able, in Arabic, to muster evidence that he had a connection that was convincing to Morocco's royal elite. The terms under which his "owner" released him were more brutalization: 'Abd al-Rahman should not remain in the United States because if free, he might unsettle the old man's children, who were to remain Foster's property. Ibid.

24 Sylvia King of Marlin, Texas, recalled as a centenarian in 1937 that "I was borned in Morocco, in Africa, and was married and had three children befo' I was stoled from my husband". It is not true that she instances a paradigm of Turner and, here, Gomez, that Muslims in America regarded themselves as not racially quite like—and indeed superior to—other enslaved Africans, given her memory that she was put in France "in de bottom of a boat with a whole lot of other niggers" bound for America. Michael A. Gomez *Exchanging Our Country Marks: The Transformation of African Identity in the Colonial and Antebellum South 1526-1830* (Chapel Hill: North Carolina University Press 1996) p. 86.

25 Robert Dannin, *Black Pilgrimage to Islam* (NY: OUP 2002) pp. 20-21.

26 Turner op cit p. 34.

27 Gardell p. 33; Diouf *Servants* p. 92.

28 Turner op cit pp. 42-43.

29 See Robert J. Allison, "The Origins of African-American Culture", pp. 478-9 discussing Michael A. Gomez, *Exchanging* op. cit.

30 Austin *African Muslims* pp. 37-39.

31 Ibid p.108.

32 Samory Rashid, "Blacks and the Islamic Revival in the USA,"*Hamdard Islamicus* (26:1) January-March 2003.See also "The Gullah Wars" by Y. N. Kly in *The Legacy of Ibo Landing* edited by Marquetta L. Goodwine (Atlanta: Clarity Press 1998) pp. 19-53.

33 Austin *African Muslims* p. 99. Given his reliability, the owner left Salih Bilali in charge of the entire plantation for months at a time, without any other supervision: Gomez, *Exchanging* p. 71.

34 Austin p. 109.

35 *Malcolm X on Afro-American History* p. 40.

36 Memories of Alex Haley in his introduction to *The Autobiography of Malcolm X* (Middlesex: Penguin Books) p. 29.

37 Diouf op cit pp. 38-40, 64; Gomez op cit 85.

38 Austin op cit p. 39.

39 Austin op cit pp. 134-135, 48.

40 Quotation from an interview received from Dr. Y. N. Kly, conducted by Ms. Carlie Denstein of the Gullah-Geechee Foundation, with Cornelia Bailey, a Gullah Elder from Sapelo Island on March 5, 2005.

41 Diouf, *Servants of Allah* pp. 68-69.

42 One African talked as though he had made the *hajj* to Mecca as a matter of course along with his other duties to Islam such as prayer and almsgiving, prior to his abduction to America: Albert J. Raboteau, *Slave Religion: the "Invisible Institution" in the Antebellum South* (New York: OUP 1978) p. 47: other cases are cited by Diouf *Servants* pp. 67-68.

43 Gomez, *Exchanging Our Country Marks* pp. 263-272; Allison, "The Origins of African-American Culture" p. 480.

44 Interview with Egyptian hajj pilgrim Muhammad 'Awf, Melbourne 21 August 2001; Gomez pp. 269-270.

45 Gomez p. 265.

46 Diouf 193 and Gardell op cit p. 35; Gomez p. 266.

47 Quoted by Raboteau, *Slave Religion* p. 46.

48 Clyde-Ahmad Winters, "Afro-American Muslims—from Slavery to Freedom", *Islamic Studies* (Pakistan) v. 17:4 (Winter 1978) pp. 193-194. For the imbalance of the ratios between enslaved African men and the fewer women in North America, the selling away of children, and the consequent difficulty male Muslims faced in having families and transmitting Islam, see Diouf, *Servants* pp. 179-181.

49 Raboteau p. 46

50 Berger, "The Black Muslims" *Horizon* January 1964. During the interactions of West African Muslims with Malcolm X in 1964, this article influenced how each perceived the other party: *Autobiography* (Penguin) pp. 474-475.

51 Arthur J. Magida, *Prophet of Rage: a Life of Louis Farrakhan and his Nation of Islam* (New York: Basic Books 1996) pp. 35-6. Walley, like "Boccarey" (=Abu Bakr or Bukhari or al-Bakri), was among the names given in ads for escapees who had been brought from partly-Muslim Gambia: Gomez op cit p. 70.

52 Y.N. Kly, "The African-American Muslim Minority, 1776-1900", *Journal of the Institute of Muslim Minority Affairs* 10:1 January 1989.

53 Turner, *Experience* p. 177.

54 Louis A. DeCaro Jr, *Malcolm and the Cross: the Nation of Islam, Malcolm X, and Christianity* (New York University Press 1998) p. 80; Malcolm X, *Autobiography* p. 97

55 Lincoln 1961 p. 121; 1994 p. 114.

56 Malcolm X, *Autobiography* (Penguin) p. 278.

57 Ruby E. Maloney in communication to E.U. Essien-Udom, *Black Nationalism* (Chicago: University of Chicago Press 1962) pp. 198-199.

58 Winters, "Roots and Islam in Slave America", *loc cit* p. 18.

59 "Emam Muhammad declares: America is the Greatest Land!", *Bilalian News* 22 July 1977. Critics finally classified *Roots* in a synthesized category: it was not wholly made-up fiction (although Haley had embellished about himself and his forebears) and not just a narrative of historical facts but a compound of both—"faction".

60 Letter from Janice L. Cooke of Ann Arbor, Michigan, *Ebony* May 1977 pp. 21-22

61 *Hijrah* (Los Angeles) October-November 1985 p. 8.

62 Sulayman Shahid Mufassir, "A Short History of Masjid ul-Ummah", *The Criterion* (Karachi) November-December 1971 pp. 50-55: in its two years of existence, the mosque already had brought 100 people into Islam.

63 Ken Farid Hasan, "That Killing Image", *Hijrah* (Los Angeles) March-April 1985 pp. 20-21.

64 Louis A. DeCaro Jr, *On the Side of My People: A Religious Life of Malcolm X* (New York University Press 1996) p. 140.

65 *Malcolm X on Afro-American History* p. 45.

66 Ibid p. 25.

67 Malcolm X, *Afro-American History* p. 56.

68 *Autobiography* p. 499.

69 Hakim Abdul-Jamal, *From the Dead Level: Malcolm X and Me* (New York: Random House 1972) pp. 252-3.

70 Azim A. Nanji (ed), *The Muslim Almanac* (Detroit: Gale Research 1996) p. 151.

71 Claude Brown, *Manchild in the Promised Land* (Penguin 1969) p. 346.

72 "Oppressive Education During Slavery", *The Nkrumaist* 7:2 November-December 1991 p. 4.

73 Gerald Early, "Dreaming of a Black Christmas", *Harper's Magazine* January 1997 p. 57.

74 Gomez op cit pp. 78-79. Gomez here developed speculation from Douglass' main biographer: William S. McFeely, *Frederick Douglass* (NY: Norton 1991) pp. 3-5.

75 Douglass' retort to the organizers of the U.S. Negro "African Civilization [*sic*] Society" in Wilson Jeremiah Moses (ed), *Classical Black Nationalism* (New York University Press 1996) pp. 135-141. Ibid p. 136.

76 Philip S. Toner (ed), *Frederick Douglass on Women's Rights* (Greenwood Press

1976).

77 Vincent Harding, "Religion and Resistance Among Antebellum Negroes", in August Meier and Elliot Rudwick (ed), *The Making of Black America* (NY: Atheneum 1969 pp. 179-197.

78 Eldridge Cleaver, *Soul on Ice* (NY: Dell Publishing 1992 pp. 77-8).

79 For Malcolm's illusion that there was no fornication, drunkenness or theft—"nothing but high morals"—in the Africa from which the enslaved were taken to the States, see *Malcolm X on African-American History* p. 40. The great African-American historian, Carter G. Woodson, had romanticized that pre-European West African states "united the best in democracy and monarchy: theirs was a slave society" but their culture's healthy sentiment that all are born the same foreclosed any exploitation: Woodson, *The Negro in Our History* (Washington: Associated Publishers Inc 1922) pp. 12-13.

80 For Muslims among the Africans in these calculatedly dehumanizing slave caravans, see Diouf *Servants* pp. 41-45.

81 "Oppressive Education During Slavery", *The Nkrumaist* 7:2 November-December 1991 p. 4.

82 "The Mechanism of Colonial Control: the Psychological Dimension", *The Nkrumaist* 7:2 November-December 1991 p. 8.

83 See Muriel L. Feelings and Tom Feelings, *Moja Means One: Swahili Counting Book* (Dial Books 1992).

84 Sheila S. Walker, "What's in a Name?: Black Awareness Keeps the African Tradition of Meaningful Names Alive", *Ebony* June 1977. Beyond its Africanist ideological frame, this essay had a subtle alertness to the nuances and complexities of the variation by African-Americans of Euro-American names, including Celtic and Hispanic ones, during the changing stages of their interaction with mainstream America since 1800

85 "Festac '77", *Ebony* May 1977 pp. 40, 46-7. Festac officials said that the festival's propagation of black cultures and experiences would not entail "underrating or debasing the cultural values of other races": ibid p. 40.

86 Massino Teodori (ed), *The New Left: A Documentary History* (London: Jonathon Cape 1970) p. 277.

87 Kly, "Minority..." loc cit.

88 See Marquetta L. Goodwine, *The Legacy of Ibo Landing: Gullah Roots of African-American Culture* (Atlanta: Clarity Press 1998).

89 Such stately residences as "Tara" (a borrowing from Gaelic), grand domestic architecture that could draw on Greek buildings, were cited in retrospect as manifest proof of the "ascendancy of southern white civilization over all other civilized societies". Organized tours of such buildings, and representation of the Old South in fiction and film, diffused a myth of lost ordered happiness under slavery—which nonetheless was "the cultural reality that [into the mid-modern period] defined whites' [ascendant] social standing in Southern life" and subordinated that of the region's Negroes. Jack E. Davis, *Race Against Time: Culture and Separation in Natchez Since 1930* (Baton Rouge: Louisiana State University Press 2001) pp. 58-65. Tara is a village of eastern Ireland NW of Dublin. It was also the seat of Irish kings until the 6th century AD and thus was evoked by poet Thomas Moore (1779-1852) and then in romantic Irish nationalism.

90 Shlomo Katz (ed.), *Negro and Jew: An Encounter in America* (New York: Macmillan 1967): Jacob Glatstein p. 50; Leslie A. Fiedler p. 39; but cf. Steven S. Schwarzschild p. 109 who as a liberal wants Jews to develop more self-scrutiny than alibis of that type; and, also demurring somewhat, Katz xvii.

91 Gardell, *In the Name* p. 268; Brackman, *Ministry of Lies—The Truth behind the Nation of Islam's [Book] 'The Secret Relationship Between Blacks and Jews'* (New York: Four Walls, Eight Windows 1994).

92 See Ralph A. Austen, "The Unstable Relationship: African Enslavement in the Common History of Blacks and Jews", *Tikkun* 1995: v. 9:2 pp. 65-68, 86.

93 Internet: soc.culture.african.american, and soc.culture.jewish 26 September 1991

94 *Struggles* 68-69.

95 Margot F. Salom, *In Sure Dwellings: a Journey from Expulsion to Assimilation* (Adelaide: Seaview Press 2000) pp. 111-112; for a systematic study, Daniel M. Swetschinski, *Reluctant Cosmopolitans: the Portuguese Jews of 17th Century Amsterdam* (London and Portland: Littman Library 2000).

96 Winthrop D. Jordan, "Slavery and the Jews", *The Atlantic Monthly* September 1995 pp. 109-114.

97 Letter by Goldman, *The Atlantic Monthly* January 1996 p. 15

98 Jack Salzman and Cornel West, *Struggles in the Promised Land: Towards a History of Black-Jewish Relations in the United States* (New York: OUP 1997) p. 79.

99 Richard L. Zweigenhaft and G. William Domhoff, *Jews in the Protestant Establishment* (NY: Praeger 1982) p. 72.

100 *Struggles* 235-238; 251 fn 24; 76.

101 Salom, *Dwellings* 202-205.

102 *Struggles* pp. 73-74.

103 Playthell Benjamin, "African-Americans and Jews: a tattered alliance", *Emerge* 1990 pp. 73-8.

104 Saul S. Friedman, *Jews in the American Slave Trade* (State University of New Jersey: Transaction Publishers 1999) pp. 181, 183. Friedman highlights that Benjamin, during one meeting with pioneering Reform Rabbi Isaac Mayer Wise and a Christian versed in the Bible, did not contribute to a discussion of religious matters from any Jewish sources: p. 81. But it is unlikely that with his "renowned intellect" Benjamin really was so ignorant of even the Old Testament: rather, as a politician he was non-committal in a mixed setting.

105 For attempts by the Irish-American, Ya'qub Hussain McAteer to lobby for Palestine visiting Sinn Fein and U.S. politicians attending their functions, see "Irish-Palestinian Solidarity Comes Naturally", *New Trend* September 1997 p. 5; cf. McAteer's "Harriet Tubman Organization Remembers John Brown", ibid.

106 *Dwellings* pp. 205-206; cf. Stephen Birmingham *The Grandees: America's Sephardi Elite* (NY: Berkeley Books 1971) pp. 104-106.

107 Ralph Austen, op cit p. 68.

108 David Mills, "Half-Truths and History: The Debate Over Jews and Slavery", *Washington Post* 17 October 1993 p. C3. Mills estimated that 115 of Suriname's 400 sugar estates in 1730 worked with African labor, were owned by Jews: ibid.

109 Jordan, "Slavery and the Jews" p. 112.

110 Dr Alauddin Shabazz, "9 Out of 10 Slaves Died Aboard Jewish Ships", *New Trend* v. 19:8 Ramadan 1419/December 1998 p. 8.

111 Mills, loc cit.

112 Friedman op cit p. 249. This Jewish nationalist formulation of American society was inconsistent when it equated Farrakhan's drive to make education convey black nationality with the Nazis (ibid): Friedman and his colleagues were themselves using diverse media and new communal structures to convince as many compatriot Jews as they could that they were a separate nation in the U.S.

113 Ibid pp. 124-125.

114 Ibid p. 67.

115 In 1770 twenty-five percent of the Jews in America lived in the South, and in 1800 Charleston had more Jews than New York's developing Jewish minority. The South was "the stepping stone for many of the great American Jewish fortunes": Zweigenhaft and Domhoff (1982) pp. 71-72.

116 Mills, "Half-Truths and History…"

117 Irving Howe and Eliezer Greenberg (eds) *A Treasury of Yiddish Poetry* (New York: Schocken Books 1976) pp. 78-80, 74.

118 Hasia R. Diner in *Struggles* pp. 101, 97-98.

119 Salzman and West op cit pp. 220, 124.

120 Ibid p. 276

121 Ibid pp. 158-9

122 Harry Golden in Katz op cit p. 60.

123 J.A. Spender, *The America of Today* (London: Benn 1928) p. 141.

124 Spender pp. 149-150.

125 Ibid pp. 149-150.

126 Britain was more than a bogey for speeches by politicians. It has repeatedly manipulated its centrality in the Anglo culture it shares with key U.S. groups to finesse privileged economic relations out of them, and to draw America into the slaughter of the two world wars: see Christopher Hitchens, *Blood, Class and Nostalgia: Anglo-American Ironies* (London: Chatto and Windus 1990). William Hale Thompson (1869-1944), mayor of Chicago from 1915-23 and 1927-31, not just courting ethnic votes, fought England's abuse of her presence in U.S. culture, institutions and public space tooth and nail for decades. During WWI Thompson was unshakably pro-German, as mayor holding meetings to burn pro-British books taken from public schools; some race-Anglos gave him the nickname "Kaiser Bill" but could not faze him. Bhi se leoch mor!

127 Gilbert Osofsky, *Harlem, the Making of a Ghetto: Negro New York 1890-1930* (New York: Harper and Row 1966 pp. 175-176.

128 Spender op cit pp. 152-153.

129 Ibid p. 142.

130 Zweigenhaft and Domhoff, *Jews in the Protestant Establishment* p. 72.

131 See Lothrop Stoddard, *The New World of Islam* (London: Chapman and Hall 1921) and his *The Rising Tide of Color Against White World Supremacy* (NY: Charles Scribner's Sons 1921).

132 Y.N. Kly, *The Anti-Social Contract* (Atlanta: Clarity Press 1989) pp. 39-44.

133 Abdul Allah Muhammad, "It's gotta be this or that", *Final Call* 27 August 1996 p. 5.

134 Spender op cit p. 148.

135 George M. Fredrickson, *Black Liberation: A Comparative History of Black Ideologies in the United States and South Africa* (New York: OUP 1995) p. 71.

136 For case-studies of articulation of these three options of identification by three brilliant 20th century German-American writers, see Phyllis Keller, *States of Belonging: German-American Intellectuals and the First World War* (Cambridge, Mass.: Harvard University Press 1979).

137 For colonial America and the early USA see Noel Ignatiev, *How the Irish Became White* (New York: Routledge 1995).

138 Robert Hill (ed), *The Marcus Garvey and Universal Negro Improvement Association Papers* (University of California Press: 9 vols 1983-1990) v. 4 p. 336.

139 George E. Reedy, *From the Ward to the White House: The Irish in American Politics* (New York: Scribner's 1999) pp. 40-41, 103-105, and plates p. 7.

140 Essien-Udom, *Black Nationalism* p. 190.

141 *The Autobiography of Malcolm X* (Middlesex: Penguin Books) p. 425.

142 Nate Clay, "Chicago's Boss Daley: What is his legacy?", *Final Call* 15 January 1987 p. 12.

143 Clegg, *Original Man* pp. 164, 271.

144 Karl Evanzz, *The Messenger: The Rise and Fall of Elijah Muhammad* (New York: Pantheon Books 1999) p. 420.

145 Chapter 5 will review Harold Cruse's prescient alertness in his 1967 book to the first stirrings of a new micronationalism among Jewish-Americans in the 1960s, and his own parallel swing to Arab nationalist insurrections and polities. Both the later-1960s pro-Arab "Black Nationalists" of his type and the new Israel-drunk Jewish nationalist elite were clarifying and separating their new ideologies by arguing with each other.

146 Dr. Conrad Worrill, "Nationalism and Blacks", *Final Call* 15 January 1989 p. 23, 27. Cf. Cruse, *The Crisis of the Negro Intellectual* (NY: William Morrow Company Inc 1967).

147 Goldman, *The Death and Life of Malcolm X* (London: Gollancz 1974) p. 397.

148 Essien-Udom op cit pp. 197-198.

149 W.E.B. DuBois, *The World and Africa* (New York: Viking Press 1947) pp. 50-51.

150 Woodson, *The Negro in Our History* (Washington: Associated Publishers Inc 1922) pp. 20-21.

151 Claude A. Clegg, *An Original Man: The Life and Times of Elijah Muhammad* (NY:

Saint Martin's Press 1997) pp. 58-59; *Malcolm X on Afro-American History* p. 41: for Elijah's use of the motif, Essien-Udom pp. 132-133.

152 *Imam W. Deen Muhammad Speaks from Harlem N.Y.: Challenges that Face Man Today* (Chicago: W.D. Muhammad Publications 1985) pp. 13-14.

153 *The World and Africa* p. 186.

154 *The Negro in Our History* pp. 9-8.

155 Ibid p. 8.

156 Ibid p. 11.

157 Lorenzo Greene, *Working with Carter G. Woodson, the Father of Black History: A Diary 1928-1930* (Baton Rouge: Louisiana State University Press 1989) p. 276; Woodson *Negro in Our History* pp. 1-2; cf. DuBois *Africa and the World* p. 83—Africa's shortage of deep bays and harbors.

158 *Negro in Our History* p. 8.

159 *The World and Africa* p. 208.

160 *Negro in Our History* p. 12.

161 The Algerian legist 'Abd al-Karim al-Maghili enunciated lucid *fatwas* (legal rulings) to help guide Songhay's monarch, Muhammad Askia (r. 1493-1529) as a Muslim ruler to combat heretical innovations (*bida'*) and customs opposed to the faith, and to command his subjects to goodness. Al-Maghili was one conduit into the Songhay ruling royal and intellectual elites of the classical, very old, Islamist Arab explication of the rise and fall of regimes and states. One letter by him to Emperor Muhammad 'Askia urging him to impose Islamic dress for pre-pubescent girls had at its close a warning by the long-dead Arab Umayyad Caliph 'Umar Ibn 'Abd-al-'Aziz (r. 717-720): "the fates/judgements from God (*aqdiyah*) that befall people are in proportion to the wickedness/debauchery/impiety (*fujur*) they occasion/work (*ahdathu*). Fear God then, and scrutinize yourself before it is too late since death cannot be escaped". No doubt 'Umar, brief pietist ruler in an Umayyad dynasty afterwards ever denounced as secular, semi-pagan and hedonistic, and King Askia Muhammad in Africa seven centuries later, faced the same difficulty in imposing strict Islamic decency on an elite or population that had been formally Muslim for generations while all the while conniving (*yatawata'u*) at the offences, as al-Maghili depicted Songhay. See John O. Hunwick, *Shari'ah in Songhay: the Replies of al-Maghili to the Questions of Askia al-Hajj Muhammad* (NY/London: OUP 1985): Arabic text pp. 46-47.

162 Greene, *Working with Carter G. Woodson* pp. 256-8. It was only at the end of the 20th century that the bulk of this work was offered to English-readers by the English Arabist John O. Hunwick, *Timbuktu and the Songhay Empire: Al-Sa'di's 'Ta'rikh al-Sudan' down to 1613, and Other Contemporary Documents* (Leiden, Boston: Brill 1999). Hunwick refused to refer to French translations of the *Ta'rikh al-Sudan* and other Arabic chronicles and texts from West Africa because "I find myself so frequently disagreeing with the French translations": Hunwick, *Shari'a in Songhay* p. xv.

163 A.O. Stafford, "The Tarik El-Soudan", *Journal of Negro History* 2:2 (April 1917) pp. 139-146.

164 Greene, *Working With* p. 396.

165 *The Negro in Our History* p. 9: for the same argument but with more detail about blacks who achieved renown in Arab empires, DuBois' *The World and Africa* pp. 184-5.

166 Woodson, *African Heroes and Heroines* (1939) excerpted in James L. Conyers Jr (ed) *Carter G. Woodson: a Historical Reader* (NY: Garland Publishing Inc 2000) pp. 244-246.

167 *World and Africa* p. 176.

168 Ibid p. 183. Some classical Muslim writers—and modern pan-Arab Egyptian ideologues who drew on them—were unsure of the descent of Tariq Ibn Ziyad al-Laythi: al-Idrisi and Ibn al-'Adhari discussed if, as well as the probable Berber origin, Tariq might rather have been a Persian from Hamadhan who became a client-affiliate (*mawla*) of the Arab governor of North Africa Musa Ibn Nusayr: 'Abdallah 'Inan, *Tarajim Islamiyyah Sharqiyyah wa Andalusiyyah* (Cairo: 2nd ed,

Maktabat al-Khanji 1970) p. 131.

169 Du Bois, *World and Africa* p. 184. For al-Nadim, a dominant, expanding race can culturally absorb other races, somewhat changing in the process. A world religion such as Islam can provide the frame within which such amalgamation takes place. Concurrently with the expansions of Islam in Africa and Asia and "parts" of Europe, "the Arabs mixed/intermarried with the Persians, Syrians, Egyptians, Turks, [Byzantine] Greeks, Goths, and some Italians and French, Sudanese, the Abyssinians, the Indians, the Uigurs and others". Strengthened by a unifying religion, a new distinct "Arabized" *jins* (race/people) resulted, no members of which had any racial loyalty to external entities: "Tajadhub al-Jinsiyyat wal-Adyan" (The Constant Tugs-of-War Between Nationalities and Religions) *al-Ustadh* 14 March 1893 pp. 706-707.

170 *The World and Africa* pp. 188-9.

171 Ibid pp. 211-212.

172 Ibid p. 190. See Terrick Hamilton, *Antar: A Bedoueen Romance* (London: John Murray 1820 4 vls.

173 Lorenzo J. Greene, *Selling Black History for Carter G. Woodson: A Diary 1928-1930* (Columbia: Missouri University Press 1996) pp. 134, 138.

174 David Levering Lewis, *W.E.B. DuBois: Biography of a Race, 1868-1919* (New York: Henry Holt & Co Inc 1993) pp. 105-106. Another connection with DuBois was that she for years edited a column on music and the arts for the NAACP's magazine *The Crisis* of which DuBois was the famous editor **[-check to see if this belongs here]** Cuney, an historian of African and **black** music, collected songs in Mexico, the Virgin Islands, Puerto Rico and Cuba and indeed was the first scholar to direct attention to Creole music: her play *Antar of Araby* was staged in Boston under her direction in 1926. See Judith N. McArthur, "Maude Cuney-Hare", *The Handbook of Texas Online* update of 23 July 2001. Maude Cuney's magnum opus was her 1936 *Negro Musicians and their Music*

175 Text of Cuney-Hare's *Antar of Araby* in Willis Richardson, *Plays and Pageants from the Life of the Negro* (Great Neck, NY: Core Collection Books 1979) pp. 28-74.

176 Woodson *The Negro in Our History* p. 6. In his 1939 *African Heroes and Heroines*, Woodson categorized Queen Nefertari, wife of Ramses II (r. c. 1290-1224 BC), as among Egypt's many "Negroid rulers": however, conquests by the Persians (527 BC), Alexander (332 BC), the Romans (30 BC) and "the Mohammedan Arabs" in 638 AD all brought immigrations "that whitened the skin of the colored Egyptians": excerpt in Conyers op cit p. 242.

177 *Negro in Our History* p. 24.

178 Du Bois, *Black Reconstruction in America* (New York: Russell and Russell 1962) pp. 4-3.

179 *Negro in Our History* p. 16.

180 *The World and Africa* 194-5.

181 *The World and Africa* 69-77.

182 *The World and Africa* 224. DuBois also termed the modernizing or westernizing Sultan of Zanzibar Barghash Ibn Sa'id (r. 1870-1888) "a Negro Arab" "who actually suppressed the Zanzibar trade" *The World and Africa* p. 73.

183 Woodson reproduced a chilling 19th century (WASP?) etching recreating a slave-raid by orientally-garbed if rather dark Arabs on a peaceful African village: *Negro in Our History* p. 3; DuBois on the "blood and cruelty" that ivory occasioned in Central Africa: every scrap of ivory from an Arab trader was steeped in Negro blood: *World and Africa* p. 71.

184 Don McCurry, *The Gospel and Islam* (World Vision: Missions Advanced Research and Communication Center 1979) p. 230.

185 Harold R. Isaacs, *The New World of Negro Americans* (New York: Day 1963) pp. 214-216.

186 *The World and Africa* p. 71.

187 Ibid pp. 74-75.

188 Jacqueline Goggin, *Carter G. Woodson: A Life in Black History* (Baton Rouge:

Louisiana State University Press 1993) pp. 183-185. Cf Woodson, *The African Background Outlined, or Handbook for the Study of the Negro* (Washington: Association for the Study of Negro Life and History c. 1936)

189 Sylviane Diouf, *Servants of Allah* p. 190.

190 Ken Farid Hasan, "That Killing Image" pp. 20-21. Herskovits' non-Anglo Jewish national consciousness was expressed in his essay "Who Are the Jews?" on which he collaborated with wife Francis for the 1960 volume of L. Finkelstein (ed) *The Jews, their History and their Culture*: art. "Herskovits, Melville", *Encyclopaedia Judaica*.

191 Carter *The Negro* 5.

192 *Aut* 269.

193 *Aut* 480.

194 Dr Conrad W. Worrill, "Dr Woodson and Black History Month", *Final Call* 2 February 1999 p. 23. Cf idem "Breaking the Cycle of Miseducation", *Final Call* 15 September 1998 p. 23, which likewise pivots around Woodson's 1933 book *The Miseducation of the Negro.*

195 C. Asha Blake, "Editor's Statement", *Newscope* (student publication of Atlanta Metropolitan College), February 1992 p. 2.

196 Christy Priester, "Book Review: 'The Miseducation of the Negro'", *Newscope* February 1992 p. 7.

197 *Final Call* internet item datelined 4 December 1997.

198 John Henrik Clarke, "Africa in Early World History", *Ebony* August 1976 pp. 125-132. Other historians have rather extrapolated that most destruction after the Moroccan conquest was caused by attacks from plundering Bambara and Fulani blacks, and Tuaregs, that the small Moroccan garrison could not beat off

199 Yusuf Nuruddin in Yvonne Yazbeck Haddad and John L. Esposito (ed), *Muslims on the Americanization Path?* (OUP 2000) p. 230. Clarke was undoubtedly colored by the Islam he rejected: he frequented the Africa-orientated but Islamic bookshop of NOI intellectual Abdul Akbar Muhammad: Vibert L. White, *Inside the Nation of Islam: A Historical and Personal Testimony by a Black Muslim* (University of Florida Press: 2001) p. 64

200 Woodson (1939) in Conyers op cit p. 250.

201 Woodson 1939 in Conyers op cit pp. 250-251.

202 Imam A.A. Noah Sefullah, "Black History in Review—Keeping it Real," Muslim Journal 20 February 2004 pp. 10, 12, 27.

203 'Abd al-Malik Mohammed, "From Timbuktu to Detroit: Education remains a Priority," *Muslim Journal* 30 January 2004 pp. 3, 26.

204 Basheer Alim, "From Timbuktu to Detroit: Education remains a Priority," *Muslim Journal* 5 March 2004 pp. 1, 11, 12 22.

205 "Great Kings of Africa: Askia Muhammad Toure—King of Songhay (1493-1529" *Ebony* May 1976 pp. 78-79; "Great Kings of Africa: Shaka King of the Zulus," Ebony December 1976 pp. 78-9.

Chapter Three

The Difficult Rebirth of Islam Among African-Americans 1900-1950

This Chapter reviews social suffering of African-Americans, including racism, as the matrix within which neo-Islamic cults took shape from 1913-1945. Most analysis goes to (a) the Moorish Science Temple of North America (from 1913) and (b) the Nation of Islam of Wali Fard Muhammad and Elijah Muhammad (founded 1930). For this period, in which a dynamic Anglo-Americanist supremacist ideology had power throughout the USA, with only limited entry of Muslim discourse from the East, our focus must be on the construction of new black communities by neo-Islam. We will nonetheless assess the problems and potential the tenets of these two sects entailed for a longer-term linking of African-Americans to the Arab and Muslim worlds.

1: SOCIAL CHANGE AND THE BIRTH OF "THE MOORS"

The first serious neo-Islamic black movement in North America, the Moorish Science Temple of North America, was launched by Noble Drew 'Ali from Newark in 1913. This movement proclaimed that American blacks were really an exiled part of the "divine" "Asiatic nation", and that during a tour of the Arab world, the Sultan of Morocco had granted "Prophet" 'Ali "a commission" to reincorporate the American blacks into their original religion, Islam. The possibility that Drew was in part prompted to search for Islam as the original religion of his people by oral fragments handed down from a bygone slave-Islam has been noted by neo-Muslim blacks and Black Nationalists in the U.S. But the "Moorish" enterprise also is argued to have had links to more spurious and even commercialized sectors in mainstream American religious life. Since 1877, white Shriner freemasons in New York had claimed initiations from a Grand Sheik of Mecca, bestowed the title "Noble" on themselves, and worn fezzes on which were crescent moons and stars—all features that were to recur in the neo-Muslim sects to be headed by Noble Drew 'Ali and Elijah Muhammad, juxtaposed Turner (1997).[1] A succession of scholars, claiming to trace white American theosophical, esoteric and freemasonic writings and motifs that Drew and his deputies plagiarized without acknowledgment, has viewed the Arabic Qur'an to have had the least input into the special Moorish *Koran* that 'Ali penned. Be that as it may, Drew 'Ali did at the least give his nationalist, but politically non-confrontational, movement some trappings from Islam as white American theosophists and Shriner freemasons understood it at that time, but also from the Qur'an in an old British translation. Thus, Drew 'Ali started the ever-increasing infusion of atomized motifs from Islam into the American elements of street-level religion in African-American communities.[2]

While the focus of some in religious studies is with the Moors' religious motifs and concepts for their own sake, our concern is rather their functions within the long-term evolution of new community—at first a community fused from fellow-blacks in the U.S. itself, but later, in some spin-offs of Drew's sect at least, to include Third World Arabs and Muslims as well. How far did early "Moorish" concepts and discourse separate converts from the blacks and whites around them and from the central tenets of the Christianity that defined the thought and self-identification of most in the USA? How clear a sense could the Moors' discourse offer of the cartography of a homeland or homelands of U.S. blacks in North Africa and Islamic Asia, as a first preliminary to ultimately build real relationships with those states after they were to achieve independence following World War II?

The Social Crisis in which Indigenous Islam Took Form

The Moorish Science Temple of America and its ideology took shape and evolved in the context of a social and economic revolution in African-American history: the migration of millions of rural blacks from the South, and their crisis-dogged urbanization in the great industrial cities of the U.S. North. Economic hardships, dislocation and social disintegration worsened for the new black populations of the North's cities with the advent of the Great Depression in 1929. The teachings and community construction initiatives of the Nation of Islam—founded in the following year—responded to the heightened level of crisis that these new lumpen blacks now faced in the North.

At the turn of century, the overwhelming majority of the African-American people had lived in the South and were rural. Then, a depression in the cotton industry of those southern states, and a coinciding upturn in the industries of the great cities of the North, drew millions of blacks northwards to fill the desperate need of those factories for even unskilled labor. By 1920, about 35 percent of the African-American population had been urbanized in the North. Even after America's sectionally prosperous 1920s ended in the Great Depression, resulting in unprecedented rates of black unemployment even in the North, the migration northwards continued. By the 1970s, only 53 percent of the 28 million African-Americans still lived in America's Southern states.

Drew 'Ali, one of the migrants from Dixie, founded his sect in 1913 on the eve of the First World War. Although the manufacturing needs of that war offered some jobs in the North to the African-American immigrants, it was hard for them to establish themselves. The novel urban environments were bewildering, and while many of the migrants came from the South with limited skills and literacy, severe racism and exclusion from the white populations of the great cities into which they were moving made it much harder for them to earn legal incomes sufficient to survive.

This discrimination at a crucial point in the formation of African-American communities in the North was to figure in the 1990s in controversies about black demands for reparations not just from Anglo-Americans, who had been dominant at the time, but also from other white ethnic groups such as Jewish-, Polish-, and Catholic Irish-Americans that were expanding from 1900 as the result of ongoing mass immigration and had been simultaneously coalescing in the same cities in the period to 1930. These *ethne* had been less involved than "WASPS" (including Scottish-Americans) in earlier and segregation in the South. Racism's constriction of the opportunities and conditions of the black internal immigrants greatly increased the chances for upward social mobility of the foreign immigrants and their progeny who faced lesser prejudice from WASP Americans.

Black immigrants to Northern cities often received low wages because white-owned shops or companies or government offices mostly refused to employ them except as sweepers, porters or in other low- prestige jobs. The blending of low wages, maximum rents and segregation led to severe overcrowding in the new slums. In the 1920s, it became customary in Harlem for additional African-American tenants to sleep in shifts in bathtubs or on floors: as soon as one person woke up and rose, another would sleep on his bedding. This was wryly termed the "warm bed system" by the black immigrants .

Sometimes violent resistance from the already established white populations in those Northern cities met the arrival of the uprooted from Dixie. In Chicago, which from 1919 onwards became the center of the activities of Noble Drew 'Ali's Moors, and later those of Fard and Elijah's Nation of Islam Muslims, this white resistance was led by the Hyde Park Protection and Development Club. Headed by a prominent lawyer, Francis Harper, the Club organized boycotts of estate agents who sold or rented to blacks. The first black families that succeeded in buying or renting property were offered payments to leave: if they would not evacuate, their white neighbors would throw bricks through their windows (1909) or muster other measures to get them on the move.[3] Such Ku Klux Klan-like resistance to the arrival of Americans of the wrong complexion came from all groups of whites in New York, later the center from which Marcus Garvey was to urge African-Americans to migrate back to—Africa...

In 1910, John G. Taylor launched the Property Owners' Improvement Association in Harlem. He defined immigration by Southern blacks as an issue of whether the whiteman or the Negro would rule Harlem, and he called on the Christian and Jewish whites he represented to "drive them out" back to the slums in which colored people belonged. New York's white press in general vilified the arriving African-Americans as "the Black hordes" and "the Black plague." Taylor proposed that whites who lived close to blocks with black residents should build 24-foot-high fences.[4] The "Red Summer" of 1919 saw 26 major race riots in such major northern cities as the future Moorish and Black Muslim strongholds of Chicago, and Washington. The police looked on as white gangs slaughtered or terrorized the immigrant black populations.[5]

African-American Relations with Jews in the Early Twentieth Century

This earlier 20th century history of the painful transplantation of blacks from Dixie into the urban North provided many roots for the ethnic confrontationism between blacks and Jews that was to become so salient after 1967 in the USA's high politics and society. Crude prototypes of the parties to later full-blown conflict took form, including indigenous black neo-Muslim activists who propagated Islam by juxtaposing it against a white race enemy defined as Jewish as well as Christian. After 1967, the American Zionists, and then the Zionoid hard micronationalists, were to clamp a stifling hegemony down upon American Jewry, which they strove to forge into a political nation through a sometimes contrived polarization against African-Americans.

Yet pink and liberal Jews writing amid this pro-Zionist hegemony at the end of the twentieth century sought to discern some patterns for positive synthesis with African-American interests from the early 20th-century interaction with Jews. While acknowledging racism by some Jews, the liberal faction thus still maintained that Jews in general were kindlier or at least more neutral towards African-Americans than were Anglos or other Christian whites. Hasia R. Diner argued (1997) that "by and large, Jews did not respond violently to the increasing Black presence in their neighborhoods"—did not use intimidation, firebombs, or guns to "defend" their neighborhoods like Irish, Polish and other Christian whites had done, perhaps because their rapid rate of economic success allowed them to shift elsewhere, and because they had no "taste" for violence.

However, the grain of Diner's data can run against her arguments. Meyer Jarmulowsky, a Jewish homeowner and real estate developer, was a skilled member of the Property Owners' Improvement Association that Taylor founded. Rather than resorting to bricks through windows or bombs that were failing to block black immigration, Jarmulowsky tried to deflect yet more immigration by Blacks into Harlem by giving a talk to African-Americans at Harlem's St Philip's Church on "The Housing Problem from the Owner's Point of View." By stressing that lessor and lessee had opposite interests in the development of the suburb, Jarmulowsky—Diner allows—"clearly wanted to convince Blacks to cease any further forays into the neighborhood." While Diner stresses lower rates of home ownership among Jews in comparison to other white ethnic groups, and criticism in Jewish papers of Jews who took part in white organizations that tried to limit further arrivals of blacks, it becomes clear that communally-prominent, propertied Jews in New York did indeed fight such immigration in coordination with other white property-owners.[6]

The 1920s and 1930s saw the spread from the mid-West across the major cities of the U.S. North of "Jobs for Negroes" campaigns that reached their height in New York, now the major American city for both immigrant Yiddish Jews and blacks. To expand their ethnic group's small, shaky middle classes, African-American rights activists and clergy hit local chain stores, trucking companies, bakeries, butchers, pharmacists, cinemas, and dairies that refused to employ Negroes, with boycotts and pickets. In New York in particular, these businesses were heavily Jewish-owned.[7] There, leadership of the movement was taken by the early African-American Muslim activist, Sufi Abdul Hamid.

Despite anti-Semitism, economic interaction with Anglos in the great cities of the U.S. North opened avenues for employment and advancement to white Jews; interaction with Jews in either Jewish or WASP-owned businesses, though, seldom provided paths to bourgeois roles for immigrant blacks in New York. The Jewish component of the white race-antagonist was more than anti-Semitic imaginings. One of the most egregious discriminators against blacks seeking employment in New York was the Jewish Blumstein family who operated the largest store in Harlem. Their emporium could have become one significant nexus for the training and growth of an African-American petite-bourgeoisie, had the relationship evolved from some reciprocity between the two groups.

But even in his store that was in the heart of Harlem, where he faced few racist Anglo customers who might object, William Blumstein was resistant to employing any blacks at all. Even faced with demonstrations and boycotts organized by black militants, who included neo-Muslim Sufi Abdul Hamid, the originator of such slogans as "Share the Jobs" and "Don't Buy Where You Can't Work", he only doled out a few menial jobs. At least in the ethnic images constructed in 1943 by black journalist Roi Ottley, Blumstein was persistently resistant to granting young blacks any of the positions with bourgeois status demanded and taken by Yiddish-speaking Jews in the period—"clerical workers and salesgirls. As a sponsor of Negro charitable organizations and as the employer of Negro elevator operators, porters and maids, he explained that he had done his share for Negroes".

Thus, this obdurate enemy, not constrained in Harlem to discriminate by the racism of the Euro-American customers he had elsewhere, still had the face to ham the part of the benefactor to the very Negroes he helped to lock into harsh lumpen proletariat lives. But, paraded in the public space of Harlem, Islam was becoming a rallying-point for African-Americans against Jewish and other white traders as a towering Sufi Abdul Hamid strode down Lennox Avenue in a turban and a green velvet blouse. He claimed to know both Arabic and Pharaonic Egyptian as he "restored" a blended Afro-Islamic identity. While white businesses in the ghettoes had to cave somewhat before the unremitting black campaigns and threats and give some better jobs to African-Americans, the few black sales clerks they took on could quickly lose their jobs if the pressure let up in the slightest. Abdul Hamid's "roughnecks" responded with threats against white businesses that only gave the jobs to light-skinned African-Americans so long as they could get away with that.[8] Insofar as he was writing in 1943 for an in part Jewish readership, Ottley had sugared over the conflict he communicated with perhaps feigned dismissals of Abdul Hamid as a thug, stand-over merchant and con man—"a crude racketeering giant".[9]

However, a charlatan solely out to extract and profiteer would not have set his face against the organized government under which he would always have to live. That is what Abdul Hamid did when he defied warnings from the U.S. Attorney-General's office to the black press that it would slap $2000 fines, prison terms and possible loss of citizenship down on any Americans who left and joined the Ethiopian or Italian armies following Mussolini's invasion of Abyssinia in October 1935. Abdul Hamid became leader of the Black Legion, purportedly 3000 strong, that set up a training camp for 500 pilots and two full regiments of infantry. He said that his followers stood ready to renounce their American citizenship in order to defend their "mother country".[10] Abdul Hamid's activities for Ethiopia had a touch of the parade, the ritualistic pompousness, and also the same lack of attention to the nuts and bolts to carry tasks and functions through to completion, that had already vitiated the Garvey movement's attempts at transcontinentalism, and which was to dog the NOI and its successors after 1950. This self-styled "Amir al-Mu'minin" ("Commander of the Believers" =the term of the classical Arabs for their universal Caliph) had not shown enough realistic and hard-nosed attention to concrete difficulties and to how hard it would be to get any resources from a largely poor and hungry African-American people over to the faraway Ethiopians. Still, Abdul Hamid had courageously dramatized the Ethiopian cause to the masses of his people in New York, as well as publicizing Islam as a link for African-Americans to the political struggles of the continent of origin. Thus, the areas of inadequacy in his infant Afro-Islamic movement came in the setting of an untiring and effective organization on the ground of an internationalist protest movement of African-Americans.

Ottley characterized Sufi Abdul Hamid's Negro Industrial Clerical Alliance as made up of "hoodlums, idlers, relief recipients, and a discouraged fringe of high-school and college graduates"[11]—a blaming of the victims that implied that America was awash with jobs for all who wanted to work, which Ottley himself showed, elsewhere, was far from the case in that period. Ottley, in perhaps pro forma language, also accused followers of Abdul Hamid of extorting contributions from white small businesses in return for not pressing them on employing blacks—operating a protection racket. Yet the contributions Hamid and his followers won from whatever sources were not being consumed, but indeed being used to provide the long-term productive employment for the followers that their movement demanded: his HQ on 135 Street served as a combination meeting hall, butcher shop and grocery store.[12]

On the whole, Jewish-American works since 1970 have ignored, trivialized or criminalized the memory of Sufi Abdul Hamid, who prefigured so many patterns of the usage of Islam in the 1960s, 1970s, 1980s, and 1990s as a serious focus for national resistance and construction by African-Americans in a context that could differentiate whites, too, into plural micronations.[13] This is so even with John Kaufman, who of all the Zionist and Jewish micronationalist publicists and intellectuals who addressed relations between Blacks and Jews in the 1980s and 1990s, strove the hardest to see the points of view of the African-American side. Kaufman forgot the role of Abdul Hamid and Islam in organizing the popular resistance to Blumstein, even in a 1997 collection whose Jewish contributors all knew that they wrote in the shadow of the rise of Farrakhan. Such atomism among Jewish-American intellectuals and publicists prevented proper understanding of who the long-term parties were, leading to their grossly underrating Islam as a long-standing element in the core of the African-American nationality and struggle. In regard to his coreligionist or conational, the most Kaufman will allow is that the toxic antipathy William Blumstein pursued against black people had a touch of "condescension" in it.[14] A history that truly seeks out the long-term patterns and social logics of the reemergence of Islam among African-Americans in the 20th century will encompass the continuum in which neo-Islam has from its inception bid for converts and politico-economic leadership in Black America as a rallying-point against real, not only imagined, ill-treatment from within important strata of Jews.

The period of the simultaneous formation of huge Jewish-American and African-American populations in the North's cities saw exploitation of black women by a widening range of Jewish as well as Christian white classes that hired them as intermittent maids in a cash nexus that did not offer the longer-term securities, such as they were, of the old-time Anglo in the deep South. B.Z. Goldberg, a witness to the arrival of the masses from Dixie in a somewhat Jewish Harlem, recalled how the advent of the Depression enabled a widening gamut of white classes to impose ever more brutal terms upon poor African-American women in the 1930s and 1940s. As black men lost what jobs they had had in the North in the 1920s, middle class white women slashed the rates they paid for housework to 25 cents an hour. Negro women waited on certain corners of the lower middle-class neighborhoods to be picked up for a day's work—the "Bronx slave markets". Now, poorer Jewish and Christian white women who had never had their housework done for them also came to the slave market because of the unprecedented cheapness of the labor. "Poor themselves, they had the Negro women do the heavy work, ...and they were stern taskmasters" who enraged black women against Jews.[15] Two black women activists who ran themselves incognito through the slave market in 1935 found that after a day of often dangerous work, Bronx home employers, manipulators of the clocks, sometimes paid only a single dollar.[16] The unequal nexus of work as day-maids and cleaners also gave Jewish and other white males many chances to force desperate black women into sexual intercourse for money.

The African-American writer, Carl Offord, in 1940 perceived the Bronx street work-markets for black females as different visually but in nature the same as the auctioneering of chained half-naked Negroes in the pre-Civil

War deep South.[17] New York's Italian-American mayor, La Guardia, tried to ameliorate the misery by opening employment offices, but black activists claimed that these only "put a shed over the [slave] markets".[18] A rabbi did head an ecumenical "Bronx Committee for the Improvement of Domestic Employees" that favored unionization.[19] Some African-American domestics tried to fight back through unionism, but could not, in the Depression, soon wrest more humane conditions from their Jewish and Christian employers, given the desperation of masses of blacks to get any work, whatsoever. Yet a minority among these needy African-American women did form long-term relationships with some Jewish families in which they learned to speak Yiddish and took part in the rearing of their children: some deeper acculturation between the two groups did occur.

Farrakhan's mother, Mae Clark, supported her children by doing housework in Jewish homes in Boston in the 1930s. In his role as denouncer of the Jews after 1984, her son was to recall those risky days when the lined-up black women would be asked "You do clean windows, don't you?": "we left our homes uncleaned, yet we cleaned yours. We left our children unkempt to clean yours."[20]

A review of the history of the formation of ethnic communities in the cities of the U.S. North in the 1920s and 1930s, then, brings out the crucial help racial discrimination against African-Americans gave to the drive of non-Anglo ethnic groups, Jews among them, to make it into the middle classes. America, especially during the brutal Depression years, was nothing like a level playing field in which blacks had the same unhandicapped chance of winning the race but turned out not to have it in them (a frequent charge of the more race-focused Jewish-Americans of the liberal-Americanist 1960s, not to mention the Jewish nationalist neo-con publicists of the 1980s and 1990s). Rather, the light skins of the Jews and the equally disliked Irish and Italians at all points won them a margin of purchasing-power and opportunities from Anglos that got them through tight times and some Anglo dislike, to secure bourgeois roles, while discrimination, resources denial, exclusion, squalid segregated housing, high rents and much lesser purchasing power sank many African-Americans (and broke their family units) who also had had the needed qualities to succeed.

It is true that for WASP Americans, color difference, because it is so visible, acts a symbol that focuses the past history of and cultural distance separating these two ethne. Complexions helped make African-Americans the primary targets of discrimination, since new "white" groups might enlarge the dominance of the Anglo-American ethnos by affiliating to it, accepting the brutal bargain that they would relinquish their distinct cultures.

But at least some anti-black racism of some Jews was an active choice that evolved and burgeoned in some independence of pressures from white society at large. It served well the achievement of bourgeois prosperity by Jews as a constituent part or adjunct of the white people of Middle America now being constructed. Racism made Jewish-owned department stores significant nexii for discriminatory class formation of Jewish-Americans and

WASP-Americans at the expense of the development of African-American populations that had moved to the same great cities from the U.S. South.

Still, Jewish-American intellectuals from the 1960s argued that African-Americans fell into anti-Semitic stereotyping that did not understand Jewish experience when blacks saw as "Jewish" some WASP-owned or WASP-directed enterprises or institutions that only employed Jews as the collectors or enforcers whom the blacks then directly experienced. Arthur A. Cohen recalled (1966) a 'forties mid-West university of Anglos that owned much of the Negro slum but "diabolically" employed Jewish rent collectors who copped the hatred: "the Jew is no more nor less than he has ever been, the viator and conduit of the hatred of one section of Christendom against another."[21] Yet did immigrant or second-generation Jews really have no choice but to take such employment? Did they really have to brutalize African-Americans as the means to join the Angloid mainstream—all ethnic components of which were to be argued by Farrakhan and non-Muslim black nationalists in the later 20th century to owe reparations to African-Americans?

The North's unemployment, higher rents for blacks, and the refusal of many whites to let black immigrants leave their deteriorating quarters for better ones combined to make the poor ex-Southern Negro a prisoner of the ghetto much more than for immigrant Irish or Jews who also faced, as "foreigners", their share of grinding poverty, textile sweatshops, slums and ethnic and cultural hatred from the self-styled "native" Anglo-Saxon Americans. Such neo-American white ethnics could reach the point of economic take-off more quickly and easily than blacks born as Americans because, to cite one crucial aspect, the rents they paid were less: then, the white skin pigmentation allowed the second generation to pass as culturally integrated Americans and thus leave the slums for the rewarding if brutal American mainstream.

The Moorish neo-Islamic movement was only a part of the widespread efforts by would-be entrepreneurs among the African-American immigrants in the North to construct a black private enterprise that would serve a nationalist clientele, and be sustained by it in the face of the racist drive to rig the race to form a bourgeois echelon in each ethnos.

2: THE MOORISH SCIENCE TEMPLE OF AMERICA

Negroes who left the South had hoped to find white fellow-Americans in the North of a more open disposition than some of their recent neighbors. Instead they found Northern whites as determined to bar and pen them in as the South's worst "crackers". The Moorish "national movement" unfolded after 1913 in response to that exclusion. As an ostensible alternative to the Americanism that rebuffed, Drew 'Ali and his colleagues asserted that the American blacks belonged to an Asiatic "Moslem" civilization—a thesis viewed then and even now by some black nationalists dedicated to restore links to black Africa as an attempt to evade the shame of provenance from a continent that the USA's white culture of the period lampooned as barbaric, and the underdevelopment of which it still stresses in the 21st century.

It is true that Drew's teachings located the original homeland of the blacks outside the continent of Africa, in the formation and diversification of the various Semitic peoples. He was in part influenced by the Old Testament in that. The blacks of America are the descendants of the Moabites and the Canaanites who were expelled by Joshua from the land of Canaan during the Hebrew conquest. The Pharaohs of Egypt allowed those expelled Asiatics to settle in Egypt: they proceeded to found the Holy City of Mecca and also built for themselves great kingdoms in North Africa, namely Morocco, Algiers, Tunis, Tripoli, etc. (their empire encompassed the Americas as well). This narration of the great past and original homelands of which African-Americans have been robbed prefigured the Nation of Islam's mythologies after 1930, which also located the original homeland of the American blacks in West Asia (Mecca), from which it then had them migrate to North, and finally West, Africa.

Using the language of vivid religious fable to get it all across, Noble Drew 'Ali diffused a thesis also being developed in more rational and scholarly, historicist, terms by some secular black nationalist professional historians such as W.E.B. DuBois, who long argued the interaction and organic connectedness linking the continent of Asia to that of Africa, and the Asiatic dimension of the identity of the blacks in Africa, from among whom the forefathers of African-Americans were brought in chains to the New World.

As well as the Semitizing Bible, Drew 'Ali's MSTA in part drew its definition of African-Americans as "Moors" from Shakespeare's and white Christian Americans' orientalist conflation of black African Muslims and Maghribi Arabs as both "Moors," during the slavery era. This term functioned to help racists minimize merit to Black Africa and to enslaved Africans who had skills and could read Arabic. Yet we saw in Chapter 2 that some of the Muslims enslaved in America had had political and lineage links to the North African states that Drew evoked, defined as "Morocco" the homeland from which they were torn, and that one was able to correspond in an Arabic so excellent that he was able, from another continent, to convince Maghribi (Moorish) Arabs who had political power on that other side of the very wide Atlantic that he was their relative whom they had to help.

Drew's sect was a mechanism crafted to guide bewildered ex-rural blacks from the South to build new community in the face of the deprivations and the trauma-inducing racism that buffeted them in the unwelcoming mega-cities of the U.S. North. By imposing different types of frugality and self-discipline, the sect gave its male and female converts both the motivation and better odds to reconstruct—on patriarchal, Anglo-like lines—African-American families, which in that period faced disintegration in the inhospitable Northern urban environment. Religious rites inside the sect's temples were designed to induce thoughtfulness and to constrain romantic or sexual feelings alternative to marriage. Friday prayer services tended to proceed amid a grave-like solemnity and silences, with scant use of music and with the two sexes seated on separate sides—a contrast to Christian churches, especially to those exuberant fundamentalist black churches the converts had left in the deep South.

While in some parts of West Africa, women had a more diverse range of roles in economic activity, in society and politics, and in marriage than in patriarchal Western and Arab societies, in North America, the slave-owners had often deliberately separated the fathers from mothers and children to atomize the populations they exploited. The low wages and intermittent employment of many African-American males who had migrated to the North's mega-cities made reluctant matriarchal heroines of black women who had to scrub the floors of Christian and Jewish whites for minimal wages to somehow support their latch-key children. To transform that disintegration, the Moorish temples, encouraged by the Qur'an and accounts of Arab Islam in the U.S. press, strove to condition the adult adherents to attempt stable patriarchal families that would also have a middle-class WASP texture. The leaders urged the males to assume the main economic role in the family and wives to obey their husbands, and discouraged divorce. Food prohibitions, passing beyond abstention from pork to a quasi-vegetarianism, (a) aided accumulation of basic savings/capital and (b) were a cultural emblem of the transformation of the personality and life-style of poor blacks that Drew and his movement were attempting.

Yet the problems in maintaining families—or evolving new middle-class patriarchal families mainly modeled upon WASP Middle America—were structural to the poor performance of the American economy at the level of these unskilled immigrants, and the constriction of money and entrepreneurial opportunities due to discrimination and segregation. The African-Americans would have to launch and develop—sustained by the extra motive of the religious value that this neo-Muslim sect put upon the endeavor—their own economic circuits. By launching various collectivist shops, farms and other economic projects, the sect tried to equip the blacks to successfully compete with Euro-Americans according to their WASP patterns, as a marginal appendage to white American private enterprise (which the Moors' businesses conceivably might enter at a later stage if America were modified).

Robert Dannin (2002) has interpreted that—beneath all the MSTA's Anglo-freemasonic stage properties, contrived rituals and the fustian—some of the nostrums, herbs and charms that the Moorish movement sold, and the turbans, robes and pantaloons they donned as a "Moslem" national costume had in them some faint but real historic reference, handed down in folk-memory in the South from Muslim Africans who had been brought there as slaves.[22]

Still, the sources of the sect's formal metaphysical tenets were also at many points very American: the Moorish movement injected an infusion of upper-class Anglo-American literary culture into semi-literate African-American masses. Scholars have argued that over 19 of the 48 chapters making up Drew 'Ali's composite *Moorish Science Temple Koran* had been lifted by him with only limited changes from a well-styled apocryphal gospel penned by the white theosophist, Levi H. Dowling (1844-1911), *The Aquarian Gospel of Jesus the Christ*, published in the United States in 1908. This work, so replete with the mystical, masonic and theosophical current in the USA's white upper crust, set out claimed acts and teachings of "Jesus" in his early youth during his supposed travels in Egypt, India and other places of the ancient world before he assumes his role as a prophet in Palestine.

The scholarship has asserted that Dowling's book contains many religious ideas or attitudes later mutated, beyond the Moors, by the Black Muslim movement—most crucially, mystical themes about a unity between man and God or that God expresses himself through man—ideas which had been spread by 19th century New England Transcendentalism, which found expression in such organized American religions as Christian Science. It should also be borne in mind here that Emerson and his friends had had a lively interest in works of Persian Islamic sufism then being introduced to the West by German litterateurs and early orientalists.[23] Noble Drew 'Ali demonstrated theosophical (and possibly Druze) influence in the respect he voiced for such founders of Afro-Asian religions beyond the Middle East as Buddha and Confucius, whom he termed prophets of Islam (along with Zoroaster). [True, it is a concept in the Qur'an that Allah has sent messengers and warners to all peoples (e.g. Q 10:47)—although orthodox Muslim thinkers before the West's conquests were reluctant to apply this to such figures beyond the Middle East as Krishna]. Dowling had Jesus travel to India to learn from Brahmanical priests as well as Pharaonic ones in Egypt.[24]

Theosophism, founded by Madame Blavatsky in the United States in 1875, stresses the never-ending continuity of human life, adapting from Hinduism the idea of reincarnation of a pious individual after his death in another human individual. After the death of Noble Drew 'Ali, subsequent leaders in his fragmenting sect were to claim that they reincarnated the spirit of their late leader. This reincarnation was in the context of a collectivist quasi-nationalist movement by an "Asiatic" "Moslem" nation that had always existed. Drew's successors could also have drawn incarnationist ideas from residues from African religions in African-American folklore and from immigrant Druze Arab peddlers and shopkeepers.[25] In contrast, Elijah Muhammad's Nation of Islam from 1930 articulated the idea of a vicarious immortality that comes through the continuity of the black nation whose collective immortal life proceeds despite the deaths of individuals. This idea has affinities to early Judaism that focused upon the surviving nation without concern for afterlives for individuals (to be developed in post-classical Judaism as the *ha-Olam ha-Boah*, "the world that is to come"). More like the ideas of afterlives and immortality for individuals articulated by the Arabic Qur'an is Drew 'Ali's concept that "after death the soul goes to the abode of Allah."[26] [Ideas of the Nation as the only, vicarious, immortality for individuals were also articulated in Egypt in the 1930s as a reinvention of ancient Pharaonic thought and culture by such neo-Pharaonic nationalists as playwright Tawfiq al-Hakim when they wanted to limit or cut out homogenizing Arab, and perhaps Islamic, influences.]

Christian Science, with its mystic idealism, denied the reality of the material world and that Jesus gave his life as vicarious atonement for human sins. Mary Baker Eddy depicted Jesus as a fallible man who accommodated his preaching to the masses' illusion that there was a material world and illnesses: this prefigured the Black Muslims' matter-of-fact sense of Jesus after 1930 as a small-time preacher. Christian Scientists sometimes conceptualized God as impersonal: that might have helped to prepare African-Americans to grasp Islam's totalist monotheism when they encountered it.[27] The Moorish movement, like the Scientists, practised faith-healing of sick followers, and denied the divinity of Jesus as had the Qur'an also. The discourses of the Moorish movement never mentioned Trinity, and spoke of "the one Allah, the author, the creator, the governor of the world." Elijah Muhammad was to dismiss the trinitarian division of Godhead into a Father, Son and Holy Ghost as a "polytheist" Christian belief: thus, the Moors and the Nation of Islam both asserted an Islamic belief in God's Oneness (Arabic: *tawhid*) when they were defining their new sects against Christian America.[28]

Overall, then, the Moors inducted into then-existing African-American religious life some dislocating fringes and heterodox elements of white American intellectualism and religion. These then set off a long-term devolution in Afro-America towards such concepts of Islam as a monotheism that targeted the central tenet of Christianity. The segments of Anglo-Saxon religious discourses that Drew selected bore the first odd passages from the Qur'an that this new tradition henceforth would more and more project to African-Americans over the decades. Drew characterized his sect as believing in a single God free from defects who was Transcendent and Impersonal although He could manifest some of His perfect attributes in good humans. [Classical Islam does have an idea that the believers should cultivate in themselves the divine ethics of God]. Drew 'Ali characterized this monotheism as the first pillar of Islam upon which all its other beliefs hang: "nothing happens without [God's] knowledge and will: He neither begets nor is He begotten" [cf. Qur'an surah 112 "al-Ikhlas"—"Pure Monotheism"].[29]

In the religious vision of Drew 'Ali and his adherents, Jesus was not a person of God or the son of God, but His prophet—as the Arabic Qur'an had taught. One scene in the sect-composed Koran indicates that Jesus was merely a human being: when some people try to worship him, he rebukes them, saying that he is their brother in humanity, come solely to show them the path that leads to God—"do not worship the son of man but praise the holy God." By moving African-American discourse away from Christianity's trinitarian basis, 'Ali thus directed the minds of his 40,000 followers, and the much larger audience that received his communications without joining, towards ideas of monotheism close to those propagated by orthodox Islam. Yet some attenuated relics of Christianity lingered, for example in the motif that Jesus, the Canaanite prophet, was killed by white Romans—a motif to be carried on in the coming Nation of Islam's narration of history, although the Arabic Qur'an had stated that Jesus' enemies "neither killed him nor crucified him: rather, a likeness of that was presented to their minds/the matter was made confused to them".[30]

The MSTA and the Nation of Islam, then, still maintained vestigial crucifixion stories as they rehumanized the prophet Jesus. Christianity had sunk deep in America into a Negro minority that had once been animist or Muslims in Africa. True, a ghost of an awareness that their forefathers had had a scripture of their own before Christianity, and had not thought Jesus God, may never have quite died in areas of the South where there had been many enslaved Muslim Africans, such as Sapelo Island.

Christian, secularist and Sunni Muslim academics and writers long charged Drew with exuberant plagiarism of the theosophical writings of his white fellow-countrymen—and that some of his communications to his Black target-audience had the tone that he was entertaining them like a conjurer in circus fun whose final outcomes for them might be far from divine or stellar. Yet Orientalist concepts of plagiarism from U.S. texts have not much discredited the Moorish movements among African-Americans. Moorish ideology sees successive prophets and messengers as each having been missioned by God to use a specific language drawn from the environment and special needs of each recipient nation: the message of Islam has to be cast in local terms and local language each time to be made understandable and beneficial to each nation. Yet the message always keeps its same simple essence that comes from God.

In contrast to the focus of more accommodationist black Protestants on relief and rewards in the Afterlife, both the Moors and the first NOI invested value in this life and world: that would motivate their adherents to carry through a new black private enterprise or conduct national movements in the here-and-now. The Moorish "Koran" has Jesus say: "my brother man,... your heaven is not far away... is not a country to be reached: it is a state of mind." Thus, humans could themselves create their own heavens and hells in their lives in this world. The early "Black Muslims" who succeeded Drew depicted Heaven and Hell as not other places but earthly conditions that the individual creates for himself in his own life within social hierarchy and America's modern economy. As Elijah Muhammad put it, "the earth is our home... if we follow and obey Allah and his Prophets, we make it a heaven; if we follow the Devil [whites] we make it a hell."[31] Both the Moors and the early Nation of Islam (the "Black Muslims") fully registered white hatred in the Northern cities, and seemed to advise withdrawal or avoidance. Yet their related ideologies had a sharp focus on this life and the nuts and bolts of success in it that builds the economic Black Nation—but which might one day incorporate Blacks into the white-originated mainstream if it only opened up to them. Greater employment and business relations with whites would after 1975 pose how much assimilation to Anglomorph America that was to entail, as the era of micronationalisms got under way in America.

Drew and his Moorish movement diffused a sense of (a) deculturation and the vital need to recover the robbed authentic "national names" and (b) the immanence of a Divine judgment. Both prefigured "Black Muslim" concerns. Because of sin and disobedience, every nation suffered slavery for disrespecting the belief and principles of their forefathers. For that reason, the "nationality" of the Moors had been stripped from them in 1774 and the Asiatics now of America were given such false designations as "Negroes",

"Blacks" or "colored people." African-Americans live a constant crisis of rootlessness and moral disintegration in the United States because of the cultural aggression that the whites wage against them. The name of a people means everything: thus, when "the palefaces" (Euro-Americans) took away the name of the Moors they robbed them of their strength, their authority, their flag, their land, their God, and their name—"everything". For that reason, at a time when judgement day was very close, the Moors were handing back the church and its Christianity to the Europeans while themselves returning to the "Moslemism" [*sic*] that their forefathers founded for their salvation both in this world and the hereafter. To rectify the present painful and grotesque situation, every nation would have to worship under its own vine and fig tree, because when every racial group has its own religion appropriate to it, peace will reign in the world.[32] The Bible's fig tree and vine as symbols of African-American withdrawal and separation were to be recycled in a more political and aggressive form by the Nation of Islam orator, Malcolm X.

More than the succeeding Nation of Islam, Drew 'Ali steered his adherents away from any showdown with whites. His movement sometimes at least went through the motions of teaching allegiance to America's stars-and-stripes, while not so ambiguously having its own Morocco-derived flag. Drew's discourse, though, enraged his following by feeding the heightening sense of many that "paleface" slavery had torn away the previous cultural roots their African ancestors had had, prior to their arrival in the New World. Because they had lost their historical memory of the Islamic homeland, and the Christian European civilization of the whites had come to dominate them, they had lost any basis for a life of dignity and freedom, because for any people to get any importance they must have a land but also a national name, as Moorish discourse argued.

The growing scholarly literature has thus far presented only limited or incomplete data on interactions by Noble Drew 'Ali or his adherents with the Arab peddlers and shopkeepers who were numerous in the large Northern cities of the United States, or on any direct sources from which the sect might have derived data from Middle Eastern politics. True, the Moorish mention of the anti-imperialist Iranian Jamal al-Din al-Afghani (1838/1839-1887) as having initiated Drew's parents into his salafite pan-Islamism during a visit to the U.S. in the early 1880s, intrigues: the historical al-Afghani did voice a vision that Islam should be propagated in America and may have interacted with one or two pro-Islam WASP Americans for such a purpose.[33] Had an agent of some serious Muslim missionary circle in the Arab World/the Ottoman Empire, or Ottoman intelligence already begun to spread ideas among the generation of the parents of the young men who founded the MSTA in 1913? The Moors read the American press and thereby became aware of the names of some current Middle Eastern leaders such as Ibn Sa'ud who had seized the holy city of Mecca from Lawrence of Arabia's Hashimites in 1924.

Despite their inability to establish or re-establish historical relations with the Arab world, Drew was successful through his rhetoric in evoking a conflict between two hostile civilizations: (a) the East, which he identified with Islam and (b) the West. This rhetoric did sometimes have a sort of globalist élan that passed far beyond the parochially American nature of the real issues facing his adherents. He exaggerated the importance of the power of names in a way that obscured the other economic, social and political dimensions of oppression: it was not solely by imposing such names as "Negroes," "Ethiopians", etc., that the whites had been able to inferiorize the dark Moors living in the United States. Drew evoked important linkages with Asia and Africa as one general whole—with the gamut of that East's religious and mystical philosophies as these had been imaged and popularized by the current of theosophy in American intellectual life, not just with Islam alone.

The sect said that American blacks belong to two homelands simultaneously: their direct geographical homeland and their original Asiatic homeland in North Africa. To assert their extra-territorial identity, the followers wore "oriental" robes and fezzes modeled on photographs of North African and pre-Ataturk Turkish garb. Yet, on the whole, they steered clear of a flavor of popular American journalism and philistine freemasonic rituals. Each member had to place the suffix "el" after his name, with the title "Bey" as a special honorific—a pro forma minimum for connecting with the Middle East. Every male member had to wear a fez throughout the day, both in the open air or indoors. Some leading preachers of the sect's temples bore the title "sheik," indicating a certain knowledge of some religious ranks in the Arab East (or is this just Shriner papier maché?).

However, the sect also granted some supervisory roles in its temples to women members, who were then given a feminine version of the title, "sheikess", that stems from the linguistic patterns of English, not Arabic. The MSTA asserted an affiliation to the Islam of the Muslims of Africa and Asia centered in Mecca. Thus one edition of the "Holy Koran" penned by Drew 'Ali carried a photograph of Ibn Sa'ud after he had conquered the Hijaz and its holy cities in 1935, with some distortion of his name, and introducing him as the descendant of Hagar [the ancestor classical Arab geneologists asserted for the Arabs]: Ibn Sa'ud was now the head of the Holy City of Mecca. At least verbally, Drew asked his followers to implement the "Divine Laws" of Mecca in their daily life as part of the process of their affiliation as "true Moslems" to the wide Islamic homeland of which Ibn Sa'ud was one crucial head. We do have, in such motifs of Drew 'Ali as this and his narrative that the Sultan of Morocco commissioned him to restore African-Americans to their original Islam, at least a theoretical recognition that Arab leaders in faraway Eastern countries have custodianship of the authentic Islam and that the African-American Asiatic Moors in America, to be true Muslims, have to take a form of Islam from them that they validate. There was here a basis or impulse for affiliation by this American sect to the Islamic World that was only to be fulfilled much later when the space between America and the rest of the globe shrank towards the end of the century.

How far towards the Arab and Muslim World did Drew 'Ali and his followers advance in his lifetime? The sect handed out to each new convert an identity card which promised that he/she would, by embracing "the Divine Laws of the Koran of Mecca", win love, friendship, peace, freedom and justice. The cards carried at their top the twin symbols of the star and crescent under which was written "Islam" and the word Unity above two hands shaking. The adjustment to the norms of the Arab World's Islam was confined to a few rudiments during and for many years after the death of Drew: rather than mosques, the sect's places of worship continued to be termed temples—a term to which the black Muslim sect launched by Wali Fard Muhammad in 1930 would also long hold for its places of worship—even after its interaction with Arab states tightened from the 1950s. While the wording and movements of the prayer had not much connection with the Arabic prayers of Islam (Drew's people did not prostrate themselves), his adherents turned East to Mecca to pray standing three times every day, raising their hands as they did so. Their three prayers of sunrise, noon, and sunset[34] are like the three time-intervals to which slavery chipped down the originally five-times-daily ritual praying that Muslim Africans performed when first brought to America. Other key approaches to the practice of Islam in the East were the prohibition of alcohol, the separation of men and women during the congregational prayer, the choice of Friday for that service as in the Arab world[35] and that the sect seldom used musical instruments in its temples, although rhythmic music is a characteristic of worship among most Christianity-derived Negro sects.

During the service, the adherents used to sit on chairs and sing snatches from well-known Christian Negro spirituals with the words adapted to the themes of their new creed, in particular its assertion of an Islamic separation from Christianity. Thus, the sentence "Give me that old time religion" was changed into "Moslem's that old time religion"—which we saw it really had been for many enslaved Africans and their offspring in early America. As was the case with the places of worship of the Nation of Islam later, the presence of chairs in Moorish temples made it physically impossible to practise the prostrations of the conventional Islamic ritual prayer. As well as asserting the prophethood of Drew 'Ali, the sect further placed itself beyond the pale of the East's Islam by its assertion of reincarnation, although that was an heretical tenet of Druze-Arab and Isma'ili Indic immigrants in North America.[36] One scholar has argued from early texts of Drew's movement that his Moorish Science temples had contact with immigrant Druze in the inner areas of Newark, New Jersey and other cities in the formative period.[37] Akbar Muhammad, the highly analytical and ironically detached—but Arabic-literate—son of Elijah Muhammad, and an individualist, categorized Drew 'Ali as having founded a "pseudo-Islamic movement", albeit one that drew on the India-influenced theosophist modality of neo-Islam founded in the 1890s by Muhammad Alexander Russell Webb, an honorary consul of Turkey in New York who became the first white American convert to Islam.[38]

Overall, Drew 'Ali's sect failed in his lifetime as an attempt to reconnect the peoples of the Arab Islamic world and American blacks through a restoration of the Islamic religion among the latter. It had created fewer real avenues of communication to Muslims or Arabs in the East than its ostensible tenets promised. On the other hand, it had motivated and disciplined its converts so that they could carry through the building of a nation crafted to achieve modern economic activity. In this, with the high ambiguity of all African-American Muslim protest sects, it had made its congregations much more similar not only to Arab Muslims, but to the enemy Anglo middle-Americans. Thus, those African-Americans who had been molded into "Moors" now had some cultural affinities with a range of outsider groups with whom they might later try to construct extended relationships, depending on how those other groups looked at them.

We have not been so concerned to detail the religious rites and teachings of the Moorish Science Temple of North America in and of themselves. Instead, our focus has been on the longer-term social effects of this national movement in preparing essential conditions for African-Americans to build new Islamic community both in the Negro sectors of the U.S. population, and externally with overseas Muslims. There is no doubt that Drew's movement was successful in severing the Christian religious community that black Americans had had with their white compatriots. Drew, in his own "Holy Koran" had indeed successfully mustered enough dissident elements from the Qur'an and from such white sources as Dowling's Aquarian Gospel to sever the concepts that had bound African-Americans to American Christianity.

Long term, then, Moorish endeavors could connect African-Americans to both Third World Muslims and U.S. whites. Drew snapped the monopoly and grip that trinitarianism had had on the thinking of his people, setting them free to chose from a variety of religions and discourses, foreign and American. The MSTA had started projects to induct the followers into the mainstream private enterprise economy of the Northern cities, adding a religious motivation to the material one to increase those followers' staying-power. Drew 'Ali had held out to vulnerable African-Americans in a restored national authenticity some concepts and narratives he had ripped from the experience of U.S. whites. Yet this covert connecting in the name of revolt and authenticity of African-Americans to non-Black groups in the USA/the West and in the Third World, simultaneously, was less trickery or cynicism than a crucial function of all these neo-Muslim movements which are so dualistic in their protest against White America.

Recent and ongoing research and scholarship is showing that Drew 'Ali and his colleagues did start more preliminary interaction with real Third World Arabs and Muslims in America than previously thought—although still within one ethos in U.S. freemasonry that can deconstruct the religions it lets into its structures, emptying them of many of their previous specific meanings. While the sect had popularized as theory the cartography of a homeland or homelands of provenance in North Africa and Islamic Asia, it should be kept in mind that there were, in adjacent milieus in the northern cities of America, acculturated Arab and Muslim nationalists who could directly convey the viewpoints of actual independence movements in the colonized Third World.

3: THE GARVEYITE MOVEMENT AND ISLAM

Marcus Aurelius Garvey, a Jamaican, founded the Universal Negro Improvement Association in 1914. He hoped to make it the instrument to link all Negro populations throughout the world, aid their education and modernization, and to establish a politically sovereign "central nation for the race" to help Negroes everywhere develop. Garvey and his colleagues ambiguously urged blacks in the Americas to "return to Africa" either by physical "repatriation" or psychically through cultural reconnection and solidarity. While based in Harlem from 1916 to his expulsion by the U.S. government in 1927, Garvey recruited hundreds of thousands into the UNIA: it was a true mass movement that not just proposed an Africanist black nationalism to the whole black population in the U.S. but established chapters in Africa itself, although Garvey lacked the management skills to carry through the possible relationship of African-Americans and Africans by duplicating the West's modern instruments (e.g. shipping lines).[39]

The communications of Garvey and his colleagues were marked by religious flux. The birth of separatist black Christian churches in North America in the 1920s was patronized as well as ideologically stimulated by the Garveyite mass movement. UNIA parades in the USA had huge paintings of the Black Madonna and her Black god-child. The revolt of Garveyite clerics against mainstream Christianity's depiction of divine and holy figures as white anticipated or helped set off similar volleys by Elijah from 1930, to be carried on discreetly after 1975 by his "reformed", "neo-integrationist" son Wallace/Warith in "inter-religious dialogue" that in removing images of the divine was to assault Christian incarnationism even from within the black churches he finessed. Numerous articles were published in the Garveyite movement's newspaper, *Negro World*, with its 200,000 U.S. readers, and later in the much less circulated magazine, *The Black Man*, elaborating on the religion of Islam and disparaging established Christianity as in the control of racists hostile to Africa.

UNIA Interactions with Middle Eastern Muslims

In his early London period, the young Garvey's formative ideological mentor was the ese-Egyptian, Duse Mohammed 'Ali (b. Alexandria 1866; died Lagos 1945). While long residence in Britain had made Duse culturally perhaps more English than Arab, his lobbying journal *African Times and Orient Review* still carried a section in Arabic. Through Duse, the impressionable Garvey had access to data straight from the Egyptian independence movement launched by the France-influenced Mustafa Kamil (d. 1908), who also had tried to construct a global pan-Islamic community with modern West-patterned instruments, anticipating Garvey's drive to thread Black Americans and Black Africa together through steamers and trade. The influence could have been two-way. The Kamilist daily, *al-Liwa'*, had from Cairo covered President Theodore Roosevelt's gesture of inviting the black lecturer, Booker T. Washington, to dinner, drawing threats from the Southern states to have Roosevelt assassinated as Lincoln had been. Another item detailed lynchings, and violations by whites of black women in the USA's Southern states.[40]

Duse Mohammed 'Ali was to join Garvey in the U.S. in the early 1920s, becoming one of the editors of the movement's *Negro World* daily: his "Foreign Affairs" column in 1922 concentrated heavily on Egypt, Turkey and Islam. Drew 'Ali occasionally praised Garvey and he and at least some followers undoubtedly read *Negro World* sometimes. The Egyptian independence movement of Mustafa Kamil had formulated approaches to create a modern global Islamic trading network from Indonesia to Morocco that would cut out Western companies and steamship lines. During WWI, Duse began a series of failed attempts to establish banks in West Africa independent of Europeans, and to promote trade between Europe, sub-Saharan Africa and the USA for a combination of profit and integration of the world's Negroes. This activity anticipated, or fed into, the similar drives by Garvey and his U.S. colleagues to develop a new "black" international commerce from the U.S. as the economic expression of Africanist diaspora nationalism—which African-Americans linked to Farrakhan were again to attempt in the 1990s.[41]

The long-term aspiration of the Garveyite movement in the USA to mobilize blacks throughout the world, and in the African homeland in particular, had early imposed some constraints on how far the movement could endorse Christianity. In 1924, delegates to the 4th International Convention of the Negroes of the World declared that "as there are Moslems and other non-Christians who are Garveyites, it was not wise to declare Christianity the state religion of the organization".[42] The mixed influences from early Arab and Egyptian nationalisms, and from heterodox movements on the margin of Islam shaped by English concepts, led Garvey and his followers to sometimes substitute "Allah" for "God," and to draw inspiration for his career from the Prophet Muhammad.

We have, though, to note the fluidity of the identifications around this motif in Garvey's discourse as political and cultural contexts shifted. Thus, as he strove to hearten his followers to bear the terrible odds, persecutions and hardships they now had to face, Garvey did cite, in a January 1922 address, the refusal of "the great Mohammed" ever to give up even when nearly all the people forsook him for a time. But he juxtaposed Muhammad with such white models of perseverance as George Washington—and the Irish leaders of the last 750 years who were now wresting final independence in the 20th century. It could get ambiguous where Garvey might slot Muhammad and the Arabs, racially, in an international black-white dichotomy, towards which he sometimes groped.[43] Arnold Ford, later a founder of black Judaism in the USA, composed for the Garveyite movement a nationalist hymn, "Allahu Akbar" [It is God Who is Greatest].[44] The Garveyites were being influenced by Arab nationalisms, and also by heterodox South Asian Islam encountered in theosophical milieus, or in the neighborhood.

But Ford could also have drawn "Allahu Akbar" as a cry that for decades was to differentiate blacks from their white race-enemies in African-American protest Islam from shards of Arabic surviving from slavery times in the oral lore of African-Americans in the U.S. or in his native West Indies. That phrase in the Islamic ritual prayer was still remembered, if somewhat garbled, by some rural blacks in the U.S. South in the 1930s.

The U.S. mass media of the Garveyites became open towards Islam as one basis of the rising Asiatic entity with which blacks might well form a coalition against imperialism. Thus, the independence movement in Egypt in the 1920s, the sensational insurrection for Moroccan independence led by the Berber Abdel-Krim in September 1921 that was to kill thousands of Spanish and French soldiers, the success with which the revitalized Turkey of Mustafa Kemal beat back the Greek armies (victories bracketed by Duse with those of militant black workers in the Johannesburg gold fields), and Gandhi's movement for the independence of India, were all covered from Garvey's *Negro World*. The Garveyites toyed with the option of linking up with a perceived new pan-Islamic movement that would unfold in both Asia and Africa at one and the same time. While Middle Eastern and Arab World movements and new independent states were catching their interest, these U.S. political nationalists were also responding to Islam as an element that was rapidly expanding and extending itself in black sub-Saharan Africa in that period. They believed that Arabic translations of articles from their paper were circulating among the Muslims in Nigeria and adjacent countries [—and given the movement's links to Arab nationalists like Duse Mohammed 'Ali, it could well have produced such Arabic materials to reach traditionally Islamic black Africans].[45] The dynamic Indian Muslim missionary movement, the Ahmadiyyah, gave lectures in Garveyite institutions and settings: they urged that movement to adopt a single religion, Islam, and a single language—Arabic—so as to get "political" support from allies in China, Arabia, Africa, Turkey, Persia and India.[46]

Such offers carried some credibility in Black America. Offering forums to foreign Muslims made political sense to the Garveyites who hoped not just for sympathy but for real aid from those overseas Muslim populations and entities. Iran was the only Islamic nation represented in the post-WWI League of Nations: its representative, Prince Mirza Riza Khan Arfa ed-Dowleh, in 1922 had helped Britain get the Iranian government to intercede with Turkey on behalf of 100,000 Greeks and Armenians made homeless during Turkey's war with Greece. Immediately thereafter, the UNIA's delegation in Geneva requested the Prince to submit a petition from it to the current session of the League. The petition, requesting that the League award the UNIA a mandate over former German colonies in Africa, annoyed the governments of Belgium, Britain and France, to whom the Garveyites also conveyed it directly.[47] This early move on the international chessboard prefigured later attempts by Malcolm X and other members of the Nation of Islam in the late 1950s and early 1960s to muster pressure from Middle Eastern diplomats and governments to modify the U.S. WASP elite's treatment of African-Americans.

The letter to "Your Highness" by the UNIA Chairman of Delegation was in exquisitely modulated high Anglo English. The UNIA was showing some international effectiveness that was more than just fustian. It really did set up two branches in the former German South West Africa that gave the only focus to growing discontent among Africans there against the new British-Afrikaner overlords, although by 1925 the UNIA had already begun to decline.[48]

The Garveyites' Responses to Muslim Insurrection Overseas

Malcolm X's parents had been Garveyite activists. The Garveyites' sense in the early 1920s of the unity of political interest of "the darker peoples of the world", of what Duse was terming "the black, brown and yellow races", prefigured the terminology with which Malcolm X in the 1960s would choose "the entire East, the dark world" as Communist ese battled America. If African-Americans related to the "black, brown and yellow" nations that were now wresting independence, dreamed Malcolm, they would cease to be "a dark minority on the white American stage" and become "part of the dark majority who now prevail on the world stage." "Although we're in the West, we're from the East—you're as black as you ever were, you're just in the white world."[49]

Garvey's speeches in the 1920s oscillated between (a) a sense that certain colonized peoples were struggling against the same imperial enemies as "the Africans" for the time, and (b) some racial identification of his group with some Muslim or Hindu peoples in that temporary camp. A swift succession of anti-colonial movements above the Sahara and in Asia in 1922 gave him and other blacks in North America a galvanizing sense that now was the time for the "Africans", too, to hit *their* (often identical) white overlords.

In his first mode, Garvey could feel that the sympathy between his people and those other groups stemmed from shared subordination to the other, white, category or camp of nations. This political rather than racialized perspective enabled him to place the struggling Irish beside his own group. That fleeting quasi-community of status, though, might cease to be felt by each group once it wrested its sovereignty. "The Irish have succeeded first among the trio of Egypt, India and Ireland to become themselves masters" by ceasing to submit as "burden-bearers to the great Anglo-Saxon race." Lloyd George had granted the Irish Free State, whereas the Negroes remained in subjugation. While weak, the Irish, the Egyptians and the Hindus felt with the Negroes, but once they gain their freedom they might make themselves copartners with those nations exploiting the weaker peoples. In this category of identifications, Garvey was tracing how temporary sovereign political power or lack of it could create perhaps fleeting international groupings. In this aspect, he viewed the world bleakly as a jungle: there are few permanent friends in international relations, only the permanent interests of each state-unit or ethnic nation.

A second category of his identifications had more possibilities in it for racial and cultural identification with some Third World peoples. Muslims were active in struggles against the mighty powers in Morocco, Egypt and also in the India where Hindu Gandhi led the Indian National Congress. Garvey's oratory conveyed the main features of those movements to the African-American masses he was addressing, while missing aspects that were problematical to the model for nationalism he sought for his own people's emancipation. On 8 January 1922, Garvey told followers in New York that the British had exiled "the great leader" of the Egyptian independence movement and that that "has caused really a tumult": he did not, though, name Sa'd Zaghlul to the African-American masses. Here, Garvey had communicated the essence of Third World independence struggles—that jailings, exiling, and hangings of the leaders galvanize more often than they silence masses, in what he called "the psychology of great movements". Again conveying the essence of developments in the Arab world accurately even amid lack of details, Garvey in 1924 called Britain "the dominant power in Africa: the diamond fields belong to her and Egypt has freedom with a string tied to it." Superb skeletal condensation!

For almost powerless African-Americans, the devastating, skilled violence of the Moroccans of the Spanish-occupied Riff was even more exciting than mass protest in Egypt. Intoxicated by "the great defeat of the Spanish forces in Morocco", Garvey characterized their officers as "Caucasians," in contrast to the native soldiers they had trained and to Abdel-Krim's "other black Moroccans" to whom many only defected on the battle-plains. Garvey exultantly read out to his New York audience from the morning newspaper that only 200 had survived out of a Spanish army of 24,085: "those native Moroccans, in addition to the Spaniards they killed, captured airplanes, guns, munitions of every kind—everything". There were blacks in Morocco, as Woodson and DuBois were constructing, and Garvey here for the moment saw Abdel-Krim's Riffians as fellow-Africans and their land as part of Africa, without recording that there were some fair-skinned Berbers in those forces that were devastating white Westerners.[50] Arden A. Bryan, sometimes the foreign affairs editor of *Negro World*, in 1919 saw Egypt as "part of our fatherland, Africa" as "a handful of white troops" and the British Empire's "Hindu" soldiery fought off "thousands of rebel natives" in the countryside.[51] But some reactions by Garvey and his colleagues would conflate not just Arabic-speaking and sub-Saharan Africa but a single Africa with an Asia that included Hindus as all simultaneously rising up against Westerners

The post-WWI movements for independence by Muslim and Asian peoples offered some guidance for Garvey's own efforts to construct the global African political nation, but were problematical as well without his knowing. The New York back-to-Africa nationalists were trying to come to grips with the problems religious diversification of the globe's blacks and the sectional status of Christianity would pose for Garvey's drive to fuse Muslim and Christian blacks into one political nation. Egypt could offer hope for their drive because both Muslim and Christian Egyptians were now behind Zaghlul and the Wafd in quasi-revolt against the British, with highlighting of the sects-neutral Pharaonic golden age that also sometimes appeared in *Negro World*.

Garvey had grown up with dark Indians in the West Indies, although he and other blacks of those isles and coasts sometimes felt that those were alien competitors who harmed "Negroes,"[52] and he hoped that some sects-integrative revolt was also breaking out in India against the British: "if it is possible for Hindus and Mohammedans to come together in India, it is possible for Negroes to come together everywhere."

Garvey and his New York masses were being electrified by the uprising by Malayalam-speaking Moplah (Mapilla) Muslims that broke out in Kerala, India in August 1921. The New York paper he held up had headlined "Moplahs Revolt in India: Declare Independence: Rout British and Elect Own Ruler", and "Three Battleships Sent to Aid British Regiment—Hindus and Mohammedans Take Vows to be Free or Die": his followers cheered. Still, he faintly glimpsed the dualities in the eruption. The paper told him that the Moplahs had been goaded to revolt by British arrests but also by news of the humiliation of the Turkey-based Caliphate as the Turkish national forces under Mustafa Kemal suffered reverses at the hands of the Greeks. Garvey was rather diverse and fluid or even confused in the types of communities he derived from the skilled insurgency of the Moplahs [some of whom had soldiered in Britain's wars in 'Iraq]. Three hundred and eighty million Indians had revolted "in sympathy with the oppressed and defeated of their own race and their own religion". Garvey missed that this "religious kinship" with correligionists in the Middle East was surely distinguishing Moplahs/India's Muslims from their Hindu neighbors—and with whom was their "racial kinship"?[53]

In his hope that a huge "race war" was looming that could break the power of white states all over the world, Garvey for the moment conflated Indians and Middle Eastern Muslim groups and perhaps even African-Americans as all one racial category vis-à-vis the West. But the agrarian uprising of the Moplahs, with its class-refusal to pay taxes and dues, had been directed against local well-off caste-Hindus as much as the British: facing terrifying reprisals if they kept any interaction with the foreigner, the Hindu landlords and shopkeepers duly petitioned the British to bring in more troops and apply martial law more severely against their Muslim neighbors. The British moved quickly to widen the split between caste-Hindus and Muslims: Lord Montagu, Secretary of State for India, told parliament that the rebels had committed "shocking atrocities on their loyal Hindu fellow-subjects".[54] The quasi-official London *Times* was hoping that the Moplahs' "ferocious murders" of many Hindus in Kerala was making many in wider India now more appreciative of Britain's "strong arm" that quelled "anarchy".[55] Such hopes of the British were to be fulfilled. Gandhi and his Hindu colleagues, like Garvey imaged, had backed the drive of the "Khilafat" Muslims in India to help the Turks maintain a sovereign Islamic state with a Caliphate in the Middle East, but the killings of Kerala Hindus provided a focus by which Gandhi's conservative Hindu rivals in the Congress Party and outside it could muster the Hindu public against him and Congress' Khilafat policy.

Thus, the Moplah uprising did not turn out well for evolving the model of coalitionist nationalism through which Garvey hoped that Africans and

African-Americans too could now achieve strength and self-determination in their turn. Yet the pan-Islamic political solidarity that India's Muslims had maintained with in some ways quite different groups in the Middle East would catch the attention of Garvey, given his drive to connect "Negroes" all around the world. [The splitting of Indian nationalism along sects in the movement for Pakistan was still to come, but when he orated on January 8, 1922, Garvey surely knew the sectarian divisions that at the end of that year led to the granting of the Irish Free State in only part of Ireland: this left open the question of whether Irish nationalism too would be able to incorporate the minority sect—for it, Ulster's Protestants].

U.S. racism had always deemed as Negro anyone in whose veins even one drop of African blood flowed. Garvey was characterized by his enemies in the U.S. black elite, by agents, by his fairer-skinned target and nemesis W.E.B. DuBois, and by later 20th century scholars as injecting West Indies patterns into the U.S. by waging a sort of a war against "mulattos" there also. "Mulattos" had enjoyed some relative privileges in the West Indies from the days of the plantation onwards as a useful intermediary group for whites, but no such clear divide of skin pigmentations set aside the USA's intermediary "black bourgeoisie" from the African-American masses. Yet Garvey's swings of attraction to Muslim populations and entities shows that context—if he was thinking of the whole West and non-Western mankind, and if Muslim or Hindu peoples looked set to break Western power—could make him think of global blackness in an incorporative way like later Arabophile black Muslims.

There is no doubt that Garvey and his U.S. followers were excited not just by protest, but in particular by devastating violence, from overseas Muslims and Hindus against "whites". He hoped aloud that sub-Saharan Africans could hit those Westerners just as hard. He declared that his organization might soon send African-American troops and nurses it was training to future battlefields in Africa of which the slaughter of the Spaniards by the [Muslim] Riffians, he hoped, had only given Europe a foretaste. Whether Garvey would have ever identified with an insurgent Arabic-speaking, Muslim population enough to send UNIA troops [and blacks who had served in the U.S. and French militaries] to aid them was never to be tested: it is at any rate in question if he would have been practical enough to carry the institutions he started through to functionality for that task, also. Garvey's diaspora Black Legion and Black Cross nurses might have made a difference, had he been able to deliver them onto the battlefields in Africa.

Yet, while not himself a U.S. Negro, Garvey had soaked in the caution and the ambivalence to the U.S. system of the group he had come to head. "Wait until we get there, boys! Don't start anything over here, don't waste any energy over here; because you are bound to lose if you start anything over here".[56] It was not just a matter that whites and their system had overwhelming power. As was to be the case in a much more covert way with the black Muslims in the 1960s, Garvey—for all his black nationalist and Back-to-Africa stance—had an alert eye for more liberal impulses from within the system that could improve the conditions of African-Americans. In early

1922 he described the Dyer Anti-Lynching Bill as having been passed in response to the impact upon the statesmen of the world of the UNIA (which really was lobbying at the League of Nations). Yet, another part of his psyche also saw the Bill as "but a continuance of President Harding's advocacy for better consideration for the Negro people".[57]

Conversely, the steadfastness of the Hindus and Muslims in Asia and Africa and of the Irish could inspire Garvey and his followers to brave "sacrifice and death" from the U.S. system, if it proved obdurate: he fused their quasi-insurgencies with the domestic cry of "Give me liberty or give me death" with which the United States itself had achieved independence through violence.[58] Thus, the Garveyites had some explosive emotions (usually subordinated) about the U.S. system itself, not just against European colonialisms abroad. But all the stress on an exodus of New World "Africans" back to their "real" homeland across the seas, and the need to join fighting there, was very functional in defusing the potential of the UNIA to focus militant resistance or insurgency inside the U.S.

More militant African-Americans were not impressed by Garvey's verbal interest in Muslim or Eastern movements and insurgencies abroad because they saw him as having made a truce with even the violent racial aspects of the U.S. system. In later 1921, the African Blood Brotherhood charged that the UNIA had done little "to organize our People to the end of stopping the mob-murder of our men, women and children and fight the ever-expanding peonage system". Garvey was charged to have promised the government that his movement would stand with America in any future war even against "friendly Soviet Russia, racial Japan, China or Haiti". The Brotherhood was angry that Garvey "has ignored the Mohammedan and Ethiopian movements in Africa—the two greatest movements working for the liberation of that continent".[59] The UNIA was being further pressured on Islam from its flank by more militant African-American groups that—influenced by Lothrop Stoddard and other race-conscious Anglos—were pressing the UNIA to tighten its relations with the Islam that was rapidly spreading in such areas of sub-Saharan Africa as Malawi.[60]

Garvey and Zionism

In the period in which Garvey and his New York paper, *Negro World*, drew the attention of African-Americans to new nationalisms in the Arab World and the Middle East, he also focused his analysis on categories of Jews. Both their new Zionism and his movement were trying to construct a globally diffused nation and repatriate it to a homeland in the Third World. The veteran Yiddish and English writer, B.Z. Goldberg, recalled (1969) that when in Harlem, Garvey—at that time organizing the "Black Star Steamship Company" to ply between the West Indies, the U.S. and Africa—kept asking how the Zionists "operated".[61]

One memory of African-American nationalists in the 21st century is that a few Jews donated to Garvey's operations in Jamaica and the U.S.[62]

However, Garvey was to come to criticize some Jews when he felt their interests clashed with those of blacks; he was also to voice doubts about effects Zionism might have for the Palestinians.[63] Post-1980 Jewish-American micro-nationalism—trying to solidify itself by constructing an enemy because the group's distinctive attributes may not be enough to add up to a positive national culture—was to strive to fog Garvey's dualities towards Zionism and U.S. Jews. *Commentary* and *The New Republic* magazines in 1995, amplified by Allan Dershowitz behind hard covers in 1997, stressed Garvey's participation in the "Buy Black" campaigns of '20s Harlem and that he had thrown off some positive remarks about Hitler, too [as had some Zionists in Europe, who accepted his premise that Jews were intruders there in those goy or gentile nations who had to go]. These Jewish micronational polemicists of the 1990s charged that "many of Garvey's specific tenets [in the 1920s] foreshadowed Farrakhan's [post-1977] Black Muslimism" (*The New Republic*).[64] Jewish micronationalism in America presents simple paradigms of nationalist blacks as automatically hostile and evil down decades and generations in an unmixed way. These dichotomizing images of a demonized Other go towards the simplest paradigms of past black Muslim sects about inherently racist "white devils" who have no other potentiality but to be what they are.

The Shifts and Opening to Islam in Religion

Garveyism was understood in its American heyday to have the potential to transform the religious life of the African-American masses. It was breaking the hold on them of all established forms of Christianity, which it was set to at least deconstruct and completely reinvent into a political race-religion. The question was whether Garveyite nationalism could take the masses beyond the discourse world of Christianity to (a) Islam or (b) an amalgam of the established world religions and nationalism. The Rev R.R. Porter in 1920 speculated that Garvey, perhaps not in a fully conscious way, had "given the world a new religion" and compared his followers to the earlier adherents of Buddha, Christ, and Muhammad when they were establishing those religions. (Note the black clergyman's assumption that Islam and other "Eastern" religions were good, like Christianity and Garveyism). Porter anticipated the Nation of Islam by evoking the immanence of God in the political Negro nation: "the devout Garveyite sees God in you, [me] and the world: he knows God because he is a part of God making the kingdom of God on earth".[65] Garvey's movement had in it spiritually violent impulses to tear up and smash the symbols of mainstream Christianity. Its chaplain-general, Rev George Alexander McGuire, seceded from white-dominated Protestantism and founded a new black nationalist "Ethiopian" Orthodox church with images of black Jesuses and black Old Testament prophets. McGuire harangued African-Americans to "wipe the white gods from your hearts": the blacks had to fix a day on which they would tear from the walls of their homes all white Jesuses and Madonnas.[66]

In the 1920s, some Garveyite writers looked over Islam as a possible alternative to an established white Christianity designed to dull the resistance of the blacks to subjection and exploitation. In a 1923 speech, *Negro World* columnist John Edward Bruce suggested that Islam would be a preferable religion for Africans because of its practice of brotherhood and lack of racism. Missionary work in Africa had to be confined to African-Americans who "think black" and had not been corrupted by European culture.[67] A small number of UNIA members most alienated from the West now wanted to make Islam the religion of the movement and of diaspora blacks. A 1922 UNIA convention discussed the topic "The Future Religious Faith and Belief of the Negro": representatives of different branches of Christianity wrangled, but "several" delegates proposed that Islam be adopted as the future religion of the Negro because "the Mohammedan religion was the religion of three-fourths of the people of the Negro race in the world [and] there have been found more Christian-minded people among the Mohammedans than among professed Christians".[68] The Islamophile faction still kept some tints from Christianity, but had moved some way into a margin between the two religions or civilizations.

The greater number of Garveyite writers, though, could not advance quite that far towards snapping the symbol of Christianity that affiliated African-Americans in subjected community with white Americans and Europe: their in comparison modest opening to Islam was more to address the pragmatic realities that its spread in Africa posed for pan-Africanism. Amy Jacques Garvey, the wife of Marcus Garvey, in an article published in the mass circulation *Negro World* in 1924, was concerned that the accelerating Islamization of many populations in black Africa might further hamper the Garveyite movement's drive to unite Africans and the Negroes of the overwhelmingly Christian Americas. Her concerns were more the practicalities of organizing a political nationalist movement across the continents, although she kept a residue of religious preference for Christianity.

Thus, Mrs Garvey ascribed the spread of Islam in black Africa to Christianity's links as an official world religion to the economic interests of the whites and to racism and imperialism specifically. The white Christian missionaries in black Africa are hypocritical "forerunners of traders": they abuse the confidence the native Africans place in them by teaching them the hymn "Take all the world, but give me Jesus" in order to drug their nerves as the whites plunder their continent. (Malcolm would take up this motif in the 1950s and 1960s). It was this linkage, she expounded, that by contrast highlighted the lack of color bar or segregation in Islam to the eyes of the Negroes of Africa, so that the teaching of Mohammed was winning more converts than Christianity. Her fear was that those continuing mass conversions of animist Africans to Islam would only "create a further breach" between the "Africans at home" and the other Africans in the Negro diaspora across the seas. Mrs Garvey called on U.S. Negroes to forestall such a religious divergence by sending their own black missionaries to Africa to bring "education and progress [that would] satisfy the material needs of the people" along with "a Christianity that will satisfy their spiritual wants." The duty of the blacks of America as Christians was to teach their brethren in

Africa things that could prepare them for a progressive life in this world and also for the hereafter—a discreet synthesis of the modernism as well as the Christianity of the Western World in which the minds of the Garveyites had been formed.

While realistic about backwardness in Africa in education in particular, Amy Jacques Garvey in 1924 was attuned to a new much more politically conscious reaction of Africans against the West's imperialism: this new attitude now was giving the preaching of Islam an unprecedented hearing. The participation of Negro Africans from villages in the British and French war effort against Germany's colonies in the continent and on the European fronts had broken down localist insularities, and made the Africans participants in macro-history through that "World War." With his new sense of having become a member along with Westerners in an incipient world community, the African now expected those "brothers" to elevate him into better things at once: if they did not, he would turn to Islam, Mrs Garvey pointed out, quoting a white missionary's warning.

Amy Garvey remained a Christian to a considerable degree in this item. True, given her concern for material progress for Africans, she also may have been manipulating alarmist images of Islam triumphing in Africa in order to galvanize African-Americans into "missionary" involvement in that continent for non-religious purposes. Certainly, she wanted to structure missions by African-Americans to make them integrate transcontinental political community and in particular bring opportunities for modernization to the Africans. Yet it is likelier that as a product of the deeply Christian New World, she sincerely pursued the interests of Christianity in tandem. Amy Garvey did accept that Islam as a force integrating new wider societies in sub-Saharan Africa was surpassing the level of behavior of Christianity's white followers who preached "the fatherhood of God and the brotherhood of man" without practising it because "this material, sordid world" had robbed them of their spiritual ideals and ethics. But Amy Garvey remained firm that, at the level of the theories, "Christianity as taught by our Lord and Savior Jesus Christ" was still the most ethically elevated among the world's creeds [–not Islam]. The weakness of Christianity, then, stemmed not from the principles of the religion but from the racist practices of its white adherents who reduced it to "a farce and a mockery." Mrs Garvey resented that whites made up "the majority" who controlled and defined Christianity, but there remained an attenuated affect, in this article at least, to a general Christian global community: better treatment and chances might quickly revitalize this category of black nationalists' commitment to a multi-racial world Christianity.[69]

Another—Afro-Asianist—article by Amy Garvey in the next year moved further away from Christianity, objectifying it as just one option for blacks alongside Islam and perhaps other religions in the East. The context was the awakening of the Eastern Giant as illustrated by the bloody insurrection for Moroccan independence conducted by 'Abdel-Krim from 1921, and the difficult birth of the modern national state in China. The wider global perspective was offering a greater range of comparative instances of exploitation that further disillusioned Amy Garvey against white-led Christianity. The awakening Easterner has realized that the white missionaries never had any intention to implement their teaching "do unto others as ye would that they do unto you": when he unmasks them "he sees a common land thief whose sole purpose is to exploit and rule." Soon the Eastern Giant will "stalk forth to sovereignty and power." "Whether we be black Mohammedans or black Christians... our racial interests are identical... By the help of God, Allah, the First Cause or the Omnipotent, we will join forces, and throw off the common oppressor." Amy Garvey here accepted that Christians and Muslims were now to be two long-term categories among black Africans, and her emotions of community with black African Muslims then blurred them out into the wider chain of Muslim populations in the whole East, of which all non-white races are now accepted as not just racial but in a broad way religious kin vis-à-vis the white West. She was starting to imbibe Islamic religious terms and motifs.

Despite her increased rejection of Christianity, Amy Garvey praised President Woodrow Wilson's "principle of self-determination" as liable to usher in a new era of political and economic freedom for the darker peoples if the "avaricious, selfish whiteman" only allowed it to apply to people of color. She remained somewhat open here to ideology among the Anglo-Saxons and Westerners who had contributed so much to her personality and with whom she would therefore have welcomed the humane community few of them wanted.[70] As the USA's war-time president, Wilson had been instrumental in instituting the practice of racial segregation in federal employment and in public facilities in Washington, DC.[71]

Marcus Garvey himself did not intervene clearly in the debates among UNIA delegates and members about what primary religion, if any, the world's "Africans" should have. He was mainly influenced by changes of international relations and by the pragmatic issues his wife descried in the growth of Islam in Africa. In one manifesto he wrote for distribution among "the blacks of the French, English and Italian colonies", Garvey identified with Kemal Ataturk's defeat of Greek forces because it looked set to destroy the post-WWI "European Peace" with which four hundred million Negroes were also dissatisfied. He wanted all Negroes ruled by Great Britain not to fight in European armies against Turkey, as they had in WWI. But neither did he want them to fight on the side of the Turks in a holy war between the cross and the crescent because "many of our race are believers in Muhammad's faith and millions of others are disciples of Christ's religion": the Negroes had to be careful not to let foreigners' quarrels divide "our people into enemy camps". Rather, all Negroes together had to drive the Europeans out of Africa.[72]

Not all followers of Garvey were happy with Islam's steady penetration of the movement's discourse and its following. FBI intelligence agents thought that Garvey in 1922 had tried to control Duse's use of the UNIA's newspapers to propagandize on behalf of "Egyptians in Wall Street" who were paying him.[73] At a 1924 Convention of the UNIA, G.A. Western from

New York complained that the British, determined to divide and rule, had insidiously "employed Turkish agents to preach Islamism to members" [Duse had moved to the States from London]. A 1924 editorial in *Negro World* had stated that both British colonialism and Turkish Islam were white forces alien to Africa, although the writer was sympathetic to the "African and Asiatic Moslems" whose interests Turkey had long manipulated as a bogey to strengthen itself vis-à-vis the expanding Western powers. This in some ways accurate retrospect of Istanbul-centered pan-Islamism makes one wonder if someone with area knowledge of the Middle East such as Duse Mohammed 'Ali might not have penned it in an Afro-Arabist twinge. It looks more likely to have been a burst of partial Christian American nativism from somebody born in the Americas who had interacted with some Muslims.[74]

After all account is taken of Christian survivals in the psyches of these Garveyite writers, these types of articles by them in the movement's mass-circulation newspaper could orientate some U.S. adherents to convert to neo-Islamic movements. Both the Moorish Science Temple of North America and then the Nation of Islam were able to use Garveyite vocabulary: Drew 'Ali termed Garvey the "John the Baptist" of his sect. These Garveyite *Negro World* communications spasmodically depicted Islam as a positive force that was integrating African society more effectively than the Christianity of an exploitative, materialist white West. They diffused the assertions of Muslims, and of the Islamophiles among Anglo-Saxon writers, that Islam had really integrated and united believers of the most diverse races. Many Garveyite writings did accept without discussion that the relationships between (a) Berber or Arab Muslims and (b) newly converted blacks in equatorial Africa were positive for the most part. Above all, this variety of Garveyite writings directed condemnations at the Christian church that were to be heightened by the Nation of Islam in its preachings and journalism.

The Moors and Political Black Nationalism

The Moorish Science Temple of North America had been nourished by—and had it itself contributed to?—the many positive articles appearing in *Negro World* that glorified the empires of the Moors in North Africa and in particular in Arab Spain. Such items argued the blackness of many of the Africans who took part in Islam-emblemed conquests in the Iberian peninsula. Yet after the American government expelled Garvey in 1927, U.S. Garveyite journalists criticized such new religious movements for winning away converts from the disintegrating mass nationalist political movement that Garvey had built up in the USA. Movements such as those of the Moors or Father Divine or Bishop Grace, *Negro World* writer Samuel Haynes argued in 1933 had leaders who "reincarnated" Garvey's leadership to some extent: they could not, though, leave any impression on the governments of the world because their program was to console the followers as individuals by teaching them an emotional, spiritual self-satisfaction or "mysticism".[75] In contrast—so this line of argument still runs—Marcus Garvey's international African nationalism had been organizing its converts into a collectivist political movement that could empower them to address the sources of their disadvantage, and had been bringing (or over a longer period might have brought) the blacks back into the processes of wide global history.

Some American academic observers close to the period, though, did consider whether the Moorish movements at least, among those cults, might have some potential to usher in a political nationalism centered in the USA. Such a U.S.-attuned activism had perhaps been ruled out for Garvey's movement by its obsession with a mother-continent of origin across the seas that drew so much time, thought and energy away from the American needs of ordinary blacks. The comparatively much more concocted and imaginary character of the overseas entities of provenance that the Moors evoked could give African-Americans more leeway to serve their own interests in America.

Dr Arthur Huff Fauset in 1944 tried to assess how many constituents the ideas of Drew 'Ali's sectarian movement had to prepare the blacks of America to mount political action on the basis of a distinct nationhood over the longer term. Fauset argued two preconditions for political action by any national group: namely (1) political concepts centered around a specific national identity or a specific national homeland of the said group, and (2) a political instrument such as a political party or other political organization. These two elements together could equip a national group to enter into political struggles. Fauset assessed that the Moorish Science Temple had indeed evoked some of the characteristics required for a continuous national identity, which he argued was precisely what the psyche of the Negroes in America had long lacked in contrast to other major ethnic groups in the USA.

Fauset contended that the Black Jews and the Moorish Americans understood something of what had been taken from, or denied, the blacks in North America by the racist system that had so thoroughly obliterated even the faintest memories of previous ethnic origins, regions of origin and culture in Africa. The two sects strove to remind their people of their ancient name and their ancient land on the grounds that no people can have a future without a national name. The Moorish Americans even went so far as to claim the American continent for themselves on the basis that it was merely an extension of Africa: the Moroccan Empire had in its glorious heyday not just encompassed all of Africa but extended over North, Central and South America, before the Moors in the eighteenth century through sin and disobedience caused God to place them in slavery. In different circumstances, it might have been conducive to a scenario of political action that, from its inception, Drew and his movement praised Garvey's simultaneous UNIA. As a mass political movement, the UNIA was something like the "political organ or organism" that Fauset foresaw might "utilize the religious organization as one means of bringing about the desired end." [The movement for civil rights in the South would in the 1970s install in Congress Black professional politicians who tried to define an enclave-nation through African issues.] Fauset believed that the ratio of power between racial groups in North America explained the failure of the Moors to develop their potential for political action. The sect of the Moors lacked the means to make their theoretical beliefs of community real.[76]

Garvey's mass movement achieved some successes in the international outreach its ideology imaged that it should conduct. The smaller following of the Moorish "national movement" did place structural constraints on the options that its leadership had vis-à-vis the American system, and on any world stage. Millenarianism could become the safety valve to drain away tensions about U.S. institutions or, conversely, the myths might give the masses' recruits enough confidence to take on the system. The tension between the confrontationism that a firmer sense of continuous identity and God could spark, and avoidance vis-à-vis the white system by the leadership, has recurred in the history of Moorish sects. The sense of the followers that the sect had reconnected them with overseas homelands and divine power released billowing energy and self-assertion against whites that were hard for the early leaders to control. Drew 'Ali used to end his identity cards with the cautious formula "I am a citizen of the United States": his confinement of his followers to religious avoidance/escapism and entrepreneurial self-improvement before the possibility of a clash between the two races was pure covert realism about the position of the Negroes as a minority in the midst of white American populations that often hated them.

Yet, like the Black Muslims later, the Noble Drew 'Ali taught his followers that he had come in the leadup to the end of time. Accordingly, his followers scanned the heavens of nights, and made out there the sign of a star within a crescent—a clear omen that the day of the Asiatics was nearing in which "the Europeans", America's whites, would be destroyed. Having recovered their usurped Moorish identity, followers began arguing and clashing with whites in many of the industrial cities of the northern USA, especially in those of the mid-West where the movement became a real plague to the police as its adherents marched through the streets accosting white passers-by and producing their "Asiatic" identity cards as tokens that the Noble Drew 'Ali had freed them from the domination of the Europeans. When the Moors were showing signs of breaking out of the escapist religious rituals that kept them awaiting their day of divine liberation from an outer margin, the "Prophet" Drew 'Ali duly warned "all Moors" to "cease all radical or agitating speeches" in their work-places, houses or in the streets: he and his colleagues had not come to create disturbances but to lift up the Nation. The followers were almost escaping their God-tinted leaders as the dynamic of collectivity-formation that the leaders' motifs about glories in the East had triggered almost surged out of their control.

It was also clear that the Chicago city police forces meant to crush Drew's sect at some time of their choosing. Drew and his businessman colleagues were able to clamp down control on factional unrest but, weakened by tuberculosis, he died after a bout in police custody in 1929. Since then, most Moorish sectlets have maintained Drew 'Ali's rejection of activist political engagement, or as he termed it, "radicalism"—a term that successor-leaders in the late 1970s were still applying against, for instance, efforts by pro-Palestinian activists to circulate PLO English-language publications among the Moorish adherents. For all the mordant home-truths the sect had articulated about the "pale-faces", and although the movement had adopted the Moroccan flag of green star on a red background, most Moorish leaders plumped to respect the U.S. flag, and—striving to establish "peace on earth" and that love that is the guiding principle of the universe—urged the adherents to play the part of quiet-spoken respect towards their unpleasant white masters (whom the religion and its businesses helped them avoid).

Yet the Moorish movement, in extending the racial distinctness of African-Americans from whites into its religious separation, and by the national vocabulary it sanctified with religion—its specific claim to America for its homeland—had taken major strides towards the articulation of African-American enclave-nationhood and micronationality in America. Garvey and his colleagues had not been as able to integrate America into their Africanist national ideology. The ferment of ideas among the masses of the Moorish adherents had been as significant as the wary compromises its leaders made. Fauset in 1944 quoted one ordinary adherent that every free people has a free national homeland with its own distinct national flag—as would be confirmed by any German born in America who would at once identify Germany and its flag as what defined him[77] [which did not take account of the cumulative Anglicization of many "Germans" described in Chapter 2].

This view shows how white ethnic groups in the U.S. and their patterns of affiliation to homelands in outside continents of provenance already had input into the national thought and social culture of followers of the Moorish Science Temple, as was to be the case also with the Nation of Islam from 1930. Some Moors were groping towards a duality of identity or status in which the plural nationalities of Americans are on one plane and the political citizenship, determined by homeland of residence, on another: "We're from a great national country... All free people have a national country"[78]—implying that the Moors might become exactly like the other *ethne* in America that observed its citizenship but bore another continent in heart and mind. The structure of America's system, society and thought until 1950, and the grip of imperialism throughout Africa and Asia, did constrict the capacity of African-Americans to affiliate to overseas political power centers much more than it deformed and eviscerated other impulses to enclave-nationhood among such non-Anglo "white" nationalities as German-, Polish- and Irish-Americans, which had much clearer ideas of their homelands of provenance. But the formalistic and mythological nature of the motifs of linkage to Muslim North Africa and Arabia in the MSTA's discourse serviced what was possible in the unitarist white nationalist era of U.S. history, with its theory of the "melting pot" that preceded the articulation and rise of political ethnic micronationalisms from the late 1960s.

4: THE MOORS EVOLVE

As Elijah had already tried in the 1950s, Farrakhan's revival of the

Nation of Islam in the 1980s and 1990s sought to tap legitimacy from the awareness growing independently among ordinary African-Americans of the role that Drew 'Ali had played as the founder of neo-Islam in North America. Farrakhan's media publicized it when continuing large Moorish-American communities prompted administrations of several major U.S. cities to proclaim Noble Drew 'Ali Centennial Days in 1986. The proclamation of the—African-American—mayor of Los Angeles, Tom Bradley, almost accepted Ali's title to be a prophet [a violation of the U.S. state's secularism], and that he really had brought "Moorish Nationality... to thousands of Americans of African descent". The duality of all these proto-Islamic movements in simultaneously (a) asserting difference and extra-territorializing America's blacks and (b) in Anglicizing or Americanizing the black masses was, though, caught in Bradley's sense that 'Ali "taught his followers to become better citizens through his principles of Love, Truth, Peace, Freedom and Justice".

The Ambassador of Morocco, Maati Jorio, had been a key-speaker at the Washington celebrations.[79] Jorio's 1986 discourse voiced a calculatedly vague friendliness containing no recognition that U.S. "Moors" were fellow-Muslims as yet: "Morocco welcomes your interest and your work for better understanding between us": the Moroccan government would strive to "make our relation a vibrant and special one".[80] The burgeoning interest of young African-Americans in Drew 'Ali and the ongoing successor-sects in the 1990s was often based on an image that they were "an anti-government Black militia": there were multiplying groups of people calling themselves Moors, playing up to that fierce image, and dismaying the old-timers.[81]

The early political potential the Moorish movement had to connect into international pan-Islamic or pan-Africanist movements was not fulfilled during Drew's leadership, or in its aftermath. 'Ali's definition of Islam and the global community of African-Americans had also encompassed the Buddhist and Mongolian worlds; following his death, the temples directed the drive for global community more to resurgent Japan than to the Middle East or Black Africa. From the 1930s, the fifty Moorish temples in 25 major American cities, along with Fard's newer Black Muslims, were made the targets of a systematic campaign by the FBI and other U.S. agencies to "break up" black neo-Islamic movements in America for good. In the case of the Moors, the arrests of male leaders for pro-Japanese statements or sympathies during World War II meant that their women had to carry on the pounded Moorish and Nation of Islam movements as best as they could on their own. Articles by female adherents now dominated the pages of the *Moorish Voice* newspaper.

But after World War II, the fragmented Moorish movements began to buy more farmland for a separated micronationalist economy. These attempts prefigured the efforts of Elijah's Nation of Islam in the 1960s and 1970s to build an autonomous "national" black economy in America under which agricultural lands were to be bought in a South that loathed blacks and fought the NOI ventures. Still, given the structural damage that the sweeping repression of the 1940s had wreaked, it wasn't until the 1980s that the Moorish movements again established a diverse press and again could attempt to recruit widely among African-Americans.[82]

Leaders of the successor-sectlets that proliferated after WWII reinvented the Noble Drew 'Ali's teachings in diverse directions. Hakim Bey tried to secularize: he kept the name "Islam" for the collective social identity that the Moors were wresting back, but said that the religions were for the ignorant people who could not read—fine Anglo-Masonic *batini* hierarchism! Drew's long-bygone ambiguity towards the U.S. political system did recur. Charles Mosley Bey (d. 1974) had been kicked out of a Moorish temple in the 1930s. A mason and a lawyer, he claimed that the African-Americans had drawn up the U.S. constitution and formed the first U.S. government, but that "the Europeans" then took it all over. His young followers in the 1950s tried to avoid serving in U.S. forces in Korea and payment of taxes. He said he was not interested in the God no one ever saw, only in solving the economic problem: this, too, extended the secular potential in the old MSTA's concern to transform the material lives of the believers. So, are the Moors, then, trying to get out or get in? The discourse of Moors of the 21st century still proudly recounts that the House of Representatives for the state of Philadelphia in 1933 recognized the right of the Moors to use their Islamic name suffixes.[83] Thus, dualities vis-à-vis the Anglo-American system are the tension that the Moorish sects are still seeking to synthesize after so many decades.

Increased Awareness of Third World Muslim Countries and Concepts

Although the Moors lacked access under Drew 'Ali to any Muslim translation of the Arabic Qur'an, after his death, translations by Mawlana Muhammad 'Ali (heretical Ahmadi) and Yusuf 'Ali (a Sunni Indian) were increasingly read at Moorish temples as these became available. After 1960, members in some of the sects began to observe Ramadan and its 'Id al-Fitr (festival-day of the breaking of the fast), although not as congregations but as individuals, and sometimes with immigrant Muslims from the Third World: the idea of the Moors' membership in the large family of the world's Muslims was to strengthen over the decades.[84]

The main formal thesis of Noble Drew 'Ali—the need to reunite the blacks of America with the populations of Africa and Asia around a core of common Islamic religion or culture—was to survive, grow and expand in the harsh American environment over the coming decades. Some Arabs who came much later to do da'wah (propagation of Islam) in America, saw the Islamism of Drew's sect as having been very limited—at most times concocted, mythical and unreal, and on occasion certainly *pro forma* in its use of a few slivers of vocabulary from the Middle East to evoke a reconnecting by the followers to that region.

It is odd that Arabic-scriptured schools of Islamic thought of the East did not have more play in the texture of the movement's worship and its *Moorish Science Temple Koran*, given that Drew had studied Islam under a (heterodox) Ahmadiyyah missionary in New York in 1912-1913, shortly before he seized the writings of the white spiritualist, Levy H. Dowling.[85] Drew's own Moorish Koran did not represent the totality of his teaching in his sect's temples: a 21st century memory in these sects is that he taught from George Sale's very old translation of the Qur'an as early as 1913, and that he continued to use and teach from it after the publishing of his own scripture.[86] Third World Islam was communicated to Drew 'Ali with an African as well as Arab ambience by a ese propagator of Islam in the U.S., Satti Majid.[87] While his American characteristics filtered out many concepts that foreign Muslims offered, Drew 'Ali's movement had long-term historical significance for the international relations of the African-American Nation that was forming: the MSTA began the modern quest of humbly-born Black Americans to affirm and develop some sort of community with the Arab and Islamic world.

Lomax Bey/ Muhammad Ezaldeen

There were one or two attempts to integrate pan-Muslim community after the death of the Noble Drew 'Ali. Teacher James Lomax Bey (later 'Ali Mohammed Bey and then Muhammad Ezaldeen: died 1957) sidestepped the final internal struggle of 1929 between Drew 'Ali and Sheik Claude Green by going instead to Egypt to study Arabic. Lomax Bey had been head of a flourishing Moorish temple in Detroit, the city that had the largest concentration of Arabs in all the USA. In 1930, under the name of 'Ali Mohammed Bey, he arrived in Turkey, and delivered a petition to Kemal Ataturk on behalf of 28,000 Negroes facing prejudice in America, requesting that his sect be allowed to found a colony in Anatolia, Angora or any other under-populated farming area. Turkish officials, though, were merely polite. For J. Edgar Hoover, the attempt to relocate to Turkey was a subversive act, harmful to America's international image.[88]

Throughout the various changes of his long career as a leader of African-Americans (1913-1957), Lomax Bey/'Ali Mohammed/Sheik Ezaldeen showed ability as a business manager and evidenced a strong drive to express nationality through a separate economics and agricultural settlements. In 1929, Lomax had challenged the authority of the Noble Drew 'Ali, partly over funds. Governor J. Lomax Bey had built up Temple #4 in Detroit into one of the largest in the movement, with 1,500 members and four businesses—two grocery shops, a laundry and a printing press. By March 1929, Lomax was claiming that Prophet Drew 'Ali had no more power and that the finance from Detroit should be in his charge: he would send none on to Prophet Drew. He had yelled defiance to Drew's face before over 1,000 people on February 15, 1929 so the Prophet had issued a letter booting him out. It was at this point that Lomax changed his name to 'Ali Mohammed Bey. But Mohammed's journey to Turkey in the end petered away into the picaresque: after the rebuff there, he found it hard to get back into the States.[89] There is no doubt that 'Ali Mohammed/Lomax/Ezaldeen went much farther than Drew would in trying to take the Moors outside the ambit of the U.S. National Government.

On his return to the USA, Lomax/'Ali Mohammed/Ezaldeen founded a "Universal Arabic Association." He continued his drive to express nationality through agriculture: he built self-governing Islamic rural communities, one as far away as Jacksonville, Florida, in which attempts were made to teach Arabic.[90] While Ezaldeen opened his followers to Arabic influences beyond any intention of Drew 'Ali, he also very much carried forward over decades the movement's concern to acquire rural lands and there build small separated "national" communities around agriculture—the fragmented "homeland" of a new religio-ethnic micronation that would always remain scattered throughout America. Under the Islamic idea of *hijrah* (withdrawal from corrupt pagan societies), followers of Ezaldeen founded the 100-acre agricultural settlement of Jabul Arabiyyah in the state of New York in 1938. Some members had been unemployed until then: but others among the new farmers continued to commute to factory jobs as well. The members built up the financial knowledge to negotiate loans and building supplies. After WWII, some Arab immigrants had offered to put together a joint cluster of farms and to help market the produce, in collaboration with Jabul Arabiyya: veteran Dawud Ghani ill-advisedly turned down such offers lest new parties take his Moors over. By 1992, the population of Jabul Arabiyyah had dwindled away to twelve. Farrakhan offered to pay a bill in the settlement's final decline.[91]

The preachings of Moorish and neo-Sunni cults in Newark from 1913 over decades cumulatively proposed Islam as an option to a large number of ordinary blacks down generations. Ezaldeen had been one of the members of the original Moorish temple of 1913 in Newark, and he and his followers were active there up to his death in 1957. When Elijah's Nation of Islam finally organized a proper branch in Newark in 1958, this came late, and drew its membership from a stratum already long steeped in the ideas and Arabic motifs of older, somewhat more Arabic-tinged, sects like Ezaldeen's. The NOI had been first implanted by a "Council of the Brothers" that exalted, but was not run by, the NOI until Elijah founded one of his temples in 1958. Up to then, the Council in Newark was socially and politically activist among blacks in general beyond what the NOI allowed, although bringing NOI Minister Malcolm X (himself on the far edge of his sect) onto its broadcasts. Council members used to sit down in his Newark HQ with Ezaldeen—"because he was learned"—old, but still ever-eager to teach his Egypt-influenced mutation of Moorish Islam.[92]

In the perspective of our new century, Muhammad Ezaldeen/Lomax stands tall among the leaders of the Islam-influenced stream in African-American identity. His efforts to combine international diplomacy, a distinct national business community within the U.S., and some self-Arabization in culture by those little communities, showed vision as well as resolve. If a divide of cultures, languages, classes, differences of races and origins, etc., stretch between (a) immigrant Muslim professionals and their progeny and (b) the African-American Islamic experience, Ezaldeen is becoming among the symbols now bridging that gap in discourse.

The idea of a limited *hijrah*—half-withdrawal in residential concentrations from an unfriendly mainstream—is one of the aspects of the African-American

Islams that most interest U.S. Arab- and other immigrant-descended Muslim youth today, despite a class difference. That America's strong materialist civilization can carry off new generations of East-descended Muslims from worried parents puts the spotlight on the separated Muslim communities achieved by African-Americans. Ezaldeen's nationalist businesses and farm-communities speak to the micronationalizing impulses that have been growing among many U.S. ethnic communities since the late 1970s. He did repeatedly set in place the nuts and bolts for such a venture that still suggest possibly viable approaches 50 years later in the 21st century. Thus, Ezaldeen's life and projects, and even those of Drew 'Ali and Elijah Muhammad, routinely appear now in the chronologies and historical reviews of U.S. Islam carried by mainstream Muslim-American websites that are broadminded about differences of tenets. Academic collections and works on the comprehensive history of Islam in America will henceforth direct America-born Muslims of Eastern extractions more and more to the works of such Moorish leaders as Drew 'Ali, Ezaldeen and Turner-El.

The narrative of 21st century orthodox-liberal Muslim groups stresses that Muhammad Ezaldeen converted to Sunni Islam of an Arab type after he parted from Noble Drew 'Ali in 1929. But the fragments of Arabic that his followers used to distinguish his faith-community in public space or in economics on occasion look a bit garbled. Ezaldeen was in Egypt and Turkey for too short a time to have mastered classical Arabic there, although he kept studying back home. He seems to have maintained some theosophical tendencies from the earlier discourse of Drew 'Ali. He and his followers were relatively more Arabic-influenced if compared with other early Moorish sects and movements, but still of that tradition.

Arabist and pan-Muslim impulses among "Moors" before the later 1950s were typically aborted or limited by the American focus of most of these sects. But with Muslim translations of the real Qur'an circulating more from the late 1950s, mythological or distinctive aspects of this tradition's early teachings became less and less able to separate the adherents from the Arabs and Muslims from Asia and Africa. It was an age of globalization in which various Moorish temples established relations with Muslim diplomats in the USA and indeed with one or two Arab Heads of State, and attended conferences in the Arab world.

Grand Sheik Frederick Turner-El

Among the stalwarts who kept the split Moorish movements going during WWII was Grand Sheik Frederick Turner-El (born c. 1910). Sects opposed to Turner in the fragmented post-WWII Moorish sector of Afro-America still confirm in the 21st century that he converted as many as 20,000 to his reinvention of Moorish Islam.[93] Sheik Turner worked to actualize the compound drive of Drew 'Ali to achieve an economic self-determination of the nation and link up to Third World Muslims. Based in Brooklyn, he was at the fore of some Moors' purchase of a 500-acre tract at Becket, Massachusetts in 1944: the farm would be an addition to others the sect had on Long Island and at Woodstock, Connecticut. Grand Sheik Turner-El planned for a new "Moorish Berkshire National Home," to ultimately include a university for the Moors of America to "be modeled after that of al-Azhar in Cairo". Summer camps for boys and girls from the New York area would direct them away from delinquency.[94]

Turner had a comprehensive vision for autonomous development of his small proto-people, and at 34 years of age in 1944 was already energetic in drawing Africans and Asians into its public rituals. In 1944, a princess of the royal house of Ethiopia sang before a religious meeting of 300 delegates from most of the East coast states held at the Massachusetts homestead. But Turner-El represented himself, and his followers represented him to the mainstream press, as "educated in Egypt where he was ordained to the divine ministry". His claim might have exaggerated a true visit or been a mythological repetition of one made for the Noble Drew 'Ali: whichever, it did tend to make Turner-El's East Coast Moors receptive when in the 1950s and 1960s, they met real Egyptians linked to al-Azhar who wanted to integrate in Islamic community with their sect. In the other, latent-integrationist, facet of the sect, Turner-El defined the Moors as "pro-Americans" who were contributing to America's armed forces and war effort; a representative of the governor of Massachusetts attended one of this series of functions in 1944.[95]

The numerous Moorish sectlets of the 1950s and 1960s that claimed to be carrying forward the teachings of the Noble Drew 'Ali present two patterns. One, isolationist, believed that the teachings and writings of Drew were all the religious discourse African-Americans needed: thus, it tried to keep the adherents away from "radical" (=political) Arab and Muslim movements in the post-World War II era of the decolonization of the Third World. The other model manifested a readiness to read religious texts from overseas Muslims and verbally stand with their political movements: that offered the possibility of a future ethnic lobby in U.S. politics and life to foreign Arab nationalists. Both modalities show increasing if diffused influence from the Arab and Muslim countries in ideas and culture upon the sects descended from Drew's original Moorish movement.

Turner-El met General 'Abd al-Hamid Ghalib, head of the Egyptian delegation at the United Nations, and Dr Mahmud Yusuf al-Shawaribi, an Egyptian science lecturer who in the 1950s was a visiting professor in two U.S. universities, at religious functions organized by foreign Muslims in America. His particular group of the diverse and badly fragmented Moors did voice solidarity with the political changes taking place in the Arabic-speaking North Africa that they reiterated was their homeland of provenance. In visiting the headquarters of Turner's East Coast Moorish sect, al-Shawaribi was struck to see a portrait of the King of Morocco, Muhammad V, who at that time was still in the exile imposed on him by the French, and of 'Allal al-Fasi, the main conservative nationalist leader in Morocco. Al-Shawaribi left with the impression that the sect had "constantly advocated the independence of Morocco at every opportunity" despite their scant resources.

In comparison to his rejection of non-Islamic heresies of Elijah and his followers, al-Shawaribi tended to take Turner on face value as a teacher of true Islam, although he did sense that "correct Islamic guidance" was needed for "a small number of individuals [in his sect] who are not adherents of Islam or who know nothing about it or who know of it only some things that have been corrupted/deformed." Al-Shawaribi provided this receptive Moorish sectlet with English-language Islamic propagation pamphlets from the Arab World. He perhaps made no attempt to read the English-language literature that the Moorish movement[s] had been publishing since the era of Drew 'Ali. He urged the Arab-world Islamic institutions to send teachers of Islam and Arabic who would rotate around those Moorish associations affiliated to Turner to carry out the formation in each of a vanguard of young Moors equipped to later guide and teach all the ordinary members in each town. Al-Shawaribi expected that the "large and organized force" of the Moors of the U.S. North East could be equipped and motivated to propagate Arab-style Sunni Islam among African-Americans in general. He urged his government to invite Turner-El to visit the United Arab Republic "to renew his knowledge" (=replace his particularistic tenets) and to motivate him to step up his propagatory activities among African-Americans.[96]

Purist Rejection of Arab Authority in Islam

The more purist successors to Drew 'Ali's teachings, though, had no particular wish to visit, or be remolded by, Third World Muslims. One narrative is that an Arab immigrant who appeared in Newark in 1918 and taught orthodox Islam among African-Americans posed one of the problems that made Drew 'Ali move to Chicago.[97] By the close of the 20th century, Arabic-scriptured Islam of the Middle East's Sunni and Shi'ite Muslims had become one contender for the loyalties of all African-Americans who want a particularist non-Anglo national or religious identity. Some Moors such as Turner-El had engaged more and more with Middle Easterners in the 1950s while others in the tradition of the Noble Drew 'Ali resisted deep affiliation to the Middle East: but paradoxically, their skilled questioning of Arab claims to religious leadership showed widening acculturation to the Middle Eastern Muslims they strove to keep at a distance.

The movement of Ra Saadi El-Sheik and Sheik of Islam Waleed Abdul Naeem Bey-Sheik in 2002 narrated that Prophet Drew 'Ali had taught that the original Islam of Muhammad has nothing to do with the trappings of Arab culture grafted onto it over the past 1400 years. Pure Islam is the realization of the reality of Man's return to Allah, the surety that Man will regain Deific Life. Al-Mustaqim, the Straight Path, requires acknowledging that God is closer than your jugular vein [cf. Qur'an 50:16]. Each Prophet of Allah has never brought anything new, but only distinctive social prescriptions to deal with their nation's unique social ills: hence the difference in the manner in which the various nations approach the Divine.

As spokesman Sheik Sharif 'Ali Bey expounded it, "contrary to current 'orthodox' Islamic belief and practice, facing the East to pray is not an Islamic requirement (2:148, 2:177 Noble Qur'an)". The practice of Islam by the Arab nations perpetuates the identity crisis of the African-American/Negro/Blackman/colored man, for he again accepts second-class status in a community that cannot see him as an equal—he cannot become an Arab. Without the national identity of his forefathers, he accepts gratefully the names, issues, language, culture, etc., of another people. "Prophet Mohammed stated that the third generation would not be of him, and history has proven him right, especially with the works of 'Uthman, the third Caliph. Prophet Drew 'Ali taught us that his followers would have to straighten out the Moslems in the East with his teachings" when immigrants charged he was unorthodox.[98]

Sharif 'Ali Bey's 2002 stance had an admirably sharp focus on Arab Muslims that rejected compliance with them in ritual, thus ruling out the acceptance upon the margin of international Islam that Farrakhan had been able to build up through orthopraxy [adoption of Muslim World rituals more than its tenets]. Although he and his 21st century group of Moors grappled with some details of the history of the long-gone classical Arabs, this was to make them function within a nativist effort to fend off any new Arab claims to hegemony or leadership over the Moors. Yet, even if just to foreclose any detailed golden-age civilization of Islam to which African-Americans would have to adjust, Sharif Ali's citation of tensions in the Arabs' initial post-prophetic period of the Rightly-Guided Caliphs, along with his real knowledge of Qur'anic Arabic vocabulary, and now the Arabic personal names of more and more leaders in this successor-sect — all added up to substantial tinting of the new Moors from Middle Eastern history and Arab culture that looks set to deepen in the 21st century.

In ideology, though, the leaders under Chief Minister Ra Saadi El-Sheik see themselves as "intelligent enough and rightly-guided enough" to engage with the macro-history of Islam critically, as able to identify those who deviated from the Pure Faith in whatever place, period or clime. They want to keep "the teachings of the Prophet Drew 'Ali [as] our link back to the pure Islam, not Arabs for whom the world would have to be made Arabs to get Islam." [In his farewell speech at his last pilgrimage, shortly before his death in 632, the Arabian Prophet Muhammad Ibn 'Abdallah had told his followers that no Arab or non-Arab nor white man or black was to win precedence over the other through anything else than greater piety]. In classical Arab-led Islam, these latter-day Moors focus on "the spiritual Bilal [ibn Rabah: an Abyssinian convert] who (while not being Arab) was the FIRST to declare [proclaim] publicly the Faith of Mohammed" [in Arabia]. Nonetheless, this 21st century Moorish school does have some impulse towards building "more meaningful" community with the Islamic world while distinguishing that from getting subordinated in culture to Arabs specifically.[99]

Elijah Muhammad in the 1950s and 1960s was to pay tribute to all Marcus Garvey and the Noble Drew 'Ali had done to prepare the African-American psyche for his movement: "both men were fine Muslims whose followers should now follow me... because we are only trying to finish up what those before us started".[100]

5: JEWISH-BLACK INTERACTION AND THE EARLY NOI

Black-Jewish Cultural Relations

Thus far, our data has shown the record of "the Jewish people in America" towards African-Americans to have been mixed. Up to the end of the 19th century, America's Jewish populations had in them a fair proportion who trafficked in, enslaved and hunted blacks for profit and/or to win prestige among and admission into a prospective "white [Euro-American] people." After the great migrations of European Jews and "Negroes" from the rural South met in the great cities of the U.S. North, many more Jews ill-treated blacks—although they were not more prone to do so than other whites, a wrong suggestion of some communications linked to Farrakhan's new Nation of Islam. Moreover, even interactions deformed by severe racism had in them some aesthetic exchanges, in music and in experiences, and some missed possibilities that a new American nationhood could have blended African-Americans, Jews and Christian Euro-Americans if the social and political structure had been somewhat different.

Anglo philanthropists like Andrew Carnegie and such Jewish ones as Julius (1862-1932) were spending large funds to help run institutions dedicated to improving the lives of African-Americans. , a multi-millionaire with a mail-order firm, was matching with money the thrusts for black collective self-improvement started by Booker T. Washington: he helped finance the Institute. The Julius Fund over thirty years provided many scholarships that enabled large numbers of gifted African-Americans to complete secondary and tertiary education; it also contributed to social welfare institutions that served blacks. 's roles instance institutions-building on an imaginative scale by Jews, Anglos and African-Americans working together. DuBois objected that such whites continued to "adhere to the policy of restricting [Blacks] to subordinate positions" in such joint institutions, in which they were always kept under intense surveillance [= racism? or the transparent accountability that has made American institutions work?].[101]

WASP and Jewish Distortion of African-American Culture

Store front cinemas were pervasively owned by Jews in New York before WWI: the developing national chain showed such WASP films as *Birth of a Nation* (1915: depicting blacks as oppressors of whites in the post-Civil War South) to other immigrants, inducting them into standard U.S. racism and promoting the notion that blacks, American or African, had to be put in their place with violence. Even the best interactions of Jews and African-Americans could be dogged by inequality and patronization, yet the two cultures were also flowing into each other in some respects. One Jew, Mezz Mezzrow, was among the earliest Euro-Americans to become interested in a serious way in African-American music. Mezzrow had early come to feel that blacks were "cooler" than whites, and chose to live in Harlem, flourishing there as a good jazz clarinetist in the 1920s and 1930s—the Louis Armstrong era. He was one of the early "white Negroes" later to include Norman Mailer, who as a critic of the American system was to be dubbed "the White Black Muslim" by rightists in the turbulent 1960s.[102]

More liberal or leftist Jews who in the 1980s and 1990s continued to work for community between Jews and Blacks within the America they shared, evoked anew as "intense cultural bonding" the bygone syntheses by such figures as Al Jolson in his 1927 movie "The Jazz Singer" (Hasia R. Diner: 1997). This film reviewed the life of the son of a Jewish cantor—which Jolson had himself been—who runs away from home and the synagogue to become a jazz singer. He is about to achieve decisive success on Broadway when his heartbroken father dies: thereupon, Jake Rabinowitz gives up that career and comes back to the synagogue to assume his duties as cantor. This 1927 film had many scenes of Jolson in black face singing songs and scenes ascribed to Negroes. Some have objected that just as minstrelsy had distinguished Irish or other "ethnic" Americans from blacks and got them closer towards Anglos, so too Jewish-scripted/Jewish-acted and films whose characters interacted with African-Americans or evoked them shifted Jews from a margin between blacks and Anglos towards the Anglos.[103] (The Al Jolson story recurs from the very bedrock of Judeo-Anglo mass-culture: Larry Parkes starred in two film reprises made in 1946 and 1949, as did Jewish-American Neil Diamond in 1981, although the shallow Diamond pulled the jazz towards rock-and-roll). On the other hand, the twists of suffering undergone by sons of Yiddish migrants when they passed themselves off as WASPs for livelihoods in the brutal bargains, made Jewish Hollywood sensitive to the tensions of U.S. Negroes who also passed at greater risk.

It is clear that few of even the better films in which Jewish scriptwriters, directors and actors depicted blacks or their culture before 1960 ever got completely out of reach of burlesque and hoary WASP assumptions that Blacks have some defect that prevents them from achieving competence or success. Many communications from all sects of "Black Islam" in the U.S. have denounced and the Hollywood mass cinema of the 20th century as having carried forward the stereotypes of 19th and early 20th century WASP stage-minstrelsy: all were one continuous racist assault against the culture and dignity of African-Americans. The pro-Warith Ken Farid Hasan in 1985 reviewed the elements from diverse African cultures that slavery and the plantation had damaged and constricted before Emancipation, but from which the early African-Americans still constructed a coherent new culture to manage their new environment. Hasan validated "Negro-English" or Gullah as retaining the "bones" of the original African languages while covering them with the "flesh" of English. He also argued that authentic features from African musics which the enslaved kept in their minds contributed crucial distinctive rhythms to the music blacks evolved in America. For Hasan, the 19th century WASP "blackface" minstrels took the "mask" of shuffling, happy-go-lucky subservience with which the slaves fobbed off the master class, and exaggerated it into a grotesque comic type to devalue African-Americans in the period in which they had won emancipation and were set to become workers in a new urban industrial economy [and a few of them small-bourgeois].

From the viewpoint of this Islamist analysis of U.S. cultures, the [heavily Jewish] directors, script-writers and actors of the subsequent 20th century Americanist cinema from Hollywood were not moving mass portrayal towards a conjunction and synthesis of the various cultures in America, and away from the earlier WASP minstrelsy's devaluation of African-Americans. Rather, Hollywood films in their turn demeaned blacks as cowardly, ineluctably incompetent, drunks, gamblers and layabouts. "The image of the African-American in film was a carryover from [early WASP] stage minstrelsy". Vis-à-vis this stage and screen tradition, Hasan, even under Warith, still kept a touch of the old totalist dichotomies of Elijah's pre-1975 sect that all whites (not distinguishing Christians and Jews) were devils soon to be incinerated by God: as Emancipation came "some clever devil took our survival techniques" and reversed them into the anti-black weapon of minstrelsy. In the other, post-Elijah, integrationist direction, though, this deformation was in part to "nullify the serious concern in the society for us"—i.e. a humanitarian or integrationist tradition among mainstream whites that could at least attempt to deliver an American citizenship without discrimination.

Hasan conceded that from the fifties, Sidney Poitier movies got beyond Step-n-Fetchit and Amos-'n-Andy stereotypes, yet Hollywood would long show itself unable to depict blacks as credible human beings. For Hasan in his 1985 retrospect, the riots and urban revolts of the 1960s prodded Hollywood to put on the screen "Black Heroes"—really "Super-Niggers as unreal as any coon-type: they were not people, they were black."[104] Thus, Hasan did not focus that post-1900 blackface and films that most conveyed minstrel-like images of African-Americans to tens of millions of Americans were mostly the product, not just of whites, but of Jewish script-writers, singers, musicians and actors.[105] Apart from Elijah's old lack of much specific animus against Jewish whites, Warith's successor sect also was concentrating its fire away onto Israelis in the far-off Middle East while seeking to integrate with all groups in America, Jewish-Americans included.

In the 1980s and 1990s, Farrakhan and his restored Nation of Islam were to spearhead a sort of moral uprising by the black bourgeoisie against the cumulative portrayal of Black Americans by "Jewish Hollywood" over the 20th century. Yet, while much was deformed in mass-projection of black culture and history by Jewish-Americans, it did make U.S. whites more open towards the African-American segment of the potential American people, and opened up some degree of employment to black actors—after World War II launching the cinema careers of Harry Belafonte and Sidney Poitier. Hollywood's Jewish film-moguls had been born in small rural towns in Poland or Russia where their parents had had poor livelihoods and faced dislike or violence from Christian Slavic peasants. Thus, some of the moguls made some films sympathetic to Negroes who tried to integrate into the mainstream of American life and its Dream in the face of resistance from Anglo Christians.

Disregarding the left-Jewish auspices under which Poitier acted in Hollywood, Malcolm X held him up as standing for a determined Afro-American authenticity in contrast to the bulk of Black actors who straightened their hair.[106] Engagement with African-American culture by pre-1960 Hollywood has to be viewed in the context of what the range of openings for black identities and thus for black professionals themselves otherwise would have been in the U.S. mass culture that modern technologies had to bring into existence. Even the oft-refilmed story of the jazz-singer had once been inclusive for its time insofar as it defined the larger, mainstream American culture sought as in part drawn from forms of music African-Americans had originated, and in which urban blacks were portrayed as still active.

Some *real* liberalism in this construction from the 1920s of a larger American identity from its Jewish minority is highlighted when we take account of America's more culturally hard-line Anglo elements: even in the 1960s, some in America's governing elite had themselves wanted to end the jazz programs that the Voice of America broadcast to a Soviet Union whose own ruling-class feared subversion from that music—which really did make its fans indifferent to the ideologies and tasks laid down by the elites of both superpowers.[107] The new mass-culture drew in some good things from African-Americans, if along with presumption and quasi-insults from such as Jolson; it sometimes fostered a reception by leftist Jews in particular to cultural creations by blacks themselves, for example in theatre: historian W.E.B. DuBois already tried to seize this opening for his people in a 1923 interview to the left-Jewish *Forward*.[108] Still, the photo of the skinny Jolson in blackface popping his eyes that Ken Farid Hasan carried in 1985 looks insultingly grotesque by any standards.

The tapping by Anglos and Jews of African-American folk-culture varied in levels of authenticity: DuBose Hayward's novel *Porgy and Bess* and George Gershwin's opera adaption of it had a drive to make money, but did get some real Negro culture from the South across to millions of northern Euro-Americans, and opened chances for black actors. But even here, Jolson maintained his drive to leave nothing for real African-Americans: he was determined that he was going to play Porgy in blackface in a musical version, and therefore had bought the stage rights to the Anglo Hayward's novel in 1929.[109]

In summing up minstrelsy as a "wholesale theft and perversion of our newly-born African-American culture" by "Caucasians",[110] Ken Farid Hasan glimpsed the duality of the contribution by this cultural form and its Hollywood reincarnation to the invention of American national identity. Hasan blasted Mark Twain's fondness for blackface minstrelsy [e.g. the childlike "yassuh" nature of Jim], without attention to the contribution real African-American but also Celtic oral styles made to a work like *Huckleberry Finn*. Minstrelsy and (Jewish-scripted) Shirley Temple vented a very Anglo-Saxon friendly contempt and ridicule towards blacks that had to devastate those African-Americans who could not close their psyches to it: it all served as a racist negation of possible Americanist community across the races. On the other hand, such and then mass cinema did synthesize a new expanded (but still basically Anglomorph) culture from African-American songs and ethos that—however much many Euro-Americans could twist and lampoon it, even as they plundered it—they could not stop, as Americans, from becoming part of their own being.

As a follower of Imam Warith/Wallace, the stance of Ken Farid Hasan in 1985 was that U.S. whites exhibited a mixture of liberalism and racism towards their black compatriots, whom they were tending to grant liberty, but that a cultural form—minstrelsy and its Hollywood successor—sometimes swung the balance against that nation-building. Following Elijah Muhammad around 1960, Warith's rival Farrakhan denied in 1984 that Abraham Lincoln ever had wanted to draw blacks into a single social community with whites. Lincoln called some black leaders to the White House and told them that Negroes and whites suffered when they lived together because they were such disparate races: "we should be separated." Farrakhan agreed with this more racial Abe Lincoln that the black intellectuals or bourgeoisie were "extremely selfish" to reject separation, then and in the 1980s: an end to integration was needed so that the poor Black masses could realize their distinct interests. The context from which Farrakhan spoke, though, was significant: he had just emerged from the 1983-1984 presidential primaries in which Jessie, with Farrakhan at his side, had made a serious attempt to incorporate African-Americans into the USA's electoral political mainstream.[111] Each camp, Warith's and Farrakhan's, after 1975 thus maintained its inner dividedness and vacillation about whether to thrust into a U.S. culture and system that was good on balance, or shun it as malevolent and devilish.

Overall, Islamic movements, motifs and themes have provided a sort of rallying-ground from which those blacks open to them have tried to wrest popularizing reconstruction of African-American culture away from the WASP and Jewish groups that have dominated the stage and the cinema in America. Neo-Muslim and Arabophile blacks in the 20th century have striven to give the folk-culture a radically different structure as a precondition for installing it in a new separate African-American nationhood in the USA.

The Anglomorph mass culture over which sets of Jewish-Americans presided was a blend of good and bad. It unfolded under, and was thus tinted by, the modernist self-confidence and race-arrogance of the dynamic Anglo castes who ruled America in the 20th century. Hollywood often advanced the inclusion of certain Jewish-American strata, yet such Americanism could constrict their projection of their own Jewish cultural specificities more than of African-American ones. In the 1950s, various American Jews helped U.S. theatre and mass cinema portray Ann Frank's period of hiding and her death at the hands of the Nazis in Holland in ways that "de-Judaized" and universalized her. Her participation in Hebrew Hanukah prayers was kept off her Hollywood screen to fit her into WASP-American tastes. Hollywood's imaging of her family's segregated hiding from the police, and her final betrayal by an informer, justified left-Americanist or liberal opposition to the segregation of Negroes, and to the thrust of McCarthyism towards a totalitarian polity.[112]

Ameliorism by Jews and Black American Self-Formation of Identity

In various ways, work by rich Jews for better rights, conditions and opportunities for blacks might indirectly remove key restrictions and barriers constraining Jews in American life. Yet aid by wealthy New York German-Jewish individuals for African-Americans, much more reviled than Jews, could easily have made Anglos much more hostile to all Jews in the country—the exact fear that long kept some major Jewish organizations away from the black struggles for equal American rights. A genuine altruism and sympathy tipped the scale for some wealthy and leftist Jews who broke ranks with their general sect-ethnos to aid African-Americans over the half-century to 1950.

There is no doubt that charitable, rich German Jews—very different from the huge bulk of Jews more recently arrived from the Slavic lands of Central and East Europe—had skills that could help people born poorer, and from much less developed rural environments, to urbanize, modernize, organize and win rights. Donations from New York's German Jews, and Jewish lawyers, enabled the NAACP to develop legal programs to defend or aid blacks who had been framed or hit by violence or otherwise victimized in the deep South, and to constitutionally break down segregation and discrimination in government employment and the armed forces.

Some have faulted an "unnuanced" admiration for the figure of the Jewish-Communist defense lawyer of Bigger in Book III of Richard Wright's 1940 novel *Native Son.* The section is a good measure of the aid Left Jews offered hard-pressed African-Americans in a lynch-prone era just before the Islam of Elijah Muhammad and subsequent black nationalist movements overshadowed Marxism of a pure type within African-American communities. Here, the novel brings us to the same conjunction between angry African-Americans and leftist Jews through which ex-Communist Harold Cruse ran his furious scalpel in the 1960s as he moved to the nationalist, Third World, anti-Israel, pro-Arab position that was to typify U.S. black nationalists from the mid-1960s. Lawyer Boris Max tries to convince the doomed Bigger that a category of whites hates him as a Jew, and also white trade-unionists, as much as they do blacks. The novel gives more weight to Bigger's response that Euro-Americans hate his people more.[113]

But Wright in 1940 also left no doubt that, more than had "Bigger" [=the lumpens?], his mind had at least been engaged by the lawyer's Marxism as a prototype for some wider analytical frame that could help African-Americans understand not only their own subordination alone but that of a wider range of groups in America's life in general. The novel disappoints in its failure to flesh out the ethnic and cultural impulses in Boris Max's opposition to the U.S. system, which Wright could have done, given all his socialization with Jewish Communists—yet this also may be because the vision Wright was developing in *Native Son* here went beyond all human groups, and their interactions. The novel makes it clear that Bigger's life as an often unemployed lumpen proletarian—and also the counter-racism and undirected violence it detonates from within him—can't be subsumed under Max's ideology that looked for a well-integrated and articulate wage-proletariat among the warring classes and nationalities. In their final meeting before the execution, this Red alien lawyer who almost carries the name of Marx both (a) recoils from Bigger as the product of an American hatred and chaos that Marxism cannot frame or redirect and (b) has some inkling that, overall, he does not understand life and death more than "the Negro" he has just defended. At its final climax, *Native Son* did transcend issues of nationalities and classes to address religious or existential questions such as why and how individuals can choose to somehow live out their lives when every Individual without exception has to die alone.[114]

Throughout his life, Richard Wright was dismissive of nationalisms and of such trans-continental mega-ideologies as pan-Africanism or Afro-Asian solidarity or the world community of color, or Islam, as much as their pan-white equivalents. His voice thus runs against impulses that have pushed African-Americans to Africanist or neo-Islamist micronationalisms, to "pan-Africanism" and to a Third World orientation that highlights Muslims and Arabs (Wright saw the 1955 Bandung Conference). He had earlier repudiated the past attraction of African-Americans towards supra-racial Communisms. He skeptically insisted that the individual should build his or her own nourishing autonomy in the face of hate and bloodshed and all the universalist but diseased and dangerous ideologies swirling around and buffeting him. Nonetheless, Wright and a generation of African-American writers did indeed look over Communism, or Socialism or various other secularist-ameliorist ideologies that some much more institutionalized and advanced Jewish-Americans held out. Such blacks and that category of Jews who were also trying to de-ethnicize themselves for a time had the chance to become friends as well as co-citizens in a shared America—Boris Max, potential father-confessor of Bigger, who can't quite carry that through. It is clear that the sometimes patronizing Jewish Marxists, philanthropists and anthropologists gave African-Americans some judicious literate weapons with which to critique the American system. These were to resurface in the pinkish tint of some careful and well-focused as well as acidic items to be carried in the 1960s and 1970s by the Nation of Islam's newspaper, *Muhammad Speaks.*

Both the rich German Jews and the small active black bourgeoisie had ambiguous attitudes towards the great masses of their respective coreligionists that they strove to improve and uplift. Some "German" Jewish philanthropists, deeply anglicized, detested—and were determined to iron out—various cultural traits and behaviors of the sub-literate, ill-mannered Ashkenazi immigrants from the Slavic lands—a caste distaste which was radiated back at the memory of those "Germans" by the immigrants' children and grandchildren as they penned the micronationalist historiography of the Jewish enclave-people in America decades later. Ben Freedman, a soap-manufacturer of German Jewish extraction, paid for full-page advertisements placed by the Arab Information Office in America, an organization linked to Palestinian nationalists, in a 1946-1948 press campaign to persuade Americans not to support the foundation of a Jewish state of Israel. His Arab committee colleague, Cecil Hourani, became convinced that Freedman was motivated by an obsessive hatred of Russian and Polish Jews.[115]

Julius supplied $3.4 million towards building or improving ten thousand schools in the deep South attended by Blacks.[116] A [Christian Lebanese?] Arabic immigrant in 1932 could only voice his admiration for this "feat" of the late "for which every liberal person has to thank him." However, the Arabic writer wondered if one motive of such Jewish philanthropists may not have been fears that Negro and other Christian masses in the U.S. could turn anti-Semitic if not placated with benefits and development.[117] The philanthropy of Julius towards African-Americans has a distinguished Americanist WASP-like texture, more than a Judaic one. He financed the construction and improvement of YMCA buildings that would continue the development of poor blacks along (watered-down Christian) Anglicizing lines, in his Americanist vision that financed development would lead poor groups into "good American citizenship." That, of course, would foster social peace that would make all Americans minimally prosperous, and thus provide a widened pool of purchasers and personnel for the nation's entrepreneurs and capitalists.

6: THE NATION OF ISLAM

The initial Nation of Islam that Wali Fard Muhammad founded in 1930 in Detroit had as its target-constituency the 250,000 blacks who had become resident in that city. We examine the first NOI's doctrines to assess two possibilities. How far could they separate blacks from America and from their own ethnos to fuse the believers into a new community in the USA? And could the tenets and motifs evolve enough to really connect African-Americans to the Arabs and Muslims of "the East?"

The mysterious Wali Fard Muhammad was assured of a hearing for his preaching that whites were devil-oppressors by the mass unemployment that the Great Depression had inflicted upon poor blacks from the South. However, while the suffering population he targeted had a high rate of illiteracy, it already had been exposed to trans-national data, contacts and experiences that could contribute to a new political and international consciousness, before Fard arrived. Throughout the 1920s, Garvey's movement, now dying, had publicized Islam not only in Africa but in a much wider East. Detroit was home to the largest immigrant Arab community in America, consisting of Sunni Muslims, Christians and Druze, some of whom had livelihoods as peddlers like Fard or who conducted small shops. There were thus multiple sources of information for Detroit's blacks about overseas Muslims and Islam.

Many of the religious and ethnic institutions that Arabic immigrants built in Detroit and elsewhere were concerned to provide socialization so as to keep the ethnic group in existence, to foster mutual help, and to offer some Arab culture that would relieve the sense of exile and of having been uprooted. Such migrant bodies might not have been urgently intended to propagate Islam outside the ethnos. Elijah Muhammad's son, Akbar, though, has speculated that there was intense informal preaching from some individual immigrants: "African-American contact with Arabic-speaking immigrants accounts for the establishment and spread of... the famous Nation of Islam in 1931." Dr Akbar Muhammad has also speculated that some Arabs who migrated before and after WWI had been sent by organized Islamic missionary circles in the East. He also hints at involvement of Middle Eastern intelligence agencies for "subversive" aims.[118] [Certainly, Mohammed Dus 'Ali had had close connections to the Ottoman elite, which decorated him: however, Ataturk ended pan-Islamism abroad after WWI, and few colonized Arab populations had any intelligence agencies with which to Islamize overseas groups for political aims]. Wallace/Warith ud-Din Muhammad, the son of Elijah Muhammad, who since 1975 has been the leader of the main sect that propagates among the blacks something like orthodox Sunni Islam as practised in the Arab countries, observed in 2002 that he was born in 1933 in a Dearborn, Michigan street that had so many immigrants from the Middle East living in it that it had by popular consensus been renamed "Yemen Street." Thus, he had been interacting with Arabs from birth.

The exchange of discourses between immigrant Arabs and African-American immigrants in Detroit and Dearborn up to 1930 laid the basis of a consciousness of an (Islamic) "East" that made ordinary blacks able to follow Wali Fard Muhammad, the founder of the Nation of Islam, when he came to convert them in 1930. The memory of Fard bequeathed by poor strata of Michigan blacks was that he came to them as a peddler of silks, second-hand raincoats and used clothing, although he said that he was a prince come from Mecca in Arabia. This image of him as eking out a precarious, roving living among even more desperate unemployed masses fits the Great Depression context, and would not detract from the dignity of either Fard as a human or of those he converted. However decades later, after 1960, Elijah's Nation of Islam tried to soften the details of the early extreme poverty so as to help award Fard the status of God incarnate.[119]

Fard's images that he could reconnect those blacks who gave him a hearing to homelands in the East was one element in his appeal. In the decayed tenement houses of Paradise Valley, he spread out for them robes which he said came from the homeland of their forefathers in the East whose glories he then began to describe. With a tactful gradualism over several meetings, Fard would carefully select Biblical verses with which he gradually drew his poverty-stricken black hosts to a condemnation of Christianity as an instrument by which the white devils had imposed their authority and oppression on the blacks. Then he drew his audience to the next step—to embrace his rather special Islam. The standard photograph of Fard that the Nation of Islam diffused after his disappearance showed him reading a large (Ahmadi?) Qur'an.

One Zionoid or post-Zionist historian, though, argued that the black nationalist mythologies Fard preached as Islam were less an exposition of that Islam known in the East than a "brilliant invention" he "fabricated out of whole cloth" to meet black needs.[120] Still, Fard taught his listeners that the real name of God is Allah, that His true religion is Islam, that "Muslim" is the true name of the followers of that religion, and that the Qur'an had been revealed to "our Prophet" Muhammad, the son of 'Abdallah in Arabia. Thus the nomeclature. How specifically Fard taught them motifs of the numerous sectors of the Qur'an that demand justice for the oppressed, so clearly applicable to their situation, still needs to be reconstructed.

As with Drew 'Ali's Moorish movement earlier, establishing community with an international Islamic religion and nation—the new (or "restored") authenticity—would separate the converts from black popular culture and habits regarded in America as central in being "Negro." Once more, "Islam" was being used as a clinical instrument to lance out the subculture that ordinary Detroit Blacks had carried with them from the USA's rural South. Although he used to eat everything that his hosts in Detroit would place before him during his rounds, once the meal was over, Fard would forbid them to eat certain foods because people in their black homeland across the seas did not, explaining that those foods were harmful to their health in contrast to the robust health that their brethren back in the East enjoyed. Here, as well as the pork banned in orthodox Sunni Islam in the Middle East, Fard prohibited such healthy foods as cornbread and collard greens which have been associated with rural blacks in the South—symbols in his drive to shift the culture of his black following away from their previous social patterns and identity.

The identity of Wali Fard Muhammad, the founder of the Nation of Islam, later proclaimed God by Elijah Muhammad, was to remain mysterious. One contention—ascribed to FBI agents in the field in the 1930s—identified Fard as a persona of a New Zealand-born [half-Maori? half-South Asian?] petty pass-white con man and former drug-peddler—a theme seized, with muffled doubts, by Ziono-American Arthur J. Magida, in his scrappy 1996 biography of Farrakhan.[121] Gardell (1996) rejected the FBI's contention on the grounds that Fard's and the con man's sometimes fuzzy photos from the period do not match. Furthermore, he pointed out, the FBI had cynically abused the American press since the 1950s to destroy the "Black Muslim movement"—orchestrated disinformation that must long render doubtful any document which that Bureau may "release" about any Muslim or Arab groups it has targeted.[122] It is to be noted that in 1959, among a battery of measures it took to stop Elijah Muhammad from communicating to Middle Eastern and African peoples during his travels, the FBI forged a demented warning from a concocted Arab father to his son and "all true Muslims" to stay away from the non-Muslim Elijah when he reached their countries.[123] (This "letter" shows that U.S. intelligence agencies were sometimes still primitive in manipulating Arabs and outside Muslims in the 1950s.)

After his assumption of leadership of the NOI in 1975, Wallace Muhammad told a Pakistani scholar he liked that he believed Fard to have been from the Indo-Pakistan subcontinent and been of Qadiyani (Ahmadiyyah) background.[124] Gardell speculated from his review of the early doctrines and practices of the Nation of Islam under Fard and Elijah Muhammad that some kind of Druze from Syria-Lebanon-Palestine—or perhaps the second-generation scion of an immigrant family?—had been the founder.[125] Evanzz (1999) tried to synthesize (a) the New Zealand/half-Polynesian con man motif emanating from the FBI with (b) an hypothesis that Fard was also a relatively fair-skinned son of an Isma'ili from Gujarat or Punjab with a "Pakistani heritage" who had married a white woman in New Zealand. Most of the evidence that Evanzz offered was shaky, although he did muster one or two virulent Islamic condemnations by Fard and his subordinates of "the Hindu" for polytheism and incarnationism, and equation of Hindus with the white devils as both enemies of Islam.

Such themes could have come from the communalist cauldron of the Punjab and Sind of the later nineteenth and earlier twentieth centuries—and are ironical motifs in that the Nation of Islam would itself shortly stumble into anthropomorphic, and some Third World Muslims felt, quasi-polytheist, tenets under Elijah. It is also true that Fard designated "Shabazz" as the original name of the black Islamic nation in West Africa from which African-Americans were torn and that "Shahbaz" is a personal name in the areas that now form Pakistan [although also in Iran and Syria].[126] However, Fard could have picked up such Pakistani-like motifs from South Asian immigrant Muslims who were skillfully courting African-Americans. True, Druzism has some positive images of Hinduism and the Hindus, with whom it shares the reincarnation tenet. The pre-1975 Nation of Islam and its successor-sects seldom vented anti-Indian motifs. During Bangladesh's struggle for independence, *Muhammad Speaks* was to stand with the darker-skinned Bengalis, whom Hindu India aided, against the more Middle Eastern West Pakistan. It is true that in the 1950s, 1960s and 1970s, Elijah and his sect were to cite the development plans of Pakistan as one source of the NOI's own Plan to build a separate black nationalist economy in the U.S. In the 1980s and 1990s, Farrakhan's *Final Call* was to give some publicity to India's Dalit (Untouchable) enclave nationalists, perceived as "Black" victims of fairer-skinned "Aryan" upper-caste Hindus, but that was the outcome of personal contact with untouchables in Libya and elsewhere rather than a development from within the religion's classical theology.

To some extent, Fard and his new sect were carrying forward and transforming beliefs that Drew 'Ali and his so-called "Moorish national movement" had diffused in the previous decade of the 1920s. After Drew 'Ali's 1929 death, some of his local leaders broke away to establish their own movements and many observers and scholars have characterized Fard as one such.[127] Whether Fard himself was or was not a former follower of Drew, he and Elijah drew upon former Moors and Moorish motifs while also recruiting ex-Garveyites. The unemployed Elijah Poole had been hitting the bottle in 1930: it was Abdul Muhammad, a former follower of Drew, who inducted him into Fard's cult. Yet, an intriguing aspect of Elijah's 1931 conversion was that it had first been set in train by his clergyman father, William, who was a friend of Abdul Muhammad and spoke respectfully to son Elijah of the accounts that the latter had given him of Fard's teachings.[128] This openness to a virulently anti-Christian reinvention of Islam is surprising, coming from a middle-aged Negro clergyman, and may indicate that Elijah's father was indeed heir to an orally-transmitted memory of a scriptural religion of African-Americans—Islam—that had preceded their christianization in North America.

The more anthropomorphic and quasi-polytheist motifs that crop up in Elijah's and Fard's religious black nationalism may have had their origin in Isma'ili or/and Druze ideas that were themselves in part fed from esoteric gnosticism that predated Islam in Egypt. In Gardell's speculation, Isma'ili dichotomization of (a) believers with angelic potential against (b) humans who are reflections of Iblis, the devil, could have provided the archetype of the Nation of Islam's dichotomization of potentially divine blacks versus white devils. Way-out, extremist, Isma'ilism's motifs of emanations of God conducting successive creations may have contributed to the early NOI's development of images of God creating Himself, or manifesting as a series of black human-like incarnations—all so offensive to Sunni Muslims who draw their tenets from the plain sense of the Qur'an's verses.[129] (Mormonism could have been another, ultra-American source of images of a destructive judgment of the devil whites, as well as of polytheistic and incarnationist errors into which "the Black Muslims" admittedly sometimes did stumble in their long march to the construction of an authentic Islamic belief-system in North America.)

Sunni Muslim writers from the East have understandably bridled at the tinctures of anthropomorphism in the early NOI's themes of the divine potential of individual U.S. blacks or of the oppressed Black Nation as a collectivity. They were, though, more or less forced on the Nation of Islam by the American environment's severe racism: the idea of the Black Man's semi-divine potential functioned as a "psychological lever" crafted to break the mental chain of inferiorization that for so long kept African-Americans at the bottom rung of society, sapped of initiative. The heresies were "an extreme version of positive thinking" (Gardell), a therapy that gave the black poor the boost of morale and hopeful outlook they needed to transform their lives against the rather heavy odds.[130]

Any Arabist reader could add on his or her account a complex of parallels that bear out lay Druze in America as one crucial source in some of the doctrines that are most distinctive of the Nation of Islam. The classical Sevener Shi'ites or Isma'ilis, the Twelver Shi'ites who currently rule Iran, and the Druze who separated from Isma'ilism early in the eleventh century all developed doctrines that there is an Imam who never died but only vanished or occulted: he will one day return to destroy oppressive governments and inaugurate a golden age on earth. It prefigured the doctrine of the Farrakhanist Muslims that "the Mahdi," the God-guided or incarnate founder Wali Fard Muhammad, and the Messenger Elijah Muhammad, have never died but only temporarily withdrawn or occulted above our globe: shortly, they will return in a gigantic spaceship to judge and destroy this wicked world. Then they will usher in the New Islam of eternal prosperity and peace on an earth that will never again have any whites. There was similarly a Druze-like flavor (with some Christian millenarian influences) to the expectations of Farrakhan and his adherents in 1991 that the savage fighting between 'Iraqis and Americans in the Gulf (Farrakhan left Baghdad just before it started), and between Muslims and Orthodox Christian whites in Bosnia and the Caucasus, was the start of the Armageddon that would soon usher in God's final judgement and incineration of the whole white-dominated world.[131]

Ordinary Druze have for centuries believed that the Day of God's Judgment of all humanity could be very close: a lay Lebanese Druze told me in 1997 that it will be preluded by a worldwide war between human groups so savage it will destroy all the soldiers' mounts, vehicles and weapons, leaving the survivors to fight out their final battle on foot with only the shattered swords they grip in their hands. It is like the nation rising against nation in Elijah and Farrakhan's Armageddon that can precede God's incineration of the world. Some lay Druze also voice the sense that Satan ("Iblis") and his adherent devils have forms indistinguishable from humans, enabling them to be active in, if not control, politics and power in the lead-up to Judgment Day. For militant Lebanese lay Druze, the Chief Devil may be Lebanon's Maronite Patriarch or its Christian state-president, whereas for some "Black Muslims" he has traditionally been the President of the United States![132] Lay Druze of the type who could have had peddler and shop-keeper interaction with the desperate blacks of Paradise Valley also believe in the awaited deliverer *Mahdi*, a title that was applied to Fard before Elijah declared him God incarnate. However, Gardell and Essien-Udom (1962) also traced Nation of Islam doctrines of the divine potential of the Black Nation and God's impending destruction of the whites to such North American sources as Christian, theosophical, Freemasonic and Mormon writings that had been articulating a sense that humans are fallen gods long before Wali Fard Muhammad or his disciple Elijah.

DeCaro (1998) has characterized the first Nation of Islam that Fard founded as (perhaps like Drew 'Ali's Moors) only "pseudo-Islamic": it did not have or bequeath the "DNA" of anything genuinely from the Arabo-Islamic world—Fard's discourse "lacked the gene of orthodoxy".[133] Yet slivers of Middle Eastern DNAs do crop up in Fard's admittedly highly eclectic discourse, even at those points where it diverged most from some Qur'anic perspectives. Several recent scholars have been struck by Fard's rejection of the prescriptive views which Christians and Third World Muslims have held in regard to the birth of Jesus: for Fard, Jesus was not an incarnational miracle (New Testament) or a creational miracle (Qur'an) of God through a virgin Mary, but the illegitimate son of the ghetto-like unskilled carpenter, Joseph, who got Mary pregnant while her father was away on business. The prophet Jesus was betrayed for the reward by a Jewish shopkeeper in Jerusalem: white Roman cops then stabbed him to death against a board as he held his arms out—a naturalist residue of Christianity's grand crucifixion narrative.

While Fard meant this reconstruction to speak to the quotidian life of lumpen African-Americans in their Northern U.S. ghettoes, it did have some Middle Eastern DNA in it. It took further the Qur'an's rehumanization of

Jesus back into a prophet, and had some Sunni-like functions in that Fard, Elijah Muhammad and Farrakhan always used the story to dismiss such central Christian doctrines as that Jesus was the son of God and a person in Godhead, with his narrated crucifixion and resurrection as self-sacrifice by God to redeem humanity. For Fard, Jesus was a prophet who mainly drew small audiences of 25 on street corners rather than multitudes.

Fard's narrative is also very like Middle Eastern Isma'ilism or Druzism in maintaining—even while denying that the events the gospels image actually happened to Jesus—the New Testament's images of a crucifixion, a tomb, a stone and resurrection as symbolic, prophetic images of the whites' mental, social, spiritual, economic and political murder of the Black Nation. The stone in front of the shallow grave symbolized the stone-heartedness with which the nation of the white devils today strives to block the national resurrection of the reawakening blacks.[134] While it was Biblical materials that Fard, Elijah and Farrakhan here deconstruct and turn to their own use, their Isma'ili and Druze precursors in the Arab world had long often allegorized Qur'anic narratives about the lives of prophets in their esoteric *tafsir* with much the same freedom—that Noah's ark denotes the knowledge from the imam or divine leader with which the adherents escaped or escape the flood of the ignorance of the common people.

Fard's rejection of Christianity's incarnationist ideology and myth showed worn-down slivers of transported disintegrated motifs taken from Sunni Muslim, Druze, and Arab Christian immigrants to America being put into a new structure designed to serve the blacks. That could happen to such materials if transmitted by oral tradition only to a second-generation Arab-American who had never learned to read literary Arabic properly. Fard argued that "Mary's father was a rich man who refused to give Mary in marriage to her greatest lover, Joseph el-Nejjar" [i.e. "the carpenter"] because he was a poor man with nothing but a saw and a hammer: that Joseph then impregnated Mary is "very reasonable and scientific".[135] Here, we see the street-level conjunction in ethnically-mixed U.S. cities of hearsay atoms carried by winds from a range of American and overseas Arab and Muslim traditions, all then fused into a new made-in-America religion by an autodidact ethnic who could read only English. The Qur'an does not apply "al-najjar" or carpenter in Arabic to that Joseph, but Fard could have picked the term up from Christian Arab-Americans if he had a smattering of spoken Arabic, perhaps from immigrant parents or grandparents. Conversely, his use of the Arabic word may have been his conscious device to connect himself in an unbroken tradition to an Islam about which he may have learnt little from his childhood and adolescence.

A naturalist view that Jesus was an ordinary bastard is a commonplace hint when uneducated Anglo and African-American chat, while "realistic" counter-interpretations of events narrated in the Qur'an, or promises it holds out, are voiced in double entendres among friends by sub-literate peasant or working-class Arab Sunnis, from whom Fard's elders could have come: and a Druze would have been held much less to the literal courses of events set out in the

Qur'an. Slivers of Arabic in part from Christian Arab immigrants, folk-hatred of Christian incarnationism among poor Sunni Americans, Isma'ilism's corrosion of historicity by reducing exoteric events into allegories, contempt for Jesus among Jewish-American ghetto merchants, the class resentments of marginalized poor immigrant or black Americans, ghetto street-wiseness, African-American hatred of racist law-enforcing authorities (Roman cops bump off Jesus), and the post-Christian post-Enlightenment "Rationalist" scientism of America—all in a twinkling run together into a new creed in Fard's remarks about Jesus.

The birth of the Nation of Islam in the 1930s, then, brings us to the disintegration and assimilation of a U.S. community of immigrant Arabs made up of Sunnis, Druze and Christians from the Fertile Crescent. As that transient minority dissolved into the African-American and Anglomorph-American nations, the immigrants yet achieved a vicarious survival in the shards of their dying language and creeds that Black Americans seize and now turn to the purposes of their own self-interest and self-liberation. With the discourse of Fard, we meet flotsam from cultures disintegrating on a margin between races and civilizations far removed from the literate centers of those traditions (although Elijah accessed materials on the Prophet Muhammad Ibn 'Abdallah, and the Qur'an in English, at the Library of Congress when following Fard's old reading list in 1939).[136] The cohering of this reinvented "Islamic" ideology from Arab and American fragments within a new social, political and religious life by the end of the 20th century would propose Islam to most U.S. blacks.

As data stands, the Nation of Islam looks to have been founded by a second-generation son of a Druze or Isma'ili Muslim, but using only the Qur'an (in an heretical or deviant Qadiyani/Ahmadi translation) as the non-Christian native scripture to be recovered. As well as incarnationist Christianities, Druzism too could have been one source of the status of God incarnate that Elijah awarded to Wali Fard Muhammad in the 1930s.[137] If, conversely, someone without any Arabo-Muslim background did found the sect, "Fard" would have moved among a stratum of African-Americans that already had been interacting regularly with Sunni, Christian and Druze Arabs settled in Detroit: he would have given a final ideological structure to Muslim World motifs they already were in the process of synthesizing before He came to Paradise Valley disguised as a peddler of used clothes. Fard openly drew on the chiliasm of the Jehovah's Witnesses. But the cornered desperation of the early Druze—massacred by Sunnis and Shi'ah alike—and their foul-mouthed denunciations of those ruling "devils" as marked to be exterminated, would run well into Fard's vituperative discourse and the situation of poor African-Americans in 1930.

African-Americans and Arab shopkeepers were seeing a lot of each other in the Detroit slum where Fard Muhammad first preached in 1930. But an assessment of how much political and social relationship the earlier converts expected that their new creed would entail with Arabs awaits a serious scanning of pre-1950 Nation of Islam and Moorish publications.

Initial Entry into the U.S. System

The glamour of the NOI for many disaffected African-Americans, and from the 1960s for many Third World Muslims, has been as a movement of protest against Euro-Americans that hopefully could turn violent. But the sect's teachings, discipline and drive for money could equally lead the adherents towards—and perhaps into?—America's central Euro system. But that would depend on whether white Americans would be prepared to make room for the Muslims and loosen up the unspoken codes of their interaction with African-Americans.

Analysts affiliated to the U.S. system understood from its outset in the 1930s that the sect was as hostile, or more, to popular black mores as to whites and was withdrawing from the Afro-American populations from which it sprung. In his pioneer 1938 study, Erdmann Beynon noted the techniques by which Fard's movement led the initial 8,000 converts to sever or minimize their contacts with the Negro community of Detroit among whom they lived. It was religion that enabled them to make the break: Beynon equated their isolation from fellow-blacks with that of "members of agricultural religious communities who migrated to new homes". And even as the sect withdrew from the African-American masses whom it defined as the nation it was missioned to save, it in a further paradox won jobs from "devil" whites for the adherents.

The entrepreneurial thrust is in all sects of black Islam, but Beynon was struck in 1938 that "their [the early NOI's] principal occupational adjustment has been factory labor, and thus the cult members have [set up and] maintained a functional relationship with the metropolitan economy outside of the Negro community." The sect's inculcation of literacy, avoidance of alcohol and debauchery, elaborate courtesy, precision, hygiene, and presentable clothing bought from savings enabled by the food restrictions—all in tandem made the disciplined members win more jobs from automobile and other factories than black Christian applicants, who were prone to booze and drugs, etc.

Ideologically, NOI members also fitted well into the modern mass-production factories of U.S. capitalism, in that early NOI members talked against unions and union organizers as enemies of Allah who had to be removed from the Planet Earth. This rejection of unions by some early NOI Muslims had a context. In the early 20th century, racist pressure from s on employers not to hire less skilled blacks who would work for less at the outset, made even the left-leaning W.E.B. DuBois a unions critic.[138] Facing exclusion from unions, the NOI's converts applied their religion to delegitimize them, and steel their own will to conduct long-term conflict with the white organized working class. Converts to Islam were trying to turn the enraging function of Blacks as temporary strike breakers into a long-term niche in factories through which to pass into the mainstream system and its wealth. As long-term workers, members could save up the basic capital they needed to then start out as small businessmen. It was working as WWII neared.

The asceticism of the converts had been meant to start them out as contenders in private enterprise: as the recovery from the Depression speeded up, the factory-workers of the NOI moved from the terrible slums into the best areas in which Negroes had settled. Then, risking living beyond their means, the Muslim workers, who only rented their homes, challenged their Negro bourgeois neighbors by buying clothes, automobiles and furniture that matched theirs.[139] In the later era of the 1960s and 1970s, also, premature conspicuous consumption was to become a temptation that could set the capitalist venture of the Nation of Islam of Elijah up for failure.

In the late 1950s, the NOI would still discourage meaningful participation by members in s, although the idea of such a multi-racial class interest organization had tantalized some before they joined, and although some ex-Communists wrote for *Muhammad Speaks*. One ex-unionist of the 1950s had been as turned off by the low class consciousness of the apathetic Negro workers he had been trying to organize as by feral bosses and by the white officials who controlled the corrupt s.[140]

The material success that the NOI brought paradoxically threatened its ideology and membership. The gains from the thrust of NOI followers to middle class status and careers, put in question for some members the anti-white tenets and hope of Judgement upon whites that had fired the initial effort. Was the white-directed world really so irredeemable and doomed, when some Muslims were now finding ways to flourish in it? Abdul Muhammad withdrew from the NOI and declared loyalty to the U.S. flag and constitution, dropping the teaching of the sect's schools that followers were citizens of the Holy City of Mecca who had their own Muslim national flag of star and crescent, and their original "national" Arabic language that they should recover.

Although the sect's workers were becoming fine anti-unionist long-term employees, by 1939 the U.S. system was preparing its most serious campaign to finish the NOI.

Repression of the NOI

The various governmental, political and judicial institutions of the American system in Detroit soon vented impulses to crush Fard's fledgling Nation of Islam. The neo-Muslim sects were early a test case of how much diversity Anglo-American enterprise would truly tolerate beyond its veneer of high-sounding freemasonic pluralist clichés. The U.S. ruling ethnos had sometimes shown greater toleration of diversity when religious in form—towards Catholics or Jews—as against modalities more likely to become frankly nationalist. (Jews and Irish-Americans were well aware of this WASP preference). But the U.S. system also had in it quasi-totalitarian drives not to allow groups that could transmit compound religious, political or cultural difference, and any autonomist collectivity based on such differences, to new generations.

Such institutions in Detroit as the police special squad justified their open drive to dismantle "the Allah Temple of Islam" from the ritual sacrifice of an African-American male on a wooden alter by adherent Robert Karriem on 20 November 1932. Karriem's rationale was that the ritual had been predestined in a previous millennium as a means to produce a "Savior" for blacks. The Swedish comparative religionist, Mattius Gardell, found no trace of such a Christianity-patterned doctrine in such fragments of the first teachings of the Nation of Islam as have survived from that period: rather, Karriem could have been made unhinged when he and his family were removed from eligibility for welfare at the height of the Great Depression by white social workers.[141] Ten days later, in an incident that anticipated the Soviet Union's incarceration of religious dissidents in psychiatric wards in the 1960s and 1970s, the police put Wali Fard Muhammad and his colleague Ugan 'Ali in padded cells of a psychopathic ward from which they were released only when both agreed to dismantle the sect and Fard agreed to leave Michigan forever.

In the days after the cops put Fard on the train, the police and a range of white American institutions orchestrated a semi-totalitarian campaign designed to make it almost impossible for any Afro-Muslim community to continue in Detroit. To publicly degrade the adherents and take away their livelihoods, 100 Muslims were arrested on blatant pretexts on the streets of Detroit, or at their jobs to get them fired. Those who were could expect no food safety-net for their children from the American system henceforth: white social workers now calmly ended welfare payments to one third of Fard's Depression-devastated followers in Michigan. Despite family food pools and the "Poor Fund" Fard established, males over thirteen often had only three slices of bread per day.[142] In 1934, the Detroit authorities were to separate two of the adolescent pupils from their parents, detaining them in a juvenile detention center as state's witnesses.[143] One sees here how America could have turned in a twinkling into a totalitarian ethnic-cleansing state that might separate the sexes and generations of whole religio-national groups marked to be ended. Yet the Detroit personnel stopped short of that abyss.

In face of the drive of white authorities to deny jobs, livelihoods and food to the fledgling sect's members and families, the leadership changed the names and signboards of its institutions. This charade that the sect had dissolved itself, though, was blown when Fard in 1933 launched a separate educational system: the withdrawal of the 400 juveniles from Detroit schools was noticed and in early 1934, the State's judiciary and police jailed the NOI leaders, and boarded up the schools and temples. While the educational officials did cite some ostensibly rational concerns about the qualifications of teachers and the curricula at these first NOI schools, Americanist intolerance pervaded their reports. The innovative potential of this new alternative educational system to critique Christianity and falsity in the American system was simply ignored by white officials who had lost capacity for hypothetical thinking and brusquely repressed the experiment. NOI education could have evolved into a modest corrective mechanism had it been attached to a liberalized American system that would have regulated (rather than crushed) diversity. Angloid officialdom over decades were to repeatedly strike at "Black Muslim" attempts to establish their own school system. In 1967, Division 5 of Washington, DC attempted to close a Muslim grade school by unleashing the local zoning, tax, health and safety bureaucracy, and by opening files on the parents of each of the around 150 children enrolled in the school.[144]

The representatives of the Christian religious elite among the Negroes from whose churches Fard was taking converts vented much the same quasi-totalitarian hatred of difference as the white institutions in whose assault they were now awarded bit parts. Evangelist Rev. Jeremiah , as spokesman for the established Negro groups in Detroit, in an affidavit to the white judge, called the sect a "reversion to paganism [that] ought to be halted at once".[145] The eagerness of African-American clergy to serve in the destruction of the first NOI surely helped fuel the virulence with which the Muslims were to continue to denounce Christianity as an instrument of the white race-enemies of blacks up to Elijah's death in 1975 (see Ch. 4).

The persistent harassment and repression by white instrumentalities was effective: Wali Fard Muhammad left the believers to "return to Mecca" in 1934, opening the way for leadership disputes and disorder that Elijah Muhammad was still bringing under control when the American authorities jailed him and his colleagues in 1942 for their anti-white, Japan-friendly sentiments: Elijah was only released the year after the U.S. defeated Japan, in 1946.

The 1942-1946 repression showed the same alternation by whites as that of the 1930s, between (a) a totalitarian drive not to allow a non-Christian minority that questioned even verbally the bases of the American system and (b) a more laid-back Anglo-American impulse that, while often contemptuous of blacks, wanted to spare itself the bother of regimenting them—and was prepared to let them worship in the ways they wanted so long as these did not frontally strike at Anglo rule. The Rev. Jeremiah had specifically denounced the Nation of Islam as a "reversion to paganism" in the calculation that the white authorities would dismantle the sect as therefore beyond anything America's Anglo-Christian system could ever allow. He was broadly right for the early 1930s. Then, whatever the letter of the U.S. constitution and other documents said, the USA's Angloid elite in practice was barely prepared to tolerate a range of Euro-Christian sects. Black churches were to be a segregated adjunct, with the Jews gripping the outside of the pale.

The formal grounds on which the U.S. intelligence and legal agencies arrested and tried 65 NOI adherents in 1942 were refusal to register for the draft, and charges of sedition and conspiracy to promote victory for the Japanese. Clegg's data suggests the U.S. agencies cynically concocted the charges to whip up press hysteria so as to highlight the FBI as those Defenders America could never do without. One variety of whites that Elijah and other Muslims interacted with in this period drove home that many Anglomorphs would not allow Islam in America. When his interrogators refused to believe his declaration that no Muslims had cached arms to aid the Japanese as a fifth column, Elijah requested a copy of the Qur'an so that he could spend his time behind bars constructively. The warden laughingly refused access to the Islamic scripture, advising Elijah rather to "read the Bible" because "that is what we put them in prison for."[146] After the sentences, a guard from the other variant of the WASPs did try in vain to procure a Qur'an, but the type of whites who hated to allow a non-Christian religion were thicker in the penitentiaries. Milan prison long refused to grant its incarcerated Muslims time and space for collective worship equivalent to its services for Protestants, Catholics and Jews—or to allow pork-free cooking, thereby forcing Elijah to subsist on bread and potatoes, which probably caused the bronchial asthma that would wrack him for the next three decades.[147]

The reports of the psychologists and psychiatrists who interrogated Elijah et al raise issues of the perversion of modern sciences by governing elites in Anglomorph states. Prison psychiatrist Dr W.S. Kennison in mid-1943 assessed Elijah as having "paranoid-type" delusions that he and his race were being systematically persecuted, "the feeling that he is being followed and that people are talking about him"—which Kennison's pages indeed were—to those with power.[148] That period had no confidentiality of psychiatric information, and any report could be dovetailed from the outset, as would occur in the USSR later, for media planting to discredit any individual or group marked for destruction. Yet, taken literally, this white psychiatrist himself would have to be assessed as clinically insane if madness were to be defined to include the inability of an apparatchik to see his own crucial functions and the day-to-day effects prescribed by the job he carries out for his livelihood. That Fard thought himself a deity was classified as insane and among the grounds for which the psychiatrists locked him in the padded cell. They ignored themes of the U.S. elite's freemasonry that its elect individuals as they built power and wealth could restore self-divinity, that cultivating the techniques of that Brotherhood elevates adherents to become creator "architects" of other "profane" humans and indeed even whole groups under the Great Architect God. Indeed, overseas, American officials would go on to create a whole "nation"—"South "—and prefabricated cultures, clergies and parties for Muslim and Third World peoples after they won political independence. Among the devoted masons was the disturbed J. Edgar Hoover, director of the FBI, whose agents had shadowed Elijah and his adherents. The FBI was among the agencies on whose behalf the psychiatrists now had to analyze the arrested Islamic black nationalists they refused to classify as political prisoners.

The U.S. has not tried to eliminate groups with the same sustained single-mindedness as Communist polities, although its recurring deportations of Amerindian populations across climatic zones into the 1920s read like Stalin's deportations of dissatisfied Caucasus Muslim "criminal nationalities" to Central Asia during and after WWII and could move in the direction of Hitler's genocide against Jews.[149] The 25%-50% death rates of resistant natives during deportations have been similar in the U.S. and Soviet experience: 400 Amerindian nations were interned en masse. Although the FBI sometimes evinced the meticulous obsession of Communist agencies to monitor, the U.S. system as a whole has not kept up the *unremitting* regimentation by the USSR's Slavic elite of non-Aryan nationalities and religions it hit and tyrannized for 50 years, but which were empowered to survive –like the black Muslims—by the hatred of their race oppressors that they sustained in their hearts. More people were allowed to exercise freedom of speech, including in print-media, in the USA than in the USSR, although the latter provided free health care not delivered to many lumpen blacks, Hispanics and some Euros in the USA.

There was always the other type of easier-going white, also: when a parole officer released Elijah in Chicago, he told him to "teach what you always have been teaching and nobody will bother you anymore".[150] This was not to be fulfilled in Hoover's and the FBI's drives to harass, subvert, sabotage and destroy the Nation of Islam throughout the 1950s, 1960s and 1970s. In the American practice, money, political power, ethnic support, lawsuits and discreet threats or bursts of violence have been prerequisites which enabled minority religions and races to wrest the rights that American theory purports to offer to all individuals. The early history of the Nation of Islam from 1930-1950 bore out the Africanist nationalist Conrad Worrill's 1989 observations that only a well-organized and institutionalized ethnic group can enable the individual to impose his rights evoked by the Constitution in the U.S.[151]

The skill with which Fard bribed local police officers to look the other way may have saved his sect from having been destroyed before it even started in the 1930s. The frozen contempt that Muslim prisoners radiated to the white authorities they were brought before in the 1930s and 1940s, with the frequent "fanatical" demonstrations and outbreaks of brawling and gunfire in and around the courts,[152] unnerved many whites and were very important in securing what leeway American bodies came to allow for the evolution of an autonomous Nation of Islam school system in the USA. Still, if the Muslims had had educated adherents, they might have been able, by a more meticulous synthesis of money, threats and an orientated use of the law, to win more leeway and quiet in the USA's mean cities.

Overall, the experiences of African-American Muslims imprisoned during WWII prefigured the U.S. prisons of the 1980s and 1990s where the courts sometimes endorsed treatment of black Muslim convicts as not entitled by the U.S. constitution to the spaces for group worship or to the pork-free diets that Jewish fellow-prisoners received.[153] On the plane of theory, the USA—in this, like the Soviet opponent it finally destroyed—holds out rights of free speech, assembly, belief and worship that are elaborately codified, even as, in regard to African-Americans who converted to Middle East-patterned Islam in prisons, Muslims were further penalized for their faith in prison. El-Aswad Abdus Salaam recalled (1973) that "prior to 1968, if anyone said he was Muslim he was sent to the mental institution or placed in isolation. There were only three religious classifications allowed then: Protestant, Catholic or Jewish" [thereby excluding converts to NOI as well as Sunni Islam]. Abdus Salaam charged that, following permission for an Islamic program for prisoners at Ohio penitentiary in 1969, Islamic literature and visiting Third World Muslim religious instructors were under tight control from a freemasonic Protestant Minister and then from a Jewish employee of the prison. When Islam spread in the prison, "the Qur'an was burned up, urinated upon [the case for NOI prisoners also], while Muslims were whipped by guards because they wouldn't eat pork sandwiches—we are even blamed for Colonel Qadhafi's actions against America in relation to the oil crisis."[154] There is no doubt, though, that converts to Islam in the (Gulag-vast) prisons network in the USA since the late twentieth century have had incomparably better chances of being allowed Qur'ans and space to do their prayers, and diets free of pork, than had Elijah Muhammad and his detained colleagues in the 1930s and 1940s. From the early 1970s, the U.S. prison system gradually allowed more access and facilities to Islam—Sunnite and Shi'ite, Warithite and Farrakhanist—because of the low rates of recidivism by converts after their release.

NOI Reconstruction of Families

From 1930 onwards, the NOI followed in the footsteps of the Moorish movements in trying to construct two-parent households of a middle-WASP texture amid very bad conditions of social disintegration in the black ghettos of the great cities. For pro-Warith academic, Dr Na'im Akbar, in 1982, this was the project of the old NOI that still had stronger appeal than ever as modern technologies and the relativism of the social scientists destroyed family among all races. The four decades history of the Nation of Islam under Elijah "stands as a unique example of an effective effort to restitute family life for African-Americans" after long-term devastation of it by slavery, systemic racist oppression and by poverty. Na'im Akbar, quasi-post-modernist in 1982 in his sense of time-periods, cited Elijah Muhammad's old "rather basic language" that African-Americans had to learn to respect and protect their women and their mothers to make themselves a fit and recognized people on the earth.

Dr Akbar was sharply aware that the old NOI here was not quite "grafting" together the "nuclear family structure" traditionally fostered in middle America up to the breakdown of the 1970s. NOI family-building differed from the middle-WASP model, Na'im Akbar contended, in that the new two-parent households could be sustained because they had additional "protection" from the wider kins and "community" (for Fard and Elijah=the Nation). In Fard and Elijah's NOI, the local leader of the women's organization and of the men's organization in the mosque had to authorize all selections of partners or the marriages could not take place. Thus, the old Islamic families constructed by Fard and Elijah were less delimitated from the wider community (extended kin, sect, Black Nation) than were middle-class WASP nuclear families from 1930-c. 1965 [although militaristic Americanist statal-nationalism also tried to harness "the Family" to its projects]. Even under

Warith from 1975, the local Imam (mosque minister) was still required to endorse the financial solvency of the bridegroom before the marriage.[155]

Although Fard's special Islam constructed patriarchal families and businesses, these enterprises were felt by many in them as extensions of a religious experience centered around that man-god. Negro women who exited from sexual anarchy in ghetto streets into a sect that called for families felt that they could not have made that break if Fard had not "answered their prayers". One female convert was delighted that the sect's puritan restrictions and the strictly "domestic" roles to which the sewing lessons, etc., pointed its women drew in non-predatory, respectful black men, and then marriage in new durable nationalist families. But while "becoming an independent nation is important," the most important need was for a God, which Blacks had never truly had in America, she felt, during their Christian delusion. The "Arab" Fard as the embodiment of Allah who was occulted up into the heavens was felt by converts as their first true—liberating—encounter with the Divine.[156] The NOI's regimentation of women went far beyond that of conservative middle-Anglo families, but its incarnate man-god Fard had more in common than they supposed with the white "Jesus"-god they were ditching. Under Imam Warith/Wallace Mohammed from 1975, the adherents of both sexes would move to a non-personal, non-corporeal, non-human concept of godhood coming from the Middle East that was to be far from Anglo-American ideas.

For Dr Na'im Akbar in 1982, the old NOI's construction of male-headed families with safeguarded mothers and children was a new direction in black social evolution. But others who had grown up in those pre-1975 Nation of Islam families thought them spiritless and gray, with "emotions always restrained, cool" (Ken Farid Hasan in 1988). Hasan recalled an NOI activist father who impressed on his wife and kids the sect's promises that the Mother Plane would soon destroy the world's white devils and non-Muslim blacks, but lift the believers to a royal paradise. Hasan thought this blend of terrorization and promises of never-ending bliss "a marvelously crafted whip" by which his father kept his followers and his family on the move to ever-greater sacrifices and efforts for the sect [—a whip that higher-up NOI leaders were also lashing down upon him, too?]. The hope of the Mother Plane made Hasan and his mother before 1975 "accept the blank, flat, two dimensional life that so many in 'the Nation' lived" because the Judgment would at last give back to family members "time and energy to spend with each other" and restore their youth that they were giving to the NOI. Hasan charged that the non-stop campaigns to convert more and more Blacks ("new suckers"), selling the sect's newspapers to the black masses, and collecting money for it, made the followers not invest much in their children and neglect some with problems, so that "most of the children left 'the Nation' in their teens, never to return." For him, the pre-1975 Nation's collectivist activism made it impossible to carry through its construction of two-parent petite-bourgeois families—his own somber family was "blown apart by one of the bombing planes like so many of the marriages established or nourished under that mess." The sect's schools misdirected children to wrong destinations—and it made those who had to attend the devils' mainstream schools "schizophrenic" and thus debilitated there. Still, it is clear that Hasan was arguing against a strong group within Warith's sect in the 1980s which still felt that the energy Fard and Elijah's ideology mobilized, and their demanding institutions, had welded coherent community out of once-atomized people.[157]

Hasan's father who went back in to read or study while his wife and children scanned the night skies for the Mother Plane, reads like a young middle-class pan-Arab patriarch of the 1950s or 1960s: Nasser's incitatory broadcasts led some converts to even read old books of the truly great classical Arabs. In repudiating Fard's old ideology but staying with the sect, the son Hasan lived a further stage in the bourgeoisification of African-American Muslims. It was taking them under Warith towards a conservative individualism that cherished personal relations much more, attempting nuclear families that would function less as units within a Nation. Under Fard and Elijah, the parents had a safety-net of nourishing support and welfare services from the Nation-collective, but in return had had to live by that Nation's requirements and projects. Pre-1975 "Black Muslim" families were not full individuals by Anglomorph middle-bourgeois criteria, but rather had affinities with those in the Jehovah's Witnesses, or among Stalinist Communists, or in quasi-totalitarian Ba'thist pan-Arabism in 'Iraq and Syria, or in Muslim fundamentalist salafist movements and regimes after WWII where someone always has an eye on you—and can harm as well as help. There was no privacy for ordinary members. The original NOI had succeeded in building nationalist two-parent Black families welded together by a religious-nationalist ideology—permanent marriage was imposed by God—and by sect-structures. During campaigns by the system to destroy the NOI and the Moorish sects during the 1930s and in particular during World War II, the women, likewise dedicated to the NOI ideology, themselves at once took on the functions of their jailed menfolk so that the sects did survive.

Early Nation of Islam Beliefs

In the American neo-Islam that crystallized among working-class African-Americans in Detroit from 1930, Islam's standard Book and teachings were mediated through America's social realities and ingrained religious concepts—and by the urgent interests of the dirt-poor converts. The Nation of Islam's not very educated first leaders and converts seized verses and motifs of the Qur'an that spoke to their socio-political tensions with the ascendant whites, tore them out of their original contexts in that scripture, and wove them into a new ideological structure designed to construct space for autonomous African-American development in American life. This new, pervasively American, NOI religion was to bequeath three tendencies in beliefs that would long turn away many Arab and other Third World Muslims who had the impulse to aid the Nation. These three doctrines—(a) the concept that Elijah Muhammad was a contemporary further "Messenger" of God succeeding the Prophet Muhammad Ibn 'Abdallah of Arabia; (b) the anthropomorphic blurring of the Qur'an-affirmed transcendent God into the created ("Black") humans, and (c) the lack of a doctrine of an afterlife with enough affinities to that held by Muslims in the Third World—were to be revived in watered-down form by Louis Farrakhan after he broke with Elijah's Sunnifying, Arabizing son, Imam Warith, in 1977. Although primarily an attempt to wrest mental autonomy from the Christian whites who surrounded them, the three tenets would—not just in the 1960s but again for the whole of the 1990s under Farrakhan—pose very serious difficulties for all attempts to affiliate the old and the revived Nation of Islam to the Arab and Muslim worlds.

In his authoritative 1981 review of the pre-1975 Nation of Islam doctrines, the tri-cultured Pakistani academic, Zafar Ishaq Ansari, noted with deep empathy for the sect's U.S. context, its deviations from key concepts of orthodox Islam. In regard to the Hereafter, the clear sense of the Qur'an is that an all-knowing, all-powerful, absolutely just and merciful, formless God far exalted above humans will reward all who were righteous in this world by resurrecting them as individuals to eternal bliss after the grave in Paradise. Simultaneously on the Day of Judgment, He will punish the unrighteous as resurrected individuals with eternal torment in Hell. In Sunni and Shi'i Islam, then, those who die will be resurrected by God after He destroys the present cosmic order, and then judged. The "Hereafter" that the Nation of Islam of Elijah projected was not that. The 6000 years the white devils have been granted to rule over the earth was termed by that old "Nation of Islam" as "this world" or "this world of sin". The "Hereafter" is the period that will follow God's destruction of the White man, a period that would initiate the never-ending "government" of the Original righteous blacks. Instead of a "life of the spirits up somewhere in the sky", the Nation of Islam Hereafter will rather be life on this earth and people will continue to be flesh-and-blood beings who would live forever. Crucially, those good black individuals who had died in earlier ages would not be resurrected by God to be included among the blacks who will have eternal bliss and youth.[158] However, the Qur'an was tapped for some images of the eternal adolescence those elect NOI saved would enjoy.[159]

The concepts of Heaven and Hell for the pre-1975 NOI signified conditions of earthly life rather than states of super-terrestrial/post-judgement existence. Heaven and Hell are determined on earth by how much money and power the individuals in question command in this life. The old Nation of Islam described Heaven as "the condition the white man now has," while Hell was the poverty and oppression to which the Negroes were simultaneously being subjected in the USA. Thus, the suffering Blackman did not have to wait for his death and an ensuing physical resurrection to experience Heaven. If, in the mental process of conversion termed "Resurrection", he were to accept his God, acquire knowledge of the basic truths about himself, his nation, and his religion and history, he would enjoy Heaven here on this earth right now. Heaven is described in banal masonry-tinged terms as consisting of "freedom, justice, equality, money, good houses, and friendships in all walks of life." These sects can deliver real benefits though, which turn out to be more ordinary than an extermination by God that brings immortality in an everlasting Paradise on earth after it. Thus, Resurrection and Heaven in the Nation of Islam from 1930-1975 boiled down to the Dead Nation's acceptance of Elijah's religious black nationalism and construction under his leadership of a collectivist nationalist private enterprise that would confer (Anglo-like...) prosperity, health and two-parent families in good suburbs.[160]

The original Nation of Islam denial of after-life in the sense in which that term is generally understood in the Arab and Muslim states shocked many from those countries. However, the Muslim states that achieved political independence in the wake of World War II did not fail to produce more generous-minded scholars and leaders abler to assess NOI doctrines with sensitivity to the context of the sufferings of those who now converted. In regard to the period of Elijah's leadership, Pakistani Sunni scholar Zafar Ishaq Ansari had the empathy to view the Elijahist interpretation of "the Hereafter" in relation to its context in the excessive other-worldliness of the Negro Christian church in twentieth century America, a drug that the Black Nation had to shake off to be able to perceive socio-economic reality and thereby prosper. Many black nationalists had come to look upon black Christianity's excessive emphasis on the after-world as one technique by whites to divert the attention of African-Americans from their sordid state of existence. The emphatic promises of a postponed pie in the heaven implied that the blacks should be satisfied with their poor-quality, unbuttered bread on earth, Ansari assessed.[161] Thus, some acculturated intellectuals at least from the Muslim World were able to see African-American engagement with the Qur'an from the perspective of the blacks' own needs in the crisis of self-determination they faced amid the oppression and disintegration of the later 1920s and the 1930s—the starting-point of their journey to Islam.

The Islamic concept of God reiterated throughout the Qur'an is that the Omnipotent Creator of this universe is beyond human sense-perception and unbounded by both time and space. He is One, and "there is nothing like Him": no one and nothing gave birth to Him, nor has he ever given birth to any being (Qur'an surah 112). In contrast, from early in the development of the sect, Elijah and his followers projected strongly anthropomorphic concepts of God—that, as Elijah Muhammad argued it, "God is a [Black] man, a flesh and blood being like ourselves". Elijah Muhammad condemned the concept of a non-material, formless "spook God" as a deception by the white devils. Running against the Qur'an's argument that God is self-sufficient and is not bound by the form of anything He creates, Elijah argued in *The Supreme Wisdom* that a formless, self-independent God was impossible because the spirit had to be nourished by air, water and food to maintain life.[162] Master Wali Fard Muhammad's teachings had resurrected the previously mentally dead Negroes "into Reality, and not into some kind of spooky, or spirit, or ghost-like teaching". He was at once the All-Wise and Living God: a divine Human Being and not something beyond the family of human beings—spookisms. "We could never ask a formless spirit to lead us because we are not a formless spirit ourselves: man cannot listen to other than man."[163] Ansari, though, did locate a statement of Elijah that did toy with the idea of a formless God independent of matter: "The belief in a God other than man (a spirit) Allah has taught me goes into the millions of years—long before Yakub, the father [i.e. creator or breeder] of the devils".[164]

Druze theology holds that we cannot know a God who is beyond the first heaven: God has to incarnate Himself into human form in order to make us understand the monotheistic unity of His Godhood. Beyond the celebration of Fard as God-in-Person, Elijah Muhammad's concept of God was also marked by corporateness as well as corporeality. "Allah" as conceived in the pre-1975 Nation of Islam was not a godhead complete in Himself: rather, in Elijah's nationalist religion, God or Allah could be constituted of the collectivity of the Original People, the Black Nation whose fathers created the heavens and the earth and then the White or Caucasian race or devils. All members of Elijah's Islam had the potential to grow towards divinity, he argued: the bygone first God who created the heavens and earth did beget since the twentieth-century Blacks are his biological descendants, who can all partake of divinity, although one of them (Fard) is the Supreme Being. In accordance with its pre-1975 conceptualization of God as necessarily human, Elijah's sect sometimes viewed Him, at least in part, as the most powerful Black scientist living in a particular age.[165] Early Druze theology blurred that sect's human leaderships into God: it evoked five *hudud* or "borders" who are something between God and humans: each *hadd* is an incarnation of God who reveals what he is a number of times—which is like the Wali Fard Muhammad who functioned for the masses of his followers as a human deliverer but was said after his 1933 occultation to have murmured from time to time to Elijah and one or two other close lieutenants that he was more than that.

Given that Nation of Islam theology did not rigorously distinguish black individuals from God, it was easy for Elijah to give mounting hints in his last years that he was being fused into his incarnate god-master Fard.[166] Yet such ultra-American ideologies as New England Transcendentalism, WASP freemasonry and Christianity's sense of the Church members as the "body of God" had also nourished this sense of We the Divine in the first Nation of Islam.

"Doomed Devils" Themes

No tenet of NOI religion has enraged Euro-Americans so much as Fard's portrayal of whites as a race of artificially-bred devils whose inherent evil was to call down their final incineration by God in the not-too-distant future. In contrast, this theme disconcerted the Muslim World much less. The officials in Nasser's Egypt and other new Arab and Muslim states with whom the Pakistani 'Abd al-Basit Na'im put Malcolm X, Elijah and other black Muslim leaders in contact in the 1950s and 1960s had themselves recently struggled against, or were still fighting, white Western colonialists: African-American hatred—or, rather, counter-hatred—of Christian whites seemed as natural to them as their own. The Pakistani Ishaq Ansari was understanding towards the early NOI's sense that the white man was the devil and that black men collectively had the potential to become divine. He did not put the responsibility for this dichotomization on the blacks who in 1930 scanned the Qur'an for guidance in the crisis that whites had inflicted upon them. The Pakistani scholar instead saw Elijah Muhammad's demonology as imposed by "the common belief in White America that the Negro is biologically deficient, that he is a born savage, that he has no glorious past to boast of, and that as the descendant of Ham, he is under the unending curse of God"—the counter-demonization from Fard and Elijah was an almost inevitable retort.[167] His fellow-Pakistani, Na'im, had not been disconcerted by this counter-demonization and the other distinctive NOI tenets as he strove in the 1950s and 1960s to keep the sect in interaction with Third World Muslim people, governments and their causes—to help Nasser but also in part to get black nationalist-type American tourists for an African-American travel agent to whom he was a consultant.[168]

The NOI's 1930 demonization of whites and their millenarian hope that God would soon incinerate the last one sound extreme, but were really as American as cherry pie. Most mainstream sects in America had long hoped—and some still were to hope into the late 20th and early 21st centuries—that God would quickly burn those who thought or looked different. Adherents of the Nation of Islam have always been well aware of how much their own yearning for an eschatological final solution had in common with the religions of their white enemies. In 1973, the too-suave John X 'Ali, from the very apex of the sect's Chicago leadership, gently reminded whites not to condemn the Muslims for hate themes like those their own churches had long articulated. It was true that Elijah taught that "the so-called Negroes are the chosen of Allah and that all others are among the non-chosen and that nothing they can do will alter that fact" (=the inherent devilishness of the doomed whites). But Elijah's demand that the blacks withdraw from the whites, and his warnings that God would soon incinerate the latter, gave no grounds to accuse him of unusual racism, refuted 'Ali, because so many more established creeds voiced parallel attitudes to other Americans. Jews claim that they are Jehovah's elect, the Catholic Church taught that it is the only church and made it very hard for its members to intermarry with non-Catholics, while Protestant sects rejected Catholics in the same way. Those white sects taught that their spiritual insight is the only one worth holding, as did Elijah Muhammad. True, Elijah predicted the early end of the non-Muslims, but then "the New Testament is laced with promises that the non-Christians will be destroyed in a fiery death, soon to come." If every U.S. religion has predicted God's early destruction of its enemies in a Day of Judgment, then "why the uproar when Mr. Muhammad teaches Black men that they are the elect and that their opponents will soon be destroyed" by God?[169]

John 'Ali in 1973, then, denied that Elijah was an abnormal racist who wished on his white fellow Americans any more harm than many of the pious among those same white Americans wished upon each other. He could have easily mustered communications from Protestant sects denouncing Catholics as in the grip of the Devil and the targets of the imminent wrath of God—not motifs liable to encourage any WASPs to welcome any Irish-, Italian-, and Hispanic-Americans into the mainstream or into jobs with them. Popular U.S. Christianity had sometimes associated the black race with the Devil: however, they had linked the Jews much less to that anti-God than had popular Catholic and Orthodox Christianity back in the old Europe. The Jewish-American enclave-nationalists of the 1980s and 1990s were to remain sensitive to atavistic tendencies to demonize Jews in Europe's Christianity, but have yet to voice much self-insight about the proclivity that a range of Zionist, integrationist and micronationalist groups in U.S. Jewry have had to so demonize white Christians and blacks who clash with Jews.

This demonizing discourse of some in American Jewry has recurred and accumulated over decades. There already was a touch of muted Devil slurs even in Shlomo Katz' 1966 collection on the encounter between Blacks and Jews, a book that was Americanist and integrationist overall, given the period. In it, Arthur A. Cohen's religious speculation that God ordered the roles of the Jews in a hostile human history for "ahistorical purpose" already prefigured desecularization of history in the more and more fundamentalizing Jewish micronationalism that was to burgeon in American Jewry after the 1967 war in the Middle East. The insistence of Cohen and co-contributors on fusing their local "Negro" opponents out into a murderous "Christendom" across the seas echoed that old anti-Semitic Europe's charges of a unitary globe-circling "International Jewry." Cohen had some feel for new "anti-Christian sectors of the Negro Community": he himself charged that use by propertied Anglos of Jews in the exploitation of Negroes was "diabolical": and in another ambiguous twinge he veered towards the Nation of Islam's identification of all [Christian] whites around the globe as the collective devil-enemy in objecting that "the white and Christian 'devil' is the origin of oppression for both the black and the Jew".[170] Images of Satan, and of all Christians as a murderous enemy of the "Christ-killers" that the Ashkenazi Jews brought with them from Central and East Europe, in the 1970s and 1980s fueled and tinged early demonization of blacks in mass media directed to Jews, in particular in films.[171]

The post-Zionist Jewish-American micronationalists of the 1990s demonized more widely within an ideology that was taking its mature form. The civil libertarian, Allan Dershowitz, was one case. Like Lucy S. Dawidowicz and Cohen so many years before in Katz' 1966 collection, Dershowitz in 1997 relentlessly conflated (a) the murderousness of the Christian peasantries of Europe vis-a-vis Jews since the Middle Ages with (b) the nationalist sectors of African-Americans with which his stratum of American Jews had been brawling since the 1960s. Dershowitz' assaults on the pogrom-prone Poles, Ukrainians, Russians, Germans, etc., seldom conceded to them or to Christianity any redeeming qualities or meritorious individuals, or that Jews had had any positive interactions with them—unmistakably like traditional Black Muslim denunciation of the lynch-prone white devils, except that Elijah and Farrakhan left barely veiled openings for their followers to appropriate creative and managerial patterns and knowledge of the devil-whites, those covert models for a "resurrected" Black national life in the USA.

A problematic for Jewish-American enclavist political particularism is whether professed atheists of Dershowitz' ultra-Westernized type could muster enough elements of a religious belief to demonize Farrakhan and other African-Americans in a sustained way. Dershowitz' secularist frames of reference do seem to buckle and snap when facing the mystery of Hitler, with a resultant demonization that he could extend to Farrakhan at least among his Black fellow-Americans. Dershowitz veered towards religious problems and a religious theodicy like that of the Nation of Islam when he mused that Hitler made himself into "a counter-god, creator of the Holocaust, most powerful being in the universe—for a time." This mutation in Dershowitz' America-centered Jewish nationalist thought elevated Hitler into an anti-Yahweh who "exercised greater power over the Jews of Europe than any deity did. He was All—a god to some, but a devil to all good men".[172] Such identification of Hitler as the Devil becomes ominous for the America enterprise when Dershowitz and other Jewish-American micronationalists dub Farrakhan (or other black Muslim leaders from Sufi Abdul Hamid in the 1930s) the Hitler of the blacks. It was as impossible for Jewish communal political nationalists in the 1980s and 1990s U.S. to concede that a neo-Muslim nationalist like Farrakhan can ever have offered anything positive to African-Americans and America as it was for Nazi or Slav anti-Semitic polemicists to depict any Jewish politician or entrepreneur as anything other than malevolent and diabolic.

This incapacity comes out in the terminology of Dershowitz' responses to moves by mainstream African-American politicians for a coalition with the Nation of Islam to tap their skills in reversing the decay and disintegration in poor African-American areas. All he would concede was that the NOI "has learned from past bigots" such as Hitler's German Nazi Party and the Ku Klux Klan that "for its scapegoating hate message to be heard, it must be accompanied by the positive work the group is now doing" in fighting drugs etc. "But if it is to retain its soul, the NAACP [National Association for the Advancement of Colored People] cannot make a pact with the devil".[173] Dershowitz's love of Israel, and refusal to regard those in conflict with Jews as human, would after September 11 make it easy for him as a legist to seek to install into America's legal system the arbitrary use of torture against Muslim peoples, proposing that a judge would sign for that only as a formality before it went ahead.

Overall, Dershowitz exemplifies a sector of Jewish-American micronationalist discourse that swiftly demonizes any non-Jewish group that gets in the way of his group in America. As Jewish political nationalists increasingly inject irrational—but functional because energizing—religiosity into their political activism, they find more and more areas for joint action with the born-again Christian right that cherishes Israel as the work of God. The demonizing Dershowitz, though, warns that neo-conservative Jews who defend that Christian right "are playing with fire and brimstone".[174] Farrakhan feared (1990) that the Jewish micronationalists' repeated reference to him as "a black Hitler" might plant the seed of his murder in the hearts of young "New Jews" determined "Never Again" to allow a repeat of the horrors of the Holocaust.[175] Farrakhan, though, had been ready to risk that when he used his pretend anti-Semitism and mock-confusions about Hitler to make the Jewish micronationalists into the unpaid PR agents who catapulted him into mainstream media visibility as one key leader of Black America during the 1984 presidential primaries.

The above comparisons establish that a fair range of Christian and Jewish whites in America have shared (although using more code-words) the spiritual violence with which the Nation of Islam from 1930 dismissed all whites as inherently devilish anti-humans who merit to be soon destroyed in a fiery death by God. The sense of many Jews and some African-Americans that their Christian race-enemies of European descent are almost inherently hostile and murderous devils has stemmed from the past ill-treatment to which those two American groups were subjected in very traumatic histories. It might be objected that the NOI's demonization of whites here went further than U.S. white Protestant sects that, in their theory at least, see the devilishness of those who are to be hit by God's fire as an acquired trait or subordination out of which individuals can opt by embracing truths that would then incorporate them into the congregations of the righteous who will be saved. Yet many white churches historically and today would bar African-Americans who wanted to join—as some streams of U.S. Judaism still block black converts more on halakhic principle. It also seems that much "religious" WASP rejection and constriction of Irish-Americans had deeper ethnic currents (which drew on culture motifs bequeathed from historic socio-political oppression of the Irish by the WASPs' mother country) coursing under it. Some pious WASPs were no more trying to convert the God-doomed Irish or Hispanics than Fard or Elijah were, the NOI's doomed white devils. Irish, Italian and Hispanic converts might not be much more welcomed at some WASP churches and social settings than Negro Protestants. The black Muslims' and some American Jews' demonization of neighborhood enemies, the NOI's eschatological millenarianism, and the insistence on endogamy by such religio-nationalist groups are all very ordinary within a U.S. pluralist system long structured out of bruising economic competition, and out of conflict and hatred between ethnic groups focused by religions. The formal tenets of the religions are violent and can get developed to justify genocides—but in various ways mainly help the various clawing ethne to relate to each other as constructively as the ethos of the segregatory U.S. system, with its feral competition, will ever allow.

Pre-1975 Interaction with Muslim World

Perhaps in accord with the ethnicity of its founder, the NOI's first mythologies painted Asia and Africa as one. In some impulses, Fard's 1930 ideology gave preference to West Asia over West Africa in identity. Mecca and Arabia were the original national home of the blacks: there they spoke their original Arabic and had "silken" lank hair: when they migrated to sub-Saharan Africa, Fard imaged, they "strayed away from civilization and are living a jungle life," and their hair got curled. Fard's comparative grading of Asia and Africa in identity early fostered a substantial drive to adopt some elements from Arab culture. In the late 1940s, ill-educated NOI members were eager to learn Arabic, listened to Arabic music records, and in their homes kept pictures of architecture in the Islamic East and the word Allah in Arabic calligraphy, and later, of course, photos of President Gamal Abd al-Nasser. Algernon Austin (2003) assessed the first ideology as having sustained a serious pursuit by NOI members of some acculturation to Arabs, and of touristic and local contact with Muslim and other non-African "Easterners" up to Elijah's death in 1975: the theme of an Asiatic origin put some limits on how far they would connect to sub-Saharan Africans.[176]

Up to the death of Elijah in 1975, few NOI members were aware of Nasser's crushing of the "Muslim Brotherhood" Islamists from early 1954. Elijah praised Nasser's modernization drives on his 1970 death. Khalid Ahmad Tawfiq, soon to found the Mosque of the Islamic Brotherhood in Harlem, while studying in al-Azhar mosque-university took part in Islamist demonstrations there against Nasser before or perhaps after his 1967 defeat by Israel: Tawfiq's scholarship there, though, had been arranged by the later, anti-Elijah, Malcolm X. The Egyptian operative and Africanist Muhammad Fa'iq recalled in 2005 that Akbar Muhammad, Elijah's son who studied at al-Azhar with Tawfiq, gifted his American car to the Egyptian war-effort before flying home to America in the wake of that disaster, which he lamented as a blow to the [secular] liberation movements of both the Arabs and the Africans that Nasser had promoted. Akbar continued to attend the Nasserite elite's functions until he left Egypt.[177] It was under Warith's leadership from mid-1975 that a forming "Black Muslim" intelligentsia came to criticize Nasser's secularism and his repression of such Islamists as Sayyid Qutb (executed 1965).

(It was shared interest in sub-Saharan Africa, not some counter-lobby, that brought Muhammad Fa'iq and Akbar Muhammad together: Fa'iq told me in 2005 that communicating to African-Americans was not among his priorities while at various times Minister of Information, and Minister of State for Foreign Affairs, from 1966 under Nasser and as Minister for Information under Sadat. This though mustering support in Afro-America could have helped prise Israel out of the one-fifth of Egypt's land it seized in 1967).

The incarnationist beliefs of the original Nation of Islam in the 1960s would repeatedly spark tensions with the multiplying Arab migrants in the great American cities and the Arab World press. In the 1980s, with increased Sunnification in the Islam-influenced sector of the African-American minority in America, the motif of incarnate or plural Black gods was no longer an issue just between African-Americans who claimed Islam and some Arab Muslims. Now, Sunnified African-Americans themselves, including Warith and his successor-sect to his father's NOI, cited the motif with a view to denying Farrakhan any role as a spokesman of Islam as he entered American parliamentarist politics through the 1984 presidential primaries. In courting desperately-needed solidarity by Arab and other Eastern Muslims for his small sect in 1999, Farrakhan betrayed an awareness that his new NOI would somehow have to cast off its image among Sunni Muslims of being prone to incarnationist *shirk* (polytheism).

Although the pre-1975 black Muslims adapted motifs from various American religions to make them speak to urgent needs of poor African-Americans, the identification of those doctrines with Islam and its overseas world also attracted those converting. The impulse of the black poor in the great cities of the U.S. to leap spiritually over the confines of the America that oppressed them to connect to a non-Western tradition and overseas world had already expressed itself in Noble Drew 'Ali's Moorish Science Temple of America. The capacity to truly grasp and accept tenets of Islam with no connection at all to some crucial assumptions of Christianity ran far behind this drive to extraterritorialize that was itself still only symbolic at most points. Yet the claim of Elijah's Muslims to affiliate converts to a major global religion beyond the white world and Christianity resonated with the "Negro" masses. It was a subordinated aspiration in the psyche of the adherents that would cumulatively color their personality with atomized motifs and vocabulary from the Arab world over decades.

Elijah Muhammad, coldly practical and often insular, evinced inconsistent attitudes to Muslim countries. In the direction of reconnection, he made it a point to publicize letters and cables he got from such ultra-political Muslim World dignitaries as Gamal 'Abd al-Nasser. Such contacts helped legitimize Elijah's leadership among the wider black public in a period in which many African-Americans did not rigorously distinguish between independence movements in the Arab World and those in sub-Saharan Africa. In publicizing those carefully-limited relations, Elijah fostered the black Muslims' sense of belonging to the Muslim *ummah* (international supra-nation), subordinate though that remained to their pride of membership in the American "Nation of Islam". On the other hand, it remained in the interest of Elijah's absolutist leadership for him to insulate his sect's distinguishing doctrines from those of the "Muslims of the East" and their concepts. Yet that became harder as more and more Muslims entered America from the East, and founded organizations that expounded Islam to the U.S. media, and as NOI members visited or studied in the Muslim countries. But the conversion of two of his sons and Malcolm X to "orthodox" Islam long before his death resulted not just from interactions with those Eastern Muslims but also from a ferment of concepts and from progressive Arabization within the sect under Elijah.

The tension between (a) the impulse to affiliate to the Arab World, and (b) adhesion to doctrines at variance with that world's beliefs, recurred in the history of the Black Muslim movements over the half-century from 1950. The issue brought out certain blind-spots in both the Black bourgeoisie and American Jewry's intelligentsia. Lincoln in 1961 as a specialist in religious studies caught the corporate nationalist essence of the NOI's conceptualization of the Divine. But he already saw the sect's survival in a hostile USA as strongly pushing Elijah and his Nation to doctrinally connect much more with the Muslim states: international repercussions of the harassment or suppression of the NOI would be extremely grave if the world's Muslims saw it as Islamic. Lincoln's impression as the 1960s opened was that Elijah "craves this immunity and ...seems willing to moderate his program" to persuade the Arabs to recognize him.[178] Lincoln was optimistic that relations were expanding with the Arab countries and that the Nation of Islam would in due course be "sheltered" into the Arabo-Islamic world as a Muslim sect, albeit a somewhat heretical one.[179] The Zionist publicist, Joel Carmichael, in 1967 sweepingly dismissed any possibility that African-Americans could have any continuous links to Africa or Islam, and categorized the differences between Black Muslim tenets and the Third World's orthodox Islam as "so much Greek" to even those American Negroes who had become "Muslim", to say nothing of to ordinary U.S. blacks in the ghettoes.[180] True, the latter formulation had some truth in the 1960s for even a bourgeois African-American intellectual like Lincoln.

Lincoln was half-wrong in 1961 to pattern a precedent for recognition from Islamic countries from the case of the Ahmadiyyah, founded in India by the "prophet" Mirza Ghulam Ahmad of Qadiyan (1839-1908).[181] The Lahore-based splinter-section of the Qadiyanis had indeed accommodated to Sunni orthodoxy in the leadup to partition, and the creation of Pakistan; one of their members had been ambassador of Pakistan at the United Nations where he argued a pro-Palestinian rejection as Israel was created. Yet in 1953 Sunni mass protest and violence against Ahmadis already had threatened the rule of Pakistan's ineffective Westernized elite, and in the 1980s the Ziaul-Haqq regime predictably had to define Ahmadis/Qadiyanis as a non-Muslim minority.[182] The claim that Elijah Muhammad had the status and function of "the Messenger of Allah" repeatedly aborted readiness of Sunni Muslims in Asia and Africa to open real relations with both Elijah's followers and, after 1978, with Farrakhan's successor-sect. Muslim populations and governments throughout the Third World, not just in Arabic-speaking countries, have always held very tightly to the tenet that Muhammad, the son of 'Abdallah of Hijaz, Arabia, was God's last prophet to humanity, and the Qur'an the final revelation from God.

At the century's close, Farrakhan, aware how badly his small sect would need support from the Arab World if the U.S. government moved to crush it on his demise, would still be wrestling with the dilemma of how to bridge its doctrinal disparity from the Third World's Muslims.

Pre-1975 Attitudes to the Prophet Muhammad of Arabia

The central doctrine of Sunni Islam—the dominant belief in the Arabo-Muslim World of Africa and Asia—is that there is no God but a non-corporeal Allah, and that Muhammad Ibn 'Abdallah of Arabia is His greatest and final prophet. Among all divergent tenets of the old Nation of Islam, the Arab and

Muslim Worlds were earliest and most furiously aware of its refusal to accept that prophecy ended in Arabia with Muhammad's death in 632AD.

Prior to 1975, the use of conventional formulas with the name Muhammad by the Nation of Islam had had some ambiguity since they could be applied to mean Elijah Muhammad more than Muhammad Ibn 'Abdallah, although the latter's prophethood was always validated at the least as a prototype that was to find its fulfillment and its interpretation in the career of Elijah. The Nation of Islam also shared with the Arab and Muslim countries a belief in the prophethood of the earlier Hebrew-speaking prophets such as Noah, Abraham, Moses, Solomon, and Jesus: in using the careers and acts and situations of these figures as clarifying images or signs or portents of the roles of Fard and Elijah—and, after 1977, of Farrakhan—NOI preachers, orators and writers referred as much or somewhat more to the Bible as to the Qur'an. While well aware that the Qur'an was revealed to Muhammad Ibn 'Abdallah in another language and country over 1300 years before, the Black Muslims of the NOI have consistently awarded the leader of the day—Fard, or Elijah, and sometimes Farrakhan still—the crucial role of the Qur'an's sole authoritative interpreter, and perhaps the superhuman in whose life the possibilities prophesied in the Qur'an are fulfilled, rather than assigning that to Muhammad Ibn 'Abdallah.

The pre-1975 "Nation of Islam", then, saw Muhammad Ibn 'Abdallah, in Elijah Muhammad's words, as "a sign of the real Muhammad" to come—i.e. Elijah.[183]

Immigrant Muslim Reassessment of Elijah and His NOI

During the career of Elijah Muhammad, his sect's more distinctive tenets made most foreign or immigrant Muslims and Middle Easterners deny any link with it. But by the end of the 20th century, not just individual Arabs or one or two sympathetic Pakistanis, but some whole groups of activists in the, by then, huge immigrant U.S. Muslim minority were coming to grasp the breakthroughs Elijah Muhammad achieved for *all* Muslims in American life. The small Jama'at al-Muslimin's alliance with Farrakhan and the Nation of Islam had its greatest resonance in Arab-, Muslim-, and Jewish-America during the 1995 Million Man March; and again when the immigrant-led but mixed group functioned as a key element in the July 1997 World Islamic Conference in Chicago, with which Farrakhan promoted his sect's acceptance into the world community (*ummah*) of Islam. Although rueful at the high cost of all the condemnations that its openness to the NOI tradition were drawing from "many" immigrant Muslims, the Jama'at's paper in 1999 daringly endorsed not only Farrakhan but even the old pre-1975 NOI and its ultra-heretical leader, Elijah Muhammad.

Hollywood-incited racism against America's immigrant Arabs and Muslims was making their militants feel some oneness of fate with the African-Americans: "a whole segment of humanity was dragged to America and robbed of language, culture, religion, and livelihood". The argument of the

Jama'at here was that, after 440 years, Islam could not have been revived among such downtrodden people by the fragile non-American Muslims who had migrated to the Midwest because most of those foreigners had dropped the practice of their Islamic religion. In this vacuum, it was Master Farad Muhammad and the Honorable Elijah Muhammad who gradually "transformed the deaf, dumb, and blind into a living example of Muslims". One consideration that drove some immigrant Muslims to embrace Elijah here was a traumatized sense of how fragile Islam, and its transmission to any new generation, was for immigrants beset by a much more powerful culture they aped.

It was this context—the high odds against *any* ethno-religious survival, fears that even successive waves of immigrant Muslims on their own could not construct a long-term community able to last—that above everything else make Elijah and the NOI a source of morale and a model that *some* immigrant populists have had to seize since the 1980s. Elijah's capacity to construct from atomized individuals a defiant sect-"nation" that flaunts motifs from Arabic and Islam in public space now becomes a part-antidote against the Americanization and dissolution of immigrant communities. In Chicago in the 1930s and afterwards, many immigrant Muslims had been afraid to even use the holy greeting of as-Salamu 'Alaykum (Peace be Upon You), went one retrospect: "Mr Muhammad boldly would express salam to people publicly" in the communal rituals of his sect before the media. "It was only when Mr Muhammad changed Muhammad 'Ali's name [from Cassius Clay: this is the 1960s] that many [immigrant] Muslims in the West began de-anglicizing their names": "Mike" once more became Muhammad, Abe was corrected back to Abdul. Thus, at least this South Asian immigrant Muslim had by 1999 come to a view like Benjamin Goodman's in 1971: it was Elijah Muhammad's use of pieces of Arabic in public identity that destroyed the Anglo-conformist limits upon construction of Islamic difference, and other cultural nationality, for both African-Americans and new groups from the Muslim World.

By the 21st century, then, some aesthetic Arabic and some shared rites now overshadowed the old divergences of beliefs. With any group survival at risk amidst the Euro-Americans, Elijah Muhammad acquired icon status for desperate Muslim immigrants as the 20th century closed. He had shown that small groups with willpower could transform sectors of U.S. society. Conniving at divergent tenets of the new NOI he did not mention, the Jama'at writer innuendoed that "very few people today"— i.e. not those in petro-funded conservative immigrant Muslim organizations who still questioned if Farrakhan were Muslim—"can say they have transformed life". Elijah Muhammad held on to Islam in the face of endless pressures, indignities and imprisonment: how many immigrant Muslim scholars of the 1990s had done as much? (This was a reference to the refusal of America's big-name Muslim associations to call for the release of the blind Egyptian Shaykh 'Umar 'Abd al-Rahman, jailed under charges of having plotted to blow up the World Trade Center in 1993). "The number of leaders that this teacher produced still lead us today: Malcolm X, Muhammad 'Ali, Louis Farrakhan, Warithuddin Muhammad, Silas

Muhammad, Tynetta Muhammad, Clara Muhammad and the list goes on". Ather Masood even wanted to place Elijah among the shuhada' (martyrs) and salihin (pious leaders) of Islam's macro-history because he was a "teacher who went through great suffering to achieve what we have today".

The sense of community with the NOI took this militant writer's mind outside his own cluster of immigrant ethnic minorities. "No one has appointed us judges and executioners over the Lost and Found Nation of Islam under Minister Louis Farrakhan. Before we rush to jump on anyone we must jump on ourselves, our desires, and our own misgivings". Many immigrant Muslims in 1999 still refused to work in the black community. "As a result, Black people rarely venture out among other [Muslim] ethnicities". Masood taunted some immigrant leaders as having internalized Anglo racism ("the Willie Lynch syndrome") when they denounced Farrakhan—he challenged them to construct one undivided belief-community with African-Americans.[184]

The 1990s struggle-to-the-death between the Jama'at al-Muslimin radicals and such oil-funded immigrant bodies as ISNA and ICNA that wanted to get into parties at the White House and into the U.S. system, was venomous for years. But by early 1999, ISNA representatives attended the Saviors' Day reconciliation of Farrakhan and Imam Warithuddin Muhammad. Farrakhan—and his shrill little Jama'at ally?—were now themselves getting mainstreamed into the U.S. Muslim establishment that shakes the hands of Hilary and "the great white father in the White House".[185]

Patterns and Assessment

The above data showed the coming together of elements for a new African-American Islam within, or on the margin of, the protest politics of early Africanist nationalism (elite as well as popular) in America. The three movements reviewed in this chapter—the Africanist Garveyites, "the Moors" and the NOI—overlapped in membership, with an accumulation of some shared themes or motifs. It was ambiguous how far any of these movements really meant to separate those they converted from America in general. All neo-Islamic sects strove to launch an ethnic private enterprise for "national" self-determination, if in an America that itself had separated them. Yet they were adopting many features of Anglo-American self-organization and ideas, and could acquire linkages of interests with the U.S. system over the long term. The symbolic or highly functional elements from Orthodox Islam that the black Muslim movements in America have highlighted have been as much directed to excise the pre-Islamic subculture of African-Americans, as against the whites. Qur'anic elements and bits of Arabic from the Third World function symbiotically within a process that draws poor African-Americans in the direction of the norms of the white American middle-classes that the ideology ostensibly demonizes. These were new black religions that can make converts more like the middle-Anglos from whom they proclaim withdrawal. The same taut ambiguity also already characterized their relationship to the faraway Arabo-Muslim world from which they borrowed, but kept many of their tenets distinct.

ENDNOTES

1 Richard Brent Turner, *Islam in the African-American Experience* (Bloomington: Indiana University Press 1997) p. 95.

2 Mattius Gardell, *In the Name of Elijah Muhammad: Louis Farrakhan and the Nation of Islam* (Carolina: Duke University Press and London: Hurst 1996) pp. 37-46.

3 Allan H. Spear, *Black Chicago: The Making of a Negro Ghetto 1890-1920* (University of Chicago Press 1967) p. 22.

4 Gilbert Osofsky, *Harlem, the Making of a Ghetto: Negro New York 1890-1930* (New York: Harper and Row 1966 pp. 107-108.

5 Alphonso Pinkney, *Red, Black and Green: Black Nationalism in the United States* (New York: Cambridge University Press 1978) pp. 38-39.

6 Jack Salzman and Cornel West, *Struggles in the Promised Land: Towards a History of Black-Jewish Relations in the United States* (New York: OUP 1997) pp. 96-98.

7 Roi Ottley *New World Acoming* (New York: Houghton Mifflin 1943) pp. 112-116.

8 Ottley op cit pp. 114-118, 124-126.

9 Ottley pp. 116-119. The man's activism simply lacks that texture. Building from the materials coming his way, Abdul Hamid had showed real devotion to "Arabian rites" in leading a struggle against those who favored Ethiopian ones in the Prince Hall Masonic order: Robert Dannin, *Black Pilgrimage to Islam* (NY: OUP 2002) p. 278. Congress investigated this power struggle.

10 William R. Scott, "Black Nationalism and the Italo-Ethiopian Conflict 1934-1936", *Journal of Negro History* 63:2 (April 1978) p. 129. Ethiopian nationals and diplomats in the USA skillfully fanned and linked up with street-level organizations and movements of African-Americans in all U.S. areas, although the charlatans skimmed from the donations. The State Department instructed the Ethiopian Consul-General to cease all recruitment activities in the country. Ibid.

11 Ottley p. 117.

12 Ottley p. 117.

13 Even in 1974, B'nai B'rith ADL officials Arnold Foster and Benjamin R. Epstein did still take a swipe at the long-dead Abdul Hamid. Hamid usefully illustrated that that "anti-Semitism of an earlier day in the black community was"—as it ineluctably had to remain in the 1970s—"the trademark of the 'con man,' the manipulator, the professional bigot": Epstein and Forster, *The New Anti-Semitism* (New York: McGraw-Hill 1974) p. 176.

14 Kaufman in *Struggles in the Promised Land* p. 110.

15 Goldberg in Shlomo Katz (ed.), *Negro and Jew: An Encounter in America* (New York: Macmillan 1967) p. 57.

16 Ella Baker and Marvel Cook excerpted in Robert G. Weisbord and Arthur Stein "Negro Perceptions of Jews Between the World Wars", *Judaism* 18:1969 pp. 434-435. Jewish women employers were the same in Chicago: ibid p. 435.

17 Offord writing in *Nation*: "You don't see the husky auctioneers; you don't see a line of half-naked Negroes in chains about their wrists and ankles. But you see hundreds of Negro women, thin, tattered, haggard, sitting on soap boxes or leaning against lamp posts, begging some white woman to buy their services for as little as 15 cents an hour." Florence Hamlish Levinsohn, *Looking for Farrakhan* (Chicago: Ivan R. Dee 1997) p. 170.

18 Ottley *New World Acoming* p. 127.

19 Levinsohn op cit p. 172.

20 Arthur J. Magida, *Prophet of Rage: a Life of Louis Farrakhan and his Nation of Islam* (New York: Basic Books 1996) p. 152.

21 Katz, *Negro and Jew* p. 8; cf. Harry Golden in ibid p. 58.

22 Dannin, *Black Pilgrimage to Islam* pp. 29, 27.

23 For the conventional reconstruction of the sources of Drew 'Ali's Koran and the text and ideas contributed by Dowling's apocryphal gospel in particular see Frank

T. Simpson, "The Moorish Science Temple and its Koran" *The Moslem World* January-April 1947 pp. 56-61; Abbie White, "Christian Elements in Negro American Muslim Religious Beliefs", *Phylon* 25:4 1964 pp. 382-388; and Gardell, *In the Name of Elijah Muhammad* pp. 37-43.

24 Gardell p. 40.

25 Gomez notes that some Bambara and Sierra Leonians brought to North America by the slave merchants had doctrines of reincarnation that he argues were perpetuated or even spread in "shout" ring ceremonies in America: Michael A. Gomez, *Exchanging Our Country Marks: The Transformation of African Identity in the Colonial and Antebellum South 1526-1830* (Chapel Hill: North Carolina University Press 1996) p. 271.

26 Arthur Huff Fauset, *Black Gods of the Metropolis: Negro Cults of the Urban North* (1944) (2nd ed.: University of Pennsylvania Press 1971) p. 102.

27 Mary Baker Eddy and her Scientists on one occasion repudiated Christianity's Trinitarian incarnationism as "polytheism" that fogged "the One ever-present" God. Their theology tended to split (a) the human Jesus from (b) "the Christ" which is the idea of God or of spirit that he bore of which the Christian Scientists are now the custodians. Eddy once said that "if there had never existed such a person as the Galilean prophet it would make no difference to me". Anthony A. Hoekeme, *The Four Major Cults: Christian Science, Jehovah's Witnesses, Mormonism, Seventh-Day Adventism* (London: The Paternoster Press 1963) pp. 200-207.

28 Whyte p. 386.

29 McCloud, *African-American Islam* pp. 12-13. Drew in this communication characterized Islam as "a very simple faith" in its monotheism and may have been wary of too much from Arabic texts coming into his sect.

30 "wa ma qataluhu wa ma sallabuhu walakin shubbiha lahum" (Qur'an 4:157).

31 Abbie Whyte, op cit p. 386.

32 Excerpted Simpson op cit pp. 59-60.

33 Gardell p. 37. Salafite movements are a Protestant-like reformation of Islam: the Ummah or global Muslim nation must purge the religion of post-classical accretions by returning to the codes and ways of the first (Arab or Arab-led) generations of the pious *salaf* (early forefathers). The unconventional young Syrian 'Abd al-Qadir al-Jaza'iri heard al-Afghani say in his final period as a seething constricted pensioner of Sultan Abdul-Hamid in Constantinople that the people of Europe might accept Islam "if it is presented with skill". They had compared Islam with other religions and found it much more accessible and clear in its tenets: by this phrase al-Afghani seems to have been thinking of a cultivated minority of writers, scholars and (relativist freemasonic?) politicians such as he had interacted with while in England and France. But the people of America were "likelier than the Europeans to accept Islam because they had no inherited vendettas with the Islamic nations and harbored no sub-conscious grudges against them as is the case between the Muslims and Europeans": al-Maghribi, *Jamal al-Din al-Afghani: Dhikrayat wa Ahadith* (Cairo: Dar al-Ma'arif, "Iqra" series 1948) p. 57. It is hard to tell how much substance there was to a narrative from this last Istanbul period of al-Afghani's life that an American diplomat sent to China inclined in India to Islam and wanted to propagate it back in his homeland: he wrote to Jamal al-Din and to the Islamic society in Liverpool under the British convert 'Abdallah William who wanted the trio to go to the States as an Islamic mission to be headed by al-Afghani: ibid. p. 49-50.

34 Fauset in Yinger p. 506.

35 Dannin op cit p. 27.

36 We took most above data about "Moorish" beliefs and rituals before 1950 from Arthur H. Fauset, "Moorish Science Temple of America" in J. Milton Yinger, *Religion, Society and the Individual: an Introduction to the Sociology of Religion* (NY: MacMillan 1957) pp. 498-507.

37 Muhammad al-Ahari in Aminah Beverly McCloud, *African-American Islam* (New

York and London: Routledge 1995) p. 20.

38 Akbar Muhammad, "Interaction Between 'Indigenous' and 'Immigrant' Muslims in the United States: some Positive Trends", *Hijrah* (Los Angeles) March-April 1985 p. 14.

39 Alphonso Pinkney, *Red, Black and Green: Black Nationalism in the United States* (New York: Cambridge University Press 1978) pp. 40-56.

40 *al-Liwa'* 8 March 1903, p. 1 and 25 July 1904 p. 1. In London, Garvey through Duse had regularly met Asian as well as African students and leaders, and Indian adherents of the West-accommodating Ahmadi/Qadiani missionary movement in Islam—the heresy that was to tint the Nation of Islam and the young Malcolm X [Turner, *Exp* 85].

41 See Ian Duffield, *Duse Mohamed 'Ali and the Development of pan-Africanism 1866-1945* (University of Edinburgh PhD 1971), and his "The Business Activities of Duse Mohamed Ali: An Explanation of the Economic Dimension of Pan-Africanism", *Journal of the Historical Society of Nigeria* (4:4) June 1969. Cf Ahati N.N. Toure, "Duse Mohamed Ali: Egyptian Nationalist and Pan-African Journalist," *Global African Community* (Texas: San Antonio) August 2002.

42 Turner *Exp* p. 83.

43 Robert Hill (ed), *The Marcus Garvey and Universal Negro Improvement Association Papers* (University of California Press: 9 vols 1983-1990) v. 4 p. 467.

44 *Exp* 88.

45 *Exp* 89-90.

46 *Exp* 29.

47 *Marcus Garvey and Universal Negro Improvement Association Papers* v. 5 pp. 32-33.

48 Zedekiah Ngavirue, "On Wearing the Victor's Uniforms and Replacing their Churches: Southwest Africa (Namibia) 1920-1950", in G. W. Trompf (ed), *Cargo Cults and Millenarian Movements: Transoceanic Comparisons of New Religious Movements* (Berlin: Mouton De Gruyter 1990) pp. 390-399.

49 *Malcolm X on Afro-American History* pp. 14-15, 22.

50 Speeches by Garvey in New York on 11 September 1921 and 8 January 1922 in *The Marcus Garvey and Universal Negro Improvement Association Papers* v. 4, pp. 51-55, 332-337, and ibid v. 6 p. 13 for quotation of Garvey from the *New York Times* 14 September 1924.

51 Bryan, letter dated 14 June 1919 to *Negro World*, Hill (ed), *Papers* v. 1, pp. 424-423. As with Garvey, Ireland sharpened Bryan's hope that the Africans now could wrest independence from Western empires. Bryan was a sales manager in Garvey's Black Star Line: he was born in Barbados.

52 In a 1924 UNIA convention, Baxter of Jamaica said that the British were pursuing a policy of "destruction by starvation": they had introduced cheap labor from India against which the Negro could not compete. Hill (ed) *Papers* v. 5 p. 679.

53 Gandhi may never have shared the illusion of the U.S. press and the Negro nationalists who read it that the Moplah uprising was part of a united drive for independence by Indians of all sects. In a December 1921 call to the British to suspend their attacks against the Moplahs, he was to observe that the Moplahs saw themselves as fighting for a religion with methods they considered religious: Yogesh Chadha, *Rediscovering Gandhi* (London: Century 1997) p. 254.

54 "House of Commons: the Situation in Malabar", *The Times* 9 November 1921 p. 16a.

55 Discussion of petition by Kerala Hindus to Lord Reading, new Viceroy of India, in "The Situation in India" (editorial), London *Times* 16 November 1921 p. 11b. By later November 1921, local Kerala Hindus and the British press were propagating rumors that Moplah leader Kunya Hammad al-Hajj had passed sentences of beheading upon collaborators of whom 34 were Hindus and 2 Moplahs: "Outrages by Rebels", *Times* 5 October 1921 p. 9b. Thus, these particular reprisals were not wholly the anti-Hindu communalism some imaged: the insurgents punished Muslims who collaborated as well.

56 Speeches by Garvey in New York 11 September 1921 in *The Marcus Garvey and Universal Negro Improvement Association Papers* v. 4, pp. 51-54.

57 Garvey, speech of 29 January 1922 *Papers* p. 465.

58 Speech by Garvey 11 September 1921 in Hill (ed), *Papers* v. 4 pp. 54.

59 ABB, "Mr Garvey and the ABB" (c. 23 September 1921), Hill (ed), *Papers* v. 4 pp. 74-76.

60 Ibid v. 4 p. 77.

61 Katz p. 56.

62 Named are "Jewish financiers" William Ritter in the U.S. and Abraham Judah and Lewis Ashenheim in Jamaica: Robin Kelly in "Online Forum: Marcus Garvey and Nationalism," http://www.pbs.org/wgbh/amex/garvey/sfeature/sf_forum_10.html 11 December 2003. William Ritter (1872-1934) was a Hungarian-born banker who financed, and worked with, the Israel Zion Hospital and the Young Man's Hebrew Association. He made at least one minor donation to Garvey's Back-to-Africa projects: "The Colonization Programme for the Universal Negro Improvement Association Raising Fund of 2 Million Dollars for Building First Colony in Liberia", *Negro World* 7 June 1924; http://www.marcusgarvey.com/nw1.htm 12 December 2003.

63 I have not seen Garvey's "The Jews in Palestine", *The Black Man* July-August 1936.

64 "Facing Up to Black Antisemitism", *Commentary* December 1990 p. 26; "Echoes of Marcus Garvey", *New Republic* November 1995 p. 16; Allan Dershowitz, *The Disappearing American Jew* (Boston: Little Brown 1997) pp. 121, 360.

65 Porter, "Garveyism: A Religion", *Negro World* 22 November 1920 in Theodore G. Vincent, *Voices of a Black Nation: Political Journalism in the Harlem Renaissance* (San Francisco: Ramparts Press 1973) pp. 364-5.

66 C. Eric Lincoln, *The Black Muslims in America* (Boston: Beacon Press 1973) pp. 64-65.

67 Turner, *Exp* p. 90. Ahmadiyyah missionary Mufti Muhammad Sadiq (South Asian) helped convert over 40 members of Garvey's UNIA: Khalid Fattah Griggs, "Islamic Party of North America: A Quiet Storm of Political Activism" in Yvonne Yazbeck Haddad and Jane I. Smith *Muslim Minorities in the West, Visible and Invisible* (Walnutt Creek: Altamira Press 2002) p. 78.

68 Hill (ed), *Papers* v. 4 pp. 991-992.

69 Amy Jacques Garvey, "Christianity in Africa", *Negro World* 15 November 1924, in Vincent, *Voices of a Black Nation* pp. 365-6.

70 Amy Jacques Garvey, "The Tidal Wave of Oppressed Peoples Beats Against the Color Line", *Negro World* 18 July 1925; Vincent, *Voices* pp. 375-6.

71 Pinkney, *Red, Black and Green* p. 39.

72 Hill, *Papers* v. 9 pp. 638-639. This manifesto was noted by the French media, which thought that France's moderation towards the Kemalists in comparison to Britain would make her Muslim Senegalese unlikely to revolt at Garvey's call: ibid p. 640.

73 FBI reports of Andrew M. Battle in Hill (ed) *Papers* v. 5 pp. 30-31. Information provided by Africanist nationalists to intelligence agents or other Anglo-Saxon government departments, though, was often manipulative: thus, while still in Britain in 1921, Duse termed Garvey a "lazy" ex-messenger he had had to fire, to U.S. diplomats from whom he was trying to get a visa. Duse threatened, if he got to the United States, to sue Garvey for libel because he had hinted in an article that his movement had some link to him: the American consul-general wrote Washington that 'Ali's commercial projects "appear to have no relation to political matters of any character": ibid v. 3 pp. 337-339. 'Ali may also have deceived MI5, too, into thinking that Garvey and the UNIA irritated him: ibid v. 1 pp. 223-224.

74 Convention minutes for 7 August 1924 in Hill (ed), *Papers* v. 5 p. 679. The editorial "White Leadership of Islam a Delusion and a Snare" of *Negro World* 1 November 1924 is summarized: ibid v. 5 p. 681. This editorial respected the Mahdist insurgency and state in the but noted it had been defunct since the 1898 Battle of Umdurman. This item was correct that "the Turkish authorities have always used [pan-Islam]

more in their own interest in dealing with European powers than in the interests of the African and Asiatic Moslems": ibid. This had been true even under the "pan-Islamic", "conservative" Sultan-Caliph 'Abdul-Hamid (ruled 1876-1908): see Dennis Walker, "Pan-Islam As a Modern Ideology in the Egyptian Independence Movement of Mustafa Kamil", *Hamdard Islamicus* 17:1 (Spring 1994) pp. 74-75, 98: cf. Kemal H. Karpat, "Pan-Islamism: Imperial Plot or Muslim Popular Resistance to Imperialism?", paper for ICOPS conference on Ottoman Studies, June 30-July 4 1981, Madrid. It was the Muslims in Africa and Asia under rule by Westerners who wanted to build up the Ottoman Empire through pan-Islamism as a power-center to counter the imperial powers. It has to be noted that Duse Mohammed 'Ali had been awarded the Majidiyyah order by the Ottoman Sultan for all his lobbying on behalf of the Ottoman State in Britain, and had indeed been one founder of the Anglo-Ottoman Society: biodata on Duse in Hill, *Papers* v. 1 pp. 519-521

75 Articles by Samuel Haynes in *Negro World* 15 April 1933 and 6 May 1933, excerpted in Vincent 368-9, 218.

76 Arthur Huff Fauset, *Black Gods of the Metropolis: Negro Cults of the Urban North* (1944) (2nd ed.: University of Pennsylvania Press 1971) pp. 98-100; for America as part of the Moorish Empire, Gardell op cit pp. 37-38.

77 Fauset pp. 115-116.

78 Fauset p. 116.

79 "Noble Drew 'Ali honored: L.A. mayor proclaims day to Moors", *Final Call* 30 September 1986 p. 13.

80 Turner, *Experience* p. 107.

81 Conversation with Sheik Sharif Aneal 'Ali Bey, Grand Sheik of Subordinate Temple #4 at Syracuse, 15 July 2002. Sheik Sharif in this movement represents MSTA veteran Chief Minister Ra Saadi El-Sheik.

82 Turner, *Experience* pp. 101-106. In 1942, a Moorish "national home" was developing in Virginia in which 50 adherents lived in a compound of homes from which they pursued farming: ibid p. 106.

83 Conversation with Sheik Sharif Aneal 'Ali Bey 15 July 2002; for Mosley Bey cf Dannin, *Black Pilgrimage to Islam* p. 32.

84 McCloud, *African-American Islam* pp. 17, 55.

85 Karl Evanzz, *The Messenger: The Rise and Fall of Elijah Muhammad* (New York: Pantheon Books 1999) p. 64.

86 Email from Sharif Aneal 'Ali Bey, Grand Sheik of Subordinate Temple #4 under the leadership of Chief Minister Ra Saadi El-Sheik 23 February 2004.

87 See Ahmed I. Abu Shouk, John O. Hunwick and R.X. O'Faye, "Satti Majid, Shaykh al-Islam in North America and his Encounter with Noble Drew 'Ali, Prophet of the Moorish Science Temple Movement", *ic Africa: A Journal of Historical Sources* 8 (1997) pp. 137-191.

88 Evanzz op cit pp. 69, 79.

89 Xerox of letter of Drew dated 11 March 1929, and the report of the costs, income and assets of Detroit Temple #4 that Lomax/Mohammed Bey had published in *Moorish Guide* 17 October 1928. Documents supplied by Sheik Sharif 'Ali Bey of the Syracuse Subordinate Temple on behalf of Chief Minister Ra Saadi El-Sheik, 2002.

90 Robert Dannin *Black Pilgrimage* pp. 33-4. Influences from experiences of the modern Arab World had been prefigured by others from ancient Egypt through Garvey's UNIA as well as Drew 'Ali.

91 Dannin, "The Greatest Migration" in Yvonne Yazbeck Haddad and Jane I. Smith (ed) *Muslim Minorities in the West: Visible and Invisible* (Walnutt Creek: Altamira Press 2002) pp. 59-76. Dawud Ghani, outstanding leader of the original pioneers of this farm-area, had had contact with the Prince Hall Masons in youth, which underscores how theosophical attitudes in U.S. freemasonry helped broaden faith-community discourses to a point where Islam might become accessible as an alternative to African-Americans.

92 Michael Nash, " 'The Son of Thunder': Who Was Minister James 3X Shabazz? Nation of Islam History in Newark, N.J.", *Muslim Journal* 1 November 2002 pp. 11,

27; 8 November 2002, p. 11. Elijah Muhammad brought in the steel-willed James 3X Shabazz from Baltimore as Minister for the 1958 Temple: still, the congregations Shabazz assumed in New Jersey had been colored in advance by discourse and Arabic from Moorish and other non-NOI sources.

93 Conversation with Sharif Aneal Bey 15 July 2002.

94 "Will Establish Moorish University in Becket; Grand Sheik of Moorish Science Temple Tells of Plans for Newly Acquired Property", *Berkshire Evening Eagle* 2 October 1944: these cuttings were sent to me from Sheik Sharif Aneal 'Ali Bey of the Syracuse Moorish Temple of the movement of Ra Saadi El-Sheik and Sheik of Islam Waleed Abdul Naeem Bey-Sheik.

95 "Princess is Among Moors at Convention: 300 Delegates Gather at Former Pearl Farm", *Berkshire Evening Eagle* 18 September 1944; "Moorish Convention is Scheduled for Becket: Three Hundred Mohammedan Laymen to Meet at Former Pearl Farm, Including West Africa Prince", *Berkshire Evening Eagle* 30 August 1944: cuttings from Sheik Sharif Bey.

96 Dr Mahmud Yusuf al-Shawaribi, *al-Islam fi Amrika* (Cairo: c. 1960) pp. 74-77—xerox of this book provided from Palestinian-American Layla Diyab. Yet, "renew his knowledge": had Turner-El truly visited or studied in Egypt years before, and thus been able to muster enough fragments of Arabic to make al-Shawaribi accept that he had indeed been in his country for a time—that there was something in Turner-El upon which to build?

97 Unsourced report of Dannin, *Black Pilgrimage to Islam* p. 28. 'Ali's move to Chicago is set in 1925 by Sharif 'Ali Bey, Grand Sheik of Subordinate Temple #4: email 23 February 2004.

98 Letter from Sharif 'Ali Bey, Grand Sheik of Subordinate Temple #4 of Syracuse, New York, June 2002.

99 Email from Sharif Aneal 'Ali Bey of Subordinate Moorish Temple #4, 23 February 2004.

100 E.U. Essien-Udom, *Black Nationalism* (Chicago: University of Chicago Press 1962) p. 63.

101 W.E.B. DuBois, *The World and Africa* (New York: Viking Press 1947) p. 291

102 See Mezz Mezzrow and Bernard Wolfe, *Really the Blues* (New York: Citadel Press 1990).

103 *Struggles* pp. 90, 263.

104 Ken Farid Hasan, "That Killing Image", *Hijrah* (Los Angeles: pro-Warith ud-Din Mohammed) March-April 1985 pp. 20-22, and idem "Film Over Our Eyes", *Hijrah* October-November 1985 pp. 20-22.

105 Irving Howe wrote that by 1910 or so, Jews had more or less taken over blackface entertainment in the national marketplace of popular culture. Mark Slobin thought that "virtually every Jewish-American stage personality from Weber and Fields through Al Jolson, Sophie Tucker and Eddie Cantor first reached out to American audiences from behind a mask of burned cork". See Jeffrey Paul Melnick, *Right to Sing the Blues: African-Americans, Jews and American Popular Song* (Harvard University Press 1999) pp. 37-38.

106 *Aut* 138.

107 Willis Conover from 1955-1995 presided with low-key Brahman Anglo-American gravitas over the VOA's nightly Jazz Hour. Eastern European Communist regimes, fearing the spontaneity and self-contained individuality, and good feelings about America that African-American music fostered, sometimes jammed his program. "A voice of jazz heard by 100 million around the world", Melbourne *Age* 18 May 1996.

108 *Struggles* pp. 89-90.

109 Melnick op cit 122-123. This study charges a sort of commodifying disposable primitivism in Gershwin's trip to the South islands where he briefly "went native" as a colonial "shareholder in American whiteness": pp. 122-3, 127-136.

110 Hasan, "That Killing Image" p. 20.

111 "The Nation of Islam and the Racial Question," *The Green March* (Melbourne) issue 7, 1987 p. 10.

112 Tim Cole, *Selling the Holocaust from Auschwitz to Schindler: How History is Bought, Packaged and Sold* (NY: Routledge 1990) pp. 28-33.

113 Richard Wright, *Native Son* (New York: Signet Classics 1964) pp. 321-324.

114 See Donald B. Gibson, "Wright's Invisible Native Son", in Houston A. Baker (ed) *Twentieth Century Interpretations of Native Son* (Eaglewood Cliffs, NJ: Prentice Hall 1972) pp. 96-108. While *Native Son* came at the tail-end of a long Naturalistic tradition in American literature, it has been noted that Paris-based Wright published the novel two years before Camus did *The Outsider*: in at least its treatment of Bigger's trial and death, then, *Native Son* innovatively pointed forward to the Existentialism that was long to dominate Western high literatures.

115 Cecil Hourani, *An Unfinished Odyssey: Lebanon and Beyond* (London:Weidenfeld and Nicolson c. 1984) pp. 61-62. Freedman argued that the Slavic World's Jews were for the most part not descended from ancient Hebrews but from the Turkic tribe of the Khazars. He fed detailed data for this argument to Syria's Foreign Minister Faris al-Khuri, who mustered it in a long and scholarly speech before the UN to deny any title of the Zionists to set up a Jewish state in the Arab world—a speech that infuriated Chaim Weizman: ibid

116 Friedman, *Jews in the American Slave Trade* p. 316.

117 "al-Yahud wa Hurubuhum al-'Asriyyah" (The Jews and their Contemporary Wars) *al-Huda* (New York) 13 January 1932.

118 Syed Z. Abedin and Ziauddin Sardar, *Muslim Minorities in the West* (London: Grey Seal 1995) p. 167.

119 See, for example, the broadcast in which Elijah contended that Fard "was not a peddler of the kind that you [African-Americans] heard that he was. He got among us by taking of orders of made-to-measure suits for men folks". Elijah Muhammad, "Master Fard Muhammad Not a Silk Peddler", http://www.muhammadspeaks.com 25 February 2004.

120 Magida, *Prophet of Rage: a Life of Louis Farrakhan* p. 53.

121 Ibid pp. 47-52, 218.

122 Gardell op cit pp. 52-53. Magida's characterization that Fard was a cynical con-artist and jailbird does mainly cite a set of 1963 newspaper articles that many might well dismiss as inspired by other motives: Magida op cit p. 218.

123 Evanzz, *The Messenger* p. 207.

124 Zafar Ishaq Ansari, "Aspects of Black Muslim Theology", *Studia Islamica* v. 53 (1981) p. 142.

125 Gardell pp. 181-182.

126 Karl Evanzz, *The Messenger: The Rise and Fall of Elijah Muhammad* (New York: Pantheon Books 1999) pp. 82-83, 400-403: cf. this book's photographic section, including those claimed to be of Fard. The name Kallat among his followers (Elijah's younger brother had been dubbed so) need not tie him and them to the town of that name in present-day Pakistan as Evanzz contends (pp. 409-411), because Khallat is a common Lebanese Christian name that the Detroit Black population Fard targeted could already have copied from immigrant Arab shopkeepers. Clegg (pp. 112-113) argued that Fard borrowed the name Shabazz from the Lal Shahbaz Qalandar mosque in Pakistan—but "Shahbaz" is current in all lands that Persian influenced. The Druze Syrian Akram Qar'uni told me (14 December 2003) that "Shahbaz" is a name among Sunni Muslims, although not Druze or 'Alawites, in Syria. For hostility from Fard to polytheist Hindus cf. Clegg p. 47.

127 Essien-Udom p. 35; Whyte p. 383; Alex Haley and Alfred Balk, "Black Merchants of Hate", *Saturday Evening Post* 26 January 1962 pp. 71-75.

128 Claude A. Clegg, *An Original Man: The Life and Times of Elijah Muhammad* (New York: St Martin's 1997) p. 17.

129 Gardell pp. 182-184.

130 Gardell p. 348.

131 Gardell pp. 162-164.

132 Interview with Lebanese Druze Riyad ———, Melbourne, 1 December 1997. My lay Druze informants in the late 1990s did not assume that the devils active in

current politics are as numerous as the devils—all the whites—imaged by Wali Fard Muhammad and Elijah, and their followers up to 1975. It is to be noted, though, that some secret early Druze texts, written when massacres by orthodox Sunni Muslims were at their height, formulated that all Sunni followers of Muhammad were non-human devils, which is heading towards the scope that devil-hood had in the old Nation of Islam.

133 Louis A. DeCaro Jr, *Malcolm and the Cross: the Nation of Islam, Malcolm X, and Christianity* (New York University Press 1998) p. 3.

134 Gardell pp. 233-237; cf Clegg, *An Original Man* pp. 54-56.

135 DeCaro, *Cross* p.15.

136 Elijah, who was avoiding his violent opponents back in Chicago, did this in the leadup to his establishment of Temple no. 4 in Washington in 1939: Clegg p. 80. Ch. 4 will suggest that the sources Fard and Elijah read or taught from may have included Washington Irving's mid-19th century *The Life of Mahomet*: it was a dated study whose simple, clear narrative was suitable to teach a group of ex-rural African-Americans who knew little about Islam.

137 The founder of Druze doctrines, Hamzah Ibn 'Ali, had raised the status of the Fatimid Caliph al-Hakim bi-Amrillah (r. 996-1021) to that of the embodiment of the Ultimate Godhead who created the Total Intellect: al-Hakim is the locus (*maqam*) of the Creator, the manifestation of God in history in this theology: art. "Duruz" *EI2*. Early Druze writings present a religion of payback that often toxically abused the Sunni and Shi'i Muslims who slaughtered its followers as "devils" ("shayatin") who would be wiped out. The early Druze dismissed the concept of a purely non-spatial God who had not manifested in the figure of al-Hakim bi-Amrillah as *ilahu 'adam*, "a God of non-existence": it sounds like the "spook God" with which some NOI members ridiculed the eastern Muslims' conception that there could be a formless God without any need for an incarnation in Wali Fard Muhammad.

138 Black radical Conservative/Republican Walter E. Williams in 1981 put himself in the line of DuBois and Booker T. Washington's denunciations of unions as "the black workingman's worst enemy". Even when not prompted by racism, the unions' pursuit of closed labor markets of skilled workers with high wages had always closed possible points of entry into employment to African-Americans, who were starting out from fewer skills, this somewhat pro-Reagan argument ran: Williams, *America: A Minority Viewpoint* (California: Stanford University Press 1982 pp. 45-46, 44.

139 Erdmann D. Beynon, "The Voodoo Cult Among Negro Migrants in Detroit", *The American Journal of Sociology* 43:6 May 1938 pp. 894-907.

140 Thomas 5X (Drake) had been a zealous steward of the AFL-CIO Meat Packers' Union but resigned when he converted. The union gave "unity" with which the members could hold off "the wrath of the boss" but was white-controlled—and "ignorant" Negro members had been apathetic, he noted with resentment: Essien-Udom, op cit p. 274

141 Gardell pp. 55-56.

142 Evanzz p. 91.

143 Ibid p. 99.

144 Kenneth O'Reilly, *'Racial Matters': The FBI's Secret File on Black America 1960-1972* (NY: Free Press 1989) p. 278.

145 Evanzz p. 98.

146 Clegg op cit p. 91.

147 Clegg p. 96.

148 Evannz p. 150; Clegg p. 95.

149 For Stalin's WWII deportations of the Turkicized-Muslim Karachai and Balkars, the Chechens, Ingush, Crimean Tatars, and Meskhetians and the Buddhist Kalmyks and Volga Germans and Greeks, see Robert Conquest, *The Nation Killers: The Soviet Deportation of Nationalities* (London: MacMillan 1970) pp. 101-111. In the 1870s and 1880s the U.S. government deported the entire population of Chiricahua Apaches from New Mexico in the country's South West to military prisons in Florida and Alabama on the continent's other side: the alien climate wreaked a

death toll of 50% of the deportees. In 1913-914 there was an Anglo change of heart about transporting Amerindian nations, and the survivors of the Chiricahua were transferred to a reservation in Oklahoma. But involuntary segregation and sterilization of Amerindians and seizure of their children by WASPs continued.

150 Clegg op cit p. 97.

151 Worrill, "Nationalism and Blacks", *Final Call* 15 January 1989 pp. 23, 27.

152 Clegg p. 39.

153 Gardell pp. 307-8.

154 el-Aswad Abdus Salaam, "How Islam Came to Ohio Prison", *The Criterion* (Karachi) October 1973 pp. 37-40. For desecration of the Qur'an and other NOI literature by guards, and the isolation and strip cells, cf Gardell op cit p. 426. However, some U.S. prisons were becoming more liberal in the earlier 1970s. The Masjid Saffat (Mosque) in Baltimore, which sought guidance from Pakistan's Jama'at-i-Islami, and from Muslim Brotherhood Egyptians who taught it Arabic, was allowed to conduct classes two days a week in a local prison, and on Muslim holy days to take in special food that non-Muslim inmates, guards and prison officials also ate. See Taifa Abdullah, "Masjid Saffat, Baltimore", *The Criterion* August 1973/Sha'ban 1393 pp. 22-24.

155 Dr Na'im Akbar, "The Restitution of Family as Natural Order", paper read before Unification Church conference on "Family Values and Spirituality: the Unification Model and Other Traditions in Contrast", Montego Bay Jamaica, 17-21 February 1982. To the Anglo-American and Qur'anic motifs that had influenced Fard and Elijah, Na'im Akbar tried to add traditional African concepts of extended, rather than nuclear, family as re-imagined by African philosopher J. Mbiti: thus, this 1982 paper reflected the widening of African elements in African-American life since the late 1960s

156 See the reflections of Sister Levinia X (Adrine) in Essien-Udom op cit pp. 85-87.

157 Ken Farid Hassan, "Remembering the Motherplane: reflections on the Nation of Islam", in *Hijrah: Exodus to Enlightenment* (Los Angeles) Fall 1988 pp. 14-15.

158 Ansari, "Aspects of Black Muslim Theology", *Studia Islamica* v. 53 (1981) pp. 156-157.

159 "You will be clothed in silk interwoven with gold, and eat the best of food you desire": Ansari, "Aspects" p. 159; cf. Gardell pp. 164-165. Silk garments and bracelets of gold in immortal life in paradise are promised to those who do good deeds by Qur'an 22:23 and 35:33.

160 Ansari, "Aspects" p. 158.

161 Ansari, "Aspects" pp. 170-171.

162 Ibid pp. 142-143.

163 Elijah Muhammad, *The Fall of America* (Chicago: Muhammad's Temple of Islam No. 2 1973) p. 38.

164 *Message to the Blackman* p. 9: quoted Ansari, "Aspects" p. 143.

165 Lincoln 1961: pp. 73-4; 1994 pp. 144-145.

166 Ansari, "Aspects" p. 153. This would make Elijah like a Druze *hadd.*

167 Ansari, "Aspects" pp. 169-171.

168 Louis A. DeCaro Jr, *On the Side of My People: A Religious Life of Malcolm X* (New York University Press 1996) pp. 137-139.

169 John X 'Ali in introduction to Elijah Muhammad *The Fall of America* (Chicago: Muhammad 's Temple of Islam No. 2 1973) pp. iv-v.

170 Cohen in Katz pp. 8-9.

171 Richard Schickel in a 1979 review of Stephen Verona's film *Boardwalk*, which sought to spin a buck from recent fears felt by Jews of newly-arrived blacks in transitional neighborhoods, objected that it depicted the gang who harassed the sweet old Jewish hero-victim "like vengeful demons in some old-fashioned religious lithograph": Schickel, "Clean Old Man", *Time* 10 December 1979.

172 Dershowitz *Vanishing* p. 184.

173 Dershowitz *Vanishing* pp. 125-6. This exact configuration of Devil and Hitler motifs to bar both Negro organizations and whites from "deals" with Farrakhan was voiced in the same year from a Likud-like Jewish micronationalist magazine

(with which the highly liberal Dershowitz surely would seldom have been in accord?!): see disturbed psychiatrist David Shore Cohan, "Souls of Blacks Not Immune" [to Hatred], *Midstream* January 1997 pp. 24-25.

174 Dershowitz *Vanishing* p. 159.

175 Gardell pp. 270-271.

176 Algernon Austin, "Rethinking Race and the Nation of Islam, 1930-1975", *Ethnic and Racial Studies* (26:1) January 2003 pp. 57, 61.

177 Nanji's version is that Akbar Muhammad was arrested and transferred out of Egypt along with Tawfiq by the Nasser regime during the 1967 war: Azim A. Nanji, *The Muslim Almanac: A Reference Work About the History, Faith, Culture and Peoples of Islam* (New York: Gale Research 1995) p. 151. Akbar Muhammad's articles on African history and Islamic theology show his grasp of literary Arabic, but how *actively* fluent was he in speaking it? Fa'iq told me that Akbar usually spoke with him in English. However, in my conversation with him, Fa'iq would have preferred had I spoken in English instead of the inflected book-Arabic I obliged him to speak: interview of Muhammad Fa'iq, Cairo, mid-February 2005. Of course, Akbar had since the late 1950s translated between his father Elijah and visiting Arabs, and his old teacher Jamil Diyab assessed him as able to speak it well. On the other hand, Diyab in conversations with me overestimated the Arabic of his other old student, Warith ud-Din Mohammed, who became Chief Imam from 1975.

178 Lincoln (1961) pp. 211-212.

179 Lincoln (1961) pp. 211-213, 218-221.

180 Katz (ed.) *Negro and Jew* pp. 4-5.

181 [Lincoln (1961) pp. 220-1.

182 Wilfred Cantwell-Smith explicated 1953's pogrom-like agitation against the Qadiyanis and Ahmadis as not just over whether the latter could be allowed within the pale of Islam with the opportunities from that in public life, but also as a focus that ignited the mounting popular discontent over the decay and loss of direction of Pakistan after its early promise: Cantwell-Smith, *Islam in Modern History* (Princeton University Press: 1957) pp. 229-231. Somewhat as Lincoln imaged, the dropping of the doctrine that Ghulam Ahmad had been a prophet, and movement towards ordinary liberal Islam by the sect's Lahore Ahmadiyyah wing for a while won the latter some acceptance from educated Indian/Pakistani Sunni Muslims as "an energetic and worthy Muslim missionary society": Cantwell-Smith, *Modern Islam in India: A Social Analysis* (Lahore: Shaikh Muhammad Ashraf 1969) p. 369.

183 *Muhammad Speaks* 16 July 1972 quoted Ansari, "Aspects" p. 150 fn.

184 Ather Masood (Chicago), "What Many Muslims Don't Know About Elijah Muhammad", *New Trend* September 1999 p. 3; idem "In Defense of Minister Louis Farrakhan", *New Trend* September 1997 p. 3. This Islamist tabloid, alienated from both America and its coopted immigrant Muslim organizations, carried a facing article by an immigrant in Philadelphia denouncing the U.S. legal system as having long prevented blacks from practising law, and for offering quality legal representation only to the rich, not immigrant Muslims: Amin Abdullah, "How Much Justice Can You Afford?", *New Trend* September 1999 p. 3. For the traumatizing struggle of the immigrants to transmit Islam to their offspring amid American mass-culture, see Sister Bilquis, "Allah is the Leader for Muslim Children, *not* Muppets, Mickey Mouse, Bugs Bunny or Daffy Duck", *New Trend* Jumada I 1418/September 1997.

185 Masood, "Nation of Islam Gathering Unites with Imam Warith Deen", *New Trend* March 1999.

Chapter Four

The Heyday of Elijah: His Articulation of Ideology in the 1960s and 1970s

This chapter reviews the evolution of Elijah Muhammad's religious thought and the bearing his attitudes towards Christianity had for the construction of a single African-American political nation. It addresses the improving social status of Blacks in general and of his micro-Nation in the 1960s and 1970s, and resultant to-and-fro fluctuation in the NOI between its old millenarian-religious protest themes and its growing acculturation to the Anglo-American system. The next chapter will set the Muslims of the 1960s and 1970s in their context of the full spectrum of protest groups and protest figures in the African-American people. Assessing the extent to which the NOI under Elijah could, for example, help integrate closer relations between the African-American people and the Third World's Muslims and Africans has to take into account the views and efforts other African-American groups were developing about international relations.

The thought of Elijah Muhammad was religious and nationalist at the same time. Up to his death in 1975, he formally argued for secession of African-Americans from the USA. His serious political articulation of nationality, though, was moving towards an enclave-nationalism in which "Black" areas in cities would be distinct economic and political units within the U.S. central economy and electoral system. But the practical activities to which he directed his followers were scattering the members of the sect while knitting it together by its distinct economic circuit, a special press and culture etc. This loss of territoriality in nationalism I term "micronationalism": the homeland can be broken up into tiny units of territory, but the nation itself remains numerous and integrated as a unit in American life.[1] Elijah was pioneering something to be attempted by several U.S. ethnic groups in the 1980s.

Our preceding chapter set out the social crisis and the ideological context in which the first Nation of Islam took form in the 1930s. We examined certain particularistic tenets of that decade of the NOI's theology likely to pose problems for efforts to affiliate the sect to the Muslim countries in the Third World. This chapter now moves to examine (a) the post-1950 period in African-American history and (b) the mature discourse that Elijah Muhammad articulated in that heyday of his leadership in the 1960s and 1970s. The directions towards which the discourse could point his adherents after his death is an issue. How radical—or how covertly constructive as well as accommodating—could Elijah and his ideas become towards America's central system? Was the NOI more likely to develop into a political nationalist protest movement over the longer term, or to continue as a religious protest that side-stepped and avoided white power—but which one day might seek entry into the system after it had equipped its adherents to compete against whites? Given that Elijah did not orate or develop policies in a vacuum, any analysis has to bear in mind the context of "white" institutions and actions and the full spectrum of Euro-American groups, as well as the wider range of African-American groups and movements, that shaped the era of civil rights and Americanist liberalism in the USA. The influx of bourgeois and student converts into Elijah's sect in the 1960s and 1970s was fostered by wider developments of America and African-Americans in that period.

Like his teacher Wali Fard Muhammad, the Honorable Elijah Muhammad has to rate highly among the charismatic leaders of a religio-political type thrown up by desperate subordinated peoples. The unemployment, hunger and breakage of old social links in a new city environment that semi-literate Black migrants from the South faced during the Great Depression was the kind of crisis that has typically opened the way for such leaders to emerge in Muslim and other history. After 1930, Fard and Elijah's emotionalist claims to have special access to the Divine helped pull together into community poor individuals who could not count on leadership or help from the now-propertied Black churches and the few Blacks in city governments and electoral politics in the North. (Rev. Adam Clayton Powell, 1908-1972, did organize rent strikes, demonstrations and boycotts against segregation and for jobs and housing in the 1930s, but he did not become a member of Congress until 1945.) The lack of institutions that have functions to defend the masses' vital interests necessitates a charismatic leader who had little more than God and his personal spirit and commitment with which to start organizing the atomized victims. But God, apocalypse, the prophets or Messengers, and Judgement Day must—if charismatic leaders or the groups their ideologies bequeath are to last—become balanced by a more sober attunedness to changes in the oppressing group: skills for negotiating some resolutions of conflict and benefits from that system can be developed. Elijah's chance to routinize his charisma into a day-to-day normal leadership accepted by African-Americans, and build institutions in America, came in 1946 on his release from jail. His principled refusal to serve in the US army against other peoples of color gave him status that overshadowed all rivals who had stayed out.[2] Yet by the 1950s and 1960s, Elijah's religious charisma and institutions-building strategy was competing with multiplying civil rights and governmental bodies that were at last delivering real resources to African-Americans.

1. ELIJAH'S PERIOD CONTEXT

The civil rights movement was a mass movement mounted by African-Americans in the segregationist South from the mid-1950s that achieved the first breakthrough in civil rights legislation since the aborted [post-Civil War]

Reconstruction period of 1865-1877. Martin Luther King, Jr. and other leaders of his Southern Christian Leadership Conference (SCLC)—most of whom had some formal tertiary education—were able to structure the spontaneous protest of the Negro masses against segregation into an orchestrated resistance movement coordinated across several Southern states. The civil rights movement challenged Euro-Americans' consolidation of power through systemic discrimination and segregation by using non-violent techniques that gave the protesters the high ground according to Christian morality. These theoretical shared values of most Americans held open the option of constructive Christian-Americanist community to those whites who relented. The integrationist movement in the South began and continued with crucial support in the North from similarly highly-educated African-Americans active in the National Association for the Advancement of Colored People (NAACP). With support in money and personnel from the Jewish-American community in particular, they pressed a series of important cases before the Supreme Court. By May 1954, the NAACP won a decision on the crucial *Brown-vs-Board of Education* ruling of Topeka, Kansas, which declared that separate educational facilities were inherently unequal and therefore unconstitutional.

In 1960 the sit-in movement began at Greensboro, North Carolina, which forced desegregation of department stores, supermarkets, restaurants, libraries and cinemas across the South. It was led by the Student Nonviolent Coordinating Committee (SNCC) formed in April 1960. As had King and his SCLC, SNCC started with some links to the decolonizing Third World by virtue of its use of the *ahimsa* "non-violent" techniques of political protest that it had borrowed from Gandhi and his Indian independence movement, led by caste Hindus. While some whites were now marching with the blacks demanding desegregation and voting rights, a good range of Euro-Americans from both the North and the South coordinated rearguard resistance. The chief of the Birmingham FBI office in 1961 notified a known Ku Klux Klan informant in the Birmingham Police Department of the routes that civil rights buses would take through the South. This enabled Klansmen to attack civil rights workers and reporters with chains, pipes and baseball bats at terminals, with the police "arriving too late".[3]

SNCC would become much more nationalistic in its protest as the years passed and identify accordingly with African and Arab movements struggling for national independence. This would lead its adherents into conflict with Zionist and early micronationalist bodies and movements among U.S. Jews, a fair number of whom had worked in common organizations with African-Americans during the struggle for civil rights. Culturally and in world view, civil rights activists in SNCC and more discreetly in Martin Luther King, Jr.'s more staid SCLC were moving in the direction of the Nation of Islam with its relatively strong identification with Third World populations, and its pessimistic view of whites and the U.S. polity.

Mass media attacks on Elijah and the Muslims, FBI-planted or not, helped his drive for recruits in the face of the growing integrationist civil rights movement. When the front page of a San Francisco paper screamed "Black

Muslims Invade San Francisco" in 1960, Elijah smilingly told his in-house biographer, Bernard Cushmeer, that "if they took out whole pages in the *New York Times*, and cussed us out line by line, they would help us"--as the Jewish micronationalists were to do for Farrakhan from 1984.[4] It is still uncertain what exact mixed motives impelled Jewish-American broadcasters, TV figures and journalists to image to millions of white Americans that Elijah's Muslims ranked as equal contenders for Black support with the growing civil rights movement. Some Jewish-American media-persons were riding the fears of Anglo-Americans in order to achieve their own acceptance as loyal comrade-Americans against the blacks; some used shock-images of Elijah's Muslims to terrorize the Anglos into serious negotiation with such radical Christianity-masked "moderates" as Martin Luther King, Jr. with a view to building a new equal America for everybody—and most of them were out for a buck.

FBI chief Edgar Hoover was determined to prevent any major Black organization—whether nationalist or integrationist—from developing in the USA in this period. The FBI's creation of paper Negro organizations, and inventive use of incitative forgeries, infiltrators, and violent suppression destroyed the Black Panthers, debilitated the Republic of New Afrika and gravely harmed integrationist black Christian leader, Martin Luther King, Jr.—but, after a full decade, had not ruined the Black Muslims or Elijah Muhammad, an internal FBI document lamented.[5]

However, some white Americans in power were reacting flexibly and constructively to the pressure from the masses of African-Americans in the South, and with a view to forestall the diplomatic problems that would flow from maintaining segregation in a world in which new independent African and Asian states were emerging. In 1964, Lyndon B. Johnson (President from 1963-1969) got Congress to pass the most wide-ranging civil rights bill in U.S. history: it outlawed discrimination in public accommodations and threatened to withhold federal funds from communities that continued to maintain segregated schools. Johnson's sincerity was credible: as Majority Leader from 1955-1960 he had been largely responsible for the passing of the Civil Rights bills of 1957 and 1960. The whites who protested that such legislation was unconstitutional and had few affinities to any concepts of equality that the Founding Fathers had ever dreamed of, were not far from the truth. Johnson followed the bill with his Great Society program that inducted millions of impoverished Blacks who had wanted to improve themselves into a large new stratum of neo-bourgeois and skilled working-class African-Americans.

Residual paternalism continued to dog and deform the progress that such liberal whites strove to confer on their non-white compatriots. Johnson assumed that Blacks should be moulded into black copies of productive Anglos at a speed that left little time to hear out their wishes. Still, all the widening opportunities and prosperity made it very hard for Elijah Muhammad's Muslims to maintain their charges that all whites were malevolent devils without exception. While President Richard Nixon scaled down the anomalous intervention of big government to assist blacks, he too knew that at least a portion of African-Americans had to be inducted into the system.

He therefore influenced the private sector to give more opportunities to Black businessmen, and encouraged quotas in education and in hiring by private firms as well as government. (In the 1990s, some neo-conservative polemicists would charge that Nixon was a sort of father of the affirmative action they were determined to erase from society and history.) While some buckling of Elijah's separatist ideology occurred in the face of all these new openings into the American mainstream, the assassination of Martin Luther King, Jr. in April 1968 had led to the disintegration of the Americanist front of Negro people, giving heightened stature and more opportunities to lead Black America to Elijah and his Muslims.

The Nation of Islam in the 1950s and 1960s did not affect America to the same extent that the Negro civil rights movement led by Martin Luther King, Jr. did. While they look complementary in retrospect, the two pursued separate strategies for empowerment and incorporation into America, and drew their strength from two separate regions of the country. While the bourgeois civil rights movement sought to open a doorway for the South's Blacks by changing America's electoral system (parliamentarism) and the laws, the Muslims under religio-nationalist slogans were transforming poor urban blacks into middle class Americans. Some Muslims were already discreetly hoping that such self-modernization and entry into America's modern economy might get the NOI as a recognized sector into some future version of the American people, still to be defined by Anglos, well down the line. Still, King was clearly speaking for the aspirations of more African-Americans with regard to participation in the American mainstream, and more directly, than did Elijah. But then in the late 1960s, shifts in African-American life and moods made Elijah and the Muslims a lot more relevant, and to a much wider cross-section of Blacks, than before. The shifts encompassed (a) changes in, and new policies by, white America's political elite; and (b) changes in the ways African-Americans saw the world beyond America, in particular Africa and the Middle East.

On the whole, the spirit of the era ran against all ideologies that formally demanded separation of blacks and whites: a good proportion of both groups realized that now was the time to make America work as a unitary polity and community if ever it were to do so, and a fair number of Euro-Americans who held power or were trying to wrest it from the system, were making determined efforts to integrate all citizens into a single American people. A lot could be said against the Civil Rights movement—and was said, by a range of Black nationalists and radicals as the problems persisted—whether viewed as an approach to self-empowerment by Blacks or subsequently in coalition with various groups of Euro-Americans. African-Americans who were becoming radicalized increasingly charged that the drive by the Christian wing of the Negro movement in the South to get into real exercise of American citizenship was meant in the first place to serve the interests of a "Black bourgeoisie" that had formed or was forming there. There was some truth in such critiques from the later 1960s onwards. Moreover, although the African-American masses had been mobilized or involved to some extent, the outcome from the outset had had to depend on how well Martin Luther King, Jr. and his colleagues could build alliances and coalitions with sectors of the white majority—a key endeavor for any minority seeking influence, prosperity or power in America.

King's image declined among Afro-American youth in his last years, although his early openness to Arab as well as African nationalists and his later demands that the U.S. end its war against Vietnam voiced a discreet radicalism that would win him the deepest respect in all Muslim and nationalist movements after his death. The real Martin Luther King, Jr. believed that construction of counter-power by minorities and the proletariat—not Christian charity alone—would make America's central institutions and corporations concede interests of the subordinated poor. If King nourished the growth of Third Worldism, engagement with Arabs and Muslims, and leftism among black youth almost without their knowing, he was still working to integrate Black and White workers within one Americanist proletariat in turn to be empowered within one new unitary Americanist people.[6]

The texture of the relations that the Black civil rights activists evolved with more liberal categories of whites was far from flawless. Jewish students at Northern universities came South and improvised classes where they taught young blacks, in "Freedom Schools" outside formal educational systems, some of what they themselves had just been taught about sociology, politics, etc. A touch of white hierarchism still dogged it, but in an embarrassing way insofar as many of those activists were only two lessons ahead of their African-American classes. Yet these young, impressionable Euro-American activists in their turn were imbibing some of the rich oral culture and experience of Southern African-Americans, in a process in which U.S. ethnic partitions fell for the time and it became a possibility that one American people might form down the line. Many of the white activists from the North were youth who spoke a liberal or pink language that urged inclusive Americanist community. Yet many such whites who risked life and limb to some degree in the South were themselves marginal, ideologically or ethnically, to the central American system of that era and to their own ethnic groups. Civil rights activism offered a chance of a new start to American life in which all protesting groups felt they could slough off the old ethnic communities of their parents that kept America partitioned.

Few Jewish activists who came South were motivated by any inherited ethnic ideology or religion. Rather, vague impulses from Communism or Socialism or Western ideas of amelioration and progress fuelled their Americanist integrationism. Goodman and Schwerner, killed along with their Black comrade, James Earl Chaney, in Mississippi in the summer of 1964, were not motivated by either Judaic religion nor any Zionist nationalist successor to it. Goodman's Communist parents had often held fundraisers in the 1950s in their Manhattan apartment for professors accused of links to Communism. Schwerner was an atheist who believed in the infinite perfectibility of man: he had decided at thirteen not to have a bar mitzvah because he considered himself a human much more than a Jew.[7]

It is clear in retrospect that some of the South's African-American Christian activists who came together with such pink Northerners in the 1950s and 1960s had themselves been influenced by Communist ideas. Thus, highly diverse margins to the American system were being mustered to try to somehow make it work as an inclusive community. When Martin Luther King, Jr. declared his "dream that one day all Americans will be equal" he meant not only his people but that lower-class whites would also get inducted in their turn into a radically restructured system. Malcolm X realized very well in his last year that the shift of some cultural media to a more sympathetic portrayal of African-Americans, and some politicians' readiness now to let African-Americans truly exercise full citizenship, really might usher in substantial change in the interest of his people—now to be pursued through a normalized participation in the electoral political process that King had striven to open (parliamentarism). The pressure from the militant African-American masses was now unremitting. From within the Nation of Islam, a young Farrakhan was also trying to assess if elite white Americans really would muster the will, money and resources to transform the lives of African-Americans. He read the report of the 1967 Advisory Commission on Civil Disorders chaired by Governor Otto Kerner of Illinois, but doubted that the system really would muster all the money that report calculated was needed to decisively improve the conditions of Blacks in those igniting cities. Yet we shall argue that in the 1970s, even Elijah Muhammad may also sometimes have pondered the new chances opening up for his people.

Faced with mounting discontent from millions of African-Americans, Presidents Kennedy and Johnson had extended U.S. government intervention, functions and institutions in order to lift hundreds of thousands in the ghettoes to bourgeois status. The Great Society programs were a responsible, large scale, and in part successful, effort by the Democratic Party administrations to eliminate poverty imposed on millions of black people by generations of racist segregation, exploitation and cumulative structural inequality. The programs brought progress because they tapped self-enhancing energies in poor African-Americans that had previously withered. However, although they enabled segments of young Blacks to make themselves upwardly mobile and escape the ghettoes, the communities which these left behind did not benefit so much, qua communities, from all the progress.

However, President Richard Nixon was philosophically less prepared to extend the functions and size of government, while still sharply aware—unlike that veteran FBI chief he had impulses to fire—that Blacks could not simply be crushed any more. Overall, Nixon favored de-politicizing the problem somewhat. He preferred that government, in its ongoing role, rather guide or subsidize the private efforts of American capitalists to bring industries to Negro areas, and stimulate the spontaneous growth of the slowly emerging sector of middle class Negro businessmen and merchants in the ghetto areas. He had no generous or utopian drive to fundamentally change the dehumanizing conditions in which most working class Negroes carried on their daily battle for survival, nor did he savor the increased role African-

American politicians emerging from the matrix of Civil Rights would from now on play in a restructured USA's parliamentarist elections and institutions (congressional, city and local). He did, though, respect all forms of power in America. Nixon's plans for a "black capitalism" to bring economic emancipation to the Negroes trapped in segregated ghettos was in part electoral pursuit of the votes of the white backlash against the Democratic Party regime's direct expenditures and programs for the ghettoes, and against the retaliatory violence that emerging black militants were now evoking or even initiating. Yet Nixon's "black capitalist" project had in it a certain real respect for the resilience and determination of the category of African-Americans who wanted to become much more like the white business classes and reap profits. The project required Black forces that pursued private enterprise outside politics: Elijah's Nation of Islam was one clear candidate.

Nixon stood for most of white America in 1969. Moreover, a section of the more liberal Democratic Party component of the U.S. elite had reacted against LBJ's integrationist (albeit paternalistic) liberal Americanism, and therefore actively aided Nixon's changes vis-à-vis African-Americans. Daniel P. Moynihan, a renegade Democrat administrator from the Johnson era, wormed his way into Nixon's new cabinet as Advisor on Urban Affairs. His book *Maximum Feasible Misunderstanding: Community Action in the War on Poverty*[8] amounted to a savage attack on Johnson's attempts at social engineering by government as the approach to integrate Americans. Disregarding the poverty and bias he had known as a young Irish-American, Moynihan's neo-conservative writings would thenceforth radiate contempt for black Americans, suggesting that they be returned to old-style "benevolent neglect" and left to decay in their ghettoes. Thereafter, Moynihan would champion Israel; and many once-integrationist Jewish liberals, such as his collaborator Nathan Glazer, would put themselves at the fore of neo-conservative drives to take away corrective provisions and facilities for African-Americans in education, the civil service, business, and in parliamentarism.

The new Republican power structure wanted to sideline the crude power structure for mainstream electoral and public office for Negroes that had been emerging from civil rights in the South. Following the assassination of Martin Luther King, Jr. in April 1968, the civil rights activists were acquiring (or now revealing?) all-U.S. policy orientations that sought to impact the American mainstream, as well as nationalistic drives that jarred the Republicans. King's calls from April 1967 for U.S. withdrawal from Vietnam in the leadup to his death had been an internationalization of the struggle—perhaps always latent as an option among the non-violent Southern activists from the early 1950s—that took him beyond the pale. The situation was becoming dangerously fluid. Black Nationalist ideas based in the North were encouraging the construction of nationhood in new alliances of diverse black classes across the whole extent of the United States.

Young bourgeois activists in the South joined in the break-up of the Jewish-Negro coalition that had brought both resources and meddling to the civil rights movement. Some culturist activists who had emerged from the middle classes, at least in rhetoric and declamation, linked up to the black nationalistic masses in the ghettos of the North who with riots and violence were now breaking the economic hold of Euro-American, including Jewish, merchants on their neighborhoods. The economic ambition of the shaky new, expanding black middle-classes made them try to push established Jewish competitors off the rungs above that they wanted to climb in teaching, social work, the civil service and other professions. Still, exclusionist rackets by some Jewish-Americans had long fed much of the resentment in New York, for instance in the education of African-American children and the obstruction of the appointment of African-American teachers to the public schools. The labyrinths of standardized tests developed by Jewish and other white teachers in the New York public schools from the 1950s would be ruled by the courts later to have had little to do with functional requirements for teaching or administration there. They had more to do with the formation, and the self-perpetuation through patronage-systems, of a new ethnic clique now determined to keep power and livelihoods through the generations to come. White—often Jewish—teachers, principals, and administrators, designed and ran cram courses. They then made sure no prospective or employed white teacher would fail once he or she signed up.[9]

The quest of some civil rights organizations to extend integrationism into a country-wide drive to build a coalition of Black and deprived white sectors across America perhaps alarmed Nixon's new conservative regime the most. The Southern Christian Leadership Conference, victor of the great civil rights battles at Selma and Montgomery, was elaborating the dead Martin Luther King, Jr.'s insistence that civil rights go beyond voting rights for Negroes in the South. Dr Ralph Abernathy, King's successor as head of the SCLC, now organized a Poor People's March on Washington that inducted some white groups. While it was doubtful if the old civil rights movement could have leaped out of its first regional base in the South and built up such a coalition over the long term, the cold reception by Nixon and mainstream congressmen for Abernathy and his colleagues when they reached Washington, made it clear that the Republican U.S. governments would thenceforth contain and starve any attempt by the drifting civil rights leaders to try to alter U.S. society as a whole. Many Jews who had been at the forefront of integrationist Americanism were defecting to an Israel-obsessed Zionism and new micronationalism following the 1967 war, while the new U.S. political establishment would henceforth not allow bourgeois African-American leaders to help extend Americanist improvements to other disadvantaged sectors of Americans in general.

The South's African-American integrationists (to say nothing of the ex-integrationist new Black Power advocates) had stepped outside the bounds of action laid down by white America. The Nixon administration, in its quest for an alternative black power-structure, tried to deal with Roy Wilkins' multi-racial NAACP (National Association for the Advancement of Colored People) and Whitney Young's Urban League. Such large, impressive-looking organizations in the North had bargaining power not because they had mass roots among African-Americans there, but due to the funds lavished on them by wealthy white communities appreciative of what had hitherto been their moderate, conciliatory, gradualist approach. Financial dependence would long hamper these two organizations from articulating some important concerns and needs of black people in general.

But the new African-American bourgeoisie, advancing and expanding in the face of unremitting insults from some of their new white colleagues and neighbors, was turning towards a nationalism into which the world view of the Nation of Islam could dovetail.

The Emergence of Bourgeois Nationalism Among African-Americans

From the later 1960s, an emerging mood of Black Nationalism was working to unite the 22 million-strong African-American people, too long fragmented by class and geographical divisions. Livingston L. Wingate expressed this burgeoning realization of middle-class Negroes that they were inherently involved in the aspirations and struggles of a broad Black nation spanning the classes. He reflected that the ghetto, psychologically and physically, was in many respects as separate and distinct from the larger community as is a separate nation. Seventy percent of urban blacks were in segregated areas because they were kept there by the white power that precluded them from moving into the larger outer community either due to lack of money or to other barriers. Such an analysis, Wingate conceded to whites, was close to Black Nationalism, but there was no alternative to such a nationalism because "the black man is psychologically and physically in a pit". On the surface of that pit stretched the greater society that held "the mainstreams of the economic and cultural life":

> They were all put in a pit merely because of color, and they will have to come out collectively. Before there can be any effective participation in the outer wider society, there must be a banding of the black man together in the pit. As long as there exists substantially in the mind of white Americans a distinction between black and white, any black man who might happen to escape out of the pit to the outer society is condemned by the state of mind that the whites have about all of us. I'm saying that the black man must not dilute his power by running out of the pit in small numbers.[10]

The new nationalist black bourgeois ideologies remained ambiguous, like "Black Islam". Wingate's demand for unity of the whole Black (not yet an "African-American") nation in the pit regardless of the diverging classes to be spanned implied that such united action was a stage prefiguring later integration of African-Americans into the still unfriendly mainstream above. In attributing the blacks' existence as a coherent group as due to white exclusion, he did not much consider that some distinctive, nourishing cultural traits might be holding them together as a discrete positive nationality. The same ambivalence and equivocation dogged Stokely Carmichael's militant-sounding 1967 *Black Power: The Politics of Liberation in America.* In it, Carmichael wrote that "the concept of Black Power rests on a fundamental premise: before a group can enter the open society, it must first close ranks. Group solidarity is necessary before a group can operate effectively from a bargaining position of strength in a pluralistic society."[11] (Secession, autonomy or long-term integration?!) Carmichael did sense the functions that the Black, Jewish and other non-Anglo micronations now being constructed could acquire as foci or units that might eventually induct those peoples into a single American polity and society over the longer term.

For the most part, American pluralism in that period was little more than veneers over a shared adopted Anglo ethos, as we see for example with much of the "Jewish culture" evoked by *Commentary.* Still, in the 1960s, a new and distinguished generation of Black American artists explored the bustling surface of popular ghetto life. These artists and their art were consciously "African-American" to the extent that they calculatingly recycled some aesthetic forms and concerns of West African animist art into their somewhat abstractized recreations of crowded black communities. Yet those canvasses too perhaps derived as much or more from Picasso, Matisse and the Dutch genre paintings that had dyed these, after all, deeply Western, deeply American, artists. The African-American Romare (Howard) Bearden (1914-1988) abstracted only mildly to give coherence to his canvasses that captured the activity and joys of living Harlem, expressing visually the creativity and vitality of traditional high jazz. From a range of Western and African arts, these painters created in high culture a sense of a distinctive people that still maintained some African elements, expressing in a more celebratory manner the concern for community that also underlay some of the much more abstract and elegiac exploration of the American condition by such white artists as Andy Warhol.[12] Bearden's 1969 canvas, *Black Madonna and Child,* was perhaps really able to speak for a race as its title claimed: the simplifying effect of his vivid collages yet again makes one more subject—here the mother and child—embody a collective African-American nation. In their simple vivid clothing, the pair have an African ambience: statuesque, calm and eternal—they have been moved beyond the reach of all the pain, and the hate of racism.

Bearden's blending of interest in religious issues and family paralleled their centrality in the special nationalism the Black Muslims were projecting in the 1950s and 1960s during the period in which his art won its maximum audience among African-Americans. His impulse towards a nationalist reinvention in art of traditional Christian religious subjects also reached back even further to the Garveyite movement in the 1920s, whose chaplain-general, Rev. George Alexander McGuire, had founded the new separated "Ethiopian" Orthodox church. Tearing up white images of the divine and saints, McGuire had put black images of the Madonna, Jesus and Old Testament prophets in place of white ones. Young people in or around the Black Muslim movement were carrying Bearden forward in the 1960s and 1970s by evolving an Islamic religio-nationalist Black protest art intended to reach a more popular audience than Bearden won. From a studio in

New York, one admirer of the Honorable Elijah Muhammad turned out paintings and sculptures of a black Abraham, black Moses, a black Jesus and of lynchings—which still distinguished ethnic identity while keeping within the Abrahamic discourse-tradition of Judaism-Christianity-Islam.[13] In 1969, a Black Academy of Arts and Letters was formed by African-American artists and writers of various nationalist tendencies who wanted to make aesthetic works contribute to raising the consciousness of their people for self-liberation as a political nationality.[14]

The new nationalist outlook inspired some generous, serious drives in a Black bourgeoisie now determined to build nationhood. Negroes of some position and wealth who were formerly most orientated to integration into middle-class America were now returning, often physically, to their parent black communities. They were no longer prepared to surrender their black identity as the price of being absorbed into middle-class respectability, nor to accept the psychologically healing accumulation of wealth of the suburbs as a basis for community with upper-bourgeois white neighbors.

The post-1965 shift in identity of Blacks who had been orientated towards achievement within capitalist America was apparent in Andrew Billingsley's *Black Families in White America.*[15] The search for a new black identity was not confined to a minority of black extremists who were making sensational headlines. Professor Billingsley described upper-class and middle-class Negroes who were forming discussion groups and seminars to carry on a continuing dialogue with wider African-American classes about their common condition, common destiny and potential for change.[16] The alternative international community towards which it groped was Arabophile as well as Africa-centered: the seminars discussed the writings of Franz Fanon, Malcolm X, and W.E.B. Dubois, who all in some way had had connections to Arab North Africa and its struggles to break free from the yoke of French colonialism.

While some bourgeois blacks were quietly moving back into the ghettos which they or their parents had left, which might have reversed a brain-drain, it proved difficult to revitalize those ghettos. Ghetto lumpens suspected that part of the African-American bourgeoisie was using outreach to them in order to legitimize a new class hegemony: that their sudden nationalist stance was crafted to project an image of angry masses which would help the new class pressure more jobs, resources and business roles or welfare positions from the white system that had been fostering its growth. Still, the nationalist impulse to reconnect with the masses took away much of the stigma that their limited education had long given the NOI's ex-lumpens among the bourgeoisie. It became socially acceptable in the 1970s to ally with the Muslims and even join them, which many middle class Blacks now did.

The impulse among the bourgeoisie to connect to all other African-American classes on a basis of nationhood was to recur over decades: Farrakhan would tap it in 1995 when he organized the Million Man March on Washington and its White House throughout the whole African-American nation.

The admission of the new Black elite into mainstream U.S. academia in the 1970s sparked conflicts with the white intellectual elite that was there to receive them. In reaction, the conferences of the African-American academics and lumpen-academics soon came to parallel Elijah's racist (or, rather, counter-racist) views of whites. In 1974, Harold 4X of *Muhammad Speaks* exulted that if any Black student is serious about the study of skin color and human behavior, then credit is first due to the Honorable Elijah Muhammad, who had been teaching Blacks for more than 40 years on the origin of all races. The 7th Annual Convention of the National Association of Black Psychologists had reviewed scholarly theses from the bourgeoisie that could indeed fit into Elijah's theories. Black people, Elijah had argued, have the greatest color-determined potential, with brown, red and yellow people possessing lesser quantities.[17] The theses of Dr Francis Cress Welsing and of Dubois McGee of the African Psychology Team were discussed at the Conference: both agreed that the absence of color in white people is a genetic deficiency. The Cress theory stated that the white or color-deficient Europeans responded psychologically to their numerical inadequacy in the context of the global population—and to their inferior inability to produce melanin—by violent confrontations with the massive majority made up of the world's color-producing people. Yet, exactly these elite affirmations of black superiority, too, like those of the NOI, were yet more sleight-of-hand to cloak a resolute drive to eliminate many specificities of African-Americans and make them more like middle-class Anglos and Jews. McGee asserted that the more refined nervous system of Black people had been "distorted by their present eating, living and thinking habits". It was a comprehensive rejection so typical of these Islamic and Black nationalist movements that all strove to transform African-Americans, excise Black folk culture, folk-ways and diets and spontaneity as they then were, in order to resist in double-edged or ambiguous ways the whites they denounced pro forma.[18]

The history of African-Americans in general in the later 1960s and the early 1970s, then, saw a reduction of the system's aid to liberal parliamentarist integrationism among Blacks: the civil rights movement was becoming less credible an alternative to Elijah and his Muslims in the contest for leadership of African-Americans. More stress by the American ruling elite on the marketplace rather than politics also could work to legitimize the Nation of Islam and its Black capitalism as a vehicle for an ongoing resistant effort by African-Americans to achieve prosperity in America. The increased nationalism of the bourgeoisie prepared them to consider Elijah's own nationalist motifs, although these had some distinctive religious sources and had been kept outside political action since 1945. The Africa or "return to Africa" high scholarship or high ideology that the bourgeoisie were now seizing highlighted Arabs, Muslims and Muslim-led independence movements overseas that were also projected by the Muslims' newspaper, *Muhammad Speaks*. Thus, there was high congruence between the directions America and most African-American classes were taking and some themes central to NOI discourse.

2. NOI PROTEST RELIGION

A serious review of Elijah's discourse has to bring out its originality as an uncommonly unitary system of meaning that assayed to cover and knit together widely-separated experiences of African-Americans—even though Elijah often covered sectors in a skeletal or basic way. The issues included (a) the origins of Blacks and whites and of their relationship, for which Elijah offered a religious explication; (b) some specifics of the recent economic and social interactions of Blacks and whites in North America; (c) the endeavor to collectively found a bourgeois prosperity that the religion made sacred; (d) the correct stance to be adopted towards the U.S. polity and (e) a God-directed resolution of the conflict between Blacks and whites. Would the solution come through incineration of whites? Or affiliation/incorporation into their system via construction of wealth and power? Wali Fard Muhammad and Elijah's discourses, in being conveyed to aggrieved black masses at the grass roots, did threaten the survival of Christianity as the ideology of most African-Americans and of the civil rights movement. The Muslims caught attention through their confrontational vilification of whites, and of Christianity as a psychological weapon of white control. The ambitious scope of Elijah's discourse also forced the activist bourgeois Christians to consider it amid the crisis. In the 1960s and 1970s, formal Christian theology among African-Americans offered few interpretations of religion in terms of the vital social and economic interests of Blacks—which was exactly what NOI theology claimed to provide in those crucial times. Black theologian Gayraud Wilmore noted (1979) that "the only distinctively Black theological reflection in written form that anyone was aware of prior to 1964 was that produced by the Nation of Islam".[19] (Yet Martin Luther King, Jr. had drawn on Gandhism as much as Christian theology to achieve Black needs, and his veiled Third Worldism was suspect to a pietist category of African-American Christians.)

Among scholars, Gardell (1995), in his overview-synthesis of Nation of Islam discourse, tended to accept the claim of Elijah or Farrakhan to have evolved consistent systems covering all reality, as the Nigerian Essien-Udom already sometimes had argued in 1962.[20] But in this chapter we likewise seek out areas of Elijah's discourse that failed to pull and bind things together into a *final* religious closure of meaning. Our focus has to be more on Elijah Muhammad's human side—his occasional doubts about the direction or the prospects of some of his enterprises, his disappointments, imprecisions in his discourses, and ambiguities that could bring in alternative directions among which his "Nation" could choose after his death. This chapter attempts a deconstruction of Elijah's religion and social critique that—while respecting his grand enterprise—shows other outlooks growing within the discourse, constricted and deformed though these may be for the time, due to the race-focused and traditional patterns so central in America, working in tandem with the preset structure of Elijah's worldview.

Whites who met Elijah and his adherents of the 1950s, 1960s and 1970s found them in the flesh startlingly unlike their media image of deadly enemies of whites and America. The Jewish-American Peter Goldman, as a reporter assigned to Negro affairs, found them not nearly so fearsome as Malcolm X's predilection for tossing in an incendiary phrase implied. For a threat to America's security, the NOI's rank and file he met turned out to be an "oddly bourgeois lot": Goldman noted the paradox that their rejection of whlte America expressed itself in economic activity on a margin that white America left for minorities at the edge of its private enterprise. Allah's children wanted to become a nation of shopkeepers with a burgher life-style that included abstinence from pork. Goldman and the Rev. Martin Luther King, Jr. both speculated the NOI shopkeepers were influenced by Jewish small-merchant neighbors pre-established in those ghettoes, although the abstinence from pork then also came to be prescribed by Islamic tenets.[21] The borrowing from neighborhood Jews could become conscious and overt. As a newly recruited NOI Minister, Farrakhan had been a flashy over-dresser: Elijah advised him to consider "the mohair suits those Jewish rabbis wear—dignified clothes".[22]

The Threat to White America

In the period of Elijah's leadership, there always remained some question whether the millenarian theology of Armageddon would release and channel self-uplift dynamism or explode into violence or even insurgency. For the majority of members, the sect offered the oppressed a cathartic verbal violence that evaded civil war. The fantasies of God's destruction of the whites rebuilt self-confidence and hopes that deliverance from outside themselves was close, while draining off the counter-hatred that many segregated Blacks pent up within themselves to the harm of their self-esteem and growth. Saved from self-hatred and unrealistic expectations of help from any whites by this eschatology, the believers could modernize themselves with energy, leaving the destruction of the white devils to God.

The initial Muslim Elijah had been a hyper-activist eager to at least verbally confront the white devil system. Following his expulsion from Detroit on May 26, 1933, and harassed from city to city, a worn-down Fard had to try, by exhausting correspondence, to rein in this still-young disciple who had stayed on in that city and was initiating so many actions without clearing them in advance for "guidance." Wali Fard Muhammad in 1933 prized the potential of his energetic, youthful disciple. But Elijah's bent in 1933 was, Fard faulted, "to get out on the street and on the top of all the high buildings, yell out your wisdom"—but "the time is not right yet, how many times have I told you this?" Elijah had to understand that he was "a long way from home and your own kind" (the Arab World and Africa) in the cave of the savage who could cut him in two if he were not discreet for the time. (This advice appeared in a letter dated 18 December 1933 from the Southwest USA ascribed to Fard by http://www.muhammadspeaks.com, downloaded 29 September 2003. I believe this ill-punctuated letter to be genuine. It has the gritty texture of a human hard-pressed by unremitting blows from a range of Anglo agencies, and even more deeply disheartened by "my own people" so badly "poisoned by the devil" that they continued to reject the unique wisdom the now peripatetic Fard Muhammad kept offering them day after day.) Fard in 1933 had sized Elijah up sharply. Elijah's solely verbal, but resounding, solidarity with Japan during World War II, met by muffled misgivings from his congregations, was to enable white authorities to arrest him and almost destroy the NOI during that conflict. That burst of repression, though, made the weakened Elijah more cautious when he got out.

Usually, Elijah's preaching, while catering to—and containing and diverting—African-American hatred against whites, depicted Allah as the Being who would do the fighting: African-Americans could live in "peace" with the ruling ["white people" constructed] ethnos until God incinerated them all. Still, his discourse did have in it crude elements that might rather go with settlement of the conflict through—or beginning with—a clash between populations, or what he and his ministers termed "Armageddon." Elijah observed that America's doom had been predicted by "the prophets of the Bible", for instance when Joel predicted "as the morning spreads abroad upon the mountains, a great and strong people set in battle array" (2:2). For Elijah this was the setting off of the nations for a final "showdown to determine who will live on earth". The surviving side would build a nation of peace to rule the people of the earth forever under the guidance of Almighty God.[23] Here, there is more scope for direct action by oppressed Blacks against the neighboring enemy-populations.

The pattern manifested in the downfall of the proud King Nebuchadnezzar in the Bible was that God smashes an oppressive people at the height of its kingdom and rejoicing. So it was with the coming of Allah (God) in the Person of Master Fard Muhammad, on the 4th of July 1930. His arrival on the day of white America's celebration of its independence meant "the destruction of the independence of the white race, and especially America" over the Black slave sitting at his feet. After four hundred years of servitude-slavery, "Allah (God) came to give justice and freedom to us and to make us equal members in the society of the new powerful, strong, and wise people of the earth"—the "Black People of the Earth" now achieving liberation. African-Americans should accordingly celebrate the destruction of the whiteman that was now occurring and the—perhaps illusory or only symbolic?— "independence" and "equality" vis-à-vis Euro-Americans that they had won on the 4th of July 1930.[24]

Allah could annihilate America at any moment but loopholes were always left. America refused to break her fall when she could have: Babylon could have been healed, but it refused (Je. 51:9). America refused to accept her chance for forgiveness "for she never offered to do anything favorable toward her Black slaves, that would make them free of her power to rule them".[25]

The later 1960s and the 1970s, the period of Elijah's mature power and teaching, was one in which some motifs for insurgency were being articulated in the broader Islamic sector of Black America and by other competitors among the secular Black nationalists. The Black American poet, Lefty Sims, wrote: "Send me O Allah as a/Rampaging fire to consume/ Your enemy as I praise your name./Turning myself to Thee, palms/Upward, arms outstretched facing/Eastwards, I seek only your command./O Allah strengthen my chest/To repel a thousand bullets, to/Live a moment in glory before even/I die." Although sustained by a truly religious belief in Allah, even this jihadist poet did not hope that he himself, personally, as an individual, would live to see any victory. But most in Elijah's sect chose life with its chances for money and prosperity.

The scholarly literature early highlighted Elijah's furious and perhaps violence-inciting imagery of white oppression and aggression against African-Americans. Elijah charged that America used the lapdog-like African-Americans as cannon fodder to defeat her enemies in Europe and around the globe but gave them no share of the spoils when they meekly returned home.[26] After the Black soldier killed Germans for the whites, "our sons and daughters are lynched, kicked, beaten, hung up in the sun, drowned in the river, in ponds and lakes, their bodies are found in the streets and the highways". "If we continue to accept these injustices, we are nothing but cowards. If we are cowards, then we ought to go home, kill our wives and then commit suicide."[27]

And, indeed, there were militants in the sect who looked forward to taking an active part of their own in Armageddon, or who might pre-empt it if it took too long coming. Thus, the chain of random so-called "Zebra" killings of whites was undertaken by an informal group in the Nation of Islam in the San Francisco Bay area in late 1973 and early 1974. The small cult-group that termed itself the "Death Angels" kept their activities secret from the rest of the San Francisco temple, but assumed that they had been brought together on directives from the top Muslim leadership in Chicago. They viewed their selection and shooting of white victims as the practical application of their sect's denunciations of whites as all satanic enemies of blacks—in actuality an aberrant extension of Elijah's teachings because their vengeance pre-empted Allah. There was no evidence that Elijah Muhammad and/or the formal leadership of the Nation of Islam ever authorized or knew of the group. On March 29 1976, four Muslim blacks found guilty of murder and conspiracy to commit murder in the San Francisco area were sentenced to life in prison.[28]

Another militant extension or mutation of Elijah's teachings occurred when an impatient Muslim splinter group took on the white police in Baton Rouge, Louisiana, in January 1972. Two on each side were killed and a fair number of police officers as well as African-Americans were injured. The Mayor said the blacks were Black Muslims from Chicago who boasted they were taking over Baton Rouge. The clash won the Muslims great admiration among secular black nationalists and militants but, consistent with the ambiguous nature of his hatred of whites, Elijah waffled on whether the splinter group had membership in his sect. He was truthful in that the malcontents had long before broken with extractive corruption in the Chicago leadership.[29] In a press conference soon after the events, Elijah ambiguously described the insurgents as "not on our register as good Muslims... Their names, some of them, are foreign to us altogether".[30]

Elijah could sometimes orate or write with electrifying imagery that sounded highly incitatory. Even in his final period when he had become very rich, he imaged that "the powerful, rich world of Christianity—especially America—[looked] as immovable as the mountains", but that high explosives could remove mountains: "so wealth and power also can be reduced to nothing". Nonetheless, the NOI's frank articulation of the race hatred most African-Americans felt towards their white oppressors could seem—to intelligence agencies, and indeed to some Negro social scientists who were covertly inflammatory themselves—as though it posed a threat of violence or insurrection against America's system. But Elijah here was explicitly responding to the unremitting drive of such American institutions as the FBI with its "evil eye" not just to monitor but to harm or destroy his sect in a quasi-totalitarian manner, during a vulnerable early stage of his organizing "the resurrection of our people". "America must be taken and destroyed, " Elijah proclaimed—yet even in this outburst he was still thinking for the most part of intervention by God rather than a violent initiative by his people.[31]

Elijah's verbal confrontationism against whites and Christianity at some points was just papier mâché veiling a more modest resistance. He toyed with a watery threat that the blacks could become a diplomatic embarrassment or fifth column in international power politics if America ill-treated them too much: "you could never win against anyone outside or inside of America as long as you seek to mistreat us". Taking a bloodcurdling Biblical passage, Elijah projected that God might give the Blacks "their [the whites'] blood to drink like sweet wine"—but this was still within the frame of God intervening at some indeterminate point in the future to do the fighting for those wronged Blacks. His parochialist, sect-centered discourse, for all its metaphysics, amounted to little more in the short term than a scenario under which the Muslims and the American authorities would keep to separate turfs. As "the people of Allah (God), the Muslims would make no trouble with anyone, but Allah (God) Will retaliate against anyone who makes trouble for us, or who seeks to do us harm".[32] This passage does not clearly state that the Muslims would resist attacks by U.S. government forces against their adherents and mosques with counter-violence, although they were to do so on occasion. Under both Elijah and Farrakhan, let alone Warith, the Black Muslims have repeatedly failed to show up when street showdowns began or threatened between Blacks and Anglos or Blacks and Jews in America. In Elijah's era, a local NOI chief in Buffalo said that it would be better to be out of town when trouble breaks out in the ghetto.[33]

Anti-Christianity

The virulent antipathy that Malcolm X voiced towards Christianity throughout his career as a Black nationalist, though phrased with his special vividness of imagery, sprang from the teaching of his sect. In the 19th century, the African-American clergy had been active in abolitionism, back-to-Africa currents and early pan-Africanism, articulating crude liberation theologies—and indeed, lecture-circuit Islamophilia. It has been argued that the anti-Christianity voiced by the Black Muslims from 1930 was in response to the temporary context of the black clergy's turn to accommodation to the white

American system as it became harsher and more segregationist towards the end of the 19th century. The black churches were accumulating property, and impressing on the masses the image of a non-violent, patiently suffering, otherworldly Jesus, arguing that white hostility and narrow opportunities here had to be borne to win bliss in a better world to come. This deradicalization of the black church was almost complete by the time of the mass migration north of African-Americans and the advent of the Great Depression—the exact point at which the Nation of Islam crystallized in the cities of the North.

In contrast, after World War II, the clergy of the Negro Protestant churches became more active in trying to reform and integrate (but not overthrow) the existing social order, mainly through the movement for equal civil rights led by Rev. Martin Luther King, Jr. Then, from the late 1960s, in response to the challenge of Black Muslim theological discourse, a fair number of Black Protestant clergymen and academics began to develop a liberation theology that now made possible a convergence of the two Christian and Muslim confessions in a joint struggle or nationalist coalition to achieve the vital interest of African-Americans under the leadership of Farrakhan from 1978. With some inputs from the Middle East's Islam, Farrakhan said he regarded all three religions that uphold the legacy of Abraham to be one faith under different labels: accordingly, Muslim and Christian blacks have to be reunified in a single movement reflecting the Oneness of God (tawhid).[34]

After 1975, Farrakhan at least changed his approaches. But not all American clergy are agreed that he ever in his heart truly broke with the old pre-1975 Nation of Islam's hatred of Christianity as irredeemably an instrument concocted by whites to paralyze the resistance of the blacks they victimize and thereby to maintain their race-hegemony.

We now examine Elijah's old pre-1975 images and analysis of Christianity and its clergies to determine how central or inherent hatred of it was in the sect's ideology, how much potential there was for a shift, and how diversely Elijah could conceive the religion and its clergies. How far was he able to perceive the depth of the change already under way in Black Christianity's shift from the old quietism and avoidance of the socio-economic inequality of blacks to the new drive to confront and change society through the civil rights movement, and then through a Black "Liberation Theology" that sounded more radical.

Despite the civil rights revolution black Christians had headed for some time, Elijah's 1973 collection, *The Fall of America*, was still voicing his fervent hope that Allah would incinerate the Black clergy along with the whites they served and who had manufactured them.[35] Christianity was the key instrument white America applied to keep her black slaves mentally debilitated and thus in her control. America had reared African-Americans for the past 400 years and thus knew how they were thinking and how they were reacting to her teachings: she knew their fear of her. But the slaves did not know America—their slavemaster—nor the doom now at the doors and windows of America and its church. "As long as Christianity worked, America thought she was safe, because... everything in the religion of Christianity is designed to make a slave out of Black people." If Christianity was in a wet rag and wrung out, every drop would write slavery for the Black man. All the world now knew that—except the spiritually blinded American so-called Negroes, who held tight to that religion in the face of Elijah's calling them to the "reason" of his special Islam.[36]

But Christianity was not just misused by whites as a lethal weapon with which to befuddle the blacks—it was nonsense in itself. The truth that would set free was not Jesus' birth and narrated death: Jesus had not been the final word of truth, he had promised that God would send one who would reveal the ultimate truth to the people who were lying in the mud of ignorance and shame, not to the wise of this world. In NOI discourse, the refutation of the Trinity opened the way for Wali Fard Muhammad and Elijah Muhammad to assume primacy in history.

In developing the theme of Christianity as a weapon of white hegemony, Elijah, like his disciple Malcolm X when he spoke on the subject, had a rationalist tone that evoked the economic interests of blacks that had to be realized in the present, without distractions engineered by the enemies. Christianity is a white man's tool that contains no salvation for the Black man: that is why the prayers of the black preachers to the government, the Father, the Son, and the Holy Ghost have fallen on deaf ears. What good is Christianity to Blacks if that religion and the God of that religion will not defend them against lynching and rape? Christianity offers salvation after death: first you must go down into the earth and rot. Any man who will work hard all his life praying to God to take him and bestow a home beyond the grave is a fool.[37] "There is no life beyond the grave! There is no justice in the sweet bye and bye! Immortality is now, here!" Blacks could be the blessed of God: this required that they exert every means to protect themselves and build a holy prosperity now in this life.[38]

As Pharaoh tried to stop Moses teaching the gospel of justice in this world, America's oppressors were determined to keep the eyes of the blacks in the sky while controlling the land under their feet. They wanted to bog their black victims down in "an impractical ethic of turning the other cheek [while they] rob our pockets." The Negroes had not come to their own natural religion that would achieve their interest because they were still weeping and moaning over the death of Jesus two thousand years before. "Yet, you don't weep, moan and go insane over the rapes and lynchings of your own people in your own time."[39] Whites unite to aid their own kind against common enemies, but that was not allowed for Blacks. "If you listen well, you can hear the screams of a Negro co-ed in Tallahassee as she vainly begs her four white abductors to leave her virtue intact."[40]

Elijah hated not just the whites and the Christianity they had fashioned as their weapon, but also—with few nuances—the black clergy class who conveyed Christianity to the masses. The white slave-master, the devil, who has deceived all human beings and civilizations around the world excepting the angels of heaven, has deceived the "reverends" [that he has made] so that they will not accept Islam. Elijah extrapolated from the Book of Revelation in the Bible that John there "sees the preachers burning in hell-fire with the devil, the white slave-masters." Yet he did have an iota of empathy for those clerics even as he simplified the Black Christian clergy into a pure instrument. Elijah was attuned to the emotionally-starved social desperation of the Black clerical class in an American culture that so exalted Anglos: the cleric will walk right into the lake of hell-fire with the devil, as long as the devil calls him "reverend" or "father".[41]

Elijah's discourse depicted American Anglo whites as hellish architects of men who had evolved an ever more intricate technology of the soul to keep the black minority enslaved. "The white man has been very clever in the making of the Black man." In the days of servitude slavery, the white "slavemaster" did not even give his slaves good food. Now, in the 1960s and 1970s, blacks with the money could buy quality food that had, however, been mostly poisoned by the chemicals used to produce and preserve it. In Elijah's analysis, the material or psychological payoffs that whites offered a minority of the African-Americans in the 20th century still were meant to mould them into a sub-elite that would be a tool in controlling the people from whom they had sprung. During slavery times, the cruder slavemaster would offer a piece of fried chicken and a biscuit with a little butter on it to a so-called Negro as an inducement for him to preach what the slavemaster wanted to the other slaves on Sunday morning so as to make those other brothers spiritually blind, deaf and dumb. The Christian clergy of his day were no better in Elijah's unnuanced, homogenizing condemnation: like their fathers, they wanted the white "master" to give them better positions in return for which they were to offer to cut off the heads of their Black brothers. Even into the post-WWII era, whites were still offering high positions and money to Negro intellectual politicians prepared to work as puppets against the good of the black millions sprawled in the mud of civilization. "They are content as long as they eat the buttered biscuit and the fried chicken as their [clergy] slave-fathers did."[42]

In his public discourse at least, Elijah dismissed the "reverends" as the enemies of their Black People. He did sense some resentment festering in the clerical Christian elite: he warned them that "the devil kills those whom he sent and who will not obey him—so be careful, 'reverend', for the white slavemaster had killed even Rev. Martin Luther King, Jr." Elijah claimed that when King "talked with me at my home... he admitted [to me] that the white man is the devil." But the devil kept him in his power through fear. If Rev. Martin Luther King, Jr. had survived, he might have moved into "the same corner" with Elijah. After Elijah told a mass-meeting that he had hit it off with King at his home, the white enemy quickly set the latter up for his death.[43]

Historical retrospect leaves no doubt that, in choosing the shared Christianity as the ground on which African-Americans might challenge white control, Elijah and his Nation of Islam had both identified a crucial aspect of the American system, and tapped a long, if sub-surface, tradition of Islamic separateness maintained by a portion of the continent's blacks since the formative period of British rule. Yet Elijah and Malcolm's denunciations of African-American Christianity by the mid-1980s came to appear as a onedimensionalizing and fanatical distortion of the historical reality, even to African-Americans who had converted to Islam. The prominent journalist Salim Muwakkil admitted that slavery in North America had bequeathed an "historically unique legacy" that had in it religious and other adaptations to white supremacy that were, in some aspects at least, serious strategies devised by a subordinated people to survive and get resources while developing some distinct culture. To Muwakkil in his 1991 retrospect, the pre-1975 Muslims seemed crass, and needlessly destructive of some good things that African-Americans had evolved.

> The Nation of Islam tries to take a shortcut to cultural development through a totalitarian method, coercing people toward a certain kind of behavior. In many ways, they were disrespectful of the black people's ingenious adaptations to the situation. The Nation of Islam simply rejected it as being a slave response: the nuances of the black experience were lost to them.[44]

Muwakkil had got close, here, to the Muslims'—in effect Anglicizing—hatred of popular black ways and sub-culture. Their drive to coerce the Black masses from some popular evolved ethnic traditions and beliefs might indeed have soon turned dictatorial and violent, had the NOI won the power.

The Elijah-era denunciations of Christianity left a legacy of resentment that endures into the 21st century among even those black Christian leaders who collaborate with Farrakhan in endeavors that are cast as coalitions for the welfare of the African-American "nation" as a whole. From the early 1980s, Farrakhan developed a more conciliatory line that there is little real contradiction between Islam and Christianity and that each flows into the other—although he may well have in mind the movement of adherents mainly in his direction. He has indeed succeeded in blurring Christianity into Islam in the minds of some in the black public. DeCaro (1998) was alarmed that Benjamin Chavis, after his 1997 conversion to Islam, had tried to maintain his credentials in the United Church of Christ in accordance with Farrakhan's line that Islam and Christianity were a continuum or a unity—would Christian African-Americans let Chavis and his ilk get away with even that? A New York rabbi mounted a divisive argument that the Million Man March and the World's Day of Atonement were really about getting Blacks to attach to Farrakhan religiously. The religious buttons of power Farrakhan strove to seize in such mass rituals were not really any held by Jews but those held by the Black Christian leaders; Farrakhan was "after Jesus: Jews are just the effigy", argued this shrewder Jewish-American leader as he sidestepped Farrakhan's ploy to make American Jewry highlight him to the Blacks.

Yet Elijah's cannonades had weakened the standing the African-American clergy could command among the masses they addressed and had striven to control through civil rights movements and Democratic Party politics. An open letter from Southern Christian clergyman-activist Wyatt T.

Walker, who long before had fenced with Malcolm X, demanded that Farrakhan truly disown the 25 years of constant vilification of the Christian faith by the Muslims, arguing that if unity were his real goal, then reconciliation had to precede it. DeCaro, though, did not expect that Farrakhan would convert many African-Americans: while Elijah had assailed Christianity as the "slave-making lie" that whites concocted to control Blacks, African-Americans at the time had held to Jesus regardless, because they had always felt that there was "an irreconcilable difference" between their Christianity and that which white people structured to maintain their interests.[45]

The pre-1975 Muslims' denunciations of Christianity had a certain macro-historical sweep of vision—which sometimes drew on clear WASP themes. Only a minority of Black Americans were Catholics, yet Elijah went out of his way to denounce the global Catholic Church. "Some of the devil's disciples are called 'father' after the pope, the chief father of Satan's religion, Christianity." The pope claims that according to the Bible, "he will sit in the sides of the north and be like the Most High" (Isa. 14:13,14). And yet Allah (God) promised to pull him down to hell (Isa. 14:15), and will do so soon.[46]

The pre-1975 condemnations of Roman Catholicism was one of those areas where the Muslims not only bore their closest resemblance to a Protestant and American orientation, but avowed that they did so. In the early 1930s, Fard had advised his followers to listen to the broadcasts of Rutherford and the Jehovah's Witnesses, given that they were an American sect close, in their denial of Jesus' divinity, to Sunni Islam and his own. This sect on the very fringe of Christianity that denounced the churches of "Christendom" helped him finally snap his Black audiences' attenuating links to Christian beliefs and churches. In his mode of drawing on the Bible as a book of prophecies whose time was now, Elijah noted that Revelation refers to the destruction of the Beast and his chief instructor, the dragon. Elijah's exegesis of that Beast, there, as "not referring to four-footed animals but to a people whose rule is like that of a savage beast", turned to his own racial-nationalist purposes this New Testament motif that U.S. WASPs had long directed against Catholic fellow-whites. Following Fard, Elijah evinced high awareness that "theologians from the time of Martin Luther" applied Revelation's "beast" and "dragon" to the Roman Catholic Church: "the late Pastor Russell and Judge Rutherford [founders of the Jehovah's Witness sect] especially take the term 'dragon' to refer to the pope of Rome, the father of the Christian church and the Christian religion".[47]

Important here is Elijah's sharp sense of Christianity as a constantly mutating diverse tradition, almost a plurality of religions, and of the fact that some recent Euro-American sects of it in the neighborhood had, in some ways prefigured some motifs of the 1930 NOI. Had the emergence of his sect had more to it than just an Arab savior who came from Mecca to reveal Divine knowledge from outside America's ways of thought? This awareness in an ill-educated Black leader of the incessant mutation of Biblical motifs by whites may suggest that a part of Elijah's psyche may have guessed that his own sect was, in the main, one more human mutation of way-out margins in the diverse white Christo-American discourses, albeit one that added other borrowings from the Qur'an useful for his people's needs. Were Elijah's teachings really the claimed authoritative, unprecedented exegesis of those scriptures by God-Allah incarnate? Elijah was furious when two members of his own family circle, his two sons Akbar and Wallace, influenced by Arabic, came to doubt that he had been taught a revelation from outside America and its concepts by Allah in the person of Fard. But was there also a deeper Elijah who recognized that his beliefs-system too, like the others in America, had rather been constructed by many hands, and in part from much the same pool? Still, some recent post-modern heirs in the Moorish-NOI tradition go too far when they wonder if there might rather have been a small, sharp, off-stage Elijah Muhammad who kept the whole rigmarole going cynically for self-gain. The matter is more psychologically, politically and spiritually complex than that.

The Black Muslims have changed greatly over decades on many tenets and themes, and it is not always easy to decide the precise motives behind the given shifts of these masters of Isma'ili- or Druze-like esoteric sleight of hand and layers of meaning. Still, both Elijah's denunciations of Christianity and Farrakhan's (and Warith's?!) wooing and blurring in effect act as serious assaults upon Christianity's title to survive as a belief-system with its own clearly-marked borders among African-Americans.

Arabic and Islamic Elements in the Hybrid, Composite Religion

Elijah and his bygone pre-1975 Nation of Islam swung between two poles in relation to the Qur'an, a vacillation that was to continue in Farrakhan's successor-sect after 1977. On one hand, Elijah recommended the Qur'an to his followers as "the Book for the American so-called Negroes". In this modality, Elijah voiced conventional Sunni-like ideas that the Qur'an is superior to other Scriptures, which are perceived to have been tampered with. Yet, Elijah elsewhere conjectured that the validity of the Qur'an was bound by time—it could guide man to the threshold of the Judgment and the Hereafter, but not beyond—and by the ethnic specificity of "the Arab World" to which it was first revealed. In view of these limitations, argued Elijah Muhammad, the Islam optimized in the Qur'an had to give way to a new Islam set out in a new book which God would give to guide the Blacks into the Hereafter, i.e. the period to follow God's destruction of the whites.[48] Moving into Elijah's role, Farrakhan in the 1980s and 1990s was to speak of a divine "scroll" within himself that in the right circumstances will come forth from him for the benefit of the entire world, not just of his own community,[49] although these formulations are vague and have difficulties for pre-1975 NOI tenets and categories.

The Nation of Islam's acceptance of the Qur'an—which, whatever role they gave to Elijah Muhammad as its God-missioned interpreter and fulfilment, they had to allow had been revealed to someone else long before—has placed persisting limits on the growth of Nation of Islam theology into an independent American religion that would be as much a thing apart as made-in-America Mormonism, and would have its distinctive scripture.

In his dualistic vein—not just attunedness to the cultural limitations of his Christian black audiences—Elijah leaped between Qur'an and Bible to assess, for instance, the decline of America's system that had been so murderous, both imperially and at home. Before, America surrounded the countries of other peoples and blew their cities to pieces. Now, as America had done, it was being done to her [Pearl Harbor? The Communist bloc?]: Elijah quoted Qur'an 13:14 that God was curtailing the land from its sides and that none could repel Allah's retributive doom. But to convey America's murderousness to Blacks within her territories, Elijah cited condemnation from Psalm 10:8 of the wicked who from the lurking places of the villages murder the innocent poor. (The psalm ended with an appeal to Yahweh to "break thou the arm of the wicked".)[50]

In general, Elijah quoted more from the Bible to explicate the plight of African-Americans and the prospects for their liberation through intervention by God. He did quote from the Qur'anic surah (chapter) 101: 1-4, applying its "terrible calamity" as an analytical frame from which to argue that it was the doom now taking place in the current destruction of the USA. The Qur'an's warning of that "day wherein men will be as scattered moths" was being fulfilled in "these great calamities that are now striking America: the chronic divisions and murder of men, the widespread raping and murdering of girls, incessant robbery and thieving, the ominous great storms and adverse weather", earth tremors, the experiments by U.S. scientists for weapons to kill millions and wipe out whole continents. All these symptoms would soon open up into the "total destruction of America". Here the texture of the Arabic Qur'an is woven into the detail of later modern America as seen from the situations of poorer African-Americans.[51]

Elijah's religious nationalism mustered the Qur'an and the Bible to focus the suffering of poor black strata in America. Daniel's description of ribs between the teeth of the beast referred to America's ill treatment of the blacks she incarcerated. America prowls the streets at night in wait for an excuse to wreak her ruthlessness on her poor prey (the Black man). If the Black man raises a hand to protect himself, he is shot dead or faces trumped-up charges he does not have the means to contest. "The Black man's wages are calculated by white wicked accountants, preventing the so-called Negro from saving by skyrocketing (in the view of the poor) the prices of the necessities of life." This white beast prosecutes, imprisons and kills those who preach freedom and justice for the poor so-called Negroes. As the judgement that white America's cruelty is incurring unfolds, "the time will grow so troublesome that (according to the Holy Qur'an) children will become gray headed".[52]

On occasion, one feels that the aesthetic and rhetorical presence of the Bible is stronger than that of the Qur'an in Elijah's apocalyptic analyses of America. The Qur'anic aspect sometimes feels as though it is an afterthought, something added on to a discussion that would have mostly been viable with just the Bible and the sect's original ideas. Yet sometimes the Qur'an has a dynamic and vivid presence equal to the American phenomena to which Elijah Muhammad attaches its verses. Thus, Elijah tried to argue the imminent fall of America, and separation of the races as the answer for Blacks who wanted to sidestep the destruction, from Qur'an 81:1, 6, 7, 12: "when the cities are set afire, when men are brought together, and when hell is kindled, when the sun is folded up". For Elijah, the symbolic "folding up" will, Isma'ili-like, be of the record of what people have done. For Elijah, the chapter (surah) prophesies that one party will be recorded as beginning, while the other party (whites) is discontinued. Already, as he wrote, wars were destroying civilizations, and the cities and towns of a nation—fulfilling surah 81 of the Qur'an. While Elijah greatly metaphoricized that surah's images of sun and the stars, mountains, camels and wild animals, so as to make them apply to America, his use of all these images imparted some feel for the Arabian context in which the Qur'an was first articulated.[53] The fulfilment of such Arabic-medium elements, though, would come in the longer term in the explosion of Sunnifying doctrines and practises, and of pan-Islamic identification with the Middle East, under Elijah Muhammad's son Warith ud-Din (Wallace) in the decades following Elijah's 1975 death.

There is no question that during the lifetime of Elijah, the Nation of Islam did not have many doctrines that the world of Islam could have recognized as Islamic. The Arab and Islamic torn-away elements and practices were present in NOI religion rather as emblems: these psychologically triggered a radical dislocation and shift in the American elements, and some disengagement from them that gave a sense of being freed and empowered. Arabic's role in opening up and pluralizing the conceptualization of the world by African-Americans would finally lead most of the adherents out altogether of the American thought-world still pervasive in the 1930-1975 NOI religion, and onto the plane of standard Islamic tenets. Breaking the grip of some norms of ghetto sub-culture, Islamic cultural traits had encouraged the adherents to become industrious, productive and entrepreneurial—drives that went well with the WASP acquisitive work ethic. The Islam that gradually made African-Americans distinct in culture also helped direct them to some points of entry into at least the margin of the U.S. bourgeois system. Thus, before 1975, the Arabic and Islamic motifs focused parochial victimizations and needs quite differently from the separate conditions that influenced how Third World Muslims read the Qur'an, the hadiths of the Prophet Muhammad and other classical Islamic writings. True, Islam has for both African-Americans and Arabs provided rallying-points against highly local situations of godless injustice. Precisely because Qur'anic principles of justice spoke with such relevance to local situations of oppression, these Arabic motifs were implanted at the emotional heart of Black American experience at street level in the ghettos.

This was clear in a clash that took place between the Los Angeles police and members of the NOI outside Mosque 27 in April 1962. The white police saw two Muslims unloading some dry-cleaned clothes from their car and stopped them, claiming that the clothes were stolen. One of the policemen pushed one of the Muslims against the car and by his own later testimony "hit the gentleman over his head" with his revolver. An angry black crowd, mostly black-suited worshippers coming out of the mosque, gathered and disarmed the policemen when one of them drew his revolver. As police reinforcements came and pistol-whipped or shot down some of the angry Muslims, the swelling Muslim crowds stood chanting "*Allahu Akbar*" (God is Greatest) in Arabic—derision of the corrupt worldly authority of the police by comparing it to the greater, righteous power of God. Even today, such cries supplicating or portending justice are vented by subordinated Muslims the world over. The Los Angeles Muslims backed off only after 75 well-armed policemen had arrived.

At the subsequent trial, one of the police officers testified that the alien chanting unnerved him and helped detonate the police violence.[54] Splinters from Arabic in such situations had a catalytic function as rallying-points around which a qualified African-American resistance or defiance took form. They also served as dangerous triggers for more violent expression of the sense some layers in Angloid-American society always had of Blacks as alien. Clearly, the interaction of all these languages and cultures was catalytic in social conflict and violence. That this particular group of Blacks bore the name "Muslims" that it shared with radical Arab nationalists whom the U.S. press assailed, heightened the tensions.

The structure of white repression of Muslim and Black Nationalist movements in the period also has to be explored. A post-modern African-American scholar, possibly a Black micronationalist, was to characterize the force that engaged the Muslims as under the command of an intelligence section of the Los Angeles Police Department. This "Red squad" had been built up by L.A. mayor Sam Yorty (who had sat on McCarthy's Committee for Un-American Activities) as a highly politicized outfit that kept thousands of left as well as Negro activists—although no far-right organization—under unremitting surveillance.[55] Did the police whose gunfire killed one Muslim and wounded six others, then, come directed in advance to find a pretext for violence, rather than as apolitical officers carrying out routine functions? The reconstruction of Kofi Natambu tends to view the police violence, and their oppression when they invaded the LA mosque, more as a venting of spontaneous race-hate. One white officer told another that he had been "looking for ten years to kill the Black Muslims". But the hate also came from the top: LA Police Chief William H. Parker on May 1, 1962, told a grand jury that unless something was done about the Black Muslims there were bound to be more frequent clashes between the police and the NOI, a sentiment Mayor Yorty also voiced.[56]

The degree of the borrowings from Qur'anic patterns of thought and Arabic rhetoric varied from plane to plane. They came naturally or casually and thus often were not sourced as such by Elijah and his ministers so that African-American and Euro-American scholars have often missed the provenance. The Arabia-derived Qur'anic elements increased where they functioned in the emotional or self-imaged withdrawal or nominal separation from whites. Elijah urged the African-Americans to "try and be ourselves first and stop trying to be white. If you see the hell-fire God has prepared for the white slave-master, the devil, you will run from the devil. The Holy Qur'an teaches that the Black man will wish that between him and the devil was the distance between east and west" [cf Qur'an 43:38]. African-Americans should follow Elijah because "I have the God with me—the God who says [in the Qur'an] that there is no fear for the one who believes in Him, nor shall you grieve".[57]

Although acutely aware that Christianity pervaded the culture of the lumpen blacks whom he sought to address in ways they would comprehend, Elijah Muhammad drew from the Qur'an as well as Bible in order to argue his ideology and leadership. In arguing that the old world would prove unable to stop the beginning of the new world under his leadership, Elijah pointed to the annihilation of previous obdurate groups. "According to the Bible and Holy Qur'an, Noah was called a liar and crazy person". As ever, the Middle East's bygone prophets were signs of patterns Elijah brought to their culminating fulfilment in his functions and the situations he faced. "Some of the members of Noah's family joined the mockers and disbelievers of Allah and His Messenger, and met the same fate as the others who disbelieved" —a scarcely-veiled threat that Elijah might prove ruthless even to family and relatives now being influenced in his sect in the 1970s by the insidious neo-Sunnism that denied his prophethood and Fard's divinity. The Qur'an rather than the Bible is the source of Elijah's adaption of Noah motifs. Using the King James Bible's spelling of the names of joint prophets of Islam and Christianity, rather than their Qur'anic representation, Elijah referred to the time of Abraham (rather than Ibrahim) and his nephew Lot (Lut) before the birth of Ishmael and Isaac, Abraham's two sons. The haters of righteousness in the cities of Sodom and Gomorrah even threatened the life of the preacher of righteousness, Lot. As he had them, God would similarly annihilate the opponents of the Messenger of Allah today in America.[58] Here, the Bible has more presence. But there is no mention in Genesis 6-7 of relatives ridiculing Noah: God orders him "come thou and all thy house into the ark" (7:1) into which his sons and their wives duly step up. But the Qur'an does have a narrative depicting a son of Noah who refused to come into the ark although implored and was therefore drowned by God, as were all the other disbelievers, before that prophet's eyes (Q 11:42-47). In this case, again, a Bible-citing communication by Elijah simultaneously has unattributed Qur'an-derived motifs that would be missed by both white and black American authors who did not bother to go through the Qur'an before they began writing.

In the same retort to those who rejected his credentials to lead U.S. Blacks on the grounds of his poor education, Elijah Muhammad noted that "messengers are never sent: they always are raised in the midst of those whom Allah would warn so they cannot claim that they did not understand the language of the Messenger, or say that he was a foreigner or a stranger." Similar to the prophets of yore, Elijah met rejection from many of his own people as well as enemy groups, he compared.[59] While Elijah did not indicate it, his defense adapted that in the Qur'an of the Prophet Muhammad, the son of ‘Abdallah (PBUH), who had brought a scripture in the local clear Arabic rather than one in a less-clear foreign language (Syriac with which Hijazi merchants traded in Syria-‘Iraq? Hebrew? The Greek of the Byzantine Christians and the New Testament?)[60] The pattern in the mission of Muhammad of Arabia in the Qur'an was to find its full, definitive application in the mission of Elijah: "the Holy Qur'an repeatedly prophesies a miserable, shameful, and disgraceful defeat for the disbelievers and hypocrites in their campaign against the last Messenger of Allah, whom Allah would raise in the time of the resurrection of the dead people".[61]

The analyses of African-American and Caucasian scholars, then, have underestimated the motifs from Middle Eastern Islam in Nation of Islam thought and culture that Elijah and his followers casually took from sources like the Ahmadiyyah translation of the Qur'an. They are nonetheless right that Elijah and his colleagues were eclectic and were wont to swiftly alternate Biblical and Qur'anic phrases and motifs. Within one paragraph, Elijah noted a prophecy in the Epistles of Paul that "the devil [with his kingdom] was made for fuel for the fire." Elijah then swiftly zags to the Qur'an which for him carries forward Paul's prophecy with its words that "the fuel of the fire is men and stones" (Q 2:24; 66:6). With a feel for the Qur'anic rhetoric, or out of a touch of Isma'ili-like or Druze-like esotericism, Elijah wrote that "we do not know why stones are put [in Hell] with men—it could be referring to the hardness of the heart of the wicked against truth and righteousness".[62]

Monotheism

The Qur'an's rejection of the Trinity provided another rallying-point for Elijah against his people's white enemy. America has filled up her country with [all] evil people; America did not allow Islam, nor a preacher of Islam, to come into her [country]; America did not want a good religion taught, prefering a religion that she could rule and control herself—that there were three Gods instead of Moses' and the prophets' teaching of one God. America makes it possible in her Godhead that if one of them does not like you, you may plead to another and if one does not let you by, one of the three will. But even in America's own mathematics, it is not possible to put three (3) into one (1). Because America had propagated that religion opposed to truth, the Author of Truth was now about to destroy her foul, nudism-loving, society, just as He had Babylon.[63] The Qur'anic and Arab Muslim hatred of Trinitarianism here focuses Elijah's resistance to white America. However, the special Islam of Fard and Elijah fell into its own incarnationism and anthropomorphisms that smacked of polytheism (*shirk* or associating partners with Allah) to more than a few Middle Easterners.

Elijah placed his conflict with Malcolm within the pattern of historical repetition or recurrence, as he did so many other things, underscoring the multiplicity of the international discourses to which this sect was heir from the outset. Malcolm's attempts to take power from Elijah Muhammad had been written and prophesied in the life of the Prophet Muhammad of Arabia. "His name is not written there in the name of Malcolm in the history—another name is used but his work is there in the history of the hypocrites in the life of Muhammad [of Arabia]. He tried to take advantage while Muhammad was sick [as Elijah was in the early 1960s]. You find this in the writings of Washington Irving and even some science writers of Islam. They can tell you Malcolm's history". Malcolm was not able to change that history of Elijah, which he knew.[64] When Muhammad Ibn 'Abdallah was weakened in his last extended illness and busy organizing military action against the Byzantine Empire, Irving had narrated in 1850, former adherent Musaylimah had proclaimed himself a co-prophet of Allah, and written Muhammad to propose that they "partition the world" between them. But the Muslims finished him in appropriate time.[65] Devoid of the traditional Western animus, Irving's *Life of Mahomet* could have been on the reading lists or curricula Fard drew up to ground his ill-educated converts in Islam and its history. The style of Irving's work was clear, crisp but also rather basic, as was his analysis of early Arabia and Muhammad's prophetic career. Without many studies by Muslims to draw on, Fard or Elijah had improvised cleverly, to direct their converts to this clear book.

While Fard and Elijah in 1930 started with their converts from where they found them, the way Islam was being projected could carry some later generation to more than one high culture or intellectualism. Muhammad of Arabia's life is seen here at third remove through a bygone WASP American belletrist, Irving, who could not read Arabic, only German. This academically primitive but also ultra-American work had predisposed some of Elijah's followers after his 1975 death to explore the serious biographies that had by then come out in English of Prophet Muhammad Ibn 'Abdallah, and English translations of the classical collections of his *ahadith* (sayings). As well as providing a path to the history and civilization of classical Islam, Irving's book could also offer one start in equipping those poverty-stricken pioneer Black Muslims to read and understand the high literature and more tolerant intellectualism of Anglo-Americans quite apart from Islam. It was ambiguous whether NOI culture under Fard and Elijah would make Muslims or Anglo-Americans out of the converts—probably its new men and women today blend both cultures.

The "Black Muslims" under Elijah gradually came to understand and apply aspects of Arabic grammar, not just its vocabulary. In the last year of his life, Malcolm resolved that if the coming child that his wife was bearing turned out to be male, he would name it Lumumba, and if female Lumumbah—formalistically modifying even the African name with the Arabic feminine noun suffix, "h". The full name that Malcolm gave his third daughter was Gamilah Lamumbah. "Gamilah" is also in Arabic's feminine form but pronounced in the dialect of the Egypt of anti-imperialist Gamal Nasser.[66] The Arabic names, words, phrases and patterns being chosen were often those linked with political decolonization in the Third World. Transcriptions of the Arabic terms for the functions of given Black Muslim stores or enterprises were sometimes included in their signs under Elijah: thus, the holy language of the Middle Eastern heartlands of the faith was already emblemic of the sect's neo-capitalist enterprise, too.

Although Elijah did not want his followers to interact too much with Third World Muslim countries that might modify their concepts of Islam, encounters and joint rituals continued. These consolidated fragments of Arabic that Elijah and other top leaders already had, gave them impressions of Sunni Islamic rituals that the NOI media then duly diffused to the followers. In 1960, *Salaam* magazine covered the Messenger's pilgrimage to Mecca. Elijah did not mention any racial difference of the old Saudi *mutawwif* (pilgrim's guide) who, father-like, led him through the Arabic rites: the worshippers in the Ka'bah from all over the Muslim world were "sincere worshippers of God". Elijah told his readers that "Allahu Akbar" in the prayers meant "God is the Greatest". He hinted at a special national significance of the Black Stone for African-Americans, and might also have seen himself as foreshadowed in the Arabic formula "There is no God but Allah and Muhammad is His prophet" as he repeated it there.[67] In the article, Elijah thanked his poor followers for collecting for his ticket to the hajj that they could never afford. A Saudi official car took him from Jeddah to Mecca: there are reports that Saudi government figures were aware of Elijah's tenets that clashed with Wahhabi Sunnism, but wanted to "show [NOI figures] around the Holy Places" so as to point them in the direction of "true [=Sunni] Islam" [Conversation with Arab academic: 1978].

While the atoms or fragments from Arabic installed at the center of NOI ritual life had yet to transform beliefs and worship, they did function before 1976 to sharpen the group-separateness that Elijah's people were evoking between their sect and Christian African-Americans. When Elijah Muhammad died in 1975, the actual 25-minute service consisted of an Islamic prayer recited in English by Minister James Shabazz and repeated in Arabic by American-Palestinian activist Professor 'Ali Baghdadi. The funeral service's "quiet dignity defied the traditional display of excessive emotionalism common to funerals for figures venerated by masses of blacks".[68] These Muslims could be staid as cold WASPs. The distribution of sweets at the service still was given the meaning that this was the final death and dissolution of one more Black, without any hope that God would restore him to a new individual life later. This was the complete reverse of a Third World Muslim funeral. But the linkages to Arabic phrases and individual Arabs were being applied to further underline non-connection with the ordinary Christian Negroes whom the NOI disdained as "the dead" in a national-spiritual sense, even as they lived out futile subordinated lives.

Secession from Islam?

While the old Nation of Islam had some Muslim and Arab DNA in it, if usually set within American ideas and projects, the interaction that Black

Muslims had with the Sunni and Shi'ite Muslims of the East was limited under Elijah. Still, there was sufficient contact to reveal great gulfs of beliefs and life-styles. Some African-American laymen and scholars wondered if the Nation might not come to formally snap its tenuous affiliation to the global community of Islam. In 1972, Elijah predicted that God would one day usher in "a New Islam to what the old Orthodox [Islam] is today. The Old Islam was led by white people, white Muslims, but this one will be established and led by Black Muslims only". In more positive terms that swung between defining Arabs as whites or as related "brothers" of Blacks, an adherent reflected that "99% of our Muslim brothers from the East have been deceived one way or another" because they could not understand Elijah and held to their "conventional" "spook" god, rejecting the man-god, Fard.[69]

While the dominant trend in *Muhammad Speaks* was to blend the Arabs into the international Black Nation, some items did see the Arabs as whites and juxtaposed them, perhaps correctly, with the Jews, also seen as white in this variety of communications. Allah sent warners to the whites from generation to generation, notably "Abraham, Noah, Mussa [Musa= Moses], Jesus and Muhammad of 1,400 years ago. It is a scientific fact that these great reformers were unable to reform the white race into righteousness". The item took up the Qur'an's teaching that "out of His mercy and benevolence, God raised men from among their own people to whom he imparted Divine knowledge of Himself". This formulation legitimized Elijah as a representative of African-Americans not bound by the stipulations, thinking or interests of outsiders, such as the Arabs. Potentially, some ultra-isolationist followers might also extend it to state that if Muhammad of Arabia addressed whites, that *he* was white—and whites had been defined as devils in Fard and Elijah's theory.

Yet this was not to be the direction in which most of Elijah's Muslims headed. The NOI saw the Qur'an as prescriptive Divine guidance destined to find its fulfilment in the Black Nation in America, much more than in the classical or modern Arabs. Most Nation of Islam discourse at least affirmed a privileged status to the Qur'an over the Bible. *Muhammad Speaks* termed the Holy Qur'an as "the word of Allah". In comparison, "the present Bible that you and I read is the words of the white man" because it had been "diluted". When the white enemies understood that the Bible was for the Blacks, they slew all truthful translators of the original Bible, and hired a bunch of wicked translators: through them they took out some of the truth and added lies to some parts. The part which they *did* publish was put in symbolic words. While this perspective is close to the Qur'anic characterization of the Hebrew and Christian holy books as corruptions of real revelations from God, the Nation of Islam did continue to cite and decode that corrupted Bible in their discourse alongside the Qur'an to an extent that no Middle Eastern Muslims would accept.[70]

The gap in tenets between the sect's followers and the Arabo-Islamic world at times looked set to widen irreparably as the dominant group in the leadership exalted Elijah Muhammad more and more during the sixties and the seventies. In his work, *This is the One,* Bernard Cushmeer described Elijah Muhammad as "the second greatest person in the universe" because the greatest, Allah, had given him the utmost knowledge of truth and the keys to eternal life. Cushmeer placed Elijah "in the company of those illustrious men, the Prophets"—which in itself was costing the sect chances for support in the Arab world—but then hinted that his growth to divinity took him beyond prophethood. "To say that He [sic] comes in their tradition is true, but... incomplete".[71] Elijah Muhammad was also sometimes argued during his lifetime to have won a comprehension superior to the past prophets through his perceived direct contact with Allah (i.e. Fard).

On the whole, Nation of Islam discourses under Elijah more often associated African-Americans with [imaged] Arabs. The Arab links had many simultaneous functions: (a) to fend off sub-Saharan Africa and its cultures, (b) to delegitimize or sideline cultural specificities of Black America that the Muslims wanted to excise from their identity (eg. in language: Gullah), (c) to snap community with the non-Muslim U.S. Negroes whom God would incinerate with whites, (d) to snap the psychological bondedness of the converts to the Christianity, and thereby to the political power, of white Americans, while (e) in the process covertly setting the converts free to adopt the lucrative, prosperity-building skills of middle Anglo-Americans. The intermittent mustering of motifs that distanced Arabs were like the use of Arabs and Arabia elsewhere to distance Negroes, Africanist rivals, and whites: all usages maximized the power, authority and independence of Elijah. (He and his ministers were not often a security risk whom outside Arab or African movements or states could manipulate.) Yet the old NOI's quick alternations of motifs for converse purposes also sprang from tensions in the heterogeneous cultural materials that had gone into the make-up of Fard and Elijah's religion. The dualities, though, may have had a deeper affinity to the elastic ambiguity of all meanings in the esoteric Druzism or Isma'ilism from which Wali Fard Muhammad, the sect's founder, could have come.

3: RESISTANCE AND ACCOMMODATION TO WHITE AMERICA

Attraction to Creativity by Whites

Insisting that he was the messenger of Allah in the last days, Elijah usually painted contemporary society in a closed and final-sounding way as evil and doomed: he hoped that his dichotomization of devil whites and potentially divine Blacks—a notable binary opposition even for his modernist era—would be resolved by God's execution of one of the warring parties. Yet even Elijah showed slight signs at intervals that he too was being influenced by the new bourgeois prosperity that was mellowing his ex-lumpen adherents. One or two of these cases even come from the 1960s. When the integrationist leader, Martin Luther King. Jr., met Elijah, he asked him if he really believed his teaching that *all* whites were devils without exception. Elijah had replied that, as two farm boys from Georgia, both of them knew there were many different kinds of snakes: there were highly poisonous rattlesnakes but there were other non-poisonous species that could be friendly. Yet all were snakes—Isma'ili- or Druze-like allegorical imagery so rubbery as to eviscerate any fixed long-term meaning out of formal tenets.[72] It does seem to be the case with Elijah that we are in the presence of a self-appointed and esoteric proto-elite already given, before 1975, to the double truth and the double language that holds out one binary meaning to urge on the masses, while concealing the possibility of a different agenda or fulfilment or synthesis for the leading stratum that could become integrationist.

As he became richer, Elijah drifted towards a more pluralizing vision of whites. He had always been at least somewhat ambivalent to America. When predicting America's imminent destruction by God as a new "Babylon", Elijah nonetheless had barely veiled his admiration for the economic enterprise and technology that had made her "the great country of America":

> Her great richness, great [scientific] institutions, and her great towns and cities, spread out like a blanket over the surface of the Western Hemisphere with her tall buildings going upward over a hundred stories! America's land is everywhere shadowed with the wings of her many planes. Her great mighty fleets on the high seas (on the surface and below the surface), her great scientific mechanical communications system!

Yet, for all this might and skill in engineering or building, "the country of America displays and practices more savagery than any civilized [sic] country on the earth"—ambiguous terminology that did not foster the fusion with Africans that was becoming more and more practicable for Black Americans. All of her educational institutions could not dissuade Americans from brutal violence: "murdering, killing, robbery, raping, and drug addiction are the only law and order that is respected in the streets of the vast towns and cities of America," ran this—rightwing Republican-like?—condemnation by Elijah.[73]

A similar sub-text of admiration for a technologically-advanced, albeit violent and racist, America also underlay a discussion by Elijah of America's destruction that took Revelation 18:19 as its point of departure. Like the religious Protestant poet, Spencer, Revelation ambiguously drew aesthetic energy from the color and corruption of the kingdom being denounced as vile and doomed—here, Babylon's merchant ships that ploughed the high seas bearing her costly merchandise throughout the populations of the earth, as Elijah recycled the motif. Elijah's discussion of God's coming destruction of America here had a similar repressed duality: it vividly depicted the naval and air might with which America threatened the nations with destruction, yet there is some respect in the notion that America "shoots herself out into space by means of the most modern rockets".[74] Malcolm X veiled his admiration less: "you can hardly name a scientific problem the [race-blinded]

White man can't solve, [even] sending men exploring into outer space" and back.[75] Goaded by competition from the USSR, the U.S. in the 1960s and 1970s developed a formidable arsenal of space rockets and space probes that impressed most humans, including—mutedly—Elijah. He could not but have noted the creativity as well as the might of America after Neil Armstrong became the first man to walk upon the moon in July 1969. Yet for all their achievements in the modernist age of those scientific transformations, Anglo-Americans were slow to make that final breakthrough to a new color-blind commitment to all humanity. Sixteen years later, moon astronaut Edwin ("Buzz") Aldrin, tipsy in a bar, told an Australian journalist that "for just a minute we really pulled the earth together... [Earth was just] an island in space...—all the wars... stupidity". But he then inquired about migration to Australia because he had heard that down there, "you don't let Blacks in".[76]

When Elijah Muhammad was a kid in America's Deep South, he hid in the bushes as approaching whites lynched a Negro from a tree; the victim's blood then dripped down onto that terrified beholder's neck.[77] It would not be surprising if Elijah never achieved empathy with victimized categories of poorer whites who migrated to America. His words of regret for the assassinated Celt, John Fitzgerald Kennedy, was an isolated burst of empathy towards one elite individual who had become a symbol of all America, not towards an ethnos. Elijah's pent-up hatred for the America enterprise prevented him from registering for the time how the diversity of its constructed, ever-widening community had already started to incorporate other than white races before his eyes—or from seeing how pluralist aspects of the system that he moralistically condemned in themselves could be extended into protections and margins that might enable his sect to survive, grow and flourish.

Hierarchical like his Isma'ili and Druze precursors with their chains of divinity-tinted infallible leaders of lineage, Elijah voiced horror that the American people from its very beginning had been heavily drawn "from the lower class of European people—their first ruler (President Washington) was a fugitive from England". Elijah, this victim of racism elsewhere so alert to the power of discourse-stereotypes to paralyse victims and legitimize their attackers, here echoed the English ruling classes' criminalization of "the Americans" who were the poor who broke away. The "common, dissatisfied and lower grade of European people" were the followers who boosted George Washington's authority. Elijah voiced little openness here to prospects that the induction of a much more diverse range of whites into politics might loosen and enrich the Anglo-Saxon system in ways that later might offer points of entry for African-Americans over the longer term.

As well as incoming low-class Europeans, the transported Africans too began to mix with the low-based, evil-minded, real citizens (whites) of the Western Hemisphere. As her economic power and needs grew, America even had to admit "underprivileged laborers in overpopulated countries such as China, Japan, and in Europe" who later could seek citizenship in America. Elijah was appalled that the resultant almost uniquely composite American people were granted freedom to live and worship as they chose: "they were not forced to serve the God of the universe who made heaven and earth nor any religion", making "America a haven for any people who wished to be free of the compellers of religious and just rule and authority"— in other words, the very Catholic Church he denounced elsewhere! For five hundred years, Americans had put into practice every evil imaginable, including luxuriant sub-cultures of homosexuality in the schools and streets from childhood onwards.

This particular extreme rejection of most people in America, though, let slip Elijah's alienation from animist Africans: the low class American whites "went into Africa and purchased slaves from among our people who were also uneducated, most of them; but there were a few who were highly educated" --probably a reference from folk-memory to the fifteen percent minority of Arabic-literate Muslims among America's enslaved Africans.[78] That Chinese and Japanese groups were now getting within sight of citizenship and its entitlements was a margin where the old strict Caucasian racial definition of America and what could be American could start to broaden out and break down. The America of the 1960s and 1970s already had an evolving albeit flawed religious pluralism, and some freedom of speech that Farrakhan, in the 1980s and 1990s, would come to clearly understand as one redeeming feature in that tense polity crucial for the survival of his sect.

Elijah's apparent lack of sympathy, here, for uneducated people, Africans as well as whites, was in accord with the high ambiguity of his sect. The NOI was populist in some of the terms and images with which it tried to recruit lumpen ghetto blacks, but it then directed the converts to something like standard literary English and to neo-bourgeois pursuits that would make them much more like America's Angloid white ruling class as they competed against it. Elijah's refusal to see that non-literate Anglos, Celts, Slavs, to say nothing of Japanese and Africans, could indeed have brought with them vital oral cultures to contribute to a new American stock, fitted well with his refusal to take time out from building wealth to seriously explore African pasts and cultures or the spoken cultures of African-Americans. (Nor were Farrakhan's media to diffuse them after 1975.) Elijah's occasional sympathy for some of the more authoritarian regimes of Western history instanced the influence of the white devils' elite systems upon Black Muslim social aims, which was barely veiled even under Elijah. Yet Farrakhan, as he faced Jewish-American groups out to destroy his sect in the 1980s and 1990s, would become much more sharply aware of what a protection for him was the extreme religious, ethnic and ideological diversity of America, the fact that there was no majority group in it with enough weight to put decisive limits on the freedom of discourses and beliefs that the fugitive founding father, Washington, and his colleagues already had guaranteed as a theory and a principle.

Economic Affiliation to America?

In the 1950s, 1960s and 1970s, the Nation of Islam opted for the construction of a network of businesses across the USA as the main organizational expression of the sect's Black nationalism. This collectivist economic self-development had a broader politico-cultural aim than individualist U.S. capitalism: while formal wages could get low, the NOI enterprises provided some degree of a social safety net, opportunity, sharing of benefits, cultural development and spiritual reclamation. However, after Elijah's death, Warith was to make the businesses individually owned (as in the U.S. mainstream): this privatization was to devastate the holdings of the Nation.

Whatever Elijah's exact intentions, this distinct road for black collective empowerment made him a more credible rival to the bourgeois African-American leaderships that rather strove to bring American prosperity to Blacks in the mainstream through non-discrimination and the ballot box. Many non-Muslim blacks were watching what results would come of the Messenger's appeals for community self-development in economics. In his formal rhetoric, Elijah was calling for an enterprise by and for all Blacks rather than the Muslim core only. He urged blacks to "pool our resources, physically and financially, stop wanton criticism of everything that is black-owned and black-operated, build your own homes, schools, hospitals, and factories", and to "spend your money among yourselves." Here Elijah was the conscious successor to ideas of black economic nationalism that had been developing since the mid-nineteenth century, and had been manifested in the industrial education and self-help doctrines of Booker T. Washington and the (ill-organized) financial ventures of Marcus Garvey. Given the economic decline facing African-Americans amid rising expectations, the NOI looked to be constructively addressing the plight of blacks without begging from whites à la Martin Luther King, Jr.[79]

Anglo-American influences were more crucial, but a collective, nationalist private enterprise by this minority [micro-]Nation also had roots in Muslim world traditions. The Qur'an—pervaded by issues and images of trade and urban life as inescapable components in broad human aspirations and experience, not that of Arabia only—also pushed the blended sensibility of the NOI in the direction of economic enterprise and professional status, advocated, too, by the culture of the Anglo-American middle classes. In the early years of the NOI, South Asian missionaries of Qadiyani/Ahmadi heretical Islam had contact with both the founder, Wali Fard Muhammad, and Elijah. The Qadiyani movement had awarded its founder Mirza Ghulam Ahmad (d. 1908) the function of a prophet of Allah after Muhammad Ibn 'Abdallah of Arabia (PBUH), and also showed signs of linking him to Krishna and other Hindu incarnations, which has affinities to what was proclaimed for Fard after his 1933 Druze-like occultation, and with Elijah's status as "the [last] Messenger of Allah." As a minority amid hostile Sunni Muslims in the Punjab, the Qadiyanis/Ahmadis developed into a micronation clustered in enclaves that expressed its identity through collectivist economic self-development, a rural-urban separate economic circuit, and self-enrichment somewhat like the collectivist-nationalist small-capitalism with which Fard and Elijah tried to uplift their followers.[80]

The advance of the Muslims in the early 1960s towards a business and real estate empire had ambiguities and tensions. Were they working towards an economy for the Nation of Islam only or for a general Black nation—i.e. how many business or economic opportunities for non-Muslim blacks would the enterprise open? Elijah also made white business enterprise the acculturating model for his small businessmen: would NOI business separate Blacks more from white America or affiliate them in the end?

Race-hate and polarization between Blacks and whites in America—that galvanizing devil-enemy in the next block—was one stake the NOI's leadership used to motivate poor followers to carry through its economic enterprises against bleak odds. Yet, even from the outset, the use of economic development to give the Black Nation more substance and capacity for independent decision vis-à-vis the enemy around it was also connecting the Nation's adherents into at least the economic activity of the USA in general.

The Nation of Islam's tabloid, *Muhammad Speaks*, instanced Elijah's pragmatism and perhaps an expectation that mutual financial benefit could weld a trans-racial cold community of sorts: he chose a Jewish-headed firm, the Lerners, to help his sect bring the tabloid out, although it carried a stream of anti-Israel articles and materials from Arab-American quasi-intellectuals. Some Black nationalists were querying why whites were getting such a number of the new jobs in the NOI, but Elijah was ruthlessly pragmatic where skills could affect his sect's drive to make money, the basis for it to survive and prosper over a long term.[81] A part of Elijah may have hoped that his white compatriots would change, develop constructive interactions with his sect of profit to both sides, and thereby prove the tenets wrong. During his presidency, Richard Nixon had not fostered greater roles for African-American voters or politicians in American parliamentarism—rather, during elections he promised his white constituency to get tough on "rioters" (=blatant code for poor blacks). Yet his acute antennae caught acquisitive drives in black social groups that he might foster to lead them away from militant black nationalism. Nixon offered the prospect of government-aided enterprise zones as the solution to the underdevelopment of America's slums. NOI emissaries approached federal officers in July 1970 for tens of millions of dollars to train tradesmen in mechanics, automobiles, and in printing and other trades.[82] (Farrakhan's successor Nation of Islam again was to direct its adherents and African-Americans in general to such skilled blue-collar occupations in the 1990s, as America's changing economy made it harder for anyone to stay or become bourgeois in the USA.) Elijah hoped that the city of Chicago might help finance the low-cost housing he was planning to build for African-Americans on its south side.[83]

The U.S. mainstream's "legal-rational" institutions had failed to deliver resources to counter racism and poverty to blacks during the crisis that ushered in charismatic neo-Muslim leaders and the Nation of Islam in the 1920s and 1930s. Yet, presidents Kennedy, Johnson and Nixon—galvanized by fear of international scrutiny and by African-American riots in American cities—were in various ways again extending those institutions and economy anew to lessen the Black groups' deprivation as long-marginalized colonial enclaves. This revitalization of the U.S. system offered a way out of the circuit of despair that had previously brought to the fore leaders from the masses who offered a charismatic counter-authority from their personal link to an Allah who could destroy. Elijah and his top counsellors may have tried in the 1960s and 1970s to contain or finesse the growth of new institutions in the NOI that, while routinizing his religious charisma and prominence, also could channel and constrain his decisions. A new compound business bureaucracy inevitably would have to improvise innumerable decisions of its own. The NOI was becoming a nationwide business conglomerate having more and more constructive exchanges with both government institutions and those of the Euro-American economy. Would a more positive U.S. system now make the sect modern and integrative of America? Would Islamic/ Black nationalist and the mainstream structures now modernize African-Americans in unison?

Given his hopes for a normal business affiliation with whites, Elijah was furious when those he linked up with proved to be motivated after all only by the old destructive race-hate of veritable devils. [It was all so non-rational for the chances of Blacks and whites to prosper together!] The Muslims hired the Anglo-Southerner, James H. Bishop, when the sect first went to farm in Alabama. Bishop worked digging holes to help the Muslims to get set up on the land they had bought, and so long as the Muslims were paying him, he did not charge them with being there illegally, as he was to do. But by late 1969 the "devil" James Bishop was now styling himself a "Christian missionary" and had started to attack Muslim property and lives in that state of America's deep South. Whipped up by this preacher of the Gospel against the enemy race, the section of whites dominant in the area had shot-gunned Muslim cattle. "[If] the gas-attendant sells us the gasoline we are arrested and charged with a crime for buying the gasoline, instead of charging the man who sold it to us"—a thinly-veiled expectation from Elijah that America might have, or develop, some neutral law or some color-blind economic transactions that could build up not just opportunities and wealth but a sort of cold community with whites. "We, the Muslims, are a people of peace and have been and are proving ourselves to be just that all over America." The materialist side of Elijah, so repelled by the destruction he prophesied, led him to protest that such violent rejection by whites of more equal, more diverse exchanges—albeit foreseen by his own formal ideology—was "very ignorant and silly" in that it got in the way of mutual profit: "we have bought land and cattle in Alabama to get the profit out of what we bought." If the government of Alabama now intended to "drive us out from our property they will have to buy us out, not drive us out."

The violence had returned Elijah to square one—back to the old exclusion from wealthy America, the millenarian ideology of 1930 and to the consolations of its empty eschatological threats against the excluders. "This demon, Mr. James H. Bishop, seeks to bring himself and the American people into a war with Allah (God) and the righteous." He was "playing with a very hot fire; for he is not attacking Elijah Muhammad and his followers; but he is attacking Allah [God—explicitly Wali Fard Muhammad here] Who welcomes the attack for this is what He came for" [=to incinerate all of America's white devils]. Even this level of Elijah's generalizing rage hid a wistful chagrin that some American institutions were not acting against his eschatology, to protect the NOI: "if the government of Alabama is in agreement with the white people of Alabama in what they are doing against the Muslims, then I want to say to the whole of white America that we have Allah (God) on our side to retaliate against anyone who mistreats us." [— against all American whites around the globe, not in America only].

Elijah Muhammad had on one occasion warned white America that he was "backed up by 500 million people, who are lifting their voices to Allah five times a day." [84] Yet Elijah's implied threats of being able to activate a world religion—international Islam—as counter-might on the NOI's behalf would hardly have fazed those now mustering the real instruments of power to harm his people. Had Elijah contacted Arab and Muslim diplomatic missions during the Alabama turmoil, and been rebuffed? While he affirmed that his adherents were "Muslims and the brother of Muslims", he deflated whatever caution some ruling whites might have felt about reprisals from overseas Arab and Muslim states when he allowed that his people might not be "accepted by our brother Muslims", although certainly accepted by his little cult's distinctive incarnate "Allah Whose proper name is Master Fard Muhammad"-–the very heresy that would long sap most support from the Muslim World so long as he clung to it in the face of white attacks. By the criteria of the political might they exercised, Alabama's Anglo-Celts had little reason to fear Elijah's followers, whom their system enabled them to ill-treat as much as they liked, and as long.

The adherents would have to wait for Fard and the Mother Ship to come down from the heavens. But while waiting they would continue to labor to build a small nationalist/collectivist neo-capitalism which at the same time served as a recruiting tool, as did all the publicity from white attacks on those enterprises. "The Nation of Islam's idea again is to build better country homes for the Black people. As sure as Allah (God) lives, we will convert every Black man in America to his or her own, and this includes those in Alabama"[85]—to be sure, a less idle threat than incineration. Combined with the mismanagement the inexperienced Muslims themselves had shown on their Georgia farm, the destruction of their farm in Pell City, Alabama, by racists brought severe economic loss to Elijah and the sect. Yet, extravagance and corruption by the NOI's elite families had consumed a margin of finance that might have carried the farms, and the projects to establish an NOI hospital and a real Islamic University, through to success.[86]

Elijah's at least occasional attunedness to white psychology and concerns made him point out how the construction of a separate ethnic community by the Nation of Islam could serve white America's own interest. He played on the sense among many whites that Blacks were an unmodern burden and that trying to integrate them into America would be more trouble than it would prove worth:

> Why should the master continue to deceive his slave? He teaches the slave that he is a free citizen with equality. Why do you (slavemasters) want to hold them: for hostages [or] prey? You do not need them. Your machines do the labor that the slaves used to do. Why not let them go?[87]

While Elijah here sought to finesse Anglo-American acquiescence to his separatist project, such attempts to strike a bargain with the Devil could one day become truly constructive proposals of cooperation with mainstream institutions that would then carry out their formal functions. Resultant deals would offer peace and progress to both races, simultaneously. Imam Warithuddin's Americanist reinvention of the Nation of Islam after 1975 would carry through this integrationist potential sometimes latent even in Elijah's most separatist formulations. And, constructive (rather than, at that stage still, integrationist) offers to white Americans for the new NOI to take charge of the superfluous blacks and make them productive—save the system money—were to recur in 1989 and 1993 in Farrakhan's more militant rhetoric and programs.[88]

When warning African-Americans that the Final Judgment might be only days away, Elijah Muhammad urged "the so-called Negro to be stripped completely of the white man's way of life, his name and Christianity." Yet even this rejectionist communication by him acculturatedly mustered Biblical motifs ("prophesies") to convince the Christian Blacks he was targeting, albeit with contempt for their beliefs.

Elijah also drew on popularized forms of white liberal discourse that had been reacting to the collapse of European imperial rule in Africa and Asia and the terror and insecurity that Westerners now universally felt in the shadow of the nuclear bombs. "The world of scholars and scientists", Elijah noted, supplementing his own divine sources, knew that Christianity would soon meet its doom because "Islam is the only religion that will survive the destruction of this wicked civilization."[89] (Already heartened here by the Ivy League liberal whites' loss of confidence and simplicity after the two world wars, the Black Muslims after Elijah's 1975 death were to shred, reinvent and recycle more and more strands and indeed sectors of that scholarship into the neo-Islamic thought-structure.) America boasted of being able to destroy the people of the earth thirty times, exulted Elijah, but God would destroy her along with those Blacks (his constituency's black haute bourgeois enemies) who looked to white Americans for salvation and prosperity. White liberal scholars and scientists confirmed for Elijah that America had no hope to win the war in Vietnam since she would be defeated not just by Russia, China, Vietnam and Korea, but by God acting in tandem with those states.[90] Yet he, unlike some adherents, did not much focus Vietnamese [Communist, atheistic] nationalism with its drive to reunite the country France and America partitioned.

In one of his most acute, decolonized formulations, Elijah in the late 1950s derided the illusion of Negroes that Abraham Lincoln had been their friend who set them free. The issue of slavery was just the "weapon" or pretext Lincoln used in a conflict with Southern whites over the relative power of the two white groups—"to bring his brother into submission to his idea of a United States and one President". The abolition of slavery had not ended the subjugated condition of Blacks, who halfway in the 20th century, Elijah stated, still faced violence and oppression [and indeed, persisting politico-legal segregation]. Yet somewhat later communications by Elijah show that his attitudes to white America were diversifying beneath the surface of his ongoing hopes for a millenarian incineration.

In 1963, Elijah Muhammad suspended Malcolm X from his post as National Representative—i.e. the second highest formal post in the Nation after himself—on the grounds that he had called the assassination of President Kennedy "a case of chickens coming home to roost" to a violent America. Since the suspension and ensuing expulsion followed a long period of mounting tensions between Malcolm X, so often highlighted by the media, and some other Black Muslim clerics—Elijah himself may have been among the jealous—various African-American and white observers saw the grounds as a pretext, masking a struggle over power and relative status between Elijah and his much younger, dynamic Minister, a contest recently charged to have been fanned by the FBI.[91]

However, Elijah's readiness to discreetly fund the inducting of Black civil rights activists into the Democratic Party shows that part of him was flexibly scrutinizing the changes, and the new chances, for Blacks in America's society, for all his ongoing millenarian rhetoric calling upon God to destroy it as satanic. As he and his followers became richer, he was identifying more with central American institutions and hoping that a neutral law could check the slide to the chaos his millenarianism still craved, but which could harm the NOI's bank accounts. He called the assassins of U.S. presidents Abraham Lincoln, William McKinley and John F. Kennedy "outlaws [who] overruled legal authority." He went even further to suggest that some U.S. leaders had had the interests of African-Americans at heart: "it seems very strange that every President who says something favorable for the so-called Negro pays for it with his life." Thus, Elijah's reactions to the murder of John F. Kennedy were already starting to draw distinctions between various categories of whites and of the institutions they conducted.

Elijah's new empathy for a few white devils at America's political apex was also fed by his worries about who next might be blown away in violent America: "any Negro who wants to lead the so-called Negro to a better life and towards true peace, freedom, justice and equality—which he is entitled to enjoy" [perhaps an allusion to the USA's Constitution and laws]—also faced the same possibility of attempted assassination. The "tragic death of President Kennedy" was "a warning to all rulers and people of value" [=including himself], and Elijah gave what advice he could to Euro-Americans holding high office about ways to tighten their security. "Spiritual teachers" such as messengers of God, one of whom he claimed to be, had been murdered in history. That such outlaw action was permitted in America outraged Elijah in this quasi-integrationist moment as "a disgrace and shame to the government and to people who are recognized as world leaders and [models] in the way of friendship and co-operation." (Perhaps he had in mind here the Marshall Plan? the Peace Corps? the Alliance for Progress in Latin America?) Here, Elijah was as acutely aware, as Farrakhan and his adherents would remain after 1978, of new modernity—"the great scientific advancement that America has made" that should have ruled out the assassination [and perhaps the absurd constriction of his people in America]. However, he then reverted to his millenarian stance that all categories of whites were equally bad. The assassination had again shown the world that the government of America and its people were given to violent and outlaw actions.[92]

America's "great progress has been made by the work of iniquity". Yet a part of Elijah wanted a cut of all that education, wisdom, science and wealth that he did not want Allah to destroy just yet. He voiced dismay that "the lawless people" were killing not just their rulers but that they arrest, prosecute and murder "anyone who opens his mouth for justice for the poor prey" (African-Americans)—which might encompass whites, including Jews, in or around the biracial Civil Rights movement, such as Goodman or Schwerner. Regardless of the people's choice of a ruler, Elijah reflected, "if chosen he should be obeyed and given a chance to serve the people until that people dispossesses him for another." In general, this swing, this spate of images, from Elijah could justify his Muslims somehow becoming involved in Civil Rights and American electoral politics according to a dawning ameliorist and pragmatic stance towards America.

Most of this communication from Elijah, though, did not expect that "the due process of law" he craved could muster enough strength in so violent a country as to bring justice for the so-called Negroes. Law and justice were impossible under "a government whose citizens are free to kill until satisfied and then turn upon their rulers and slay them"—not far from Malcolm's view of violence as inherent to white America for which he had sacked him. Anticipating a course that Farrakhan was to consider in the 1990s, Elijah broached populist white politicians on the margins of the white system by tacking onto those presidents who paid with their lives for doing something for Blacks, the populist Louisiana Senator, Huey P. Long, U.S. Senator of Louisiana, who preached "share the wealth" and was assassinated for that in 1935 in Baton Rouge. A concept of poor Blacks and poor whites as having common justice interests and perhaps a common opponent in America is latent, here, as in the more private, pink, Rev Martin Luther King, Jr..

Most of Elijah's commentary, though, saw "no justice for the poor, the so-called Negroes in America as long as they are subjects under the American flag". Forced integration through the passage of Civil Rights bills—the whites' social equality through the same treatment under the law for all—"is only a trap for us. To accept it will make us enemies of God and our Black people of Africa and Asia" [an integration of Arabs, Pakistanis, Indonesians with Africans under the rubric, "Black"] "who are our true friends." Integration would make African-Americans share white America's "doom",[93] by having shared in the wealth that had accrued from America's global exploitation of "black" peoples, Elijah implied. Yet the breakdown of traditional patterns of segregation was now more and more blurring the line between the two groups in ways that struck at the heart of all of the NOI's traditional assumptions about community. As the 1960s passed, Elijah had to admit that previously inconceivable intermarriage was now taking place. But America could not repay her past evil against the Blacks with another evil of trying to tempt the Black slaves by offering them its white women.[94] America could not fend off God's annihilation with such a vile bait to keep the Blacks with her to share her doom. Yet intermarriage was not just something taking place within the greater African-American community: it now was occurring within the sect, itself. In 1975, Elijah's son Wallace/Warith Mohammed consequently had to redefine religious community on race-neutral and Americanist lines.

Parliamentarism, U.S. Institutions

Most communications by Elijah ruled out the American political system as a road to empowerment for African-Americans—yet at a few points, he tantalizingly sniffed the wind and balanced the pros and cons. Ignoring the long efforts of racists to disenfranchise his people, Elijah dismissed the privilege the slavemasters' children had granted blacks for the last century: the right to vote for whites for the offices to judge and rule. This freedom to vote had made the Black man in America unrealistically "proud of himself [as] he goes to the polls to vote for a white ruler." Elijah did recognize that "he is gradually changing to a desire to vote for his own kind for such offices of authority", but on the whole this article or sermon saw the vote as of little benefit to Blacks. "After the election and the victory [of a white candidate] there are very few favors that come from his office to the Black voters who aided him in getting in the office." Had Elijah's interactions with Chicago's [Irish-American] mayor Richard Daley, for example, not turned out as fruitful as hoped? In contrast to Farrakhan's recognition long after, in the 1980s, that the vote can be made a form of power in America, Elijah thought that no white politician would "owe the Black voter anything as long as he has to feed, clothe, and shelter him"—i.e. if he had no economic power of his own—which did grasp the attitude of many Euro-Americans in the era. Given that, in this worldview, strength in American society flows from economic resources and thus status, it might make little difference if the Black vote could be cast or not cast: the white majority was going to win and continue to rule in its own interest, anyway. For a while, Elijah elsewhere considered forthcoming presidential elections. Yet, neither Republicans nor Democrats had done much for Blacks in the last century. Regardless of which party of corrupt politicians won, the die would always be set against the Black people in America. Prior to Judgement Day and its Great Incineration, this was ineluctable in the unchangeable nature of the group that ruled the world: Adam—progenitor of the white race in this formulation—was the first political crook.

Yet a part of Elijah was attentive and constructive here: "this election is one of the most serious in the history of American government, because [whichever party won would be] faced with the problem of saving the lives of the people of America." Elijah does seem in this communication to have at least toyed for an instant with the idea that a better outcome might produce "a lull before the storm" of chaos and Judgement, and that every hour and day by which it could be delayed would yield some widening benefits to Blacks. On one hand, Elijah hoped that the "Black man should be very serious and careful about his voting because 90 per cent of the Black votes are cast by ones who do not have the knowledge of what they are casting their vote for." On the other extreme of this pendulum, the elections did not matter because "I have said for many years [to] vote for Allah (God) to be your ruler and come follow me" out of the American system, as Elijah here imaged the choice.[95]

Elijah Muhammad—not just his protégé Malcolm—harbored some unspoken respect not only for the likewise vulnerable "Reverend" Martin Luther King, Jr., but also for Congressman Rev. Adam Clayton Powell, Jr. and for the gains they were winning for blacks by engaging with the U.S. system and institutions. Although Elijah at most points in time dismissed taking part in the American political system as it stood, the Muslims before 1975 never explicitly ruled out future participation in electoral politics. In a sense, the sect's slanging-matches and media conflicts with integrationist Negro leaders had already drawn the NOI into parliamentarism to some extent by the early 1960s: in 1964, Elijah urged the election of "black representatives dedicated to the advancement and welfare of their people" as the means to dislodge "black political puppets". He did not at that point, though, call on his followers to join in—or help muster—such a vote. Social scientists early detected such waverings or significant silences about electoral politics during Elijah's lifetime, which they related to his sect's increasing accommodationism as it accumulated more and more property. They speculated that its growing economic stake in America might one day bring the NOI openly into the U.S. political system.[96]

A few veteran African-American politicians and Elijah's Muslims were moving towards each other as the "civil rights" revolution became more and more radical. Adam Clayton Powell, Jr. (1908-1972) had achieved more in working through the U.S. parliamentarist political system than any other African-American politician in recent memory. As pastor of the Abyssinian Baptist Church in Harlem after doing well at Columbia University, Powell had been a skilled populist agitator for civil rights, jobs and housing for Blacks who yet strove for reasonable relations with Anglo- and Jewish-Americans in his city (he condemned even the pre-1939 Hitler). As the powerful, judicious Chairman of the House Committee on Education and Labor from 1960-1967, Powell helped get through more than 48 pieces of social legislation for desegregation of education, man-power training, including the ending of discrimination by organized labor in apprenticeship training programs [Elijah wanted to get his youth into trades], and for minimum wages and the treatment of juvenile delinquency, under Kennedy and then Johnson.

As a Christian clergyman, Powell was of a stratum that had tried to help U.S. institutions strangle the NOI from its beginnings. From 1961, though—because he had his ear to the ground, wanted to renew his faded political appeal among the young African-Americans, and because he again saw, as he had when young, that strength within U.S. parliamentarism had to be supplemented by the street—the aging Powell also began stressing the economic interests of his people, and the idea of mass direct action, including boycotts. Powell had drifted into a conflict over relative standing with the stridently anti-NOI NAACP, going as far as to dissuade Robert Kennedy from appointing a good NAACP lawyer, Robert L. Carter, to a federal judgeship. Although a Negro in a position of institutional power in Congress, Powell became at risk of being left behind by the dramatic protest campaigns of Martin Luther King, Jr. in the South and by Malcolm X's electrifying anti-white oratory to ghetto masses in cities across the North.

In 1963, from a platform shared with Malcolm X, Powell told a massive outdoor rally in Harlem that he was "very close to agreeing almost completely with Malcolm X's analysis of our present Negro organizations". He called for more collective effort in education, economic enterprises and political bloc voting, calling on whites to be barred from leadership positions in the NAACP, which he felt should finance itself from the black masses instead of by donations from Euro-Americans. In this speech, Powell was influenced, as Malcolm too sometimes was, by sub-nationalist or ethnicist Euro-American bodies and populations. The media and white leaders charged that he was swinging to "black nationalism", but why was such [sub-]nationalism "only a dirty word when applied to Negro people?" The B'nai B'rith, the Italian or Polish or Irish ethnic organizations did not draw their leaders from outside the group: why should the NAACP or the National Urban League? "The Negro" would have to "fight" to get more out of the white man.

Powell may have been harboring apprehensions that, if the NOI came to run candidates, Malcolm X might one day take his Congress seat from him: he could not let the Muslims outflank him.[97] Malcolm respected Powell for the skills with which he achieved some truly major interests of African-Americans through the American political system, and for his youthful pressure on Edison and the New York Telephone Company to hire Negroes.[98] However, whether due to a Christian distaste for Islam, or from fear of angering whites who could harm his career and lifestyle, or of annoying Elijah, or because he and Malcolm always had been disguised rivals—or from some blend of such motives—Powell's church was among those in Harlem that refused to accept the non-Christian funeral of Malcolm X after he was assassinated in 1965.[99] Powell in his later years accomplished much for radical Black Nationalism, serving as convener of the first Black Power conference in 1966.

As with most white millenarian cults also, Elijah conceived his life and that of his sect as almost desperate resistance to a vivid neighborhood devil-enemy who is ever pawing at the front door. "Our future is at stake and 99% of us do not know it. They seek any kind of charge to place against us to get revenge for our preaching the truth. They tap our telephones, eavesdrop and follow us around from place to place, and use tape recording machines;

and the hypocrites and stool pigeons keep them up to date on what we say and do. They are bold enough to even ask your own relatives to do you evil—and due to fear and ignorance on the part of my poor people, the enemies hire them to destroy themselves".[100]

For years after he built wealth and power in America, Elijah still vented his detestation of the Black Negro middle classes that had so long despised and harmed his—in their eyes, disreputable—lumpen movement. Without having read Gramsci, he had an acute focus on the precariousness, psychological fragility, and lack of much bargaining power of a (in this case, Black) new bourgeoisie that sought to validate itself within a culture and discourse originated and structured by another group to maintain hegemony. Such stool-pigeons, boot-lickers and Uncle Toms with advanced education did not want the praise and exaltation of their own Black people but that of the slavemasters' children. The slavemaster would give it to them as long as they reject themselves and kind and their heritage, and instead worshipped and exalted the white people. In his view, they did not get the real integration they craved for their services and self-abnegation. White people did not like bourgeois blacks to "come into their neighborhood, jumping on them and licking them in the mouth like a puppy. They do not want their friends to think that they are taking you for an equal. He will talk to you as a friend when he is not in the presence of members of his society." Clearly, a part of Elijah exulted at the discomfort or tragedy of the Black bourgeoisie that had hated him as much as whites did. In his puritanical mode, he toyed with the idea that the corrupt middle class blacks had fully deserved the retribution of social rejection by the group for which they had opted. Whites "do not like you coming into the block beating your wife or girl friend and drinking in front of their houses", which "no decent or intelligent person" would. In this instance, Islamic values and those of the Anglo middle-brow devils corresponded, facilitating the latter's influence as a covert model for the transformation of other African-Americans whose lumpen-derived ethos the NOI activists detested.

While a part of his makeup had always somewhat envied and wanted to attain some of the comforts—and the mainly white suburbs of residence—of the Black businessmen, politicians and high clergy who lambasted him, Elijah and his sect's sanctity had always come from his claim to stand for the oppressed poor black masses. That dichotomy was now crumbling with the bourgeoisification and growing wealth of at least some in his NOI. He was not now living with the pure wretched lumpens for whom he claimed to be speaking fearlessly: the places of residence they chose were taking him and his top ministers in the opposite direction from their paradigm of community, towards whites. "Although I live in a neighborhood with white neighbors, I do so for the purpose of proving that I can live in their neighborhood just as cleanly and noiselessly as they do"—vintage Black Muslim contempt for the ways of the rowdy, vital, poor Christian blacks amid whom they emerged, and one more slip revealing the middle and rich whites as a veiled model of the Muslims who denounced those devils.[101]

Some *Muhammad Speaks* items showed the Nation of Islam moving from being (a) the "crackpot" sect mouthing religious menaces against the U.S. system from outside in a way that might not always discriminate between its components and diverse actors to (b) becoming one of the net of counter-institutions for appeal or review that provide the checks and balances needed to make any Anglomorph polity truly work as a liberal democracy. The Nation of Islam press, with its mass circulation among nominally Christian Blacks, could become the vehicle for these sects to assume such a review role for African-Americans in general in affiliation to the system they criticized. A late 1974 item of *Muhammad Speaks* on alleged brain control experiments by some medical institutions linked to the U.S. government shows the paper assuming appeal functions as one intermediary between African-Americans and the U.S. government. A man rang *Muhammad Speaks* claiming that government-funded research facilities located near "the Nation's capital" [=Americanist habits of thought] were conducting "brain-implant" and mind-control techniques. When the skeptical paper checked it out, though, the list of facilities and medical personnel the caller named looked reasonably accurate. When *Muhammad Speaks* paid a visit to the institutions it found a culture of secrecy: it was not allowed to talk with scientists charged with having participated in "inter-disciplinary" genetic and medical experimentation at the facilities. African-Americans had come by their paranoia honestly: the Muslim paper had been at the fore of the U.S. press exposure of immoral experimentation by institutionalized authorities, notably the Tuskegee experiment with blacks whose syphilis was left untreated, and the sterilization of two Black teenage girls in Alabama. Now, the Congressional Committee on the Judiciary had released a report entitled *Individual Rights and the Federal Role in Behavior Modification*, which found that the U.S. federal government "is heavily involved in a variety of behavior modification programs ranging from simple reinforcement techniques to psychosurgery" through a wide range of its departments.[102]

Here we have an ongoing critical stance by the new Muslim proto-intelligentsia that nonetheless now gets a very sharp focus on white Americans that finds their institutions—and the "Caucasian" Americans themselves—acting in both bad and good ways vis-à-vis minorities. While *Muhammad Speaks* here was acting as an avenue of appeal for African-Americans against a sector of the U.S. government, it was also tantalizingly helping a committee of America's Congress to carry out its own same function of scrutiny. Perhaps Elijah had become too rich to want God or himself to destroy the system very quickly. The new hopeful and ameliorist view forming among his adherents that the system had diverse types of whites and institutions in it, and that informed involvement by Blacks could change it to the benefit of the race, began to intermittently tint the views of Elijah as well. As the civil rights revolution opened the way to the induction of a new African-American political class into the American polity, Elijah would aid them at an early point with crucial money despite all the ideological words he had ever uttered.

Perhaps to spare the young politicians Elijah helped from Anglo and Zionist fury that could have destroyed them—and to keep up an image of his own ideological consistency—his sect's media did not mention this support while he lived. It was put in the public domain in the late 1990s by the now-established mainstream politicians who had taken that money three decades before, and was then taken up by members of Farrakhan's new Nation of Islam to justify its entry into U.S. parliamentarism against Elijah's repeated prohibition against participating in white-run elections prior to 1975.

In 1996, the veteran black congressman, Julian Bond, recalled the days of his youth when he, with other neo-bourgeois blacks, had just begun his career in Democratic Party politics, a possibility that opened to blacks in the South during the collapse of the authority of its old-time white racists, who could no longer deform that Party into their local instrument. Bond had come up with another Democrat friend from Georgia to Chicago to somehow clear the way for attendance by a radical delegation of 16 blacks and whites at the 1968 Democratic Party Convention due to be held there in one week. In view of their impoverished backgrounds in the South, and given that the Democratic Party would not be bearing any of their costs, the proposed delegation might not have been able even to meet the expenses of traveling to Chicago from Georgia, let alone decent hotel accommodation near the Convention. In his desperation, Bond agreed to dine with Messenger Elijah Muhammad and ask his help, an effort he felt was useless considering that whites were to make up the majority of his delegation. Elijah and the two delegates from Georgia duly met. When Bond and his companion left the building, the NOI ministers discussed whether to cover the expenses of travel and accommodation for the sixteen delegates. Some of the ministers opposed the request on the grounds that the NOI's religious teachings forbade taking part in white politics in the Last Days; some of the males and all of the Muslim women opposed giving any help to a delegation made up mainly of whites. However, Elijah Muhammad cut short the talk, called in the two youths, and gave them $3000 to get the delegation to Chicago and help pay their bills. "He literally changed the face of the Democratic Party", wrote Julian Bond in 1996, "and I have wondered, from that day to this, why he did it". Perhaps Elijah had foreseen the eventual entry of the Black Muslims into mainstream politics from 1983 under Farrakhan?

In 1968, the American Democratic Party was being transformed from a white heavily Anglo-Saxon and Protestant organization to one whose membership would henceforth more and more encompass all races in the United States, though this inclusion was not always to find reflection in its electoral platform and policies. [The new compromise, though, would not draw leadership from all classes in a given ethnic group, briefly a possibility after ordinary blacks, in taking part in the mass protest movement in the southern states for civil rights, attempted to register as members of the Democratic Party.] Elijah's decision in 1968 was one step in the process of expanding the representativeness of America's central political institutions: the incomparably greater number of Latino and black faces amongst the conferees of the two major American parties by the 1990s had made both resemble American society as it really existed in all its diversity.[103] The Democratic Party henceforth would act as a key setting for the upward mobility of bourgeois or young educated Blacks.

Elijah was usually a shrewd ideologue who was adaptable and swift about the means he seized to make his aims realities. This incident, though, was far outside any preceding NOI ideological framework. Despite his advanced years in 1968, Elijah had grasped the depth and speed of the political and social transformations taking place in America in the era of the collapse of her war effort in Vietnam: he no longer underestimated the movement to win civil rights. Throwing the preconceptions of his own ideology to the winds, he aided the parliamentarist aspect of integration that one day might provide opportunities and resources both to his followers and to the masses of poor blacks in which his sect had crystallized. Elijah's high alertness to the growing ethnic inclusiveness of U.S. institutions was like his farsightedness in ordering that Spanish be taught in his schools, because he foresaw how demographically significant Hispanics one day would become in the USA.

In the 1980s, the media of Farrakhan's successor NOI would fault established Black machine-politicians in the Democratic Party for not giving enough openings to younger black politicians. Overall, though, the second NOI was to publicize economic opportunities wrested for the Black bourgeoisie by the Black-headed city administrations that the Civil Rights revolution ushered in throughout the USA.[104]

Not only did Elijah increasingly try to avoid any clash with the system—he was actually trying to make that polity work and really integrate the races in some sense. A press conference he gave after some followers or ex-followers or ex-sympathizers took on the cops in Baton Rouge in 1972 showed how split from his early ideology and rhetoric Elijah's later vision could have been becoming. In it, the old side of him yet again read into *Genesis* the manufacture of the progenitor of a white race whose individuals henceforth would slaughter each other unrestrained by any sense of collectivity. But in reply to a white American journalist who asked "what would be an out for me?" Elijah replied that "there would be no such thing as the elimination of all white people from the earth, at the present time or at the break out of the Holy War." This was because some of them are "not born or created Muslims but they have faith in what the Muslims are trying to live". "It is only through Islam that white people can be saved."[105]

In his last years, city mayors both white and black across America were proclaiming Honorable Elijah Muhammad Days in their cities, and engaging in joint public rituals with the NOI. Elijah's deputies took part in and thus validated those rituals of the changing America. As a figure in Black consciousness, though, Elijah had for decades been a symbol of the antagonism between working class blacks resolved to rise, and bourgeois blacks determined to keep them down in their place. This durable class ill-feeling was nearly as strong as Elijah's hatred of whites. When the mayors of Berkeley and Oakland proclaimed Honorable Elijah Muhammad Days, his

National Representative, Louis Farrakhan, found it "significant" recognition of "this man who was so hated, so despised and so rejected by our people [i.e. the Black bourgeoisie] and, of course, by the dominant white American society." "The Honorable Elijah Muhammad works for the poor, and it is the poor who have elevated him," not the [Black] intellectuals or bourgeoisie. Farrakhan was in accord with the past, pre-prosperity Elijah when he warned in 1975 that most Blacks were still struggling for survival in America. All the recognition of Elijah from the mainstream could be just one more subtle "subterfuge" to throw the Blacks off guard while the system prepared to dismantle the NOI, as it already had the Student Non-Violent Coordinating Committee and the other "so-called Black protest organizations," Farrakhan cautioned.[106] Elijah and his top colleagues were moving away from the poor whose support had raised the sect towards the looser, more inclusive mainstream America that Anglo-Saxons dominated. Yet his long-standing, ingrained perceptions of class categories among Blacks and his decades-old ideological baggage would prevent him from carrying through affiliating to even just the Black bourgeoisie while he lived.

Overall, subtexts and acts by Elijah or followers before 1975 that pointed forward to efforts thereafter by Warith or Farrakhan to enter the U.S. political system appear to be atypical. The stronger drive of the sect was to keep outside politics and seek wealth and empowerment within economic endeavors and religion. Elijah's ideology that the sect was a religious instrument to socially reform Blacks and make them productive in economics lingered in the 1980s and 1990s in the new NOI of Farrakhan. It created a duality that might sap Farrakhan's will to carry through the transfer of the NOI to the forefront of an African-American ethnic politics within the U.S.'s representative political system [parliamentarism], giving rise to the question whether African-American Muslim sects really can make themselves positive system-challengers to a widened U.S. majoritarian system or a new component of it within American national politics.

Southern Background, Regionalism

Although the Nation of Islam unfolded in the great industrial cities of the USA's North, many of its recruits were under-educated blacks, the "unwanted of Dixie" who had originally migrated there from the deep South. Some NOI leaders readily allowed that they knew little of the South, but the harsh, special contours of racism there always structured the view of whites of those of its leaders who had originally been formed in it. Elijah's reminiscences from his prosperous stronghold in the North were of an Old South straight out of William Faulkner and Richard Wright. The Black people in the South had been brought up for centuries to fear white people. It was "pitiful to go in the South's rural districts, and see how, after four hundred years, the wicked, sun-burned, keen-nosed, tobacco juice-mouthed, and blue-eyed devils" [the part-Celtic "white trash" the South's genteel Anglos loathed almost as much as they did Blacks] "are buckling our poor people down to such slavery conditions; crushing them to death, and diseasing them." Their children grow up suffering from malnutrition. Untreated diseases send the Blacks off to their crude pine box graves or undignified hole in the ground. In some places "the Black people" were forced to walk to a drugstore and ask a supercilious white drugstore owner for their mail although he was not really giving something for free because the senders of the mail have paid taxes and bought the stamps for a real mail service.[107]

The Black people were cowed by this vicious enemy who kept his gun loaded. A happy policeman or sheriff was seeking just the slightest chance to kill a Negro. He only had to say to his judge, the brother devil, that he "had to kill a Negro" to get a handshake. Elijah had heard from their mouths when he lived in the South [many decades before] that "there were more Negroes than whites in the South and white people should kill off some." But Allah in the Person of Master Fard Muhammad, "to Whom praise is due forever, has come to deliver the Black man in America and to kill our oppressors."[108]

Provoked by the vicious oppression of the South that had formed his youthful personality, Elijah's fury did not often register the plurality of either the attitudes or the class and ethnic texture of its whites and blacks. His pain could blind him and his colleagues to new chances opening up to blacks. In this communication at any rate, Elijah put no value on the vote that the South's Blacks were wresting from their race-enemies. Instead, his assessment was that the Black Man of the South would be a fool to vote for any white man there to rule him. "He should stay away from the polls, because the white man for whom he votes is an enemy and is bound to tighten the shackles more than ever" and to continue to enforce the unjust laws he designed to harm the Black Man. Instead, Elijah urged the Blacks rather to vote for Allah and for His servant Elijah Muhammad to bring to pass "all the prophecies of the Bible of what He will do in freeing the Black man of America."[109]

Even the fire-eating Malcolm X had years before grasped that universal suffrage would quickly modify the behavior of even the most racist Southerner congressmen, who would have to deliver real benefits to blacks to get re-elected. [True, gerrymandering was to recur in the south in a new century in an effort to thwart African-American voting.] "Why else is it that racist politicians fight to keep black men [sic] from the polls?"—lucidity from Malcolm not as urgently concerned to integrate Black women into America's political mainstream. The white vote is always evenly divided and an ethnic group that voted in a bloc could decide the outcome: "a ten-million black vote bloc could be the deciding balance of power in American politics". Malcolm focused the detail of all the units that had input into the U.S. system and won back benefits: not just long-disliked Irish Americans whose votes made one of their own President by 1960, but the special interest lobbies—Labor, Big Oil, the farmers, doctors, etc.—who had all moved into Washington to make sure that new laws by Congress served the interests of their groups. He wanted every black to give a dollar to build a skyscraper lobby in

Washington, D.C. that would force the government to set up a massive department directed only to ending the problems of the blacks, which, in a way, President Johnson would do for his "Great Society".[110] In 1983-1984, Farrakhan, too, was sometimes to strive to induct African-Americans into left-Democratic Party politics as a means to build some ethnic power.

Yet Elijah most often—true, not always—failed to see that electoral politics would nourish the emergence of a new class of Black politicians in the South with some will to help their ethnic group in general. Overall, Elijah was at risk of misleading his people to miss a range of new opportunities. Yet, he paradoxically fostered constructive optimism when preaching that God would shortly incinerate all members of the white enemy-group. With their hopefulness, and thus their initiative, boosted, in the brief or even prolonged leadup to Judgement Day, the blacks could "live in peace with money, in good homes, and with the friendship of God and the righteous"[111] — an implicit sub-text from Elijah that the setting of the devil-ruled society or polity was not equally oppressive at all points and that his Muslim sub-nation could carve a rewarding niche of their own in it through economic self-determination. Jewish-Americans and Irish-Americans had faced lesser hatred from the dominant ethnos, which they too had—more discreetly—stereotyped as a Satanic enemy in order to redirect their fury into a fuel for the grueling endeavor of carving out niches or creating jobs in a system reluctant to grant them. Sonia Sanchez caught the ambiguity in at least some of even Malcolm's protest discourse which could open up into either a showdown or a modest constructive dream like that voiced by King: that "it's possible to get an education and not sell your soul; it's possible to work in a job without demeaning yourself," i.e. to become an equal—ordinary—American among the others that the system employed.[112]

The above communication by Elijah on the South was substantially accurate. It was stereotypical in that it did not differentiate poorer from some richer Blacks or poor whites from other whites who, with relaxed old-world southern charm towards each other, systematically finessed and wrung wealth from all the poor. Yet the item differentiated even the poorest Southern Blacks, and certainly America as a whole, from the underdevelopment of the Mother Continent, Africa. Carefully keeping the Blacks terrorized into submission, "the white man" gets rich: "he builds himself a fine luxurious home on the plantation and as far as he can see he claims that the land is his" [=allusion to dispossessed Native Americans?] The poor slaves living in the leaking shacks in winter have "the worst living conditions of human beings that could even be in the jungles of Africa where they do not have sawmills or brick kilns to saw timber into lumber and to mold bricks"—a considerable underestimation of the state of development of the Mother Continent by Elijah.[113] Martin Luther King, Jr. won through to a richer understanding (which had a tint of Marxism to it) of how poverty, lack of education and inequality among whites in his native South aggravated a racism that was manipulated by elites to maintain their lucrative hegemony over society as a whole: the two poorer groups could only rise if they did that together.

U.S. Prisons

Elijah Muhammad's modality of Islam was a protest language that African-Americans in the U.S. prisons system easily grasped. Thus, his Islam spread rapidly in American penitentiaries in the 1950s, 1960s and 1970s.

Even after he slipped out of the straitjacket of Elijah's counter-racism, Eldridge Cleaver still interpreted events in part through the lens of Elijah's reinvention of Bible characters to make them speak to oppression of Blacks. Cleaver wrongly gave Muhammad 'Ali a nationalist liberatory seriousness equal to that of a W.E.B. DuBois driven into Ghana exile, or the assassinated Malcolm X, when the boxer floored the hyper-Catholic, Floyd Patterson. Cleaver's mind at once jumped to Elijah's reinvention of the story of Lazarus, whom Elijah Muhammad had made symbolize the breaking and systematic dehumanization of the Negro in America. The enslavers had "killed the black man—killed him mentally, culturally, spiritually, economically, politically and morally—transforming him into a 'Negro', the symbolic Lazarus left in the 'graveyard' of segregation and second-class citizenship". Elijah Muhammad had been summoned by Allah to raise up the modern Lazarus, the Negro, from his grave by a nationalist rebirth. After adopting with his holy Arabic names a new identity in place of that which America gave him, the boxer Muhammad 'Ali had pounded the die-hard Lazarus, Floyd Patterson, into submission. Such fragments of Elijah's ideology still from time to time could focus Cleaver's anger against America, although he now thought "the hand of man" rather than God's would execute the old America that had jailed him.[114]

During the early attempts of various authorities and agencies to suppress the NOI in the 1930s and 1940s, not all whites had treated Elijah with equal harshness. The increased prosperity in the 1970s of himself, his clique and indeed his followers in general moderated Elijah's hatred of whites so that he saw them more plurally. What then appeared to Elijah to be a final weakening of America's global economic and political power was the context for him. The nonplussed U.S. officials had been unable to stop the fall of their money market and widening unemployment: the nations were laughingly turning down America's peace offerings as Goliath staggered, stabbed by the sword within and the sword without. The weakened white man more deceptively than ever offered his free Black slave some crumbs of freedom, justice, and equality to somehow keep hold on him as the dissatisfied world struck back. Yet some of the more intelligent whites were now behaving almost satisfactorily: a warden at a Texas prison-house was sending the believers (Muslims) to the Temple so that "they may listen to the truth which is their salvation today. I think that this is a very wise warden" comparable to Ahab's general who "knew that Ahab was wrong and [the earlier] Elijah was right" and so fed his followers whom Ahab held captive.[115]

A changing America began granting more and more jobs to reliable Black Muslims as warders. In some prisons both most minders and most of the Black incarcerated now adhered to Elijah's more and more ambiguous, although not yet integrationist, protest Islam.

Stateville penitentiary in the 1960s prohibited NOI chaplains and services, and any entry of *Muhammad Speaks*, the Qur'an, and books to teach Arabic. U.S. courts upheld that exclusion of a religion on grounds that conversion to Elijah Muhammad's creed would make prisoners not inclined to obey America's non-Muslim authorities.[116] However, the hatred that many prison officials had vented against the NOI's Islam and its propagation in some prisons tapered off as it became clear that it could help calm the Black prisoners, properly handled. The converts at Marion Correctional Institution, Ohio, wrote to *Muhammad Speaks* that they were actualizing the drive to be clean internally and externally, and to achieve a sense of dignity, all so central to the teachings of the Honorable Elijah Muhammad. Superintendent E.P. Perini and his officers, and an amiable clergyman, had made it possible for Muslims to eat pork-free food at M.C.I in Chicago. The Superintendent had commended the Messenger's followers for their discipline, and for being respectful to officers and staff members: that was "why the administration could take a positive view of the Muslim program".[117] The new Black bourgeois elite were connecting the now-cleansed Muslims and the unwilling system into each other. Senator Rudolph Clay was a member of the Task Force on Corrections of the Indiana Criminal Justice Planning Agency. After his repeated insistence, *Muhammad Speaks* was placed in all Indiana prisons to achieve "the positive self-rehabilitation that the Nation of Islam, the Islamic religion, and the Honorable Elijah Muhammad teach".[118]

Muhammad Speaks covered even more incredible changes in the U.S. police and prison systems. In Atlanta, the new Black mayor, Maynard Jackson, appointed an African-American chief of police. On his first day, Chief Eaves "busted" 52 officers involved in corruption or in the mid-1974 firing on Black demonstrators demanding the dismissal of his white predecessor.[119]

Even under Elijah, then, as the Nation of Islam became richer and more conservative, its ministers were establishing a live-and-let-live relationship with the authorities in the huge network of U.S. prisons. The scene was being set for the installation of Muslim prison chaplains from both Warith and Farrakhan's successor-sects after 1975, some of them to be salaried by the prisons and the U.S. government. The ambiguity and alternation of roles of NOI Islam as a protest religion for prisoners in the USA instances the recurring dual functionalism of the net of creeds that were founded by [the Isma'ili- or Druze-like] Wali Fard Muhammad in 1930.

The stances of Elijah and his Muslims to America's mainstream economy and society and to the USA's electoral political system were still salient for elite African-Americans as the 20th century closed. Hyper-integrationist Blacks, intent to deny any role for Farrakhan in mainstream life, found it hard to view the Muslims from more than one angle, so they missed the constant, multiple ambiguities of Elijah and his sect's stances of protest against White America. The linguist, John McWhorter, in a 2000 book critiqued the cult of victimhood and the condemnations of white intellectualism that, so he contended, were still demotivating those Blacks now getting higher educations. McWhorter could register nothing positive about Elijah Muhammad, while obscuring the many ways in which Elijah had anticipated McWorter's own Anglicizing enterprises, subtly or overtly. McWhorter carried forward the hoary dichotomization of the Black Muslim movement against the civil rights integrationist tradition incarnated by Martin Luther King, Jr.. Against biographer Clegg's modest celebration, McWhorter objected that Elijah had had adherents who stepped out of line beaten, or in the case of Malcolm X, killed, and that he womanized—"moral issues". Elijah "scorned the Civil Rights Movement, considering Martin Luther King, Jr. a 'fool', scoffing at young blacks' participation in sit-ins, and played no part in paving the way for blacks' successes today".[120]

This persistent dichotomy from hardline integrationist Blacks collapses, given (a) the data that came to light in the 1990s of Elijah's bankrolling the civil rights activists' entry into American parliamentarism, and given (b) the growing understanding among Islamic African-Americans of the radical design for American society that King pursued beneath his accommodationist phraseologies. Given Elijah's conservative reverence for the traditional pedagogy and learning of America's white-run universities, his Anglicizing teachings or drives would not encourage the type of slacking that McWhorter blasted in his Black bourgeois students of the 1990s. There is too much money, and to be sure potential collective prosperity, at stake in an education for Americans who think like the good WASP, Elijah!

4: THE IMPACT OF ARABS AND MIDDLE EAST ISLAMS

Middle Easterners and the Borders of World "Black" Community to 1975

Decolonization and the development of new independent Muslim, African, and Asian states did register with Elijah, but through many filters of his ideology and his people's U.S. situation. The question was if the accessions of Afro-Asians to political power could make him and thus his followers more optimistic about the more inclusive political parliamentarism now unfolding in America, or hearten them to confront the U.S. system.

Decolonization in other places in the globe demonstrated the capacity of "Black people" to become independent actors in hopeful, ameliorative political change without God having to destroy the world. Such "Black" Africans and Asians provided an imaged model that Elijah cited to try to change the Americanism of "the average so-called Negro" whom he assessed as wanting to acquire white flesh and blood. Instead, "the Black people of the earth are seeking independence for their own, not integration into white society": would his words here truly impel African-Americans to demand political separation from the USA? "In what other country on this earth will you find 22 million people within the framework of another people's government seeking to become qualified citizens joyously singing the songs of integration?" Integration, which had been designed to destroy the USA's so-called Negroes, had made them "the fools of the nations".

Knowing that the independence movements of the non-white peoples had caught the attention of African-Americans, Elijah now tried to make them highlight and validate his leadership and program to the Black lumpen-bourgeoisie, the wannabies and the established professionals. In "Of Land and Nation",[121] Elijah used decolonization abroad to discredit his integrationist factional opponents in the African-American population. But this (again skeletal) communication did not manifest much detailed interest in the specificities of the movements and states in Afro-Asia he was holding up for his parochial purposes. "In order to build a Nation you must first have some land": the 400 year-old enemy had mentally poisoned his people since the slavery era to divert them from "uniting and acquiring some land of our own". Elijah's rhetoric urged purchase of agricultural land as a means to separate and articulate the U.S. Black nation (or just the Nation of Islam?) vis-à-vis the U.S. state and Euro-Americans. How far would the Asians' and Africans' achievement of independent states take him and his followers towards a real political break or independence in statehood from the USA?

On the whole, the interest of Elijah in Muslims and Africans across the seas was not strong enough for him to seek out and apply details of their decolonization drives, organization, ideologies and new state structures to the Blacks in America. The overwhelming numbers of Euro-Americans ruled out African-Americans duplicating the nationalist movements of "Black people" in Algeria, West Africa, etc. Rather, those Afro-Asians primarily served as images fired back and forth between the Black Muslims and the other groups in Black America. Only a total collapse and disintegration of the USA or indeed intervention by Almighty God Himself could have made it practicable for African-Americans to establish an independent territorial nation on some part of the existing U.S. territory. The example of the new Asians and Africans was not to push Elijah and the NOI much beyond their localistic use in projection of an internal enclave-nationality or micronationalism to be built in America. It anticipated those micronationalisms that were to develop later in America among many groups in the post-modern era, not least in the American application of struggling motherlands across the oceans. But his millenarianism denied Elijah some analytical tools needed to conceptualize a determined enclave-nationhood that conceivably might one day be legally structured into the American system of government. Nonetheless, Elijah's thrust in the 1960s and 1970s to set up new self-managing rural enclaves within a total nationalist sub-economy or circuit went beyond what even nationalist Jewish-Americans were ever to conceive or attempt.

Some of Elijah's followers and journalists were less skeletal than he about the Third World. Chapter 5 will sample efforts from the NOI's media to get to grips with the unfolding contemporary histories of the peoples/states of Asia, Africa and Latin America, fleshing out their specific outlines much more than did Elijah. However, in the period leading up to Elijah's death in 1975, NOI ideologues such as Malcolm X and other writers did not show much interest in finding malfunctions and structural problematics in the "Black" new societies overseas: to view change there in a critical modern way in turn could have led to more skilled understanding of the needs of African-Americans themselves, and of strategies to achieve them.

However, more and more cultural elements coming in from the Middle East entered the casual daily life of the adherents under Elijah. A Saudi sociology student in 1950 taught NOI women how to cook Middle Eastern dishes, which the sect's restaurants came to offer in the early 1970s.[122] The pattern in 1962 was that adherents played some jazz records in their homes but balanced them with other records from Arab pop-culture: compared to non-Muslim African-Americans, they did not seem very responsive to the jazz.[123] This was a puritanical policy that came down from the leadership of the movement. As Minister of the sect's main New York mosque, Malcolm X banned blues songs from the Nation's juke boxes there because the genre fostered regretful nostalgia that only sapped energy. He did allow some less unsettling jazz records, balanced with Arab and African disks.[124] In a way, then, the Nation of Islam leadership under Elijah did use recorded music and song as a conduit that injected enough intimate culture of Arabs and Black Africans into their sector of Black America to distinguish it, in combination with ideology, as a separate—pious—ethnos or micronation from the other Blacks.

The occasional ambiguity or wariness of Elijah and his followers towards Africa put them at odds with the fervent drive of many Afro-American youth outside the sect to re-fuse Black America with Africa in the 1960s, 1970s and 1980s. Similarly, Elijah and colleagues in swings voiced reservations about Arab and Middle Eastern Muslims. Elijah Muhammad and Farrakhan, though, had developed no fixed position on the pan-Muslim option for community by 1975: they never really developed any systematic ideology about the various planes of human bonding and interaction. Rather, they alternated between two views of the Arabs: (a) that they were a key component of a global "Black" community that would include African-Americans, as against (b) rarer perceptions of Arabs as white in contexts of theological, social or political tensions with them. This inconsistency was an instance of the ambivalence and covert duality of scenarios that underlay most positions taken by NOI discourse to 1975.

Arabs who criticized the theology of the Nation before 1975—for example, its refusal to accept that Muhammad Ibn 'Abdallah of Arabia was the last Messenger of God—were sometimes dismissed under Elijah as whites who could only be believers by faith, not by nature: one 1967 insult even speculated that peninsular Arabians are half-caste descendants of stray female white devils left behind when the Blacks of Mecca drove the grafted white devils off into exile in Europe six thousand years ago.[125]

Such racial rejection of Middle-Eastern Arabs and Muslims under Elijah and Farrakhan was, though, only one extreme of the pendulum of NOI attitudes. The other point to which this U.S. psyche more regularly swung was a wide definition of "blackness" that incorporated their Middle Eastern coreligionists while diluting away Africa beyond the Sahara. Farrakhan's media in the 1980s and 1990s reprinted communications by Elijah that gave the international Black Nation flexible borders that could encompass Arabs, Pakistanis and even Turks, and were very open to ideological influence from them, although with some uncertainty or vacillation that there might be plural race or color categories, or sub-categories, within that "East" (Third World).

Elijah's aspect of openness to Middle Easterners as fellow-"Blacks" was brought out by his drive to restructure relations between the two sexes of African-Americans as a central aspect of nation-building in North America. Influenced by wives as *harth* (cultivable land, tilth) in Qur'an 2:223, he defined the Black woman as "man's field to produce his nation: if he does not keep the enemy out of his field, he won't produce a good nation". Essien-Udom (1962) traced the sense of lumpen ghetto males who opted for Elijah in the 1950s that white males, who had money and social standing, could casually access most Black American women to whom they took a fancy, which left fewer meaningful relationships to the Black male.[126] Blacks, warned Elijah Muhammad, had to go out into those fields to carefully seek and destroy the worms and enemies bent on destroying their crops. "You are not careful about your women. You don't love them: you have allowed visitors to run in and out of your house" who had destroyed the love Black men and women might have had for each other in North America.However, the Middle East's Muslims patterned to Elijah how "the Black man" might bar whites from access to his women in North America.

Elijah's sense that there was no race break between his people and Middle Easterners was fostered by his travels. In late 1959, he visited Turkey, Egypt, the Sudan, Ethiopia, Mecca and Medina in Arabia, and Pakistan with a couple of his sons. "We returned home from Lahore, Pakistan, on about the 6th of January 1960. Everywhere we went, the Black man recognized his woman. He had great respect for her. We dined in the homes of some of the most influential people of these countries—government people. In some of their homes, we never did see any of their family, only men. The waiter was a man or boy, not any woman".

The racist sexual abuse of African-American women in North America, miscegenation and the loss of the racial integrity of Black Americans as a potential political nation thus confronted Elijah and his colleagues with a crisis in which radical counter-patterns from Middle Eastern societies would receive consideration. When perception of pathologies in Black life in America, the neo-Muslim nation-building drive, and gripping images of social purpose in Third World Muslim societies worked in tandem, U.S. "Black Muslims" can lose any sense of a racial divide separating their minority from Muslims in the alternative power-centers of the Middle East.

But in a nativist patch in the same text, Elijah distinguished "brown" or "yellow" as well as more strictly "black" groups in the non-white world, as outgroups in the face of whom African-Americans have to hold themselves with self-respect. As Elijah put it, "the brown man [and the yellow man and the white man] will never recognize you until you protect your woman."[127] In his report on his African-Asian tour to the NOI's 1960 Convention, Elijah bracketed those countries of the two continents as the region where "Islam is the dominant religion of the black man." He and his two sons were met with "brotherly love in Turkey when it was learned that we were Muslims... We could live and go anywhere over there without thinking someone was going to throw a stone because we were in the wrong place." Thus, the socio-political relationship of Euro-Americans with their black neighbors, when contrasted to a sense of new greater "freedom" in Asia as well as Africa, made Elijah see Turks, Egyptians and Arabs there, too, as "black" without his differentiating them from African-Americans in that context.[128]

Elijah Muhammad's pre-1975 stress that Black women were "your first nurse", and an informal but crucial teacher in the household—"your first lesson comes from your mother"—whose protection and control was a central task of his nationalism ran parallel with similar themes in the Egyptian movement for independence from British colonial rule conducted by Mustafa Kamil (died 1908). Elijah had been influenced in youth by the writings of the Sudanese-Egyptian publicist, Duse Mohammed 'Ali, who had lobbied for Kamil and his successor Muhammad Farid from London, and who subsequently migrated to the USA where he wrote for the media of Marcus Garvey.

Louis Farrakhan was a mass popularizer during the era of the leadership of Elijah Muhammad of the Nation of Islam's blurring of the lines of racial separation between Africans/Blacks and Arabs/Asians. His early calypso record, "Whiteman's Heaven is a Black Man's Hell", diluted the African component of the international "Black Nation" in part in response to the dynamism of Arab World and Muslim World movements for political decolonization and pan-Arab unity in that era: "The Black Man everywhere/ is on the rise./ He has kicked the white man/ out of Asia/ And he's going fast out of Africa."[129]

Essien-Udom (1962) stressed tactics by which Elijah kept his sect independent of Arabs and Eastern Muslims who strove to involve it too closely in Nasser's Egypt and the struggles of Arab nationalisms against various Western nationalities, such as in Algeria.[130] However, the 1990s brought out data about interaction by Elijah and his ministers with Nasser's Egypt in particular that suggest he looked the Egyptians over in a more serious way than Essien-Udom considered. In 1959, Nasser offered Elijah a palace if he moved his base to the Mother Continent: the Egyptian leader had analysed that Elijah would gain a following in the millions if he taught in French West Africa. When Nasser died in 1970, Elijah wrote in an obituary that Nasser had been "a great friend" of the NOI who through his industrialization drive strove to help the poor of Egypt and Africa "do something for themselves in a modern way", his skeletal insight ran.

Farrakhan's close long-term relationship with al-Qadhafi's Libya after 1978 was a successor of the relationship Elijah Muhammad founded with Nasser's Egypt, the original model of the young al-Qadhafi [Qadhdhafi/ Gaddafi].[131] Some Black observers tended to see Elijah as senile and demented in his latter years, and thus an instrument of subordinate leaders around him in the sect. But Elijah Muhammad flew with other top Nation of Islam leaders to Libya in 1972 to negotiate the coming relationship with the young al-Qadhafi early in his rule.[132] Since Elijah was around 75 at the time, it testifies to the fact (a) that despite his advanced age, he had the stamina to keep control of the NOI to his 1975 death; and (b) that Elijah gave more meticulous importance to developing relations with Arabs in the 1950s and 1960's than some figured.

Whatever his particularistic swings about Arabs in other contexts, aid or expressions of sympathy from Arab states or elites modified both Elijah's demarcation of intimate community and his millenarianism. Libya's brash new revolutionary leader, Mu'ammar al-Qadhafi, in 1972 gave a $3 million loan that turned into a grant so that the NOI could purchase a magnificent Orthodox church for its national headquarters in Chicago. The occasion led Elijah and *Muhammad Speaks* to again envisage a broad international "Black" community that might distract adherents from sub-Saharan Africa as the area of provenance with which African-Americans now had much better chances to reconnect in the 1970s. The $3 million showed that "the Libyan people remember that we Black people in America are their brothers—the love between the Black Man in the Western Hemisphere and the Black Man around the earth which takes in Africa, number one, and reaches around Asia and the Isles of the Pacific back to America". God would ultimately incinerate the whites. But such God-decreed aid from "the rich world of our Black Brothers" would help those in the USA towards "getting united and doing something for Black Self in America". Yet Elijah's language left no doubt that for him the God that now was employing the, here, Black Arabs for that purpose was still Wali Fard Muhammad "who found us".[133]

Elijah sensed that if he could get additional financial support from Third World Muslim states for Black economic development in North America, it would mobilize African-Americans in general around his sect. Wider Christian and secular African-American groups were to have similar hopes that Farrakhan might win trade benefits from the Third World when he set off on his World Friendship tours following his organization of the 1995 Million Man March on Washington.

The sense of Middle Eastern Muslims as non-whites—which in part developed some long-standing Anglo-American racial concepts—continued in coverage of the Middle East by the media of Farrakhan's new reconstructed Nation of Islam in the 1980s and the 1990s. When President Bush Sr told the U.S. Congress that the world "now recognizes one sole and pre-eminent power", *Final Call* described Congress as "responsible for wreaking havoc and destruction upon the darker peoples of the earth". Here, the Farrakhan tabloid in a way racially identified with Iran, as articulated by its clerical hardliner, President Khamenei, as among the "nations who are fighting to lift the boot of oppression worn by the U.S."[134] In a 1986 speech to a conference in Libya, Farrakhan equated Patrice Lumumba, Nasser, Nkrumah, Amilcar Cabral, Castro, al-Qadhafi and Khomeini as all leaders of enslaved nations whom the imperialists fought:[135] this juxtaposition of Black Africans and Middle Easterners (and even anti-U.S. Latin Americans) resembled the Nation's pre-1975 swings towards a global Black nation or community made up of Asians, Africans and perhaps Latin Americans.

Elijah's outbursts of racial rejection or distance against Middle Eastern Muslims were a function of the incompatibility of some of his religious tenets with those accepted by Third World Muslims. Although important, such outbursts under Elijah—or Farrakhan after 1978—do have to be relativized against the multiple-texted NOI discourse that could come to blur and bracket Blacks and Arabs/Turks/Persians/Pakistanis/Indonesians into intimate community in at least a broad sense. Analysis of the pendulum also has to include the recurring ambivalence and reservations of all sects of Muslim African-Americans, including Farrakhan's, to sub-Saharan Africans.

The Black Muslims' somewhat greater identification with Arab-led or Muslim movements or governments in Africa could sometimes alienate them from Black African movements and states led by Christian-educated elements. The millenarian sense of the dawning of a new historical era of sovereignty that could suddenly usher in very great prosperity for the world's long-enslaved blacks was evident in Elijah Muhammad's message to Kwame Nkrumah when Ghana became independent in March 1957. Ghana was inhabited by animists and Christians with a smaller but substantial African Muslim minority of over twelve per cent.[136] Elijah Muhammad headed his message, "The Muslims of America Salute Ghana". He used astronomical imagery to evoke the age of sovereign well being that he and his followers wished for the Ghanaians now. The letter reflected his strong awareness that many of the USA's blacks were descended from enslaved Africans who had been brought from Ghana and West Africa generally: he expressed the hope that outsiders would never again be able to take "Black Gold" from Ghana. Nonetheless, irrepressibly, Elijah wrote to Nkrumah and the predominantly non-Muslim newly-independent Ghanaians: "May the One God Allah be thy God".[137] [That ideological exhortation was at clear variance with the pluralist demography and pink-secular political structure of the country, Ghana, as it then stood.]

In the most positive vein, the achievement of independence by nationalists in Africa was held up as a morale-building model for the emancipation U.S. Negroes could achieve with similar techniques. In 1961, Elijah Muhammad lashed the USA's Black bourgeois elite for their satisfaction with education their white enemies had designed to keep the Blacks in servitude, an education that left Blacks unable to inquire into their proud past prior to slavery or to have a desire to become independent economically or otherwise. As a counter-model, Elijah lauded [non-Muslim] black African leaders who came to America for higher education resolved to use the knowledge they gained there to win independence for their peoples back in Africa: he cited the return of Kwame Nkrumah to Ghana, Dr Hastings Banda to [in part Muslim] Nyasaland (Malawi) and Dr Azikiwe to Nigeria. Elijah in this address made the model of those tertiary-educated black non-Muslim Africans function to inspire U.S. Blacks to build a parallel nationalist black capitalist economy in America and to support and attend a separatist Black Muslim school system. The latter, though, would inculcate "the daily Muslim duties, the teaching of Arabic", with which the nominally Christian Africans he had named were unlikely to sympathize.[138]

Decolonization in Africa was broadening the horizons of the millenarian nationalism advanced by Elijah and his followers in America, but they continued to find it hard to fit the sect's emblematic Islam into Christian-led or secular nationalist movements in Black Africa.

Despite their provenance from West Africa, Elijah's Black Muslims on some significant occasions showed that they did not feel comfortable identifying with black African countries in which Christians or animists were the majority or had political leadership over black Islamic elements. When Essien-Udom in 1958 visited the auditorium of "the University of Islam", the sect's secondary school in Chicago, it was decorated with the flags of all countries in the world inhabited by Muslim majorities, with accompanying captions summarizing their histories, populations and resources. Non-African Muslim countries like Pakistan, Turkey and peninsular Arabian states were there, as were such Arabic-speaking African countries as Egypt, Morocco and the Sudan. However, the flags of important black African countries with non-Muslim leaderships—for instance, the flags of Ethiopia, Liberia and Ghana—were absent, although Liberia's then-ruling establishment was descended from American Negroes who returned to Africa. It revealed the U.S. Black Muslims' considerable identification with Arab anti-imperialist nationalism that the flag of the FLN's provisional Algerian government-in-exile hung in the auditorium in 1958, although it wasn't until 1962 that the French were finally driven from Algeria.[139] Elijah Muhammad swung away from the orthodox Islamic heartlands to some extent in his last period, reflecting his view that the Black Man of America and the Black Man of Africa had to re-unite, although his ambiguous language there may still have diluted the Africans with the "Blacks" of the whole globe as a loophole out from any deep community with Africans.[140]

As late as 1976, the Afro-American black nationalist, Kasisi Jetu Weusi, assailed the Black Muslims' mythology (which they were dropping by then) that American Blacks were descended from Africans who had originally migrated to Africa from the Arabian peninsula (Mecca) and that "the so-called Negro" was thus really "the Asiatic Black Man". For *Black News* this mythology of an Asiatic origin fostered low self-esteem and a low regard for black Africa: it implicitly denied that all blacks everywhere in the world in reality were Africans.[141]

Although Elijah and his followers celebrated Arab and African political nationalisms as motifs in their millenarian optimism, Elijah carefully limited the Black Muslims' contacts with Arab and Black-African Muslims. He made sure few of his followers migrated back to Africa or the Arab world, the "East" from which Black Americans had been brought in chains, or even went there for temporary studies. The progress and emancipation of Africa and Asia was for him a means to build his followers' morale for economic and communal self-improvement in America, not a potential destination or homeland. He kept his sect well outside the growing political activism by U.S. Blacks, despite his own secret financial assistance mentioned above.

Resident Arabs: Jamil Diyab, Palestinian

Shaykh Jamil Shakir Diyab, a Palestinian, immigrated in 1948 and in 1949 became one of the early principals of the "University of Islam", the NOI's secondary school in Chicago: he also taught as its instructor in Arabic. How he got the job again instances how small shops provided a long-standing nexus between Arabs and Islamizing African-Americans in U.S. cities. A green grocer from Diyab's home village near Jerusalem had been impressed with the honesty and cleanliness of his Chicago NOI customers: they had told him that Elijah's school needed a good Arabic teacher, and he recommended Diyab, a star pupil in Palestine Matriculation Arabic who had gained a diploma of education from the Mandatory Government there. The friend had at the outset told Diyab that those African-American Muslims "differ from us in some beliefs."[142]

In his pioneering 1962 study, a Nigerian, Essien-Udom, related that there was grumbling in the Chicago congregation that Diyab, while principal, never attended a single temple meeting, and that another subsequent Egyptian principal showed the same "disinterest in religion": "the [Black] Muslims feel that the Arabs are not interested in identifying with them". The separate congregation that Diyab established in Chicago after he left the NOI in 1956 as "a mixed group of Negroes and whites" (Arabs) was argued to have therefore looked "prestigious" to some African-American recruits from the heretical Ahmadiyyah or from the fringes of the NOI. When principal, Diyab had been earning $100 a week: Essien-Udom tended to see his efforts to incorporate African-Americans into a new composite Muslim congregation after he left Elijah as instrumental, for example, to the inroads he was making as a real estate agent into the Negro housing market in Chicago. Essien-Udom wondered if Diyab was not one more conman "exploiting the gullibility of the Negro lower class, who run from place to place seeking to escape from being black!"

Essien-Udom's characterizations resounded within African-American ideological politics, which were under swift transformation in the 1960s, because those restless middle class African-Americans were reading his book as one of the very first broad-gauge analyses of the NOI.[143] No doubt, some immigrant Arabs, like the more gifted recruits to the Nation of Islam, tried to build livelihoods around or within being Muslim in America, as, similarly, Christians and Jews have often applied their religions in U.S. life. Perhaps Diyab finessed a good salary, but his professionalism as a pedagogue led him to eschew Arab politics in order to teach his pupils knowledge that would equip them to win good American livelihoods in their turn. Essien-Udom never considered that, beyond individuals, two ethnic groups might be starting to develop a humane, cooperative relationship in America.

Diyab may have contributed some motifs from Sunni Islam to ideological materials being grafted by Elijah, but this was brief. It was Elijah and his lieutenants who had not encouraged participation by Diyab or other Arabs in the sect's religious life, because they wanted to contain foreign influences on it: thus, they did not allow Diyab to teach religion or the Qur'an while principal. Diyab struck his pupil, Wallace/Warith, as a "firm, rational believer in the teachings of the Holy Prophet". In the many private conversations the teenage Warith had with him, Diyab took care not to argue against or undermine his father, Elijah. Appointed to teach science, mathematics and Arabic rather than religion, Diyab did, though, slip fragments of information about Arab Sunni Islam into his Arabic and science classes, and equipped and encouraged Warith to read the Qur'an.[144] Diyab's version of Islam did fit in with America's modernist "rationality": he believed that only the Qur'an, the word of God revealed to the Prophet Muhammad (PBUH), had to be followed: the *hadith* or collections of sayings attributed to the Prophet had only been put down on paper 200 years after his death and were thus always "suspect". On a range of grounds, Diyab dismissed severe ("ugly") *hudud* punishments for adultery, theft, etc., as not compulsory in Islam. This slimmed-down post-orthodox Islam would be slower to clash with that of Elijah or with Anglo-American norms. Diyab lasted as a teacher of Arabic in the sect's Chicago school from late 1949 to 1956.[145] After 1975, Farrakhan was to condemn Islam's doctors of the shari'ah law for making the hadith equal to the Qur'an as sources, with his in-house Palestinian journalist, 'Ali Baghdadi, attacking the majority of the traditional *'ulama* for that in unison, as had al-Qadhafi.[146] Diyab's modernized Sunnist input was long-term: in 1996, Warith's tabloid publicized his new book, *Modern Interpretation of the Qur'an: Interpretations to Reflect Our Changing Times*, directed to whites as well as African-Americans.[147]

True, after he left Elijah, Diyab did at least once harshly challenge the credentials of the NOI to be Islamic in the eyes of African- and Euro-Americans. Elijah's "cult... have different religious books, prayers, fasts", and did not meet the criteria by which all Muslims and non-Muslims judge an organization or group to be Islamic or not. Elijah's followers had turned "the very cornerstone of Islam, universal brotherhood of man, black as well as white, into hatred": this had attached an "insidious stigma" to all Islamic societies in America.[148] Insofar as NOI divergences from Islam on these points would have been well-known to him over the years, Diyab may have been jockeying here for Anglo preference or toleration as a rival Muslim leader in Chicago's south side. However, his cast of mind did avoid nationality in relation to most issues.

Diyab's departure or expulsion from the NOI milieu indicated specificities that Elijah wanted to maintain, but this was only one early episode in the long story of Arab-NOI interaction. Diyab continued to seek, for the rest of his life, a truly Islamic religious relationship with those in the Nation of Islam tradition. Long after, in the next, 21st, century, and by then very old, Jamil Diyab was still teaching Arabic to children and adolescents at the Jawharat al-Islam mosque of Elijah's son, Warith, in Phoenix, California. His memory was that NOI members and juveniles with whom he had interacted in the 1950s, 1960s and 1970s had "shown no serious interest" in the cause of his people of Palestine or the pan-Arab nationalism of Nasser, neither of which he had promoted because "politics was not my aim". Nor did they show much interest in American politics. His concern was "to teach true Islam". Piercing below the denunciatory surface of Elijah's protest Islam, Diyab had assessed in the 1950s that the followers felt "their only nation is America" (*ummatuhum ul-wahidah hiya Amrika*). (He did, though, recall that Israel's attacks on Egypt in 1956 and 1967 aroused some concern in the ranks of the NOI and other neo-Muslim African-Americans.) Diyab gradually drew away from the Arab-American community, noting ironically in 2002 that immigrants' habit of seeking political support for their varying homelands of origin from the other Muslims after Friday congregational prayers was unlikely to get anyone anywhere either from or in faraway America. Islamic Black Americans may have gradually become his community.

Diyab saw his efforts—in the 1950s as an NOI teacher and then as a frank Sunni Muslim missionary to African-Americans in his own right—as having borne long-term fruit in Elijah's son, Wallace/Warith, who subsequent to his father's death in 1975 had rapidly attached the sect to international Sunni Islam. Diyab had remained a friend over all those decades with the son: he assessed Warith as able to converse well in Arabic and to accurately interpret the meaning of Arabic verses of the Qur'an. In 2001, in his 80s, he was exultant that the great split in the NOI tradition after 1978 had mended after Warith and Farrakhan reconciled: now, members of Farrakhan's 100,000-strong group who found themselves too far from one of his mosques simply went to the local mosque of Warith where they now prayed the same international Arabic ritual prayers with his adherents, and indeed took part in Islamic studies. Here Diyab [—this time around in 2001—] was more doctrinally welcoming of a still somewhat divergent Farrakhan than were some young immigrant Muslims in America: were Arabic prayers and shibboleths now becoming enough for him as an old Arab in a mighty Anglo-America? As we age, we may tend to overrate our effect on others and become more easily satisfied by mere forms in which we had some hand. Diyab set Farrakhan's following by the 21st century at fifty thousand to one hundred thousand, and Warith's as approaching one million. My impression from Diyab's superb classical Arabic was that he really may have been a "shaykh" (religious scholar) who immersed himself in Islam's classical Arabic texts, as some admiring Arab students rated him in the 1960s.[149]

Diyab may have been truly motivated by Islamic evangelizing drives in the 1950s and not been drawn into the pan-Arab nationalism that fired most Palestinians in the era: he at the time dismissed charges by eminent NAACP civil rights lawyer, Thurgood Marshall, that Elijah Muhammad was supported by Nasser[150]. Gamal Abdel Nasser became most vivid in the Middle East and in American mass consciousness only following the 1956 Suez crisis, the point at which Diyab left the "University of Islam". The Egyptian Mahmud Yusuf al-Shawaribi would develop programs to bring young adherents of Elijah to Egyptian universities, although Elijah was to contain them. Al-Shawaribi, too, probably had religion-centered priorities like Diyab.

Immigrant Arabs who interacted in depth with the NOI in the 1950s and 1960s, such as Diyab and the sect's in-house journalist, 'Ali Baghdadi, should be viewed not just as atomized individuals but as representing a more long-term conjunction between two groups—African-Americans and Arab-Americans—both under construction. There was a larger social meaning to Diyab's roles than $100 per week or a hustle by him to buy and sell real estate. His cousin, Layla Diyab, also was to build close social relations with the NOI's Sunnified successor-sect under Imam Warith ud-Din Muhammad. By the 21st century, equal encounter and symbiosis between African-Americans and Palestinian-Americans had become a genre in Arab-American cultural productions. The 2000 independent film, *Adrift in the Heartland,* by Brigid Mahar, a Palestinian, traced the blossoming of friendship between a successful female African-American social worker and a female Palestinian Muslim immigrant. Starting from their shared love of jazz and American movies, the African-American social worker becomes sensitized to 'A'ishah's uprooting from Palestine, and her devout Islamic faith, overcoming U.S. stereotypes about Islam. Thus, instead of one-sided Americanization, two different religious, political and cultural worlds met in a partial acculturation.[151] Another independent film production, *American Colors*, produced in Chicago by writer and director, Khaled Barakat (32 years old, born in Ramallah, Palestine) also traced the mingled life of African-American and Arab-American communities. Set in one of Chicago's most economically depressed African-American neighborhoods, it traced the daily lives of two Arab-American brothers who are owners of a neighborhood grocery store, and their interaction with various members of the African-American community, including Cleo, an African-American female activist. The film showed the poverty and prejudice inhibiting the development of both groups in America.[152]

Although the roles of Palestinian-Americans as shopkeepers in ghettoes who sometimes sell liquor have created some strains with African-American Muslims since the period of Elijah from the 1950s, these two groups have exchanged cultures, ideas and some political solidarity with each other that over time have mounted up.

Egyptian Interactions with the Nation of Islam

In accordance with the NOI's ideology of progressive historical recurrence, Elijah preached that Fard and he, himself, were the highest-degree or culminating articulators of Islam, while Middle Easterners and their prophets had just been their "foresigns." Arab Muslims strove to alter this ideology of the Black Muslims in the 1950s, 1960s and early 1970s. In the same period, many in the NOI were seeking Arabs out to actively explore Islam's world community, which the Nation of Islam had promised them at conversion.

The Egyptian, Mahmud Yusuf al-Shawaribi, a visiting lecturer of soil science at two U.S. universities, was chosen to be director of the new Islamic Center of New York in 1955, with heads of the UN delegations of the Islamic countries making up its advisory council.[153] In the 1950s, al-Shawaribi interacted with Elijah's Black Muslims well before the mainstream U.S. mass media made them known to Euro-Americans. His introduction had not come by way of immigrant Arabs or Muslims but through an ordinary member of Elijah's NOI and had delicately-balanced dualities. A passing African-American taxi driver in Washington recognized from his deportment that al-Shawaribi was a Muslim. The driver then mentioned that he himself was a member of a Muslim society with branches in various cities. When al-Shawaribi invited the taxi driver to come with him to the Washington mosque, he said he could not, but would meet him again anywhere else. At that second meeting, al-Shawaribi introduced him to the director of that same Washington Islamic Cultural Center! At the meeting, the African-American mentioned that members of his special Islamic association had been strictly instructed not to mix with any other Islamic societies, in particular not those that had any white American members, which was indeed the case with al-Shawaribi's Center.[154]

The original Nation of Islam had formed in 1930 in a Detroit with many Muslim and Druze Arab shopkeepers. Not surprisingly, by the 1950s, Elijah's restrictions on interaction with foreign Arabs were only being obeyed in a minimalist and pro forma way, with initiatives for encounters being taken by ordinary members who were working around the rules of their leader. Clearly, the adherents had long known immigrant Arabs, their facial features and their mannerisms well enough to recognize them on sight. The long-standing interactions, which dated back to years before Wali Fard Muhammad even founded the sect in 1930, could take place outside formal institutions. By not quite going inside al-Shawaribi's Islamic Center, the adherent met the letter of Elijah's prohibition while nonetheless still interacting with the personnel of a structure whose ideas about Islam had to challenge those of his sect's leader. To talk with Arabs was a very important need in his psyche.

Al-Shawaribi emotionally responded to NOI members from the Arab side: "their women's garb and covering their heads [in NOI meetings he attended] screens all sensitive areas of females that Islamic religious law prescribes be covered." When visiting the sect in Chicago, al-Shawaribi was electrified by its school there: "we imagined in it that we were addressing Egyptian pupils who read and write in Arabic." Many of the pupils read out whole surahs of the Qur'an to him and adequately answered his questions on the rituals of hajj and other matters. Diyab had really got Arabic going in that system![155] For resident Arabs who knew how dynamic Anglo-American culture was, and how precarious if the U.S. system would allow Islam or Arab culture or identity, or institutions to transmit them in public space, the Black Muslims offered hope that Muslim Arabs, too, could construct long-term community in America.

Sometime in the 1950s, al-Shawaribi "insisted" on meeting Elijah Muhammad to ascertain how far he shared beliefs ascribed to some of his followers, such as that he was a prophet. He found Elijah "a handsome-featured brown man, slender-built and of sharp intelligence." Elijah's view of his own and Wali Fard Muhammad's functions grated on the Egyptian Sunni who nonetheless saw the quasi-greatness of the personality of the small Messenger, whom many Euro-Americans and some blacks found unprepossessing on first encounter. "The man exercises an enormous spiritual hold over his followers, and he in person strikes me as a strong and energetic man with great ability in organizing things." Al-Shawaribi drew from Elijah unambiguous statements of his tenets that the "Hijazi" whose picture hung from his wall was God incarnate (Shawaribi did not name Fard), and that that God still directly gave him directions for his work in propagating Islam in America, in the face of al-Shawaribi's arguments that the Qur'an and the prophetic sunnah (practice) of Muhammad of Arabia were God's final guidance to humans. However, the existence of fringe elements that claimed direct access to God in Arab Sufi Islam predisposed al-Shawaribi to see Elijah's tenets as amusing rather than as any radical threat for the long term.[156]

Elijah had refused to change his tenets in discourse with the Egyptian. But the intrusive, hyper-energetic al-Shawaribi thought that he was able to convince other NOI leaders in many cities over the years that God is One with no associate (a reference to Fard and to the NOI concept that individual blacks can make themselves gods) and that "the noble Arab prophet is the last of the prophets and apostles... and that whoever believes in a prophethood of anyone after Muhammad is an unbeliever (kafir) without any link to Islam."[157] "The head of the mosque [of the NOI] in Washington and that in New York formed branches in their cities of the [Cairo-centered] Association for the Publicization of Islam" that al-Shawaribi had come to represent in the USA.[158] (They were at least passing around his pamphlets, at any rate.) Al-Shawaribi *had* appeared with New York's Malcolm X on the NOI's national radio program, aired in over eighty cities nationwide by 1960. On October 22, 1960, a New York black newspaper carried a government-planted story that Dr al-Shawaribi of the World Federation of Islamic Missions had criticized the Black Muslims for distorting Islam. At a November Afro-Asian Bazaar that drew Third World diplomats, al-Shawaribi, who had accompanied Malcolm X there, denied that he had ever denounced fellow-Muslims [=skilful phrasing?]. "I thank Allah that once a week the teaching of our faith can be heard on the air in this area." While FBI equipment could have caught private outbursts by al-Shawaribi against tenets of Elijah, the Arab had installed himself into NOI mass media that Malcolm controlled, and therefore kept up a united front.[159]

Elijah himself allowed al-Shawaribi to pass through a wide range of NOI centers despite his preaching Sunni Islam. He does seem to have been looking Arab Muslims over in a serious way and waiting to see how much input he should allow them, their culture, and their concerns (e.g. Palestine) into the NOI system. Overall, al-Shawaribi's book documents that a wider range of members of Elijah's sect wanted more and closer interaction with Arab and other non-American Muslims in the 1950s than the West-published scholarly literature has perceived. At the age of 42 in 1964, al-Shawaribi had been visited by Malcolm X, just out of the Nation of Islam, who was moved by al-Shawaribi's rather basic and chirpy *Readers' Digest*–like presentation of Islam as the religion of peace and love: all Muslims were brothers regardless of color or race, al-Shawaribi expounded from the Qur'an. A long-standing narrative in U.S. books runs that after Malcolm left Elijah in 1964, al-Shawaribi led him over several weeks from his ongoing condemnations of all whites as devils to the view of Islam as a multi-racial religion of "democracy" compatible with science within modernity, the standard view in Nasser's Egypt. Two letters of recommendation from al-Shawaribi got Malcolm into Mecca with accommodation from the former Secretary-General of the League o Arab States, 'Abd al-Rahman 'Azzam, and his family, all, like al-Shawaribi, politically conservative, Islam-minded, Egyptians who did not always love the Leader, Gamal 'Abd al-Nasser, a social upstart.[160] In reality, Malcolm had met al-Shawaribi, and been soaking up ideas from Sunni Arabs, long before 1964. Malcolm's conversion to a universalist Sunni Islam was no sudden leap but a late culmination of many years of interaction with foreign Muslims of a good caliber stationed in the States.

In a way an admirer of modernist Anglo-America, the Nasser-era technocrat al-Shawaribi saw sharply that African-Americans were being incorporated into the U.S. mainstream in the 1950s. He saw them less as victims or disadvantaged or poor, and more as an element that was already strong in American life and becoming more so: and he was concerned to affiliate Islam, Egypt and the Arabs to that strength. "The brown Americans ... have gradually entered in notable numbers into the great cities of America, especially into Washington, New York and Chicago, and now occupy leading positions in diverse governmental departments." Al-Shawaribi was attuned to the rise of African-American professional classes who were getting specialized education: he considered Howard University in Washington "among the greatest universities in America." He had too rosy a view of how much desegregation America had really been able to actualize as the 1950s closed, positing that now (1959) African-Americans had "absolutely" equal access to education "following the Supreme Court's [1954] decision prohibiting any form of discrimination in education."[161]

Al-Shawaribi's calculations of the imminent strength of African-Americans in the U.S. mainstream makes us wonder if he did not have political motives in addition to the religious imperative to spread correct Islam that, for him, was primary. FBI agents visited him in New York. Awareness that he and other Arab lecturers and officials in America had to operate in an environment where the government and its agencies could turn hostile at any moment may have inhibited political activity by him in America, and even what he spoke or wrote in the Arabic language (of which American agencies as yet only had a primitive grasp). But he, like the Palestinian Jami Diyab—and 'Abd al-Rahman 'Azzam in Sa'udi Arabia?—was critical of 'Abd al-Nasser, whom he viewed as an inexperienced young officer who was long incompetent in administration and lacked any broader culture. Instead of truly uniting the Arabs, Nasser was dividing them though his personality clashes with the established, experienced Arab leaders. These were Arabs intent to spread their standardized (but post-traditional, slimmed) Islam in America but who would put little hope in any activities by the post-1952 Nasser regime to build up a political alliance (the counter-lobby) with African-Americans.[162]

Al-Shawaribi could have had more empathy for NOI anger at aspects of American reality. Unlike Sadat and other political officials Malcolm X met in Egypt, he felt, or at least wrote, that the NOI's denunciations of "white devils" deformed Islam. He could have made some allowances for the African-

Americans' sustained brutalization by Euro-Americans that made them look inhuman to blacks, whom that trauma then turned towards an alternative, justice-based non-Western religion. Al-Shawaribi was also disturbed by the refusal of "a section" of the NOI to be conscripted into the armed forces, which he felt "infuriated [U.S.] governmental institutions", while the "inimical posture that the NOI adopts to other religions [Christianity, Judaism] ... is something Islam can never validate."[163] His concern here—similar to denunciations by Jamil Diyab of the "devils" tenet after he left Elijah—appears to have been to present an image of Islam as a religion of almost theosophical harmony. That was to fit Arabs and other Muslims coming from abroad for quick acceptance in an American society that already in theory had in it a supra-Christian ethos affirmed, for example, by Freemasonry, theosophism and by the literary tradition of Transcendentalism.

In al-Shawaribi's view, elements in their own cultural make-up or self-identification were pushing the Black Muslims towards the Arab and Muslim countries. However, al-Shawaribi intended a process designed not to absorb the sect but to reconstruct the identity it already had put together: the group would continue and always govern itself. He hoped study in Egypt would Sunnify NOI youth, and planned for seven NOI students to go to Egypt to form "a core" for a stratum of scholars and technical graduates in the sect, who then would themselves "guide their people and their relatives on their return after they complete their tasks in Egypt."[164] The memory of Diyab was that Elijah was opposed to sending even his son, Akbar, to the mosque-university of al-Azhar because of "his fear that his son would learn of the mistakes in which they had been brought up."[165]

Al-Shawaribi projected in the late 1950s that Arab missionary outreach, if well-planned, "in a very short time will lead the overwhelming majority of this sector of the American population into Islam."[166]

Elijah tried to prevent at least one follower from going to study in Egypt, and his Chicago temple sometimes turned away Arab students and scholars from visiting.[167] The failure of Elijah Muhammad to stop Arabs and foreign Muslims from changing his followers illustrates the limited power of the discourses of charismatic leaders even over sects whose ideologies give divine authority to those leaders' dictatorships. Frequent NOI denunciations of "hypocrites" under Elijah show adherents carving out a discreet initiative in their own lives and thoughts. But who was two-faced? When he converted them, Elijah had promised them humane exchanges with overseas Muslims: "you are not a Negro from this day on, but a free independent Asiatic Muslim with Allah, and a billion of brothers and sisters throughout the world, on your side as friends."[168] The converts duly made sure that their membership delivered on that covenant. They bent and stepped around some empty images, fictions and mythologies of Elijah to forge a real transcontinental community of Islam.

The Patterns of Ideology and Discourse to 1975

Although they do not rise to the brilliant oratory of a Malcolm X,

Elijah's writings hang together well even in our new century. The faint echoes of Gullah creole syntax created an impression of folk-belief, of something immemorial and wholesome resurging—lost family now regained—which many African-American intellectuals, too, took away from meetings with Elijah, although in his discourse it concealed the newness of the religion that Fard and he innovated. Elijah's simple food made James Baldwin "feel extremely decadent," and back in his father's natural, modest house, although he was really in the mansion of a religio-political leader. Elijah had a way of making educated Blacks feel guilty that they smoked and sipped.[169] Elijah had his own aesthetic and individual presence as he recycled, broke down, mixed, fused and blended in a new structure (a) eschatalogical materials from the Old and New Testaments; (b) images or emotive phrases atomized or taken in fragments from the Qur'an; (c) shocking, vivid or sensational images of past U.S. realities; (e) self-enriching and scientific-modernist drives covertly seized from middle-class American ideologies of the white devils; and (f) materials from earlier Black nationalist ideologies, especially that around Garvey.

Elijah could passionately preach the imminence of God's destruction of the whites. Yet suddenly a reductionist tone recurs that focuses upon quickly-changing realities of U.S. society, and sounds rational or pragmatic for a charismatic quasi-prophet by the simple fact that it is so turned-off from any emotion. In such passages, he offers in very succinct Anglo-Saxon vocabulary the simple essence of some white behavior or attitudes or groups where these threatened the vital interests of U.S. blacks—or sometimes about opportunities and ways they left open for Blacks to exit from their low socio-economic status. Elijah's employment of basic, flat rational language to analyze the oppression against African-Americans would likely have come as a shock to Euro-Americans; after all, they had stressed Elijah's painfully limited education and assessed his IQ as at the level of a twelve-year-old's when they had him in jail. For a Negro to analyze Euro-Americans astutely and with clarity would be a disturbing turn of events for them.

Elijah's more basic or unadorned formulations also chilled some African-Americans who vaguely felt him to be evil: they sensed him as a pseudo-parent manipulating a repertoire when he first drew an emotionally needy Malcolm X into the sect. Yet Malcolm X would not have become a protest leader of Blacks without Elijah and his teaching. Any potential problem of toxicity with al-Hajj Elijah Muhammad might well inhere in many political leaders or heads of institutions, anywhere.

Elijah's more laconic, stripped-down formulations—about black opposition groups, not whites only—had affinities to the similarly skeletal, not quite human, reports of white U.S. agencies in those years, narrowly concerned to ferret out things about enemy humans that might help to undo them, or break them up, or rub them out, or take them over. On the other hand, altruistic or at least wide national streaks in Elijah—who to be sure set an almost religious value on the liberation afforded by money—are clear in his bursts of concern to secure the interests not just of his sect-members but also of wider strata of African-Americans that unabashedly sought integration. His often was a sect with real solidarity of communities, Black or Islamic, a nationalist movement intent to advance the whole African-American struggle: this old Nation of Islam was far more than a personal wealth-accumulating sect structured to enrich and empower a Leader (or a clique of cronies).

Elijah could be generous with money when he wanted to be. Both the disturbing and the shrewd tones of some of his more stripped-down communications, just like his more altruistic, nationalist, impulses, may well have proceeded from his very Anglo-originated American-ness, although Islam and the Arabs too provided some distinctive tints. Elijah's skeletal, analytical impulse reads as highly modern as against post-modern assumptions that there usually can be no simple essence because most human things and *courants* have deeper multiplicities that are all at the essence of their being—which we saw was somewhat so of some of the NOI's followers vis-à-vis America, and to a lesser extent of even the discourse of Elijah that could become ambiguous or constructive to whites at odd places.

Charisma theory may come to categorize Elijah Muhammad alongside the cold, legalistic, skeletal Muhammad 'Ali Jinnah, the founding father who carved Muslim Pakistan out of a mainly Hindu India. Both men felt remote in their thinly-veiled Westernist-modernizing projects from the cultures and languages of the masses they tried to galvanize by evoking the Divine and Islam. Elijah's Nation of Islam and the movement to carve Pakistan from India were alike to the extent that both chose separatism (albeit territorial separatism in Pakistan's case) as a means to create, from a desperate starting-point, a private-enterprise economy. Each was crafted to become a self-sustaining circuit apart from the economies of India's much more developed Anglos and Hindu majority, or that of the U.S. WASPs. Each movement gave an Islamic religious value to a separated economy and to the imminent prosperity it was promised to be bringing. Both movements unfolded in continent-wide states that had tendencies to become systems with segregated castes. On one plane, both these Islam-based movements were playing with fire: the religious history each evoked could detonate massive communal violence with two opposed groups that were much more numerous. Yet somehow each movement inducted many from rising urban-professional classes intent to build banks and businesses that needed stability.[170]

On the whole, Elijah's religio-political discourse of the 1960s and 1970s did provide an energizing account of the situation of African-Americans, often cast in religious myths. His non-passionate mode, though, also identified some very cautious economic lines on which they could develop out of their inferiorized condition and imposed undevelopment. While such strategies of Elijah sound considerably like the discourses of some non-Anglo Euro-American groups that gained entry from the margins of the American system, he usually blended the broad range of elements that he cut out from America's Angloid mainstream culture, from Christianity, and from the Arabs and Islam so seamlessly that few African-Americans he targeted ever guessed how syncretic the whole system was. He had made a new structure that served the urgent interests of African-Americans in America. Despite this, his discourse has a disturbing texture joltingly unlike the structure of either of the two great world religions on which he drew. One feels, in reading his speeches and articles, that one is confronted with a new and unfamiliar ethos, like Mormonism—although Elijah failed to pen or dictate any convincing new successor-scripture to the Qur'an and Bible that would have made his sect an independent religion for the long term.

Elijah Muhammad had a seminal influence upon all Black protest movements articulated by a new generation of African-Americans in the 1960s and 1970s. Eldridge Cleaver's initial protest personality formed in prison at a time in the early 1960s when Elijah Muhammad was winning many converts in prisons across the USA: they soon became the single most powerful group among California's convicts. Elijah Muhammad's campaigns to restore family by purging the ghettoes of drugs, alcohol and the resultant brawls and jail-terms that together served to destroy home life did appeal to these atomized Blacks' yearning for community. Cleaver reminisced that this sector of Elijah's thought was subsequently carried forward by the future Black Panther Party when it took up its guns to run drug syndicates out of the ghetto areas. Yet, as an imprisoned Muslim, Cleaver already preferred Malcolm X's concentration upon politics in contrast to Elijah's "love of theologizing", and as he graduated to Mao and hung Stalin's picture on his wall, voiced less and less comprehension of Elijah's strategy of construction of a black private enterprise by new middle-American families as a strategy towards viable autonomy and liberation.[171] Yet even Elijah's theology left its mark on the now emerging Black Panther movement: his application of images of "the Beast" and Babylon from the Book of Revelation to America was reiterated by Cleaver while in exile in Algeria in the 1970s.[172]

Yet Cleaver—like some Ministers of Elijah's mosques in private—could not assent to the Messenger's "white devils" tenet. Some Panthers hated whites almost to a similar degree, but the impulses in the Panthers for community with whites—at first just with the liberals and the leftists—were much stronger. Marx and Engels' socio-political and economic categories made leftist Panthers more narrowly rather oppose a ruling white clique that enslaved some whites as well as blacks. Cleaver refused to "make wild generalizations à la Muslims".[173]

In the end, Elijah Muhammad could not truly make his system a complete closed circuit that might have offered clear and inescapable solutions to the major problems. His throbbing prophesies of Divine incineration of the race-enemy ruled out whites ever accepting him as a political leader of Blacks who could ever negotiate any conceivable settlement with the opposed dominant group. Elijah sometimes very faintly toyed with the idea that whites might take on humane qualities or be granted loopholes and reprieves, and therefore grant his sect a modest niche in America. But he was too bound by his decades of millenarian warnings, the original source of his nationalist authority—by God and God's incineration—to make too many deals without imploding his leadership.

ENDNOTES

1 Another term in common international-legal usage for this phenomenon is "non-territorial minorities".

2 Classic characterizations of charisma and charismatic leaders in societies are to be found throughout Max Weber, *The Theory of Social and Economic Organization* tsd and edt by A.M. Henderson and Talcott Parsons (New York: Free Press 1947), and in *From Max Weber: Essays in Sociology*, tsd and edt by H.H. Gerth and C. Wright Mills ((New York: OUP 1958). See also Ann Ruth Willner, *Charismatic Political Leadership: A Theory* (Princeton University: Center for International Studies 1968) and idem *The Spellbinders: Charismatic Political Leadership* (Yale University Press 1984).

3 Summary of 3000 FBI letters, memos and teletypes released to the American Civil Liberties Union in "FBI 'helped Klan to fight protests'", Melbourne *Age* 21 August 1978 p. 8.

4 Jabril Muhammad, "Repentance of the accuser: the ADL's attack on Farrakhan," *Final Call* 10 November 1998 pp. 26-7.

5 Mattius Gardell, *In the Name of Elijah Muhammad: Louis Farrakhan and the Nation of Islam* (Carolina: Duke University Press and London: Hurst 1996) p. 96.

6 King did not formally use Marxist class terminology in the address to striking sanitation workers in Memphis that he gave shortly before his assassination. As well as wages and securities, the workers before him were fighting for the right to organize: "we can all get more together than we can apart". King quoted Walter Reuther that power is the ability of a labor union to make the most powerful corporation in the world, General Motors, say yes when it wants to say no. Freedom and equality were never "voluntarily given by the oppressor; it is something that must be demanded by the oppressed." "In Remembrance of Martin Luther King, Jr.", Service Employees Union 6:1 (Winter 1992) pp. 28-29. Walter Reuther (1907-1970) began his career as a trade unionist after a 3-year tour of Europe in which he worked in the Gorky automobile plant in the Soviet Union for a time. He progressively organized automobile workers throughout the USA, wresting important benefits from the Ford company. Reuther worked with the U.S. system in the mass production of aircraft during WWII but organized a strike of automobile workers in 1945 as the War ended. He became impatient with the sluggish pace with which U.S. unions' federations were winning better conditions for the workers in the post-War 1950s and 1960s.

7 Seth Forman, *Blacks in the Jewish Mind: A Crisis of Liberalism* (NYUP 1998) p. 70.

8 (New York: Free Press 1969).

9 Jonathon Kaufman, *Broken Alliance: The Turbulent Times between Blacks and Jews in America* (New York: Scribner's Sons 1988) p. 133.

10 Quoted Fred Powledge, *Black Power, White Resistance: Notes on the New Civil War* (Cleveland: World Publishing Co 1967) p. 11.

11 Stokely Carmichael and Charles Hamilton, *Black Power: The Politics of Liberation in America* (New York: Random House 1967) p. 44.

12 Ted Hughes, *American Visions* (BBC-Time 1996), televised Australian Broadcasting Commission 7 May 2000.

13 Account of neo-Muslim Floyd Saks in Claude Brown, *Manchild in the Promised Land* (Penguin Books 1969) pp. 342-343.

14 Alphonso Pinkney *Red, Black and Green: Black Nationalism in the United States* (CUP: 1978) p. 77.

15 (New Jersey: Prentice Hall 1968).

16 Powledge, *Black Power* p. 11.

17 *Message To the Blackman in America.*

18 Harold 4X, "Psychologists study relationship of skin color and behavior", *Muhammad Speaks* 20 December 1974 p. 18.

19 Gardell, *In the Name of Elijah Muhammad: Louis Farrakhan and the Nation of*

Islam pp. 239-241.

20 Gardell, *In the Name of Elijah Muhammad* passim; E.U. Essien-Udom, *Black Nationalism: A Search for an Identity in America* (Chicago: University of Chicago Press 1962).

21 Peter Goldman, *The Death and Life of Malcolm X* (London: Gollancz 1974) p. 397.

22 Arthur J. Magida, *Prophet of Rage: a Life of Louis Farrakhan and his Nation of Islam* (New York: Basic Books 1996) p. 104.

23 Elijah Muhammad, *The Fall of America* (Chicago: Muhammad's Temple of Islam No. 2 1973) pp. 175-6.

24 Elijah Muhammad, *The Fall of America* pp. 58-72.

25 *Fall* p. 71.

26 *Fall* p. 72.

27 *Fall* p. 6.

28 J. Gordon Melton, *Encyclopaedic Handbook of Cults in America* (New York: Garland Publishing Inc 1986) pp.249-250; Clark Howard, *Zebra* (New York: Berkely Books 1980).

29 Lincoln, *The Black Muslims in America* (1973) pp. 5-6; 1994 pp. 3-4

30 "Muhammad Meets the Press", *Muhammad Speaks* 28 January 1972. The fighters had come to the NOI's Baton Rouge mosque expecting aid.

31 *Fall* pp. 44-45.

32 *Fall* p. 100.

33 Magida p. 104.

34 Gardell pp. 238-244.

35 *Fall* pp. 20-21.

36 *Fall* pp. 199-200.

37 *Fall* pp. 3-4.

38 *Fall* p. 13.

39 *Fall* pp. 13-14.

40 *Fall* pp. 14-15.

41 *Fall* p. 21.

42 *Fall* pp. 60-61.

43 *Fall* pp. 22-25.

44 Studs Terkel, *Race: How Blacks and Whites Think and Feel About the American Obsession* (New York: The New Press 1992) p. 167.

45 Louis A. DeCaro Jr, *Malcolm and the Cross: the Nation of Islam, Christianity and Malcolm X* (New York: OUP 1998) pp. 5-7.

46 *Fall* p. 22.

47 *Fall* p.165. For the tenets of Judgement that the first NOI borrowed from the Witnesses, see Claude A. Clegg, *An Original Man: The Life and Times of Elijah Muhammad* (New York: Saint Martin's Press 1997) pp. 72 and 56.

48 Elijah Muhammad, *Message to the Blackman* (1965) summarized by Zafar Ishaq Ansari, "Aspects of Black Muslim Theology", *Studia Islamica* v. 53 (1981) p. 155.

49 Gardell op cit p. 135.

50 *Fall* p. 161.

51 *Fall* pp. 221-222.

52 cf Qu'ran 73:17 *Fall* p. 151-2.

53 *Fall* p. 164.

54 Goldman p. 97; cf Arna Bontemps and Jack Conroy, *Anyplace But Here* (New York: Hill and Wang 1966) pp. 236-237. Our second chapter established that the "Allahu Akbar" —the recurring cry that "Allah is the Greatest" in the face of white power —was one of the Arabic phrases of Islamic prayer brought from Africa that had survived faintly in African-American folk memory into the 1940s. Calligraphic representations in Arabic letters maintained the phrase among the ministers leading Elijah's sect in the 1950s: see Essien-Udom op cit p. 81.

55 Clegg *Original Man* pp. 169-171.

56 Kofi Natambu, *The Life and Work of Malcolm X* (Indianapolis: Alpha 2002) pp. 251-255.

57 cf Qur'an 5:69 *Fall* pp. 24-25. The phrase "la khawfa 'alayhim wa la yahzanun"

(they shall not know fear nor shall they grieve [in the outcome]) is often applied to the believers who hold firmly to God by Qur'an: cf 2:38, 2:62, 2:112, 2:262, 2:274, 2:277, 3:170, 6:48, 35, 10:62, 43:68.

58 "Resurrection of Our People", *Fall* p. 43.

59 *Fall* p. 44.

60 Qur'an 41:44: "had we made it a scripture in a foreign language, they would have said 'why have its verses not been made clear—what! a non-Arabic scripture and an Arab prophet!'": Qur'an 43:3: "We have made it an Arabic Qur'an in order that you will understand": Qur'an 41:3;13:37; 20:113; 46:12; 26:192-199; 39:28; 42:7.

61 *Fall* p. 44.

62 *Fall* pp. 138-139.

63 *Fall* p. 141.

64 *Fall* p. 206.

65 Washington Irving, *The Life of Mahomet* (London: John Murray 1850) pp. 310-313. For a bi-cultural pairing by Elijah of Judas and Musaylimah as both the embodiments of supreme treachery, see *Fall* p. 83—which could make Elijah Jesus and Muhammad Ibn 'Abdallah both in one.

66 See Bruce Perry, *Malcolm: The Life of a Man who Changed Black America* (New York: Station Hill 1991) p. 328.

67 "Messenger Elijah Muhammad's Pilgrimage to Mecca", *Salaam* July 1960; www.Muhammadspeaks.com 6 March 2002.

68 "Reverent Dignity at Muhammad's Rites", *Muhammad Speaks* 21 March 1975 p. 5.

69 Lincoln, *The Black Muslims in America* (1st ed) pp. 234-5.

70 "Faith and Obedience in Allah and His Messenger", *Muhammad Speaks* 28 February 1975. While this item's usage of "Mussa" for Moses is close to a bilingual Qur'an such as that of the Ahmadi Muhammad 'Ali, the name—with this spelling—also turned up in advertisements for the recapture of runaways under slavery as one of the African "country names" that some enslaved Africans kept up alongside the Western names imposed on them. See Sheila S. Walker, "What's in a Name?: Black Awareness Keeps the African Tradition of Meaningful Names Alive", *Ebony* June 1977.

71 Cushmeer cited Ansari, "Theology" p. 151.

72 Goldman op cit p. 65.

73 Elijah Muhammad, *Fall* pp. 99-100.

74 *Fall* p.124.

75 Malcolm X, *Autobiography,* p. 373.

76 Derryn Hinch, "Heroes come down to Earth—with a thud", *Herald* (Melbourne) 2-3 November 1985 p. 7.

77 Gardell, *Farrakhan* p. 47; DeCaro, *Malcolm and the Cross* pp. 24-25; a somewhat different lynch narrative is offered by Clegg, *Original Man* p. 10.

78 *Fall* 88-89.

79 Clegg p. 158.

80 Wilfred Cantwell-Smith in 1943/1946 found that Madiyan, the movement's headquarters, once a village, had become "a thriving town undergoing a minor capitalist boom". The sect was founding industries there and had bought farmland to provide work for its peasant members, which Elijah was to attempt in the USA's Deep South. See Smith, *Modern Islam in India: A Social Analysis* (Lahore: S.M. Ashraf 1969) p. 371.

81 Clegg 374: this employment of whites was also noted by the African-American left-nationalist Alphonso Pinkney (1976) in his *Red, Black and Green* p. 161, where it is interpreted as pragmatism and a "policy of separating religion from business".

82 Clegg, *Original Man* 256.

83 "Muhammad Meets the Press", *Muhammad Speaks* 28 January 1972.

84 Louis A. DeCaro Jr, *On the Side of my People: A Religious Life of Malcolm X* (New York University Press 1996) p 135.

85 *Fall* pp. 84-86. An article from the *Wall Street Journal* to which Elijah referred

was by staff reporter Neil Maxwell and published in the issue of 25 November 1969.

86 Clegg, *An Original Man* pp. 253-254: the Nation lost $682,000 in failed agricultural schemes.

87 *Fall* p.165.

88 Gardell p. 309.

89 *Fall* p.19.

90 *Fall* pp. 233-4.

91 Gardell pp. 78-79.

92 Elijah Muhammad , "When Abe Lincoln, J.F. Kennedy Spoke Out for Negroes," reprinted as chapter 7, *Fall* pp. 33-35.

93 Elijah Muhammad, "Is Modern America as Merciless as Ancient Ninevah?" *Fall* pp. 116-118.

94 *Fall* p. 151.

95 *Fall* pp. 36-37.

96 Edgar Litt, *Beyond Pluralism: Ethnic Politics in America* (Glenview, Illinois: Scott Foreman and Company 1970) p. 87: for the overall process of accommodation, pp. 85-90.

97 Charles V. Hamilton, *Adam Clayton Powell Jr: the Political Biography of an American Dilemma* (New York: Atheneum-MacMillan 1963) pp. 354-365. It should be checked how far Powell in the 1930s was influenced by Muslim protest cults in Harlem as well as by the Jewish organizations that gave him fora and funds.

98 *Autobiography* p. 202.

99 Alex Haley in introduction, Malcolm X *Autobiography* p. 66. Nonetheless, Powell must have been one source of more Americanist statements by the evolving Malcolm X that African-Americans should institutionalize their power as a lobby within U.S. parliamentarism. Only, the more like seasoned U.S. politician Powell that Malcolm became, the abler he could be to run against him

100 *Fall* p. 47.

101 *Fall* pp. 60-62.

102 Lonnie Kashif (Washington bureau), "Government avows brain control experiments: Behavior modification more prevalent than ever", *Muhammad Speaks* 20 December 1974 p. 4.

103 Abdul Allah Muhammad, "Eleven Fifty-Five: It's Gotta Be This or That", *Final Call* 3 September 1996 p. 5. The [*Chicago Tribune*] article "Now let the Democrats praise Elijah Muhammad" that had just been published in the *Chicago Tribune* giving Bond's account had appeared in its 23 August 1996 edition.

104 Atlanta Mayor Maynard Jackson's affirmative action program raised the minorities' share of city contracts from less than 1% to 38% within 5 years and produced 25 new Black millionaires: "Former Atlanta mayor dies", *Final Call* 1 July 2003 p. 38.

105 "Messenger of Allah Meets the Press", *Muhammad Speaks* 11 February 1972; www.Muhammadspeaks.com 6 March 2002.

106 Lawrence C. X and James Hoard Smith, "Farrakhan warns Blacks 'stay vigilant'", *Muhammad Speaks* 14 September 1975 p. 7.

107 *Fall* p. 80.

108 *Fall* pp. 80-81.

109 *Fall* pp. 81-82.

110 *Autobiography* p. 425.

111 *Fall* p. 82.

112 David Gallen, *Malcolm A to X: The Man and His Ideas* (New York: Carroll & Graf 1992) p. 42.

113 *Fall* p. 79.

114 Eldridge Cleaver, *Soul on Ice* (New York: Dell Publishing 1992) pp. 94-95

115 *Fall* pp. 255-257.

116 Perry, *Malcolm* p. 243.

117 Joe X (Flake), acting minister at M.C.I, "Prison officials commend Muslim's deportment", *Muhammad Speaks* 20 December 1974 p. 15.

118 "Indiana senator demands *Muhammad Speaks* in prison", *Muhammad Speaks* 14

February 1975 p. 21.

119 Harold 4X, "Black Chief of police overcomes many obstacles: Atlanta's 'Super Chief' scores high with Blacks", *Muhammad Speaks* 20 December 1974 p. 21.

120 John H. McWhorter, *Losing the Race: Self-Sabotage in Black America* (New York: The Free Press 2000) pp. 66-67.

121 Unsourced excerpt from Elijah in "Of Land and Nation" at www.Muhammadspeaks.com 22 February 2002.

122 Algernon Austin, "Rethinking Race and the Nation of Islam, 1930-1975", *Ethnic and Racial Studies* (26:1) January 2003 pp. 63, 60.

123 Essien-Udom p. 119.

124 Memories of Malcolm's deputy Benjamin Karim in Gallen, *Malcolm A to X* p. 98.

125 Gardell p. 194.

126 Essien-Udom, *Black Nationalism* pp. 89-90 Sexual predation by Euro-Americans was particularly glaring in the small towns and countryside of the Deep South, from which many who converted to the NOI in the North's cities hailed.

127 Reprinted from Elijah's 1965 *Message to the Blackman*: Elijah Muhammad "The Black Woman", *Final Call* 20 August 1996 p. 19.

128 Essien-Udom, p. 275.

129 Magida *Prophet of Rage* p. 68.

130 Essien-Udom, op cit pp. 291-297.

131 Gardell p. 206. The probability is that Nasser put Elijah Muhammad up while he was in Egypt.

132 Gardell op cit p. 206.

133 "Thank the Libyan People in Africa for loaning $3,000,000", *Muhammad Speaks* 19 May 1972.

134 (Editorial) "Pride goeth before destruction", *Final Call* 24 February 1992 p. 16.

135 Gardell p. 393.

136 The 1960 census had set Muslims at 12% of the Ghanaian population, "Christians" at 42.8% and animists at 38.2%. There were important Muslim communities in the North in particular, and Muslim quarters or zongos in the towns of the South as well as in Ashantiland.

137 Essien-Udom p. 280.

138 Essien-Udom p. 233. Dr Nnamdi Azikiwe (1905-1996) was editor of the *West African Pilot*, a tribune of feverish Nigerian nationalists: he became President of Nigeria on its independence in 1960. Although of the Christianized Ibo ethnos, he only reluctantly supported the Biafran secession in 1966: as a young man, he had studied Islam as a potential ideology for Nigerian independence, but did not opt for it.

139 Essien-Udom p. 234.

140 Eric C. Lincoln, *The Black Muslims in America* (Michigan; Eerdmons and New York: Africa World Press 1994) pp. 211-212.

141 Kasisi Weusi, "A View from the East: the New Nation of Islam", *Black News* March 1976 p. 14.

142 Phone conversation with Jamil Diyab 24 March 2002.

143 Essien-Udom, pp. 238, 318-319.

144 Zafar Ishaq Ansari, "W. D. Muhammad: the Making of a 'Black Muslim' Leader (1933-1961)", *American Journal of Islamic Social Sciences* (v. 2:2) pp. 255-6.

145 Phone conversation with Jamil Diyab 24 March 2002. Diyab's Palestine teachers' diploma blended Western and Arabo-Islamic components, consisting of psychology, pedagogy, Islamic religion and the Arabic language.

146 Gardell p. 195.

147 Layla Diyab, "Modern Day Islamic Thought Through the Eyes of Jamil Diab: A Time for Transition and Reflection", *Muslim Journal* 10 May 1996.

148 Essien-Udom p. 318; Lincoln (1961) p. 170.

149 Telephone conversations with Jamil Diyab in Phoenix, 27 February 2001 and 24 March 2002.

150 Essien-Udom op cit p. 319.

151 *Adrift In the Heartland*, ninety-minutes long and filmed in Chicago and Palestine

with a volunteer cast of actors and students, had its debut screening on November 29th, 2000 on the Day of International Solidarity with Palestine. It was screened in community and religious centers throughout the city of Chicago during the winter and spring of 2001. Brigid Mahar held a Master in Fine Arts from Northwestern University and was teaching film production at Columbia College. Data from Layla Diyab, Chicago.

152 Data from Layla Diyab.

153 "An Islamic Center is Organized Here", *NYT* 24 March 1955 p. 41. al-Shawaribi was at Fordham and Maryland universities.

154 Dr Mahmud Yusuf al-Shawaribi, *al-Islam fi Amrika* (Cairo 1960) pp. 127-128.

155 Ibid pp. 128, 130.

156 Ibid p. 131.

157 Ibid p. 132.

158 Ibid p. 132.

159 Kofi Natambu, *The Life and Work of Malcolm X* (Indianapolis: Alpha 2002) pp. 234-235.

160 Peter Goldman, *The Death and Life of Malcolm X* (London: Gollancz 1974) pp. 164-5.

161 al-Shawaribi, *al-Islam fi Amrika* p. 134.

162 Phone conversation of 28 December 2003 with Dr Jamil Diyab. A relative of al-Shawaribi may have suffered under the Nasserite regime. It was untrue that Nasser lacked broad culture since he had in his youth written an anti-imperialist novel modeled on Tawfiq al-Hakim's neo-Pharaonist nationalist novel *The Return of the Spirit ('Awdat al-Ruh*: 1933), in which the charismatic Sa'd Zaghlul mobilizes the Egyptian masses for independence from the British as a new Pharaoh whom their ancient identity conditions them to obey. Nasser's Minister of Culture Tharwat 'Ukasha presided over a vast program of translations to diffuse the masterpieces of Western literatures among the whole range of literate classes in the Arab world. Nasser's land reforms were the most effective in modern Middle Eastern history: possible feudal class links of al-Shawaribi, the 'Azzam family and Diyab certainly should be explored.

163 Ibid p. 129.

164 Ibid p. 135.

165 Telephone conversation with Jamil Diyab 24 March 2002.

166 al-Shawaribi, *al-Islam fi Amrika* 134.

167 Essien-Udom pp. 263, 184-5.

168 Essien-Udom p. 200.

169 James Baldwin, *The Fire Next Time* (New York: Dial Press 1963) pp. 71-86.

170 For the case of Jinnah see Dr Sikandar Hayat, "Charisma, Crisis and the Emergence of Quaid-i-Azam" *Journal of the Pakistan Historical Society* 50:1-2 pp. 31-46.

171 Cleaver, *Soul on Fire* (Waco: Ward Books 1978; London: Hodder and Stroughton 1979) pp. 74-77.

172 Lee Lockwood, *Conversations with Eldridge Cleaver* (New York: McGraw-Hill 1970) p. 53, excerpted *Soul on Fire* p. 92.

173 *Soul on Fire* p. 93.

Chapter Five

Elijah Muhammad's Muslims in a Changing America

Elijah Muhammad's Nation of Islam had been the only serious (if ambiguous) Black Nationalist movement in America in the 1950s and early 1960s. After 1965, though, African-American groups with sharpening nationalistic outlooks multiplied, as did the class components of the African-American minority. Clearly, the NOI's thought widely tinged those newer groups even when they argued with it. An issue here, though, was how far the wider strata and their reception of Elijah would modify the NOI's activities and concepts, or retard the sect's expansion.

Black Nationalism became the dominant identification among African-Americans after 1965. The lack of any wide area with a black majority was more and more seen to rule out classical secessionist Nationalism as a strategy for self-determination. As economic change and speeding admission into the central society scattered Blacks and Jews and more individuals lost continuous "national" territory, the homeland could become only the land under such individuals' feet at a given moment—the "micro-homeland." Elijah strove to integrate that separated, atomized Black Nation through a collective economy, media and modernist lines of communication that could cross continents. Thus, U.S. Blacks and Jews were both at that same time heading towards deterritorialized micronationalisms where new instruments knit together a particularistic micronation that can be millions strong without any sizeable homeland.

1. THE NOI IN ECONOMIC MODERNIZATION OF BLACKS

From 1964-1975, the last decade of Elijah's life, the movements and power-centers proliferating among African-Americans increasingly defined America's Negro minority as an "Afro-American" or "Black" "nation." These expanding groups' shift to nationality made African-Americans more open to the NOI's themes, and to its leadership claims. While the NOI duly recruited many from the new currents, it was not modernizing fast enough to achieve hegemony over that whole spectrum. Elijah and his colleagues now had to engage with (a) the now-seasoned "civil rights" politicians and their followers in the new bourgeoisie; (b) new Black nationalist, "Black Power", spin-offs from civil rights that responded—but with reservations—to the NOI tradition;

(c) young neo-bourgeois blacks falling under the influence of the campus whites' New Left, including its permissiveness, and of Marxist or Maoist scriptures; (d) neo-Sunni African-Americans in and outside his sect and (e) a phenomenally expanding stratum of young professional blacks who, like Elijah, were fired by the premises of the American dream and capitalist private enterprise—the would-be entrepreneurs and the parastatal white-collar employees.

As they reviewed the now-dead Elijah and the old particularist Nation of Islam after 1975, the sect's drive to express African-American nationhood in economic enterprises rather than achieve it through insurrection was one legacy that struck a range of African-American groups beyond the sect. Among the Africanist nationalists, Randy Simmons (1976) evaluated that the Nation of Islam had demonstrated "something to the rest of Black people that was unprecedented: that by sticking together and putting its members' money together, the Nation could make important social and economic gains." Elijah's NOI had proved that blacks could do well in small and medium-sized businesses.[1]

Class Status Shifts through Conversion

Elijah sharply caught the torn feelings and dilemma of the post-World War II black bourgeoisie who wanted to live at the standard of living of the white middle classes, but doubted that they would be given enough jobs and opportunities to sustain that. He tried to project a continuity of ill-treatment throughout African-American history, but was uneasily aware of recent ambiguities and shifts. For four hundred years, America had prospered from the labor of her Black slaves. Now, though, she sometimes "pays the Black man high wages and salaries and then takes them back from him through the high cost of living". [Not a problem faced by Black employees only!] Elijah's situation-driven, and perhaps only temporary, asceticism condemned the conspicuous consumption that stopped blacks who wanted to succeed from accumulating the initial capital needed to start them out in business, and for community development. It was "trying to live according to the way the white man lives [that] keeps the Black man down." In the mid-20th century, the continuing drive of the white man to keep the Black man in a condition of poverty and inequality nullified the promise the whites' Constitution held out to all human beings in America. The bourgeois blacks had acquired the education of the white man, but when made unable to compete with him, create trouble to find a way to self-prosperity. Elijah Muhammad had sharp insights into this opposed, self-interested, bourgeois class that had been expanding in the 1950s and 1960s as America boomed. It now was raising Black nationalist trouble on TV in order to get further in and earn more money.[2] Many members of the class had long felt the position they had painfully won was threatened by destabilizing rhetoric from Elijah. But now some were advancing some of the same themes as Elijah and TV super-star Malcolm to blackmail their personal or class advancement from the governing whites—"Mau-mauing the flak-catchers", as Tom Wolfe, a popular white southern writer of the period, put it.[3]

Elijah's condemnation of the bourgeoisie's consumptionism was astute pragmatism more than a fixed dogma: he condemned their living beyond their and their nation's means *at that stage in time*. His sect's asceticism had always been crafted to get the blacks out of underdevelop-ment, and could lapse when that condition did. One day it might become practicable even for adherents of the NOI to embark upon bourgeois consumerism. Indeed, Elijah himself already owned Cadillacs. In formulations of this type, Elijah was alertly abreast of the improved opportunities and every swing of mood and tactics of that bourgeoisie. He was far from the senile, disorientated, "drooling" old man, serving as a Mao-like aged ventriloquist's dummy for advisers around him churning out press statements under his name, that the young Eldridge Cleaver, who inclined to al-Hajj Malcolm, perceived from his prison.[4]

Many NOI activists whom non-Muslim Blacks encountered in the 1970s had skilled upper working-class status, and hopes to ascend further from that to middle-class roles. Yet hatred of whites as a fuel to integrate a black nation—the sense of new Black community under construction—could be more prominent in the recruitment drive. Lawrence Moten, who later became a Christian lay-preacher, was in the mid-1970s just out of the Armed Forces and working for a wholesale book company. As a lonely and still "illiterate" young man who had come to New York and "had no outlook in life, was not doing anything", he still did not go for "the rap-type mentality" of a city that encouraged "getting drunk and acting like a fool." A highly paid, highly skilled NOI welder of tankers and U.S. gunships, and another Muslim, tried to put into Moten's head that they were "buddies" bound by a nationalist brotherhood of Islam, to which they would welcome any Black whom they could persuade to join. This promise of an integrated community was what mainly drew uprooted, atomized African-Americans. Instead of just working for the whiteman, why couldn't Moten join the NOI and bring the fruits of his efforts back into the community? The idea of an economic circuit, of a proud and self-independent new Black nation, appealed. The two demonstrated their concern for fellow-blacks by warning Moten and other targets to separate and not be caught in God's extermination of whites.

Moten felt that his two Muslim friends "were not making anything up about the white man." They did not, in the mid-1970s, much hold out better economic prospects in the NOI, although he had an idea that he might be called upon to manage "projects." Although not yet a curious reader, the young Moten may have also had at the back of his mind faint images of the brilliance of Islam's history and contributions to world civilization, inter alia to architecture: that world-history backdrop later made Farrakhan resonate more to him in the 1980s and 1990s, though he was by then a devout Christian.

In the end, Moten did not succumb and convert in that heyday of Elijah. The Incineration could free blacks from the initiative-sapping fear they had long had of the whites who had always exercised power in America. Yet his two friends' repeated imaging that "when the blood flows the white women and children will go too", stuck in Moten's craw. He protested that "man [African-Americans as well as humans in general] would not allow that." Fard and Elijah do seem to have made a mistake about how far African-

Americans could be brought to hate neighboring whites who had harshly oppressed them but with whom they had American bonds as well. Yet for all the spiritual violence of the NOI's millenarianism, Moten also noted that its converts "kept their noses clean" after they joined up: the millenarianism's draining off of both their hate and fear of their race-enemies paradoxically was making them clash less with law enforcement agencies, as they now directed their energies to positive endeavors. [But how revealing that the upward-bound Muslim tradesmen who wanted Almighty God to incinerate U.S. whites, for wages repaired their ships that bore guns able to incinerate some non-whites in Vietnam or elsewhere!]

The huge number of Blacks to whom the NOI were getting across their invitation in the 1960s and 1970s had a sharp eye for the human texture of those who were pressing Elijah's special Islam upon them. Moten's welder friend, already a skilled tradesman before he became a Muslim, had very fair movie-star looks and was an immaculate dresser. The Muslims promised almost *Reader's Digest*-like tight, happy nuclear families, but this fair friend did not always seem in harmony religiously and otherwise with the dark-skinned Christian woman he would pick up from the houses in which she did cleaning work for white mistresses—and he had two other women. Once, when his friend went to the kitchen to make tea, Moten uneasily opened the draw of his dresser and found it full of pictures of nude white women.[5]

Many African-Americans in the 1960s and 1970s held back—they wanted to test if the Muslims were serious about the severe moral code and ethic of reconstructing families that Elijah proclaimed. Some converts seemed unable to quite live up to the sect's formal puritanism, which banned non-marital sexuality, alcohol, drugs, and many small pleasures.[6] Could Elijah? Did he? What were the real attitudes of Elijah's Muslims to the other blacks? They promised brotherhood and a new integrated Black nation, but did they feel oneness with wider African-American population, or were some trying to profit from them as a distinct Islamic micronation? Where the NOI was really heading was similarly ambiguous: was it separating the adherents from whites, or with the skills it imparted, preparing them to link into or enter America's white mainstream at a later stage? Were the Muslims truly a vanguard for a coming African-American Nation or simply a smaller new religious micronation, self-segregating and contemptuous towards the surrounding black populations that refused to join or to live by their norms?

Openings for Affiliating Neo-Bourgeois Muslims to America and Success

The widening chances for a modernist institutionalization of the Nation of Islam as its professional neo-bourgeoisie took shape were clear at a late 1974 seminar-workshop held in Chicago to outline a program for a college division of the sect's schools. For decades, those bodies of primary and secondary teaching had been gauchely termed "the University of Islam." Now, though, a shaky and inexperienced, but fresh-faced and dynamic, cadre of real university-educated professionals was forming within, or joining, the sect. Could they extend the parochial schools of the sect up into tertiary education, in the footsteps of Irish- and Italian-Americans ("the Catholics") and of the Jews, all of whom had built up their private-sector schools and universities to maintain their ethnic and religious identities in American life?

This 1974 seminar on education had been coordinated by Arthur Majied Muhammad, the Nation's General Business Manager. The project, still at a very preliminary stage, was part of the growing prospects for the NOI to affiliate to elite universities, governmental institutions and business enterprises in the American system, which were now prepared to foster the growth of the Black bourgeois classes seeking to affiliate to that mainstream. The workshop drew more than 150 participants from throughout the country. These prospective members of a possible future educational elite were primarily graduates or students in business and the sciences, more than from the humanities. It was a forming elite that already had a fair mix of male and female professionals, though as yet few graduates in apex PhD degrees. Professionals or proto-professionals who used Arabic names or had studied Arabic, were few among those in attendance, although the coming College was to offer, in addition to the teachings of the Messenger Elijah, "mathematics, science, languages and history".

Throughout the 1950s and 1960s, the Nation of Islam had grown in acrimonious polarization against a Black bourgeoisie that detested the presumption of the sect's uppity lumpens and its Muslim, non-American patina. While a fair number of the Muslims had now entered the ranks of the bourgeoisie, the shades of old class tensions remained. Many neo-bourgeois adherents themselves were mutedly wondering if the decades-old "National" cult-teachings of Elijah could incorporate bourgeois modernity, based on specialization, without disintegrating. As Dr Octavius X (Rowe), president of the Roxbury (Massachussets) Medical Training Institute, had to stress: "most of the participants were holders of post-graduate degrees, but readily acknowledged the limits of their academic training as it compared to the knowledge given to them by the Messenger—there is only one expert and that's the Honorable Elijah Muhammad." Most of the seminar sessions were chaired by Clark X, Director of the sect's New York school. Clark held a Masters in biology and was billed in announcements as having done extensive work in cancer research. "This meeting is the first attempt to formalize a curriculum out of the basic concepts given by Messenger Muhammad" in the first part of his mission. The attendees at the NOI conference had not been like the general professional bourgeoisie of "degree-laden Blacks, most of [whose] discussions when they gather tend to revolve around the colleges they attended or their level of attainment."

The seminar was projected to be the first of a series of conferences. Its organizer, Majied Muhammad, was to "turn over our findings and conclusions to the Honorable Elijah Muhammad and wait for his word on what our next step will be." The new bourgeois elite forming within the Nation of Islam was deprecating itself and its specializations, but it was also taking over.[7]

By the late 1950s, the Nation of Islam had the makings for a crude business empire: a bakery, restaurant, grocery store, a car-repair and paint shop, a laundry, a dress shop, and a haberdashery. A large portion of the profits were used to support elderly members, for some of whom homes were opened—a micronationalism's effort to provide a system of social security—as well as to underwrite the sect's schools and the activities of the Chicago headquarters and smaller temples. Already, then, the movement had shown that it was able to mobilize the financial capacities of cash-strapped lower-class blacks. But the economic and class composition of the Nation's membership changed as the Nation of Islam, overwhelmingly lower-class in the early years, increasingly recruited professionals and educated individuals. Diffident neo-bourgeois recruits who had positions in the white world were (like many Jews in that period) mainly there incognito, only "coming out" as Muslims when they entered the mosques at night. All the while, Elijah continued to denounce non-Muslim bourgeois blacks as just "free slaves" of the whites.[8]

Elijah's theory sought to build a collective, self-contained, national economic enterprise. In urging ordinary African-Americans to therefore "buy Black" wherever they could, the NOI was helping black businessmen through an initial stage in which they would have to charge more than white businesses. Elijah gave free exhibition space to Negro businesses—banks, insurance, retail stores and service enterprises—at the NOI's 1960 Annual Convention, at which Third World African and Muslim commodities were also displayed.[9] But the venom the Muslims still sometimes felt against the black middle-classes that had long derided and excluded them could burst out at any time, costing their best chances to win over that bourgeoisie. In October 1972, black professionals chartered six planes to Chicago for a "unity meeting". College drop-out Louis Farrakhan assured that they would not have to join the NOI in order to enjoy financial relationships with it. But the meeting turned out to be "a complete disaster" (Dr Leonard Jeffries)—instead of pleading for their cooperation, the Muslims denounced their bourgeois guests for two hours for their indifference to collective African-American well being.[10] (Some of Farrakhan's communications to the African-American bourgeoisie in the 1980s and 1990s would again take that turn but be outweighed for them by the *frisson* of his rhetorical denunciations of Judaism and the Jewish nationalist "enemy" that had so widely publicized him for its own purposes).

By the 1970s, Elijah's economic empire was looking impressive: farms, private home construction, rental housing and real estate, food processing centers, restaurants, clothing factories, banking, import and export businesses, aviation, health care, administrative offices and shipping on both land, sea and air. The mainstream institutions of the bourgeois classes wanted to test how far the Muslims' "national" private enterprise could help employ their own new graduates. Representatives of the Community Colleges of Chicago (CCC) met with the Nation to discuss how Black graduates could be absorbed into Muslim enterprises. Very much part of the shift of ideologies occurring in America's general black bourgeoisie in this period, the educators too had been acquiring nationalist impulses that drew them towards the Muslims. The Black Nation could become an economic community: "many students are simply not aware that business opportunities exist within the

Black community", said Timuel Black of the CCC. He felt it "vital" that Black graduates be absorbed into black businesses, rather than those of the whites, so that they would "upgrade" the total Black community. The Muslim representatives present explained that the NOI had established its enterprises "to benefit the total Black community [in] nation-building."

The mainstream educators in attendance tried to connect the NOI into a system of mutual benefits which events would soon show the sect's businesses were not well-managed enough to sustain. They proposed a study arrangement between the colleges and Muslim businesses, which would also later funnel some of the prospective graduates into the businesses. Under this proposal, work-study students who attended NOI businesses would receive financial compensation as well as class credits, along with the practical experience that would enhance their value to the black business community. The Nation of Islam would have first option to hire them after graduation. As a further exchange, Muslim business personnel could enhance their skills through college courses.

Some lumpen-bourgeois blacks cut their teeth on business administration or journalism in the NOI empire, and then moved on to professional careers in the white-run mainstream. But the NOI also attracted some employees who did not need the Nation to prove to the mainstream that they had skills. Charles 67X (Moreland) had received advanced education in journalism in the State of California, and served as a correspondent in the Los Angeles Bureau of *Newsweek* magazine, and as Information Officer for the Economic Opportunity Commission before becoming editor of the newspaper in 1972 at age 27. Before entering the Nation of Islam, he had published many poems and short stories. These were dynamic, young, skilled, budding professionals, the pick of the crop of Afro-America. They represented the Nation well in the American center's institutions. Charles 67X was elected to the Board of Directors of the federally funded agency that reviewed health facility proposals for Chicago's South Side. That made him well placed to facilitate future acquisition of a hospital for the Nation of Islam. Charles 67X was aware that lack of articulate representation at the highest level had doomed an earlier NOI attempt to build a hospital.[11]

By the 1970s, an Islam-colored Nation was being constructed out of many black classes. The Black bourgeoisie was throwing itself with zest into the induction of the ex-lumpen Muslims (whom they could still patronize as rough diamonds) into America's central life. The "Black" elite's shift to the NOI's nationalism in part stemmed from its desperation about where the American economy was heading as oil prices soared. The backdrop was "widespread economic failure, wholesale layoffs from the country's industries, and dwindling career opportunities for Black college graduates." Most American graduates after 1973 faced the recession, but persisting racial discrimination lessened the chances for black ones. As the credibility of the American system lessened, so Elijah's economic counter-Nation won a hearing from more and more frustrated elite Blacks.[12]

African-American politicians who had been inducted into high office in the wake of the triumph of the civil rights movement were equally eager to draw Muslim private enterprise even into regions remote from the NOI's traditional centers. Mayor Johnny Ford of Tuskegee, Alabama, presented Elijah with the key to his City, having written a letter to him voicing the desire for "industrial entry" by the NOI into the Tuskegee-Macon County area. Academics and officials from both the famous Tuskegee Institute and the City of Tuskegee told NOI representatives that they wanted to see the Messenger come into the area to build industries, factories, and foundries in accordance with the Messenger's drive to set up a "Black Economy."

Tuskegee City took thought-out steps to get economic collaboration with the Nation of Islam up and started from the outset. The keys ceremony already displayed inventions by a NOI member, and farm items produced by the sect. A group of specialists from Tuskegee Institute would assess their marketability, and the potential for local manufacture in the Tuskegee-Macon County Area. The Tuskegee experts attending considered the Nation of Islam "the number one Black economic enterprise in the country, having amassed massive assets throughout North America, the Caribbean, and in Japan".[13]

It now seemed conceivable that white America itself might usher Elijah's Nation of Islam into the central American economy. Nixon's men were still finding the Muslims' ethnicism too much to stomach, but *Time* tried to welcome the sect into America as "the Original Black Capitalists", a title that got close to their constructive essence. *Time* reflected that in recent years, the "Black Muslim" movement had "been saddled with a falsely fierce image," deepened by the murder of apostate Malcolm X four years before. But beneath their façade-denunciations of "white devils", the magazine pointed out, the Muslims had always been "the bourgeoisie of the black militant movement." Now, the sect's dogged adherence to the notion of "build black, buy black" was paying dividends. The "Black Muslims" had become the nation's leading exponents of the "black capitalism" for which Nixon now called. The aged Elijah Muhammad's energies were now totally concentrated on building a Muslim-owned financial empire that he predicted would lead to a separate self-sufficient "Black Islam" nation within the continental United States.

Time presented the apparent breakthrough towards a Muslim business empire as only recent. Elijah conceded "we didn't have the money to go into business before now." In 1968, the Muslims had sunk an estimated $6 million into businesses and real estate, two-thirds of it in Chicago, the base of the sect. Muhammad's goal of ten times that amount in 1969 was rightly doubted by black businessmen whom *Time* interviewed, but the newsmagazine toyed with the possibility the sect could double their investment in 1969-1971.

The *Time* article left the impression that the sect's Chicago warehouse, apartment houses, bakeries, clothing store, restaurants and two supermarkets, and the dairy and poultry farms in other states that supplied them, were well-run. On the whole, *Time* had given the Muslims the kind of coverage that was likely to help them move beyond the tithing of members to negotiate the $20 million loan they sought from various banks.[14]

Under Elijah, the development of a compound, somewhat self-contained, private enterprise within the USA at one and the same time radiated the religion, and linked African-Americans to Third World peoples. As the business empire developed in the 1970s, the Nation of Islam was developing a community with the black customers of the whiting and other fish it imported from Peru that was at once economic, propagational-religious, nationalist and international. The shipments would arrive at a Georgia port and be distributed out by the Muslim truck fleet to outlets in Washington, Baltimore, Richmond and Norfolk (Virginia). Demand for the whiting fish had increased with the growing inflation, making it a staple dish for some black areas of Washington. The truck drivers would invite African-Americans they interacted with during their drives to mosque meetings ("fishing" for souls). "The 'fish' program, 'fishing' [for converts] and the selling of *Muhammad Speaks* represent an integrated three-pronged thrust by the followers of the Honorable Elijah Muhammad to uplift the Black people in America."[15] Sales returns on the fish were outpacing expenses by $1 million in 1975.[16]

After assuming the leadership in 1975, Warith disparaged his father's business projects and enterprises as pro forma and designed for non-economic, religious aims. He charged that no economic circuit had been truly routinized: the 5,000 acre farm in the South only occasionally trucked up to *one* store in Chicago some beans that somehow never got canned as the promised constant "Salaam" brand, and a few watermelons: most products that that store sold had been purchased from a wholesaler in Chicago. Large NOI buildings built from the fund-raising campaigns had no tenants. Imam Warith explicated the enterprises as not meant for profit by Elijah but as a nationalist bait to draw in converts with the promise of facilities and careers. And the more the adherents donated, the more they were psychologically bonded to the sect.[17] However, Warith's run-ins with his father had put him outside the sect for long periods prior to 1975: he was not a charitable analyst of either his father or the hardened clique in charge of the businesses who had tried to block his succession and whom he duly later drove from the sect. Warith was finding enterprises his father bequeathed not lucrative: he did not take into account new global macro-economic determinants, such as the 1973 hike in oil prices, or a range of American factors, some of them political, which might have impacted them negatively. Some U.S. agencies had been determined to prevent the NOI from establishing new exchanges with U.S. businesses and in particular with overseas companies and governments.

After 1967, Elijah Muhammad at last caught the attention of the new expanding middle classes with his thesis that African-Americans could achieve a nationality and self-determination in America by blending a discrete economic circuit/grid with an apparently alien religion that could focus the followers' constructive tension with America. After 1975, though, the greater scrutiny under Elijah's more utilitarian, low-key, son, who also directed the followers more to religious studies, brought out that some of the businesses had been corroded and sapped by off-stage corruption, nepotism, cronyism and mismanagement. Thus, Warith privatized or sold off the businesses. Some around Farrakhan and among the secular Black nationalists equated the disposal of much of the NOI's collective economic assets as, like the termination of Reconstruction, a destruction by race-enemies of a major remedial path that had been taken by African-Americans toward restoring their well-being. Government intervention in relation to taxes and demands for a breakup of the collective nature of the estate, plus the expensive legal wrangling among the inheritors, were to be denounced as more efforts by the U.S. system to break up collective entities so as to atomize African-Americans and leave them defenseless. But representation of Warith as a puppet of the U.S. system by citing "released FBI documents" could not convince most blacks, given that the FBI in the same decade of the 1970s concocted "internal documents" that it released to make Black Panther personalities suspect and fight each other.[18]

Overall, from a management perspective, the NOI had not been able under Elijah Muhammad to assume the major role that the development of America's national ideologies, society and economy, and its own great efforts of construction, all together had opened up for it in the early 1970s. The U.S. economy sank more and more into recession: but elite consumption and skimming had flourished under Elijah's authoritarian regime where it was depraved to "plant seeds" — ie. scrutinize any of the ruling demigods, the interlocking ascendant cliques who put themselves beyond discussion or accountability as the collective reflection of God.

2. RISING ETHNIC TENSIONS IN THE 1960S BETWEEN "THE BLACKS" AND "THE JEWS"

Growing ill-feelings between African-Americans and Jewish-Americans were sharpest in New York City, which in the 1960s had more Jews (1.8 million) and more blacks (1.5 million) than any other city in the world. New York was the political capital city of both Jewish and African-American nationalists in the USA.

In many cities of the U.S. North, black children were often taught in crumbling public schools by Jewish teachers, some of whom just went through the motions on their road to the American dream. Neighborhood welfare centers, heavily staffed by Jewish social workers and bureaucrats, looked like "welfare colonialism" by two other, white, "nations" to more and more ordinary African-Americans who were turning to nationalisms as a means to at last bring some "empowerment" to ghetto people. Bayard Rustin, executive director of the A. Philip Randolph Institute and a recipient of Zionist largesse, warned that many poor ghetto Negroes were seeing only four kinds of white people—the policeman, the businessman, the teacher and the welfare worker. "In many cities, three of those four are Jewish."

As their minds turned more and more to entities in other continents, Stokely Carmichael and other proponents of Black Power were denounced in the 1960s for losing sight of opportunities for integrating Americanist community in the U.S. Yet they were hardly alone in that. Many of the more Israel-directed Jews connected with civil rights had little sense that Jewish-Americans had automatic duties to blacks for the construction of a reciprocal, more equal, American community without which the U.S. would never become a successful society, and without which Jewish-Americans would not be observing the American citizenship they had gained. Some Jewish-American ideologues had always thought of the civil rights milieu in terms of a quid pro quo of support for Israel. Accordingly, after the Arab-Israeli War of 1967, they branded criticisms of Israel by SNCC and others as betrayals of previous Jewish support for the movement for civil rights. In contrast, neo-bourgeois blacks regarded civil rights as their inherent unconditional entitlement as Americans, rather than simply a political trade-off. Yet the extraterritorial false consciousness that was increasingly defining each "people" did now also serve the local ethnic-class interests of each in America. Each side seized the galvanizing Palestine-Israel symbolism at the onset of battles between black activists and Jewish teachers over community control of New York City schools that ensued in 1968.

"Blacks and Jews" were being differentiated more and more as to identities and also interests in the 1960s as the ideology of the melting-pot faded, and the mainstream U.S. ethos itself shifted to "roots" and the resultant micronations. White ethnic groups and media, beneath their formal lamentations, were complicit in the breakdown of relations. *Time* magazine's 1969 cover story on "Black versus Jew: a Tragic Confrontation," despite some integrationist-Americanist phrases, assumed in places at least that the ethnic groups in America never could blend and fuse, against occasional evidence in U.S. social development that all of them might, over the long term. Martin Open of Boston's New Urban League charged that some lay and religious Jewish leaders were not so much reacting out of a paranoia understandable for their ethnos as exaggerating "Negro anti-Semitism" as one instrument to reconstruct their own community on post-Americanist lines. They calculatingly "fanned the fires of dormant anti-Semitism in this country as a means of establishing a rebirth of Jewish awareness, identity and unity".[19]

The blacks copped the heat by spearheading the return in American mainstream discourse back to "roots" and all those overseas homelands of provenance. In making the U.S. better able to tolerate national diversity, they thereby set a layer of Jews free to imply discrete nationhood for the ethnos they envisaged. Thus, the Islam-friendly blacks trying to construct an "Afro-American" nation, and the post-1967 Zionoid particularist militants who emerged at the end of the civil rights movement, from the outset legitimized each other's roles in the new U.S. ethnic politics. As these two elites tried to clamp down their respective hegemonies on African-Americans and Jewish-Americans, they nourished each other's growth, foreshadowing the polarization and rowdy shadow-boxing that was to come between Farrakhan's new Nation of Islam and the new Zionoids after 1978.

Affinities between "Blacks" and "Jews"

In contrast to other negative imaging, African-American Islamophile theologian C. Eric Lincoln in the 1960s recalled that a Jewish protagonist often figured in black "vocal folklore" as a neutral buffer between white Christians and the blacks, not as an enemy. In some African-American jokes, "John Henry" and "Mr. Goldberg" would work together to outwit "Mr. Charley".[20] Such lore reflected how, from the mid-19th century, the growing success, wealth and influence of Jews in American life beyond its WASP strata, created some margins, gaps and openings into which African-Americans too could move. According to some Jewish-American intellectuals, some African-Americans had a sense of the Jews as "almost being black": because they too had been mistreated, "their hearts go out to black people." "They will socialize with you when the Irish and Italians will not"[21] —although Malcolm X had the opposite impression that when blacks moved into transitional neighborhoods, the Jews there were the first to leave, while some Irish Catholics and Italians stayed. But Malcolm, too, was aware, here in the early 1960s, that "Jews themselves often still have trouble being accepted".[22]

At first, the ragged Jews in the great cities of the North offered a vivid model for self-bourgeoisification to the much more desperate African-American families who had come up from the South. Bayard Rustin, one of the African-Americans who tried to relate his people and himself constructively to the Jewish neighbors, in 1968 recalled black mothers urging their sons to study hard in the way the neighborhood Jewish boy did, and "get ahead instead of dropping out of school".[23] The Black Muslims ambiguously concentrated that tradition, mixing in competitiveness and polarization. Jewish activists in the early 1960s would overhear Malcolm X denounce "Jewish slumlords" and then, without noticeable protest from his audience, urge African-Americans to respect and aid each other "the way the Jews do".[24] A 1964 study of Negro attitudes by the University of California Survey Research Center found African-Americans less likely than white gentiles to see Jews as "clannish" or "conspiratorial".[25] African-Americans knew too well that the formation of exclusionist ethnic cliques and networks that secretly pre-planned sharp no-holds-barred actions, the pursuit of positions for race patronage, and the roles of extended families had always been at the very heart of social, political and economic power in America, rather than unique to Jewish whites.

The feelings of Islamizing blacks, specifically, had been mixed. Elijah's followers in the late 1950s empathized with the fact that Jews had been "roasted like peanuts by the white man in Europe." Some in the NOI wondered if the Jews as "Semites" or "Asiatics" should be placed with the Arabs in the wider "Black Nation." Others argued that the Jew is accepted as a white man, "and that's how he likes it."[26] Hardball by Americanizing Jews determined to make it up the economic echelons and the professions, though, had long fostered mixed feelings in the Muslim group that was itself determined to become bourgeois. Overall, the Muslim cults before 1967 had at least some more positive attitudes towards Jews as quasi-colored and co-victims of the white Christian devils. In the 1960s, some Jewish-American activists may have themselves been ambiguous about how far the (diverse) Jews were one white race with "Japhet" (Christian Euro-Americans).[27] As Christians, Negroes could identify with the Old Testament's narrative of the children of Israel's exodus from Pharaonic slavery to statehood—but also see modern Jews as heirs to a deicide committed against "Jesus."

The Blacks' Struggle to Win Control Over Their Education

The New York teachers' union, two thirds Jewish, was led by Albert Shanker, a Jewish liberal who had been in civil rights but was a life-long advocate for the Jewish state of Israel in the Middle East. Now he would be a key architect of the movement by Jewish middle classes that were winning power and wealth from the Americanism that had gained them acceptance as quasi-equals in America, to a Jewish micronation in American life that would keep the old Zionism's symbol of Israel as its flag.

The decentralization project in the Ocean Hill-Brownsville school district was an adaptation by the system to the reality that ordinary blacks in the North's cities had now been politicized outside its own institutions. That had established them as an important interest that needed to be brought in and awarded responsibility. Financed in part by the Ford Foundation, the experiment gave a community-elected neighborhood board and its African-American administrator, Rhody McCoy, a measure of local control over policies in the area's eight schools. McCoy, a possible closet Muslim, had been a friend of the late Malcolm X and rejected the integrationist Americanism of Martin Luther King, Jr.. McCoy's stance had long been nationalist rather than individualist. He had sacrificed his own admission into a regular career in teaching when he refused an offer to be guided through the intricate mazes of tests and training, which were little more than rackets whereby interlocked cliques of Jewish, Irish and Anglo teachers had blocked recruitment of blacks into the public education system. McCoy would not let them make him one of the token blacks to legitimize their charade that the profession they had taken over gave equal opportunity to all races.[28]

The decentralization project triggered a power struggle between the forming African-American elite in public education, determined to wrest control over courses and the hiring and firing of teachers, and Jewish teachers equally resolved to widen their control over curricula and the schools in which they taught (and for Shanker, already, to win control of all teachers in the USA, overall). The predominantly Jewish United Federation of Teachers (UFT) feared that decentralization, if applied to the entire system, would destroy the union's bargaining power. After the black local governing board summarily ousted ten teachers accused of sabotaging the project, the UFT-led teachers went out on strike, crushing McCoy's drive to set up a Black-run educational system covering primary school to college.[29] The Islam-influenced McCoy and his board had been dismissed as a result of an illegal strike and one million New York school children had had their educations interrupted. The issue had degenerated into ethnic conflict on a massive scale. The emerging micronationalist elite controlling the teachers' union had been able to panic ordinary, confused New York Jews into a regimented and potentially violent enclave nation by calling the Ocean Hill-Brownsville activists "black Nazis"—

and by running off thousands of "reprints" of "Black anti-Semitic leaflets" being distributed (whoever wrote them) in or near the area's schools.[30] A fair number of Jews, and other Euro-Americans in the state, had been divided about community control and decentralization in education. The mass printing changed the debate to Black anti-Semitism, which swung most Jews and teachers behind Shanker, enabling him to crush McCoy and the de-centralization.[31]

Shanker was fired by both personal and ethnic motives. He had been leader of the union only since 1964: the 1968 ethnic polarization enabled him to clamp a firm grip on it which he would tighten over the decades. As the ethnicist leader of a body most of whose members were Jewish-Americans, he used ethnic confrontation as a means to tighten those with his features and residual smattering of Yiddish into a sort of micronation-union, with himself as that tribe's leader. He always took positions that maximized opportunities for his race-group. He opposed busing and quotas for blacks in the North, and vented frank race hatred when he demanded: "why not just confer an MA at birth on Blacks and minorities?" He was one of those Jewish-American liberals of the North whose radicalism for the South's WASPs quite melted away when integration began to bear in the least on the chances or life of their own group in the areas where they lived in the North. Indeed, some Euro-Americans and their media were getting worried that Shanker and his clique were starting to freeze a key sector of America into a dangerously inflexible, stratified society. By 1975, one white unionist, by no means the only one, voiced impatience that "as the new face in the American labor movement [Shanker] adheres to the status quo"—he was not alive to the need and possibilities for innovation and reform. But by then, Shanker's reach had become national.[32]

During 1968's polarization between Jews and Blacks across New York, some African-Americans likened their inability to wrest control over their and their children's lives and education to the dispossession of the "black" Palestinians by Israel. Yet some parents had wrested input into their children's destinies, smashing down Shanker's barriers and locks to get their children inside a few schools where they and non-striking teachers kept teaching some pupils. Aware now that the blacks could rise, New York Mayor John Lindsay tried in vain to block demands from Shanker that the whole decentralization experiment be not merely modified, but ended.[33] But Shanker was resolved not just to bargain with or subordinate but to end the other party.

And not just in education. *Muhammad Speaks* went on to publish articles that tried to block Shanker's drive to make himself the successor of "George Meany, the racist and reactionary president of the AFL-CIO", which would have given him even huger power over the lives of African-Americans. *Muhammad Speaks* highlighted Shanker's aid to the campaigns by neo-conservative whites—wherever in America they might be—to roll back as "reverse bias" the reparative quotas instituted to induct minorities into the law schools, the trade unions and the USA's two major political parties.[34] Like Shanker, the Jewish neo-cons were identifying more with Israel as post-1967 micronationalization spread in the Jewish-American minority, just as, in the same period, African-American militants tightened their links with the African and Arab states.

Until the mid-1960s, a wide range of blacks—not just the educated Christian activists of the civil rights movement in the South who knew some Jews at close quarters, but also the NOI's lumpen recruits—had often regarded Jews as fellow victims of White Christian racism. By the end of that decade, there was a widespread feeling that American Jews had become part of the Establishment [an actual sociological consequence of their upward mobility], and were joining in WASP ill-treatment of African-Americans. The charges of "hypocrisy" and "betrayal" now leveled against Jews by such Black activists as Daniel Watts, editor of the vocal monthly *Liberator*, show how influenced they had been in the civil rights movement by pink-liberal integrationist discourse from Jews who truly had helped them. An opportunity for "brotherhood" had been missed: Watts observed in high emotion that "we expect more [from Jews], and when it's not forthcoming that love turns to rage." "The liberal Jew has been in the forefront telling the South to integrate, while he lived in lily-white communities in the North. That hurts more than a Wallace, who is at least honest".[35]

The network of government schools were a main focus of ethnic conflict between Blacks and Jewish-/Italian- and Anglo-Americans in New York over decades. In a 1976 machine gun-like review, Africanist nationalist, Kasisi Jitu Weusi, recalled that in the late civil rights period, young white men and women attacked buses bringing 10-13 years-old Black children to schools in the Italian and Jewish, still somewhat working-class, suburb of Canarsie: the riot police had to quell those attacks. Now in 1976, local [Euro] politicians and police were encouraging more violence in and around the mixed schools, Weusi alleged. He was placing the 1976 tensions within an ethnic continuum that focused on Jewish teachers already active back in the 1968 conflict. "Canarsie High School principal, I.S. Rosenman, a Jew... [was] in 1968 principal of Boys High School located in the Black community of Bedford Stuyvesant." Under his inept administration then, half the students dropped out and only 20 diplomas were awarded in a graduating class of 400. Rage from students and parents caused Rosenman's transfer to Canarsie.

Weusi charged that "Jewish administrators" now controlling the civil service, education and [Shanker's] UFT were "mechanical mice" intent on implementing their union rules and regulations for their own interests as an ethnic stratum. Incapable employees were never dismissed "but kept on ice for a year or two until the headlines die down and then they are transferred to another school to continue their destruction of the minds of our children." In the New York City public school system, Rosenman's trademark was "liberalism. Kids are smoking, drinking beer: smooching and looseness is everywhere." Weusi set out the functions of the mixed schools as one primary battlefield nexus within which the nationalities were now defining themselves against each other. Yet, in the main, because he so carefully caught the detailed functioning of the New York public educational system, Weusi's spirited article did not sink into a pathological anti-Semitism that would cloud reality. He was able to see things from the perspective of the other party also, mentioning the economic and class dimensions that were triggering a lot of the racial ill-feelings in New York: unemployment, miseducation, high rents, high taxes, crumbling real estate markets and a parasitic civil service—all these were causing the frustrations that "whites" were now taking out on "blacks."[36]

Kasisi Jitu Weusi's transitional 1976 article could have viewed the "Jews" and "Italians" in Canarsie more richly, including more in class terms. He was right that the Jewish-Anglo-Irish teachers' stratum [although often from working-class parents or grandparents] had become a bourgeois economic interest group: his detailed description of it was needed to focus answering self-assertion from his own group. Within the USA's corrective mechanism of pluralism, Weusi's print-speech was mobilizing his people to stand up to Euro forces that were deforming the education system into a set-up for hereditary ethnic patronage: quality in education was coming in last. Although Weusi mentioned Jewish ethnicity in the elite abusing the schools, and thus Black kids there, he did not condemn any Jewish ideology as motivating them. [True, the permissive anything-goes liberalism for which he rapped Rosenman was being developed by a range of white groups together in the core America of that period]. This nationalist writer's dislike of the beer and smooching carried forward the Nation of Islam's drive to turn *their* African American pupils into humorless WASP-like 1930s Gradgrinds, who were left little time indeed for depraved pleasures in their study-packed adolescences. The Muslim and Africanist nationalists of the 1970s sought for Black kids, so they could lift themselves above the class into which they were born, something like the unremitting earnestness Dalits (Untouchables) have needed in India to claw their way up educational systems they could not afford and which snarled at them. Reform Jews were indeed votaries of the permissive society in the 1960s and 1970s. The NOI and the new Africanist nationalists stood against it with their blend of Islam's hatred of fornication and booze, and the solid old middle-WASP love of work. Then in the 1980s these bourgeois ethnic elites and the newer (Black, Hispanic etc) elites all became like each other as once-Westernized Jewish professionals, too, put slivers from a traditional religion into their ethnic and professional life: all were building parallel religio-political micronationalisms.

Economic Foci of Conflict

In the 1960s, the liberal sector of the self-styled "Zionist" community, always prepared to do many things for Israel except to go to live there, was passing through ideological flux. While it and the U.S. system toyed with measures to forestall Jewish-Black conflict, these came as too little, too late. Lucy S. Dawidowicz (1967) and historian Joseph Boskin suggested that Jewish capital might underwrite an "exodus" of Jewish merchants from the ghettos of the North by buying their property and reselling it to local petty-bourgeois blacks. Once Blacks and Jews were meeting, Dawidowicz wanted to involve such U.S. institutions as the Small Business Administration, since governmental rent subsidies were already helping the poor pay their ghetto landlords.[37] In Boston, the Department of Commerce made a grant to a Small Business Development Center to arrange for the transfer of several dozen shops from Jewish to black ownership. Such measures could fit into President Nixon's plans for a "black capitalism" that the federal government would subsidize and supervise.[38]

There thus was little magnanimous or generous or hopeful in Jewish-American ideas for transfer of small concerns to black businessmen. American Jews were bankrolling the welfare budget of Israel almost without limits to somehow keep its construction of its ethnically-tense society going. But the proposals to transfer some ghetto businesses from Jews to Blacks mostly assumed that the U.S. government would foot the bill, with the Jewish "charitable organizations" merely coordinating the process. "Such a gesture" might "meet the demands of the Black Power-ites at their face" [—but, with non-nationalist ("responsible") Negroes to be selected in their turn paying "reduced rates" along with the WASP regime, perhaps they might even turn yet another profit for the departing Jewish businessmen?][39]

It was not only a question of to which communities—Israeli or American—these Zionist discourse-groups gave priority. Dawidowicz' communal hatred flamed up in her relentless conflation of by now well-urbanized poor African-Americans with Slavic anti-Semites who had of old attacked Jews in Central and Eastern Europe. Dawidowicz responded to efforts by a range of blacks, not just militant groups, to start cooperatives for the ghetto poor, with "how doth the Black Panther resemble the White Eagle!"—a reference to the pre-1939 anti-Semitic Polish governments' subsidization of consumer cooperatives to provide breaks for the slowly-growing Slavic lumpen-bourgoisie under definitions of nationhood that marginalized the country's Jews, who thus tended to leave. Had she known in advance how likely her parallel was to inflame anyone of Polish-Jewish extraction in America against almost all the Black groups there? Dawidowicz seized on Black Power advocates like Stokely Carmichael who ascribed ghetto dislike of Jewish merchants and landlords to the economic relationship, not Judaism: she likened them to Pavolaki Krushevan who "wrote similar things in his paper in Kishinev for five years; then, in 1903, came the pogrom".[40]

Such writings could serve to justify "pre-emptive" violence against blacks. When African-American students, led by a Black Jew who once attended Hebrew teacher's college, held a sit-in at Brandeis University, one way-out Jewish leader in the area suggested that "Brandeis should be made *Schwarzenrein* (cleared of blacks) the way Hitler made Germany *Judenrein*."[41] Some once-traumatized groups can unthinkingly pass on the violence and massacres they themselves once suffered to other groups with no connection to it.

Dawidowicz in 1967 had been ahead of her Americanist era as a budding Jewish-American micronationalist when she made the USA's ghetto blacks reincarnate Europe's old Nazis and Slavic pogromski. Such micronationalist movements lack sufficiently coherent non-Anglo cultures through which to bring together and integrate a nation. To stampede the masses into their ideological corral, the movements must always evoke some lethal race-enemy who is always clawing at the door. Was the maturing young Farrakhan monitoring this technique of the forming Jewish nationalist elite he was to depict as the deadly enemy to the Black bourgeoisie of the 1980s and 1990s?

Not all the Jews were the same: the good and the bad and the in-betweens bought and sold and scribbled and orated at the fork in the road between Americanism and micronationalities that Jewish-Americans and black Americans had now reached. Some of the Jewish writers wanted to carry through to completion the construction of the inclusive American nation, which they knew would still be tough and risky to finalize. No mere validating banner over the interests of the in-group's elite and its gains, this drive to put together a composite American nationhood could overarch and transcend all the ethnic groups—so as then to clamp scrutiny and demands down upon one's own as well. An example of an Americanist ability to scrutinize one's own group was Roland B. Gittelsohn's critique of those of his own ethnos who did not share his drive to build seriously inclusive American community. He already noticed in 1966 how "some Jews are fond of holding up to the Negro—either in chastisement or challenge—our own example of self-help" in an America that had not always welcomed non-WASPs. "The implication is: if we could lift ourselves up so dramatically in two or three generations by our own bootstraps, why can't you do the same?" Gittelsohn rejected this excuse to do nothing for a group of fellow-Americans. The Negroes had been brought to America in chains that were to deny them any initiative for a long time, while the European Jews had come willingly and been allowed more choices and chances, despite facing some dislike.[42]

To those who ironized that no one had ever legislated a war on poverty or the defense of civil rights for Irish, Italian and Jewish migrants at the turn of the 20th century, Ben B. Seligman retorted that the old poverty of the immigrants had been "surrounded by a layer of hope." The newcomer could be absorbed by burgeoning industries—steel, railroads, textiles, clothing—that demanded no special skills, offering an "internal ladder of opportunity" to him and his offspring.[43] Negroes in the mid-1960s were making their most serious drive to become skilled workers or middle-class "in an economy whose unskilled sector is contracting under the impact of automation" (Gittelsohn). [Chapter 2 showed that, whatever some Jewish communalists of the 1960s and 1970s said, Irish- and Italian-American politicians had early in the twentieth century time and again appealed to their own ethnic groups to help get them into, and keep them in, local and city government, and that they had duly used such political offices to bring services and opportunities to those groups that had begat them—which both "Blacks" and "Jews" now were about to do in their turn.] Gittelsohn called for the mustering of "communal authority" to control those Jewish property owners and merchants who behaved unscrupulously in the ghettoes. He also observed that if Jews could be the scapegoat against whom some African-Americans voiced what was really a hatred of whites in general, some Jews could conversely inflict the same scapegoat status upon blacks: "some Jews can with impunity voice their resentment of all Christians only against the most helpless of them in this country, Negroes." Gittelsohn himself articulated a frank hatred of the "evil" WASP power-structure that he believed had encouraged its Negro and Jewish victims to fight each other.[44]

Gittelsohn's worries on this point were soon to be over-fulfilled as many liberal or left Jews leapt over to the New Right that was taking first shape. In the 1970s and 1980s, the Jewish-American neo-cons in its ranks were to be the most fertile in devising ingenious expedients to slash opportunities and facilities for blacks—far beyond anything their awed Anglo colleagues could ever have bothered to conceive, or think through. But now fusion of elite Jews and WASPs came through intermarriage.

Gittelsohn's fears back in 1966 that expressing anti-Semitism would become a way for Christian blacks to get closer to the USA's Euro-Christian majority were to prove misplaced. As Jacob Cohen already pointed out, "a pogrom, by proper definition, takes place with the permission and often at the instigation of the police and administration." In America's ghetto riots, the rioters would have torched or looted Jewish businesses had Christian whites owned them, while the police, fire-brigades and other American institutions tried equally hard to save *all* properties owned by any Euro-Americans "which shows what an advantage it is for a Jew to be a white man in this country".[45]

The Failure and Waning of Jewish-American Liberalism

From the mid-1960s, American groups were diverging from each other by evoking and aiding extraterritorial motherlands (Israel, Pan-Africa, Poland, Ireland) much more, by the systematic formation of micronations, or through new interest in folk or popular religions that America's rationalist liberalism had so rightly downgraded. Attempts by liberals among Jewish-Americans to get to grips with the Black-Jewish tensions often only showed them, themselves, getting entangled in this process of self-differentiation that was now working to widen the gap between African-Americans and Jews. The Boston sociologist, Leonard Fein, had been in the category of the most Americanized Jews for whom loss of belief and living in Tradition, and outmarriage, would not cost membership in the group, while open criticism of Israel, especially after 1967, would.[46] Still, the shift towards extraterritorial motherlands across the seas, and to communal differentiation, if not confrontation, among both blacks and Jews following the Six Day War was turning the thoughts of even the most secularized American Jews back to old, decrepit religious institutions. Fein argued in 1968 that intervention from the U.S. central government's institutions, and Jewish communal ones of a quintessentially American type, was not the only approach to improve Black-Jewish relations: "the Jew has ample resources within his religious tradition to eliminate inequities that cause interracial tension." At the suggestion of some Boston Jews, including Fein, a group of Negro tenement dwellers presented their grievances against their Jewish landlord to a beth din, or

Jewish religious court. "This was a bunch of very old guys who haven't read James Baldwin or Rap Brown." The landlord agreed to make overdue repairs, while his tenants promised better housekeeping.[47] The rabbis involved had psychologically pressured the slumlord by depicting that Judaism and its law ran against his misdeeds but would confer on him a "good name" if he stopped, Fein recalled in 1981.[48] (Yet threatening demonstrations by blacks and the glare of the press photographers and television, too, had brought the slumlord to a situation in which he might listen to such a reinvention of Judaic morality that could enable him to keep his business going while getting him off the hook.)

There were practices and concepts in the old Judaism of Europe that could have been restructured and extended to bring African-Americans and Jewish-Americans closer: both had, after all, shared the Torah. Overall, though, the shift of both groups from c. 1967 onward to micronationalisms in which religious motifs, tenets and clergies were to be given more prominence, did not help reconciliation. Providing largesse to Israel had long been a sort of substitute religion for Jewish-Americans, but now they were to become steadily more religious in their ethos as their interest in foreign affairs soared. Recurring execution by the Israeli military of Egyptian-African and Arab prisoners of war was among concerns of the new Islamophile African-American nationalisms under development in 1967. But a Zionoid like Fein, however temperate and decent, still had to argue in 1981 that the Israeli army had by and large maintained its unusual "purity of arms" (*tohar haneshek*) in all its wars—a bloody younger Ariel Sharon being but the sole "exception" who proved that rule.[49]

In early 1969, *Time* magazine carried a strained and not always wholehearted dialogue between the quasi-Muslim or crypto-Muslim educator Rhody McCoy, the administrator of Ocean Hill-Brownsville's experimental school district, who was 46, and Fein, at that time aged 34. McCoy gave as good as he got; neither of the two looked for flaws in his own group. Fein was complacent about "the Jewish community's history of many creative relationships with blacks" although he evidenced some fellow-feeling in his sense that his and McCoy's grandparents had been simultaneous victims of two white Christian racisms. But he also depicted blacks as saying among themselves: "look, the Jews have gotten it in the neck, too: how do I explain their success and black nonsuccess [in America]?" The blacks inevitably would "just assert that the Jews were successful only by cheating" blacks. Not deepening that Jewish community self-introspection by Jews of which he too was capable, Fein characterized "a lot of Jews" as fine liberals who obviously were not gougers or cheaters or bigots. Hostile blacks therefore denounced them as hypocrites as a ploy to make them, also, finally turn against the blacks so that the nationalists could then sit back and say, "See, everybody's a racist."

Here Fein risked acquiescing to the coarse-grained stereotype of Jewish bigots and ideologues: that the blacks had failed to make it in a hostile America as had the Jews, and hence did not merit special treatment or facilities. In reality, relative Black "non-success" in America had been mainly in private enterprise economics. It would take time before they would have, to further their development, a "Black capital" pool like the "Jewish capital" to which, as Dawidowicz pointed out, her people could resort in New York. Since the end of the civil war, African-Americans had made determined strides towards mass literacy through self-education, through the government schools that were shacks into the 1940s, and through both their integrationist and Islam-tinted nationalist press. Fein was right that money from Jewish philanthropists and Jewish personnel had been central for helping African-American leaders develop such institutions as the NAACP and the Urban League and in keeping historically black institutions of higher education afloat. The Muslim and Black nationalist segments of African-Americans now wanted solely Black institutions. Yet the integrationist black bourgeoisie, shaky as it was, had always been—and would remain—much more skilled in structuring the growth of such Euro-promoted institutions to serve its own development and the interests of African-Americans as a whole than either their white collaborators or their black critics conceived.

McCoy denied that anti-Semitism had a special role in the reaction against a diverse range of whites in the late 1960s. He replied that most black people were "still enslaved" in one way or another, and less concerned to make Jews into scapegoats as to blame conditions on the total American scene: "it's an anti-white attitude period." McCoy ascribed their anger to economics: some Jews were now practising the same discrimination with which some gentile whites had once constricted *them.* Blacks who wanted to make their start "can't even get a job as a dishwasher in certain areas they inhabit." He was farsighted for 1968 in saying that blacks who wanted the parochial oppressors off their backs would resist Italian as much as Jewish ones: Jewish and Italian communalists would be banding together against African-Americans and any particular facilities for them in New York by the 1980s.[50]

Rhody McCoy had fewer integrative Americanist impulses in 1968 than the liberal "Zionist" Fein. Fein was at least prepared to concede in theory that the Jewish community might have some bigots and exploiters whom "the organized Jewish community" should isolate. As still basically an Americanist, Fein knew some sort of mutual communication of their disparate cultures and religions had to take place between these two American groups that had to live together in New York and elsewhere as either good or bad neighbors in a single country. McCoy was languid about mutual community education: anyway, it could be just a ploy to evade "a process of doing" that would free blacks from exploitation. McCoy had had to claw his way up a brutal teaching profession: but here he lost sight of the urgency of making less hostile to each other two huge communities that could do one another real harm. And more exchanges of quality culture materials might have enriched both groups—although enclave-nationalisms tend to resist acculturation.

It is understandable that Fein felt he might be patronizing blacks to tolerate anti-Semitism from them more than from the other sectors of Christian

America. This stance, though, ignored McCoy's repeated point that Jewish individuals had exercised degrees of power over blacks—economic and other— of which few white Christians had to complain. Hence, the resentment from African-Americans was more a response to actual abuse than that of white gentiles, whose Christian culture fueled *their* hostility. And a part of Fein was linking up to fellow white gentiles when he hinted that "racism" was almost as much a contrived bogey in the minds of African-Americans as was their anti-Semitism: both were a "copout." He put before the black community a choice: was it going to be, like many other ethnic communities, introverted and hostile to other groups, or would it build for itself a capacity to relate to others productively? Fein's Americanist stance here took inadequate account of the much greater systemic racism that African-Americans had faced, and still did, in comparison to Jews. And he did not foresee that the Jewish-American community now developing would also fulfil his fears as it evolved into a regimented micronation in which any scrutiny of Israeli actions in the Middle East brought debarment from the group in America, as he was to concede in 1981.[51]

Some of the early Jewish micronationalists' shafts hit home, but not just on the African-American targets. In her conflation, Dawidowicz mocked a certain type of ghetto Negro migrated from the deep South as, like the Slavic Christian peasants who became the pogromists, prone to "a primitive religiosity embedded in superstition and a distrust of urban mercantile society and a money economy".[52] Still, many of the sub-literate Jews who migrated to the USA's big cities from tiny settlements in Slavic countrysides had brought with them similar superstitious wariness about non-correligionists. Then secularization through the modernist Yiddish newspapers and literature by which the immigrants became literate, and later through New York's Anglophone rationalist left-liberalism, downgraded superstition and its functions for constructing community. Yet primordial irrationality was coming back from the later 1960s, reflected in the forming Jewish-American nationalist discourse now fusing African-Americans with bygone Slavic and Nazi murderers. The new Jewish-American micronationalists would in the 1970s and 1980s install the dimly-remembered old religious superstitions in their new nationhood with in-your-face contempt for the liberal rationalism that New York Jewish writers had so much shaped in its distinguished heyday. Things that had once distinguished and separated Jews now had to be restored, whatever the cost to all parties.[53]

Nation of Islam Activists and Tensions of Black Ghettoes with Jews.

New nationalistic African-Americans could lack self-insight quite as much as their micronationalizing Jewish opponents. In the African-American intellectual elite, Harold Cruse griped that "the emergence of Israel as a world-power-in-minuscule meant that the Jewish question in America was no longer purely a domestic minority problem": many American Jews began to function as "an organic part of a distant nation-state." He depicted the

Zionists as mustering orchestrated blackmail on the U.S. parliamentarist system: the Chairman of the Democratic National Committee warned that failing to support the birth of Israel might cost the states of New York, Pennsylvania and California. The USA (with the USSR) had created a Jewish state in the heart of the Arab world that did violence to the UN Charter's promise of equal self-determination for all peoples.[54] This rejection of Jewish-American input into foreign policy came from an author who by then was at the fore of connecting African-Americans not just to sub-Saharan Black Africans but to a range of anti-West Arab and Muslim insurrections and regimes! Cruse resented the much greater skills and institutions with which American Jewry had achieved a connection with, and indeed—as concerned money—built, a faraway state of provenance because that was a need his category of African-Americans were increasingly feeling, themselves. At the same time, his rebuke also brought out his ongoing veiled Americanism which was somewhat similar to Anglo-American insularism—the discreet choice Africanist ultras repeatedly make not to carry their reconnections with Africans and Muslims to the same lengths as Zionist Jewish-Americans towards Israel. There were limits to how much the U.S. "Zionists" would do for Israel, but the neo-Africanists harbored much greater unease about extending extra-continental identity so far that it could hamper African American incorporation into the American mainstream—a goal that ethnic sub-nationalisms sometimes subtly help minorities to achieve in the USA.

How far and how explicitly did the Nation of Islam take part in the Black-Jewish ethnic conflict that was spreading in the 1960s and 1970s?

Considering how much unequal contact African-Americans had with Jewish whites—and not just in their two sub-nationalisms' capital city, New York—communalist denunciations of U.S. Jews were not a strong feature of the NOI's print-media in the 1960s and 1970s. Most *Muhammad Speaks* sniping was against whites in general. But at street level, the oral communications by ill-supervised speakers could fan parochial dislike of Jews as one technique to recruit from the atomized black masses. NOI picketers and speakers in New York would stand in front of Euro-owned stores to urge the gathering African-Americans to buy "Black only": it frightened Jewish white shopkeepers who compared the Muslims to Hitler when he was starting out. The police, however, could not stop free speech that did not call for illegal violence outright.

The Muslim missionaries were channeling ethnic rage to corner a clientele for a new black nationalist small-business stratum—the NOI's. They whipped up outrage that whites owned the butchershops, bakeries, grocery stores, fishmarkets and pawnshops that extracted needed money out of the ghettos, leaving only the barbershops for blacks who wanted to get into private enterprise. Elijah's evangelists perfectly blended Islam's religious requirements (prohibition of pork and alcohol) and the rage of the poor African-Americans, into NOI economic interests and a covert onslaught on lumpen black culture: the white shops retailed to the blacks comic pigs' tails and pigs' feet they would never put on sale in white areas. If in New York, the Muslims' denunciations could become like Jew-baiting, the black Christian target-audience equally colored it thus from their own tradition. One pavement NOI orator condemned "Mr Goldberg" the butcher: his old meat had been growing blue in the refrigerator but Goldberg had coated shellac over it to make it look still fresh enough to buy. One member of the audience then added that the Jews "killed our Jesus too!"

Thus, the NOI validated from Islam their drive to squeeze an ethnic group out from the ghettos, to win money and customers. A sense that a New York group were successors to ancient Hijaz Jews denounced in the Qur'an could lock into a traditional Christian pietism among ill-educated poor Negroes. Yet that residual faith in Jesus among the listeners was perhaps more the NOI's target than "Mr Goldberg": the NOI orators were fishing for exactly those blacks in Harlem who yearned to break with African-American popular traditions and become bourgeois. Quite as much as the Anglo white "devils", Jewish ones provided the covert model for becoming an entrepreneur, and building a constructive, productive nationalist community. They were monitoring more than the Jews in the ghettos. The Harlem NOI kept their telescope focused on separated Jewish neighborhoods, too, which, their reconnaissance by car had revealed, did not have a whole lot of bars and liquor stores: the Jews "know how to get that money" while minimizing spending it. Their quarters did have synagogues, bakeries and grocery stores [—Black areas had Muslim mosques, Muslim bakeries and NOI grocery stores].[55] The NOI's drive for an initial period of asceticism as the tactic to accumulate the capital for a later period of prosperity through private enterprise was also like that of Sunni Arabs overseas in the Malay world as well as in the ghettos, or like Druze peddlers among blacks in Detroit or New York. Still, while focusing on private enterprise, the Qur'an had denounced fraudulent, heartless merchants in Mecca. But New York's Jewish shopkeepers too provided another model for the techniques through which the NOI's activists could make themselves traders and achieve prosperity through businesses.

However, the pre-1975 NOI also has to be assessed as one source or conduit that pumped out pro-Arab, anti-Israel data and themes among African-Americans, both masses and bourgeois, as Jewish-Black relations deteriorated in America after 1967.

3. THE WIDENING DIVERSITY OF AFRICAN-AMERICAN GROUPS

The Black Panthers

The rise of the Black Panther Party (BPP: founded in 1967) appeared for a time to offer a more politics-engaged (and insurgent?) alternative to the NOI, one that was getting across to the same poverty-stricken groups from which the Muslims had for so long recruited. The Panthers made themselves an unprecedented rallying-point for deep rage among ill-educated lumpens at police brutality in the Northern ghettos. At every level, Panther communications either developed Nation of Islam ideas or defined the new "self-defense" organization against them, charging that the NOI never turned up for the showdowns in the ghettoes. The ambiguous theme that was the Panthers' first rallying point—arming a vanguard for the self-defense of poor blacks—they had taken from the dead al-Hajj Malik al-Shabazz' call for blacks to form rifle clubs, which were legal under the U.S. Constitution. Eldridge Cleaver had begun his ideological life as an NOI convert and organizer in prison. Then he felt relief, in explosive San Quentin penitentiary, when Malcolm's adoption of a more open Sunni Islam freed him from having to argue that all whites by their race were inferior devils inherently doomed to be slaughtered by God—an equivalent for blacks of the terrible "white man's burden" of supremacism and race-hate. It was Malcolm's letter from Mecca describing white blue-eyed Muslims eating from the same plate with Black ones—universalism under Islam's unifying pilgrimage—that set Cleaver free to attempt to integrate a left-Americanist community with the protesting white college kids.[56]

A tenet of the NOI that had early attracted Eldridge Cleaver to it had been Elijah's call for several states of the USA to be set aside for African-Americans, although by 1968 Eldridge, as the BPP's "Minister for Information", was repudiating it on somewhat ambiguous grounds that Elijah had been "not able to implement this," just as Garvey had not had the means to truly get his masses back to Africa in the 1920s. Cleaver's dropping of his "separatism" was pragmatic but could also open up support from those Jewish and Anglo whites whose class-based analysis opposed ethnic nationalism.

Militancy that the Panthers took from foreign ideologies could be applied in incompatible ways. The Panthers were occasionally violent integrationists who hoped Mao's Little Red Book could make America work, and get "Black people" in. Most of their statements had two faces that looked in opposite directions: incorporation as well as separation. The Party's Program held the U.S. federal government "responsible and obligated to give every man employment or a guaranteed income" [=FDR as hale as ever—but what about women?]. If the capitalist system wouldn't deliver full employment, though, the community would have to take the means of production from the white businessmen to "employ all of its people and give a high standard of living".[57] The Panthers initially presented themselves as wanting "non-violence just like Martin Luther King, Jr.—but we must defend ourselves [when attacked] as Malcolm X said" [drawing on Qur'an 2:190-194: the believers have to fight when they or a holy mosque are under attack, but must not aggress, and have to conclude peace with those who attack once they withdraw to their own patch of turf].

The Panthers' study of "the specifics of the law" as the basis on which they then, guns in hand, followed and monitored the police, had from the start showed a duality towards the American system. Forcing the police to live up to the functions set by official ideology harbored a liking for some aspects of that system. The Panthers' policing of the police could end in shootouts—or make American law-keeping more just at street-level in the ghettos. The BPP's idea of "revolutionizing the court systems" was likely to turn out to be ameliorist and Americanist rather than revolutionary. In their concern that laws be democratic and justly implemented, the Panthers could become very American. Appealing to long-standing protections stated in the American system itself, the Panther paper objected loudly when a bill was presented to Congress in 1975 to silence widening "national" objections to corporate privilege and growth "as hardship engulfs wider and wider sections of the American people" [*sic*]. The Panthers were resisting the fake "fight against crime" bill in defense of the freedoms of speech, assembly and association offered by America's Declaration of Independence.[58] However, confronted with an existential situation of savage attacks from police departments and agencies determined to destroy them, the Panthers did develop militants like Assata Shakur and Kathleen Cleaver who could fight superbly with weapons.

Nationalists?

On another plane, the Panthers certainly focused nationalist secessionist feelings among the black populations at large. The Party had initially been titled "The Black Panther Party for Self-Determination": but after a while the additional phrase with its quasi-secessionist undertone was excised. Some in the Party spoke of it as a revolutionary nationalist organization following on the late Malcolm X, and this image mustered a lot of the support the Party drew from the wider Black public. While he was briefly in the BPP, Stokely Carmichael was termed "the Prime Minister of the Afro-American Nation": of all the militant young leaders, he perhaps articulated the concepts closest to full classical ethnic/cultural nationalism, extra-territorializing many of those impulses to Africa. Muslim convert Dhoruba Bin Wahad recalled the drive of the Panthers to establish "a relevant education that would teach us who we were." BPP rhetoric often seemed to promise violent confrontation with the American system. Speaking like the calm head of a middle-rank independent state, Huey Newton proclaimed that "we're going to commit troops in the spirit of internationalist solidarity" to fight with the Viet Cong against U.S. forces in Vietnam. The Panthers would make their position known at the Paris Peace talks—one more proposal designed to infuriate top U.S. officials and keep the TV cameras rolling. Such gestures—loudmouthed support for the Palestinians against Israel may be another instance—were dysfunctionally provocative, given that the Panthers almost never followed them up with detailed action. The public grandstanding only helped American agencies build up a public mood permitting them to grind the Panthers down with waves of arrests and shootouts.

At least sometimes, Panther spokesmen gave an impression of indifference to any specific national culture of, or for, U.S. blacks. Thus, despite all they had taken from Malcolm X, perhaps most of their communications failed to define their group as an Afro-American or African-American or Africanist nation—and occasionally even as a discrete nation of any sort. They spoke more often of "black people in America" than of the black people or any Black Nation. Eldridge Cleaver in 1968 refused to choose between (a) those who wanted only action moving solely around "our national consciousness" [=particularism that included some nationalists who had been in the SNCC, such as Stokely]; and the other option of (b) the formal status of black people as "so-called American citizens" which some wanted to now make real through a Communist-like class struggle in which the blacks were supposed to serve as the vanguard of a wider proletarian revolution.

Cleaver wanted the Panthers to "make use of both" analyses. He more and more came to view his ethnic group as without much active cultural distinctiveness: it had been formed and defined by the attitudes and ill-treatment of groups of whites bent on capitalism's economic exploitation. Nonetheless, Cleaver endorsed a UN-supervised plebiscite through which "black people" could decide if they wanted separation from America or citizenship in it. In saying so, he did not say with which group the BPP would campaign. He used a throw-away phrase about "individuals and splinter organizations" that had been sounding off "for too long now" about nationality: this was meant to apply to the radical Africanist cultural nationalists—including Stokely with whose SNCC the Panthers had just "merged"?—rather than against Martin Luther King, Jr. and his "one America" nation dream. Cleaver may have hoped to simply use a plebiscite, like participation in mainstream parliamentarism, as one more instrument to politicize urban lumpen masses whom he knew were "illiterate" and often debilitated. (The Panthers waved guns at the cameras as though all African-Americans would rise tomorrow, but their intent may just have been to try to image to the most atomized in the ghettoes that they *could* assert themselves, enter politics, and even change things. But the Panthers had to scream just to get heard on the stoned-out streets). Cleaver may even have been planning to use the plebiscite as a means to finish the Africanist nationalists. It could all as easily end in some form of local community input into law-keeping and city-level policies, a modest devolution, as in the break-up of the state: "the political structure of this country has to be totally rearranged so that black people can have some control over the implementation of the sovereignty of this country".[59] Yet, the BPP was equivocating on *any* separate territoriality for "black people" even at city-municipal level.

In the 1970s, the Panthers and the Nation of Islam kept up strict policies that slowed an increase in their card-carrying members. Still, each of these two often-competing vanguards was getting its communications across to whole strata of blacks. In San Diego, California, Fruit of Islam juveniles, and their Panther equivalents with some of their parents, were selling their movements' two newspapers outside the entrances to all government schools. Many of the pupils' parents already bought *Muhammad Speaks* from time to time, but a new generation of adolescents were doing so much more often. In California churches, the Negro clergy were vainly warning that kids who went near either group could burn in hell. The NOI paperboys saw themselves as budding "soldiers of Allah." The FBI fanned tensions across the U.S. between the NOI and the Panthers over the turfs from which each could sell their papers. But one Muslim adolescent felt friendly to his Panther peers who brought their little Red Books to school—it was just that he could not understand what the hell Mao was writing about.[60] Thus, a sort of community of youth wider than the sect or parties did form around contiguous Black protest discourses in California during the 1970s—conversations and print-Islam that would cumulatively draw many ex-Panthers across into (Sunni) Islam in the 1980s and 1990s.

The glamour of the papers stemmed from their expression of counter-identities. But in hindsight from the post-modern era, the Panthers and Muslims rather look to have served as auxiliaries of the schools that barred them. The schools were teaching the adolescents how to read, and the Muslim and Panther texts then made reading that same literary Anglo-English attractive as a medium for a particularist identity and self-interest. In the vocabulary and styles of their print-language, *Muhammad Speaks* and *The Black Panther* were on balance like Middle America, and propagated many concepts borrowed from various categories of Euro-Americans. They tended to detach the youth from traditional oral Black culture and language forms.

Multi-Racial Community?

The Black Panthers built up significant community with white and other non-African-Americans. After the Martin Luther King, Jr. and Bobby Kennedy assassinations, the Panthers found themselves getting more and more response from Latino and Amerindian groups. The Panthers were able to link up with young Appalachian whites. They had high awareness of the desperate origins of poor whites from "the Oklahoma dust bowl", and the skills with which the American upper classes put such youth in police uniforms and pitted them against blacks. While those in the BPP gained a sense of importance from the fear they aroused in the police, its rhetoric denouncing "the pigs" opened no path to dialogue with more popular white classes. And in hindsight, the contributions by wealthy Euro-American actors and socialites to such ventures as the Huey Newton Defence Fund were a sort of vicarious playing with a revolution. When Martin Luther King, Jr. was assassinated, the last tango's aging Marlon Brando told his secretary to order up rifles and pistols so he could shoot his way to Washington. Could these black and white cliques have ever stumbled into a real uprising?

In the non-revolutionary, integrative-ameliorist direction, the Panthers mixed charm and implied vague threats in order to get donations of commodities or money from white-owned businesses in the ghettoes so that they could launch and sustain health clinics and free lunches for children there.[61] Yet Hollywood-like celebrity status and all the cocaine and liberated white women that now duly beset them in high society ate away the anger and the commitment of many of the most charismatic Panthers. It became ever more ambiguous whether the Panthers were organizing an alternative to the American government or just challenging it into genuinely governing in the ghettoes by extending its social services to those there. Would the "community control" they sought really "empower Black communities", or rather make the Panthers, the other Black nationalists, the reformed gang-leaders—perhaps even the Nation of Islam?—intermediary agencies between the black masses and a WASP elite and entrepreneurs now working to soothe and affiliate malcontented populations? Had some U.S. administrations or at least out-of-control agencies and police not been so hell-bent to crush them, the Panthers could perhaps have become among the architects of an integrated Americanist community in its left-liberal sector.

The Panthers from the streets were getting drawn into university life and the student revolution at a time in which many upwardly mobile followers of Elijah were also embarking on an American higher education. The Panthers were competing with the changing NOI to recruit young members of the new bourgeoisie that was forming out of the traditional black petite-bourgeoisie and the Great Society programs, in institutions of higher education and in the civil services.

On the Berkeley campus, the young middle class woman who was to become Fahizah Alim helped in the Panthers' breakfast and other programs among inner-city children and youth, albeit wincing at all those "showings of arms" directed to the TV cameras. Her boyfriend of the time was a "loud, angry, Panther wannabe, a middle-class revolutionary stamping around in combat boots and sporting a wild Afro." Most in the class recited strident poems denouncing the pigs but she felt drawn to a quiet, neat, somber Muslim who read a poem about the role of "the Black Man" [*sic*] in creating a safe world for his family. Her "middle-class" aspect had not warmed to the "unkempt vulgarity and disorder" of the Panthers. At the other end of the options, she had considered but rejected the integrationist movement headed by Martin Luther King, Jr. as too passive in the protest it dramatized. By Christmas 1969 she had decided not to carry a gun or let any man rotate her around his comrades "for the revolution." Elijah and the Nation of Islam had appeal somewhere between those two options.

Fahizah was struck when the NOI adherent in her class, having carefully put her in touch with the NOI, then cut the contact because he was married, sidestepping any romantic involvement [=like a moral bourgeois WASP young man stepped straight from some 1953 issue of *The Reader's Digest,* or from a popularizing Islamic magazine of Nasser's modernist-nationalist Egypt]. The Nation of Islam gave a sense of security to Fahizah Alim as to other women converts of the time through its unquestioning submission to a highly disciplined line of authorities that were "Black" after a lifetime of white power, particularly in a period in which all things looked to be falling apart. For her, the Nation of Islam under Elijah was a sheltering "womb" in which she and other members could develop in a directed way but which she was to outgrow. The dignity of the "regal", focused, non-sexual personality that the sect fostered in its women members blinded her for the time to the restricted range of roles and opportunities it offered females. The chaste fine manners of the young male Muslims offered respect to women and the hope that sex would be personal and mean something lasting when it did come through marriage. Fahizah exulted at the success with which the Nation transformed drug-addicts, thugs, convicts and prostitutes into productive parents with stable families. Yet she gradually realized that not all had been completely remade. Some Fruit of Islam retained the violent habits of their pasts, the stress on authority and submission could enable those higher up in the system to impose quasi-totalitarian controls on ordinary members and end privacy, and anyone who tried to correct malfunctions by a critique was branded a hypocrite or an enemy and could face a ritual beating.

The Nation's denunciations of white culture and its claims that it was restoring to Black people in America the civilization and culture of which their forefathers had been robbed at enslavement satisfied Alim as a restoration of authentic identity that would now make the converts energetic in their daily lives. When Elijah died in 1975, Fahizah Alim made the transition to orthodox international Islam and Arabic prayers under Warith, and then her Islam all seems to have come to an end—albeit leaving some good memories with her. In her 1998 retrospective, she saw that while a student she had not been as great a "liberator" as she had thought with her work tutoring inner-city kids or enrolling voters: such activities had left less time for the educational opportunities that her world-class university, Berkeley, offered. She seems in 1998 to have still not understood how similar to U.S. middle class values were the family patterns and social attitudes her Muslims so painstakingly rebuilt behind a symbolic racial separation with Arabic clichés, or how modest an autonomy the Muslims or Panthers sought from whites behind all that shouting. The voting rights, Mao-validated integration and even the fashionable, tawdry, sexual liberation that the Panthers imitated, had been similarly American.

For all the strident poems and TV guns, she and the Panthers had constructively extended the system, and worked for the integration of Americans, by pressuring Berkeley to move forward from narrow Anglo-centrism to offer academic courses that would henceforth cover the range of the populations in America. Her conversion to Elijah's Islam was in a setting in which diverse classes and groups of African-Americans were coming together in a mainstream modernity: a rather middle-class woman even in her origins, Alim's community work among the Black poor near Berkeley showed the drive of many young people at the time to transcend classes and construct "Black" or "Afro-American" Nationhood in America.[62]

A deeper assessment of the NOI in the 1960s and 1970s as a neo-bourgeois movement in such specific settings as the colleges and universities, must indeed not just sample mosque-attending confirmed Muslims but trace the influence of all U.S. groups on each other and the turnover from each. Many times more Blacks passed through the NOI—but were altered by it—or through the Panthers, than stayed in either group. We saw in chapters 3 and 4 that Anglo radical rationalism, and the denial of divinity to Jesus by the Jehovah's Witnesses and their proclaiming of an imminent Judgement Day, made blacks likelier to hear out Fard and Elijah's rejection of the crucified Jesus as God.

Virgil Dugue, born in 1954 in Louisiana, once wanted to become a Catholic priest but found that the clergy in his seminary were drunkards, with one a homosexual and another who got his niece pregnant. Meeting with discrimination in secondary school, he read *The Autobiography of Malcolm X* and books about the African slave trade and took part in boycotts. In college, Dugue felt attracted to the Panthers who shouted about winning power from the barrel of the gun: he did not join but hawked their newspaper and shared joints—but not their atheism—with them. When the Nation of Islam came to his campus, their teaching that the White Man is the Devil explained to him why whites enslaved and murdered millions of blacks and Amerindians: he duly converted. He became a tense neo-bourgeois with a "secular job at a community center" who spent all his remaining time (save four hours for sleep) outside selling *Muhammad Speaks*. Then he became disillusioned on seeing that all the proceeds were going to NOI headquarters; and that a Euro-American lawyer who had defended him well did not fit into other devil-like whites he had known.

But the NOI had skillfully cited the New Testament to impress upon Dugue that Jesus was not God. This was the Islamic teaching that stuck for him: heading towards a nervous breakdown, he converted to the Jehovah's Witnesses because they too said Jesus was not to be worshipped, and like the NOI, did not celebrate Christmas and the other pagan holidays of the so-called Christian churches. White guides and an African-American bride awaited him with the New Orleans Witnesses.[63] Here we see how the Panthers, the Nation of Islam and the perhaps non-Christian Jehovah's Witnesses in succession saved the sanity of one oppressed minority youth and guided him to relate constructively to other Americans through offering them print-literacy—although the newspapers he hawked changed.

At their worst, the Black Panthers were a sort of ghetto put-on, evoking degrees of resistance or alternative parallel government they simply had neither the means nor any wish to actualize—often just feigning fierceness to trick resources or concessions out of the white system. Yet, the Panthers identified and dramatized important issues to America. They publicized black health problems, like sickle cell anemia, years before even most black media did so (although *Ebony* did), forcing the general American health system to act.[64]

Leaders and members of the Student Nonviolent Coordinating Committee (SNCC), ex-integrationists who had been radicalized by the struggle for civil rights in the South in which they had had Euro-Christian and Jewish partners, developed more elements for a positive cultural nationalism than had the Panthers.[65] Stokely may have vociferated that the struggle of his people was a "black thing", cutting out the whites and Jews amidst whom his personality had formed in New York, but he saw the need to reconnect to more than "the threads of resistance that our ancestors laid down for us." Much more than the Panthers, he refused to let "geography" determine "the question of community." He had an Africanist sense of exile as intense as Malcolm's—and as open-bordered. His aim was the "survival [of] a people whose entire culture, whose entire history, whose entire way of life has been destroyed." Carmichael certainly always defined Africa to include its Arabs and Berbers in the "blood of the same blood and flesh of the same flesh" into which African-Americans now had to re-fuse. His drive to internationalize his people's struggle to connect out into all West-colonized peoples of color in Africa, Asia and Latin America further worked to blur the borders of the more intimate "nation" comprised of (a) blacks in the Americas and (b) the Africans of their areas of origin. His drive for the broad global community of color carried forward the not uniformly-featured globe-scattered "Black Nation" of Elijah's Muslims, which in its turn may have come from the faint ghosts of assumptions from a bygone old African Islam handed down in African-American folklore.[66]

Cleaver frankly left "in abeyance" the "insoluble" question of "land" (continuous territorial homeland), although correctly pointing out that in this ambiguity he was just like all the major currents of Black Nationalism and Black Power, past (Garvey: Back to Africa) and present, in America.[67] [The purchases of land by the Moors and the Nation of Islam, and after WWII by the Republic of New Afrika, had not amounted to even enclave-homelands]. The Panthers' formal positions—that a world-wide uprising by peoples of color to overthrow capitalism would set blacks free to achieve sovereignty or devolution in the U.S.—unmistakably postponed insurrection. But they glimpsed the real dialectic unfolding between (a) the shifting relations between the states of the globe as direct colonialism ended and (b) the increasing chances for some new form of African-American nationalism as America headed towards its post-modern era. Cleaver in 1968 grasped how globalization was beginning to diversify the possibilities for distinctness now opening before African-Americans: true, he was too hopeful about the potentialities of the shaky emerging independent states, given the limitations of their elites and their resources:

> I say that the world is becoming such a small community that the whole question of [continuous] geographic homelands does seem to dwindle in importance. A lot of black people do want a geographical homeland of their own... The primary function of black people now is to get organizational power. Once they get that power they can relate to the Third World powers throughout the world, and through this coalition we can force the type of settlement upon the U.S. that we decide we want.[68]

This again typified the usual Panther refusal to choose a clear course or option. But their era only offered so much understanding or resources. It was from c. 1973 that the decisive globalization, the growth of the black bourgeoisie and the devolution of resources from the thinning central government of America were to open the way for the emergence of full micronations in America. Continuous territoriality was not to be a problem for them in the age of PCs and the internet. Farrakhan was to spearhead the wider connection of the Black enclave-nation or micronation out into African, Muslim and Asian polities overseas, in unprecedented engagement by the Nation of Islam tradition with U.S. mainstream representative politics.

Elijah Muhammad on the New Left and the Campus Revolts

The sudden jarring changes that weakened the authority of America's elite in many campuses in the 1960s led to an opening-up of the system from which African-American Muslims could benefit, as the Panthers did. However, Elijah Muhammad only reacted cautiously to the campus "revolution." Overall, he sounded closer to the U.S. educational establishment and voiced the cautious horror of real social destruction, when it comes, that recurs in his conservative sect and its descendants.

In his conservative mode, the revolt of mainly white students appalled his covert admiration for American institutions and mainstream—white—creativity and wealth. He urged "the philosophers and scientists" [of what race or mix of races?] to look into the destruction of America's educational system that was in turn destroying "their wisdom to educate the people." Although to him, as a millenarian, it was a perhaps deserved "curse" brought by Allah/God, he was not among the "many [who] look without taking a second thought on the destruction of America's education." Here Elijah condemned the white new left and white journalists in sympathy with it, but perhaps also the Black Panthers and other more secular black nationalists who were projecting themselves and their issues within the campuses as well as on the streets—overshadowing the NOI. On and off, Elijah did develop a constructive vision, as, though, did the Panthers, also in *their* veiled way. Education was the guide enabling "the people to keep and maintain a civilized life." In this twinge of identification, Elijah was appalled to see "the American people" coming to a point where they were destroying the very libraries housing their textbooks of education, fighting their teachers, setting fire to schools, colleges and universities. Elijah here was thinking like Nixon—and indeed like Ronald Reagan!—although he often condemned American militarism abroad.

Elijah had become aware that some "Black people of today"—the new more secular black nationalists active on campuses—"are blindly helping the white people to destroy this civilization." They were like Samson who in his day pulled the building down just to get even, without considering the future of his people and those people he was destroying. Here, Elijah sharply grasped the linkages of interest and ideology that he and his stratum had acquired to America's central institutions in which his youth now were enrolling and getting jobs. His limited Nation, through the upward mobility he had directed over decades, was too close to winning through to all those institutions offered, for him to endorse their wholesale destruction.

That millenarian side of him that wanted the destruction of America and whites, though, felt vindicated that "her colleges, her universities and her teachers are in danger", that "the students no longer want old world guidance. But in their mad destruction of the old world they do not know how to prepare for a new world civilization [because] they refuse to hear a teacher teaching of an educational system of a better civilization... the civilization of the Blackman." This coming superior educational system of the aboriginal Black Man of the earth had never been known to this world, in which God put the Black Man to sleep in order to let the white man try his hand at ruling. In this millenarian mode, his vocal persona, Elijah regarded the "100 per cent" dissatisfaction and disintegration in America as no loss because Allah (God) would soon come to "guide another people into setting up a better educational system for the people of whom He Himself is the Head." In this swing to his millenarian, eschatological side, Elijah exulted in God's destruction of America's dying world educational system that "only kept us slaves to the white man." America was crashing and bursting asunder in its final end: "Allah (God) will destroy her for she is the most evil one of the white race, more evil than Europe, worse than her father England".[69]

However, Elijah was wrong in fearing that the Black Panthers or Africanist nationalists around Stokely Carmichael and the Black Power movement could have much harmed America, given their scant resources, their disorientation and the ambiguity of their social and ideological interactions with the diverse Euro-Americans. The macho guns were a playing to the media that deluded white New Leftists that they were joining in a multi-racial "revolution" that in reality was only adjusting the landscape of the actual possibilities in American society and politics. In their symbiotic relationship, the Panthers, in confirming that a revolutionary movement had to be led by a black vanguard, "got the white radicals off the hook" of having to build a unified society. The civil rights movement, in sending young Northern Jews off to the South to take on "the crackers", had earlier freed them from confronting their own elders and strata back home who also could ill-treat blacks.

Still, Elijah was right that revolution seemed to be in the air among the privileged young from 1965. The world was unraveling: black people had wrested the right to be taught their history in the mainstream's top educational institutions, and the budding women's movement now followed suit. (Nation of Islam media vented contempt against the white new women who were asserting their right to bed any race or any sex: they were trying to inveigle young blacks away from their Nation's women and were just another new face of the old supremacist Devil). Although contained and then eviscerated, the radical student movements in which the Black Nationalists served as an emblem made it impossible for the U.S. elite to carry through in Vietnam the imperial tendencies in the foreign policy it had been pursuing since WWII.[70] In a modest way, those campus movements did help induct into the apex bodies of learning African-American students and budding academics who went on to consider the Marxist ideas the New Left proposed, ideas which the resourceful "Blacks", as always, turned to their own needs. Overall, though, the new young Afro-American leftists and secular nationalists were a limited ideological threat to the NOI, with little capacity to really take over leadership of African-Americans in general.

Elijah on the Factionalization of Blacks

At least in his public discourse in the leadup to his death, Elijah Muhammad kept up his sect's traditional fire against Black middle-class clergy and political leaders. But sometimes he had a shrill tone that let slip that he felt himself to be facing serious challengers or being left behind by the new forces among African-Americans who were now raising Malcolm and King as icons for ideologies now being evolved. Elijah had been rattled by the new youthful black nationalists who evoked Malcolm X to his face and that of his members—"you come around trying to argue with us" [was he fearing that their armed or rhetorical radicalism made his sect look like passé wimps?]. "You may be able to wreck the whole of America", retorted Elijah, accepting here the value that the new generation of black nationalists put upon their resources and strength, "but you have nothing to replace it with." As ever, Elijah said he was waiting for God to come and to fight on behalf of the Blacks: "vengeance is Mine saith the Lord, I will repay." His rain, snow, hail and earthquakes could "destroy America at once, but He brings her destruction upon her gradually, as the Holy Qur'an teaches".[71]

To again highlight the Nation of Islam to blacks as the radicals who were working for their "independence", Elijah equated his great opponent in Islam, Malcolm X, with the "turn-the-other cheek" Martin Luther King, Jr.: both had been integrationists and slavish instruments of whites. In this communication, which said little that was positive about any African-American outside his sect, Elijah charged that the devil was brilliantly spreading division among African-Americans by getting the Black people to idolize other Black leaders. Martin Luther King, Jr. was not the disciple of any Black man: he had urged Black Americans to integrate with white people and become white folk, and then the white man killed him—which could be the fate, warned Elijah, of any Blacks who continued to worship the white man after King's fashion. Rev. Martin Luther King, Jr. had not sought an independent home for Blacks as Moses had for Israel after oppression in Egypt, and as Elijah continued to do. Here, Elijah let slip his assessment that the largest single group among African-Americans still supported integrationism of the type taught by Martin Luther King, Jr..[72]

Malcolm X was the same. In Elijah's view, Malcolm left the NOI as a hypocrite. He went and joined white people and worshipped them, and he got the same recompense as King. The white man was naming colleges after Malcolm only to entice black audiences to join in the philosophy which he bequeathed—"that white people are good." Malcolm had acquired that doctrine in the Arab World: he went to Mecca where he saw white people, was excited to eat from the same plate with them, and decided to join in with the white man, although he had been taught the history of the grafted white man's birth and impending collective execution.

This attack by Elijah on Malcolm brought out that the Arab states had exercised some power in African-American religious and political life from the early 1950s: if that heartland of Islam had rejected the claim of any black in America to be a Muslim, then, given the globalizing revolution in mass media, especially TV, that was taking place, that black American would lose legitimacy in that aspect among even local ghetto populations.[73] Malcolm's consistent strategy ever since his prison conversion of appealing for support from Arab and Islamic states finally became a real threat to the standing of Elijah, Elijah's anger now revealed, years later. Malcolm had "[sought] my place over the people by going over the earth and making a mockery of me." Even after Malcolm was well dead, this maneuver still activated duality and ambivalence in Elijah towards the Arab countries. On one hand it irritated him into a sense that some Muslims present in Mecca—perhaps some Arabs—were white, i.e. were ideologically aligned with the white supremacy manifested in America, and thus might well corrupt some Black American Muslims into collaboration with the U.S. white overlords. But Elijah's more pan-Islamic side countered with his sense that "the very people of Mecca and Egypt and other places he [Malcolm] went are with me today." Nonetheless, the competition with other African-American leaders for followers in America remained the primary contest: "here, in the United States of America, today, I have more followers than I had before Malcolm said a word".[74]

At his more inflexible, Elijah Muhammad in the late 1960s and 1970s failed to grasp or capitalize on his and the NOI's position as part of the DNA in the new generation: some of his themes had been built into their new movements from their outset. He did not like the sometimes very close interactions emerging young Left black radicals were having with the educated Jews and other whites who were teaching them so much. Here, Elijah was not realizing that those on-campus African-Americans held up the Nation of Islam to those Euro-Americans as one almost immemorial component at the heart of their radical Black protest movement. At the invitation of the New Left's David Horowitz, a Jewish-American, Donald Warden, a young black law student who loved Castro, contributed an article in which he denied that civil rights or the liberal white Northerners [heavily Jewish] around it would solve "the Negro problem." Against Martin Luther King, Jr., Warden held up the analysis of "the psychological oppression of blacks by white values" articulated by the Nation of Islam, who were "virtually unknown" for Horowitz—which only showed that that youth-Left now had a leader who mainly listened to or read himself and his white clique. Warden's stress that Black Americans' "internal colony" had to link up with revolutionary movements in the Third World drew upon coverage in *Muhammad Speaks* of Arab movements that the coming Black Panthers, for whom Warden was to be a mentor, would befriend.[75]

Clearly, Elijah was being too rigid. That the new black nationalist and black leftist youth came round to argue with NOI figures stemmed from Elijah and the NOI's ideology being a part of their being. Elijah and his colleagues could have been more friendly, more concerned to learn new things themselves, which might have enabled them to deepen their influence on those pro-Arab youth through joint activities—e.g. exchanges between the schools both movements built to reclaim blacks. Under Elijah, however, the Nation of Islam was a closed ideology and social group that too often sought no dialogue with anyone. Farrakhan, though, was learning the lesson: after he built a new NOI, in 1978 he was to invite Left, Africanist and Christian blacks to write in his newspaper as a united front organ.

Elijah was coming to grips with the paradoxical reality that their status as dead tragic martyrs gave his rivals, Martin and Malcolm, more appeal, and over a broader spectrum, and thus in a way more power, than they had had while still alive. Elijah retorted that he would still have the same power and protection from Allah (God) "regardless to whether every one of you rejects following me—I mean the whole thirty million of you." This perceived unresponsiveness of most U.S. Blacks did not matter because "we have a world of Black people that I can continue to teach, and they are anxious for me to come and teach them." Perhaps Elijah was remembering the old offer from Nasser for him to base himself in Egypt so as to reap converts "in the millions" in West Africa [which might further Egypt's influence there].[76] "I do not give two cents for you following Malcolm if you want. You will get divine death and destruction with no one to give you any honor and respect ... only the devil whom you serve." The rejecting African-Americans could have a world full of devils aiding them as they scrabbled to get what the devil offered: but Allah (God) had already come to put an end to the enemy devils and their power to rule.[77]

Having depicted all his serious opponents as having little positive to offer African Americans, and most African-Americans as ingrates, Elijah then offered to weld a united front—one with little enough give-and-take about it. "If all the little Black organizations who are trying to do something for self would unite with me and make a complete body of one, we will most certainly have salvation in our hands at once." He expected, though, that the egos of others would prove too big: each would be "like Christianity, with each one sitting and enjoying his little part" which would finally cost each the part he had built up. The other groups and movements would have to come to him for a unification, simply because, from his point of view, "you do not have anything for me to unite with you for. You have nothing but a chain carrying it around that any wise civilized [*sic*] man can take and bind you with" There was almost a relish on his part here that the dominant civilized devil-Anglos continued to use up and ill-treat both the civil rights activists and the new black nationalists who in various ways all strove, much as Elijah imaged, to get into America under a variety of protest-discourses.[78] The skills in exercising control and hegemony that his white race-enemies had developed may have struck the innermost Elijah as a wise civilized technology from which he himself was borrowing on his humbler plane, as he readied his sect to lead the as yet "non-civilized" masses of African-Americans in general.

America was being torn to pieces politically as the political party of Pharaoh had been when it confined the Hebrews. Yet the conservative

Elijah, in his ameliorist aspect, leaned more to the old black career politicians than to the new sensational radicals. The cowardly spiritual leaders were the ones whom the devils were using to confuse the blacks, more than "the political leaders of Black America".[79] Elijah's ingrained hatred of Christianity left a tiny gap for the conservative African-American career politicians to agree on joint actions with him in the era of rapid change. But then he urged the foolish so-called Negroes to "unite and ask the government for a portion of America"—purportedly a separate statelet—in which to live in peace.[80]

A purely religious spiritual violence that leaves the incineration to God could always suddenly jump to fighting between the two human groups. Elijah warned whites who wanted to go to war against Allah and the freedom Allah came to grant the slaves, that Pharaoh before them had not wanted Israel to go free in a land to themselves, only to be drowned by God in the Red Sea. "The [white American] losers of this war will land in a lake of fire, not water." Thus far, God was the one who does the fighting for the oppressed and carries out last judgements. But then Elijah reflected that if white America wanted to free her slaves, she could easily do so. "This would be simpler and easier than what she is doing: killing and provoking them through police force, national guards and finally the U.S. Army, as we see in Detroit, Michigan." Now Elijah shifts the focus again to the possibility that the Blacks might fight back. There was a continuum between the refusal of the slave-masters to approach their unarmed slave unless armed, and America's current display of many deadly weapons in the ghettoes "to cause fear among the so-called Negroes, but Allah is removing the fear".[81]

In the 1970s, Elijah sometimes sensed that events in America and the ideological development of the African-American people had passed him by. He thought America was succeeding in tricking many African-Americans to follow "hypocrites"—one-time followers who had moved on to new discreet or announced movements or agendas—to "doom." The general body of black Americans was not supporting his sect's attempts at collectivist economic self-development. If led by him, Black Americans "could buy hospitals and places to educate and train our people into the superior education of the nations of earth" [=Judgement Day or no, this remained a porous sect very quick to seize all patterns for ameliorist secular development that it saw anywhere in the Third World—and in the "white" West much more]. But African-Americans instead preferred to give their money over to white Americans and let them spend it on what they wanted so long as "they pay you a little interest: we offer interest too, the highest of interest, but you do not trust us." Elijah's Muslims would build on, regardless, and be the winners, as the scriptures had prophesied for those who would believe.[82] Black men in America had been so divided against each other that they constantly did evil to each other. The Muslims gave the predominantly black Midway Technical School in Chicago $30,000 to clear them of their debts. In return, they only tried to wreck all the beautiful businesses the Muslims had set up for them on the south side of Chicago, Illinois.[83]

***Muhammad Speaks*' Coverage of Internal America**

In the 1960s and 1970s, only the Nation of Islam among the ideological groups in Afro-America [and perhaps the NAACP] had the media instruments to transmit a self-contained, sustained discourse across to the African American masses. The social, international and religious ideas of *Muhammad Speaks* had an incomparably wider, and more cumulative, influence on the ghetto masses and the petite bourgeoisie: the media of new more secular groups had much smaller circulations, at least until the Panthers took off in the 1970s. *The Liberator*, launched in 1961, was a forum for would-be civil rights politicians who attacked Martin Luther King, Jr.: despite its racially mixed editorial board, its staff sometimes called for protest and revolution and explored the unfulfilled legacy of al-Hajj Malik El Shabazz (Malcolm X). But the journal's circulation was small, totaling only 200 in the Harlem stronghold. With hundreds of thousands buying *Muhammad Speaks*, observed pro-Arab secularist Harold Cruse (1969), the NOI was able throughout the 1960s to recruit many from the unaffiliated, anti-integrationist, nationalist youth whose numbers were growing steadily throughout the decade.[84]

As the premier mass-circulation African-American tabloid of the 1960s and 1970s, *Muhammad Speaks* may have drawn to its editorial staff a few crypto-Communists or ex-Communists. As the Cold War intensified, the Communist bloc won a certain luster for some African-Americans in search of a protest that white America would notice. To a minor extent, this was the case with Elijah, also. In an isolated sentence, he considered whether "we would worship China and Russia against them?" But his sect would not, for it had the support of Allah (God), who was more mighty than all those nations.[85]

Input from Marxism and Marxists may have helped the *Muhammad Speaks* writers evolve their meticulously-focused, highly professional, reportages of the sufferings of the poorest classes of blacks across the countryside. A 1974 piece by Harold 4X and Joe Delaney of its Atlanta Bureau starkly conveyed the pain in the Mississippi Delta, "a stretch of rich, black soil where Black people by the thousands are slowly starving to death." It did not project that blacks there had many chances to progress and build wealth like those Elijah promised the North's ghettos. Tourists could observe "Blacks" bending to pick "scrap" cotton on a plantation in 1974 for $2.5O per hundred pounds: in the 1940's that had brought $2. The development of cotton picking machines and chemical weed killers had shrunk the need for functions black laborers had once had, in the cotton fields.

With Gorky-like sharpness, the item traced the sufferings of Mrs Bonnie Staten of Marks, Mississippi, "a typical victim in the land of despair." Married at the age of 14, she went into the hospital in 1940 and the doctor advised her never to work again: she underwent three major operations. As a young girl, Mrs. Staten had to do a great deal of plowing, carrying 100-pound fertilizer sacks on her back and picking cotton for her widowed mother who later died. Now, in 1974, her body was wracked with rheumatism and arthritis. In 1968, following the advice of civil rights leaders she would come to despise as sellouts with few real programs of benefit to ordinary people, she took a trip to Jackson to hear the soon-to-be-assassinated Senator Robert Kennedy speak at a Democratic Party rally. When she returned to Marks, she and her family were evicted from the Posey Mount Plantation on a three-day notice. Her husband could not find work in the county, and eventually fled to Chicago for work. On 1 May 1974, Black women who worked as maids on plantations were given cuts in their working time of three and four hours a day to avoid paying them the minimum wage. The item showed how the operation of private enterprise and the markets increased the sufferings of Mississippi blacks: little food was planted in the rich soil of the Delta because of commercial cotton, milk was scarcely available for babies because cattle or dairy farming were rare: the few factories such as cottonseed oil mills were laying off people.[86] This item then, tended to see black suffering as structural to a capitalism that would not leave them the margin for self-development for which Elijah hoped.

It was in its focused dissections of social suffering such as this that *Muhammad Speaks* drew closest to America's (traditional rather than New) Left, and the Nation of Islam sounded like it might have some potential, after all, to be at the head of an active revolution from the ranks of the poor in America, rather than the projector of doom to whites from the flying saucers that never quite arrive.

4. POSSIBILITIES FOR RELATIONSHIP WITH THIRD WORLD PEOPLES

Elijah's Muslims in the 1960s and 1970s had widening interaction with immigrant Arabs and Muslims, and with Muslim countries in the Third World. The contacts were fed by the unfolding of the Middle Eastern elements inherent in the hybrid culture and religion with which the NOI had started out in 1930. Yet the interests in Third World Muslims and their states that Elijah's Muslims were developing were also nourished by new expectations about the Arabo-Muslim World among a wider range of groups and currents in the African-American people.

Growing African-American Cultural Attraction to Sub-Saharan Africa

Muhammad Speaks carried frequent articles on resistance to apartheid in South Africa, and on the struggle of Africans against Portuguese colonialism and the white supremacists of Rhodesia.[87] From around 1965, real knowledge of and identification with Black Africa spread among young conscious African-Americans, in the ghettoes and in the colleges and universities alike: in particular, they studied, and with some success, Arabic-strewn Swahili, which was easier than tonal languages of the ancestral West Africa. This new generation of Afro-centrists affirmed, at grass-roots level in the North's ghettoes, real threads detached out from African cultures: the Mother-Continent Africa was no more something far away from these African-American mass audiences. Although most of them were not Muslim, many of these populist black nationalists either had passed through or been on the fringes of the Nation of Islam, and certainly respected it as the most cohesive and sustained black protest movement that 20th century America had seen. The secular black nationalists around New York's *Black News* accepted that Islam was a deep-rooted element in the sub-Saharan black Africa with which they wanted African Americans to relink themselves. Accordingly, standard literary Arabic was one of the languages that the new secular Black Nationalists, too, were learning.[88]

It is not so easy, though, to unite continents long socially separated one from another. Not alert to the opportunities for a new international community with benefits to both parties, some African visitors to the USA were amused at what they saw as the superficial unevenness of this recovery of African identity. At the end of the 1960s, the Washington Black Power leader, Rev. Douglas Moore, asked a touring Kenyan the Swahili equivalent of "I will crush you like flour", which he in a speech that night duly applied against "those playing with our rights." This visitor, Martin Njoroge, concluded that "their [African-Americans'] 'Afro shops'—supposed to sell African clothing and works of art—make you realize that they have a petty, visionary Africa in mind, not the one that I came from." Njoroge argued that most Kenyan and other African leaders considered black Americans in Africa as much foreigners as the white Americans who came there. However, the Kenyan MP, Mark Mithwaga, had undertaken a "Let the Negro return to Africa" campaign.[89]

Most of the new Africanist Black Nationalists respected the Muslims' long-standing affirmations of some relationship of Afro-Americans with a dark humanity of an "East" that would extend far beyond Africa, south of the Sahara. They, too, knew that Islam and even Arabic had a living presence in the Negro African countries. Some of these young Black nationalists would have accepted Elijah's Muslims as collaborators or perhaps guides in the enterprise of reconnecting Black Americans to the diverse Mother Continent—and indeed to Arabs beyond it. (Rev. Douglas Moore was also the mover of a resolution condemning Israel for violating Palestinian rights and cooperating with South Africa passed by the mainstream first National Black Political Convention held in Gary, Indiana, in March 1972; Moore had in 1971 also protested the efforts of the Zionist ADL to halt federal funding for the anti-drug clinic of Moorish leader, Hassan Jeru-Ahmed).[90] In the upshot, however, the Nation of Islam voiced American separateness from, as well as relationship with, sub-Saharan Africa.

In the 1970s, the Nation of Islam's national representative, Minister Louis Farrakhan, told an Africanist nationalist audience in blunt language that the Nation of Islam now considered Blacks in North America irreversibly separated from Black Africa. American blacks now could never again be made a constituent of the African community while resident in another continent, as the secular Afro-nationalists in vain were hoping. In assailing re-Africanization, Farrakhan—somewhat like Elijah—vented irritation that the Africanist nationalists were putting their atomized African cultural elements on parade in public space, as successfully as the NOI had when highlighted its Islam for two decades using similar parades:

> You play the drums and dance up and down the street, and get all sweaty... and then what have you accomplished? Nothing! 'But I get an African culture, I'm really going home' they often reply. Well, Elijah Muhammad teaches us that culture is the outgrowth of knowledge at a particular period in history. Whatever a man's culture was, as he evolves and he gets a new knowledge, he develops a new tradition—new culture, new ideas, new way of life. That traditional African was our culture, but today we're in a new day and we're getting a new wisdom. And we must bring forth a totally new culture.

Farrakhan's rebuke showed that the Black Muslims in the 1970s were grasping more the separateness and diversity of the wide range of groups that comprised darker humanity. But it was more than pragmatic adjustment to the reality that America's blacks had acquired a separate history and become a separate socio-cultural unit or spatial community that the NOI now had to build into a new discrete belief-Nation. More, Farrakhan spoke here with sharp affect to the specificities of American blacks [and to the American way?]. New links with far-off Black Africans were not to be allowed to become far-reaching enough to eliminate the American particularities that the U.S. Negroes had acquired. Farrakhan didn't lament the Afro-Americans' distinctness that separated them from Africa because he believed those Black American patterns—[in part patterns and motifs that they had adapted from their Anglo neighbors]—were superior:

> We are something unique and, therefore, what we speak of must be unique... [If we go and pattern ourselves after] Africa, then you cannot be guided right because Africa today is looking for a better way, and you are the better way for Africa.

Thus, intact African culture not only could not be restored in the American environment, it should not be. Too much time had passed since blacks in America lost the viable African cultures that they had once had.

Farrakhan's speech to the African nationalists of "the East", i.e. Brooklyn, was another surge of the layer of America-directedness that recurs in the personality of all sects of African American Muslims. The priority that Muslims of the NOI tradition have always given to solving specific grass-roots American problems facing the poor urban African-Americans they address, to realizing self-uplift and prosperity without wasting time, has time and again limited the demands and inputs they allow from their continents-spanning Islamic or African connections. Moreover, Farrakhan's speech had not only a pride in the achievements of U.S. blacks but a tacit sharp respect for white-directed America's unequalled modernity and richness. The priority goes to actualizing prosperity for underprivileged African Americans by the duplication of sectors of American capitalism's ethos and techniques, which are however given a blended black nationalist and Islamic tint.[91]

The conventional American-ness of these Islamic African-Americans should never be underestimated. Opposite this speech in which Farrakhan distanced Africa, the paper carried a denunciation of Marxism: Black Socialist Worker Party members who advocated "revolutionary consciousness and worker solidarity" might "mislead Black people from taking the only intelligent action they can take in this day and time." Capitalism with its "enormous mutability" readily accommodated itself to "novel situations," as had been illustrated by "the New Dealism of the Roosevelt era, the welfare capitalism resulting from the transformation of unionized threats into hard-hat accomplices, etc." The Black masses consistently had rejected the alien [Marxist] concepts of "Jewish intellectuals." The potential to disrupt society was latent in the Black Muslim movement, but commitment to some of the ideology of white America's capitalist system, and a discreet search for some niche in it, had been early built in the 1930s into the Nation of Islam's protest rhetoric. Black Muslim ministers and *Muhammad Speaks* and other organs—although often tacitly or in muted language—have regularly conveyed to their African American audiences that capitalist America, despite white evil in it, posed the requirements of modernity that everyone has to meet.

Elijah did not think—or at least sometimes would not admit—that he had anything to learn from the new generation of youth, either white or black. The hippies' symbolic revolt and the white "return to nature" horrified him. Some of the white people were coming out again with the long, straggly hair of their cave-ancestors, which a few foolish, unlearned black people imitated. Elijah was similarly unsympathetic to the new black generation's linking up with animist Africa and its traditions. He had for nearly forty years been urging the Black Man in America "that we should accept our own": but instead of going to the decent side of his own [Islam? Arabia? Muslim areas of sub-Saharan Africa?], he goes back seeking the traditional Africa of the "jungle life" still to be viewed "in some uncivilized parts of Africa today." Non-shaving blacks in America who cultivated "savage dress" would not win the love of their brothers and sisters in Africa because the dignified people of Africa are either Muslim or educated Christians—except that Africa today does not want Christianity. To "get a home in Africa after the war", blacks from America would have to have accepted Islam to be let in.[92] The Nation of Islam's media were offering abundant data on the oppression and struggles of Africans, but usually did not have an open and exploratory stance to African beliefs and cultures. *Muhammad Speaks* exulted in 1964—prematurely for most of the continent—that expanding Islam was breaking the control of Christianity on Africans as they became politically independent.[93]

For their part, the USA's new secular Africanist nationalists had a love-hate relationship to the Nation of Islam, which had long registered on their psyches as an option they had all considered at some time in their lives—but rejected. *Black News* noted in the wake of the February 1975 death of "the Honorable Messenger of Allah, Mr Elijah Muhammad" that "many hearts in our communities skipped a beat", feeling an era had ended. The Africanist magazine revered Elijah because he "had built a little of nothing into a massive [business] empire"—sustaining "the most orderly, disciplined, and successful organization Blacks have constructed and kept alive since their arrival in America." But the admiration was blended with deep rage at the materialist stance of superiority and "extreme isolation" that the adherents struck [as an Islamic micronation within the African-American enclave-nation] towards other black Americans in the 1960s and 1970s. As more and more Mercedes-Benzes and Cadillacs lined the blocks around the temples, and larger and more elaborate edifices were constructed for all of the enterprises of the Nation, the Muslims' general attitude became "since we got the wealth that shows we got all the answers." Lashing back, *Black News* alluded to rumors that the Nation, which had preached so hard and long against all immoral activities, was actually trafficking drugs into the black communities.

The Africanist magazine charged that the "Asiatic Blackman" theme the NOI had kept up since its emergence in 1930 had "always smacked with denial that all Black people are in fact Afrikans"—"self-hatred" that veiled true experience and true identity. It hoped that Warith Muhammad's renaming of blacks as "Bilalians" [after the Arabian Prophet Muhammad's Abyssinian adherent, Bilal Ibn Rabah] at last defined them as Africans so that new followers "could openly side with their Brothers in struggle all over the globe and truly understand that we are one" and, in regard to culture and ideology, at last "explore, hopefully freely, the vast storehouse of African culture" [which neither Wallace nor Farrakhan's successor "Nations" would truly fulfil after Elijah].

The Arab and orthodox Islamic atoms percolating and spreading through the NOI under Elijah had led naturally to the further step of the (more politicized) neo-Sunnism of a Malcolm X and a Wallace/Warith. The Africanists of *Black News* hoped that the new leader, Imam Warith, would control a trend that had been affiliating interested African-Americans to "racist" Arab and Asian elements that exercised power within the international Islamic community. By talking so positively about Mecca, Sa'udi Arabia, and Egypt on his return from them, *Black News* argued, al-Hajj Malik el-Shabazz (Malcolm X) caused many African-Americans to lose sight of the racism found within all institutional religions—Malcolm never got a chance to Africanize Islam. Just because Mecca is located in the [Arabic] "East" was no good reason that every Islamic authority has to be an Arab [—a view the Prophet Muhammad himself had stated in Arabia in his farewell speech to his followers before his death]. *Black News* allowed that Islam had to be a component in a new Africanist identity for African-Americans because "Islam has deep cultural roots amidst the peoples of Black Africa." But the magazine half predicted that the "nationalist" Arab and Asian leadership in international Islam, because of racism, now still would not recognize their African religious Brothers in the West although Wallace had made changes so that he could get into their conferences. [However, the swiftness with which Sa'udi Arabia and the Gulf states recognized Warith as perhaps the main Islamic leader in the USA took the wind out of such Africanists' demands that African-American and African Muslims be sealed off from the Arab and Asian Muslim countries and their prescriptive articulations of Islam.]

Wallace Muhammad's renaming of his followers after an Ethiopian—but Arabia-resident—companion of the Prophet Muhammad was dualistic and ambiguous. It did recognize some racial difference between African-Americans or Africans and most West Asian Arabs—yet in conceding the varying physiognomies at one and the same time symbolically placed the Blacks in the Arab lands, or in his people's case in those lands' standard Sunni Islam. As had been the case with Elijah before, Warith and his colleagues after 1975 would publicize political and economic issues of the sub-Saharan African peoples without much regard to their cultures or languages. Warith's early decision to welcome white members into the successor-sect, while meeting the non-racial ideology of Arab-led Sunni Islam, also was given impetus by the heavy rise in the 1970s of interracial marriages among upwardly mobile African-Americans, an expanding neo-bourgeois class to which the no-longer-so-lumpen Muslims with the Benzes more and more belonged.[94]

On the whole, up to 1975, Elijah and his colleagues had, as charged, side-stepped emotional fusion with sub-Saharan Africa alone, through their rather catholic and diffused definition of the global Black nation. Elijah voiced a rather skeletal awareness of decolonization and independence movements in sub-Saharan Africa as these picked up: "the white race has been disgracing the entire Black nation of the earth. Africa is suffering under the same wicked power of the white race and having an awful time trying to rid herself of such a demon. She will do so—and soon."[95] Yet, although "the Black Man in Africa is our brother, our central responsibility is with the Black man here in the wilderness of North America". His sect would not become a lobby, "expend our energies pleading for the cause of Africa"—not just yet.[96] Elijah projected that the endeavors of his sect to revive and uplift colored people in America would one day encompass all darker peoples of the world. Under the guidance of God, the NOI would unite the Black Nation[s] of the earth "who are leaving in search of us" now they had learnt that the black Americans had been abducted in the chains of slavery off to the Western Hemisphere.[97] Clearly, making Black Africans just one component in a worldwide "Black Nation" could diffuse the sect's energies away from their domestic goals into building a global, loose, "Black" community—or, conversely, for a time spare the U.S. black micronation being constructed the hard tasks that linking to those Black Africans had to entail.

Sometimes, though, in the 1960s and 1970s, Elijah saw that the maximal global mother-community for African-Americans had too much diversity in it for the concept of one wide Black Nation to encompass. The American Black man had lost many lives in the Pacific "while helping the white man to conquer the people of Japan who are the brown half-brother of the Black man" (like the Arabs?).[98]

The new rigorous Africanists, then, were right that the protean drives of Elijah and his ministers and journalists to connect African-Americans, black Africans, East Asians, South Asians and Arabs together as racially interrelated—and bursts of engaged coverage of Arab affairs from *Muhammad Speaks*—could harm focusing on Africa as the Mother Continent and on the non-Islamic nationalisms unfolding there. Yet that could save time and energy for lifting African-Americans, whom Elijah perhaps thought would not be in much shape to help others in other continents for a long time to come.

Attitudes to Arabs Among Americanist Integrationists and Secular Black Nationalists

After World War II, as in the 1920s and 1930s, lumpen-originated quasi-Muslim cults were growing in parallel with widening sympathy for Muslim states and liberation movements among bourgeois African-Americans. Thus, if the ghetto-based Muslim movements linked up politically with Third World Arabs and Muslims, such a pan-Islam would make their movements appeal more, not less, to educated Negroes, who in their turn could offer skills of their own to make such an international political bloc-community effective, although they identified less with the Islamic religious symbols of those cults.

Overall, the Arab World achieved quasi-independent states or launched insurrections for independence somewhat before populations in Africa below the Sahara did. The African—but in particular the African Arab—revolutions that followed World War II interested the vulnerable African-American bourgeoisie, integrationist and "separatist" alike, as replies to White Western power that Black America could never match as an outnumbered minority. That the Arab insurgents blended their armed revolt or resistance with cultural repudiation of Westerners appealed to African-American intellectuals. This attraction held for both middle-class civil rights integrationists and the new more radical "Black nationalist" intellectuals who became their critics. Harold Cruse excerpted 1956 acid from P.L.Prattis that if integration were put to a vote among South Africa's Blacks, they would reject it, as would the Arabs in North Africa who were fighting precisely against France's efforts to integrate or assimilate the eight million Algerians, to make Frenchmen out of them. These Arabs were fighting integration to establish "their own culture, their own religion, their own language" in independence from France, Prattis accurately analyzed. In contrast, he followed this for U.S. blacks with the chillingly realistic scenario that, given the disappearance of the Amerindians who had resisted, "integration is a must with us": African-Americans had to "help this white man in the time when the tide of war and civilization may change." Prattis' article had incendiary ambiguities and dualisms (which the angry Cruse missed). If an integrationist, Prattis was a ruthlessly clear-sighted one. He left no doubt about the violent past and the ingrained supremacism of many Anglo-Americans, who would come to terms with African-Americans only under heavy pressure from a shift of global power to Africans and Muslims through violence in decolonization.

Nationalist Harold Cruse had that same hope. He had been in the Anglo-French landings in Oran in November 1942: it struck him that French prejudice against Arabs in Algeria had the same intensity as Anglo-American antipathy to Negroes. Two Arab women asked his group of African-American troops if they were Arab: perhaps they might not quite know given that their fathers had been stolen from Africa so long ago. [Algerians become darker the farther South one goes]. To those Arabs and Africans—and the whole "colonial world"—fighting for cultural and political separation, Cruse disparagingly contrasted the struggle of the millions of Negroes in the southern part of the United States for integration. Here we see how the yearning of the most alienated educated African-Americans for a wide and varied, self-contained, national culture, denied to them by America, could highlight Islam and a literary Arabic, politically active within modernity. Written indigenous languages were much less salient in sub-Saharan struggles and new states, and lacked Arabic's universalist claims and roles endowed by the Qur'an.

The rebellious, radical Cruse charged that Arab models for liberation were being obscured—deliberately or from warped vision—by the forming civil rights establishment incarnate in Martin Luther King, Jr., who had achieved national and world fame as the young leader of the Montgomery, Atlanta, public bus boycott.

Here Cruse cited a December 1956 speech by King that had been published in the first quarter 1957 issue of *Phylon* magazine, "sponsored by Atlanta University, an all-Negro [*sic*] school". Such vitriol from Cruse in a following decade did not perceive the carefully-worded empathy for Africans and Asians that King, and many of his Civil Rights colleagues, always kept up, in this 1956 speech as in others. The "speech" had had a fair bit of cloaked radical granite in it. King placed "the nationalistic longings of Egypt" [=as now led by radical pan-Arab, Nasser] alongside "uprisings in Africa" [=undoubtedly including the independence struggle of Algeria's Muslims that had broken out two years earlier], discontent in Asia and the uprising against the Russians in Hungary, and all of those next to the struggle for civil rights amid the "racial tensions in America." The pains entailed in all those cases were the birth-pangs of a new world order that would benefit America's "Negroes." While King here named Hegel and may have implied the dialectic of the likewise German Marx who came after him, he voiced a strong identification, racial and thus more positive than a mere solidarity of a shared subjected status, with "the colored peoples of the world," 1.3 billion of whom had now become free as France, Britain and other colonial powers withdrew [=decolonization]. As well as Muslim nationalist movements in Africa and Asia, King was also endorsing the Indian nationalism of non-Christian Hindus and possibly Red China and Communists in Vietnam as all reconquering dignity and sovereignty for non-white people, the majority of humans, who had been "dominated politically, exploited economically, segregated and humiliated." Reverend King's equation of the system of satellite states that Stalin's Russia set up in Central and East Europe after WWII—insurgent "Hungary" —with colonialism, and racism in the U.S. showed that his sympathy for Asian and African movements challenging the West derived from emotions other than Marxism. It was hardly a compliment to the anti-Communist USA of the 1950s, though, to equate its treatment of blacks to subjugation by Russia against which the Hungarians had title to revolt with guns. [It was unfortunate that King could not in 1956 critique the non-white Mao or the Hindu caste-supremacist aspect of Congress Party nationalism and state rule in India.]

This stylized, calculated essay of Martin Luther King, Jr.—we clearly have more than a passing speech here!—fifty years later stands up as a multi-faceted and nuanced response to a stage in human (not just U.S. or "Negro") history. King in 1956 refused to allow himself to be confined to the freeing of African-Americans within a reformed parochial U.S. system. He wrote outright that colonialism and imperialism in Africa and Asia were "the international aspect" of "an old order" of which racist oppression in America was a connected part: all had to be ended. King was very like Cruse, the 1960s Black nationalist, in refusing to allow Anglo-Americans to box his people within America, or even "Black Africa": perhaps out of pan-Muslim DNA bequeathed by America's first enslaved Africans, King like Cruse, wanted a much wider community with the full range of peoples in Afro-Asia. In this speech at least, the Reverend King, although Christian as always in the constructive strategies he set out to reach a settlement with Anglo-Americans internally in the U.S., did not refer to the rivalry between Islam and Christianity not only in Africa and Asia, but also in the USA, now again sharpening in the age of decolonization. Nothing in his essay would make young African-Americans cold towards the Muslims of Egypt, North Africa, Pakistan and Indonesia, all of which he named as among the exhilarating instances of the wresting of independence, along with Indians and Chinese, etc.

King had written—but at this point only using a Biblical motif "Egypt" to span Asians and Africans, and African-Americans, in general?—that they "have broken loose from the Egypt of colonialism and imperialism, and they are now moving from the wilderness of adjustment toward the promised land of cultural integration. As they look back, they see the old order of colonialism and imperialism passing away and the new order of freedom and justice coming into being." A decade later, Harold Cruse wanted African Americans to focus much more on Arabs specifically, and to take patterns from them. Cruse assailed King's perceived characterization that "cultural integration" was an aim of Egyptians under Nasser: only an integrationist intellectual of the Black bourgeoisie could be that ignorant of the Third World's anti-colonial revolutions, he fumed. In Cruse's vocal left-nationalist world-view, Nasser's Egypt was not struggling to become "culturally integrated" with any Westerners [although the reality indeed was that Nasser, modifying a long Egyptian liberal tradition of acculturation to Western high literatures and intellectualism, was seeking at least technological and cultural borrowings from even the Anglo-Saxon countries, if within a framework of greater political equality than under the pre-1952 monarchy]. In reality, King, although Cruse missed it, had himself savored the construction through state power of high cultures drawing on indigenous elements by nations in Africa and Asia that were now winning independence: they had set up "their own governments, their own economic systems, and their own educational systems."[99] King in 1956 was much more like the pro-Third World Cruse than the latter grasped.

King's 1956 essay was the richer in its sensibility. But we can see how King's wealth of universalist quotations from Donne, Emerson, etc., gave some passages an air of genteel belles lettres, a liking of shimmering fine language for itself, patches of a pleasant ease and calm, intellectual wisdom, that could not but infuriate impatient militants like Cruse. Yet this controversy is one tantalizing meeting, as much as divergence, in the 1950s-1960s between (a) Arabophile Black Nationalists who were becoming quasi-secessionist, at least in emotions, and (b) the Afro-American middle-class "revolution" in the United States that despite some constructive stances towards whites was indeed much more like a revolution than it let itself look at the outset. Although he could give his words a sleek accommodationist surface, King's integrationist protest discourse has since the mid-1980s been accepted by Black Muslim, Black nationalist, and Black Marxist analysts as well as by unaligned academics, to have harbored wide-ranging rejection of many aspects of the U.S. and international West-dominated systems as they stood—what Eric Dyson (1995) termed "the masked radicalism" of the South's new Black Christian politicians.[100] Like the NOI's press, King was voicing sympathy in 1957, although without naming him outright as Cruse did, for a Nasser detested by Anglo-American rightists for accepting Soviet-bloc arms in 1955 to ward off Israel, not to speak of the racially-specific loathing that a few Jewish-American journalists and spokesmen whipped up against such Arab opponents of their homeland of the mind, Israel—with which Nasser had just fought a war. Foreign Secretary Dulles had meant to bring down Nasser when he withdrew the U.S. loan offer for building the High Dam in mid-1956. King voiced only a muted interest in Nasser's regime at the close of 1956: he may have feared that more could risk badly-needed support and funds from both Anglo and Jewish fellow-Americans. (Similarly, his opposition to the war in Vietnam in the 1960s was to draw fury from Anglo-America and such central U.S. institutions as the FBI.)

True, for years, King was to hail Israel, condemn the "Arab nationalist" states, and—in the wake of the 1967 Arab-Israeli war—warn emerging young black militants that any criticism of "Zionism" was really anti-Semitism against Jewish-Americans that he would not allow.[101] Such stances by King predisposed left-nationalist media in the Arab World to cover and interview his young militant enemies such as Stokely Carmichael and some Panthers. King's movement had needed Jewish donations and media support from the North to break the grip of the local racists in the South. It is to be noted, though, that in one statement in ostensible support of Israel that he made in the wake of Israel's 1967 expansion in the Six Days' War, King implied an indictment of U.S. policy at least, and probably of Israel. In a September 1967 letter to Rabbi Jacob M. Rothschild, he warned that while Israel's right to exist as a state in security was "incontestable", the great powers were obligated to end the "imposed poverty and backwardness" of the Arabs that caused threats to the peace. King here was outspoken that the Arabs had not caused most of the backwardness that had been "imposed" on them by others (by whom?), and perhaps implied that one-sided aid to Israel's interests had enabled it to harm justified interests of the Arab countries. His call for "a concerted and democratic program of assistance" to heal Arab-Israel tensions was ambiguous: "concerted" implied that the U.S. and the Soviet Union both had been worsening the Middle East by competitively shipping arms to regimes, none of which [including Israel?] were real liberal democracies, and that both those Great Powers should work together in the Middle East for the welfare of the Arabs—the antithesis of Cold War ideology.[102] It remains a matter for speculation whether King suspected that Israel had sought expansion against Egypt, Jordan and Syria from as early as 1947, which in turn had forced the Arab states to waste money they needed for development on arms and helped destroy parliamentarism (potential democracy).[103]

King's suggestive views on the Middle East and Israel again bear out the need not to dichotomize African-Americans in Americanist movements, against those who were more Islamist or nationalist or Africanist or alienated, in the 20th century. As was so often the case, King in 1957 and 1967 was bent on helping African-Americans think for themselves beyond the conventional analyses by Anglo and Jewish-Americans by making those much more open-ended, without himself spelling out exactly what he meant. It is clear that King and his colleagues in the SCLC did not share the triumphalist glee of the U.S. Zionists and Anglomorph America's media that Israel in 1967 had smashed a hopelessly dysfunctional and vile group that was the enemy of both the two white states. True, the civil rights Americanists in some ways were diverging from black nationalists now linking to the Third World, including its Arabs and Palestinians. The African-American integrationists were trying to balance their sympathy and imminent interaction with those Arabs with their drive to widen positive relations with their Jewish fellow-Americans. King's rather public letter to the rabbi in 1967 tried to synthesize the interests and the aspirations of (a) Israeli Jews, (b) Arabs/ Muslims, (c) African-Americans and (d) the U.S. polity so as to make all of them prosper together.

In the discourse of Martin Luther King, Jr. and other colleagues in the civil rights movement, it is the slivers that do not fit in—the barely audible phrases—that point to the real concerns, or at least some deep concerns, of these Americanists who seldom forgot that their ancestors had come from an Africa that overlapped into the Arab World. The Rev. Jesse Jackson, who became a lightning-rod for Black-Jewish tensions in U.S. politics from 1983, saw his conjunction with Middle Eastern states and nationalism not as a departure from the civil rights movement but as fulfilling it. Jackson recalled that Martin Luther King, Jr. told him before his murder that the conflict between Israel and the Palestinians was to become "the next big new tension in the world." While Jackson could sometimes be insensitive to the feelings of

U.S. and Israeli Jews, he nonetheless sincerely sought to aid a constructive solution in the Middle East in which both sides would win peace. Jews needed their homeland after 2,000 years but the Palestinians needed one too: if "those two moral rights are not reconciled then nobody, including Israel, is going to be secure",[104] which fully stated what his mentor, King, had hinted back in 1967. Jackson's simultaneous engagement with Palestinians/Arabs and Israel really was in the tradition of the peace-making radicalism of his first model, Martin Luther King, Jr.

The discreet or outspoken empathy of diverse African-Americans in 1967 for the Arabs in their grimmest hour might have stemmed from more than either anti-Semitism or from the similar vilification and racism to which African-Americans and Arabs had been subjected by mainstream U.S. film and print media in which Jewish-Americans had flourished alongside Anglos. The hyper-active Zionists in the U.S. neighborhood made the Middle East vivid to Blacks, but the 1967 war also confronted all peoples with the issues of relative justice between Arabs and Israel in the Middle East. But some subconscious folk memory that some of their grandparents and forefathers had had strong Islamic links to Arabs, Muslims and "the East" prior to enslavement may have helped attune African-Americans of all factions to the interests, sufferings and resilient struggles of the Arabs and Iranians.

The Internationalization of SNCC

The interest of Prattis, Cruse and probably King in Nasser, the Algerian independence movement and other Arab nationalists had successors. After 1964, recruits from the North who had been in the NOI, and publications that blended a focus on "black" or African liberation with sympathy for Algerians, Arabs and Palestinians, were flowing into SNCC, especially its Atlanta Project office. The black separatist concepts being woven into the street-level black southern struggle drew on the writings of the orthodox-Sunni Muslim, Malcolm X, with his Arab linkages, and those of the Francophone psychiatrist Franz Fanon, a diaspora "Negro", whose *Wretched of the Earth* imparted data about the Algerian Revolution, for which he had done work. When staff members of the Student Non-Violent Coordinating Committee in mid-1967 elected as chairman Rap Brown (who later became a Muslim with the name Jamal al-Amin), they announced that SNCC would "encourage and support liberation struggles against colonialism, racism, and economic exploitation" around the world, and would meet with left Third World governments and liberation groups. They authorized an application for NGO consultative status with the United Nations Economic and Social Council (ECOSOC). SNCC militants were responding to real possibilities for community with the Arab, African and Islamic worlds now opening up. Stokely Carmichael stated that SNCC was viewed "around the world and particularly the Third World" as the American organization that was most prepared "to lay the foundation for a revolution." He was not just fantasizing here: translations of his speeches were to be published in *al-Hurriyyah*, the Beirut organ of George Habash's pro-Nasser

Arab Nationalist Movement, which after 1967 became the Popular Front for the Liberation of Palestine (PFLP), while Beirut's liberal-Nasserist al-Adab publishing house brought out an Arabic translation of Carmichael's 1967 book, *Black Power: The Politics of Liberation in America* that he co-authored with Charles Hamilton, along with another translation of Malcolm X's autobiography.

SNCC's top leaders were linking up with Muslim groups in America. When calling for "Black Power" in Chicago on 28 July 1967, Stokely Carmichael said he planned to meet with Elijah to discuss joint goals.[105] The NOI from then on provided his bodyguards. Carmichael and the still fairly young NOI Minister Farrakhan were friendly from 1966 onwards. At the May 1982 observance of African Liberation Day, Carmichael (by then Kwame Toure), was to urge African-Americans to join either his All-African Peoples Revolutionary Party (AAPRP) or Farrakhan's new successor Nation of Islam as the instruments through which to work towards the liberation of black people. His movement came to work with Farrakhan's across America by 1992.[106] Farrakhan was to attend on the death-bed of Carmichael/Kwame Toure as a revered veteran Africanist nationalist who to his 1998 demise voiced love to Africa's Libya and its ever-helpful great Leader, al-Qadhafi.[107]

As it groped towards a particularistic ethnic nationalism, SNCC wanted to prove its independence from its dwindling body of white—and especially Jewish—financial backers. Accordingly, in 1967 a group of SNCC staff members published an article of solidarity with the left-tinted Arab regimes and the Palestinian populations, all at that time reeling from their devastating defeat in the Six Days' War. However, some staff members who would discreetly agree with the pro-Nasser, pro-Arab article, feared the Jewish-American rage it would trigger. Jim Forman, the head of SNCC's International Program, had recently met with Arab leaders, but calculated that SNCC might not withstand the external pressures, especially those in New York, that an anti-Israel stand was sure to detonate.

SNCC's explosive 1967 article blended traditions of left, Africanist and Muslim Arabophilia that had been unfolding for decades among African-Americans:

- *Left Africanism*: Eleven years earlier, when Nasser nationalized the Suez Canal in 1956, Israel, in coordination with a French-British attack, seized Egypt's Sinai. As U.S. Jewish Communists called for "Arms for Israel", their African-American pro-Bandung comrades had supported Egyptian President Gamal 'Abd al-Nasser, for which they were dubbed anti-Semites. Benjamin Davis Jr condemned Jewish self-styled "liberals" for pressuring Black newspaper editors into defense of Israel.[108]

- *Islam*: Ethel Minor, the editor of SNCC's newsletter who volunteered for the task of writing the article that SNCC's central committee wanted in 1967, had been friendly with Palestinian students during college, and had been a member of Elijah's Nation of Islam. Minor's article in *SNCC Newsletter*, a listing of thirty-two "documented facts" regarding "the Palestine Problem", was a distinguished forerunner of the new conjunction between the African-American and Arab revolutions. For an original Black perspective on the havoc in the Middle East, it recycled too many ill-digested motifs from the more tired, cliché-ridden discourse of the radical Arab bourgeois nationalists who were now facing their moment of truth. The unnuanced SNCC article contended that the initial Arab-Israeli war of 1947-1949 was an Arab effort to regain Palestinian land and that during it "Zionists conquered the Arab homes and land through terror, force, and massacres." Still, the journalistic shock treatment by Minor and her collaborators in some ways really did, as they intended, get African-Americans beyond pro-Israel motifs of "the white American press" to important aspects of human suffering in the Middle East. It was an early instance of Israel's loss of the moral high ground in the world media following its 1967 expansion. One central charge of the SNCC newsletter—that of mass executions by Israeli soldiers of disarmed Arabs in the first three Arab-Israeli wars—made a comparison with Nazi death-camps, and was branded anti-Semitic defamation by furious Zionist organizations in America. But the charge was to be confirmed decades later by revisionist Israeli historians—and very reluctantly by Israel's politicians and military in August 1995.[109]

Facing pandemonium across the U.S. and even in the world media, workers at SNCC headquarters called a press conference at which Program Director Ralph Featherstone denied that the organization's new frank anti-Israel stance was anti-Semitic. However, he further enraged many American Jews by criticizing Jewish store owners in America's black ghettoes.

One must feel a certain suspicion about the motives of Jewish-American organizations and journalists that took Minor's article from a newsletter that only had a circulation of a few hundred, and then used global news agencies to diffuse its anti-Israel stances out among tens of millions in America and around the world. As they themselves moved away from integrationism and liberalism, some Jewish-American leaders were trying to panic all American Jews out of their wits so that they could regiment them into a micronationality that they would lead. Jewish micronationalist leaders would utilize "Farrakhan" as a similar neighborhood bogey in the 1980s and 1990s. By their reciprocal denunciations, Arab-tinted black nationalists and Zionoid micronationalists from mid-1967 have repeatedly highlighted the "opponent" elite and thus their claim to lead in the opposite community it threatens: each leadership group thereby legitimates itself as the defenders of "our people." The ploy has garnered invaluable popular support for both self-appointed elites. These "warring" pro-Muslim black and Jewish micronationalists have so helped each others' growth that neither may have lasted without the other.

The conjunction of black nationalists formed within SNCC with the Middle East's Arabs and Islam had its built-in limitations from the outset. Minor herself realized that non-Muslim staff taking the stand lacked the commitment to educate themselves about Middle Eastern history well enough to discuss the issue intelligently before America's media.[110]

During and in the wake of the controversy, while arguing that African-Americans had to stand with the Palestinian Arabs whom the Zionists expelled, Carmichael repeatedly imaged that Egypt had been a crucial center in Africa for 4,000 years and that African-Americans therefore had to help fight Israel's occupation of the Sinai of Africa's Egypt—which was also the stance of the OAU. This stance took up Pharaonic motifs in traditional U.S. pan-Africanism that Carmichael now applied in a secular way to circumvent the Christian/Muslim divide between his people and those Muslim areas of the Third World to which he wanted to link them. Alongside such motifs in modern thought, though, Carmichael/Toure may have been carrying forward other folk motifs that ran the Arab countries and Africa together, transmitted by mouth from the days when many of the Africans enslaved in North America and its islands did indeed read Arabic.

The Manichaean dichotomizations of good Arabs and evil Israelis that Stokely Carmichael, the Black Panthers, and other nationalist and left African-Americans retailed for decades after 1967 did not research the specificities of the Arab countries enough to equip Black Americans to surmount the practical difficulties of affiliating to that world. Uniting Arabs and African-Americans would not be the automatic fusion the U.S. black nationalists daydreamed it might—and yet real elements had now come into place to carry it through with hard work and realism. Carmichael had shown signs of becoming serious when he had, through the columns of Beirut's left-Nasserist *al-Hurriyyah*, appealed to the Arab states to grant scholarships for young African-Americans to come to study Arabic at their institutions [a language of manuscripts that would also have equipped the African-American intelligentsia to envision and analyze the history of widened stretches of sub-Saharan Africa much more sharply].

The conditions for the Arab world and Afro-America to connect and devise joint enterprises of mutual benefit were now better than ever before. Elijah Muhammad had discouraged followers from emigrating to such Muslim countries in Africa as the Sudan or Egypt.[111] However, his son, Akbar, did receive an excellent education at Cairo's al-Azhar mosque-university, where President Nasser cultivated him (and Akbar cultivated the regime: the eminent Egyptian Africanist Muhammad Fa'iq recalled in 2005 that Akbar was a socially skilled charismatic who won responsiveness to his own concerns and interests at functions of the Egyptian governing elite). One veteran adherent in the early 1960s, Karimullah, who had been jailed by the American government during the Second World War, hoped that his son would go to study at al-Azhar as a preliminary to becoming a Minister.[112] Clearly, from 1965-1975, the NOI leaders and rank-and-file were having increased exposure to Arab-American leaders, officials in the Arab countries, and to the Arabic language—which was more and more tinting most currents of Black nationalism in the U.S., not the NOI only.

The Sunnifying effects of residence and study in Cairo and other Arab capitals in the 1960s and early 1970s entered African-American high literature, notably David G. DuBois' mordant novel, *...And Bid Them Sing,* which was publicized by the Panthers' paper. Its author placed Americanist limits upon this simultaneous impact of Islam and Africa on the small Arabic-literate intelligentsia now in formation. Malcolm X, visiting Cairo in 1963, had impressed upon the students that one of their main tasks was to educate Egyptians about the plight of their Black People in America. For one of David DuBois' ex-Nation of Islam characters, Arabic and Sunni Islam are just a fad. For another ex-NOI, "Suliman Ibn Rashid" (based on Khalid Ahmad Tawfiq, whose father had been with the Moors, and who helped found the American Muslim Students Association in Cairo), the Islam he takes from the Arabs furthers his much more serious drive to eliminate from his being everything that points to his American background. He is one of those who in that era were re-Africanizing themselves, although in his case with an Islamized Euro-American wife as well as an Egyptian wife for company, and while working in a U.S. food aid program. (Even the most militant African-Americans who leave to the Third World must carry always their Americanism within them, wherever they go). This Du Bois approved when, following the 1967 defeat of the Arab countries, the characters return to America where, he implies, their true community and struggle await them.[113]

What of the Arab side? Active English skills would help a broad range of Egyptian institutions construct long-term interactions with African-Americans, while the Nasser regime's stress had been on inculcating Arabic in education. Still, Egyptian officials and lay-people had enough texts in Arabic as a starting-point to enable them to interact skillfully as well as sympathetically with African-Americans. The institutions of the Nasser regime had sponsored Arabic translations of U.S. studies and African-American texts on such subjects as the life of W.E.B. DuBois, the post-World War II protest roles of the NAACP, the Civil Rights movement and the developing Islamic movements among African-Americans. All the articles of a special issue of *Freedomways* about Blacks in the deep South "and the subjugation which the government and the white population practise against them" were brought out as an Arabic book.[114] These Arabic translations of U.S. works sponsored by the Nasser regime had been read widely throughout the Arab countries. When Malcolm X made his 1964 *hajj* (pilgrimage) to Mecca, Arabs voiced to him how "frightening" they had found the Arabic translation of *Black Like Me*, written by the white American, John Griffin, who had dyed his skin and then traveled for two months across America to find out how his Black fellow-countrymen were treated. The images of Elijah's NOI adherents and their deviating tenets that Sa'udi Prince Faysal knew when he received Malcolm X in 1964 came from accurate articles by Egyptian journalists.[115] Egyptians attempted serious study of NOI institutions. In 1965, an Egyptian professor from al-Azhar University came to the United States to study the schools of

Elijah's small Nation.[116] A Beirut publisher in 1962 brought out a truncated, and in places garbled, Arabic translation of C. Eric Lincoln's 1961 *The Black Muslims in America.*[117]

As Egypt's President Nasser and Jordan's King Husayn after 1967 edged towards peace with Israel, which would set up a compromise Palestinian statelet in the West Bank and Gaza strip, the PLO in August 1970 conducted a congress at 'Amman's al-Wahdah refugee camp to wreck any such settlement. Stokely Carmichael, at that time briefly with the Black Panthers, was among the 50 invited foreign observers. Over Baghdad radio, Stokely said: "The Palestinian people have only one solution, which has all our support: elimination of the Zionist entity from Palestinian soil".[118] The Black Power militants had projected themselves and the U.S. cause they voiced into the discourse of the Arab world as endorsers of its struggle against Israel: it would take longer for African-Americans to convey material aid or manpower to the Palestinian nationalists in their faraway region of the globe, to lobby for such Arab causes in America, or to get aid themselves from the Arab states.

Interaction with Jewish fellow-pupils had helped form Carmichael's personality in adolescence in New York. Jewish communists first inducted him into the city's left-wing politics. His leap from a pro-Israel to a pro-Palestinian stance helped him outflank factional enemies in SNCC and in other organizations in the 1960s and 1970s who could cite that they had never had such linkages to Jews.[119] "Palestine" and "Israel" had now become emblems clarifying the separate identities and interests of Jewish and African-American groups in New York and other American cities in this period. However, non-Muslim militants of these neo-nationalist African-American sectors were more and more interacting with Muslim black Americans and Arab students and immigrants on American soil. This had led to the transmission of the new leftist and nationalist thought of Carmichael and Panther leaders into Arabic publications in the Middle East, and to their subsequent extensive travels there.

Solidarity with the Palestinians in 1967 was a turning point in the pursuit by African-American militants of a Third World-linked identity within the cultural and political world their ethnos shared with Jews and other Euro-American quasi-nationalities. As a drive to construct a real bloc in international relations, the solidarity bore fruit slowly. Kwame Toure tried the longest and hardest to carry through community with Africans and Arabs, moving to Muslim Guinea as his base for a "pan-Africanism" that he made more and more committed and real.

In 1979, Toure met PLO leaders and journalists in Lebanon, where he toured the South in which Israel was using bullets, bombs, shells and airplanes to crush the PLO. Yet in the face of all that was thrown at them, he found, "the Palestinians are alive ...the most alive in the Arab nation [for] the Palestinian Revolution is the spark for the entire Arab revolutionary movement." Carmichael's statements to the PLO media had some micronationalist-Americanist dualities. On his Black Nationalist side, he depicted "the African masses" in North America as from first enslavement throwing themselves in repeated uprisings against the U.S. capitalist system, "just as the Palestinians hurl themselves against the Zionist machine." He likened African-Americans to the Puerto Rican groups struggling for independence from the U.S. Now, by 1979, the capitalist system had taken back all concessions it had had to make to "the Africans" when tied down in Vietnam. Yet other of Carmichael's points to the Arabs did not dichotomize African- and Euro-Americans as much he did the Zionists and Palestinians, who were out to kill each other. U.S. policy after Sadat's peace remained total collusion with Israel. But Carmichael somewhat let non-Jewish white Americans off the hook. "The Zionists effectively control the U.S. policy through the U.S. tax dollars which support the Zionist state of Israel." But "the American people" would turn against the government on the question of Zionism, as it had against the Vietnam War, Carmichael assured the Palestinians and Arabs. To the extent that his argument was anti-Semitic, exaggerating the capacities, will and unity of Jews in America, Carmichael in this aberration viewed Christian Euro-Americans as manipulated by them and thus less responsible: "the American people" was for that instant a terminology formally open to Blacks, although not to Zionists. But Carmichael was too alienated from the U.S. system and all its whites to visualize African-Americans lobbying to the USA's white "masses" for Africans and Arabs. Such a role would have shifted his thinking and that of his group. Pro-Arab or pro-Africa lobbying could have inducted the black tendency for which Kwame spoke into a sort of membership in "the American people." Speaking for a foreign cause on U.S. television amounts to various groups of Americans coming together to talk, and can be just the beginning.

A decade had passed, and the compound community that would span the oceans was proving slow to come about. Carmichael was right that "since the 1960s, the Black Power movement has been unique in its [total] support of the Palestinian movement": he lamented, though, that after twelve years "there has not been much direct contact between the PLO and these groups." "Direct contact is necessary so that we can better support the struggle of the PLO" for the Democratic Palestinian State in place of Israel.[120]

Panther Responses to Africa, the Arabs and Islam

In contrast to Carmichael and his kind were Black Panthers who had more mixed attitudes to the African countries and their histories and cultures. Black groups tinged by Communism might well sometimes deride the new Africanist individuals and groups as incompatible with being on the left or "revolutionary." Still, even while on that other side, the Panthers more often felt themselves to be fighting for the interests of blacks specifically in the USA than for a single community of diverse American masses (Marxist class-struggle).

Huey P. Newton voiced mixed feelings towards Africa and the Arab countries in 1968. He dichotomized his Panthers as a "revolutionary movement" intent on bringing socialism to the black people, against "cultural nationalists"/ "reactionary nationalists." Huey rejected the Africanist nationalists with virulent language: the "end goal" of the "reactionary nationalist is the oppression of the people." Newton here vented a purely negative view of African cultures or history that had not been transformed by the West or by communist ideas coming from it—thus his insult that "Papa Doc" Duvalier really did represent "the African culture" when he oppressed the Haitians he confused by evoking it. "He merely kicked out the racists and replaced them with himself as the oppressor. Many of the [Africanist cultural] nationalists in this country seem to desire the same ends." "As far as returning to the old African culture, it's not advantageous"—"culture itself will not liberate us." Newton dismissed Africa-citing cultural nationalism among African-Americans as "pork chop nationalism" [=more of the DNA of the old dichotomy of halal-haram—Islam-allowed vs Islam-prohibited foods—surging up from the African-American historical subconscious?] While the Panthers sometimes did not properly understand where their orientation might lead, they were clearing the way for some Americanist community.

Still, the pragmatic need of their minority for outside power-centers in the face of Anglo domestic power, and co-victim affinity to some likewise ill-treated Third World peoples, in tandem made the Panthers build political alliances with Muslim and Asian as well as African states. Rejecting "the old [sub-Saharan] African culture" with one breath freed Newton to then hold up the "revolutionary nationalism" of "the revolution in Algeria when Ben Bella took over". There, the people ended up in power after they kicked out the French. It was still early in the history of independent Algeria, but Newton was already too uncritical in asserting that the post-colonial leaders who took over were "not interested in the profit motive where they could exploit the people": at any rate, a new class of a statal bourgeoisie was to evolve under them in Algeria that would not be exactly "in office strictly on the leave of the people" as Newton hoped in 1968. The Algerian leadership had nationalized industry and plowed its profits back into the people—"socialism in a nutshell".[121] The movement's paper relayed out at face value the Algerian government's statements that it was energetically constructing at the UN and in other fora of international relations a new "Third World" bloc that would command influence and respect in world politics. Having started as an uprising [as the Panthers still were?], the Algerian leadership was at the fore of the Third World governments that won a quasi-Head of State hearing for guerrilla 'Arafat at the UN in 1975.[122]

Acculturated Algerian and Palestinian Islamists were in this period making direct input into other self-Islamizing strata in Black America. The important Algerian Islamist thinker, Malik Ben Nabi, lectured in 1971 to the new Islamic Party of North America (IPNA), which was also in contact with the Palestinian Islamist group Hizb al-Tahrir. IPNA was an outgrowth of Washington's "Community Mosque" (Masjid ul-Ummah) founded in 1969, and its leader, Muzaffaruddin Hamid, had passed through many Muslim societies in Asia and Africa.

The Panthers used to like to romanticize themselves as an heroic revolutionary insurgency striking to destroy both racism and capitalism simultaneously. That stance, in conjunction with drives by U.S. agencies to smash or kill them or drive them into exile, pushed them toward Left-Arab regimes, Vietnam, Cuba and Red China, in the Third World. Another reality, though, was the Panthers' ambiguous community with the New Left sons and daughters of the richer white classes who were at the universities. These strata gave the Panthers the money and public support needed to carry on in the face of repression. Newton rapped the cultural nationalists who could not accept the "white revolutionaries" [=campus kids, left-Jewish movie stars] who had sincerely turned against the system. Newton was acute in assessing that the anti-war whites had sapped the U.S. government's capacity to wage war in Vietnam, and the cultural nationalists (into whom he obliquely ran some SNCC figures who refused any contact with whites) myopic not to see that. While the young protest whites were a bit "abstract" as revolutionaries, as he saw, the fact remains that Newton (and Cleaver) wanted social relations with them more than with black cultural nationalists.[123] Such community in turn gave some scope for input by more pro-Israel New Leftists that could slow conjunction by the Panthers with Arab regimes and independence movements such as the PLO.

The conjunction of the Black Panthers with Palestinian and Arab nationalisms influenced or expressed long-term culture. In *The Black Panther* of 30 August 1969, Don Cox argued that Zionism's "Kosher Nationalism" was a form of fascism. He called for Israel to pay reparations to all those who had been displaced in the Middle East: "all properties stolen must be returned to the people of Palestine." Cox raised slogans for victory for al-Fatah and the people of Palestine in their struggle against Moshe Dayan's "storm troopers." He did so again in the name of the Black Panther Party to the 1971 Palestinian Students' Conference in Kuwait.

The multiple ways the Panthers maligned diverse white entities (and ideas among blacks they didn't like) as swine have a cultural resonance separate from any of the discourses in or from the West, such as Marxism, that were also influencing them. An issue of *The Black Panther* showed two pigs—U.S. Imperialism and Zionism—kissing, snout to snout: the pig labeled Zionism wore Moshe Dayan's eye-patch. Another cartoon showed a massive pig labeled "USA" suckling two piglets labeled Israel and West Germany.[124] Fard and Elijah's Muslims, in their esoteric Druze- or Isma'ili-like style, had already extended Islam's exoteric dislike of the pig as a forbidden meat into an energizing simile for the polluting whites' collective Evil. The NOI [and Drew 'Ali's Moors even earlier] had been teaching Islam over decades. Eldridge Cleaver was highly aware that the campaigns of Elijah Muhammad against pork had pre-disposed imprisoned converts like himself, and indeed "the Negro community" in general, to take up the application of the epithet "pigs" to the police by the new Black Panther discourse of the 1960s and 1970s.[125] It was not just that the Panthers dubbed cops "pigs." More: Black Panther cartoons of bullet-riddled U.S. and Zionist dead pigs project an almost religious ethos in which the swine expands into a representation of the collectivity of an undivided binary evil that is almost cosmic, in this dimension of the diverse Panther psyche. Giving battle to swine resembles the waves of red billowing through the new worldview of early Soviet Communists such as the poet Mayakovsky or the greenness and/or crescents exploding in the nationalisms of Muslim populations in the Third World. We must again wonder if the swine as all racist exploitative evil in general is not another resurfacing from a collective sub-conscious of old forgotten struggles by enslaved Muslims or their offspring not to submit to the "forbidden" (haram) cuisine of a forming Anglomorph Protestant America. In their ethnic self-definition, Hui (Chinese-speaking) Muslims have long fused resistance to the Han Chinese surrounding them on all sides with the pork the Han eat: avoidance of pork then becomes the focus fueling Islamic separation and non-participation in that national community that would pollute "religiously".[126]

The Black Panther's coverage of sub-Saharan Africa was solid and sharp, albeit concentrated upon de-colonization struggles and politics. For instance, it grounded African-Americans well in the intricate interrelations of the entities of Southern Africa in that era of the power of the apartheid regime: those neighboring states found it hard to assert themselves against a South Africa on which they were economically dependent, for instance as employer of their migrants.[127] One news item dissected not just political imprisonments in South Africa, but (drawing on WHO figures) huge disparities in that state's ratios of doctors and nurses between whites, Africans and "coloreds"/Asians.[128] The paper relayed the views of a spokesperson for South Africa's Pan-Africanist Congress who held out revolutionary struggle as the path to liberation; he had been heartened by Mozambique's independence.[129] The PAC had been a militant nationalist organization that went much less out of its way to welcome white compatriots than did the ANC, whose non-racial ideal and make-up carried further one impulse among the Panthers. *The Black Panther* reported the assassination in Zambian exile of the Chairman of the Zimbabwe African National Union (ZANU), probably by Rhodesian intelligence.[130]

One 1975 item in *The Black Panther* seemed to consider it best to break up at least one independent African state on national lines—Ethiopia, whose feudalist government since 1961 had faced an insurgency in Eritrea [that was Muslim-led in its first stage].[131] While this was a stride into critical scrutiny of African states, in Ethiopia's case one that was now mouthing Marxist slogans, the mixed ideology of the Panthers assured a hearing for the post-Selassie Addis Ababa regime when it proclaimed "socialism." *The Black Panther* carried an item hailing the Dergue regime's nationalization of all rural land in the name of a single "Ethiopian people" that did not exist.[132] Similar positive coverage of the land reforms of a "Marxist" new Ethiopia that was battling mainly Muslim secessionist forces was inserted into Warith's paper by some ex-Communist editor.

Like *Muhammad Speaks*, the Panthers' paper often connected Black Africa out into wider anti-imperialist associations that included Arabs. Left-

African and left-Arabist materials entered Black Panther discourse together. *The Black Panther* carried an interview over three pages with the leader of the Mozambique independence movement, Samora Machel, in which he charted a left-wing, populist course for his new African state being born from the Portuguese empire: he was "against capitalism" and expected help from "the socialist countries". [Machel was unwisely optimistic given low literacy, his party's shortage of cadres and the $400 million he mentioned his government would need quickly]. Or the Panther paper could convey the connections of sub-Saharan freedom movements even to such faraway [non-white] Communist states as Vietnam and China, in that era.[133]

The Panthers' articulation of friendliness towards Chinese people and their Communist regime followed late in a long-standing racial and cultural identification with China and Japan: for decades, the NOI had been affirming that Black Americans, too, were "Asiatic." In the 1960s, the Asiatic identity of one NOI adherent had made him tour Hong Kong, Tokyo, India and Pakistan as well as Egypt, Kenya and Nigeria—not Europe—so that he could get himself among "my own kind".[134] *Muhammad Speaks* in 1966 ran articles on Muslims in China.[135]

The Black Panther's criticisms of Israel, too, tended to focus less on its unequal internal societies than upon polarization of the Third World as a whole against it. In early 1975, seventeen Third World nations meeting in Havana urged the 70 non-aligned members of the UN to press for the expulsion of Israel. This would express the determination of those states to break Western domination of the UN.[136]

The Panther media did not always foster a simplistic or knee-jerk pro-Arab view of the Middle East among the lumpen and wannabe African-Americans it reached. Sometimes it could give two sides. Huey Newton for a time valued the ideas and resources that the Jewish-American left-activist David Horowitz contributed to the Panthers' school and other programs. This emboldened the young white American to object to a Black Panther article that attacked "the Zionist, racist state of Israel" during the 1973 "Yom Kippur" (Ramadan) War. Support from Stokely and the Black Left to the Arabs in 1967 had disconcerted Horowitz, but he had only come to fear that the Arabs could threaten the survival of Israel during their 1973 "aggression" (in reality a limited counter-assault to wrest back some of their lands into which Israel had expanded in 1967). Horowitz and the other Jewish radicals who were now moving towards Zionism had not yet shrunk the virulent, complex conflict in the Middle East down into a neo-Republican paradigm. His teacher, Trotsky's biographer Isaac Deutscher, had believed the nation-state was an anachronism that socialism would end: he advised Europe's Jews in the 1930s to join in that Revolution, while the Zionists urged them to flee to Palestine. However, the Holocaust made Deutscher swing to Israel as the "raft-state" for the Jews.

Huey let Horowitz develop these themes in a position-paper published in *The Black Panther*. It called on "the Government of Israel to recognize the claims of the Palestinian people for independent national institutions, as originally provided by the UN, and [on] the Arab states and the Palestinian liberation movement to recognize the existence of the State of Israel, as the national sovereignty of the Jewish people." The sleight of hand with which Horowitz only offered national institutions to the Palestinians but statehood to the Zionists, might leave Israel's grip on the West Bank and the Gaza Strip. His pan-Muslim-like notion that there could have been some global "Jewish people" now repatriating itself did not fit well with modern Western thinking and accurate perception of reality. Yet Newton had let him give the Panthers' African-American constituency a more diverse image of Israel and the world's Jews, and a Jewish viewpoint that tried to make itself sound ready for a constructive settlement with the Arabs.[137]

As Horowitz grew more Zionist, the insolence of his suggestions to Newton towered ever the higher. He said that he wanted to help the Panthers' programs but then proposed to Newton that the Black Panther Party disband itself because its Leninism was sterile and no conditions for a real revolution existed in the USA. The ever-polite Huey demurred that he could not dissolve the party at once because many had gone to jail to build it: the rank and file would have to be pre-persuaded gradually.[138] Such abusive interaction between Jewish leftists now adopting Israel as their emotional homeland, and left-integrationist African-Americans only fueled pro-Arab feelings in the Black Panther movement.

Simplistic politicization in the movement, and the danger under which the Panthers had to function in America, narrowed how much they could perceive of the aesthetic cultures of the Third World populations to which they reached out. Yet their wide anti-imperialism could widen the range of culture they wanted to access, out from the countries of sub-Saharan Africa to take in also at least the Arab world, and, more formally, China, Vietnam and Korea. In the era of decolonization, important institutions in Africa were threading together the new elite cultures of the countries below and above the Sahara. The Second Congress of the Pan-African Federation of Film Workers, meeting in Algiers in early 1975, called for the development of a popular, democratic and progressive African culture that *The Black Panther* hoped would produce "authentic Black and Arab films." The October before, (Francophone) Black and Arab filmmakers and critics meeting at the 5th Carthage Film Festival in Tunisia had viewed films of pan-Africanism and revolutions against colonialism and neo-colonialism. The Festival's Tunisian president, Tahar Guiga, said that "cinema is the most dangerous form of colonialism." The greater autonomy and coherence of language among the African Arabs was here fostering cultural and aesthetic self-assertion against Westerners by sub-Saharan Africans—and by militant African-Americans now passing through those all-Africa institutions.[139]

International politics that could affect America steered the Panthers beyond Africa towards other Third World populations that were also Muslim as well as "of color". Yet Islam as a culture-tincture and as an ideology also prompted and tinged their outreach. Sometimes we see the first buds for a community of belief as well as interests with Muslims in the Third World that could blur Marxist class criteria. *The Black Panther* conveyed the official honor and mass welcome Muhammad 'Ali received when he visited Malaysia in 1975, endorsing Islam as one special global link of Black Americans to that distant land. The paper accepted 'Ali's assurance that he would spend his earnings from the fight on erecting buildings all over the U.S. to help Black people.[140] A warily anonymous reply, perhaps from one of the young Muslim Malay students being influenced by Marxism in the 1970s, rebuked *The Black Panther.* He blasted Muhammad 'Ali as a class alien to all who were progressive for having $3 million in the bank: in contrast, the average Malaysian worker earned $10 per week. 'Ali had arrived at a high-point of conflict between the classes in Malaysia. The preceding year had seen the struggle of the [Malay Muslim] Tasek Utara squatters against eviction in Johor Baharu and huge peasant anti-starvation demonstrations of 30,000-50,000 in northern Malaysia, and strikes were unfolding in the cities, the Marxism-influenced writer exaggerated. He dismissed the officially-highlighted "symbolic" Islam of Muhammad 'Ali and the fanfare of the world title bout in Malaysia as a diversion and "tool of the regime to dull the growing political consciousness of the Malaysian people".[141]

The magnificent global reach of Islam as a mega-community had some appeal for the Panthers, members of a long-bullied minority in the USA. They wanted to credit Islam's claim that it integrated classes and far-flung peoples of color. The Malaysian letter writer had caught the ambiguity of the populist Panthers towards Muslim African-Americans who were openly hell-bent to get rich and climb up out of the classes they claimed to defend. The Panther movement had a similarly ambiguous posture towards generous, rich Jewish and Anglo liberals that also sat uneasily with its Mao cliches of class struggle. Concurrence with the ruling system in Malaysia would be of a piece with the Panthers' agreement in the 1970s that rightist regimes in the Arab and Muslim countries, insofar as they were acting to phase out Western control, were thus in one trench with the left regimes of the Third World—which Red China also was testing to some extent. Yet the paper had carried a more diverse array of communications than it has been credited with by neo-con and Jewish-nationalist polemicists, that sometimes equipped its readers to make more flexible, hypothetical assessments of given governments and societies. In the outcome, the West-attuned Muslim elite of Malaysia was to deliver real development and affirmative action to ordinary rural Malays, although penalized by cronyism and ongoing elite class formation, while the Red post-Muslims were to wither away from the campuses.

The Black Panthers' affection towards Muslims, African-American or overseas, often accompanied their being ordinary Americans ideologically. They sometimes dropped class severity towards rich Muslims in Afro-America or overseas—for example Muhammad 'Ali—when they showed serious philanthropy towards the poor and hungry in Africa, for example in the drought-stricken (heavily Muslim) Sahel, or elsewhere in the Third World.[142] The Panthers were a movement readier to consider ameliorism than their occasional application of class criteria to blacks as well as to the U.S. ruling class might lead some to expect. That set some Panthers free to move in the 1980s and 1990s from the Party's left-secular ethos to a protest-Islam that defined community less by economic classes.

In retrospect, the SNCC and Panthers' impulses to reach out to the Arab and Muslim as well as black African peoples were a venture they were too American to quite carry through, despite the fact that increasingly they fled to the Algiers they had hailed from afar. Certainly, daily life in the Third World countries with which the new African-American militants were now interacting could not match the goods even oppressed racial minorities got in the USA. And Cleaver thought Algiers, ruled by President Huwari Bu Madyan's military "socialist" regime, resembled something out of a Western movie: "people disappearing in broad daylight... bribery, payoffs, blackmail and smuggling... a ruthless, frequently violent, male chauvinist brotherhood ruled the country".[143] Eldridge Cleaver complained that his Cuban and Algerian hosts were racially different from, and unfriendly to, African-Americans and sub-Saharan Africans whom they wanted to control within their national territories. This while he was pressing the objecting Algerians to grant their sovereign territoriality as a base from which he and his exiles could direct acts of armed robbery, violence and hijackings in the States or Europe—which would have provided the excuse America had long sought to terminate "pro-Soviet" Algeria.[144] Further, Cleaver at least, among the exiles, could not meet the linguistic requirements of transcontinental alliances: he found it hard to endure the French language and cuisine even in Paris, and never even tried to learn so way-out a language as Arabic as a means to communicate to Algerians or Palestinians or Syrians, etc. Yet, he could have built on the splinters from Arabic and its world that the NOI had opened to him when he was a member.

There is no doubt that Eldridge Cleaver was a bit of a monolingual Anglo chauvinist vis-à-vis foreigners. The man's conversion to Jesus in a France that gave him sanctuary prompted U.S. WASP fundamentalists to bring him home and then get him out of jail quickly. Yet it had some cultural sincerity too. Cleaver's final exchange of hugs with Billy Graham and Jerry Falwell, and his exultation when the Christian millionaire-benefactor had him live a while in his wealthy white family, actualized all those rhetorical, language, ideological and dietary links to WASP fellow-Americans that had kept him an alien in the Middle East, Europe, Asia, Africa and Cuba, and even in a France that had treated him very well.[145]

Huey Newton, Eldridge Cleaver, Bobby Seale, Stokely Carmichael (later to become Kwame Toure) and Rap Brown et al were all very big on the TV screens in the 1960s—too big for the mental and moral balance of one or two of them, some colleagues had to judge in retrospect. It is in the early Panthers' sense of ordinary people and drive to reestablish low-key normal life and facilities for them in ghettos that we get close to the valid heart of their movement. If they weren't about ending the abuse of ordinary [black] people and bringing peace and services in which they could grow, what good meaning could the Panthers or Elijah's Muslims or the Moors ever have had? In 1993, from the revived *Black Panther* newspaper, the one-time Panther Kit

Kim Holder responded in the reflective way of the post-modern 1990s to the death of Huey Newton in a drugs matter. Holder brusquely dismissed attempts to pass "complete blame [onto] the government in this case." In the past, the FBI-led Counter-Intelligence Program (COINTELPRO) had targeted the BPP and Newton in particular and indeed almost every progressive movement and individual struggling for African-American liberation, and some blood had been drawn. But the Party had transformed the jailed Newton into a Messiah-like "baddest revolutionary in history": the cult of personality of its "Free Huey" movement that finally got him released in August 1970 had been a good tool to draw African-Americans into the Party. Holder's concern was all the "community programs" that the Party achieved during Newton's time in jail—self defense, free health clinics, food programs. Newton had left the Revolution many years before his death. There could be no supermen messiahs to lead drug-beset African-Americans to "the promised land" [=a side-swipe at the cults built after their deaths around Martin Luther King, Jr. and Malcolm X]. Leadership and freedom could "only come from the hard work and struggle of thousands of ordinary people," concluded Holder.[146] [These insights could also be applied to the hierarchical authoritarianism of the NOI, with it's God-missioned and God-tinted Messenger that likewise dampened initiative and feedback from ordinary members!]

The Black Panthers took the side of diverse forces in the Arab and Muslim peoples fighting against Zionism and various Western states. As their exposure to Third World Muslims and their cultures grew, many Panther members asked deeper and deeper questions about the Islam that was the bedrock that underlay those peoples' strength. Especially after Hoover shattered the Panthers, many of its veterans graduated to Islam, and became the worshippers who filled the mosques in the inner cities of California. Their engagement with not just the Muslims in the Third World but with migrants from it now constructing the new *ummah* in America, itself, has tightened. In the 1970s, ideological and social interaction with radical Arab immigrant professionals already had been close and one of the influences assimilating the Panthers to rational or scientific modernity. *The Black Panther* delightedly publicized in 1975 the new West Coast Arab-American magazine edited by an immigrant PhD that tried to measure if and how far Israel was losing support in the U.S.: the new publication attempted intellectual rigor as it dissected U.S. mainstream politics in order to start a serious Arab counter-lobby.[147] In mid-2002, African-Americans and immigrant Muslims thronged to Panther Jihad Abdul Mumit's comedy play, "Inside Fighter." It set out the violence, fear, corruption linked to drugs and the gang turf wars of the U.S. inner cities that the immigrants too had come to know so very well— "the innards of America." The play evoked the ability of the Evil Whisperer, the Devil [c.f. the "Waswas" or "slinking Whisperer" in Qur'an 114:4] to "defeat just about every defense human beings have at an institutionalized level"—only complete submission to Allah and the martial arts groups could roll back his activities in U.S. life. Pakistani Kawkab Siddiqui's modernist-jihadist *New Trend* called on all immigrant Muslim groups across the country to pay Abdul Mumit's troupe to come and perform to their masses.[148] The former

Panther Muslims were American super-optimists about the prospects for Islam in America. As Imam Abdul Alim Musa, a former jail mate of BPP founder Cleaver, put it in 2001: Clinton, the two Bushes, Putin—" all the oppressors"—could join together but Islam would still rise to dominate all other ways of life in America.[149]

There is no point denying that the student youth of SNCC, and the Panthers with their street-corner "hard blacks", bit off more than they could ever have achieved, given their limited resources, in respect to international affairs in their era. Stokely Carmichael sometimes naïvely assumed that just exchanging oratory overseas with Third World movements or regimes could thread African-Americans to peoples from whom wide oceans, time and a special racism had long separated them, as he knew in his sober moments. The early drive of Cleaver or Carmichael to define the relations of African-Americans with white groups according to whether the latter would or would not embrace Ho Chi Minh, Castro, Lumumba, Nasser or Yasir 'Arafat was an unprecedented internationalization of U.S. black identity. Yet, Carmichael's in part altruistic drive for community with non-white peoples whom imperialists brutalized around the globe was to broaden out in the 1970s to encompass some whites. He and his fellow-Africanists came to feel the pain of Ireland, whom the English ruling classes had colonized well before they set up the West Indies of his parents.

5. NOI RELATIONS WITH THE ARAB, MUSLIM AND THIRD WORLDS

Arabization and Islam's Macro-History

In the 1960s and early 1970s, elements were accumulating in the Nation of Islam that would later, after Elijah's death, provide bridges to much deeper ideological engagement with the Arab World. In the late 1950s, Sunni-like prayers in Elijah's NOI—reinterpreted to award him roles like some of the Prophet Muhammad of Arabia—were usually uttered in English but occasionally in Arabic.[150] While Arabic was atomized so as to make it address the needs of African-Americans, many of the atoms were understood in themselves and were emotionally central in the new identity the Muslims were constructing. After he was socialized into Islam in the early 1960s, Cassius Clay took the new names, Muhammad 'Ali. Questioned by white journalists as to what they could mean, he correctly identified Muhammad as meaning the object of all praises and 'Ali as meaning "the most high"—"Cassius Clay" was just another of the slave names that African-Americans were now repudiating as they restored their original names robbed under slavery. Yet the youthful Muhammad 'Ali already had a dualism, however muted, towards the hard-hitting NOI doctrine that whites were artificially-created devils. Asked in the interview how he could believe that, 'Ali retorted that he had to "believe everything he [Elijah Muhammad] preaches." Whites would have to get up and prove they're not the devil, given that "their history is the history of a devil."[151]

After his February 25, 1964, defeat of Sonny Liston, Euro-American newspapers had polarized, as foreign and violent, the Islam in which Cassius Clay now proclaimed his belief, against the Christian integrationism of his quasi-middle class father as well as of his opponent, Floyd Patterson. Yet Clay, Sr. had, as ‘Ali grew up from childhood in the murderous, segregated South, vented Garvey-influenced militancy in family dinner-table harangues—so often pent-up counter-hate festered under the accommodationism that such mild-mannered Negro Christians of the South put on for whites when they ventured outside their communities.[152] Garvey's movement had had openness to Muslim countries and movements beyond Black Africa (see chapter 3). Cassius Clay/Muhammad ‘Ali made clear to the English-speaking world, with the Middle East's Muslims overhearing, how deeply it cut him as a youth that, when he brought a gold medal for America back from the 1960 Summer Olympics in Rome to his hometown in Kentucky, a white waitress still refused to serve him a cup of coffee: now, as a Black Muslim, he had spared himself from going to such places that hated his kind, related Iranian Shi‘ite cleric Hadi Khosrow-Shahi approvingly.[153]

Malcolm X, always the internationalist, mustered old Islamic history from the Middle East already cited by Wali Fard Muhammad in the 1930s to galvanize Cassius before the match with Liston: “It's the Cross and the Crescent fighting in a prize ring… a modern Crusades—a Christian and a Muslim facing each other with television to beam it off Telstar for the whole world to see” the outcome. As early as his victory speech, and thenceforth, ‘Ali wanted the Islam he now declared to be not just Elijah's but “the same religion that is believed in by over seven hundred million dark-skinned people throughout Africa and Asia”.[154] The black bourgeoisie of the 1990s was to celebrate the boxer's Islam and insistence on Arabic names, and his roles among overseas Arabs and Muslims, as a breakthrough in his people's wresting of respect and a margin of independence from whites. One bourgeois writer looked back in 1991 to a 1965 *Sports Illustrated* article by Floyd Patterson titled “Cassius Clay must be Beaten: Why I Can't Let a Muslim be Champion.” Patterson had refused to call ‘Ali by anything other than this, his previous name, but “on November 22, 1965, ‘Ali boxed Patterson silly while asking him ‘What's my name?’ and eventually Patterson agreed that his name was ‘Ali.” For some bourgeois African-Americans after 1990, who did not all regard boxing as too elegant, ‘Ali's value was as an ideological figure of the weight of Martin Luther King, Jr., whom Malcolm X had taught to obey the law but to send menacing whites to the cemetery, and who in 1967 refused to fight in Vietnam: ‘Ali had enabled the bourgeoisie by the 1990s to “do normal things [*sic*] freely arousing only a resentful suspicion instead of mobs.” They saw his Muslim aspect as a nourishing option for blacks.[155]

The use of shards torn out from Arabic to focus a system of meaning in the daily lives of local adherents speeded up in the last years of the old NOI. World heavyweight boxing champion Muhammad ‘Ali duly called one of his children “Muhammad Ibn,” which he rightly glossed as meaning Junior or Son of. Thus, ‘Ali expected his son to be marked by his personality for the rest of his life: insensitive, given Ali's own resentment of the domination that his father had exercised over his life when he had been young. Through this Arabic name he had made his own son a junior, one writer reflected.[156]

As Malcolm had expected, and as some of the disgruntled in the Black bourgeoisie welcomed, the images of a punching, victorious Muslim Clay would henceforth install him, and thereby his national group, in the discourses of the Arab world and the Middle Eastern states. Expatriate elite Muslims from the Third World were by the 1960s reaping Black converts who wanted to study a strict, Arabic-medium Sunni intellectualism in the Middle East: some condemned Elijah and the NOI to the Arabic mass media there as non-Muslim in tenets.[157] In 1966, after Clay's electrifying conversion, the Cairo mass-circulation magazine *Minbar al-Islam* still minimized the NOI's understanding of even simple elements from true Islam, although with much less theological bitterness and fewer details of heresies than before. Yet the same issue carried a photo of Muhammad 'Ali in the ritual postures of Arabic prayer and described his latest victory in the ring in Canada as a model for long-term triumph through faith in Allah, self-possession and skilled intelligence-gathering in advance of "every international battle of our heroes": such qualities could guide the Arab youth of the 1960s, too inclined to gripe against their elders.[158]

In the 1970s, Muhammad 'Ali was to play a crucial role alongside high Nation of Islam leaders in negotiating financial aid in Libya from the young al-Qadhafi and his new military-led regime. Still, by then 'Ali was already making entertainment visits to U.S. troops in South Korea, and by the 1980s, inept U.S. officials would try to use him in their propaganda in Africa against the USSR's occupation of Afghanistan. After 11 September 2001, Ali was used to project America's beneficence towards Muslims in the Arab mass media. A seed of this Americanism had been already there in his 1964 somewhat mixed and ambiguous first declarations of his Islam.

But in the Middle East, 'Ali's impact was as a symbol who focused resentment against America in the most diverse strata in Muslim states. From two scholarly U.S. books in Beirut Arabic translations, from a few numbers of *Muhammad Speaks*, and from the Arabic and Farsi press, Iranian Shi'ite cleric, Sayyid Hadi Khosrow-Shahi put together as good an overview book about the pre-1975 NOI as his conditions allowed. In it, though, Shahi was clearly catering to the needs not just of the anti-Shah Shi'ite clergy but of secular-professional Iranians who were now feeling the full impact of America and modernity under the Shah. Drawing on wide coverage of Cassius Clay/ Muhammad 'Ali in such pro-Shah Farsi newspapers as *Kayhan* and *Ettela'at*, Shahi portrayed 'Ali's conversion to Islam as triggering great hostility from Americans. But "these threats and denunciations from Western reactionary circles had no effect on the morale of this new Muslim", whom he quoted as saying: "I am temporarily bearing weapons to protect myself".[159] The mainstream secular as well as Islamic press in Iran took seriously Muhammad 'Ali's switch to a puritan stance and life-style after his 1964 conversion: membership in Elijah's Nation of Islam had stopped him from smoking cigarettes and chasing any woman who took his fancy. The only relationship that the sect and all Islam allowed with non-related women or men was marriage.

'Ali bulked largest as a serious ideological figure in Iran in the 1960s in the wake of his 1967 refusal to serve in the American armed forces in Vietnam at the cost of his championship title and the risk of five years in jail. "Basically, I know the war in Vietnam to be unjust: I will keep up my struggle against the militarist system in America". Both the secular and Islamic media in Iran highlighted Islamic motives in Muhammad 'Ali's refusal to fight the Viet Cong, but the coverage helped even Islamist Iranians now to view Christian Americans more plurally: that enigmatic cleric, Dr Martin Luther King, Jr., soon to be assassinated, held 'Ali up to youth as a model for sacrificing fame, his championship and a huge income to satisfy his conscience [*Ettelaat* and *Kayhan*]. And 'Ali was cheered when he spoke against the war at Chicago University by the mainly white protest-kids there, the Farsi print-discourse, including the pro-Khomeinis, registered.[160] Thus, there was always some incorporative flexibility about what political communities black Muslims in the USA, and the very different ones in the Third World, were trying to imagine, conceptualize and build in the 1960s and 1970s.

'Ali did not energetically pursue his chances for a global political role. From Egypt's sphinx in 1971, he indicated that he might join in an Arab counter-attack on expansionist Israel. But would this go beyond fooling for the cameras? From the perspective of our new, 21st, century, the Hollywood bio-epic, *Ali,* read back into 'Ali's taunting-cordial exchanges with Jewish-American sports writer, Howard Cossell, beamed to the U.S. masses from TV, an augury for a new integrated nation and friendship between Americans of different colors and classes.[161] More career chances in the 1960s and 1970s were drawing more African-Americans into contact with Euro-Americans of different sub-groups and with their American dreams.[162]

Shi'ite cleric Sayyid Hadi Khosrow-Shahi had a different hope and a different polity, but he too came to straddle two discourse worlds in macro-history. He had put together his study of Elijah's pre-1975 Nation of Islam from limited reference resources and perhaps without having visited the USA or ever having met a NOI adherent. But then came Iran's Islamic revolution. He had long been close to Khomeini, who now made him ambassador for Iran to the Vatican. A royalist Iranian exile who sought to make the Europeans and the victorious Iranian republican Islamists fight each other, defamed Khosrow-Shahi in the London *Times* in 1984 as only in the Vatican as a cover from behind which to organize a terror network in France, Spain and Italy with a view to assassinating Iranian emigres, including even the Shah's dear son "Riza II."[163] But Sunni Arabs had long known Shi'ite Khosrow-Shahi as the dialoguer in gold-rimmed glasses, the scholar of obvious holiness who in his soothing, soft Arabic always strove to bring Sunni and Shi'ite Muslims, and indeed all good people, together on common ground. This gentle and broad-minded man had been a clear ideal choice as the new Islamic state's Ambassador to the Vatican. In the end, the British newspaper could only unreservedly apologize for the article and all the distress it caused the Sayyid.[164]

In 1990, Khosrow-Shahi was elected to the powerful Assembly of Experts, the institution which makes sure that Iran develops always along the Islamist path prescribed by its popular post-Shah constitution. His criticisms had long offended Israel, and officials in the Bush Jr administration were to charge that Khosrow-Shahi had had a hand in an alleged camp in Lebanon's Biqa' Valley for training Sa'udi dissidents, and thus in the attack on the U.S. Khobar Towers military complex in Dhahran, Sa'udi Arabia in the late 1990s.[165] But Sayyid Hadi Khosrow-Shahi was not on that level of anti-Americanism. In his book, he had quietly parted company with Elijah's Muslims when they depicted their race as God's "special people" or "superior" to Euro-Americans: he rapped that in at least one footnote as a "non-Islamic" belief.[166] What is true is that from 1978, Khosrow-Shahi judiciously advised the new Islamic Iran in the welcomes and resources it gave Farrakhan and his colleagues: the Islamic regime stepped adroitly around secondary variations in tenets. Matching Hadi Khosrow-Shahi's ecumenicism, Farrakhan used the recurrent interaction to try to reconcile Iran with Ba'athist 'Iraq—and both with his own American polity that he still loved despite all it had done to his people.

Religion, Economics and the Non-White States

The old NOI's focus on self-organization and self-enrichment in America up to 1976 time and again limited how far Elijah and his colleagues would apply cultural elements coming from the Middle East into building relations with Arabs and other Third World peoples. Scholars have seen Malcolm X as truly looking eastwards, and as trying to build a bridge from the old NOI mythologies and fragments of Arabic to a real conjunction with Third World states and peoples in the era of decolonization, while Elijah kept everything within a cult rhetoric.[167] Malcolm X was assassinated in early 1965, but the potentialities for transcontinental relationships with Arabs, etc., went forward in Arab-orientated impulses that were to develop in Wallace-Warith's successor-sect after 1975, and in Farrakhan's outreach to the Muslim countries after the 1995 Million Man March on Washington. Images of *current* overseas Muslims and other Third World peoples in the later discourse of Elijah and his followers before 1975 measure how much potential there already was for new relations in history with Third World groups and states, in the traditional more localistic, elite, core of the sect.

One facet of Elijah hoped new interactions with darker peoples and states out in the Third World might bring economic and political resources that could help improve the conditions of at least some African-Americans.

Cargoism

In his 1973 collection imaging the impending annihilation of America, Elijah referred to "other nations" whose populations "run into hundreds of millions of people [who] have sympathy for the Black man in America. They hope to help the Black man in America to be free to go for self." But for Elijah the phrase "go for self" often meant economic self-improvement, rather than political self-assertion or political secession. Thus, the NOI might choose to interact more with those Afro-Asian states with the economic development likeliest to bring material goods and profits to him and his people.

The richness and capitalistic prowess of non-Muslim Japan in the 1970s highlighted it as a partner with which to trade as much or more than Asian or African Muslim states. But as soon as it learned that Elijah's Muslims were trying to purchase wholesale quantities of low-priced merchandise from Japan for the benefit of all the Black people in America, white America intervened to make it hard for them to get anything from outside at a lower price than African-Americans had to pay to America: "this is evil on the part of America" which had to take account "that we the Black people in America are the brothers of the Black people, the Brown people and the Yellow people" in Asia and Africa.[168] Thus, measures from official America to block the transfers were underscoring that material exchanges could not be separated from the political in international relations. Thus Elijah too, not just Malcolm X, considered courting moral political support from the Muslim and African states or nations to win their minority some strength against the whites who pressed all around them.

Economic resources could influence with which states the Nation of Islam's leaders chose to tighten relations. But non-whiteness was a strong bond in its own right. In the 1930s and 1940s, Elijah's young sect had identified with Japan in the years in which it was politically and then militarily challenging the American government, albeit offering little in economics to blacks. This had led the WASPs to jail the NOI's male leaders: the women, who were left at large, kept the sect going, but barely. At odd times in the 1960s and 1970s, Elijah implied that his Muslims could, by diplomacy, harm America in her international relations if she moved against or constricted the sect: U.S. Blacks had as brothers the whole gamut of the globe's non-white races. The perspective here is not so different from polite letters from prison by the newly-converted young Malcolm X to U.S. authority figures that likewise had tried to use the U.S. government's relations with the emerging Muslim countries to win better treatment from white America for the black Americans, who through conversion now were linking to those states. For Elijah, the economic benefits of linking up to Muslim and Afro-Asian states had more weight than political relations for their own sake—again drawing him and his colleagues towards dynamic Japan and the Latin American states. Yet, if whites constricted his sect's economic development, he too might identify more with the Asian and African states in a political way, also.

Often, Elijah termed all of the populations of Africa and Asia (and Latin America?) a single global supra-African "Black Nation." Since white Americans, and the white race in general, have deceived the entire world of Black people and their brethren (brown, red and yellow), Allah was now causing "the darker people" to wake up and realize that the white race was really their six thousand years enemies all over the earth[169] Such formulations could be extended into an idea that African-Americans could overcome their weakness as a minority in America by linking up with the states of the globe's non-white majority in some loose economic or/and political community.

The Israel-Palestine Struggle

NOI images of Palestinians, Israelis and Zionists in the 1960s and 1970s had background in the earlier history of the sect as a semi-persecuted down-at-the-heels cult. Already, before 1950, the creation of Israel and the exile of the Palestinians could sharpen how Elijah and his Muslims saw the situation of the Black Nation in America. Palestine, Israel and the Middle East became entangled with factions in Negro America, and with relations with Anglo and Jewish compatriots, as the NOI's global view took form. Ralph Bunche, a Negro academic who served in the U.S. State Department and as a key official of the UN for more than two decades, was an exemplar of integrationism: his achievements in the U.S. mainstream challenged the avoidance of whites for which the NOI called. When internal options and factions among African-Americans connected up with the new Jewish state, the Palestinian cause was an early politicizing catalyst for the development of NOI thought. On behalf of the UN, Bunche had been able to negotiate a sort of armistice in February-May 1949 between the Jewish and Arab armies in and around Palestine.

Early NOI portrayals of Israel/Palestine made America somehow complicit in claimed transfer or cleansing of Palestinian populations in order to create Israel. It was yet one more instance of American WASP double standards. If Ralph Bunche could push aside Palestinians to create the new state of Israel, Elijah preached in the late 1940s, why couldn't he remove white people from four or five Southern states to make way for the Black Stone [Kaa'bah-symbolized African-American] Nation? Here, whatever empathy Elijah Muhammad felt for his Palestinian coreligionists was balanced by his respect for the effectiveness with which those Ashkenazi Jews had separated a new race-based state: new-born Israel spoke to the racial criteria that he wanted to determine the formation of plural states in North America. Also, Elijah's sympathy for the Palestinians and Arabs could get attenuated around this time by swings to a sense of racial difference from Middle Easterners. In one, Elijah said that Muhammad Ibn 'Abdallah of Arabia who appeared 1,400 years ago was a white man: his value was to be a sign pointing to the later real Muhammad—the God-missioned Elijah in America.[170]

But by the late 1950s, Nation of Islam spokesmen and media were excoriating UN Undersecretary Bunche as "the George Washington of Israel", even as his negotiations in the Arab-Israeli conflict brought Bunche a Nobel Prize.[171] As one eminent director of the NAACP, the bourgeois Bunche exemplified the integration option that the Muslims wanted to refute, and the roles that such African Americans were to have to play, if they were to rise to prominence in American administrations. As well as the class and ideological conflicts dividing black Americans, Palestine, Israel and the Arabs were also being given more relevance by Arabophile expectations among wider segments of the black bourgeoisie and in the quasi-intelligentsia around the NOI. For instance, a 30 July 1960 article in the *Los Angeles Herald-Dispatch* denounced Bunche as "the stooge of the Western powers" who kept the UN aside when the Christian Belgians and the South African whites shot down Africans like flies. It was Russia who saved Egypt in 1956 and ordered Israel out of the Sinai Desert and the Belgians out of the Congo. The "Christian French" had been bombing the Algerians and Tunisians supported by "the Christian United States and Britain".[172]

Such an item from a paper edited by friendly non-Muslims fitted into the NOI's Islamic concerns, which defined the racist bloc of the West as Christian as well as white, and wanted to juxtapose sub-Saharan Africans and the Arab peoples. But the *Los Angeles Herald-Dispatch* also was voicing the excitement of non-Muslim African-Americans at the protest, defiance and insurrection against the West by Arabs in Northern Africa and the Middle East as well as by black Africans, and the hope of the African-American public that something would come of that decolonization for them as well, in the longer term. A wider African-American public that wanted to build relations with Africans, Arabs and Muslims independent of the functions of someone like Bunche on behalf of the system, here pushes converted Muslims forward to focus and spearhead new international alliances. This pressure could politicize, expand and systemize the extraterritorial sympathies of Muslim African-American groups beyond what they might have reached, of themselves. The late 1950s and early 1960s already showed the interest of non-Muslim African-American media in Israel's "brutal treatment of the Palestine Arabs who had befriended the Jews in an hour of need".[173]

Muslim sects are pushed to the fore by a wider range of African-Americans to condemn Israel, but while such sects as the NOI then give an Islamic structure to the concern, the wider black anti-Israel public does not leave them much room to maneuver or moderate towards Zionists, or withdraw. In the 1980s and 1990s, Farrakhan was to face such constriction from the wider African-American bourgeoisie that had "made" his sect by highlighting it as authority for its anti-Israel and anti-Jewish sentiments.

Pre-1975 Black Muslim thought about Israel/Jews and Arabs in conflict divides into two periods: (a) less detailed interest and rarer engagement before the Six Day War of 1967 and (b) rising denunciations of Israel in *Muhammad Speaks* from 1967-1975 as that state "rampaged" in the Middle East and as relations between Jewish-Americans and African-Americans worsened. The shift among Black Muslims to deepening exploration of Arab struggles had much the same periodization as that among American Jews after the 1967 war to tighter support for Israel, Zionism, and then to an Israel-emblemed micronationalism. Palestine or Israel are among the insignias that delimit diverging peoples in the U.S.

Elijah Muhammad internalized the central idea hammered by Palestinian and Arab activists with whom his sect and its media had relations—that Israel was created after the Second World War at the expense of the original Palestinian inhabitants, whom it stripped of lands. But Elijah assimilated this broad theme to his own millenarian worldview that was preoccupied with America and its forthcoming destruction by God. In his 1973 collection, *The Fall of America* [this communication must have come from a *Muhammad Speaks* number of several, or many, years earlier], Elijah referred to the power and destruction that would very soon bring about the fall of the white man's world. "Here in America we can see nothing but the fall of America." Here Palestine occurred to his mind among movements in other countries that were telling Americans to go home. He saw Israel as a "little brother" that America and England had deposited on foreign soil: "they deprived the Arabs of their own land and sent them into exile." Elijah believed (fueled by Arabophile writers in America and Britain who were warning the West could lose the Middle East following the rise of radical pan-Arab nationalism in the 1950s) that this expulsion was about to cost America the power and authority it had once exercised in the East: "this means bloodshed and plenty of it." Elijah here hoped that foreign (Communist?) navies and planes which were neither American nor British would try to drive America out of the Middle East: "they will not be satisfied as long as Israel is in Palestine." Yet this pan-Islamist solidarity was not central for Elijah: rather, Palestine was one more illustration that the world would soon be going up in flames as demonstrated also by the explosive potential of the Cold War between the communist and western blocs on the borders between east and west Germany [=the U.S.-Russian crisis of October 1961 focused by Berlin?].

Thus, crises in the world quite apart from Muslims or any particular ethnicity diluted millenarian Elijah Muhammad's identification with Arab nationalism in the Middle East. Elijah's priorities, as well as the still-limited size of his sect, made it still unlikely to give political or material aid of any kind to the Palestinians or to other Arabs. The "foreign lands" and "the East" that Elijah evoked were blurred, non-detailed entities in his mind: for him, those peoples' expulsions of the Americans had more importance as omens of God's approaching extermination of the whites in America. Thus, God, here, would fight the main battle of Muslims for them at some time in an indefinite future without there being any need to take part in improving or transforming current politics. Elijah's millenarianism lacked a drive to construct a black Islamic or pro-Africa lobby in America to neutralize the influence of, say, the American Zionists'—or South Africa's—lobby.[174]

However, some followers felt impulses to go further than the Messenger. In the late 1950s, the NOI, in part hopeful of getting some funding, took part in, or organized, functions in New York that brought together its own representatives, the personnel of Arab delegations at the UN (notably the missions of Egypt and Syria), African-American figures from entertainment and the arts, and non-Muslim black professionals. In April 1958, the Nation hosted a conference in Los Angeles to celebrate Pakistan Republic Day that also focused on the upcoming tenth anniversary of Israel, and which featured Muhammad Mahdi from 'Iraq, a lobbyist of the immigrant-organized Arab Information Center. Mahdi argued that the return of the Arab refugees to Palestine in accordance with UN resolutions was the first vital condition for peace in that region. And in response, Malcolm X appealed to the Arab states to get around "Zionist control" of the U.S. press in order to reach "the millions of people of color in America who are related to the Arabs by blood" and ready to support them.[175] Syria's UN ambassador was in search of

American allies to help him lobby against Israel's expulsion of Arabs in the Lake Hula area and her setting up of agricultural settlements and fortifications there. Through scholarships and his diplomats, Nasser was trying to bring lumpen proletariat Muslim cults and Black nationalist bodies in the USA closer to his country so that they might come to act as a lobby to neutralize that of the Zionists in the States.

African-American media in which Elijah contributed his "Islamic World" column highlighted segregation against dark-skinned diplomats in the States. Similarly, Malcolm X evoked concern from diplomats and "outraged Muslims of the African Asian World" to give his people more strength after raiding cops traumatized his pregnant wife. However, Elijah rejected a suggestion of conversion to orthodox Islam from an adherent on the grounds that "devils" had corrupted Islam in the East.[176]

By and large, Elijah (and for the most part even Malcolm and Farrakhan) seldom felt, before 1975, that politicized animus against Jews in America and against the state of Israel in Islam's heartlands, that became more salient in the revived Nation of Islam that Farrakhan was to articulate from 1984. Jewish business figures provided Elijah's old NOI with partners in publishing and boxing.[177] Ordinary NOI members or supporters, too, had some day-to-day symbiotic interaction with Jewish fellow-Americans before 1975 which, Farrakhan's new media were to imply, might as well continue in the 1980s and 1990s. Elijah, reprinted years later by Farrakhan, was aware that some of his followers, intent on avoiding pork, "buy meats from the Jewish shops", which he permitted from the "Orthodox religious Jews, who want to follow the law of Moses and the food that he prescribed"—though he distinguished these from a more Americanized category of Christian-like Jews who would eat everything: "the merchandise of those Jews must be shunned, if you desire to live".[178] Hence, Elijah—and Farrakhan in 1987—allowed his followers to have some economic interaction with Ashkenazi Jews, not just for convenience but because he saw some affinities with them in comparison to Christian whites. Still, a report written for the American Jewish Committee monitored that *Muhammad Speaks* was often carrying "overt anti-Semitism" that blasted the global financial conspiracies of international bankers, whom it depicted as heavily Jewish.[179]

The solidarity with the wider Arab World, and specifically with Palestinians, that the Nation of Islam's newspapers (more than its ministers) voiced in the 1960s and 1970s had long-term input into how concepts of global communities evolved among African-Americans in general. But even with those taking the fore, engagement with Arabs and Israel could get refracted by the interest and construction of the African-American nation as it now cohered and sought self-determination within its U.S. polity. Malcolm's 1964 autobiography had some passages in which he, like Garvey and indeed sometimes Elijah, expressed respect for the self-organization with which a category of the Jews of the world established a territorial-nationalist state of their own on the soil of Palestine after WWII.

In one paragraph that veered close to some assumptions of Zionism, Malcolm X rejected Americanist drives to integrate the plural peoples who migrated to America into one new nationality that would ultimately reach the stage of their intermarriage and fusion inside the frame of their shared U.S. polity. Like the porous Garvey way back in the 1920s, Malcolm here in 1964 approved not just the expulsion of the English from Ireland to reverse their projects of assimilation, but also Zionist objections to the quickening integration of the Jews of Germany into the German nation in the leadup to Hitler's assumption of power. Malcolm condemned the actions of German Jews in changing their names, intermarrying with Aryans, and eagerly seizing German culture. He felt his own enclave-nationalist stance in America was vindicated by the fact that Hitler had so brusquely shown how wrong was this process of self-Germanization by integrationist Jews. Malcolm further voiced some understanding of the most extreme Zionist factions' resort to violence after the breakdown of negotiations with British mandatory authorities in Palestine. Once the Stern Gang started shooting down the British, the British had had to relent and help the Jews wrest Palestine from the Arabs. Thereafter, the Jews established their own country of Israel, "the only thing that every race of man in the world respects, and understands."[180]

For Malcolm X, here at least, and as Elijah felt in one twinge back in the late 1940s, the Zionists thus provided—in this aspect—a model for blacks in America. However, in purer pan-Islamic formulations, Malcolm came close to fusing (a) Palestinian Arabs with African-Americans and (b) Jews in the Middle East with parochial U.S. Jews. In reasoning that was to continue to resonate in the Black-Jewish ethnic polarization of the late 20th century USA, Malcolm as an NOI Minister depicted that in America, Jewish merchants in the ghettoes "sap the very life-blood of the so-called Negroes to maintain the state of Israel, its armies and its continued aggression against our brothers in the East": every "Black man" [but what about "Black" women?] "resented that." With the help of the Christian whites of America and Europe, the Jews "drove our Muslim brothers [the Palestinian Arabs] out of their homeland where they had been settled for centuries, and took over the land for themselves: this every Muslim resents." [The repeated stress by Malcolm and Elijah on "the Black Man" and Arab and Muslim males was a Middle Anglo-like lapse from Frederick Douglass' sense in the century before of Negro men and women suffering together, from feminist insights, and from the Qur'an's sense of the male and women believers as aiders of each other who build God's ethical society together: Q 9:71-72].

Here, at the start of the 1960s, Malcolm thrust towards a synthesis of (a) religion-imposed solidarity with the Palestinians and Arabs with (b) parochial conflict with some domestic American Jews. (True, many non-Muslim African-Americans after 1967 were to voice their own solidarity out of a sense of the injustices done to the Arabs, without any criteria from Islam). Another parochial-Middle Eastern parallel was Malcolm's exaggeration that Jewish-American "control" of the mass media [it was really more like virulent input by some Jewish journalists] enabled them to direct the thinking of most Americans on the [pan-Islamic-cum-pan-African] issue of Egypt's nationalization of the Suez Canal in 1956. Such 1950s-1960s unification of a domestic Islam with a global pan-Islam anticipated Farrakhan's pairing from 1978 of his very rhetorical struggle against some local U.S. Jews, with a sometimes blurred evocation of Palestine/Israel in order to take the moral high-ground over them. It is to be noted, though, that even in these condemnations, Malcolm retained a ghost of indecision about whether Jews were to be classified as among the whites. He was still respecting the fact that many recently-immigrated Jews had made their own way up towards the top in America—without begging from whites as Negro institutions did on grounds of shared Christianity.[181]

At the height of the Arab cold war between "progressive" and monarchical/"reactionary" states,[181] Malcolm X had, in the leadup to his death, kept on equally good terms at one and the same time with king-deposer, Nasser, and with his nemesis, King Faysal of Sa'udi Arabia. *Muhammad Speaks* may have been similar in the 1960s and 1970s: it never achieved a clear ideological stand with either the left or the right in the Muslim Middle East, although the Palestinian 'Ali Baghdadi, a former President of the Organization of Arab Students in the USA, tugged the readers towards the Arab left-polities or movements of such leaders as Gamal 'Abd al-Nasser. A modest preparedness to stand up to the Western states, even in only a limited or just verbal way, sufficed for Arab rulers to draw kudos from *Muhammad Speaks*. In the wake of the 1973 October (Ramadan) War in which the frontline Arab states dented and sometimes mangled Israel's war machine, Tunisia's veteran President Habib Bourguiba, speaking to his national assembly, refuted accusations made by some Western countries against the oil-producing Arab countries, and stressed the need to develop the national economy in Tunisia. Those Western countries now blaming the Arab states for the inflation in the West, Bourguiba pointed out, conveniently ignored that inflation had existed long before the increase in oil prices. The Arab states had title to use oil as a weapon, given that it was only aimed at exerting pressure on the United States and other big powers backing Israel.

Here, *Muhammad Speaks* derived modest pleasure from the new post-1973 image of the Arab states as effective on the battlefield against Israel, and as able to muster increasing economic power to pressure Western states like America into respect for a single Arab World interest. But smart African-American readers would have noted the modesty of the aims of Muslim states that were essentially trying, through war and oil, merely to pressure Israel to return to her 1967 borders, not to destroy the Jewish state. *Muhammad Speaks* quoted Bourguiba that his state "considers the Palestine cause our own."[183] [Yet in 1963, Bourguiba had proposed a Jewish and a Palestinian state according to the UN's 1947 partition plan as the solution, which most Arab World nationalists and indeed governments blasted because it would not let enough Palestinian refugees back in]. The item came from Communist China's Hsinhua news agency. The endorsement of the conservative, "liberal" Bourguiba thus came from a Red China that had for years been ready to accept right-leaning, non-white regimes or movements of the Third World that even modestly opposed the USSR and America—from a China that now had reasonable working relations with Nixon's America. Those rulers in Peking (like Elijah's Muslims who republished them) were far from being ideologically-driven revolutionaries in world affairs: they would disregard the internal politics of any ally ready to work with them.

For all their borrowings from Marxism, the Black Panthers sometimes tended to follow the NOI's lead and approve the rightist Arab governments to which, as their oil revenues mounted, influence was now flowing, away from the left-military regimes that Israel defeated in 1967. As they built their own institutions and increased their political independence from the Western powers, the lately backward oil-shaykhdoms had taken real measures to press the Western powers into a serious settlement around Palestine. Their aid to the front-line Arab governments and populations brought Sa'udi Arabia and the Gulf statelets credit among the Panthers and other secular U.S. Black Nationalists as well as the NOI. Drawing on the same Red Chinese Hsinhua news agency as had *Muhammad Speaks* the year before, *The Black Panther* hailed the 9th Arab Petroleum Congress' threat "to use oil as a defensive weapon to liberate occupied Arab territories and win the national rights of the Palestinian people." Like Bourguiba, the item ascribed the paralysis afflicting Western economies to that system's structural malfunctions, not to raised oil prices.[184] Israeli propaganda was trying to split the now-rich oil-producing Arab countries and poor African peoples who now themselves felt the pinch of higher oil prices. Against that, *The Black Panther* reported that aid given by OPEC to Third World countries totaled $17 billion in 1974, 10.2% of the GNP of those 13 states. In contrast, the industrialized states continued to violate a resolution of the UN that they allocate a minimum of 1% of their GNP to aid development by the Third World.[185]

Radical Arab nationalisms of the Nasser or Palestinian type touched some members of the NOI, and also secular "Black" movements, with a leftist tint. But the growing strength of conservative monarchies and religion in the Arab World from 1967 lost the Arabs few friends among either the religious right or the left in Black America. The rightist Arabs moved in the best PLO and Red China circles of the time, and African-Americans hoped that they might help make the white Western states more rational. *The Black Panther* covered in detail the takeovers of oil production by the—in many ways very weak—peninsular Arabian and Gulf states as part of the Third World's seizure of sovereignty from the Western powers. The paper carried a report in early 1975 that the Joint Chiefs of Staff and the CIA's director wanted to occupy the Shawar oil pipeline in Sa'udi Arabia.[186]

From 1967-1975, *Muhammad Speaks* charged that the life of an Arab in Israel differed little from that of a Black in Alabama; likened the attacks of Israeli planes and tanks against Arab civilians and refugees to Hitler's blitzkriegs; carried claims by Arabs that they had undergone torture at Israeli hands; and interviewed representatives of the al-Fatah "Palestinian liberation movement" so that they could set out their goal of a "democratic secular state" to replace Israel.[187] Those PLO spokesmen who passed through African-American protest milieus after 1967 stressed the secularist, radical-left drives of their movement, its potential for serving as a spearhead to establish a united Arab world under socialism.[188] Such coverage from the tabloid, with its above-500,000 circulation, fed the increased interest of the new Africanist youth in Palestinian nationalism. (However, some otherwise highly conscious youth in the NOI itself did skip many articles about the Middle East when reading the sacred newspaper.)[189] Such Palestinian political activism spoke to the black youth's priorities, but also modified and bent the religious withdrawal of the NOI from the oppressive society around it.

The NOI's long-standing religious explication of suffering kept its hold in the 1970s. Margery Hossain wrote in 1973: "Messenger Muhammad teaches us that we are the descendants of the Original Black God who created the heavens and the earth. An enemy put us to sleep" by purpose of God to test the Blacks. But "now it is wakeup time." "Listen to the world news. Look over the face of the earth: everywhere each nation seeks to stand on earth that he [*sic*] can call his own".[190] Thus, sub-Saharan African and Arab nationalist struggles pulled (a) Elijah's calls for African-Americans to procure land in some sense before the Solution that God would wreak on Judgment Day, towards (b) a political territorial secessionism as a secular solution. (Yet pockets of land, and prosperity through businesses in special quarters, all might in the end only affiliate the Muslims to America or even take them in.)

Arabs and Persians

Even during Elijah's comparatively insular reign, *Muhammad Speaks* was enabling Arabs to teach their somewhat secular nationalisms to American blacks. In 1971, it even carried a pan-Arab attack by the Palestinian-American 'Ali Baghdadi against the Shah of (Muslim) Iran, mocking his financially ruinous celebrations of the 2500-year anniversary of the ancient Persian Empire. This self-proclaimed "King of Kings, Light of the Aryans" was expansionist against the Arab shaykhdoms in the Gulf, as a puppet who was enabling U.S. imperialism to arm Asians to fight other Asians and thereby "guarantee the flow of oil to his imperialist masters."[191] There was a clear tone in Baghdadi's article of an Arab nationality resisting not just the Shah but, equally, a hostile Iranian nation. In the 1980s, however, the triumph of Khomeini's "Islamic Revolution" in Iran, was to change a few Black Muslim writers into rejecting these semi-secular Arab nationalisms that the sect's media had long transmitted to Black America.

Some items written by indigenous adherents of Elijah wove Arab causes into parochial American society and politics in ways that showed some potentiality of the Black Muslims to become a pro-Arab lobby in American public life. In August 1972, *Muhammad Speaks* editor, Leon Forrest, dismissed all the mainstream white candidates in the USA's 1972 presidential elections. Although a liberal who spoke for peace, "McGovern is quite anti-progressive when it comes to backing Israel"—that "mythical state" of which he and President Nixon were both lackeys. "Yet none of his Black colleagues and followers will call him on this question", although Israel-Palestine could become the new Vietnam of the mid-1970s.[192] [Would the NOI one day go into the political mainstream to do better?]

Wider Muslim World and Other Third World Countries

Attunedness to America's governing white elite and hatred of its power shaped much *Muhammad Speaks* coverage of the Middle East. The tabloid was unable, given the times and that early point in the development of the "Black Muslim" educated class, to impose any undivided ideological stance towards the overseas countries to which it was voicing some kind of community. *Muhammad Speaks* could also use materials from the Anglo-morphic mainstream with some acumen towards its own construction of a global pan-Islamic community. In 1973, it carried an article by Peter Holden from the Pacific News Service, set up in San Francisco on a non-profit basis as an alternative source of news, in particular items scrutinizing the U.S. role in Vietnam. The item concluded that the movement of the United States aircraft carrier Constellation into the oil-rich Persian Gulf—the first such since 1948—was marking a new United States commitment to military and political action in the Middle East. America was bringing the 7th Fleet onto the Mideast scene as a permanent force.

The item brought accurate and sharp images of the operations of Congress and the military, and the white factions fighting in each, to African-Americans. The question was whether the U.S. should carry through the building of a proposed base on the mid-Indian Ocean islet of Diego Garcia after the disasters of Vietnam. Opponents preferred Kissinger diplomacy around the world. Advocates in the military and Congress argued that military control of the sea lanes was necessary to maintain the USA's access to raw materials—oil, for one. The CIA had characterized the USSR as not enough of a threat to justify the move; conservative admirals, too, wanted to keep the 7th Fleet in the Western Pacific and Indo-Chinese waters. But President Gerald Ford overruled the CIA.

Until then, the *Muhammad Speaks* item pointed out, the U.S. had taken great pains to keep a low profile in the Persian Gulf, although since early 1972 it had maintained a small naval installation on Bahrain, just off-shore from some of the richest Sa'udi oil fields. The item reminded the Islam-tinged African-American readers that Nixon in 1971 had deployed the 7th Fleet in the Bay of Bengal during the India-Pakistan war in a thinly-veiled "tilt towards Pakistan" [although the U.S. though, had not intervened to stop India and the creation of Bangladesh]. The item ascribed to white America some violent impulses towards Arabs. Incensed by their threats of partial oil embargoes over Palestine-Israel, top Washington policymakers were considering moves to seize the Mideastern oil fields: Israel might seize those of Kuwait on America's behalf. [These particular Americans and Jews were not so far from the devil-whites stereotypes of Fard and Elijah].

Muhammad Speaks readers were being reminded of the "strong feelings" over the expense and bad outcome of the collapsing Vietnam commitment that had made several congressmen in 1972 object even to the modest move to Bahrain.[193] *Muhammad Speaks* was educating the readers in the procedures of Congress, the techniques the governing elite used to circumvent it, and the diversity of the international impulses of elite U.S. whites, many of whom now had become innocuous isolationists after Vietnam. But it also caught at length here, as it happened, a crucial turn in the USA's geo-military stance abroad towards oil and the Gulf which were to draw America into three wars there, with devastation and bloodshed that are with us all, still, in a new century thirty years later.

Muhammad Speaks deepened African-American understanding in the 1970s of the functioning of U.S. institutions and policymakers and of the overall structure of society. The desire of all African-Americans to understand the white power with which they had to cope every day in their lives was further focused, not blurred, by the NOI believers' religious impulse to better understand the faraway region from which their Qur'an had come. Such coverage by *Muhammad Speaks*, like other black protest papers of that era, could become constructive over the long-term since it was educating blacks to become a part of that active, politicized American public that was sufficiently knowledgeable to hold the governing WASP elite accountable in foreign as well as internal affairs using America's representative institutions (parliamentarism). It had been the hope of Nasser and other Egyptian and Arab leaders from the 1950s that an Islam-influenced African-American community would act as a pressure-group on behalf of the Arabs—and so counterbalance the Zionists' lobbying for Israel in Washington.

Elijah Muhammad had sent a message to the first Bandung Conference of Non-Aligned States in 1955. In the 1970s, *Muhammad Speaks* maintained the followers' interest in this bloc of mostly non-white and Muslim nations that strove to place itself outside the power exerted by America and the white states allied to it. Attended by 80 heads of states and governments, the 4th Summit Conference of Non-Aligned countries held in Algiers in 1973 represented 2 billion people—not all of whom, though, were as happy about their regimes as were Elijah's Muslims. The Conference held out as its goal "eliminating foreign monopolies and assuming control of national resources... [to achieve] national sovereignty against any hegemony"—a formulation that distanced it from the Soviet Union and its satellites as much as from the USA and the white states that followed it.[194] The overwhelmingly non-white and extensively Muslim non-aligned states grouping did not dichotomize humanity into two racial camps in the totalist, vocal way of Elijah and his followers. But their policy here of keeping at bay all non-Third World states (including the USSR) fitted well enough into the NOI's rejection of all whites.

The growth of the NOI drew increased publicity by journalists and the media in the Middle Eastern countries. Javad Alamir of Iran predicted that the Nation of Islam was the "nucleus" that would soon take leadership of Black Americans as "by far the most progressive of all Black movements in the country." The NOI's ex-lumpens must have felt they were rising socially in receiving such approval from that Middle Easterner who "commands easy audiences with major political and diplomatic figures throughout the world, including Secretary of State Henry Kissinger [and who] spent 12 years working for the prestigious French periodical *Le Monde*, and has published reports in the top U.S. periodicals, including Newsweek." Alamir brought an entire news crew, including camera and sound equipment, to Chicago to film Muhammad's Temple No. 2, and the Nation of Islam's business enterprises there. A tour of the *Muhammad Speaks* newspaper and plant impressed him with a modernity [and indeed, a coverage of international affairs?] that surpassed many European papers. The first-hand view of the NOI made the Iranian want to publicize in the East "how Blacks unite for the first time—be proud, and not beg, but become what they should become."

Alamir said that he first became acquainted with the Nation of Islam through the adverse coverage of the American press—the FBI's old and ongoing disinformation campaigns were as ever drawing new friends and converts to the NOI! Despite the very great gulf between the NOI's street-level recruits and highly Westernizing-educated Middle Eastern leaders like 'Abd al-Rahman 'Azzam (1891-1971: first Secretary-General of the League of Arab States), who inducted Malcolm into Sa'udi life, the toxic racism that such "Eastern" elite Muslims had met in the Western countries, and their intellectualism, made the NOI's verbal militancy resonate to them. The pleas of integrationist black spokesmen "for equal partnership in the wealth and dignity of America" were dismissed by Javad Alamir because, in his view, the Western countries would always remain basically "a civilization of apartheid." It was the frozen, distilled rage of a cosmopolitan man who had not truly been admitted into the Western societies through which he passed because of the way he looked and where he came from.[195] With Javad Alamir, the "Black Muslims" had won the friendship of an eminent international TV commentator and host with wide access to both the Middle Eastern and the U.S. media.

Even under direct colonial rule to 1922, the multi-lingual 'Abd al-Rahman 'Azzam always tried to communicate in English to the British, whose skills and technology his realism respected: he was one of the oft-rebuffed acculturated Muslims, like Javad Alamir. 'Azzam, a founder of Egyptian pan-Africanism, and in youth a follower of Mustafa Kamil, wrote in 1932 that the classical Arab race's conquests and dispersals "permitted it to mix with [and incorporate] the black people and other peoples", from which it derived new "youth" for its post-classical rebirths.[196] While here, in 1932, 'Azzam felt himself an African and an Egyptian, in part racially different from Arabic-speaking Palestinians and Syrians, Malcolm X saw him as a generous, hospitable, father-like whiteman among those Arabs: 'Azzam caused him to revise his old NOI rejection of all whites as a race. In one of their meetings in 1964, the 75-year-old 'Azzam, who had followed Malcolm in the U.S. media while working for Sa'udi Arabia at the UN, "spoke of the lineage of the descendants of Muhammad the Prophet, and he showed [Malcolm] how they were both black and white". Here, 'Azzam was developing his 1930's and 1940's sense of the Arabs as a constantly-changing composite blend of races, as well as of a wider multi-racial Muslim world. He told Malcolm that any problems of color he might encounter in the Muslim world only resulted from, and measured, influences from the West. Here 'Azzam indicated his awareness that the tribalist lands of Islam were no races-blind paradise, and was preparing Malcolm for some letdowns so that he would carry forward as a Muslim.[197]

Although 'Azzam in 1964 was aware of Malcolm's lumpen "criminal" youth when he helped him, he liked Malcolm as "a very honest, intelligent and clever man," and believed that the influences of the not-fully-Islamic Elijah Muhammad and then of true Islam had wiped away all of Malcolm's early deviance. 'Azzam's 1972 retrospect-interview suggests that Malcolm's final breakthrough engagement with Sunni Islam in Sa'udi Arabia was an outcome of chance and muddle more than of any pre-planned coordinated action by Arab leaders and officials there and back in New York. Officials at the court that judges the credentials of those bound for Mecca for the pilgrimage were (justifiably?) reluctant to let Malcolm proceed on grounds that he did not meet the ritual requirements of being a Muslim: 'Azzam intervened twice and he believed that Prince Faysal may have "sent them a message not to make much trouble about it."[198]

The 1970s brought an unprecedented spate of petrodollars to the oil-rich Arab states. Under Elijah, though, little of that wealth was donated to the Nation of Islam. In 1972, Libya's new revolutionary leader, Mu'ammar al-Qadhafi, financed the NOI's purchase of a magnificent church for its national headquarters in Chicago. But from the Gulf states and Sa'udi Arabia, Elijah got only pro forma minor donations that still ignited paranoia from the new Jewish-American micronationalists in such organizations as the B'nai B'rith Anti-Defamation League. The globe's Sunni Muslims were well aware of the distinctive tenets of Elijah by the 1970s.[199]

Relations with the Communist World

Alienated from the roles of white Westerners, *Muhammad Speaks* sometimes echoed the angry Left's acceptance of Mao, Castro and other Communist dictatorships, all made glamorous by attacks from the U.S. press. The Nation of Islam retained the respect of a semi-insurrectionary Marxism-tinted fringe among African-Americans to Elijah's death in 1975—and did not yet have enough hankering for mainstream respectability to repulse them or their leftism.

When former Revolutionary Action Movement (RAM) organizers Robert Williams and Muhammad Ahmad (Max Stanford) spoke at Boston's Tufts University in 1973, *Muhammad Speaks* carried Williams' comment that "the moment of silence given to slain Chilean leader Salvador Allende" showed that Blacks were becoming "much more aware of world situations." Williams had been an NAACP president but had then become an armed self-proclaimed "self-determinationist": he fled the United States to avoid being killed on tendentious charges of kidnapping in his hometown of Monroe, North Carolina. He had recommended the "very informative" *Muhammad Speaks* to the Red Chinese, who liked that newspaper's avoidance of fashion shows and sports for serious [=political?] issues. While Williams' call for blacks to start rifle clubs for self-defense was formally within the American ethos and Constitution, that and his residing in Red China were hateful to the boundaries set by the U.S. polity: yet *Muhammad Speaks* relayed his voice within the sect. After helping to set up RAM, Ahmad had later organized the first Black Panther Party along with others. These leftists had a puritanism like that of the NOI's Muslims: Ahmad blasted the new "penthouse-style revolutionaries being accused of having the best coke" [=eg. Huey Newton?], the sexy Black exploitation movies such as *Shaft* that harmed the Black woman's culture, and the drugs problems that had to be ended with a blend of the no-nonsense of Mao and that of Elijah Muhammad.[200]

One editor of *Muhammad Speaks* in the 1970s, Joe Walker, may have been a card-carrying Communist at some point. Walker retained a pro-Soviet orientation in some items he wrote or selected for *Muhammad Speaks*. From Alma Ata, the capital of Soviet Kazakhstan, he dilated on all the progress the Muslims there were making under the beneficent guidance of their [blue-eyed] Slavic mentors.[201] An embarrassing *Muhammad Speaks* item parroted that "national discord [in the Tsarist Empire] had only been a reflection... of social reality" [i.e. classes], and that by putting an end to exploitation of man by man, the USSR's "socialist revolution" ended national discord in the bargain, so that now all its socialist nations were drawing together.[202] While the Soviets had achieved some breakthroughs such as mass literacy (in two imposed Western alphabets) in Central Asia, Joe Walker failed his African-American readers by refusing to see and report sharpening tensions between the USSR's Slavs and Muslims, including those in the new statal elite whom the Soviet system had moulded—a trend that any African-American who wanted to keep his eyes open would have sensed, had he toured. The USSR, whose integration of whites and Asians Walker mythologized, only had two more decades of life before it: the final disintegration already looked highly likely in 1973, and would accord with NOI tenets.

Some Communist states and movements (e.g. the Vietnamese, the Chinese) were non-white nationalistic components of the forming bloc of the "East", for the NOI world-view. But Joe Walker was articulating a radically discordant fringe in NOI communications when he openly argued that whites (Slavic, here) and a non-white/Eastern group (Central Asia's Muslim populations in this case) could build a shared humane political community together, and had, under the Soviets and Communism. Yet this denial of the sect's central doctrine may have fitted into an integrationist impulse or dream growing beneath the confrontationist surface of Elijah and his colleagues. If the USSR could bring disparate races and cultures together, might America be able to do the same in the long term?

Ideology—the wide, non-uniform global "Black Nation" that the NOI had been imaging since 1930—plus the sect's responsiveness to anti-U.S.

movements in Latin America, plus the internal need for a coalition between Blacks, Latinos and Amerindians to modify the hegemony of the dominant group in the U.S.—all these together already under Elijah tugged the Nation of Islam beyond a narrow political nationhood of African-Americans alone. *Muhammad Speaks* cited the "need for a land-base for non-white people" as among the exigencies that drew noted Black, Latino and Indian scholars together at a Minority Planning Conference sponsored in Gary by Indiana University. The conference academics in agreement with the NOI defined the stake of the conflict as not so much Black, Brown, Red or Yellow power but "economic power." Like Elijah, Dr Benjamin Alexander (Chairman of Chicago State University) said minorities had to become producers and not just consumers.

Relations with Spanish-Speaking States and Hispanic Americans

The NOI's rallying in support of Puerto Rican studies in colleges and universities where they faced cutbacks was in affinity with the ambiguous Black Panthers, who had been simultaneously on the streets, and around Black Studies on campuses. Dr Frank Bonilla, an academic born in Puerto Rico, said that during the 1960s, Black militants had inspired Puerto Rican activists. Dr Jacob Carruthers of Northeastern University of Illinois lamented that desegregation was unprecedentedly funneling off neo-bourgeois blacks into once purely white suburbs: his [enclave-]nationalist project required that "a Black majority has to be somewhere," so Blacks had to stay in the inner cities to build a land-base for self-determination in unity with Hispanics there.[203]

In late 1974, more than 2,000 U.S. National Guardsmen were called out in Puerto Rico in response to a wave of strikes called by various worker groups to protest bad working conditions, low salaries, and the bans on unionization and strike action by public employees. There was more than 30% unemployment in Puerto Rico. *Muhammad Speaks* publicized demonstrations of solidarity in Chicago and New York organized by the Puerto Rican Socialist Party (PSP), the Center for Autonomous Social Action (CASA)—a Latino organization with 30,000 Mexican, Colombian and Puerto Rican members—and the African-American Solidarity Committee. The hope of *Muhammad Speaks* was that the strike and the demonstrations of support in the two Americas would speed up the liberation of all of Latin America from American dominance, and relink the USA's own traditionally separated Puerto Rican and Mexican communities.[204] All in all, the atmosphere of such items of *Muhammad Speaks* was like the militant solidarity with left Latin Americans voiced from Stokely Carmichael's Pan-African Socialist Party or the Black Panthers: the *Muhammad Speaks* item also once more fostered their tendency to construct some sort of community or political front between blacks and Spanish-speakers in U.S. cities.[205]

In the 1970s, as Farrakhan's successor tabloid, *Final Call*, would continue to do in the 1980s and 1990s, *Muhammad Speaks* denounced the readiness of U.S. white elites to massively deport Hispanic "illegal aliens", mainly undocumented Mexican workers in the Southern states of the USA, in times of economic stress.

The business linkages of the NOI conglomerate with Peru, the source of the fish retailed by Muslim stores projected that country through *Muhammad Speaks* to millions of African-Americans. The paper covered the "slight elbow wound" received by the Peruvian Fisheries Minister General Javier Tantalean, during an attempt on the life of the Prime Minister by elements unhappy with six years of military-led "revolution". The assassination attempt came just before a major Latin-American conference was to be held in Lima to coordinate "actions aimed at counteracting the U.S. economic monopoly over the hemisphere".[206] [Using Peru as the source of the fish disregarded Gullah-speaking Black fishing communities of the U.S. southeast lowlands, although the NOI orated that it was working for independent black states in the USA.]

While the Muslims were being tinted most by Arabs in the 1960s and 1970s, neighborhood relations with Hispanics, and trade with Spanish-speaking states, were also drawing the Nation of Islam to the world of Latin America and to the emergent quasi-nation of Hispanics in the USA itself. Elijah Muhammad arranged for Spanish to be taught to children alongside Arabic in his parochial schools because "one day there would be more Spanish-speaking people in America than white people and we would need to be able to communicate with them."[207] He could be pretty far-sighted! The Black Panthers too taught Spanish to some of their African-American pupils as a tool to communicate with Black people in Latin American countries, to make the Party's Chicano pupils feel at home, to stand with Hispanic co-victims of racism in the U.S., and in order to show "the interrelatedness of all cultures" [=Panther non-nationalism, also a covert enterprise of much NOI journalism].[208] Chapter Two showed that Carter Woodson, W.E.B. DuBois, and a host of other African-American nationalist authors had all stressed the roles of blacks of African origin or descent in the construction of "Moorish" Islamic civilization in Spain during the seven centuries of Muslim rule there, and the contributions of transported black Africans to many areas of Latin America. The social boundaries between Muslim African-Americans and U.S. Hispanics would further blur in the 1990s as the latter converted to Islam in droves, and Farrakhan strove to forge, or encouraged, alliances with their enclave-nationalist leaders in U.S. electoral politics.

All in all, the coverage of overseas Muslim and other Third World peoples from *Muhammad Speaks* in the 1970s was exploratory. The journal did consistently pursue a special interest in Black African and Muslim peoples in the Third World—particularly when and where those populations were in conflicts with local whites or Western powers (America included). Although overseas news was selected to dovetail somewhat into sect tenets, most of it was taken at a second remove from non-Muslim and often "white" sources. The African-American writers of the sect at that time were still a narrow circle without the capacity to systematically analyse overseas phenomena on their own account. The failure of the sect's writers and preachers to complete a closed ideological system in Elijah's lifetime meant that the items, although on the aggrieved anti-white side, did stimulate some flexible and open reflection on the Islamic and African worlds by readers. Like its successors under Warith and Farrakhan, *Muhammad Speaks* did not often print genuine news items or essays on the intimate oral and written cultures and literatures of the Africans and Middle Easterners it portrayed, although there were already some authentic English translations. The interest in Latin Americans accorded with the NOI religion's very broad definition of the global "Black nation" that could encompass so much diversity. By 1975, exactly what kind of a world community for African-Americans the unfolding discourse of the sect would finally formulate—and what exact ratio Black Africa would have in the final ensemble—was still an open question.

ENDNOTES

1 Randy Simmons, "The Nation of Islam: 1", *Black News* August-September 1976.

2 *Fall* 227-8.

3 Tom Wolfe, *Radical Chic and Mau-Mauing the Flak-Catchers* (New York: Farrar, Staus and Giroux, 1970).

4 Eldridge Cleaver, *Soul on Fire* (Waco: Ward Books 1978; London: Hodder and Stroughton 1979) pp. 76-7.

5 Conversation with Lawrence Moten, 6 April 2001.

6 Alcohol was prohibited by the Qur'an and by the "national" drive of ragged NOI recruits to save the capital needed to start up small businesses. An old friend of Claude Brown who had just converted, once he had got out of sight of "the Brothers", did agree to go for some Islam-prohibited beers with him—over which he still condemned some local Jews. Claude Brown, *Manchild in the Promised Land* (Penguin Books 1969) p. 352.

7 Alonzo 4X, "Nation of Islam plans national college: '...there is only one expert, the Honorable Elijah Muhammad'", *Muhammad Speaks* 20 December 1974 p. 5.

8 Claude A. Clegg, *An Original Man: The Life and Times of Elijah Muhammad* (New York: Saint Martin's Press 1997) pp. 111-112.

9 C. Eric Lincoln, *The Black Muslims in America* (Boston: Beacon Press 1961) pp. 93, 140-141.

10 Karl Evanzz, *The Messenger: The Rise and Fall of Elijah Muhammad* (New York: Pantheon Books 1999) p. 375.

11 "M.S. National Editor elected to hospital planning board", *Muhammad Speaks* 20 December 1974 p. 4. Cf. the account of the similarly very professional career journalist and playwright, Richard Durham, who had been a previous editor from 1964-1969, in Mattius Gardell, *In the Name of Elijah Muhammad: Louis Farrakhan and the Nation of Islam* (North Carolina: Duke University Press and London: Hurst 1996) p. 64.

12 Larry 14X, "College officials discuss possibility of student employment with Nation of Islam: Decreasing job market sends graduates towards Muslims", *Muhammad Speaks* 20 December 1974 pp. 5, 19.

13 Harold 4X and Minister Oscar X, "Tuskegee Mayor Pays Tribute to the Messenger", *Muhammad Speaks* 28 December 1973 p. 4.

14 "Races: The Original Black Capitalists", *Time* 7 March 1969 p. 15B.

15 Lonnie Kashif, "D.C. warehouse purchase sparks Muslim drive", *Muhammad Speaks* 20 December 1974 p. 10.

16 Clegg *Original Man* p. 1975. The revisionist historian Evanzz (*The Messenger* p. 378) toyed with gossip at the time that the Muslims used their thriving business importing fish from Latin American countries where cocaine was produced as cover to smuggle that drug out among all the ghettos. But who first started that

rumor long before? Those in the NOI tradition have fought all drugs over decades: the new NOI under Farrakhan was to become something of a neighborhood nuisance in its efforts to drive dealers from African-American communities.

17 *Imam W. Deen Muhammad Speaks from Harlem N.Y.: Challenges that Face Man Today* (Chicago: W.D. Muhammad Publications 1985) pp. 53-55.

18 By the time that Elijah Muhammad died in 1975, educated African-Americans were becoming distrustful of any files coming from the FBI, whether "stolen" or under "FOI." Alex Poinsett claimed from the mass-circulation *Ebony* in 1976 that J. Edgar Hoover ordered the concoction of faked FBI files naming Black Panther leaders as police informers and that those then be mailed as "stolen" documents to their factional opponents, in order to make the Panthers decimate each other. See Alex Poinsett, "Where are the Revolutionaries?: Fiery Black Militants of the 1960s have all but Disappeared", *Ebony* February 1976 p. 86

19 "Black vs. Jew", *Time* 31 January 1969 pp. 33, 37.

20 Academic C. Eric Lincoln (1966) in Shlomo Katz (ed), *Negro and Jew: An Encounter in America* (New York: Macmillan 1967) p. 90.

21 Harold E. Quinn and Charles Y. Glock, *Anti-Semitism in America* (New York: MacMillan 1979) p. 62.

22 *The Autobiography of Malcolm X* (Middlesex: Penguin Books 1976) p. 491. Malcolm read a pattern of swift flight from arriving blacks by Jews back into Harlem's transformation into an African-American ghetto after 1910: ibid pp. 167-168.

23 "Black vs. Jew", *Time* 31 January 1969 p. 35.

24 Jacob Cohen in Katz op cit p. 11.

25 *Time* 31 January 1969 p. 35.

26 Lincoln (1961) p. 165. The *Los Angeles Herald Dispatch*, a paper that the NOI sold and probably financed, equated Christianity's "fiendish gas ovens to 'scientifically' rid the world of millions of Jews" with the USA's dropping of the atomic bombs on the Japanese, and lynchings: Lincoln (1961) p. 131.

27 See Leslie A. Fiedler in Katz op cit p. 32.

28 Kaufman, *Broken Alliance* p. 133.

29 Kaufman in Jack Salzman and Cornel West, *Struggles in the Promised Land: Towards a History of Black-Jewish Relations in the United States* (New York: OUP 1997) pp. 112-116.

30 Kaufman offers an excerpt from an anonymous leaflet placed in teachers' mailboxes in *one* Junior High School denouncing tricky-liberal "Middle East Murderers of Colored People" who should not be employed for teaching African-American history and culture to black kids in need of self-esteem (Salzman and West p. 114). The excerpt does not read to me as something a less well-educated black parent or agitator would have drafted, despite use of mannerisms. Earl Lewis (1997) speculated that agent provocateurs of the FBI or other law-enforcement bodies fabricated a fictional document to finally split Jews and blacks (ibid pp. 254-255). Or did someone else concoct it? Kaufman assessed the UFT's mass printings of the handouts as "a brilliant tactical move" by Shanker to muster enough determined support from Jewish teachers, Jews in general and the media to sustain and win the strike: ibid pp. 114-115.

31 Ibid pp. 114-115.

32 "Albert Shanker: Power is Good", *Time* 22 September 1975 p. 33. This article gives Shanker credit for fostering 10,000 Hispanic and black para-staff, to whom he could offer the opportunity to become teachers over the long term.

33 Don Petersen, "Row hits new school term", *Herald* (Melbourne) 9 November 1968.

34 *Muhammad Speaks* 28 February 1975 p. 21.

35 "Black vs. Jew", *Time* 31 January 1969 p. 35.

36 Kasisi Jitu Weusi, "Amid a City Near Collapsing: Racial Warfare Grips New York City High School", *Black News* November 1976 pp. 6-7.

37 Shlomo Katz, *Negro and Jew* pp. 19-20.

38 "Black vs. Jew", *Time* 31 January 1969 p. 37.

39 The broader-minded Jacob Cohen in Katz pp. 13-14.

40 Dawidowicz in Katz, op cit pp. 15-19. The hard-line Dawidowicz was in 1966 a researcher of the American Jewish Committee and a frequent contributor to the *Commentary* journal that was to spearhead the micronationalization of American Jewry soon to come.

41 "Black vs. Jew", *Time* 31 January 1969 p. 34.

42 Katz, *Negro and Jew* pp. 45-46.

43 Ibid pp. 110-111.

44 Gittlesohn in ibid pp. 46, 44.

45 Katz op cit p. 12.

46 Leonard Fein, *Where are We: The Inner Life of America's Jews* (New York: Harper and Row 1981) pp. 86-87.

47 *Time*, "Black vs. Jew" p. 37.

48 Fein, *Where are We?* pp. 295-296.

49 Fein's argument ran that during the 1956 Sinai campaign, Matta Gur and Rafael Eitan, both later chiefs of staff, put in complaints that the young Ariel Sharon had not taken due care to protect enemy soldiers and civilians: Fein, *Where Are We* p. 89. Yet the revelations of 1995 were to implicate Eitan in these massacres of prisoners that marred all Israel's wars.

50 Jonathan Rieder, *Canarsie: The Jews and Italians of Brooklyn against Liberalism* (Harvard University Press: 2nd ed 1987).

51 Dialogue, "Black vs Jew", *Time* 31 January 1969 p. 36.

52 Katz op cit p. 16. The thesis that a Christian fundamentalist popular tradition pushed ordinary African-Americans towards hatred of Jews was also argued by Gittelsohn in *ibid* p. 43.

53 Reform Judaism had from its birth stressed the rational and modern, and rejected anything that appeared "unscientific." Tashlich was a folk ritual of unlearned Slavic World Jews in which one throws crumbs into a body of flowing water to symbolize the casting away of one's sins. In America, both secular and Orthodox Jews had cut out this purificatory rite that had not originated in Judaism's texts. But by the 1980s, Reform Jews in America "no longer care about appearing modern and up to date" and both they and the Orthodox had made Tashlich part of the festivities of their Jewish New Year in public spaces. See C.E. Silberman, *A Certain People: American Jews and their Lives Today* (New York: Summit Books 1985) p. 257. The "primitive religiosity embedded in superstition" of a lost rural Eastern European Jewry was now installed in the constructed new anti-black, anti-Arab Jewish-American micronationalism as a blood-and-feeling repudiation of reason and Americanist modernity, contrived in order to fuse into one the new Nation it set apart. For the "sheep-like" way in which newly religious Jews—former bohemians, beatniks and secular professionals—in 1979 gulped down all the "revealed truth" banalities of rabbi David Lapin at the Pacific Jewish Center, *ibid* p. 249 fn.

54 Harold Cruse, *The Crisis of the Negro Intellectual* (London: W.D. Allen 1969) pp. 480-481.

55 Claude Brown, *Manchild in the Promised Land* pp.341-354.

56 Cleaver, *Soul on Ice* pp. 62-63.

57 Massimo Teodori (ed) *The New Left: A Documentary History* (London: Jonathon Cape 1970) pp. 289, 283.

58 Edit. "Stop Senate Bill no. 1", *The Black Panther* 22 February 1975 p. 2.

59 Interview with Cleaver 13 and 20 April 1968, Teodori (ed) *The New Left* pp. 284-289. On the other hand, Cleaver had spoken in a very serious tone of "Black urban guerrillas liberating black communities with the gun by eliminating America's police power over the black colony": Cleaver, *Soul on Fire* (Waco: Ward Books 1978; London: Hodder and Stoughton 1979) pp. 96-97.

60 Memories of San Diego of Idris Michael Tobin (b. 1956), 8 March 2002, and 11 April 2003. For FBI forgeries to make Panthers and Black Muslims fight over newspapers, see Gardell, op cit pp. 90, 366.

61 Electronic News Group, "Fine Cut: All Power to the People" (1996 British documentary: ed. Ruby Yong and Lee Lew-Lee), transmitted SBS Australia 25 May

1999.

62 Fahizah Alim in Amy Alexander (ed) *The Farrakhan Factor: African-American Writers on Leadership, Nationhood and Minister Louis Farrakhan* (New York: Grove Press 1998) pp. 148-167. Another Islam-influenced bourgeois young woman who through joining the Black Panthers was moved from "the security of the college campus and the cocoon of the great American Dream Machine" into the thick of child hunger, the homeless old, police brutality and the squalid housing of inner city Black America was Safiya Bukhari-Alston. Her rose-tinted Americanist glasses for a while made it hard for her to credit a Harlem "like one of those underdeveloped Third World countries" that she was now seeing through her Panther activities. Bukhari-Alston, "We Too Are Veterans: Post-Traumatic Stress Disorders and the Black Panther Party", *The Black Panther* February 1991 p. 25.

63 Virgil Dugue, "I Tried to Change the World" *Awake!* 22 March 1990 pp. 21-25.

64 "Fine Cut: All Power to the People".

65 In all its stages, SNCC kept its office staffs minimal: most members were activists in the field who only endured the danger for one year: given such turnover, no single coherent long-term ideology developed. SNCC did have a "redemptive" sect-like nature that stressed the round-the-clock oneness of members with the black masses and with each other: Emily Stoper, "The Student Nonviolent Coordinating Committee: Rise and Fall of a Redemptive Organization", *Journal of Black Studies* 8:1 (September 1977) pp. 13-34.

66 Address by Stokely Carmichael in Teodori (ed) *The New Left* pp. 281-2.

67 Massimo Teodori (ed) *The New Left* p. 289.

68 Teodori (ed) *The New Left* p. 289.

69 *Fall* pp. 92-93.

70 Mark Kitchell, *Berkeley in the Sixties* (film) televised by SBS Australia 1 May 2000.

71 *Fall* p. 98.

72 *Fall* p. 94.

73 See *Original Man* pp. 132-134, where Clegg sees the vituperation between Elijah and more "orthodox" African-American challengers from the late 1950s as about media standing as much as about given doctrines: "the emergence of Arab Muslim nations as significant players in international affairs... embassies ... In a world shrunk by television, radio, and the media in general, the combatants could hardly have afforded to overlook the importance of image." A bland message from Nasser to Elijah Muhammad was reassurance for NOI members that their leader was not "a phony Muslim" as his critics charged: Essien-Udom *op cit* p. 297.

74 *Fall* p. 95. But an innermost Elijah remained ambivalent and nuanced in his apprehension of Malcolm: Malcolm had turned from Allah (God) and Elijah, and started to follow the ruling whites, who duly raised him up for African-Americans to follow, yet "Malcolm was no lover of white people"—he "only lied to them in order to get a chance to fight me." Instead of a "lover" of whites, Malcolm was a "double-crosser" who tried to get at Elijah with their help: *Fall* p. 206.

75 David Horowitz, *Radical Son: A Journey Through Our Times* (New York: The Free Press 1997) pp. 110-111.

76 Gardell p. 96.

77 *Fall* p. 96.

78 *Fall* pp. 96-7.

79 *Fall* p. 106.

80 *Fall* pp. 159-160.

81 *Fall* pp. 165-166.

82 *Fall* pp. 207-208.

83 *Fall* pp. 162-163.

84 Cruse, *The Crisis of the Negro Intellectual* pp. 404-410, 420-421.

85 *Fall* p. 207.

86 Harold 4X and Joe Delaney, "Land of Despair: the Mississippi Delta, the valley of hunger", *Muhammad Speaks* 20 December 1974 pp. 8, 17.

87 Calvin Williams (special report), "Rhodesia prepares for war with FRELIMO", *Muhammad Speaks* 20 December 1974 p. 22.

88 See advertisement for audio tapes: "Listen and Learn to SPEAK ARABIC (Classical), YORUBA (Nigeria), SPANISH or FRENCH using the conversational method from a New York business": *Black News* February 1979 (4:5) p. 26. The two Western languages also could prove useful to pan-Africanism, given its drive to link up to populations of color in Latin America and the importance of French in West Africa.

89 Martin Njoroge, "Afro-Americans as seen by Afro-Africans", reprinted from Nairobi *Daily Nation* in *Atlas* (New York) 3 March 1970 pp. 20-22.

90 Benjamin R. Epstein and Arnold Forster, *The New Anti-Semitism* (New York: McGraw-Hill 1974) pp. 196-197.

91 Alonzo 4X, "Seven Speeches by Min. Louis Farrakhan", *Muhammad Speaks* 6 December 1974).

92 *Fall* p. 150; for Elijah's "missionary complex" towards animist Africans' traditional religions and clothing—"I am already civilized and I am ready to civilize Africa"—see Clegg, *An Original Man* pp. 240-1.

93 "Islam Broke Christianity's Iron Grip on African Life", *Muhammad Speaks* 23 October 1964 cited Algernon Austin, "Rethinking Race and the Nation of Islam, 1930-1975", *Ethnic and Racial Studies* (26:1) January 2003 p. 60.

94 Kasisi Weusi, "A View from the East: the New Nation of Islam", *Black News* March 1976 pp. 14-15.

95 *Fall* p. 83.

96 *Fall* pp. 16-17.

97 *Fall* pp. 165, 166.

98 *Fall* p. 72.

99 Harold Cruse, *Rebellion or Revolution?* (New York: William Morrow 1968) pp. 59-61, and 171. Cf. Martin Luther King, Jr., "Facing the Challenge of a New Age," *Phylon Quarterly* 18:1 1957 pp. 25-34, especially 25-26. P.L. Prattis had published his excerpted article "Integration" in the *Pittsburg Courier* of 28 July 1956, after America and Britain withdrew finance for the High Dam and Nasser nationalized the Suez canal—to be followed by invasion of Egypt by Israel, France and Britain. The Arab East looked to be slipping out of the grasp of the Western powers, as King, too, was aware.

100 Eric Dyson, *Making Malcolm: the Myth and Meaning of Malcolm X* (New York: OUP 1995) p. 176.

101 Salzman and West, *Struggles in the Promised Land* pp. 190, 196.

102 *Struggles in the Promised Land* p. 196.

103 For the drive of the young Israel of David Ben Gurion to expand its borders at the expense of the neighboring Arab states see Stephen Green *Taking Sides: America's Secret Relations with a Militant Israel, 1948-1967* (London: Faber 1984).

104 Marshall Frady, *Jesse: the Life and Pilgrimage of Jesse Jackson* (New York: Random House 1996) p. 347.

105 Clegg pp. 330-1.

106 Toure Muhammad, *Chronology of Nation of Islam History* (NOI: 1996) p. 21. Carmichael (Kwame Ture) in 1992 was to praise Farrakhan for his efforts "for the upliftment of our community" throughout the U.S.: see C. Asha Blake, "Interview with a Revolutionary: Dr Kwame Ture", *Newscope* (student publication of Atlanta Metropolitan College), February 1992 p. 8.

107 *Final Call* 24 November 1998 pp. 20-22.

108 Salzman and West, *Struggles* pp. 214-215.

109 Israeli journalist Gabi Brun wrote that he watched Egyptian POWs being forced to dig their own graves, so that Israeli soldiers could then machine-gun them in. Military historian Aryeh Yitzhaki estimated that 1000 Egyptian POWs and Palestinian civilians were massacred, including 300-400 at al-'Arish on 6 September 1967, but his estimates and reconstructions were structured to obscure the central role in the mass murders of Rafael Eitan. Official Israeli historian Michael

Bar Zohar had seen such killings in the 1967 Six Day War, and believed they took place in all Israel's wars. Israeli ex-General Arye Biro had conceded that he killed 49 Egyptian prisoners in the 1956 war: he did not have enough men free to guard them and felt no regret. Israel's 1995 Housing Minister Binyamin Ben-Eliezer denied that he ordered such killings as commander of a special unit known as "Shaked". PM Yitzhak Rabin, one of the old Palmach ethnic cleansers in 1947-1949, issued a statement in which he "very strongly condemned such acts" although declining to prosecute Biro, no longer in the armed forces. Rabin mused that nascent Israel's armed forces were born with a lack of battle norms and poor equipment amid hard combat so that there were "exceptions": overall, "the Israeli Defence Forces earned their glory as a humane army whose soldiers are blessed with special moral values." Ross Dunn, "Rabin condemns past army killings", *The Age* (Melbourne) 18 August 1995 p. 9; Laub Karin, "New Reports of Israeli Atrocities; Journalist says he saw Troops Execute 5 Prisoners in 1967", *Seattle Post-Intelligencer* 18 August 1995 p. A20. Four days later, on 21 August, a female Palestinian suicide-bomber killed five Israelis and destroyed two buses in Jerusalem: *The Age* 22 August 1995 p. 8.

110 The preceding data about SNCC's stances towards Algerians, Palestinians, Arabs and Israelis is drawn from Clayborne Carson, *In Struggle: SNCC and the Black Awakening of the 1960s* (Cambridge: Harvard University Press 1981) pp. 266-268, 192-193; cf Carson in Salzman and West, *Struggles in the Promised Land* pp. 188-192.

111 Essien-Udom pp. 263-264.

112 Essien-Udom p. 247.

113 "Book Review: '...And Bid Him Sing': Exciting New Novel by David G. DuBois," *The Black Panther* 12 April 1975 pp. 21, 25. David G. DuBois, an admirer of Mao's China, had been a journalist in Cairo in 1960-1972. Drawn from life, this book was a sort of left-Americanist ideological argument as well as a novel.

114 See W. Haywood Burns, *Aswat Ihtijaj al-Zunuj fi Amrika* (trans. Muhammad Sa'id al-Na'na'i) (Cairo: "Fil-Ma'rakah" series 1968), an anthology of voices of protest from African-American history; *Freedomways* special issue: Muhammad Muhammad al-Ahwani and Muhammad Ahmad Karra' (trs), *al-Thawrat al-Sawda' fi Amrika: Nidal al-Zunuj fil-Wilayat al-Muttahidat al-Amrikiyyah* (The Black Revolution in America: The Struggle of the Negroes in the USA) (Cairo: "Fil-Ma'rakah" series 1968). For the data in Arabic on DuBois, see e.g. *William Edward DuBois: Dirasah fi Qiyadati Jama'at al-Aqalliyyah*, (Cairo: Mu'assasat Sijill al-'Arab 1965), a translation by Faruq 'Abd al-Qadir and Dr Muhammad Anis of Elliott M. Rudwick's *W.E.B DuBois: A Study in Minority Leadership* (Philadelphia: University of Pennsylvania Press 1960).

115 *The Autobiography of Malcolm X* (Middlesex: Penguin Books) pp. 462-463: the version of Griffin's book *Aswad Mithli* tsd Zuhayr Shakir (Cairo: "Fil-Ma'rakah" series 1970) is probably a second edition. Sa'udi media continued to cover the spread of Islam and race relations in America: 'Abdallah 'Ali al-Sani', "al-Zunuj fil-Wilayat al-Muttahidat al-Amrikiyyah" (Negroes in the United States of America) *Majallat Rabitat al-'Alam al-Islami* Muharram 1398/December 1977 pp. 29-31.

116 Algernon Austin, "Rethinking Race and the Nation of Islam" loc cit p. 64.

117 'Umar al-Dayrawi (trs.), *al-Muslimun al-Zunuj fi Amrika* (Bayrut: Dar al-'Ilm lil-Malayin 1962); I have not seen Habib Fahuli's book *Thawrat al-Zunuj fi Amrika* (The Revolution of the Negroes in America), published in Beirut in this period.

118 Sam Cooley, "Symbolic meeting site: Arab guerrillas lay antipeace strategy", *Christian Science Monitor* 27 August 1970 p. 3.

119 Clayborne Carson in Salzman and West pp. 186-191.

120 "Interview with Stokely Carmichael: Common Struggle of the Palestinian and African People", *Palestine: PLO Information Bulletin* (5:16) 1-15 September 1979 pp. 34-35.

121 Interview with Huey P. Newton in August 1968 in Teodori (ed) *The New Left* pp. 289-290.

122 See statements of Algeria's 'Abd al-'Aziz Bu Tafliqah after Yasir 'Arafat spoke

before the UN: "President of UN General Assembly Interviewed: 'Emergence of Third World No Myth' ", *The Black Panther* 22 February 1975 p. 18.

123 1968 interview with Huey P. Newton in Teodori op cit p. 291, 293-4.

124 Epstein and Forster, *The New Anti-Semitism* pp. 203-205.

125 Cleaver, *Soul on Fire* pp. 91-92.

126 See Barbara Pillsbury, Cohesion and Cleavage in a Chinese Muslim Minority (Ph.D thesis, Columbia University 1973) passim.

127 See e.g. "Lesotho Protests S. Africa's Sabotage of Miners' Pay Plan", *The Black Panther* 29 March 1975 p. 20.

128 "UN Commission Appeals for Amnesty for Apartheid Opponents", *The Black Panther* 5 April 1975 p. 19.

129 "Revolutionary Violence will Free Us: David Sibeko, Representative of the pan-Africanist Congress," *The Black Panther* 1 March 1975 pp. 19-20.

130 "International News: 'Imperialist Scheme' Charged in Murder of ZANU Leader" (Herbert Chitepo), *The Black Panther* 5 April 1975 p. 17.

131 ELF director of information Mohamed Sa'id, "We are Struggling for National Liberation in Eritrea", *The Black Panther* 2 June 1975 pp. 19, 20.

132 "Sweeping Land Reform Decreed in Ethiopia: All Rural Land shall be Collective Property of Ethiopian People", *The Black Panther* 15 March 1975 p. 19.

133 "FRELIMO delegation hailed in China: Large Crowds Shout Revolutionary Slogans of Welcome: Samora Machel's Speech", *The Black Panther* 8 March 1975 p. 17.

134 Dr Leo P. McCallum analyzed by Algernon Austin, "Rethinking Race and the Nation of Islam" loc cit p. 61.

135 Ibid p. 60.

136 "Third World Nations Recommend UN Action Against Israel," *The Black Panther* 12 April 1975 p. 19.

137 Horowitz, *Radical Son* pp. 226-228.

138 *Ibid* p. 227.

139 "Pan-African Film Workers Urge 'Progressive African Culture'", *The Black Panther* 8 March 1975 p. 21.

140 "25,000 Cheering Fans Welcome Muhammad 'Ali to Malaysia", *The Black Panther* 23 June 1975 p. 23.

141 "Sports: Did 'Ali Title Bout Shelter Troubles in Malaysia?" *The Black Panther* 14 July 1975 pp. 23, 25. The close interval between the original *Black Panther* article and the publication of the reply may locate the rebuker in America. Far more Chinese Malaysians were studying abroad in that era than Malays, although the writer's use of the term "Malaysia" may identify him as a Malay given that most Marxist Chinese of Malaysia refused to recognize that 1963 federation.

142 See "Muhammad 'Ali Pledges Aid to Needy Minorities, African Drought Victims: Meets with UN Secretary-General on World Hunger", *The Black Panther* 15 March 1975 p. 23. By 1975, a drought had for ten long years gripped the Sahel, including wide tracts of Chad, Mali, Gambia, Niger, Upper Volta and Senegal: 100,000 Africans had already died, the Panther organ noted.

143 Cleaver, *Soul on Fire* pp. 134-135.

144 To the credit of his rationality, Cleaver did stop his more "cutthroat" members in Algiers who wanted to kidnap the U.S. ambassador: *Soul on Fire* p. 143. Other of his men dated women in that embassy: dualism.

145 It reads like authentic, uncontrollable culture-shock when Cleaver in exile burst out to some anti-American French who only wanted to be sympathetic that their country was industrial and technological "trash" in comparison to the America that made the surpassing electric typewriters: *Soul on Fire* pp. 188-189. Cleaver would surely have swung a punch at any Yankee racist who inferiorized African-Americans as not up to U.S. technology to his face like that!

146 Kit Kim Holder, *The Black Panther Party and the Death of Huey P. Newton*", *The Black Panther* February 1991 p. 10.

147 "*The Arabs*: Valuable Analyses on Middle East Issues," *The Black Panther* 23 June 1975 p. 19, 25. The director of the West Coast Arab Information Center

producing the magazine was Dr Khalid I. Babaa.

148 "Artistic Endeavor to Understand and Confront Evil in American Cities... Takes Richmond, VA by Storm", *New Trend* v. 21:3 Rabi' II 1423/June 2002 p. 1. As a high school student, Jihad Abdul Mumit read books by Nkrumah, Malcolm X, Che Guevara and Mao Tse Tung. He joined the Panthers at the age of 16. In his senior year, he was elected president of the Black Student Union at Plainfield High, New Jersey, and a month later was charged with the murder of a Plainfield policeman; the group was acquitted of all charges in 1972. In 1975, Jihad was charged with two bank robberies: while in prison he embraced Islam, and on parole participated in the anti-crack watch sponsored by Masjid al-Taqwa in Brooklyn. Biodata from *ABC Federation: forever in struggle*, http://web.archive.org/web 29 January 2004.

149 Kelley Beaucar Vlahos, "Radical Black Panther Chief Blames American Leaders for Terror Attacks" in *Fox News* 3 November 2001.

150 Essien-Udom pp. 218-219.

151 BBC Manchester, *About Us: The Nation of Islam* transmitted on SBS Australia 16 April 2000.

152 David Remnick, "The Boy Who Grew Up to be Muhammad Ali", *Good Weekend* (Melbourne *Age* supplement) 28 November 1999 pp. 14-15.

153 Sayyid Hadi Khosrow-Shahi, *Nabard-i-Islam dar Amrika* (Tehran: c. 1974) pp. 150-151.

154 Malcolm X *Autobiography* pp. 417, 419. Fard installed the Crusades in his mythologies as an illustration of the aggressive nature of the whites throughout history. He reconstructed that the Muslim warriors' capture of Jerusalem in 1187 and of Constantinople in 1453 were what forced the repelled white Christians to colonize the Americas and enslave Blacks (Africans) there: see Clegg, *Original Man* p. 57.

155 Ralph Wiley, "Ali: the Man, the Hero", *Emerge* May 1991 pp. 33-34. Like the class it spoke for, this article was a mix of militancy and the determination to make it into mainstream America—the drive to wrest Anglo-like ordinary lives pepped up with quasi-Muslim motifs. The latter included the author's indulgence of the ex-Christian 'Ali's cry that "God is with me" after he floored Liston in 1964 as "ultimate truths" as well as "boasts to sell tickets." Wiley was respectful of 'Ali's divorcing his first wife when she refused to wear her dresses below the knees, of the early resonance of 'Ali's name among Arabs in Mecca, of the Muslim religious grounds on which he refused to go to Vietnam, and of his bringing American hostages home from 'Iraq on the eve of the second Gulf war.

156 Wilfred Sheed, *Muhammad Ali: a Portrait in Words and Photos* (London: Weidenfield and Nicolson 1975) pp. 193-4. 'Ali called a later daughter he bore by his wife Veronica Porche, "Hana", which "they chose because it means happiness and peace of mind": "Who is Veronica Porche?", *Ebony* July 1977 p. 68.

157 See interview with convert Muslim Fa'iz Mahmud Shuja' al-Mu'tazz (ex-Anderson Holland from Chattanooga, who had worked as a stevedore), a student at al-Azhar University, in *Minbar al-Islam* (19:3) August 1961 pp. 128-129.

158 See Riyad Khalifah, "al-Islam fil-Wilayat al-Muttahidah" (Islam in the United States) *Minbar al-Islam* (24:1) 22 April 1966 p. 290; "Lana min al-Ma'rakat al-Akhirah li-Clay Durusun... wa Durus" (The Many, Many Lessons Clay's Latest Fight Holds out for Us), in *ibid* pp. 273-274.

159 Sayyid Hadi Khosrow-Shahi, *Nabard-i-Islam dar Amrika* (Tehran: c. 1974) pp. 148-149.

160 Khosrow-Shahi *op cit* pp. 161-3.

161 Stanley Crouch, *Time* 28 January 2002 pp. 53-56. Harold Cossell presented himself to African-Americans as a Jew in a range of relationships with Blacks as a group, sportsmen the most prominent. Some African-Americans accepted him as a friend while others dismissed him as patronizing: see *Ebony* December 1976 p. 76.

162 'Ali's engagement with Ashkenazi Jews came to take in some who lived overseas as well. In the 1990s, he was to take awards from institutions in Israel,

despite some memory there of odd criticisms in his earlier years as a Muslim.

163 Amir Taheri, "Suicide Bombers Sign Up in London", *The Sunday Times* 8 January 1984 p. 10.

164 See *Sunday Times* 9 December 1984 p. 19b.

165 Jamie Dettmer, "List Fingers Iranian Cleric for Bombing", *Insight on the News* 4 June 2001.

166 *Nabard* p. 64.

167 Louis A. DeCaro Jr, *On the Side of My People: A Religious Life of Malcolm X* (New York University Press 1996) pp. 122-124, where there is detail of some Egyptian and Indonesian diplomats and politicians with whom Malcolm interacted.

168 Elijah Muhammad, *Fall* pp. 121-123.

169 *Fall* pp. 174-175.

170 Evanzz p. 159.

171 Lincoln (1961) p. 139.

172 Lincoln (1961) p. 131: we saw that Elijah briefly toyed with the idea that his movement could "worship" white Russia as well as Red China in *Fall* p. 207.

173 *Los Angeles Herald-Dispatch* article of 9 January 1960 cited Lincoln (1961) p. 132.

174 Elijah Muhammad "The Destruction and Fall", *Final Call* 11 March 1997 p. 19.

175 Evanzz pp. 183-186.

176 Evanzz pp. 184-194.

177 Gardell *Farrakhan* p. 410; Clegg p. 374.

178 Elijah Muhammad "Bad food causes us to look old", *Final Call* 1 March 1987 p. 33.

179 Evanzz, *The Messenger* p. 375.

180 Malcolm, *Autobiography* pp. 384-385.

181 Excerpts from Malcolm X interview in Lincoln (1961) pp. 166-167.

182 See Malcolm Kerr, *The Arab Cold War 1958-1964: A Study of Ideology in Politics* (London: OUP 1965).

183 "Tunisia refutes U.S. charge," *Muhammad Speaks* 20 December 1974.

184 "Arab Petroleum Congress Declares Oil 'A Defensive Weapon'", *The Black Panther* 5 April 1975 p. 18.

185 "OPEC Aid to Third World Totals $17 Billion", *The Black Panther* 5 April 1975 p. 18.

186 "Kuwait Takes Over Oil Industry", *The Black Panther* 15 March 1975 pp. 19-20; "Kiss, George Brown of the Joint Chiefs of Staff and CIA director William Colly: Occupy the Shawar Oil Pipeline in Sa'udi Arabia," *The Black Panther* 1 March 1975 p. 22.

187 List of articles in Benjamin R. Epstein and Arnold Forster *The New Anti-Semitism* p. 211.

188 "Palestinian Liberation Organization appraises Middle East struggle"—interview by Chester Sheard of Ibrahim Ebeid of the PLO at the National Anti-Imperialist Conference in Solidarity with Africa held in Chicago: *Muhammad Speaks* 9 November 1973 pp. 3, 7.

189 Information from Idris Michael Tobin, a young NOI activist in California in the early 1970s, 11 April 2003.

190 Margery Hossain, *Muhammad Speaks* 19 October 1973.

191 Lincoln, *Black Muslims* (1973) p. 235; 1993 ed. p. 213. The original article was published in *Muhammad Speaks* on 29 October 1971.

192 Cited *New Anti-Semitism* p. 209.

193 Peter Holden, "Persian Gulf penetration marks policy shift", *Muhammad Speaks* 20 December 1974 pp. 7, 10.

194 "Nonaligned nations meeting in Algiers: Seek means for world self-reliance", *Muhammad Speaks* 19 October 1973 p. 15.

195 Larry 14X, "Iranian journalist lauds Nation of Islam", *Muhammad Speaks* 7 February 1975 p. 16.

196 Extract in Robert Montagne, "L'Union Arab", *Politique Etrangere* April 1946 pp. 190-191. See also Dennis Walker, "Africanism and the Egyptian Territorial Homeland in the Thought of 'Abd al-Rahman 'Azzam (1891-1971)", *Islam and the Modern Age* (New Delhi) August 1984 pp. 133-146.

197 *Autobiography* pp. 446-449. However, the whitening of such Arabs as 'Azzam and such dichotomizing periodization of Malcolm's beliefs by his ghost-writer, Haley, could be read as an instrumental fiction to some extent.

198 Charis Waddy, *The Muslim Mind* (London-New York: Longman 1976) pp. 107-109. This 1972 interview by Waddy of 'Azzam years after his induction of Malcolm did not extract as much substance as might have been hoped and may have distorted him: that she conducted it in English might have clouded in-depth assessment by 'Azzam of his motives and perceptions of Malcolm at that time.

199 For American Zionist rage at tiny sums that Abu Dhabi, Qatar, Syria and Bahrain flicked to Elijah, see *The New Anti-Semitism* p. 211.

200 Charles Aikins, "Black leader Recalls Historic China exile", *Muhammad Speaks* 19 October 1973.

201 Joe Walker, "Central Asian Republic's phenomenal development", *Muhammad Speaks* 2 November 1973.

202 "USSR's social groups show unity", *Muhammad Speaks* 2 November 1973 p. 20.

203 James Hoard Smith, "Economic woes strengthen non-white unity", *Muhammad Speaks* 20 December 1974 p. 14.

204 Alonzo 4X, "Protests of repression [in Puerto Rico] forge new Mexican, Puerto Rican Unity", *Muhammad Speaks* 20 December 1974 pp. 14, 17.

205 For the Black Panthers' interest in Puerto Rican nationalists active on such campuses as Rutger's University, "Puerto Rican Independence Support Group Formed for North America: Calls for National Liberation, Self-Determination", *The Black Panther* 12 April 1975 p. 18.

206 Lonnie Kashif, "Gunman wounds Peruvian fish minister in murder attempt", *Muhammad Speaks* 20 December 1974 p. 20.

207 Sonsynea Tate Little X: Growing Up in the Nation of Islam (San Francisco: Harper 1997) p. 39.

208 "Youth Institute: Spanish Classes [in Oakland, California] Explore Latin American Culture", *The Black Panther* 22 February 1975 pp. 4, 14.

Chapter Six

The Rise of Farrakhan in Elijah's NOI

1. TENSIONS BETWEEN "THE BLACKS" AND "THE JEWS" OVER FOREIGN POLICY TO 1980

This chapter reviews later deterioration in Black/Jewish relations in the late 1980s that set the scene for a Muslim like Farrakhan to become the leader of African-Americans in the 1980s. It reviews the development of Farrakhan under Elijah's leadership and his relationship with Elijah's son and successor, the Sunnifying Wallace/Warith Muhammad. The role of Jewish individuals and Jewish cultures in the formation of the young Farrakhan are examined to help explicate his role as the great ethnicist champion of "the Blacks" that he crafted from 1980. The chapter offers a portrait that includes the personal side of Farrakhan, and his insecurities of identity and ambivalences towards Euro-American groups.

Andrew Young and the Shifts in African-American Relations with Jews, Israel and Arabs

The so-called "Andrew Young affair" erupted in late 1979 after Young, the first African-American to serve as U.S. ambassador to the United Nations, met the UN representatives of the Palestine Liberation Organization at the home of the Kuwaiti Ambassador to the UN. The meeting and the controversy that followed was the culmination of (a) years of mounting understanding among African-Americans of the Arab and Palestinian causes, fed by Elijah's mass media, and (b) the growing determination of the African-American educated classes to help direct U.S. foreign policy toward the ending of racist regimes in Africa and a liberal resolution of conflicts in the Middle East and Latin America. Many African-Americans regarded the drive to sack Young, the highest black official in U.S. history, as linked to the demand of Jewish Americans for "exclusivity" in the drafting of the USA's policies and programs in the Middle East, so as to make them serve their "homeland of the mind", Israel.

Young had been one of the discreet relative radicals from Martin Luther King's Southern Christian Leadership Conference. From 1972, as a Congressman, he had tried to block some allocations for the Vietnam War.

Early in his tenure at the cabinet-level UN post, Young had faced virulent pressure from the African-American media to "get brothers and sisters in crucial jobs in the State Department and allied agencies." The explosive intellectuals demanded that Young end CIA funding of "almost every major black organization or outfit dealing with Africa... They've used the black officials [and academics] just like pawns in a messy international game that, at times, may have included murder. It's shameful what they've done to black participation in African affairs... So Andy, first get the CIA off our back".[1]

During their 1979 crisis with him, Zionist media-persons and supremacist Anglos in the USA stereotyped Andrew Young as a dangerous pro-Third World firebrand at the UN. In reality, he had served well international image-spinning by the Carter administration. His UN speeches against colonialism and racism convinced some Afro-Asian delegations and leaders that America really was coming to care about the aspirations and rights of their peoples. But Carter's team had done little to change the policies of previous U.S. Republican governments. The administration had early called for U.S. companies active in apartheid South Africa to desegregate facilities, train Africans and advance them into managerial positions. Was this gradualism in pursuit of a principle, or was it simply a rationale for foreign firms and investment to stay and economically strengthen the apartheid regime that secured their own profits? Young verbally defended his administration's continuation of nuclear cooperation with South Africa, including supplying it with enriched uranium, as it developed nuclear weapons with Israeli guidance. True, the Carter government worked to prevent deaths of Africans in custody. Young argued that American investment and the spread of the market under apartheid would transform that system. Young worked against racisms in U.S. and international institutions only in a realistic, long-term way: he was part of the USSR-obsessed American system that was changing only slowly: it was still hard for U.S. officials to view any threat to apartheid apart from the will of international communism to expand.[2]

The meeting between UN figures at the house of Kuwait's ambassador fitted with Young's diplomatic functions as a facilitator of channels of communication for America at the world body, most member-states of which felt that the Palestinian nation had to be involved as a party for any Middle East settlement to have any chance of holding. The Africanist *Black News*, from New York, noted that other U.S. officials, for example America's ambassador to Austria, had likewise been meeting with PLO officials: Young was just the "fall-guy" scapegoat. Israel's influence on America's electoral politics, through an American Jewry whose activist sections still identified as "Zionist" in a simple way at that time-point, had whipped up pressure by U.S. politicians who sought reelection, and by some WASPs and American Jews in government, for the policy of exclusion of and enmity towards the "terrorist" PLO. They promoted the notion that the Palestinians were a non-existent people with whom Americans should not be allowed to talk. The Zionists and their political allies charged that the demonized "Arabists" (experts on the Middle East) at the State Department had prompted Young to meet the PLO.

After his resignation, Young stated that he had also sought to break the impasse in the Middle East because further economic upheavals caused by Arab oil policies would affect "the constituency I represent"—the African-Americans already hit by reductions of oil output following the 1973 Arab-Israeli war.[3] (He had, after all his compromises and will to do his job for the American polity in general that salaried him, a touch, himself, of the drive of the rising micro-nationalisms to make U.S. foreign policy aid either ancestral homelands or the micronation itself in America). The *Black News* Africanists exulted at the beginnings of a shift of power in the USA system, which they covertly hoped could come to incorporate African-Americans, too. "The furore from the Israelis and American Zionists derives from their fear that the USA is changing its policies... Perhaps the Israelis thought there was an oil deal in the making." President Carter had recently compared the plight of the Palestinians to the Civil Rights movement of the 1960s.[4]

Recent Zionoid historiography on Black-Jewish relations has depicted Young's dismissal after meeting some PLO individuals as an affair with which Jewish American organizations had little if any connection. The lobby organizations could indeed give a different structure to their role than usual for two reasons. Firstly, racists among the USA's Anglomorphs had reached the end of their patience with Young's UN criticisms of some of the colonialist and racist distant relatives of Euro-Americans and sometimes even of aspects of America's record with its own blacks.[5] Some in the Anglo-American elite were in no mood to protect Young. More decisively, the Israeli authorities and diplomats, apt to contemptuously use their Jewish-American lobbyists, now chose to intervene to destroy Young directly themselves with not even a pretence that any domestic American political struggle or process was taking its course. As soon as he heard that Israeli agents knew of his secret meeting with the PLO, Young warned the Israeli diplomats not to make it public— "splash" it, as he put it. In mature, quiet diplomacy, Young told Israeli representatives in New York that they could indeed exact his hide from the White House, but that adding an internal U.S. ethnic clash to the Jewish state's deteriorating press image could devastate Israel's position in America.

In the upshot, the super-confident Israeli diplomats chose not to tell President Carter in a confidential memo: instead, they telephoned *Newsweek*. Flushed with past successes, the Israeli diplomats and operatives were sure they could sink Young with effortless ease, but the publicity at once exploded into what was for them a nightmarish free-ranging debate on the Middle East by the U.S. media, as the furious African-Americans broke free of any domestic Jewish control. The newlyself-directed and galvanized African-American people were in no mood for Young to go, thereby restoring "plantation politics", without taking on Israel and its instruments. Parren Mitchell, former chairman of the Congressional Black Caucus, warned that "out on the streets, the perception is that the Israeli Government went out of its way to embarrass and humiliate a black man... When you ask who did him in, the people say 'the Israelis'."

The explosion of ethnic ill-feeling between African-Americans and Jewish Americans over Young harmed Israel at a time when it needed as much good will as it could muster from all American groups in order to finesse all negotiations with Arab states into a means to overpower and exclude the Palestinians. For almost the first time, U.S. television networks with mass audiences had sent camera crews into southern Lebanon where they photographed Israeli bombs and shells devastating Lebanese and Palestinian civilians and their homes, rather than such Palestinian guerrillas as may have survived in those smoking ruins.

The Young affair was no mere domestic tug-of-war between blacks and Jews that caught Carter and his administration in the middle. Rather, domestic American ethnicities and global politics had now become as decisively fused for African-Americans as for their Jewish compatriots. Although the man himself swiftly moved to abort it, the struggle around Young as a symbol became a watershed in the formation of opinions and images about the Middle East in the USA, as well as in the development in U.S. politics of an African-American enclave-nation, or post-modern micro-nation with no territorially continuous homeland. By the time he went, Young had indeed registered his point to millions of Euro-Americans as well as to his own people, that the policy of not speaking to the PLO was "ridiculous". In a declaration of independence from the smaller Jewish minority whose Zionist leaderships had manipulated black organizations for so long, the most diverse assemblage of black leaders since the 1960s decade of civil rights met the same PLO representative Young had spoken to: they then issued a collective call for a review of U.S. policy to consider the establishment of an independent Palestinian nation. African-Americans' efforts aside, the affair speeded up discreet shifts in the diplomacy that America's Angloid elite had commenced toward ending the Arab-Israeli conflict.[6]

As things finally went—this time—President Carter chose to sacrifice Young rather than face long-term charges and pandemonium from the formidably-organized Jewish groups that lobbied for Israel. All along, perhaps, Young may have mainly been acting out impulses circulating among non-black colleagues in the State Department. Yet his actions and comments had proposed to all Americans who could read and watched TV that the Palestinians would have to be made a key party comparable to Israel—the unspoken truth on which the U.S. establishment would not muster the nerve to act until the administration of Bush, Sr.

In reviewing this affair that has now faded into history, it would be hard to dismiss Andrew Young as just another American politician or one more complaisant black who served time in the public eye so that the American polity could convince the post-World War II world it really was reinventing itself into a single integrated, liberal nation. Young had displayed many of the qualities required of a major international statesman. He had gained enough support from African-Americans, from Arab diplomats at the UN, and from Anglos who had discreetly tired of Israel to stay and make a fight of it. An Americanist, for all his reproaches about his country's failures to live up to its ideals, he chose not to run his country through a long-term polarization of two American groups to save his own position, and took the consolation prize of becoming Mayor of Atlanta. The fact remains that Young had fatally misjudged at the outset how much input stronger American ethnic groups would allow an African-American to have in such sensitive areas of elite action as the Middle East, and its crucial oil, in that historical period.

Young's Functions in African-American Macro-Consciousness

Yet the transformation of the international identity of African-Americans went forward: Young's departure only speeded up the reaction towards Arab and Palestinian nationalisms—and to Islam. James Baldwin had had Jewish friends in adolescence, and as a young writer had once penned condemnations of African-American resentment against Jews that were routinely cited by Jewish micronationalist controversialists into the 21st century. "The state of Israel was not created for the salvation of the Jews", he wrote a month after Young's overthrow; it was created for the salvation of Western interests. Baldwin here further extended a leftist solidarity with the Third World, including the Arabs, that had already been prefigured in cruder form in his interactions with lumpen Algerians while a young man in Paris at the outbreak of the Algerian war for independence from French rule in 1954. As with Harold Cruse, what he saw—and what was said by the French with whom he conversed—quickly convinced him that many French people pursued a toxic racism against Algerians which had many parallels to that facing his own people back home. In his more poverty-stricken hours in Paris, Baldwin had forged strong friendships with, for instance, a "beautiful" so-young Algerian street vendor who then became among the disappeared, and had witnessed cops beat an old one-armed Algerian peanuts vendor to a pulp on a sidewalk. Like the sub-Saharan Africans then in Paris, Baldwin was not at physical risk, but he was building a love-hate relationship with the culture of the French—with its elements of loathing and fear of Arabs.

James Baldwin was an individualist, and eternally wary of politics, like his Paris mentor, Richard Wright. Wright kept his distance in Paris from Black Africans and Muslims and just didn't see French violence against the Algerians in the streets of that metropolis, to Baldwin's dismay. In contrast to Wright, Baldwin had to stand spiritually with the Algerian independence fighters in 1954 because "Algeria after all is a part of Africa, and France, after all, is a part of Europe: that Europe which invaded and raped the African continent, and slaughtered those Africans whom they could not enslave—that Europe from which, in sober truth, Africa had yet to liberate itself. The fact that I had never seen the Algerian Kasbah was of no more relevance than the fact that the [paler] Algerians had never seen Harlem. The Algerians and I were both, alike, victims of this history and I was still part of Africa, even though I had been carried out of it nearly four hundred years before. Their battle was not theirs alone but was my battle also." Baldwin had been unsure, before he left America, if he should go to Paris or to an Israeli kibbutz.[7]

Charles Silberman had once worked as a liberal to integrate all Americans, and won the respect of Malcolm X. But in 1986, as a hostile

Jewish micronationalist, Silberman summed up the new post-1967 leftist nationalism of African-Americans as a thesis that the nation state was no longer the primary arena within which class struggle took place: rather, there was now a worldwide struggle between have and have-not nations, with Israel being a prime instrument of Western interests [—a point her Republicanizing Zionist lobby in Washington had argued for years and still does argue]. The resignation of Andrew Young had become a metaphor for a struggle between two competing U.S. ethnic groups that had allied with two opposing camps in an international struggle for power.

Silberman stressed that this fabric of thought among African-Americans— which took extra-USA identity far beyond sub-Saharan Africa— made black bourgeois leaders and their young followers, and also young Hispanics, feel no longer a minority in America, but instead part of a worldwide majority of people of color, the Third World. Hence the stress by Jesse Jackson's 1984 campaign on foreign policy, which Silberman mused "had not previously been a major black concern."[8] Neo-Republicanizing and micro-nationalizing Jewish American organizations have, since the early 1970s, repeatedly denied the entitlement of African-American movements and organizations to have input into U.S. foreign policy on Africa as well as the Middle East on a scale anything like that lobby's input on any matter that touched any Jews anywhere around the world. Even many Africanists and pan-Muslims polarized two broad international race-camps in 1979-1980 only on one plane. Young's role had made them hope that blacks could have input into foreign policy on a wider scale, that the stances of Anglo-Americans could be changed, prying them loose from the country's Zionists.

Much protest interest in Middle East conflicts by African-Americans is discreetly constructive and moderate: it assumes that not just the UN can be made to work to establish peace abroad in the interest of all parties (including Israel), but that U.S. institutions also can, if only the U.S elite is broadened. Africanist *Black News*: "Andrew Young was right to create a better relation between the U.S. government and the PLO [for as] human beings who have been driven from their homes", they had to be made part of the peacemaking process for the final bargain to hold.[9] In effect, the *Black News* Africanists wanted to help as well as pressure Carter and his administration to carry through the policy many Americans now wanted in the Middle East.

One odd voice relayed by *Black News*, though, voiced a much greater discontent in seeking to eliminate rather than ameliorate both U.S. reality and that of Israel. R. Dhoruba Moore, a future convert to Islam, and in background a Black Panther not of the New York-centered Africanists, presented the Middle Eastern struggle as one between the Arab peoples and the European settler state of Israel. Dhoruba assailed the black middle classes' swallowing of talk about some compromise solution, speaking of how the right of America's instrument, Israel, to exist "almost automatically precludes the existence of an independent Palestine" [which may have been true in that smallish tract of land]. Israel was not a legal state because a minority of European Jewish settlers oppressed U.S. black Hebrews and the Asian and African Jews there, as well as the remaining Arab population. Dhoruba was a relentless, original analyst. He grappled with a hard issue: if Israel was one tool of the USA to control Middle Eastern oil, then might U.S. policy there—and Israel—also be of benefit to U.S. blacks, given that cheap oil acted to reduce the level of economic deprivation at home [in his Panther, Red Book-like analysis]? Dhoruba Moore was not at any rate very hopeful that the black middle class organizations he despised would soon dare "enrage" the liberal Jews who aided them by opposing the U.S.'s Mid-East policy and Israel.[10]

Dhoruba's attitude that Young was one more high bourgeoisie black who did what was asked of him, and thus had deserved to be the fall-guy, ran against the overall tenor of *Black News* and most African-American opinion in 1979 on this crisis. The Africanists of *Black News* had some sympathy for the Palestinians but it was expressed rarely and usually was almost lost in the special ethnic angle they pursued about Israel—(eg. "persecuted Black Hebrews")—on which they had only occasionally written. The paper only passingly mentioned even the part-African Palestinian nurse, Fatimah al-Birnawi, whom Israeli ill-treatment of Egyptian prisoners traumatized towards counter-violence against Zionist civilians as well as military Israelis.[11] *Black News* did not make wider relations with Arabs a priority. In 1980, it retorted to Imam Warith's campaign to remove racial images from worship [as a means to get at Christianity], with a sophisticated attack on the tenets of Islam developed by classical Arabs.[12]

U.S. Foreign Policy and African-American Identity and Institutions-Building.

In August 1983, 250,000 rallied in Washington to commemorate the 20th anniversary of Martin Luther King's "I have a dream" speech. A good range of mainstream African-American leaders headed the innocuous March in which blacks and whites again linked hands. It was, though, boycotted by many Jewish American leaders and organizations, unlike the original 1963 March in which African-American politicians like King had not thought it politic to say too much about overseas countries. The organizers of the 1983 March had drawn up a scrupulously balanced foreign policy paper that opposed "the militarization of international conflicts... encouraged by massive U.S. arms exports, in areas of the world such as the Middle East and Central America." [Israel was the largest recipient of U.S. arms in the Middle East]. Jewish groups were particularly enraged that some Arab-Americans had been consulted as well as themselves for the drafting, not grasping the changes to the U.S. landscape from immigration and the need to induct as equals into the mainstream the Arab and Muslim immigrants who faced so much Hollywood-fostered racial hatred. The organizers offered in advance to disavow any anti-Semitic or anti-Israel statements that might be made, and keep all placards to the general theme of "jobs, peace and freedom"—but could not placate the Zionoids.

Hyman Bookbinder, Washington representative of the American Jewish Committee, said that "the organizers made a serious mistake when they moved away from the 1963 civil rights goals into complicated foreign policy questions" [=with possible negative effects for some projects of the U.S. Zionoids]. The policy statements of the 1983 March were too pro-Third World and anti-American, Bookbinder's neo-conservative formulation ran. Mrs Coretta Scott King may have only enraged the Zionoids the more with a statement worthy of her ambiguous murdered husband when she reassured the Union of American Hebrew Congregations that all policy statements from the March would "highlight the goal of peace [but] we will not articulate a specific strategy for achieving it."[13] For many Likud-like Zionoid micro-nationalists in America, the word "peace" in itself—with its implication of fewer American arms for Israel—was like waving a red cloth at a bull in the 1970s and 1980s because it had to entail changes in U.S. stances, pullbacks by Israel from territories she captured in 1967 but regarded as hers by Biblical right, and of course, would set everyone free to talk with the PLO.

It was simply untrue that the original civil rights movements had had no connection to overseas issues or the Middle East since some of the Jewish-American aiding organizations had required King and other Americanist black leaders to sign a never-ending stream of statements supporting Israel and condemning Arabs as they sang for their supper. Many of the massive U.S. "sales" of arms to Israel had been on credit, with repayment unlikely given Zionist clout in Washington. It was hardly surprising that mainstream African-American leaders by the later 1970s were losing patience with those hemorrhaging billions, a resentment that was to mount as Reagan slashed allocations for the education, training, health care, and nutrition of poor African-Americans.

African-American writers, politicians and officials determined to wrest access and success for their people in America's central political institutions were more and more ready to take on the Zionoid nationalists who essentially ruled out any major input by African-Americans into foreign policy apart from support for more money and arms for Israel. They saw formulations such as those of Bookbinder or Silberman, recurrent in the discourses of Jewish-American micronationalists, as ultra-discrimination that claimed a sort of monopoly for a faction in American Jewry over U.S. Middle Eastern policy and openly stereotyped African-Americans as too stupid to be able to contribute to U.S. policies in international relations. Mainstreaming African-Americans stressed the long history of African-American attempts to wrest input into U.S. foreign policy, especially on Africa and the Middle East. John L. Waller, an African-American politician from Kansas who served as U.S. consul in Madagascar in the 1890s, had worked against France's efforts to clamp down a real protectorate on the island, trying to weave settlements and economic chances for African-Americans into American manifest destiny as it could be practised there—a clash projected to the Black intelligentsia in the 1970s.[14]

Martin Luther King, Jr., Reginal Gilliam reviewed (1975), had faced criticism from Euro-Americans for "diluting" or "overextending" the civil rights movement when he came out against the Vietnam War, while the white mass media's refusal to publicize such evolving Africa-directed activities of blacks as the 1972 Africa Liberation Day held in Washington was meant to sap the routinization of African-American interaction with the huge Mother Continent across the seas. True, some African-Americans during the earlier civil rights period acquiesced to the discrimination about foreign policy entitlements, acceding that external involvements were "romantic nonsense" or "a resource-drain when the struggle is here." In reply to both white and black Americans who argued thus, an African-American academic, Martin Kilson, traced a long and extensive history of "African concern" among the black intelligentsia and political leaders from Frederick Douglass, through DuBois, Garvey, Elijah Muhammad and secular Black Nationalists like Harold Cruse.[15] African-American colleges and universities educated many of the early post-colonial leaders of West Africa.

On the more positive side, the Jewish lobby and all its institutions offered a model for the escalating attempts by African-Americans to influence U.S. foreign policy in the 1970s and 1980s. Representative Charles Diggs and the fire-eating Stokely Carmichael had gone separate ways, but both held up the lobbying for Israel by "the Jewish American community" and by Irish-Americans for Irish nationalists in Ulster— cf. Garvey and Malcolm X long before!—as providing patterns for blacks to exert influence upon America's international relations. By mustering compound institutions and unified voting in the USA's two key cities, "Zionist" institutions produced a veritable requirement on U.S. politicians "to support a strong pro-Israeli position in all domestic politics and... on the question of Jews in Russia."

Gilliam was conscious that pressure from American Jews for Israel simultaneously helped integrate and nourish a domestic Jewish micro-nation as well: support of an overseas interest won that sector of Jews "overall responsive representation" from U.S. political institutions, which thenceforth had to take account of the Jewish community on any internal issue also. Gilliam wanted African-Americans likewise to develop their lobbying for Africans in mainstream American domestic politics to build a long-term domestic political clout they could simultaneously apply to improve the domestic black condition, as U.S. Zionism had won for American Jews. Given that Africa had large deposits of all the world's 52 most important minerals, it would have immense strategic importance to the U.S. after its development. He hoped that the new African-American political pressure on U.S. companies and institutions to withdraw their investments from white supremacist entities in Southern Africa would motivate the coming black-led governments there to develop special trade relationships with U.S. black businesses following liberation. Representative Charles Diggs had resigned from the USA's UN delegation in 1971 because of U.S. protection of colonialist Portugal and South Africa during votes and debates there, and U.S. military facilities and trade with Rhodesia, Portugal and South Africa.[16]

By the early 1980s, then, the African-American educated classes determined to make it into the American mainstream had assembled the conceptual framework for inducting their ethnos as a lobby into U.S. foreign policy and institutions. No truly representative U.S. governmental system could continue to privilege the Zionist sector of American Jewry in the formulation of American foreign policy. African-Americans for centuries had had *their* cultural links to the Middle East and to Arabic through Christianity and Islam; African-Americans would suffer the most from oil limitations in prices and through reductions in social spending; the endless aid given a modernist Israel could have made a significant difference if spent back home; and, above all, African-Americans were supposed at long last to have been granted equal citizenship and political rights. African-Americans had won their right to have their say, and not just on sub-Saharan Africa, narrowly defined.

Randall Robinson of TransAfrica questioned in 1979 why Israel, with just 3 million people, was to get $785 million in U.S. aid for 1980, while [oil-rich] Nigeria with 80 million people was to get nothing. Yet Robinson also voiced concern at the large grant to Sadat's Egypt, which had made peace with Israel (which his pro-Arab aspect saw as a sell-out of the Palestinians).[17] He was not unnuanced in a 1980 interview to *Africa Report*. He shared Gilliam's dream: the U.S. and the other Western powers were growing more dependent on Africa—thus, in helping it develop its independence and resources, the traditionally uninfluential African-Americans might gain new leverage of their own, including in domestic affairs. No one had ever questioned if the Euro-Americans who supported the Marshall Plan for Europe were loyal to the United States. Support to the PLO from the OAU, the Arab League, the United Nations and "virtually the entirety of the nations of the world" made Robinson urge the U.S. to induct the Palestinians into the Sadat-Begin peace process. Black American sympathy for Palestinian self-determination and statehood had "created a strain in the relationship between black Americans and the Jewish community." Zionoid spokesmen and media repeatedly assailed Robinson as an anti-Semite. But he had empathy for Jews as well as Palestinians: African-Americans understood "what it was like for the Oriental Jewish community living in many of the Arab countries traditionally." Like King before, and like Jesse Jackson, Robinson wanted a constructive settlement that would bring simultaneous peace and prosperity to Arabs, Israelis—and to Americans who had their own domestic needs.[18]

Israel's destruction of Andrew Young marked the end of an era in U.S. ethnic politics. It finished off the last lingering expectations of many African-Americans that their ethnos could be installed as an equal component in U.S. political life and government through the American way. The dismissal of Young "established the climate for the emergence of Nation of Islam leader Farrakhan as a major spokesman for disenchanted and distrustful blacks,"[19] a leader who would tap the new readiness for Jewish/Black conflict outside the constraints of the U.S. system. The Middle Eastern linkages this ethnic conflict now had for many African- and Jewish-Americans favored the emergence of a Muslim as the premier representative of the emotions of black Americans—a spokesperson who would move the tension from the secular discourse of a Young and the mainstreamers to a religio-political synthesis that would cultivate pan-Islamic connections or reconnections to West Asia and Africa. A parallel blending of restoration of elements from religion with political ethnicity was now forging Jewish Americans into another micro-nation of a new type in this succeeding period of America's history.

2: THE FORMATION OF MINISTER LOUIS FARRAKHAN WITHIN THE NATION OF ISLAM (1955-1980)

Louis Eugene Walcott was born on May 11, 1933, in Roxbury, Massachusetts. His Garveyite mother, originally a West Indian from St Kitts, exposed her children to such publications as *The Crisis*, published by the NAACP. Her hard work as both seamstress and housemaid for her one-parent family supported the education of Farrakhan as a violinist from age six. By age thirteen, Farrakhan had played with the Boston College Orchestra and the Boston Civic Symphony, and at fifteen, performed on national television and radio. Graduating from high school at age sixteen, he earned an athletic scholarship for his prowess as a track sprinter and attended Winston-Salem Teachers' College in North Carolina, excelling in the study of English.

Farrakhan was set to embark on a brilliant career as a vocalist, calypso singer, dancer, and violinist. However, in February 1955 he joined the Nation of Islam, and from 1956 served as the Minister of Muhammad's Temple No. 11 in Boston, Massachusetts. In May of 1965, three months after the assassination of Malcolm X, Elijah Muhammad appointed Minister Farrakhan to Temple No. 7 in New York City. When he arrived, the NOI and thus he himself faced considerable hostility in New York given the impression among some African-Americans that the NOI had had some involvement in the assassination. But Farrakhan's eloquence and energy soon restored respect for the Nation. In 1965, the Honorable Elijah Muhammad made Farrakhan the sect's National Representative.[20]

As a recruit to the Nation of Islam, Farrakhan had to engage with issues that he would later work through after he launched his own successor-NOI in 1978. These included: how much would the religious strictures of Islam separate the still not all that large sect from those African-American cultural practices—notable among them music and dance—that might best get its tenets across to the black millions? Also significant for the long-term is how much capacity for leadership of those masses did Farrakhan display in his Elijah-era ministries vis-à-vis America's authorities and institutions: did he build the fortitude and credibility to become the main leader of African-American Islam and nationalism in the 1980s and 1990s in a sustained, long-term way? A role of that expanse would have to bridge the class divisions disuniting African-Americans: to what extent did Farrakhan before the death of Elijah Muhammad become a figure with the readiness and skills to bring together the bourgeois blacks with those of a more popular background, who needed the skills of that bourgeoisie in order to cohere and progress? The issue of relations with the Arabo-Muslim heartlands was not as central in the

1960s and earlier 1970s as later, when Farrakhan was to lead a different NOI, but his attitudes towards Arab cultural elements, towards Arabs and towards Israel and local Zionists under Elijah have relevance for the future when he was to exercise leadership over hundreds of thousands of African-Americans under Reagan, Bush and Clinton. The world tours that he was to conduct in the wake of the Million Man March would expressed his realization that that vast demonstration had given him the international standing to conclude relations of a new compound depth with the Muslim states and movements of Asia and Africa.

African-American Culture and Mass Mobilization

Orthodox Sunni Islam restricts music in the Middle East, although Middle East-modeled "orthodox" modalities of Islam had spread with and through the practice of jazz by African-American musicians after WWII.[21] As one prominent young pre-1975 leader of the sect, Louis Farrakhan Muhammad intermittently had uneasy, vacillating attitudes to music that were like those of his mentor, Malcolm. After Farrakhan converted, his mother did not want him to learn that she had danced to a calypso record when it was put on in a Jewish home in which she worked. A rather long calypso-rhythmed song that Farrakhan recorded—" White Man's Heaven is a Black Man's Hell"—was played in the jukeboxes of the movement's restaurants. Although this and other songs and music-laden plays by Farrakhan were recruiting many outside blacks in the late 1950s and 1960s, Elijah Muhammad finally lost patience. He served an ultimatum: "Do you want to be a song-and-dance man or do you want to be my minister?" Farrakhan chose the Nation of Islam and his remaining musical creativity almost ended for the duration of Elijah's life and leadership.[22] After the Messenger's death, though, Farrakhan's revived Nation of Islam, from 1978 on, was to legitimize and use hip-hop and other music and song to project its special Islam to millions of U.S. blacks.

Farrakhan's Evolution as Leader from Minister of a Mosque to Deputy of Elijah

The whole of Farrakhan's career under Elijah Muhammad was marked by at least some strains in his interactions with both members who were popular in origin and with new educated bourgeois recruits, who in the 1960s and 1970s increasingly entered the movement's mosques, including his in Boston, and with the general bourgeois classes from which those recruits came. These tensions, though, should not be exaggerated. Farrakhan was not born within a "black bourgeoisie" family, but he had enough education to make himself a leader who could bridge the gap between the two classes.

Zionoid biographer Arthur Magida depicted that, while Minister at the Boston mosque, from 1956 Farrakhan had had to allow himself and his congregation to be bullied by Clarence X Gill (later Abdul Jabbar), an allegedly thug-like Captain of the paramilitary Fruit of Islam there.[23] Some Euro-Americans also have tried to smear Farrakhan as involved in the murder of Malcolm X in early 1965. The quotidian reality was more humdrum. Gardell did not rate Clarence as meriting a mention—and put furious statements by Farrakhan against Malcolm in the lead-up to the latter's 1965 murder in the context of repeated campaigns by the FBI to provoke conflict and violence between black nationalist leaders and factions.[24] In 1996, in the period of Farrakhan's leadership, *Final Call* carried a positively-phrased obituary for Clarence X Gill, stressing that the Honorable Elijah Muhammad had described Clarence as, in some areas, his best Fruit of Islam captain. The memories of Minister Don Muhammad and the later actions by Farrakhan simply don't bear out the characterization by an [FBI-installed?] "defector" and Jewish liberal biographer Magida, that Clarence Gill bullied Farrakhan and the congregation at Boston. There were some scuffles among incompletely remade recruits there, but the respectable Korean War veteran Clarence and his FOI had been the steadying influence maintaining order and discipline: hence, a trial judge placed all of the alleged law-breakers under the supervision of Clarence as part of their probation. When Farrakhan decided to rebuild the Nation of Islam, one of his first acts was to send for Clarence as a seasoned figure to advise and train young FOI Captains and regional officials. Gill died in 1996 as a "legendary" figure in NOI Islam who gave decades of his life to those two movements so that he never found time to marry.[25]

It is true that, as a greenhorn minister in the Boston mosque, Farrakhan feared he was proving unable to relate to some educated persons who joined the Boston Temple: they seemed more intelligent and he could not understand their ideas. However, Elijah refused to relieve him of his post, and as Farrakhan gained confidence, the Boston temple's membership tripled in three years. The aura of invincibility and discipline that surrounded the Boston Muslims, and their abstinence from drugs, won them the respect of the surrounding black population.[26] Still, Farrakhan had been too immersed in developing his musical talent to complete a higher education, and even when he had won wide support from bourgeois African-Americans in the 1980s and 1990s, would continue to risk alienating them by repeatedly blasting their class status and attitudes towards blacks poorer than them.

Farrakhan reached for a Malcolm-like status during a 1972 New York police attack on his Harlem Mosque. Fighting back, infuriated Muslims shot one policeman and beat others. Thousands of Harlem residents gathered to defend the mosque and torched police cars: Farrakhan adroitly controlled the resistance from the top of a sedan without giving way to the police force. While only Libya, of the Muslim governments, protested the police storming of the NOI mosque, Muhammad 'Abd al-Ra'uf, Egyptian director of the Washington Islamic Center that serviced diplomats and rich Muslim immigrants, declared that the 700 million Muslims of the world stood with Elijah Muhammad—for that, braving calls for his ouster from his immigrant flock.[27]

The mainly African-American Islamic Party of North America (IPNA), a successor to Washington's "Community Mosque" (Masjid ul-Ummah) founded in 1969, was being influenced by Egypt's Muslim Brotherhood, Pakistan's Jama'at-i-Islami and the Sa'id Nursi movement in Turkey, all moulded in conflict with quasi-secularist regimes. However, IPNA joined in the immigrants' calls for Dr 'Abd al-Ra'uf's resignation: "the 'Black Muslims' of Elijah Muhammad do not preach or practise Islam as defined by the Qur'an and Sunnah," instead claiming that God was incarnated as a black man. The sect had not established *salat* (Arabic ritual prayer), they did not pay *zakat* (Islamic charity), they did not fast in Ramadan and they did not make pilgrimage to Mecca except as a deception to cajole resources out of overseas Muslims. 'Abd al-Ra'uf's statement of solidarity with Farrakhan and Elijah legitimated such NOI heresies: hence he had to go, argued IPNA.[28]

IPNA's denunciations of Dr 'Abd al-Ra'uf were part of a thrust to take leadership of all African-American Islam from all the other organizations and sects, for which it would need immigrant Muslim allies. The attacks on 'Abd al-Ra'uf were assailed in turn by Imam 'Antar 'Abd al-Khabir of the Atlanta affiliate of the earlier-established Darul-Islam movement, itself mainly African-American. In some ways, the Darul-Islam had much of Elijah's micro-nationalist thrust: it declared itself "about having an army, having a police force, and for collecting taxes."[29] Some argue that IPNA leader Yusuf Muzaffaruddin Hamid's unremitting barrages against not just Elijah but anyone who claimed to represent Islam among African-Americans were meant to supplant them, not just for the purity of Islam's tenets and practices; the Darul-Islam had been among Hamid 's victims and now seized on the events in New York to get back at him.[30] In 1972, the Community Mosque/IPNA was sure that Islamic revivalist tracts mailed from the Middle East and Pakistan had a total truth that made Farrakhan abject. But after IPNA had dissolved, its founder was to conclude in 1991 that the "political methodologies" of the Arab Muslim Brotherhood and Pakistan's Jama'at-i-Islami had not had in them enough "spirituality" to meet the needs of black people living in a very different America.[31]

For all the question marks around the religious tenets or practices of his sect, and scant Muslim World solidarity with it at that time, Farrakhan went on to become a major spokesman of the militant sector of the African-American community. Already by 1974, he could draw 70,000 to his Black Family Memorial Day lecture in New York.[32]

The influence of Elijah on the young Farrakhan was mixed. After Elijah made Farrakhan his National Representative and allowed him to carry forward the NOI's National Broadcast, he assigned the young man subject matter for coming four-week periods. The natural bent of Farrakhan was towards drawn-out preparation and meticulous documentation from scriptures for each half-hour radio talk. But the Messenger told him to instead let Allah speak through him. Thenceforth, Farrakhan never used notes: "I started speaking on a subject and would allow God to feed me." Elijah's direction made Farrakhan develop more within the great tradition of African-American religious oratory as the mass leader of millions that he was to become in the 1980s and 1990s. On the other hand, Farrakhan's orations after 1978, some of which rambled, were to pivot around a few thin quotations from the Bible and the Qur'an. Had Elijah nourished his tendency towards documentation, Farrakhan might have articulated a denser and tighter, more precise, theological-cum-political discourse that might have guided his African-American audiences better.

Elijah's star pupil, Malcolm X, had turned self-assertive, including in ideas and policies, before leaving the NOI. Elijah wanted to test whether his current National Representative, Farrakhan, had any of Malcolm's thrust to build personal prominence and power at the expense of his mentor. After six years, Elijah told Farrakhan to let the public know that Elijah Muhammad would be coming back on the radio next week. Farrakhan prepared a tape titled "Hearken unto the voice of God" to play in advance of Elijah's first talk. Pleased, Elijah then called Farrakhan and said, "Brother, you may continue" as the radio voice of the sect.

It is not wholly clear what the full range of feelings were between the two men in Farrakhan's formative period. Elijah was a dominating personality with acute attunedness to the psychology of his followers: in this instance he tested Farrakhan's loyalty, and remained willing to cede a lot of the limelight to him as long as he was assured that that loyalty remained, so that the NOI would continue intact. Farrakhan phrased it three decades later that Elijah had made him a "baby" to whom he had given a "lollipop" to which the baby duly got used, as planned, but which Elijah then took back. This process of the training, education and testing of Farrakhan went on over years, but Farrakhan never overtly faulted, later, a paternal control and direction that could approach infantilization. Farrakhan conceded that Elijah "never would praise me in the public, as he had Malcolm", after he became National Representative, but claimed that the Messenger still was grooming him to become his successor. In 2002, Farrakhan claimed that Elijah had said on a now "lost" tape that "Allah made me to take His place among the people and I am making you to take mine".[33] But how could anyone ever have lost a tape or a document with so clear a transfer of authority as that?!

Farrakhan After Wallace Mohammed's Succession, 1975-1980

Farrakhan's years as National Representative of Elijah Muhammad gave him some claim in his own right to a leading position or to become the Leader after Elijah died in 1975. In the upshot, though, leadership passed to Elijah's son, Wallace (Warithuddin) Muhammad, who took the so-called Black Muslims very quickly in the direction of Middle Eastern Sunni Islam and integrationist Americanism. Combining Americanism with Arabophilia would henceforth entail many ideological and political strains and tensions for Warith's followers.

In the two years following Elijah's death, Warith/Wallace and his allies sidelined Farrakhan. Needlessly humiliating the man, Wallace moved him from his New York power-base to an unorganized mosque set in a loft in Chicago. Farrakhan in retrospect rationalized the experience to foreign interviewers as one designed by the Imam "to purify my heart" of pride. When his son played an old tape of Farrakhan as "National Representative of the Honorable Elijah Muhammad", Farrakhan told him to "turn him off—he's too damned arrogant."

The differences between Farrakhan and Imam Wallace (soon, Warith ud-Din) were ideological to a great extent. Farrakhan had not liked to see Elijah Muhammad and his teachings "trashed", the collective economic enterprises of the Nation being dismantled and sold off, and the believers losing their discipline as the new bourgeois individualism developed under Wallace, who dismissed the old NOI ideas and patterns as the "playpen" the Muslims no longer needed.[34] As he undertook, after 1978, to rebuild or build a new NOI that was supposed to restore the old teachings, Farrakhan would have to live down the fact that he had caved to Wallace-Warith and his new Islam for a while, and been pushed around in full view of America's mainstream mass media. Farrakhan had insisted to *Time* magazine and its millions of readers during the transition that he had not been moved to Chicago so that Wallace could keep an eye on him. No other man held "the keys to divinity" he stated: "there is no one wise enough to approach the shoelaces of Wallace Muhammad".[35]

Farrakhan was to try to avenge this loss of dignity vis-à-vis Wallace/ Warith from 1978.

Gardell tended to extrapolate from such heavily erased files or purported files as the FBI released under FOI that that Agency had in advance chosen Wallace/Warith as the best successor to his father because it had assessed that he was the only son likely to end the sect's "racist" protest function.[36] While that scenario would legitimize Farrakhan's post-1977 restoration, it may build too much on disorientated ramblings from one particular FBI agent, or swallow one more FBI forgery. As it turned out, the literate neo-Sunni anti-Zionism and extraterritorial solidarity with overseas Muslim causes to be articulated from the sect's tabloid under Warith after 1975, were not to foster acceptance of U.S. foreign policy in the black bourgeois classes. Some veteran African-American Muslims in retrospect see such "positive" assessments of Warith attributed to the pre-1975 FBI as yet more divide-and-rule forgeries from that agency, intended here to keep Farrakhan and Warith at each other's throats. Other radicals who never came to like Warith's low-key politics stress that the dismantling of the collective economic enterprises of the NOI, and thereby much of its power, could be in accord with a likely FBI ambition.

The Young Farrakhan and Jewish Culture and Groups

Much of Farrakhan's career under Elijah to 1975 unfolded in New York, where Farrakhan had grown up on the margin of a massive Jewish population. He received some strong doses of Judaism in boyhood and adolescence there, and had some Jewish friends.

Elijah Muhammad already held up rabbis' garb and Jewish merchants as positive models. After 1978, influence from the religion and culture of American Jews was to be openly stated by Farrakhan and his new NOI, even in the context of their avowal that they could, some day, organize African-Americans to stand up to Jewish-American power. In the wake of September 11, Farrakhan questioned approaches of the Bush administration that could cause the loss of hundreds of thousands of innocent lives without addressing the causes of terror. He "humbly" asked the President to draw on his own sect's very public process (through the Million Man March) of Atonement, which was "also practised among the Hebrew faith as their holiest day." All of humanity needed such a self-purging, self-redemptive process.[37]

Farrakhan recalled at a flashpoint of tension with the Zionoid micronationalists in 1996 that as a little boy, he would listen every week to Jewish cantors "sing the Torah" on radio. He may already have come to suspect in adolescence that he might be of partly Jewish descent. Many people of Iberian or part-Iberian descent in Jamaica and the West Indies have some Sephardic crypto-Jewish ancestry, and Farrakhan came to wonder if the Portuguese or in part Portuguese-descended parents of his philanderer father, a light Jamaican with lank hair, "were members of the Jewish community." The ambivalent Farrakhan was to swing towards this possibility in this 1996 interview carried to Jewish newspapers around the world. If he had some Jews in his lineage, then he hoped before his life ended to have rendered a service to the Jewish community, as well as to his own Black people. But then he rapped the international conspiracy of the Jewish bankers and the past involvement of Jews in the slave trade.[38]

The fragmentation of black families left Farrakhan's psyche vulnerable in ways that the families-restoring and Nation-building NOI ideological discourse soothed but could not heal. His mother, Sumayah Farrakhan, had lived in Bermuda, and Farrakhan in the 1990s still had vivid memories of his joyous third birthday there. Despite the fact that his white or semi-white father was killed by a construction crane on that island, there was for many years a travel ban against the Muslim leader visiting Bermuda, whose population was sixty percent black. Farrakhan was overjoyed, there in 1998, when 5,000 Bermudians came in driving rain to hear him speak. "I am not a hater of white people. I am not an anti-Semite", the racially mixed Farrakhan assured his "homecoming" audience. While in Bermuda, Farrakhan spoke as Warith had done when, after 1975, he had shrunken the NOI's old teachings about inherently evil white devils down to mere metaphors for a fleeting situation: "White color didn't put us in bad shape", Farrakhan said; it was "a sick mind in a color that put us in bad shape." He then diluted evil as exclusive to whites yet further: when Blacks prey upon one another it's because a sick mind in a Black body is causing suffering. Among the West Indian nations, Bermuda had the lowest unemployment rate of six percent, and a high standard of living, Farrakhan and his party saw. On the other hand, there were U.S. air and naval bases installed there, and Bermuda was still only autonomous from Britain, not truly independent.[39]

Notwithstanding some idiosyncratic concerns and past contacts, Farrakhan before and under Elijah's first Nation of Islam was representative of the dualism of Muslim and nationalist blacks towards local Jews in the late-modern period. Jewish traders and entrepreneurs were competitors and models who were blocking the broadening of neo-bourgeois black private enterprise in the ghettoes. Politically, the two micro-nationalizing elites were coming to be on bad terms: under Elijah, Farrakhan—monitored by the ADL—already identified Jewish leaderships as an enemy that through its [exaggerated] "control" of the mass media was fighting the expansion of the NOI.[40] The "Jewish enemy" would continue this dual stimulation—as models, as enemies—of those in the NOI tradition after Elijah's death in 1975.

Farrakhan's adolescence and his years under Elijah had attuned him to Jewish-Americans. Now, from the later 1970s, as he became a U.S. ethnic leader in his own right, the clashes between blacks and Jews in the United States were multiplying. Farrakhan's stances to the Jewish side in that conflict from 1980 would always have an unusual, intimate, not quite rational, edge to it, for all the cold calculation with which Farrakhan has often crafted his moves in advance, as a superb politician.

3: PERSPECTIVE: ISLAM AND U.S. BLACK IDENTITY TO 1980

Chapters four and five presented a sort of dialogue between (a) general African-American identity and history after 1950 and (b) movements that claimed to represent Islam—or, in the secular sector, to stand "100 per cent" with Arab causes, as Stokely Carmichael did.[41] On the whole, Elijah interacted more, and more flexibly, with the changing conditions of African-Americans and the shifts in the world view of their mainstream sector (or at least some of his colleagues did) than might have been expected from an aged religious figure who had some stern tenets to maintain.

It is hard to pin down where exactly pre-1975 NOI discourse was leading the adherents in regard to the 20th century Middle East, the Arabs, orthodox Third World Islam—and even sub-Saharan Africa. The radical newness and unorthodoxy of many of Elijah's religious tenets and practices would certainly enrage those Arabs or Iranians or Pakistanis who have strict expectations of what any Muslims had to be like. Yet the words and verses and phrases plucked out from the Qur'an and its original contexts, kept coming in, thinly but pervasively. Sometimes Elijah identified Arabs as fellow-blacks, or half brothers to the blacks—and sometimes as whites, which could have some almost inherent implications in his discourse. But the elements were coming into place for a majority of Elijah's followers to frankly Sunnify once he finally departed. The main thrust of NOI discourse before 1976 was that all the world's "Black" people—sometimes including the red, yellow or brown peoples, sometimes distinguishing while still attaching them—were theoretically eligible for membership in the sect. This preference for an international identity in part directed to sub-Saharan Africa that yet passes beyond it—an identity that brackets Africans and Asians—was to recur in Farrakhan's successor-sect into the 21st century.

Although America-bound and parochial in aspects, the old NOI by 1975 was interacting for political, economic and diplomatic purposes with a range of states around the globe, while representing a local U.S. interest. Operating as the head of a micro-nation, Elijah could not resolve ideology too tightly. The extreme flexibility and open-endedness of his religion's definition of who was "Black" and who white at any point gave Elijah a margin to be pragmatic. His acute sense of the economic needs of his nation could lead him to develop relations with Latin American states and Japan more than with dysfunctional Arab states, although pre-1939 NOI ideology had already made him stand with the Japanese "relatives" during WWII at the cost of a jail sentence that destroyed his health.[42]

We tried in our discussions of the 1960s, 1970s and early 1980s to trace ways in which (a) Elijah's Nation of Islam, (b) somewhat more secular Black Nationalists or Africanists and (c) mainstreaming civil rights integrationists, apparently rather rightist, all nourished and protected each other. Rather than dichotomizing these factions, we tried to see African-Americans in general as an evolving people that was *as a whole* being more and more tinged by Muslim and Middle Eastern influences (not just by Africa), in this period. With their mass-circulation paper, *Muhammad Speaks*, the Muslims were no doubt an unmatched focus for the further crystallization of Islamic and Arab attributes, motifs and linkages among African-Americans. But their micro-nation was from 1950 nourished by the hearing it would get from a literate black bourgeoisie that had been directed by Islamophile Africanist writers for eight decades to welcome Islam as a good aspect of the African continent of origin.

As the barriers of separate class origins crumbled with the stepped-up integration of the African-American nation, both the Nation of Islam and the new young Africanist nationalists found themselves more and more interacting with Arab nationalists. Isolationist and apolitical aspects of the NOI's religion checked its own involvement, but *Muhammad Speaks*' precise concern with the ways patterns of political power in America harmed Africans and Middle Easterners did nourish the new African-American political class's efforts to install lobbying for that Third World within electoral parliamentarism. While Elijah lived, the Muslims could not break enough with their millenarian despair of the system to attempt parliamentarism on their own account. Still, both they and the more secular African-American opponents of the new Zionoids were examining how Jewish Americans and Irish-Americans and other whites had blended transcontinental lobbying with an integration into mainstream politics that have paid off locally for American micronations whose members are not truly yearning to emigrate. There thus was a real potential for the Muslim and Africanist activists also, not just the overt integrationists, to in the end follow in the footsteps of once-hated non-Anglo white groups into the central American enterprise.

In general, Elijah's old Nation of Islam was a serious contender to lead or to transform African-Americans in the 1960s and 1970s. This was because its comprehensive discourse and activities covered multiple sectors of American life, and in ways that were often more constructive than their presentation stated. Although without as much hope and eloquence as Martin Luther King Jr, the NOI did sometimes allude to procedures or settings that could lessen white-black conflict in America, and one day perhaps integrate the two. Elijah's Nation of Islam became a contender because some resources as well as ideas it was building could help make real hopes and interests to which black, but also white, America were turning in that larger period. The NOI could have taken the lead in an effort to construct a multiple-planed alliance with the Arab World that most sections of conscious African-Americans had come to want. It could have been at the fore of a restructuring of the African-American relationship with the American Jews who were becoming the most successful and powerful minority in U.S. history: the frankness needed might over the long-term have ushered in a more equal, rational and cooperative relation between those two American "peoples." Elijah and his Muslims had shown themselves ahead of their times in their long drive to give economic expression to nationhood by building a cooperative private enterprise complex. Both the American governments and the expanding black bourgeoisie could have aided this enterprise which would have brought the Muslims into community with not just the black but the white middle classes.

The times and the Nation almost came together, but often the NOI did not seize potentialities that were not always so far from its formal aims. The campaigns of police and intelligence agencies over decades debilitated it. The human weaknesses of the NOI personnel, inherent constraints from the racist U.S. environment and the poor starting-point ensured that the business empire would not be at the level of the roles then opening in America. And Elijah was old, and thus sometimes would lapse into rigid and authoritarian stances that shut out emerging Arab-influenced groups among African-American youth with which the Nation could have exchanged insights, who respected him and who might have made productive allies, or collaborators on projects for African-Americans in general.

The Nation of Islam thus failed under Elijah to become the force directing African-Americans. Yet it had, in regard to social ideas or data about the nations of the globe, tinted most African-Americans. After Elijah's 1975 death, the Nation's composite culture and roles were to diversify and spread further in the African-American nation.

ENDNOTES

1 Simeon Booker, "Washington Notebook", *Ebony* 17 May 1977 p. 26.

2 A.M. Thomas, *The American Predicament: Apartheid and United States Foreign Policy* (Aldershot: Ashgate 1997) pp. 92-107.

3 Richard Cohen (New York), "After Andrew Young", *Australia-Israel Review* 12-26 September 1979 p. 6.

4 "Andrew Young: A Matter of Principle" (edit.), *Black News* August-September 1979 pp. 7, 27.

5 James Haskings, *Andrew Young: Man with a Mission* (New York: Lothrop, Lee and Shepard 1979) showed that the U.S. media exaggerated Young's interna-

tional criticisms of the USA's internal record vis-a-vis its blacks: p. 181.

6 See Graeme Beaton, "Young divides America", *The Weekend Australian* 1-2 September 1979 p. 12.

7 James Baldwin, *No Name in the Street* (London: Michael Joseph 1972) pp. 29-33, 39-43. Baldwin became truly close to at least one male Algerian in Paris; he grasped their and all Arabs' crucial difference from African-Americans: they had kept themselves culturally and territorially intact throughout rule by Westerners, despite some deculturization by France. Although the Algerians "had been in a sense, produced by France", they remembered a sun-lit homeland to which they would return. "But on my side of the ocean, or so it seemed to me then, we had surrendered everything, or had had everything taken away, and there was no place for us to go: we *were* home" ibid p. 30.

8 Charles E. Silberman, *A Certain People: American Jews and their Lives Today* (New York: Summit Books 1985) pp. 342-343.

9 "Andrew Young: A Matter of Principle" loc cit.

10 Dhoruba Moore, political prisoner, "Blacks and U.S. Mid-East Policy: An Unprincipled Leadership", *Black News* December 1979 pp. 22, 28, 30.

11 The magazine published a long 2-part indictment of the Israeli state's treatment of African-American "Black Hebrews" who came into the country. In the course of denouncing treatment of these co-ethnics, the article very briefly mentioned the part-African Palestinian woman Fatimah al-Birnawi: jailed for planning to plant bombs following Israel's 1967 conquests, she was alleged to have undergone ten years of torture sessions and beatings in Israeli prisons that knocked all her teeth out. "The African woman was released in November of 1977 [after ten years] and told to 'go back to Africa' ": Sekou Jahi, "Black Hebrews and Israel" - 2, *Black News* 4:15 (August 1980) pp. 13, and 12-14; instal. 1 in ibid 4:14 (July 1980) pp. 16-17, 25. *Ha-Olam Hazeh* on 14 January 1968 published an interview with al-Birnawi in which she set out her motives for trying to plant a bomb. When working as a nurse in Qilqiliyyyah, she had seen Israeli forces expel Palestinians, blowing up their houses. In Nabulus, she then had had to treat Egyptian and Jordanian prisoners burnt with Israeli napalm: however injured, the Israeli authorities had at once then sped them off to prison camps.

12 Khawaja Shabazz (Bruce Cosby), "The Christ Color Controversy: Or an Analysis of W.D. Muhammad's Position on Ethnic Imagery in Worship", *Black News* 4:16 pp. 8-11, 31. Again: our term "classical Arabs" means individuals whose native speech was Arabic or who used Arabic as their main language and identified with the Arab entity in history, up until the Mongols sacked Baghdad and murdered the last "Arab" 'Abbasid Caliph al-Musta'sim in 1258.

13 "Martin Luther King rally: Squabbles threaten civil rights dream", *London Times* 27 August 1983 p. 5; Bruce Wilson, "America revives an unfulfilled dream...", *The Sun* (Melbourne) 29 August 1983 p. 8. For Hollywood's defamation of Arabs, see Jack G. Shaheen, *Reel Bad Arabs: How Hollywood Vilifies a People* (New York: Olive Branch Press 2001).

14 Randall B. Woods, "Black America's Challenge to European Colonialism: the Waller Affair 1891-1895", *The Journal of Black Studies* 7:1 (September 1976) pp. 57-79.

15 Kilson with Adelaide Hill, *Apropos of Africa: African-American Leaders and the Romance of Africa* (New York: Anchor Books 1971).

16 Reginal E. Gilliam Jr, *Black Political Development: an Advocacy Analysis* (New York: Kennikat Press 1975) pp. 184-191.

17 William Raspberry, "One Way Benefits", *Guardian Observer* 7 October 1979 p. 15.

18 Anthony J. Hughes, "Interview: Randall Robinson, Executive Director of TransAfrica," *Africa Report* January-February 1980 pp. 9-13.

19 Salzman and West, *Struggles* p. 192.

20 Tynetta Muhammad, "An historical look at the Honorable Elijah Muhammad", 28 March 1996.

21 Robert Dannin, *Black Pilgrimage to Islam* (New York: OUP 2002) pp. 59-60.

22 Arthur J. Magida, *Prophet of Rage: a Life of Louis Farrakhan and his Nation of*

Islam (New York: Basic Books 1996) p. 71.

23 *Ibid* pp. 91-94.

24 Gardell pp. 76-85.

25 Donald Muhammad, "Remembering a soldier for Allah", *Final Call* 6 August 1996 p. 38.

26 Clegg, *Original Man* p. 62.

27 Gardell pp. 121, 385-386.

28 "Libya Seeking Contact with America's 'Black Muslims' " *al-Jihad* (Cape Town) Jumadal-Akhirah 1392H pp. 7-8.

29 Sulaiman Nyang, "Islam in the United States of America: A Review of the Sources," *Islamic Culture* (LV:2) April 1981 p. 104.

30 Dannin, *Black Pilgrimage* p. 71. For the pre-existing struggle between the Darul-Islam and IPNA from the latter's founding in 1971 see Khalid Fattah Griggs, "Islamic Party of North America: A Quiet Storm of Political Activism" in Yvonne Yazbeck Haddad and Jane I. Smith *Muslim Minorities in the West: Visible and Invisible* (Walnutt Creek: Altamira Press 2002) pp. 87-90.

31 Beverly McCloud, *African-American Islam* (New York and London: Routledge 1995) p. 68.

32 Gardell pp. 121-122.

33 Interview with Farrakhan in January 2002 in Jabril Muhammad, "A look at a man prepared for a divine mission", *Final Call* 19 March 2002 p. 26.

34 BBC Manchester, *About Us: The Nation of Islam* transmitted on SBS television Australia 16 April 2000.

35 "White Muslims", *Time* 30 June 1975.

36 Gardell pp. 100-101, 122-123.

37 James Muhammad, "Farrakhan: War can end through process of atonement", *Final Call* webcast article 17 October 2001. The Jewish Yom Kippur or Day of Atonement falls on the 10th day of the seventh month: it is a time for repentance from wrongdoing at a time when the Hebrew year is about to begin again. The Yom Kippur has had in it some ideas of abstinence and physical self-denial, and so may have indeed helped pattern the repudiations of smoking, alcohol, domestic violence etc by blacks during the Million Man March and on its subsequent anniversaries.

38 Daniel Kurtzman, "Farrakhan claims father had Jewish lineage", *Australian Jewish News* 10 May 1996.

39 Askia Muhammad, "Min. Farrakhan visits Cuba, Bermuda", *Final Call* February 1998: web-posted 22 March 1998.

40 Epstein and Forster, *New Anti-Semitism* p. 211.

41 *Palestine: PLO Information Bulletin* (5:16) 1-15 September 1979 p. 35.

42 Comments on Elijah's pragmatism as a leader, and his constructive response to Euro-American power through economic self-development instead of insurgency, Diana Collier 31 January 2001

Chapter Seven

Farrakhan's Changing Post-1990 Nation of Islam

1: RELIGIOUS THOUGHT AND CHANGE IN FARRAKHAN'S NEW NOI

Prior to 1975, some immigrant Arabs (but also some Sunnified African-Americans) managed to coax some followers of Elijah Muhammad towards orthodox Third World Islam. Once Elijah died, those so influenced devastated his teachings to reconstruct the Nation into a semi-Sunni sect. What were the limits upon Sunnification and Arab cultural and linguistic influences for Farrakhan's new—"restored", so he claimed—Nation of Islam in comparison to Warith's group?

Focusing on the new NOI's provenance as an early instance of the made-in-America "New Religious Movements", Gardell (1996) was doubtful that orthodox variants of Islam centered overseas would prove strong enough to draw Farrakhan's post-1978 sect into the moulds of Middle Eastern tenets. The influence from Middle Eastern Islam upon the post-1978 NOI amid globalization rather comes as "orthopraxy" in which the sectlet more and more in the 1980s and 1990s *practised* the Arabic prayers and rituals of the overseas Muslim power centers while maintaining its core doctrinal and social distance from Arabs, Iranians, etc.[1] But the widening of orthopraxy within the new NOI has had at its fore black African Muslims as well as Arab-Americans who have been installed in the sect or who regularly pass through it—the orthopraxy has not just been picked up during travels or put on, in anticipation of them. The cumulative injections of Third World Muslim motifs and tenets since 1978 have gone beyond some limited Arabic prayer formulas and rituals, although these might not transform the old homegrown base to the extent it has done among Warith's followers.

But even the attempts of some in the sect to keep differentiating NOI religion in tenets from the backdrop of Middle Eastern Islam is itself a deeply acculturating process that could well end in a final affiliation of the NOI with the Islamic heartlands, one day, as globalization shrinks and fuses the world. Within the worldwide ummah of Islam, many features of aesthetic culture, and some beliefs and practise distinguish one Islamic population from another, as Farrakhan and his colleagues have long known well. Thus, the new NOI will maintain and reinvent local and historical elements of the tradition on which it follows that are non-heretical.

As the new century approached, Farrakhan's small and vulnerable sect needed donations and diplomatic support to survive in a pseudo-"conservative" America which radical-right WASPs and Jewish micro-nationalists were building more and more power to devastate. The World Islamic Leadership Conference held in Chicago over 3-6 July 1997 was among the efforts made by al-Qadhafi and Farrakhan to tighten relationships with each other and also with the highly-educated immigrant Muslim professionals in America whose aid any African-American Islamic movement would need in order to transform the conditions of the black poor. Five hundred scholars and political leaders attended workshops on health, education, religion and economics. The attendees of Middle Eastern background bestowed on Farrakhan the title of "Shaykh" or Islamic religious scholar of an Arab-world, Sunni type. In his addresses to the conferees, Farrakhan recognized Muhammad Ibn 'Abdallah of Arabia as the last and greatest of God's messengers, accepting the Kalimah, "there is no God but Allah, and Muhammad is his Prophet" ("La Ilaha Illallah: Muhammadur Rasulullah"), the primary statement of Islamic faith worldwide. In so doing, he necessarily demoted Wali Fard Muhammad (until then the incarnation of God) and Elijah (hitherto the Messenger of Allah) to two great Muslim leaders through whom Allah had manifested His "healing" of African-Americans. And indeed it was al-Hajj Elijah who first had taught Farrakhan the glorious life of the Prophet Muhammad Ibn 'Abdallah of Arabia, whose *sunnah* or model behavior and sayings alone could "lead us to success in establishing Islam in America".

A few days later, Farrakhan applied the Islamic world's crucial monotheist tenet in a two-edged way. In solidarity with certain Arab benefactors, he condemned to the Conference the U.S. embargoes that were causing infants and women to die in 'Iraq and Libya, and might soon do so in the Sudan and Nigeria. Muslim governments and peoples should stop complying with the embargoes out of fear of America: "fear Allah and set up no partner with Allah: Washington D.C. is not a partner with God."[2]

A feature of this conference was the coverage that Farrakhan's *Final Call* gave to the calls of the Pakistani-American, Kawkab Siddiqi, Amir of the USA's Jama'at al-Muslimin, for liberation for women in the public institutions of the Islamic movements: NOI female leaders such as Ava Muhammad, a widow of the bygone Elijah, were grafting such motifs from those immigrants onto the central roles they were carving for their sex in Farrakhan's evolving NOI.[3] Prominent at this 1997 pan-Islamic meet was Farrakhan's Ghanaian collaborator, Shaykh Tijani Bin Umar, who was central in directing the sect's members into Arabic rituals and Sunni concepts of Divinity. Bin Umar was to carefully lead ten thousand NOI supporters through Arabic congregational prayers at the Saviors' Day celebrations of 28 February 1999 at which Warith Deen Mohammed embraced the son of a bedridden, frail Farrakhan, ending the years of polarization. In 2003, a book with a cassette or CD for the proper Arabic pronunciation was being distributed on a widened scale to teach the Arabic ritual prayer en masse. It carried a statement ascribed to Elijah urging the believers to learn the prayers "in your own language and that of your righteous foreparents—Arabic." Thereby they could serve "the One True God, Allah".[4]

There are many cultural and doctrinal aspects to the increased openness of Farrakhan's second NOI to Sunni Muslim tenets and assumptions. However, we now concentrate upon the movement from (a) the allegedly infallible leaders and leaderships of the past, who derived that authority from their claimed closeness to God, *towards* (b) increased humanization of leaders and ethical scrutiny of self and the sect in Farrakhan's NOI. The Qur'an recognized that the soul of most individuals repeatedly directs them to evil ("innal-nafsa la-'ammatun bil-su'": Q 12:53 in a self-critique by the Prophet Joseph/Yusuf), although God may intervene to check this, particularly in the case of His prophets. To view leaders as subject to scrutiny by the *Ummah* is an essential step for the movement from millenarian cults whose leaderships draw special knowledge from God, to the often low-key rationality of Sunni Islam.

Toward the Humanization of Leadership, and Self-Reflection

Farrakhan became less liable to read divine invulnerability or infallibility into NOI leaderships in the 1990s, and opened more to Sunni Islam with its humanization of prophets and current leaders, as the progress of his prostate cancer forced him and his followers to confront his mortality. They did so with much more realism and frankness than Elijah's followers had showed towards his often-denied illnesses in the leadup to his 1975 demise that a Shi'ite-like Farrakhan had argued never really happened.

By the 1990s, an educated bourgeoisie/lumpen bourgeoisie with some knowledge of Arabic had formed in and around Farrakhan's NOI. They would have to be empowered to undertake rapid innovation and quick correction and self-correction rather than be regimented by a quasi-divine leader or a kinship clique, if this sect were to survive, let alone prosper. The idea that a leader in America is a prophet or next to God, or a person in God who fires down infallible guidance and orders, could constrict the swift ad hoc initiative the adherents would need if the sect and its economy were to become compound and modern. And scrutiny and accountability—between the leaders themselves and from the wider ummah or community—had not been notable in the old NOI or any of its successor sects, in regard to leaders. Democratization and the humanization of leadership was the challenge that Warith had had to meet in 1975 for the expectations of his well-off bourgeois followers after Elijah. Yet some among them questioned if all Warith's unpredictable never-ending abolitions of institutions and his decentralization, while appearing to give locals initiative, had really been meant to preempt the growth of structures that might have made him accountable? His enemies in his successor-sect branded him a discreet dictator like Mu'ammar al-Qadhafi whose calls for "the masses" to take over administrations some saw as a ploy to slow the growth of specialized institutions that could supercede him and his clique. By pretending to give all power to popular congresses, al-

Qadhafi in fact retained veiled dictatorial powers so that he could continue to atomize the educated classes, Libyan dissidents had contended. [Both al-Qadhafi and Yasir 'Arafat had some Islamic moral stature, brilliant ideas and real long-term vision for their peoples. Yet 'Arafat's opponents in the PLO also argued that he always tried to keep the earth moving under the feet of everyone else so he could have the decisive say in Fatah—that he did not always encourage the emergence of new institutions. A good range of African-American Muslim leaders have monitored and met both Arab leaders over decades, including Warith and Farrakhan.]

All versions of the Nation to date have been inhospitable to the idea of building internal avenues for appeal against the decisions of sect personnel with authority. Those who called attention to malfunctions in the 1960s were denounced (and, in one or two cases, even roughed up) as "seed-planters" out to destroy rather than rectify the Nation. Farrakhan's gropings for a new theology conceded that even in God-directed organizations, leader-individuals are fallible humans who can clash lethally with other egos and thereby threaten the organization's survival. The development of religious introspection or mechanisms for self-criticism in his NOI could be an important step forward towards modern democratic forms of organization, where there will be a more equal back-and-forth interplay between leader and the led, as the worthwhile American tradition prescribes. Such internal democracy would stimulate local initiative, which could make economic enterprise succeed and return profits.

Farrakhan was trying to rectify destructive modes of interaction not only between the led, but also between leaders of the NOI organization directing their "resurrection". He had the tone of one who had passed over some rough ground in his own life—had himself, perhaps, not always acted ideally—but who has wrested from such experiences a painful self-knowledge that makes him a better reformer of his people.

Combating Envy as a Force for Political Fragmentation

In 1995, Farrakhan tried to come to grips with the phenomenon of "envy" [which came close to tearing the Nation of Islam to pieces back in the earlier 1960s]. He termed envy a divisive "spiritual disease" that was fragmenting the African-American political leadership and politically conscious classes "to such a degree that it makes our future success limited and doubtful": the whites had long been manipulating it. If someone sees another person with a gift or talent that gives that person honor, respect, and wealth, which is what each of us as human beings may want in life, and if we fail at that gift or talent, a desire is ignited to murder the person that is envied. Envy makes its possessor a devil: the envier can pretend to be the best friend of the person who is envied, seeking to learn everything that he or she can about the person that is envied, only to use it to bring about the destruction of that person. Farrakhan also mustered a judicious theological analysis: "envy is [indirect] hatred of Allah (God). Envy is a subtle charge that Allah

(God) is unjust and that Allah (God) has acted by the envied as He should have acted to the envier".[5]

Behind its denunciations of the whites and their system as devils, Elijah's old pre-1975 Nation of Islam also put in place a comprehensive critique of the black ghetto life-style. Yet it may be Farrakhan after 1979 who innovated a deeper ethical note that directs Muslim individuals towards a self-scrutiny of their roles within the sect itself, now seen as a possible stage for Satanic hatred and murderous behavior no longer viewed as the monopoly of doomed white devils. Could Farrakhan or his colleagues or successors advance another step and install modern institutional mechanisms to scrutinize, and then limit or correct or dismiss, those whom envy infects within the organizational structures that the sect-ethnos labors to build? He mentioned how jealousy made it to easy for Cain to slay his brother Abel in the Bible. Farrakhan also cited Joseph and his jealous brothers, also covered by the Qur'an.

The Bible came to predominate over the Qur'an and the *ahadith* in this 1995 speech of Farrakhan at one point where he depicted Jesus as a victim of the envy of the Jewish religious elite, the Roman authorities and Judas: envy leading to "the betrayal, trial, and crucifixion" [a crucifixion that the Qur'an denies ever happened: see Q 4:157].

Farrakhan did cite, as he represented from the teaching of Elijah, a saying of Arabia's Prophet Muhammad that "we cannot be considered Muslims until we love or want for our Brothers and Sisters what we love and want for ourselves". "If you can truly desire for others what you desire for yourself you will uproot the evil of envy." In this speech, Farrakhan did also cite the Qur'an that "you can tell the righteous for they walk the earth in humbleness" [="*hawnan*"/humility, Q 25:63 where these meek—rather Christian-like—pre-hijrah Muslims only return the greeting "Peace" to the ridiculing pagans who do not want to understand].[6]

Farrakhan's description of the murderous venom of envy might fit well enough his incitatory language against his former mentor, Malcolm X, in the leadup to the latter's assassination on February 21, 1965.

The texture of the articles published in *Final Call* in the second half of the 1990s is of a true disintegration and transition of beliefs, much more than of a tactical maneuvering within the U.S. ethnic landscape and international politics, where, to be sure, Farrakhan needed all the Muslim allies he could find, as his Jewish and Anglo enemies constricted his businesses and closed in.

2005: The Qur'an and the Humanization of Leadership for the United Front of all Blacks

Farrakhan remained within sight of the community ethos of the classical, pre-1975 NOI in his critique of envy and conflicts between individuals that hampered the cohering and the growth of Elijah's sect, and perhaps his own. Here he was still trying to make the closed Nation that Fard and Elijah founded work. But in 2005 he applied the Holy Qur'an to construct a united front of African-Americans that tended to recognize distinct sects and ideological tendencies among the blacks as long-term realities that had to dialogue and select from each others' ideas.

Farrakhan in 2005 implied a substantial critique of Elijah's old NOI and his own past roles while mobilizing the whole gamut of blacks for the Millions More Movement. He was aware of the piercing scrutiny he faced from African-Americans after the disappointing aftermath of his 1995 March, and had to leave no doubt that he had become a modest person, much more able to work with other blacks beyond his sect. Still, Farrakhan's shift looks self-reflective and truly religious in that the Bible and Qur'an now judge from outside the NOI among the other black leadership groups. Since the days of Caribbean plantation slavery, the slave-master's children had worked to discredit and disunite all black leaders striving to bring unity to a fragmented people. The teachings of the Honorable Elijah Muhammad and Malcolm X were able to reclaim and unify only a part, not all, of the fragmented black nation because the sect's pre-1975 leaders had a lack of understanding of the universal nature of the Message they bore. But "we were successful in uniting a segment of our people, to produce the Nation of Islam as an example of what a united people could produce in the way of providing for our necessities of life."

The united front of Black leaders and organizations for which Farrakhan was now calling in 2005 was unprecedented: "for the first time in our history, those of us of different ideologies, philosophies, methodologies, denominations, sects and religions, political and fraternal affiliations have come together." The Millions More Movement was bringing all together so as to "direct our energy, not at each other, but at the condition of the reality of the suffering of our people, that we might use all of our skills, gifts and talents to create a better world for ourselves, our children, grandchildren and great grandchildren." Now Farrakhan refused to go on faulting gays or lesbians who stood on their platform to preach their own representation of self to the world, equating them with Christian and Muslim blacks, who had the same right. "Ignorance", and the disparate ideologies or philosophies of African-Americans could not be allowed to cripple the "movement that needs all of us—and, when I say all, I mean all of us." Farrakhan quoted statements attributed to Jesus in Matthew 7:1 and Luke 6:42 warning against judging others. Black Civil Rights Advocates, Nationalists, Pan-Africanists, Christians of every denomination, Muslims of every sect, students of every fraternity, Masons, Shriners and Elks, all had to commence dialogue to shape and reshape each other's thinking. As against Elijah's preaching that Allah would soon incinerate the black clergies and Christians along with the white devils who manipulated them, Farrakhan quoted the Qur'an's command: "Remember Allah's (God's) favor to you when you were enemies, then He united your hearts so by His favor you became brethren. And you were on the brink of a pit of fire, then He saved you from it" (Q 3: 102).[7]

Farrakhan had come close in this open letter to all African-Americans to conceding that Elijah Muhammad had not properly understood or applied the universal teachings of Islam when building his sect-Nation, so that blacks had stayed disunited. Was Elijah, then, a fallible human leader who did not always have a direct line for guidance to God? Farrakhan in 2005 had also implicitly apologized for his past verbal violence against black homosexuals, as his 1995 reflections on envy had for his verbal violence against Malcolm X in the latter's last year. His at least verbal acceptance of long-term exchange of ideas between black groups that would all continue was unlike Elijah's contemptuous dismissals of Christian and secular-nationalist blacks. I believe that this sharpening sense of Farrakhan and his younger lieutenants of the human inadequacies of leaders and movements, including their own, the correction of them from the Qur'an, and that the old Nation of Islam had been part of the problem of black disunity prior to 1975, can help this cluster of African-Americans make their final transition from anthropomorphic concepts of leadership and sect to the critical, more egalitarian, stance of Sunni Islam. The plain sense of the Qur'an, the Sunnah of Muhammad the son of 'Abdallah, and the lives of the first generations of the righteous Muslims in history can make Muslim protest sects among African-Americans places where leaders are accountable and chosen by the members, and individuals are given the right to rapid innovation in a decentralization of power.

Farrakhan in his new Sunnism-tinted theological discourse does, of course, continue to maneuver to keep some scope for his sect that would award it wide freedom, and diverse roles, and title to be special. It would be surprising if he did not, given that all ethnic and sectarian groups in Third World Islam do so themselves. But engaging with Third World Sunni Muslims works to humanize and democratize concepts of leadership, and as a wider community works to impose unity of belief on essentials such as the primacy of the teaching of the Prophet Muhammad Ibn 'Abdallah of Arabia. In August 2001, Farrakhan attended "the International Islamic Symposium on the Seerat [=Model Life] of Prophet Muhammad in the Light of the New Millenium," held in Chicago by the Universal Islamic Center, whose Amir was the Ghanaian Muslim, Shaykh Tijani Bin 'Umar. 'Umar was a friend of Farrakhan's who had been active in leading the Chicago NOI to the full practise of Arabic-medium Sunni Islamic rituals. There was input into the Symposium from Arab World Sunni 'ulama' as well as from the large number of Muslim West Africans who came. In his speech, Farrakhan stated that "the prophet (PBUH) was born in Arabia, but he envisioned a nation without boundaries [offering] true brotherhood in the faith of the belief in the Oneness of God and the Oneness of the human family." This impulsion towards a global "Nation of Islam" (yes, Farrakhan applied the name of his historically ethnicist sect to its Qur'anic universalist reverse!) that was to incorporate all colors was primary in this speech by him. That integrative Nation was a possibility, a hope, in history, but one delayed by insufficiently deep, even "stagnant", understandings of the Qur'an, that left current Muslims unable to remake into the image of Islam a world that instead remade their weakened Islam into its image and likeness. Some imams and shaykhs in the Muslim countries had "watered down" Islam and the practise of the Prophet Muhammad to avoid persecution by political rulers in their country. Farrakhan quoted in full an English translation of the Qur'anic surah 'Abasa in which God faults the Prophet Muhammad for preferring to court a rich Meccan rather than answer a question by the poor blind man, 'Abdallah Ibn Ummi Maktum, who wanted to learn about Islam and purify himself. Here, Farrakhan turned this regulation by the Qur'an of Muhammad in Arabia to critique immigrant Muslims in America as languid people concerned with status who directed their teaching of Islam to those who feel free from need like that bygone rich Meccan [i.e.=Euro-Americans], but turn away from the long racism-blinded but now awakening Blacks who are tapping their way up for guidance after 400 hundred years of slavery. It was a bit of an outburst against immigrants and Third World Muslims with whom he wanted brotherhood, but Farrakhan knew now that there is no superiority of Arabs over non-Arabs or for the White over the Black, or vice versa. He was applying the Qur'an, which he now described as "the final revelation that would be given to the world before its judgement," to get a recognized place, and aid, for African-American Muslims in the tolerant mosaic of the Ummah of Islam alongside Sunnis, Isma'ilis, Sufis,and Shi'is.[8]

We now review the reinvention of old elements from the theology of Fard and Elijah in Farrakhan's new NOI, while measuring the expanding orthodox and Third World motifs and tenets coming in, which should be weighed against ongoing adjustments of the old tenets. The prospects for theological change in the Nation of Islam's composite religion are affected by globalization's connecting, across all lands, of belief-communities that were once self-contained. Also influencing change will be how ready the U.S. system proves to admit Islamic African-American groups that are now becoming more influenced by Arabs, given America's tensions with the Muslim World, now incomparably worsened by September 11 and 'Iraq.

Neo-Fardian Themes in Farrakhan's NOI

The old-timers faction in Farrakhan's new Nation of Islam has been slow to break with the sense of recurrence in history of Elijah's old precursor-sect. This aspect in NOI ideology had viewed earlier messengers of God in the Middle East as setting crude patterns that were to achieve their culmination and fulfillment only in America, in the Muslim sector of African-Americans.

This sense of Elijah and Farrakhan as the full expression of what previous prophets strove for or taught, clashed with the Third World's understanding of the finality of the prophethood of the Prophet Muhammad of Arabia. The aging, veteran faction in Farrakhan's sectlet scanned the Qur'an for confirmation of their America-centered, millenarian interpretations of history. In 1998, Jabril Muhammad stressed that he followed the Honorable Elijah Muhammad who cited the key of keys provided in the Holy Qur'an's verses that God made the son of Mary and his mother "a sign" (Q 23:30; 19:21). The "sign" function of Jesus and "others of that day" [and then, in turn, of the Prophet Muhammad and his companions in Arabia] is "his meaning for us today".

The just Allah is the author of this view of the process of history, far superior to what we have been taught by this world's best scholars or historians.[9]

Nation of Islam Minister Jabril Muhammad (formerly Minister Bernard Cushmeer under Elijah) believed his thought on Elijah and Fard had crucially convinced Farrakhan, as he stumbled out from Warith's post-1975 Arab-influenced reinvention of the NOI, not to return to show business but to restore that supplanted old-style Nation.[10] Jabril Muhammad had kept the self-confident attitude of Fard and Elijah before 1975 that is not open to formal theological counter-interpretations from Third World Muslims. But by the 1990s, the rearguing of disparate old tenets became unprecedentedly porous to atomized motifs and aestheticism from not just the Qur'an but modern Third World Muslim thinkers.

At least some veteran quasi-theologians of the new Nation of Islam strove in the 1990s to develop the pre-1975 sect's Isma'ili-like or Druze-like concepts of Time and its recurring cycles. Such cycles would relativize early Islam in Arabia and the greatness of the classical Arabs, the centrality of which is argued more than ever by Sunni Muslims in the 20th century. For example, Jabril in 1998 expounded Elijah's teaching that successive groups of 24 wise scientists or imams set up or wrote the history of the Black Nation for the next 25,000 years period over the last 66 trillion years. These men do not live for the whole 25,000 year period of time that they foresee but, Elijah Muhammad informed him, "an average of 500 years." Elijah's sense that the scientists passed their wisdom on from son to son in a specially-educated kinship group or groups was in accord with the stress on lineage in leadership from all branches and derivatives of Shi'ism. The transmission by the scientists' inner elite of their confidential wisdom and power to the youth who would take their places over trillions of years was a process of succession that Jabril saw as continuing in Elijah and Farrakhan.

Overall, the old theology of Elijah's bygone NOI, as it was adapting in Farrakhan's successor-sect, had to doctrinally jar the Arab and other foreign Muslims with whom Farrakhan and his followers were interacting more and more in the 1990s. How far back did the succession of wise leaders go? How many Qur'ans or writings of world histories did they produce over the past 66 trillion years? Neo-Fardian theology in the new NOI sought manifestations of divinity in individuals of human form. Jabril termed the scientists who prewrote the history of the present world 15,084 years ago "gods", to be succeeded by other gods. He admitted that he was trying to puzzle out things he understood only imperfectly. He at least was giving Fard back his old divine status that Warith long before had ended in a context of pressure from Sunni Arabs, as Farrakhan too had later accepted. "The hardest thing for Blacks [of America] to accept about the Honorable Elijah Muhammad is the fact that he met and was missioned by God Himself" (ie. Fard, in 1930). But Jabril's motifs about recurring tightly-knit elites of divine "scientists" again could, as it had done in Elijah's inner clique, make Farrakhan and his leadership circle like gods governing the new Nation of Islam: such a hierarchical theme might leave them less likely to administer the new NOI in an equal or democratic fashion from the base up.[11]

The sect's old anthropomorphic—and, some have objected, quasi-polytheistic—concepts of God held in the 1990s for individuals of an older generation, even while they borrowed from overseas Muslims more discourse than ever before. But even the literate neo-traditional theology that the Nation of Islam might now have been developing unfolded in widening acculturation to more and more diverse Sunni exegeses of the Qur'an. Amid such borrowing, though, a group in the new "Nation of Islam" could still keep up a discordant affinity for, say, the incarnationist or polytheist thinking of the Pharaonic enemies of Moses, to cite one biblical figure. Jabril Muhammad scoured modern Jewish and Christian translations of Exodus to seek support for an early NOI notion that a spatialized God fought Pharaoh's pursuing hosts from his space ship. (This reconstructed Fardian theology was attuning the adherents to widening learned sectors of whites—including Jews—not to the Third World's Muslims only).

The neo-Fardian Jabril dived into learned Muslim World works in order to reargue, in refutation of Warith and his adherents, that Elijah Muhammad is still alive up in a Mother Plane, which is invincible because, he thinks, it bears God incarnate in the human-like form of Wali Fard Muhammad. Conservative new-NOI theology kept up the wariness of Elijah's old Nation of Islam of Sunni Islam's formless "spook god". Farrakhan-exalting Jabril sought confirmation from the Qur'an for his sect's classical thesis that God is spatially defined and moves back and forth on land, and up and down like a human or superhuman. Jabril cited the Qur'an, surah 28:38: "And Pharaoh said: 'O chiefs, I know no god for you besides myself; so kindle a fire for me, O Haman, on [bricks of] clay, then prepare for me a lofty [tower], so that I may obtain knowledge of Moses' God, and surely I think him a liar'". [This was from Mawlana Muhammad 'Ali's somewhat heterodox Qadiyanism-tinged translation of the Qur'an, but Jabril supplemented it with other translations and exegeses by the Indo-Pakistani Sunni revivalist ideologue, Sayyid Abul-'Ala Maududi (1903-1979), and the Judeo-Austrian neo-Sunni convert, Muhammad Asad (1900-1992)].

For Muhammad Asad, a neo-Sunni, Pharaoh's order to construct a "tower, that haply I may have a look at the God of Moses" showed his contempt for "Moses' concept of God as an all-embracing Power, inconceivably high above all that exists"—a pagan monarch's incapacity to grasp the clear non-personalist nature of God. Jabril, in contrast, saw Pharaoh as perceiving more of the reality of God than the learned tradition of Sunni Islam. God, he imaged, had earlier stepped down onto the earth as a spatially-demarcated person with human form, and he was continuing to interact with Pharaoh and his people from within an air-craft defined in space. Because Moses' God, too, had a human-like form for Jabril, Pharaoh, in Jabril Muhammad's exegesis, "did not see Moses' God as superior to himself" and thus was sure that he could "get rid of [Moses'] God if he could just get high enough to get to Him."

With Jabril Muhammad's discursive articles in *Final Call* we may be seeing the beginnings of a literate theological and exegetical tradition in Elijahist "Black Islam," designed to contend with the sober Sunni Muslim discourse-tradition that has been winning over so many African-Americans. Jabril's piece showed greater affinity to the incarnationist and polytheist Middle Eastern paganisms—and indeed to contemporary fundamentalist American Christianity which was swamping the surrounding American religious communities—that both Judaism and Islam fought, supplanted and loathed. Yet, the Arab and Muslim states had turned a blind eye to the tenets of this faction within the NOI in admitting Farrakhan and members of his sect into their moots and institutions after 1980.

Bygone Middle Eastern prophets are archetypes for today's America. A juxtaposition of materials by Jabril imaged that the pagan Egyptians' fatal encounter with the God of Moses might soon find a successor in America through the ominous encounters of U.S. aircraft with the so-called "UFOs" [that in Elijahist eschatology are regularly fired out from the Mother Plane that circles the earth, being piloted by Blacks with the technology to destroy the world]. Jabril's incarnationist reading of the Qur'an and the Bible's treatment of God's destruction of the pathetic pagan Egyptians embodied in "Pharaoh" thus builds confidence in Farrakhan, as a leader in contact with a Power that can deliver the People America oppresses when he warns white Americans of the might of the Baby Planes.[12]

For Jabril in 1996, past history had two current applications: for achieving power against white America, and for the fulfillment in U.S. history of the revelation of Islam. The old concepts of divine or divinely-guided leaders still carried forward by Jabril Muhammad and other veteran thinkers, have worked against the development of compound (=diverse and mutually reinforcing, but at the same time specialized and autonomous) institutions in the Nation and in black movements in general. Still, old Druze or Isma'ili or Shi'ite ideas of an inner group of leaders illuminated by the Divine, but also defined by lineage, could legitimize the management by Farrakhan's family of much of the economic holdings of the new NOI as a sector apart from its more specifically religious bodies and framework.[13]

While old tenets held for some NOI veterans, at least for the time, the citations that thinkers among them like Jabril were making in the 1990s and after from Islamist intellectualism overseas, both fundamentalist and modernist, could corrode and end some old assumptions over the long term. The modernization and bourgeoisification of Farrakhan's sect, the influx of Latinos—and then of white members!—and openings for constructive exchanges or roles vis-à-vis the U.S. mainstream were pushing the adherents towards Sunni Islamic ideas whose rational moderation would better serve their new needs and functions.

NOI Changes and Deepening Engagement with Middle Eastern Islam

By the late 1990s, Farrakhan was moving his followers towards changes, but his language still had dualisms and ambiguities. At issue was the degree of ideological particularism he would maintain to distinguish the

NOI from Arab and other Eastern Muslims, and to continue to promote special interests of blacks in relation to the American system. In a late 1998 Harlem address, Farrakhan reviewed change in human history. Elijah's old doctrine that all whites were inherent devils was the main bar to attaching the Muslims to the U.S. system as positive challengers or a corrective lobby. Now Farrakhan was coaxing the believers away from the devil concept, and in Elijah's own name, initiating reflective self-scrutiny, as Herbert Muhammad had prefigured in the early 1960s (Ch. 1). The Honorable Elijah Muhammad, through his Minister Malcolm X, had made a generation see all white people as devils or snakes. While still "right, to a point", it was "masochistic" to keep pointing to white folk as the source of the pain without the black victims taking the responsibility for healing it on their own initiative, Farrakhan now warned the old-timers.

In this revisionist re-imagining of the sect's past, Elijah himself in his lifetime had been pointing Farrakhan away from white devilhood. Farrakhan had broadcast a radio commentary every week on his behalf "beating up the white man". Elijah curtly phoned him to tell him to "stop throwing trash in a well I am trying to get a drink of water out of"— a metaphor for the old NOI's accelerating induction into the rich U.S. mainstream. For Farrakhan in 1998 that "trash" was "a truth [that] has passed the time of its usefulness".

Farrakhan was clearly preparing traditionalists in his sect for radical breaks with some old themes of the Elijah era, as more and more Arabic rituals entered the sect. On the other hand, he was maintaining the old NOI's sense of religion as a continuous series of revelations. Could these still culminate in America with Elijah as a prophet, like and in succession to, Muhammad of Arabia, and indeed, with Farrakhan as a prophet after Elijah— concepts that would enrage Third World Muslims? After all: after God sent Abraham, He sent Noah, Lot and then Moses whose wisdom had a time value of 2,000 years. When Jesus was born, people said they didn't need him because they had Moses. Since Jesus had come to raise the development of religion to another level, the Jews, in rejecting him, corrupted Moses by holding on to that bygone prophet. Farrakhan was particularistic when he then rebuked the Christians as not having had the Messiah who was 2,000 years yet to come, a clear reference to Elijah Muhammad (—or to himself?) But the logic of this chain of evolution might only turn out to be that some key teachings of Elijah Muhammad were now obsolescent, so that Farrakhan's members now had to put them behind them.

In 1999, Farrakhan retained an Elijah-like impulse to reject the surviving Gospels in turn as having been "concocted" by the white man to confuse and subjugate the blacks. Accordingly, Allah had revealed the Qur'an to Muhammad. The Qur'an itself looks a new book but was a compilation of the best of the revealed word of God through the many Prophets that he sent, correcting the many errors that had been introduced into earlier texts. [Those Sufis and radical African-American neo-Sunnis trying to block entry of Farrakhan into world Islam argued that while he was giving the Qur'an a higher ranking than the earlier scriptures, he had yet to rule out an ongoing process that would give a new Book to some African-American. How far had Farrakhan really moved from old NOI doctrines towards Sunni Islam, they interrogated?]

Farrakhan referred ambiguously or plurally to the orthodox Muslim World's doctrine that there was no Messenger to come after Muhammad of Arabia. They had God's final Message of Qur'an, but had allowed it to lose its power to counteract the might of America by bowing down to it. Their fearfulness enabled President Clinton, a counter-godhead, to bomb 'Iraq, regardless of whatever the UN said. "The wisdom of the Qur'an needs deeper introspection so we can extract from it greater power to heal the human family. As it is now, it is weak because the" [Sunni] "scholars have not seen into its depth." Here, Farrakhan could also have been maneuvering to keep a margin for ongoing esoteric-symbolic exegesis for himself and his sect beyond Middle Eastern understanding of the Qur'an. Overall, his was the simple message that the Qur'an obligated Middle Easterners to worship God without ceding authority to worldly powers such as America, which was a form of polytheism (*shirk*).

He was not clear about how wide the margin of doctrine he wanted should stretch. By 1998 Farrakhan was conceding that on some matters the Muslim world and its orthodox representatives in the States who had criticized Elijah before 1975 had rightly represented the Qur'an. Trying to resolve the contradictions, he argued as follows: God had raised the Honorable Elijah Muhammad in the West, to produce an Islamic Community that seemed unorthodox, given that Islam doesn't teach color or race. "Islam teaches the Oneness of God, the Oneness of the Human Family" (a phrase increasingly used by Farrakhan to include white sympathizers of the NOI) "and a Universal Brotherhood, but racism and white supremacy has affected every religion and every doctrine that impresses itself on the human family"—a charge that Farrakhan on occasion had applied to fair-skinned Middle Eastern Arabs also. Farrakhan's discourse here made the point that if Wali Fard Muhammad and Elijah Muhammad had given Islam a focus on racial matters, that was only temporary to address a very special situation, a special America in a particular era.

Farrakhan further implied that the Qur'an as well as the Bible had been abused by white supremacy to "destroy your ability to perceive reality correctly". The strong "justice" and races-neutral, egalitarian current in the Qur'an was being backgrounded by the ruling elites of some *ethne* that had primacy in this area of the Muslim world or that. As the 20th century ended, Farrakhan clearly retained some misgivings about the Arab and Muslim worlds with which he was now engaging much more closely. Nonetheless, he was awarding the Qur'an a greater weight than other past scriptures revealed overseas, and was gently phasing out key old NOI tenets such as the "white devils."[14]

In this late speech of 1999, Farrakhan moved away from Elijah by characterizing him as now outdated on the nature of community and the altered American society that had come into existence. He was moving towards the Qur'an while resisting any Arab monopoly over its interpretation. He had impulses towards a multi-racial Muslim community, perhaps in his own sect, too.

The Threat of Violence and Repression of the Religion

Although less than in the long-gone era of Elijah Muhammad, Farrakhanist mosques and congregations continue to draw hostility and sometimes violence from the white police and authorities across America. While such thrusts from the mainstream fueled the potentiality for NOI militancy and withdrawal from the greater society, they have also revealed the widening array of not just African-American but also white interests that have become associated with the sect, or with which the sect wants to ally.

On August 8, 1996, in Inglewood, Los Angeles, over 100 sheriffs' deputies, police officers, and FBI agents, in a massive display of force, surrounded the NOI's local mosque to serve an eviction notice. Western Regional Representative, Minister Tony Muhammad, charged that the law-enforcement officials came to the mosque before business hours intending to start a confrontation. A black councilman observed that the Nation was being "singled out to be treated differently than would be normally the case had an eviction effort been initiated with some other religious organization": he wanted to arrange talks between the NOI and the police.

Tony Muhammad's hints that God might zap Inglewood and Los Angeles focused real hatred against a fair number of whites, but also freed the blacks of any requirement to at once fight on their own account, which would have been suicidal for them. His threat alluded to the Nation of Islam's covert efforts to dovetail into white America in a wider pan-American community—"persecution of a righteous people whose intentions and works are good for the country" [=America: would the NOI ever truly work to partition it, then?] Minister Tony's concern at "a hidden hand that's bent on destroying the reputation of the Nation of Islam and Minister Louis Farrakhan after the Million Man March" [=the Zionoids?], again hinted at the sect's drive to mainstream itself and win respectability and acceptance from the predominantly white central community.

Black Christian leaders who came to the NOI's side in Ingelwood wanted liberal whites to join in. Thus, Brotherhood Crusade President Danny Bakewell Sr [African-American] said "we should have every ethnic group, including white folks, out here [protesting] because this is an attack on religious freedom".

Farrakhan's adherents were successfully defining the issue at stake in Los Angeles as freedom for religious groups in general, and not just those run by African-Americans. The NOI's 1996 coalitionism towards U.S. institutions and wider groups passed beyond realism, manipulation, or tactical survival to the idea of a counter-"community", an alternative America, or perhaps the real America, that would include some liberal whites not out to atomize and control non-Anglo groups ("assimilation"). This type of NOI communications implied that African-American Muslims share a common "country" (Farrakhan calls it "the city") with whites and, implicitly, that they may come to share a potential common nationhood with them.[15] This weakens hopes that Allah might soon incinerate.

2: THE MILLION MAN MARCH: INDUCTION INTO ELECTORAL POLITICS?

The Million Man March of 1995

The 1995 Million Man March in Washington was mass contact by Farrakhan and the Nation of Islam with the overwhelmingly non-Muslim bourgeois masses, nominally Christian, that turned up. The March in itself symbolized the resolve of a range of black classes to reform African-American internal society. A broad-gauge account of Farrakhan's Million Man March of 1995, and the consequences for African-American political identity, will be presented in my companion volume on Islam among African-Americans after 1975. One of my concerns there will be the unfolding and conflicts of micro-nationalist movements and ideologies in the USA, notably instanced in ethnic polarization between Farrakhan/the NOI and Jewish-American nationalists. In that work, I concentrate on the high ambiguity of the March and its legacy as both (a) an affirmation of the single nationality of African-Americans and (b) a formulation of ways to relate blacks to parliamentarist activities and values of the U.S. mainstream.

The March was an Islamizing event. A range of Muslim sects were allowed to appear before the multitude and recite the Qur'an in Arabic on a basis of equality with the Christian and black Jewish clerics whom Farrakhan had inducted. It was a recognition in public space of Islam as part of the being of blacks that had had no precedent. Farrakhan led the multitude through chanting of "as-Salamu 'Alaykum", the Arabic greeting of "Peace be Upon You" between Muslims that also recurs in Islamic ritual prayer.

The March brought unprecedentedly broad ideological outreach by (a) immigrant and black Sunni Muslim groups to (b) both those Christian African-American multitudes and the thin layer of NOI cadres striving to direct and control them. Representative of the type of militant Sunni groups that came were the Jama'at al-Muslimin and its Amir, the Pakistan-born Dr Kawkab Siddiqi, who was teaching at an African-American university in Baltimore. The March measured the extent to which Farrakhan's sometimes fake condemnations of Jews and Israel now could draw orthodox immigrant Muslims, for whom some of Farrakhan's religious tenets had been worrisome.

The pro-Saddam Jama'at al-Muslimin of the immigrant students and professionals and the African-Americans who had joined them, were happy that W.D. Mohammed [whose followers still queried NOI doctrines] had not turned up "because W.D.'s love of the U.S. government, his love of the Zionists, his love for the Sa'udi Arabian monarchy, his honors received from the killer Mubarak of Egypt, his visits to the Pentagon, would have turned people against Islam. Thanks be to God that this friend of the rich, the exploiters, and the corrupt rulers did not come." A common hatred of Israel and Zionists drew one type of immigrant Sunnis, despite credal disparity with Farrakhan, to the March; and pro-Khomeini Shi'ites from Iran and Afghan mujahideen [whom Farrakhan had often endorsed in his speeches—and visited in Pakistan] also were out in force. Black American professionals attending the MMM chanted with the Jama'at that the U.S. government should free that gentle blind Egyptian cleric, 'Umar 'Abd al-Rahman, it had framed of urging the blowing-up of the twin World Trade Center towers in 1993.[16] Farrakhan was to wonder in 1996 if some future U.S. administration would not incarcerate him in a cell next to that of Shaykh 'Abd al-Rahman: they might then read the Qur'an together as two of the "militants" of a single "true Islam".[17]

Such attraction of Farrakhan and other colleagues to the insurgent salafists of Third World Islam would not help movement by the NOI towards the U.S. mainstream and system, especially after September 11. But some left-nationalists of the Arab World would not have dichotomized the Egyptian or other Arab salafists (e.g. in Algeria) against Anglo-Saxon imperialism as did some African-American Muslims. From its founding in 1929, the Muslim Brotherhood's relations with the British had ranged from initial coexistence to armed attacks in the last years of the monarchy. The Brotherhood's Secret Order ("Jihaz Sirri") had at some points been more concerned to kill "apostate" parliamentary politicians than British troops. Did 'Umar 'Abd al-Rahman follow in that pattern of priorities? Like Usamah Bin Ladin, jihadist 'Umar had helped the mujahidin fight the Russians in Afghanistan, who got money and training from America which in turn let 'Umar in to live and preach in the Big Apple. Some in Egypt's governing establishment wondered if America might have been holding 'Umar and his Jama'at al-Jihad in reserve to unleash them on its Egyptian ally if Mubarak stepped out of line on Palestine or anything else. 'Umar's group had killed Sadat earlier. Some salafist texts from Egypt postpone any strike against Israel until the "neo-pagan" Egyptian political system is overthrown. At any rate, too many Muslims fell as cannon fodder in Afghanistan, 'Umar probably tried to bite the hand that once fed him, and so he had to be put away.[18] Was 'Abd al-Rahman in the 1980s reporting to U.S. agencies on the Libyan regime that had jailed its homegrown Egyptian-style salafists?

During his overseas tours, Farrakhan glad-handed Palestinian salafist jihadists such as "Brother Khalid Mash'al" after the Mossad tried to assassinate him in 'Amman. The anti-American and anti-Israel glamour of these Arab movements pull American Muslim cults from heterodox beliefs to streamlined, ultra-political, forms of Sunni Islam.

The hatred against Arabs and Islam in U.S. mass culture has driven some immigrant students and professionals to solidarity with Third World radical Islamic movements and anti-U.S. regimes. Such political pan-Islamism put a category of immigrant Muslims in the same U.S. trench with Farrakhan, outweighing disparities in his doctrines from the Third World Arab and Muslim revivalists and governments with whom he voiced some sympathy.

Political Mobilization after the 1995 Million Man March

For the time, the March made Farrakhan the undisputed national leader of African-Americans. This raised a possibility that he could have gone on to construct a long-term mass-movement with enough of a vote-bank to compel the mainstream's white political bosses to admit his people—and, indeed, himself and his Islam—into American electoral politics in an unprecedented way. This opportunity, though, brought out the tensions as to whether even the new NOI could become a genuinely political, as opposed to a religious or entrepreneurial, group.

The potential of the black Muslim sects to help lead a deeper engagement by the Afro-American common people with the American political system was clear in the November 3 1998 American elections. Minister Benjamin Chavis Muhammad, who had been a sort of professional politician before his 1997 conversion to Farrakhan's Islam, and national director of the 1995 March, was perhaps the driving force behind the serious effort the NOI now made to lead ordinary blacks away from cynicism and avoidance into activism in electoral politics. In New York, as in Chicago, Atlanta, Houston, Washington, D.C., and other cities, NOI posters and flyers and radio broadcasts urged voters to come to the polls. A large "Get Out the Vote" rally was hosted by Farrakhan in Chicago. Minister Benjamin also took to the Big Apple's airwaves, especially on stations popular with black youth, urging them to vote for their own interests.

This 1998 "grassroots" campaign did induct many sometimes apathetic ghetto blacks into parliamentarism. Muslim volunteers were at the fore of the "Get Out the Vote" campaign. Above-average black voting helped oust House Speaker Newt Gingrich, and brought Democratic gubernatorial victories in Alabama, California, South Carolina, Georgia and Maryland. In question here, though, is whether Farrakhan and the NOI might not have had more ideological elements in common with the Republicans—reconstruct families, God, self-uplift through entrepreneurship—than with the Democrats for whom most Blacks were opting. The NOI's denunciations of injustices against blacks internally and in the Third World did defy the Republican governing system. The sect was showing that it could channel the anger it aroused at these injustices into skilled activity by blacks in the USA's parliamentary system.

There is no doubt that a few top leaders, and many volunteers, of the Nation of Islam in 1998 put the spotlight on their sect when taking part in a drive to advance African-American interests through congressional politics. On the other hand, this was a coalitional campaign in which Farrakhan was once again working with Black Christian clergy-politicians, a consistent pattern since he had founded the new NOI in 1978. Thus, the NOI of 1998 remained woven into the black professional politicians class and the clergies in the face of all Jewish micronationalist efforts to isolate and starve his sect since 1984.

But there were limits to how original the NOI could become in politics. At least nominally on the agenda of the NOI's 1998 effort in congressional, gubernatorial and city-level mayoral politics was a motif that various African-American politicians had been toying with since the 1980s—the "Third Political

Force" that Benjamin Muhammad, East Coast Regional Minister for the Nation of Islam, hoped was now emerging. The full projection of the idea in Black micro-Nationalist thought had been that African-Americans should field an independent candidate for the U.S. presidential elections. [Following the defeat of the 1984 candidacy of Jesse Jackson for President—whom Farrakhan had helped win mass support from blacks—the African-American community had deliberated such an idea]. But in 1998, Farrakhan and his supporters gave it a fluid twist that might only serve to scrutinize and adjust the U.S. two-party system as it stood: a coming Third Force would focus on registering, educating and inspiring voters to support candidates who will back an agenda that addresses the needs of blacks, other so-called minority groups and the poor. Some African-Americans had tired of putting all their eggs in the basket of the non-reciprocating Democrats.

In the 1998 elections, the upshot had only been that the NOI was giving electoral aid to African-Americans who worked with the Democratic Party at several levels. The Republicans and Farrakhan had looked each other over following the great March of 1995. Farrakhan also thought over an ad hoc approach in which blacks could opt for this or that Republican or Democratic candidate in this and that electorate according to how useful that individual politician would be for black interests. But in 1998 the black activists, politicians and churches with whom the NOI worked seemed to be fashioning the sect and its activities—just as Christian blacks had moulded the NOI in regard to ethnic conflict with U.S. Jews and Israel, once Farrakhan made that the rallying-point at which he bid for black support in the early 1980s. The small NOI's wide (if intermittent) political interactions with urban "African-Americans" in general have to be understood as a reciprocal process in which each group colors and somewhat steers the other.

The NOI's activists during the 1998 elections had some sort of a vision that their activism could open the way to "empower ourselves [Blacks] going into the next century". This required that the NOI interact with a range of other black groups with a view to building "our ability to work together" (Wendell Muhammad, Atlanta).[19] Only time will tell if all the attention and time that Farrakhan gave to connecting to overseas Muslims after the Million Man March had been fatal to the meticulous domestic focus needed for the NOI to lead the African-American people into a new parliamentarism, perhaps ethnicist only at first, that might help integrate America over the long term.

The NOI media's coverage of the 2000 presidential and congressional elections was too detailed to come from people who could still have believed that God's judgement and destruction of the world was close at hand. Itself a political act of mass consciousness-raising, the coverage again showed the impulse of Farrakhan and his followers to stand somewhat between the Democratic Party traditionally favored by blacks and the Republican Party. Here, the communications in *Final Call* were voicing the bourgeois-lumpen duality of the following of the Nation of Islam, which call into play diverging class interests.

The NOI in 2000 was striving to engage with the African-American bourgeoisie and intellectuals, and with mainstream black politicians. It remained a movement without enough resources of its own to take political leadership of the African-American masses; but established black politicians still had to court it because of its capacity to muster a significant voting force in U.S. mainstream elections. The atmosphere in *Final Call* was exploratory and pluralist as the Muslims and the black political elite, who both needed the other, groped for ways to relate following the crucial elections of 2000 that brought in George Bush, Jr. The dilemmas brought out *Final Call's* capacity for long-term thought. Ordinary Americans, black and white, were mainly preoccupied with the dispute over the uneven counting of returns in the state of Florida. In contrast, the *The Final Call* was looking beyond the final result in election 2000 to the attempts by some black leaders to define a correct posture when the 43rd president was sworn in.

The newspaper was again functioning as a forum for divergent views, and thereby fostering a capacity for hypothetical thinking in its mass readership. It did give some space to the conventional political concepts of the ethnos: 92% of black votes counted had gone to the Democratic Party and some politicians wanted to cooperate with the Democrats in Congress, hoping for a miracle that would result in a presidency for Al Gore. Here, *Final Call* carried Rev. Jessie Jackson's assertions that Bush's becoming president was creating a tyranny. "If the court rules against counting our vote it will simply cause a Civil Rights explosion", the leftist Reverend threatened. "We can afford to lose an election—you can't afford to lose your franchise."

But *Final Call* itself was far from that pseudo-explosive. It carefully put together all views among blacks. It also cited Dr Ronald Walters, Professor of Political Science at the University of Maryland, who had been a senior adviser to both "Jackson for President" campaigns in 1984 and 1988, but now was pushing the black political leadership to engage the next president, even if it were George Bush, Jr. Walters counseled blacks to test the compassionate conservatism that Bush claimed to represent. If Bush took office, Walters told a session of the National Coalition of Black Civic Participation, blacks should present him with lists of recommended appointees as well as with public policy agenda items for the next administration, not "sit back and watch the show" yet again just because a Republican had won.

Some sons and daughters of black beneficiaries of affirmative action were now climbing into wealth they might well safeguard by voting Republican. But the black strata lower down in the money scale—for instance William Lucy, President of the Coalition of Black Trade Unionists—wanted to fight a Republican Party victory. The NOI relayed the detailed steps Lucy planned to get blacks more deeply into the mainstream political system. But the sect's Chief of Staff, Leonard Muhammad, was trying to portray the NOI as able to contribute policies that it had itself originated. He noted that a comprehensive agenda addressing the concerns of the blacks and "the poor" [=poor whites as well as Hispanics?] had been presented to both presidential candidates through the Million Family March. He cautioned that this coalition of blacks and poor had to mobilize to force whoever gets into office to address the agenda. This was one more case of impulses in the Nation of Islam to move to a position between the Democratic and the Republican parties, based on ad hoc lobby-like interaction with them in which the NOI sometimes conveys the vital interests of the poor to that bi-party system. Democratic president Clinton had turned back the clock by his program of welfare "reform" and anti-affirmative action legislation against the blacks. Here, the NOI Chief of Staff was addressing both the concerns of the lumpen proletariat constituency in the ghettos and that of the harder-pressed sections of the black bourgeoisie.

Final Call projected the impulse to move to a median ad hoc position between the system's two great parties out onto even Democrats among African-American politicians, given the outcomes for their case in that party under Clinton. Representative J. C. Watts, an Oklahoma Republican, counseled the black community to be open, just as Governor Bush had to be, to forge a relationship that would work. He reassured African-Americans that Bush Jr would not punish the black community at large for its support for his opponent, Al Gore. The Congressional Black Caucus, although mainly Democrat, was—*Final Call* noted approvingly—taking as its mantra the old cold-blooded saying that there are no permanent friends and permanent enemies, just permanent interests. The Caucus would be loyal to issues of Blacks irrespective of whoever would be in the White House. The Nation of Islam's engagement with elections and parliamentarism in 2000 sought politicians geared towards legislation that would foster or deepen the middle-class status and accumulation of wealth that the sect's members pursued. It gave space to arguments of Republican representative Watts that some measures by Bush might help blacks accumulate wealth, such as his policies of tax relief, and eliminating marriage and death taxes.[20]

Final Call's stance towards the new government of George Bush Jr, then, was from the outset non-aligned—alternately as open to it, or as critical as it had been to the outgoing administration of President Bill Clinton. Its correspondents were clearly intrigued by the new Republican administration's appointment of retired General Colin Powell as Secretary for State. Under Elijah Muhammad, the old NOI's media had long dismissed appointments of blacks to high policy positions, but this appointment to such a central position was harder to dismiss. One *Final Call* item hoped that the incoming Republican administration might speed up the outgoing Democratic administration's induction of racial minorities and women into the State Department. Currently, 25 percent of the foreign service workforce were women, with only 505 blacks and 390 Hispanics amongst the 8,971 employed. *Final Call* carried Democratic Senator Charles B. Rangel's demand that the new administration give opportunity to African-Americans to become ambassadors and secretaries of Ministers—the " foot in the door".

The item meticulously assessed how effective the State Department had been, and might become, as a system for the upward class mobility of blacks. It did want U.S. administrations to help Africa. This particular item voiced no criticism of past American policies in the Third World: it did not foresee any conflict or duality of loyalties for African-Americans who took up such jobs. The paper thus sought induction of the ethnos into institutions that should be neutral for all the races and the religious groups.[21]

At the same time, the NOI had long been disturbed by aspects of official American secularism that had placed restrictions on the range of roles that the religious NOI could take up in the mainstream. Its Jewish nationalist opponents had mustered U.S. secularist restrictions to deny roles and resources to Farrakhan's sect. Republican rhetoric had long depicted the Party as more receptive to input from custodians of religious faiths in comparison to the Democrats. George Bush Jr, following his win, quickly called an interfaith gathering of around 30 members of the Christian, Jewish and Islamic communities, including some blacks, titled "Rebuilding Our Faith". One Bush policy was the loosening of federal regulation of groups that can provide social services with government grant money (the Jewish micronationalists had objected that the NOI's security agencies had tried to convert when contracted, in violation of secularism) as well as various measures to foster private religiously-based education, which the NOI conducted. *Final Call* was responsive.[22]

Those most intrigued by Farrakhan in the African-American political classes feared that he was not responding quickly enough to politically organize the huge numbers of dissatisfied blacks whose initial engagement he had won through the Million Man March. The black politicians and intellectual opinion leaders continued to aid or advise Farrakhan, though, in the hope that he could—as the charismatic leader most able to link the range of black classes—be led to actualize the promise of his sense of the vote as a form of power in America that African-Americans should seize. They would try to nudge and steer him so that he would act on this impulse to constructively take the blacks into the mainstream to restructure it from within.

Here, the constructive, and in reality integrationist, African-American opinion leaders continued to be driven to Farrakhan by their stark vision of the inhospitality of all sectors of the political mainstream to their race: their clarity on this easily matched his. A year after the March, the [relatively leftist] Earl Ofari Hutchinson shared the rage of the black leadership that Republican presidential candidate Dole had refused to address the NAACP's 1996 annual convention. The Republican Party had systematically rejected blacks for three decades.

But the ruling Democratic Party was no sanctuary for African-Americans. Hutchinson dismissed as fools the black delegates who had chanted "Four more years, four more years" before a beaming President Clinton at that NAACP convention. Clinton felt no need to give any details they could hold him to, for the promise he made there to continue the fight against racism. But pink Ofari Hutchinson was condemning Clinton's changed Democratic Party of 1996, not the bygone "Democratic Party that championed New Deal, Great Society, labor and civil rights reforms". Clinton had spent two elections trying to out-Reagan Reagan and out-Bush Bush/Perot in a chase to grab back the defecting white middle-class, ethnic and blue collar voters and distance himself from "special interests", i.e. women and minorities. Hutchinson accurately predicted that in this election, Clinton would clone the 15 to 20 percent of Republicans drawn to his positions into "Clinton Republicans."

But Hutchinson was also determined to steer Farrakhan's sect and the millions of African-Americans open to it away from the chimera of a black third parliamentarist party, with which Farrakhan and *Final Call* had sometimes toyed. Hutchinson listed independent African-American parties in the 20th century that had all crashed on the hard bedrock loyalty of black voters to the Democrats. If blacks withdrew from the political playing field, it would turn the electoral process into a white, middle-class primary, and give conservatives an even greater excuse to ignore or torpedo black needs, Hutchinson argued. Reagan had achieved that and the blacks were still paying a huge cost.

In place of (a) uncritical submission to Clinton's popularity and consequent power within the Democratic Party, or (b) self-penalizing surrender of the two mainstream parties to white neo-cons through "third party" withdrawal, Hutchinson (c) called the blacks to engage more with the two great parties. They should brandish the millions of votes of the dissatisfied to "transform Blacks into independent political power brokers to both the Democrats and Republicans". Ethnic vote threats and bloc voting had shown their capacity to make or break a candidate, campaign, and agenda before. In 1972, the Black Political Convention forced Nixon to increase minority business funding, propose non-punitive welfare reform, and strengthen affirmative action programs in the trades [—from which Elijah's Muslims tried to benefit].

Yet Hutchinson inclined more to the Democrats, who in 1984 and 1988, faced with the vote-power of Jackson's Rainbow Coalition, had given paper support to national health insurance, full employment, political redistricting, and affirmative action. Hutchinson wanted the new political front of "the Blacks" forming around Farrakhan to apply this power in parliamentarism to make the Democrats win but then direct resources to the black populations after their reelection. Yet Hutchinson also urged the blacks "as independent political brokers to lobby, challenge, and pressure both parties to support full funding for jobs, affirmative action, education, health, drug and crime prevention programs, and non-punitive welfare and criminal justice reform"—the price for getting African-American votes.[23]

Farrakhan's new 21st century NOI fits well into the ongoing Civil Rights/Democratic Party political tradition among Africans-Americans that Elijah and his old NOI once short-sightedly mocked as it took form in the 1960s. The NOI's media convey to the masses the messages of radicalized veteran "Civil Rights" leaders who are by now frankly open to Arabs under attack from the U.S. system and Israel. In the leadup to the 2003 March on the 40th anniversary of Martin Luther King, Jr.'s 1963 March on Washington, *Final Call* quoted King's son that "poverty has grown, ...racism, and militarism is the order of the day"—a condemnation of Bush's invasions of Muslim countries after September 11. Yet it also recognized that black elites had found a degree of acceptance within the system: the NOI newspaper carried the satisfaction of John Conyers, dean of the Congressional Black Caucus, at the huge increase in black mayors, elected officials, and members of Congress by 2003 from 1963. But the veteran Conyers was also happy that Muslim and Arab-American institutions, and feminists, now had their accepted place in the annual March alongside the original Black Christian organizations and trade unions.[24]

By 2003, then, even Middle Eastern Muslims and their interests and concerns had been finally incorporated into the veteran black integrationist political movement. This completed the timid August 1983 entry of Arab-Americans—and of African-American efforts for Middle East peace—into the 20th anniversary March on Washington two decades before, which had made "the Zionists" walk out. Farrakhan's restored NOI had become hard to distinguish from the black political mainstream in its approval of non-violent, constructive politics as a means to bring more social chances to blacks in general. If the NOI can last, it could work well with—in?—the black political mainstream as each influences and modifies the other.

Militants: Could the U.S. System Disintegrate?

If, overall, Farrakhan failed to carry through the mass nation-mobilization he had started in the Million Man March, others around his sect tried to build a mass movement, themselves. Khalid Muhammad, Farrakhan's young rival in the sect, in 1998 brought together a "Million Youth March" in New York. Throughout the rally, police sharpshooters and helicopters menacingly manifested themselves. They had been sent by New York's Rudolph W. Giuliani (Mayor 1994-2001), an Italian-American politician closely allied with the USA's Jewish enclave-nationalists and Israel. One hundred thousand African-Americans turned up. The March's organizer, attorney Malik Zulu Shabazz, now invited "revolutionary Arabs and [immigrant] Muslims to join the nationwide movement" that Islam could take to victory.[25]

But the mainstream of Farrakhan's revived Nation of Islam was working to contain the drift toward social explosions and U.S. system-disintegration.

One ameliorist impulse in the Nation of Islam to build power for blacks within the U.S. system instead of confrontation against it was clear in Cincinatti, Ohio, when a police killing there and three nights of rioting tore that city apart in April 2001. The funeral at New Prospect Baptist Church showed again how centrally the second NOI has installed itself in Christian structures. The NOI representative there revved up the mourning crowd by telling it to channel their rage: "Don't get angry and throw a brick. Get angry and register to vote". Compared to the clench-fisted New Black Panthers present at the funeral, the NOI's message fitted more with the pleas for peace from Martin Luther King III, NAACP president Kweisi Mfume, and the Cincinatti Mayor at the ceremony. Yet the party chairman for the Panthers who orated was now the Islam-influenced Malik Zulu Shabazz.[26]

3: GETTING RICH AND DISPARATE BLACK CLASSES: COULD THE NOI INTEGRATE THEM IN ONE CARING NATIONHOOD?

The NOI and Nationalist Private Enterprise

It is hard to assess the likely outcome of the business operations that Farrakhan and his sect tried to build up from the early 1980s. In 1998, he appealed to the followers to send checks to the Three Year Economic Program. This program was presented as the NOI's answer to unemployment, hunger, poor housing and all the other problems of the blacks. The $10 or more a month contributions of the followers had "made it possible to purchase your 1,600-acre farm", but there was still so much more to do.[27] Farrakhan tried to evoke nostalgia for the era of Elijah with projects such as bean pie restaurants, but overall he could not whip up the collective nationalist passion around his businesses that Elijah Muhammad did arouse in his followers and among African-Americans in general, in his drive to create a projected parallel, self-contained, black national economy in the 1960s and 1970s.

Farrakhan's projects did not sufficiently employ the much more sophisticated and compound non-Muslim black bourgeoisie that had developed since the era of civil rights and affirmative action. Some of his projects sought to cater to the conspicuous consumption of the upper sections of the black bourgeoisie that had become rich by such projects as a luxurious restaurant with facilities remote from the needs of ordinary African-Americans. While Farrakhan evoked the collectivist economic ethos of Elijah in advertisements in *Final Call* soliciting donations for his "economic plan", the advertisements were non-specific in detail and had a diffident tone that suggested that some in the black public had expected him to get funding for his businesses from the Arab states, not from them. While the black middle classes have liked Farrakhan, been prepared to formulate economic nationalist strategies in conjunction with his fora and media, wished his projects well, and thrown his enterprises the occasional lifeline loan, this has been with a relaxed attitude far from the awe and even obedience that Elijah was able to build up for his mini-economy even in fairly wide sectors of Christian African-Americans beyond his sect.

Farrakhan did, however, build effective security agencies whose employees proved their street-wise capacity to guard properties in crime-ridden areas and to rid black communities of crime and drugs that had formed in public housing in those areas. Here, the new Nation of Islam could fill a need not just of impoverished black communities, but of new black business classes that want security in which to develop—and of the US system itself which would benefit from security services that could understand the African-American poor. While "Jewish" denunciations of Farrakhan from 1994 never stopped in the press and even in TV cinema, some Anglomorph public servants and politicians discreetly came to see the Nation of Islam as key potential allies at street level against the flood of drugs and as an instrument for channeling dangerous or burdensome poor urban blacks into a healing, non-violent parliamentarism. Some TV depictions came to project positive images of the NOI's foot soldiers as, for all their cold alienation (rather than hatred), in effect "on the same side" as the desperate police fighting the dealers.[28] However, lobbying and pressure from U.S. Jewish micronationalist organizations soon stopped U.S. departments and local city governments from hiring NOI security agencies, cutting off a niche that could have become the entry-point of Farrakhan's Muslims into the American system.

Farrakhan's sect also tried to associate its interests with the nationalist ethos of the African-American bourgeoisie that had some money to spend by attempting a guide role for those who traveled back to the Mother Continent for identity tourism (Chapter 1).

Overall, the development of the Nation's enterprises in the late 20th century and early 21st looked to be in the doldrums. Changes in the structure of the U.S. economy as a whole since the mid-1970s have made it harder and harder to launch the modest business enterprises with which the Muslims had started out under Elijah. In that respect, though, the shift of Farrakhan's followers in the 1990s to such projects as nationalist malls in the inner cities in which they are partners with Christian Black businessmen was attuned to the openings. Clearly, though, their ethnic vendetta enemy has had some successes in blocking points at which the NOI could have entered the central U.S. economic system, causing a real attrition of resources and recruitment over the decades.

Farrakhan's NOI and the Black Bourgeoisie's Economic Nationalism

The black business classes in general—not the NOI's entrepreneurial component only—have succeeded in linking their success to sovereignty and prosperity for the African-American Nation. Farrakhan's mass-media has highlighted such tendencies beyond the NOI itself, contributing to the widespread communalization, nationalization and politicization of economics in the minds of many blacks: the NOI's ideological press and radio repeatedly muster the masses as a constituency of nationalist customers for the non-Muslim black businessmen.

In late 2000, a Chicago alderwoman refused to allow a black entrepreneur to build a hotel on land he had inherited in the community: she said she was committed to building 3,000 units of public affordable, and market-rate, housing. A *Final Call* interviewer amplified the counter-argument of the black heir, Anthony Fields, that his commercial property had never been slated for residential use and that the alderwoman was deceiving the low-to-moderate income community with hopes of attaining quality affordable homes. The NOI newspaper ran the argument of Fields that the Alderwoman's refusal to change the zoning suggested she was participating in a major prime property land grab, which would displace black voters. Fields voiced faux naïve puzzlement that he had become one of the symbols of the current black economic empowerment movement when he set out to build the Lakeview Howard Johnson hotel and Plaza.

One can understand the NOI's backing for him. Muslim and secular nationalist blacks had to support any bourgeois element in the black community who might prove a means to place local development in the hands of a member of that community. Even if low-income housing actually was built in this instance, that might merely stack the black poor in ghettoized housing warehouses. For the nationalists, the key for revival was to seize and carry through any prospects for commercial activity and further development by individuals in the community.

Fields was mustering Farrakhan's *Final Call* and another local black newspaper to help pressure the city into granting the zoning upgrade he needed to build a hotel—and a national community which might develop around it, so he said. "My promise to the community is that 80 percent of all construction and permanent jobs will go to the residents of the 4th Ward." With the hotel as an anchor, nearby black businesses would develop commercially.

Farrakhan's sect was taking Field's part in unison with black bourgeois elements who made their class economic interest a key element of nationality. The hotel was only "one battle in a struggle for the land that African-Americans could not afford to lose", argued Everloyce McCullough, chairperson of the Black Economic and Political Network (BEPAN). James Stewart of the National Economic Association hailed the hotel as only one more component in a campaign to create a significantly self-sufficient black nationalist economy. The hotel could also secure tourism, and "as the community develops would probably encourage us to spend more money in our own community." Inner-city blacks preferred to shop, view films, and get together in hotels in their own area, "not just only by the airport".[29]

The drive of Farrakhan's new Nation of Islam to make itself a partner of the wider black business classes, with nationalism serving as one nexus, has gone beyond ideological exchanges and conferences to enterprises at street level. The sect built real responsiveness among Christian businessmen and inner-city blacks to this kind of nationalist path to development. From the time of Elijah, Muslims have been credited by cross-sections of inner-city blacks as equipped to spearhead the construction of conventional businesses in run-down, violent ghettos. While the new NOI's denunciations of racism and conditions could fuel little explosions, its drive to bourgeoisify through private enterprise again brings out this tradition's duality towards the system. While the sect sharpens protest nationality as a motivating fuel to carry through the African-American "national" construction and to draw and hold the purchasing constituency it needs if it is not to fail, the more the sect and its allies build going concerns, the more they have a vested interest in the system they define blacks against.

This was brought out by the launching in Boston in 2001 of the Grove Hall neighborhood mall, called "Mecca", which in part was the product of the Neighborhood Development Corporation of Grove Hall (NDCGH), whose director was an NOI Muslim, Virginia Muhammad. The whole venture was pervaded by a sense that the Muslims could not do it on their own but would need collaboration not just with Christian black businessmen but also with the central U.S. system. Virginia Muhammad was right that the $500 billion purchasing power of urban black communities in the USA could foster the growth of a black bourgeoisie if some sort of economic circuit could be created. Even at the outset, though, the circuit was not to be self-contained and final to the extent that ultra-nationalism would demand. Virginia Muhammad noted that the nationally-known stores in the mall will be owned or managed by blacks, a formulation that sometimes would accept a role as junior partners or employees of white-dominated large American companies that have to be induced into the ghettos, which are sometimes lacking enterprises, altogether.

Since its foundation seventeen years before, NDCGH had been able to provide training opportunities for local residents, convince the city that area residents and business owners want to have a say in the future plans for the community, help area businesses to be stronger and move contractors working in the community to hire local residents. NDCGH successes included managing a $1.2 million rehabilitation project which provided 12 units of affordable housing and four commercial units in the heart of Grove Hall.

Still, NDCGH's estimate that it had created 200 jobs for community residents showed the limits to which nationalist private enterprise could provide livelihoods for poor blacks. The body had recruited the first full-service bank to Grove Hall; graduated hundreds of potential first-time homebuyers in the last three years; and assisted Grove Hall businesses in accessing over $1,890,000 in grant funding to improve storefront facades. The Muslims and their allies in Boston were, as Farrakhan's sect had been doing since the early 1980s, pressuring city-level government in a constructive way, applying the threat of black voting power to give blacks a stake in a revised status quo. The NDCGH owned the property and the land used for the mall. The financing of the project came through public funds from the city and private money from Fleet Bank. Virginia Muhammad thanked Mayor Thomas Menino "for being true to his word when he said that people should be able to live, shop and work in their own community" [=enclave nationalism]. She herself said that her group had been successful "because we have forged these partnerships with the city, private sector and community".

The success of the efforts of the new NOI and its allies was the culmination of a decades-long effort in which a continuity of leaders and of planning has been crucial. Minister Don Muhammad had headed Mosque No. 11 since 1965: he notes that "the Nation of Islam was willing to work with the community. We helped rid the neighborhood of much crime and later received the support and respect of many people across the city. Today, even Black professionals are returning to the community."

The key to the successor-NOI's continuing clout was the image it built up over time that its ideology provided by the teachings of Elijah and Farrakhan could guide it to lead a restoration of community—enclavist self-determination through economics—in areas of urban blight, unemployment and high crime, "making it a neighborhood again."[30] While the new NOI's vivid portrayal of white violence and prejudice has fueled themes of Divine retribution or Judgement Day or street rumbles among African-Americans, again, as with the old NOI, the dynamic for acquisition through private enterprise overcomes the millenarian hope that God might incinerate the race-enemies next month. The end-outcome of much NOI cosmic sound-and-fury is often modest: blacks trying to help and trade with each other, individuals taking some personal responsibility each day for kin and for other co-nationals they encounter—"a neighborhood again."

In 1999, Elijah's old drive for "luxury, money, good homes and friendship in all walks of life" was the main theme of the Economic Development workshop held during Saviors' Day weekend. Nation of Islam Chief of Staff Leonard F. Muhammad had been doing for self since the age of 13, although aware that he and the other Believers had "signed on to the hardest job in the world". Could their unique dynamic sense that every day that they got up and worked for the Nation "made history"—the collectivism of their nationalist endeavor—and their range of contacts with each other across the States, empower them to achieve wealth where atomized blacks failed?

Leonard introduced Nation One Communications, a long-distance service and telecommunications company founded by the Nation of Islam. Others from across the country gave the audience of 600 practical procedures to utilize Project Exodus, an economic program implemented by Farrakhan in 1998 as a foundation for establishing a strong economy. Daniel Muhammad, an MA in Business Administration, operated two successful businesses in Ghana, Dirt Patrol Cleaning Services and Be a Champion, a basketball camp to motivate youth. "Farrakhan is the one to link us to these nations [in order] to build an Islamic economy: build a business and bring it to your nation," said Daniel. Utilizing the customer base developed through Project Exodus, the Muslims in Los Angeles established their first food co-op, and established a partnership with black farmers throughout California to produce crops for the cooperative. A Mosque was teaching canning to the women in the African-American community. Two 18-wheelers and one 24-foot truck were donated by local black truckers to help in the distribution of the food.[31]

The 1999 national business workshop of the NOI, then, showed the pre-existing non-Muslim black bourgeoisie giving substantial help to get the Muslims' nationalist private enterprise or parallel economy off the ground. This wider community support, the Muslims' tough nationalist and religious resolve to win against all the odds, the international contacts that the new NOI had built up, the blend of collectivist altruism and the drive to get rich—all these advantages together might sustain some Believers to become wealthy within the movement, but then one day become part of the U.S. mainstream that is still not over-eager to have blacks. The tendency of African-American Muslims and Black Nationalists to leave ghettoes after they build some skills and nationalist successes there for money in the mainstream disappoints. Yet post-modern communications and technology then enable them to build cyber-linked successors to the communities they leave to live amid other ethnicities. In the era of micronationalisms, success and leaving do not cost individuals their ethnicities or their "Islam" or their "Judaism", etc. (although

45% of American Jews quizzed in a mid-2005 Harris poll did not believe in God).

Final Call's coverage of the Clinton and Bush Jr administrations, and the openings they could bring non-whites, though no doubt dualistic, was always integrationist in some way. The Muslim newspaper gave a hearing to Aida Alvarez, the first Hispanic woman to serve in Clinton's cabinets, when she publicized to black business forums the public-private partnership of the "New Markets Initiative" that was to provide tax credits, investment capital and credit, and technical assistance to stimulate the formation of minority businesses in the nation's most economically distressed rural areas and inner cities. [Acceptable as "black" by the NOI's old inclusive criteria], Alvarez as the administrator of the U.S. Small Business Administration (SBA), was in a position to aid the NOI's precarious small businesses; she was aiming at up to $15 billion in investments. She had already signed agreements with the NAACP, the National Urban League and the U.S. Hispanic Chamber.[32]

Farrakhan's media link his sect's survival to that of an overall black bourgeoisie that is incomparably more institutionalized and compound than the NOI's shaky ventures. Both the Nation of Islam and the wider bourgeoisie try to make the survival of black economic enterprises the meaning of nationalism. Farrakhan's mass media has tried to hose down concern about troubled black banks and possible white takeovers in order to keep its hundreds of thousands of lower middle-class readers within the economic circuit of those big African-American institutions, even at a margin of risk. The Nation should be autonomous economically as well as in culture and education.[33] For the ordinary blacks these communications are reaching, the nationalist aura both Muslim and non-Muslim "Black" ventures cultivate around "Black" banks and property only amounts to a marginal extra: it can catch some interest but without changing the drive to seek profit wherever it comes from, which motivates the Black public as it does the country's "whites". Yet the fascination with high finance in the NOI prosperity-religion after 1980 one day could induct some layers of blacks into the U.S. central financial system once some strength and wealth are built under a nationalist rubric. Conversely, some notable African-American successes in business could give the adherents and potential converts confidence that their Nation, in some manner, could go it alone?

Farrakhan's revived NOI has further aided the institutions and culture of the general black bourgeoisie by publicizing the threats to black-owned and even Hispanic radio stations from "white takeovers." *Final Call* amplified the calls of African-American educators, social workers, ministers, healers, community police, adoption agents, realtors, employment agencies and fundraisers who all together urged that "community wagons of protection and support [be] circled around" one endangered station. The major white corporations could not be allowed to dictate what culture and news got to air from the USA's barely 200 "black-oriented stations".[34] The item made clear that Farrakhan had an interest in the issue since he needed the access to the airwaves that only committedly African-American radio stations would offer.

Unremitting campaigns from Jewish nationalists constricted how far NOI businesses could be linked into governmental institutions in black areas across the USA. However, the sect's ecumenical stance to all Black Nationalist organizations led them to utilize the NOI's highly-regarded security services. The "NOI Security" and "NOI Professional Community Services Organization", both privately-owned businesses, provided security, assuring an atmosphere of family-like fun, for the Ujima Cincinatti-Bration African Festival on July 24-26 1998. Two hundred thousand people of almost every ethnic background turned up for the jazz [=the impossibility of partitioning America]. The Ujima Festival was mainly organized by the presidents of the Greater Cincinnati's African-American Chamber of Commerce, and its United Vendors Association, both of whom had participated in Farrakhan's Million Man March.[35]

The functions of the NOI's security firms at this 1998 Festival instanced how the sect's businesses were being sustained by the acceptance of black cultural nationalists and much more advanced black business classes that the Muslims were working for all sectors of the African-American Nation. The wide range of non-Muslim black circles whose business activity had become interwoven with that of the NOI, or legitimated by the sect's media, and the resultant friendliness (and lifeline loans) from non-Muslim nationalists, secular or Christian, made it harder for the Jewish micro-nationalists and hostile Anglos in government to starve the NOI to death by cutting off livelihoods.

Strata and Classes Beyond the Bourgeoisie

The new NOI's coverage of "Black" businesses puts in doubt whether a separate economics can deliver enough benefits to enough African-Americans to hold mass interest in that line of nationalist development. Remnants of the classical theology of the Nation continue to focus deep doubt that whites and blacks could ever coexist constructively. Amid the impasses or collapse into which Black business ventures can peter out, Left voices from general America, relayed through the NOI's newspaper, define capitalism as inherently evil—but controllable. Two [non-black?] leftists carried by NOI media in 2000 portrayed big company capitalism as able to transform its financial resources into political power via campaign contributions. How could workers negotiate with big companies? When faced with union organizing campaigns, employers threaten to close their plant and to move elsewhere. Such threats—"a union won't do you any good if you don't have a job"—often defeat drives to organize unions. During the pre-1976 period of the leadership of Elijah Muhammad, some writers and organizers in the Black Muslim movement had come of unionist and even Communist backgrounds. The item in 2000 projected drives from the U.S. union movement to lobby government to issue laws making plant-closing threats illegal, and also to issue investment and trade policies to block employers from shifting to avoid unions.[36]

Unionism resonated to the living conditions of that section of recruits to the sects of Elijah and Farrakhan who were achieving upward mobility through factory jobs and blue-collar trades. The 2000 item could confirm employment by whites as hopeless and thereby spur the adherents to seek self-employment. But the two writers' own attitude was that the best chance of prosperity for most, and the real battle, was in secure employment by large companies through the construction of trade-unionism there—an organized wage-proletariat that modifies the terms of ongoing relationship with capitalism.

The new Nation of Islam's unification of religion, nationhood, political nationalism, parliamentary politics, private enterprise and economic decisions, and international relations was a holism that would merit the term "Islamist" if that means that Islam and Arabic motifs tint all sectors of thought, although not with even strength in this NOI. The Nation has constructed this unified or intersecting ideology by porously drawing materials from an immense range of Middle Eastern, Qur'anic, African-American, Euro-American, Jewish-American, Israeli, African, Marxist and Protestant Christian sources.

Those in or attached to the Nation of Islam who prefer the American Way of private enterprise as the road to reasonable incomes have still had to come to grips with the fragmentation and harsh conditions that is the lot of many African-Americans under Republican Party administrations. Farrakhan sometimes sounded as though he shares some assumptions of Republicans about society—can tell the poor to change those of their behaviors that can worsen their condition—but his paper also carried resistance to Republican administrations' programs that make things worse for the poor. Struggling families and grassroots and economic actions from across the nation were reported in 2002 to have assailed President Bush Jr's maneuvers to cut funding assistance to one-parent families under cover of diverting funds to encourage "married-couple families".

In a meeting in April 2002 at the University of Chicago during Bush Jr's presidency, Democratic Party members of Congress agreed to help the grassroots win input into the national debate about welfare "reform": the welfare system had developed a culture of disdain and amoral decisions, they charged [although that already had been developing under Clinton]. The Democrat on the government "efficiency sub-committee" tried in her turn to involve the grassroots against "wasted dollars on military equipment that we don't need," and tax breaks for the richest, that left too little for social spending. Congressional progressives, grassroots black women and the African-American Muslims' dislike of Bush's global war on Muslim terrorists were all coming together. The ethnic make-up of the meeting had affinities to the NOI sects' quest for an Islam-tinged community of color wider than African-Americans: black, Latino and Arab women who were past or present welfare recipients "gave gripping testimonials to the legislators on how the system they relied on to help pull them out of poverty and despair [harms] them beyond belief."

The impoverished ghetto women on whom *Final Call* was now focusing were still those who shared the Muslims' thrust to make themselves bourgeois and educated through hard work and enterprise. A briefly-incarcerated black woman was told by a caseworker that transportation assistance was only provided to drug addicts attending detoxification programs: the public aid office would not fund her travel to job-sites and education that might have got her and others off the rolls after a while. On the other hand, the ethos of some of these black women—they were bent on college degrees, not marriages for Bush subsidies that they blasted as "prostitution"—ran against the NOI's construction of middle-American families. And the item gave a nuanced account of the travails of an Arab woman immigrant whose husband became disabled and whose children often had to miss school to translate for her, because the government refused to supply a professional translator. Then her assistance was cut off without explanation.[37]

Overall, Farrakhan's new NOI was a bourgeois movement striving for upward mobility and wealth, although with some impulses to address the needs of the poor among whom its prototype first took form, so long before. It fueled the upward ascent of its members with an ideology of nationalism in which it claimed to be unifying the whole of the African-American Nation in America. To some extent, Farrakhan's NOI did achieve this nationalist aim it projected. The sect's paper did achieve a coverage of the problems of a range of African-American classes, interests, ideological schools, and rural as well as urban populations over the full extent of the USA. This process was more than just coverage or analysis—rather, Farrakhan's institutions and media *were* where all these categories of African-Americans met and got to know each other; it became the nucleus of the Black or African-American Nation, with hundreds of thousands of the readers and listeners getting drawn in. Farrakhan and his followers sometimes even get across to alienated black youth and even their mass culture and to the single mothers of the ghettos. Probably, though, they still harbored the old NOI view that these were pathetic groups that had to be improved, reclaimed, and recast into middle American moulds coated with thin Arabic.

Tentative Incorporation into the System

For all their ridicule and denunciations of it, Farrakhan's Muslims deeply respected the American system after which they were modeling some of their own modest projects—and out of which they, like other African-American groups, hoped they could one day get financial aid. With their stress on urgent practical tasks related to the social uplift of the black masses, most Farrakhanists might well ditch their ideology of millenarian judgement and pro forma withdrawal if the system offered some resources and guidance for a definitive assault on African-American poverty.

Given the war that America's Zion-emblemed Jewish micro-nationalists waged from 1983-2000 to marginalize, starve and destroy Farrakhan's sectlet, the American system has not often opened to it other than at city government level. It is revealing how meticulously and with what lightning speed the Nation of Islam responded to the rare overtures or openings from the white system. In an unprecedented move, Texas Governor Ann

Richards in later 1992 extended a formal invitation to Farrakhan's local mosque minister, Robert Muhammad, to come and put the Muslim program before her office. Alarmed by all the destruction from the recent Los Angeles riots, she and her colleagues were seeking more constructive forms of interaction between the African-American community and the white power structure.

Minister Robert Muhammad quickly submitted a detailed memorandum with recommendations for addressing racial conflict across the state of Texas. A future "Governor's Citizen Action Task Force" would "assist your [Governor Richard's] office through recommendations, advocacy, and implementation of policies"—a pattern that would make the NOI a junior partner of American government at state level. The urgent meticulous memorandum wanted to knit together the pro-Islamic section of the black bourgeoisie and the structures of American government. Further incorporating the NOI's bourgeois African-American constituency into the American state, the Task Force would make recommendations for openings on boards of regents, regulatory agencies, and judiciaries. Robert Muhammad also crafted his memorandum to secure the state's patronage for black private enterprise, in which Muslim sects were active: "economic development" would foster a grassroots organizations/state government "partnership"—yes, Muhammad used the term!—"dedicated to developing community-based self-help initiatives."

The Health Care proposals of Farrakhan's minister would have been denounced as socialist-like by Republican rightists: he called for a concentrated drive to eliminate infant mortality by promoting pre-natal care and making quality health care affordable to all. The NOI had highlighted itself to the blacks as the group that was ushering in an alternative African-American education system—mouthing contempt for the white system as finished, and even for the blacks who developed particularistic ebonics or Afrocentric courses within those schools. The education component of Minister Robert Muhammad's proposals, though, was "to assist the Governor with a statewide educational initiative".

According to Minister Robert Muhammad, his reason for highlighting the above five points was to "benefit all Texans by uplifting those at the bottom while not tearing down everyone else." As they become constructive, the Muslims are developing the capacity to see a situation simultaneously from within the minds of a group or groups in conflict, or who could come into conflict, with the African-Americans (here, poor or middle American whites in a situation of recession). Growing empathy could quickly mutate into a sort of Americanism or inclusive American nationality. It seemed as if the Farrakhanists were ready to throw their counter-racist ideology out the window if whites gave the resources the African-Americans so badly needed. Minister Robert Muhammad had stated that "our emphasis is on action, not studies or finger pointing—actions leading to solutions and not just another academic study".[38]

The Transformation of NOI Pan-Islamism

My coming book pivoting around Farrakhan will document the changes in his sect's relations with overseas Muslims following the Million Man March.

Overall, Farrakhan's post-1995 tours abroad had a cautious and exploratory texture: he could even have deliberately visited too many countries as a device to postpone any specific NOI response or any action. Such heavily Muslim states in West Africa as Mali, Nigeria, Gambia and Guinea reinforced influences from the Arabic language on his delegation, but from within African settings. Farrakhan and those traveling with him were acutely aware of how coup-ridden or divided were some of the African states they were traveling through, but he adopted a triumphalist stance of pan-African support for Mugabe's efforts to seize and redistribute lands farmed by whites in Zimbabwe. In reality, *Final Call* left its hundreds of thousands of African-American readers in no doubt of the anachronistic nature of the long-established nationalist African elites, some of which had ruled some sub-Saharan states since the 1960s, and of the determination of rising new classes drawn from the younger generation to elbow them aside and usher in private enterprise and pluralist civic societies.

It had become obvious by the 21st century that Farrakhan's world tours since 1995 had failed to achieve their announced goal of constructing new compound relationships with Third World peoples and states. The interaction had always remained narrow, a matter of his meetings with heads of states and a few speeches and press conferences: Farrakhan had failed to connect institutions in the Muslim world, such as economic or academic ones, into such institutions as African-Americans had built, or into others that his own sect could have tried to build to open new dimensions of relating. In the aftermath of the 1995 Million Man March, many African-Americans had grasped that Farrakhan's tours were opening up for African-Americans yet another historical opportunity as great as all the potential for their political mobilization that the Million Man March had opened up inside the U.S. itself. If Farrakhan's Nation of Islam yet again proved not up to the chances it itself had occasioned, that put some of the blame onto the wider non-Muslim U.S. black bourgeoisie for not having supplemented the NOI's meager resources. That bourgeoisie had grasped that important economic, commercial, political and cultural resources and relations might be opened up by the tours, and duly gave Farrakhan and his delegations some slap-up sendoffs. Yet the bourgeois academics, writers and politicians set up no specialized machinery to muster diversified, organized, institutionalized resources or guidance to help entrench such connections for the long-term. Probably what the potentialities required was that the wider bourgeoisie take over Farrakhan and his colleagues—which was also what had been required for a long-term political organizing of African-Americans after the MMM. Farrakhan has always carefully maintained the separateness of the NOI, but he might have accepted some resources and the constraints that had to come with them.

The way that Farrakhan structured his breakneck world tours was not the approach of a leader intent on carrying through the drive for the alternative affiliation that diverse Afro-America wanted with those Muslim and African entities which mattered. He could not concentrate on a few important countries and finalize a link-up with them. Instead he fragmented and squandered his limited time and attention, and that of his party, over such a number of countries that it was very hard to prepare in advance or follow up. Had he wanted it to turn out like that from the start?

In Russia, Farrakhan and his companions took a dislike to the virulently anti-Muslim Slavic authorities who harassed them and tried to shake them down for money at airports. He and his party were ecstatically received by Muslim minorities that the Russians hit or repressed. Ordinary Russians called those minorities "blacks", but now the NOI simply recognized them as, and termed them, white—the dawning of a Warith-like acceptance that Islam incorporates all races of humanity, with whites now included. In "Russia", Farrakhan sharply focused the explosive hatred between Russians and the Muslims of the Caucasus. In his new frame that Islam is for all races, though, he missed criteria of colors and races in Moscow that were close to old Euro-American and NOI concepts when he termed such attacked Muslims as the Chechens, "white". An Indian correspondent in the same era of the late 1990s found that Moscow's Russians had long casually called people from the Caucasus in their city "blacks", whom explosions of Chechen bombs in Moscow now made the Russian masses eager to "destroy to the very last one."[39]

Europe's Bosnia, inhabited mainly by Slavic Muslims, and Kosovo, the home of Albanian Muslims, were a watershed in the new NOI's transition from a racial Third Worldism to a pan-Islam that could see a variety of Muslim races and thus could voice solidarity with Muslims it now perceived as "whites". The new non-racial pan-Islamism also entailed seeing some U.S. involvement overseas as positive. Farrakhan's travels in Israel, Palestine and Jordan brought interaction with Israel's most violent Islamic revivalist enemies but he kept his sect's encounters with them and with 'Arafat and the Palestinian authority symbolic.

In the discourse of Elijah Muhammad, Albanians had been one way-out margin to which the pre-1975 NOI made its global "Asiatic" Black Nation so wide-embracing that all meaning to "blackness" could break down. Once, Elijah Muhammad was seeking to recruit a black American to work for his paper *Muhammad Speaks*. One candidate, though African-American, was married to an American woman of mixed Albanian and Irish ancestry who was glaringly white by any U.S. criteria. But Elijah trusted her as an "Asiatic" because she had some link of descent to the Albanians, of whom many are Muslims: he hired her husband.[40] It might be hard to describe those who converted to Islam in Albania under rule by Ottoman Turks as anything else than Indo-Europeans and white. Elijah probably had here a sense of Islam as an irreducible conditioning that once it is imparted generations before in one Muslim-led environment will recur even in another continent in the guidance of parents with only very diluted blood-links of descent to that faraway land.

In a 1999 article of Farrakhan's successor-NOI, Ahmed Rufai mostly dismissed military threats and arguments from Russia, Greece and the overall Orthodox world, plus some Jewish-American journalists, to make the U.S. and NATO end military actions to eject Slobodan Milosevic from Kosovo, whose Albanians he was expelling and killing. The critics warned of a possible confrontation with Soviet troops in the Balkans should the bombardment continue: ground troops would put American lives at risk in a "new Vietnam".

Such arguments might appeal to some of the African-Americans most hostile to the U.S. system, but *Final Call* assailed them as excuses for opposing NATO actions against Yugoslavia that might protect its Muslim population: the opposition masked anti-Muslim racism. Rufai queried where the same "antiwar" voices, particularly in the media, had been since December 1998 when U.S. and British forces began to bomb 'Iraq? "European lives and security are apparently more valuable than those of the Middle East." While Rufai was probably also targeting Jewish-American commentators and politicians (Serbia had fought the Nazis in WWII), he was becoming ready to share with the Balkan Muslims an enemy that might turn out to be the whole Orthodox Christian world, Greek and Slavic. "President Boris Yeltsin and the Russians committed the same criminal acts against Chechnya three years ago that the Serbs commit against Albanian Muslims today." The lives of [non-diabolical] American troops now had to be risked because Milosevic had spurned diplomatic efforts by UN Secretary-General Kofi Annan to end his expulsions of ethnic Albanians from Kosovo.[41]

Ethnic cleansing touched a sensitive nerve in African-Americans, who had known transportation across continents and being barred in America. *Final Call* was happy when the three groups, Muslims, Croats and Serbs, began to reintegrate in the small Bosnian town of Brcko as the expelled Muslims returned to their homes under international supervision.[42] For many in the NOI tradition, interest in warring religions and ethnic groups in the Balkans acquires a logic that points them to a multi-racial Islam and integration of conflictual groups.

Idris Michael Tobin (b. 1956) had passed through adolescence in Elijah's old NOI, was in charge of Stokely Carmichael's security, and then converted to Sunni Islam and attended immigrant-founded mosques after he suddenly realized that "Islam has to be for all people". He had gained military experience in the U.S. army. After America crushed Milosovich, he helped the Muslims of Kosovo clear the mines the murderous Serbs left behind them. He had been received with kindness and a brotherhood of Belief by Kosovo Muslims whom he perceived as white and who perceived him to be black. However, that extent of fusion with "non-colored" Muslims remains exceptional in African-American Muslim movements.

By the end of the 20th century, Farrakhan's NOI was moving to the same non-racial or multi-racial Islam for which Warith/Wallace and his adherents had opted in 1975. Maybe an innermost part of Elijah and his colleagues had always hoped for that and set it up. They and many secular Black Nationalists had usually defined who was "Black" or "of color" or "dark" in flexible ways determined by how hostile whites with power were, for instance, to light-skinned "Easterners" whom NOI ideology appended to the "Asiatic" Black Nation. Brown eyes alone had since 1930 sufficed to admit many Third World populations, and some spouses might not have needed even that.

4: AFTER SEPTEMBER 11, 2001

The attacks by fighters from the al-Qa'idah/Jihadi tradition of Muslim revivalism on U.S. financial and political centers on 11 September 2001 struck at the heart of America. Following this international violence, Farrakhan tried as never before to synthesize the African-American tradition, America, Islam and the Middle East, in part to secure some new role for himself and his NOI.

The terrorist attacks brought the followers of Warith ud-Din Mohammed into what he called "a dangerous time" in America. A white pupil threw stones at Warith's son. The women adherents had loved the modest hijabs of the Middle East as the means to cover their heads;[43] now Warith told them just to wear long modest American clothes so as to look somewhat like anyone else in the street lest "the Christians" [=black Christians?] attack them. To dampen any reflex in his congregations to stand by such Muslim states as 'Iraq, the Imam depicted those regimes as persecuting the scholars and educators of Islam there: America could be made everybody's homeland of refuge.[44]

Now Euro-American hatred forced all who had said they were Muslim in America to state what Islam would henceforth mean for them in a transformed country in which all parties would still have to go on living with each other in some fashion. The 9/11 strike, represented as long-overdue retaliation by its perpetrators, brought the final internationalization of Islam in America. Muslim African-Americans now had to define their beliefs and aims in relation to the Middle East: the eras of parochial cults had ended forever.

Farrakhan responded with his most coherent and statesmanlike communications ever, as to what was the NOI's Islam, what was America and what to be American, and what global pan-Muslim community meant. He again showed some post-millenarian sense that political power and institutions could be ameliorated through discussion and pressure, without God having to destroy the world.

General Non-Muslim African-American Reactions

In the aftermath of the September 11 attacks, not just Muslims alone, but a wide range of established Christian African-Americans strove to formulate responses to the new international crisis that would serve the black nation's interests in the USA.

Following the September 11 attacks, Sa'udi prince al-Walid Ibn Talal offered $10 million to assist those New Yorkers in need as a result. When Mayor Rudolph Giuliani spurned the check in a ploy to win Jewish votes in New York, Congresswoman Cynthia McKinney, an African-American with a pro-Arab record, requested Talal to write a similar check for charities servicing homeless black communities in the USA with poorer life-expectancies than babies born in Bangladesh. She implied that U.S. foreign policy towards the Palestinian issue might be changed by a growing number of establishment whites who were now becoming aware of the anger of many Arabs that the U.S. had earned through its unwavering support for violent Israel (Chairman of the House International Relations Committee, Henry Hyde, and former National Security Advisor, Zbigniew Brzezinski, on CNN). In the best multicultured African-American micro-nationalist vein, McKinney cited condemnations from Israeli peace organizations like B'Tselem and the Israeli Gush Shalom that Israel's occupation of the West Bank and Gaza Strip was the root cause of the violence and hatred, while pointing out that, in 2001, 80% of people in prison in the United States were people of color.[45]

McKinney and other pinkish quasi-nationalists like her were thus maneuvering in the wake of September 11 to blend the interests of overseas Arab states and African-Americans in part in order to win the latter resources that the USA's harsh radical-right regime denied. Would they be able to construct this international counter-community? At issue was whether the sometimes intellectually under-institutionalized Arab states would even see this possibility for an alliance with which to checkmate the Zionists in U.S. life.

Non-Muslim Blacks: Al Sharpton

In moderating his sect's interactions with Jewry and Israel, Farrakhan could not move too far from the concerns, demands and expectations of the non-Muslim majority of African-Americans. There had long been sympathy among diverse sectors of that people for President Yasir 'Arafat and militant Palestinian nationalism, which grew stronger after Ariel Sharon invaded the territories of the Palestinian Authority. Non-Muslim black politicians in New York in particular were interested to address the conflict in the Middle East that was now inextricably woven into the fabric of conflicting ethnic and religious identities within the city. Al Sharpton had been a communalist opponent of the USA's Jews and whites since the early 1980s, but by the 21st century he had also been drawn towards Palestinian nationalism almost as much as had the Nation of Islam (American limitations continued for both). *Final Call* had always publicized him. In a March 2002 interview to Farrakhan's paper, Sharpton voiced concern that the events of September 11 were providing the U.S. police and the Justice Department with an excuse to carry forward the racial profiling—albeit for the time mainly against immigrant Arabs and Muslims—that African-American organizations had agitated so long to end. Beneath his tough front as an incendiary demagogue, Sharpton was fiercely loyal to the liberal and parliamentarist institutions and procedures in the U.S. system that he wanted to make protect his sub-nation. The new anti-terrorist "Patriot Act" assailed the civil liberties not only of blacks but also those of Americans in general: "to say that they have the right to detain people without charging them [means that] they have just totally torn up parts of the Constitution".

But it was not just a parochial or internal matter that African-Americans and immigrant Arabs/Muslims were now coming together as both being "colored people" against whom the country could turn inimical at any time. Far beyond America, Sharpton's discussions in Israel with both the Palestinians and the Israeli leaderships had convinced him that U.S. policy was too "unbalanced"—one-sidedly pro-Israel—for it to solve the mass violence in the region. Yet his visit had left Sharpton judicious and sober in tone. He did want, himself, and want African-Americans in general, to prod all the parties towards constructive solutions of benefit to all. The involvement of Secretary of State Colin Powell, a black American holding high office, may have suggested to Sharpton that his people, and he himself, could have input into America's Mid-East policy. He did not believe that the Bush government had enough commitment to a Palestinian state to act as mediator for a serious solution, but he did strike, as Farrakhan too was now trying to do, a positive tone to some Israelis. Sharpton took Foreign Minister Shimon Peres at face value as ready to negotiate a Palestinian state with 'Arafat: he assumed that Peres [once father of the Israeli atomic bomb and architect of Israel's alliance with the Afrikaners] had merited his Nobel Peace Prize. For the parochial inter-ethnic passions, Sharpton rapped the Jewish-American lobby for inciting the harmful situation rather than "inspiring a level playing field that could lead to a peaceful resolution to this." He also rejected any coming attack by Bush Jr on Muslim states and North Korea.[46]

In 2002, Sharpton had, on Israel, the careful tone of someone who could help found a counter-lobby that would work for a synthesis of African, Muslim, Euro-American and local African-American interests in the USA. It was a shift from the 1980s in which he and other non-Muslim black nationalists, in unison with the new NOI, had sounded off against the US system and its agencies, local Jews and against Israel like incendiary anti-Anglos and anti-Semites—sometimes only micro-nationalist vaudeville. Now marginalized black leaders stood revealed in the new century as judiciously seeking normal rights, modest opportunities and input into an America that could be made rational—rather than advancing winner-takes-all scenarios. Sharpton was enraged at the suspension of the U.S. constitution here not just because it could limit his roles and rights and that of other African-Americans but also because he ideologically believed in that document. Sharpton knew the benefits of the rule of law, and the NOI covertly had also kept within the U.S. system's rules in an attempt to improve it for blacks.

The Impact of September 11 on Farrakhan and his Sect

From his academic ivory tower, Elijah's son, Dr Akbar Muhammad (2002), assessed that the violence could be producing "an historic change in the general attitude of Muslim African-Americans towards government" as Warith ud-Din Mohammed, and Farrakhan in a fashion and to an extent, voiced solidarity with their polity against the killers. Imam Warith and his sect had started the New World Patriotism Day parades in 1977, and he at this point, with his sect, now applied the Qur'an and the sayings of the Prophet Muhammad to define al-Qa'idah as crazy animals outside the circle of Islam. As well as their killing of innocent civilians, [neo-Republican?] Warith also assailed the terrorists' destruction of the World Trade Center qua property.[47]

Overall, the Euro-American backlash against the attacks and international Islam worked to deepen the pariah status of Farrakhan and the Nation of Islam in U.S. society. The NOI was always on the far margin of what the USA's governing elite (and also, for that matter, the Muslim states) would allow. Farrakhan and his colleagues remained acutely aware that when the federal building had been bombed in Oklahoma City in 1995, some in the U.S. authorities had initially blamed members of the Nation of Islam and immigrant Muslims for that act, which turned out to have been committed by the WASP Vietnam war hero, Timothy McVeigh. In 2001, the NOI's leaders feared, the U.S. government remained eager to link Minister Farrakhan himself to terrorism as a means to silence him for good. Although some of the Nation's disparities in beliefs from Third World Muslims were continuing in 2001, and Farrakhan might have preferred to quietly build his little sect scattered in America's cities, the new war's fusion of all the countries of the world, the U.S. white media's own conflation of all Muslims everywhere, some interests of Afro-Americans in general, and the white publics—all forced him to define the NOI against the backdrop of Islam qua the global mega-religion that now pervaded the minds of everyone in the U.S.

Farrakhan tried to endorse America as a potential polity—now not just to protect his sect—in a dualistic way that would leave a margin for his followers to distance themselves from the Bush regime if it struck at too wide a range of Muslim forces and populations overseas. America could remain strong for hundreds of years if President Bush would only change its unfair policies to deal with the Middle East crisis with an even hand. Then, all the hatred among Third World Muslims would begin to diminish and dissipate and the American people would not have to worry about bombs and bio-warfare anymore.

The more positive sectors of core America that Farrakhan was now endorsing were flawed in themselves at best. Hiistory forced Farrakhan to admit that some of the founding fathers of America were slave-owners, while arguing that they had still been God-fearing men who would not be pleased with the Bush administration's current deviation from their principles that had made the country great. Farrakhan warned his followers and African-Americans that President Bush "is not satisfied with a war on Afghanistan alone but is planning a wider war to include 'Iraq, Libya and Sudan"—only, such a wide onslaught would "end the United States as it is currently known because God's judgment will visit the country."

There was an emerging sense of a certain type of elites across sects and presumably races being integrated into new American community in Farrakhan's call "upon the religious community to [now] call America's leadership to repentance." The [Christian, Muslim and Jewish] clergy would be the "spiritual watchmen and women" who under fear of God's anger now had to "deliver the message" to a "spiritually blind and morally bankrupt" U.S. leadership.

Farrakhan took a step in the direction of the ethos of Islamist groups fighting to win political power for the religion in an outburst against President Bush Jr's insistence that Islam was a religion of peace. While in some ways a religion of peace, rebutted Farrakhan, Islam, like Christianity, also had a principle of a just war for certain contexts. "Fundamentalist Christians and Muslims only want their communities to return to the purity of the word of God, and Islam is a theocracy: it strives for government under the rules and laws of God". This was a line of emotion that could lead off towards the ideologies of insurgent Muslim movements in the Third World ready to kill *some* of white fellow-Americans of the NOI.

Farrakhan was angered that the U.S. system's discourse about overseas Muslims so clearly set a much lighter value on the lives and freedom of African-Americans than on those of whites. When the Ku Klux Klan burned down churches, it was not called terrorism. When repressed citizens rise to alter or replace governments, are they then terrorists or the liberators of their people from oppression? In legitimizing insurgency against at least some Third World regimes associated with America's power, this query by Farrakhan put him outside the American mainstream's discourses, and perhaps pointed in the direction of the Third World's fundamentalist Muslim bombers.[48] The UN, argued Farrakhan, had to define terrorism so governments could be judged by some consistent correct standard, as Syria's late President Hafiz al-Asad had told him in a 3-hour interview before his death. (The UN was an institution for the secular ameliorism and restoration of an international rule of law towards which Farrakhan now leaned).

Farrakhan was yet again swinging back and forth, willy-nilly, between (a) an America that he admired but which excluded and (b) Third World holy warriors who were even angrier than his still marginalized people. His past criticism of Jewish and white Americans' treatment of Black people, including the government's, "doesn't mean I hate America". He was just, under the USA's constitutional guarantee of free speech, trying to contribute to the constructive criticisms that could assure America an even greater future. The ascendant U.S. forces should not stifle something that could cause them to reason beyond their own biases, prejudices or views.

Farrakhan here was trying to affiliate himself, as might a statesman, to more open sections of "the American people"—including establishment whites—who as time passed were themselves raising more and more questions about Bush's war. He had even seen on television white former ambassadors and men and women of conscience who spoke against ill-considered actions in the Muslim world but were cut right off, because some did not want to publicize mild views that might help Americans to think more clearly.

No amount of political skill or political money had been able to unite America behind its newly-elected President until the tragedy had done so. It had brought "the many diverse elements of society together as brothers and sisters." Yet Farrakhan had positioned himself close to the few liberals and Democrats among Euro-Americans who as yet were coming out against Bush's militarism in the Muslim countries: if Afghanistan or 'Iraq became quagmires, he and the NOI could have a role with those whites in a broad popular anti-war front like that which ended America's Vietnam war.

The other impulse of Farrakhan hinted that the September 11 suicide squads were the sword of God: God had said in the Qur'an "I give life, and am the ultimate cause of death" ["nuhyi wa numit" Q 15:23; 50:43]. But this plane of Farrakhan's responses focused not only or primarily on world geopolitics but on a position of Farrakhan and the Nation of Islam within America as the culmination of Islam's history. It was by Allah's permission that America has become the undisputed ruler of the world, having the power to destroy other nations and people by the tens of thousands and millions. To correct the spiritual lapses and moral decline of such nations, Allah (God) raises a messenger [=Farrakhan] from among the poor and the abject to guide and to warn the great and the powerful. Allah knows that the powerful will not heed a warning coming from their ex-slave or from the abject, so the Quran teaches that Allah (God) then seizes that nation with distress and affliction, that it might humble itself. Thus, Allah "used" the September 11 tragedy to bring a great nation to Himself .

Farrakhan was of two minds about the hijackers. In one impulse, they had "lost their humanity and had become like wild beasts with only one thought in mind"—to destroy the USA, with which Farrakhan for an instant felt as one: "we stand with President Bush, the government and the people of the United States, in their desire to hunt down those responsible for this heinous crime against humanity." His other impulse had been started off by the growth of the atomized slivers of Arabic in the NOI's old faith, and fueled over decades by his sect's accumulation of data about the struggles of Third World Muslim peoples, and social contact with individuals from them. In this second pan-Muslim facet of his being, he saw the hijacker-bombers less as monsters evidencing chaos, and more as stemming from the tragedy of a grievously wounded people. The Palestinians, as an instance, since 1948 have lived in refugee camps and are scattered throughout the world, finding no joy in living. It was lack of the joy of justice that was causing children to strap themselves with bombs. They care nothing for their lives, and they care nothing for the lives of others. They want others to feel the pain of what they live with every day. Thus, a few Palestinians danced in the streets at September 11.

Farrakhan had the same tense fascination for American capitalism's material construction as had Elijah before him. The perpetrators of the "crime" had turned aircraft that symbolized America's technological brilliance and mastery of the air into missiles with which they "destroyed a national symbol of this nation's financial strength and architectural genius." But Farrakhan parted from President Bush's explications that "they hate us because we're the beacon light of freedom" and from envy at the wealth the land of opportunity offered. He felt that he had to address the issue of competition between religions, and the claim that Muslims would use force to effect conversion. "Pastors and preachers and Reverend Franklin Graham said that they hate us because we're Christians and they want us all to be Muslims." Whether

Islam and Christianity had to exclude each other was a sensitive issue in relation to Farrakhan's drive as a black nationalist leader to lead all African-Americans. It required that Farrakhan address Euro-America as the representative of all Muslims in the world, not of his own sect only—which in turn gave him more political standing in his country. "On behalf of Muslims I must say that no Muslim hates a Christian because he's a Christian and believes in Jesus Christ... There are 1,250,000,000 (one billion two hundred and fifty million) Muslims, and every one of us believe in Jesus" who was mentioned in the Qur'an so many times as the son of Mary, as the Messiah. How could the perpetrators have killed "us because we're Christians" when they had also killed Muslims, Black and White, Asian and Hispanic, Jews and Christians, Agnostics, Hindus and Buddhists in the WTC "crime against humanity"? Because the escalating violence in the Middle East could trigger Armageddon, the world had to impose the peace of justice in that area—through the "religious scientists" of Judaism, Christianity and Islam, given that politicians like Bush, Jr. could not rise to that duty.

Farrakhan's response to the crisis toyed with crafting an alliance with the USA's immigrant Muslims. America as a beacon light of freedom has called many nationalities, many races, many ethnic groups to its shores. Among these are Arabs and Asians, many of whom are Muslims, who have come to this country not to destroy it, but to apply its freedom and economic wealth to make a better life for themselves and their children. They build their mosques and schools so that they can keep in touch with their religion and their culture, not to destroy America's culture and her way of life. Many of these immigrant Muslims served America in hospitals, in colleges, in universities and in research laboratories, aiding all aspects of American technology and scientific progress. They love the countries of their birth, but they greatly love their adopted country, the United States of America. The American people should not harass and beat these good citizens and destroy their mosques simply because of the evil done by others who may profess the religion of Islam: "this would only make you like the perpetrators of this crime, who attack the innocent because of their anger and their hatred."

NOI members, born in America, did not fear losing their green cards, and now would defend such migrants against injustice. "Those [immigrant Muslims] who have rejected us as non-Muslims, look at us again. We are Muslims and we love you". While Farrakhan here saw immigrant Muslims as vulnerable in the short term, he also was as acutely aware as ever of the power and resources they were building as professionals, and he wanted to connect the NOI and African-Americans over the long term to all that intelligence, resources and potential power. [In the short term, indigenous Muslims could fall victim together with the immigrants if the "war between civilizations" projected by Samuel Huntington came to pass. The agencies of American governments had already tried for decades to discredit and destroy the NOI].

As a Muslim, Farrakhan called for prayer lest "this war may take American soldiers into Muslim countries and cause the death of many, many innocent Muslims". He warned that new laws to combat terrorism could turn out to repeat the governmental crimes of 1941 when Japanese Americans were herded into concentration camps. The movie, *The Siege*, had already prefigured a similar fate for the USA's "terroristic" Muslims, and had evidently chilled Farrakhan.[49]

The 1 December 2001 letter of Farrakhan to Bush, Jr. on the one hand tried to communicate to the President on the basis of the unitary Americanist nationalism that Farrakhan and his sector of U.S. protest Islam was now starting to feel [and which some in Elijah's sect indeed already had harbored]. He wrote of his "concern" for the life of Bush and "our country". He pointed out that he had every title to use the joint possessive pronoun, "because the blood of my ancestors soaks this soil and their blood has been shed on every foreign battlefield for the preservation of this nation".

America's might was becoming so complete over the whole globe that it was hard for Farrakhan not to see it as some will of Allah. Farrakhan saw America's might as a test imposed upon it by God. "If we [*sic*] act well, He will not replace our rule; however, if we allow the power, wealth, and wisdom that we possess over Allah's (God's) servants and creation to blind us... then, He acts through the forces of nature and through peoples to overturn our rule". He warned Bush that in order for America to win from Allah the perpetuity He had not granted former international nations and empires, "you must rule according to the Will and the Way of Allah (God)". Reiterating a promise to humans in the Qur'an, Farrakhan suggested that America under Bush and the no-longer doomed or devilish whites could, if ruled in a manner that reflected the will of God, become "the Viceregent of Allah (God)—the person or nation that rules the earth [world] in the place of God."

But Bush after September 11 was pursuing for votes a drive to destroy forces of terror overseas that could increase it, Farrakhan warned. His letter fused the victimization of African-American youth in the War on Drugs with President Reagan's drives to end al-Qadhafi, and to void the Panama Canal treaty that had been signed by President Jimmy Carter to return the Canal to the Panamanians by the year 2000. America overthrew President Manuel Noriega, Farrakhan explicated, not over drugs but to place a government of America's choosing in Panama to effectively nullify the treaty returning the Panama Canal. Thus, Farrakhan at the close of 2001 was reprising the old pre-1975 Nation of Islam's sense of a global Black Nation with Arab and Latin American components. His placing of the actions of American administrations within a justice framework was in accord with global Muslim populations, but also with the stances of political progressives or leftists in the Western countries, which favored African-American radicals to form good relations with those whites.

America's foreign policy did not make Farrakhan feel at home in his own country as a Muslim: every President since the Nixon/Ford administration had taken some military action against a Muslim nation. Both President Jimmy Carter and President Reagan felt that the overthrow of the Shah Mohammed Reza Pahlavi, and his replacement with the Islamist regime of Ayatollah Khomeini, was a threat to America's vital interests. Official America's hostility rallied Muslim contrarian Farrakhan to the self-titled "Islamic revolution in Iran": Imam Khomeini had wanted "the Iranian people to return to the purity of the faith of Islam". Where 'Iraq touched Iran's interests, Farrakhan now sounded critical of Saddam Husayn: it was with America's approval that the Sa'udi government and the rulers of the United Arab Emirates bankrolled Saddam into a strong military power to use against the rise of the "fundamentalist" regime in Iran. [Against Farrakhan's assumption of an "Islamic Revolution" in Iran, the regime of the mullahs was to fail to much change such aspects of culture as the de-Arabized vocabulary of modernist print-Farsi, or the West-derived assumptions about relationships and society of elite urban youth].

But Farrakhan's attitude to the Saddam regime was the reverse when the context was the interactions between 'Iraq and America, only. Farrakhan rapped Bush Senior's "problem with Saddam Husayn and 'Iraq" in which he involved young black men (the 1991 Gulf War): he warned President Bush, Jr. not to go ahead to finish the overthrow of Saddam Husayn that his predecessors had been unable to complete. If Bush Jr made Afghanistan only a preliminary to the much wider war that was already being planned, he advised, that would unite the Muslim world in a Holy War (Jihad) against America and Great Britain, which the rise of fragmenting nationalisms had long made impossible. Bush would place the more moderate Islamic pro-American Middle Eastern regimes [=certainly Sa'udi Arabia and the Gulf statelets, and perhaps Mubarak's Egypt] at risk of being overthrown by growing Islamist forces within their countries if they reluctantly opted to side with America. "The coalition that you are gathering will fall away from you and you will have to pursue this war alone". It was advice which was to be proved prescient by 2005 as the 'Iraqi resistance gathered strength.

Farrakhan wanted Bush to seriously follow through on his statement that the Palestinians should have an independent, sovereign state. That would make terror in the Middle East subside: America's settling of the 53 year-old problem with justice would justify America's position as the Viceregent of Allah (God). It would avoid the clash of civilizations some wanted: the Muslim World has much to learn from the West and the West has much to learn from the religion of Islam through careful dialogue. America would then preside over a peaceful world.[50]

Read together, the range of Farrakhan's motifs in the wake of the annihilation of the twin towers showed yet again that he still could not resolve the contradictions in the NOI's background and makeup as a protest-outlet of an oppressed people, with the U.S. government's and policies abroad, to break through to a new symbiosis. Yet the wide Anglo- and Jewish-American hatred against Muslims and Arabs following September 11 had made it very unlikely that he could have succeeded.

Movement towards a Median Position between Arabs and Jews

The mixed signals that Farrakhan had been sending out in the late 1990s about Jewish fellow-Americans and Israel had been losing him support among angry young blacks. In 2002, he tried to soften the print-war that his bourgeois followers had waged against Jewish-Americans in his name on their own account. He pointed out that his followers had never conducted violence or commercial boycotts against U.S. Jews and misleadingly stressed that African-American researchers linked to his sect had not, in their studies of the slave-trade, tried to document a predominant Jewish role: "the involvement of Europeans, Arabs and Africans was also noted". Farrakhan here was certainly radically moderating his and his followers' past tone of ethnic denunciation of Jews in America.

During the 1980s and 1990s, both Farrakhan and his deputy-cum-rival, Khallid Muhammad, dubbed the Ashkenazi Jews with whom they were crafting ethnic conflict as Indo-Europeans, that is, convert "Johnny-come-lately Jews". Israel had never been in Egyptian bondage for 400 years: it was African-Americans who would exodus from white slavery.[51] By the 21st century, Farrakhan was presenting himself to Jews with links to Israel as accepting the Jews and their exodus as a factual episode in a single tradition of "the children of Abraham, Jews and Muslims [and Christians]" who had to reconcile in the USA through dialogue. (The motif of a broad Abrahamic religious tradition had been advanced by non-radical immigrant Muslim professionals to integrate Jews, Christians and Muslims in one pious American community when the male professionals could meet at the "dialogue" seminars, and at the fraternal and theosophical temples). In 2002 in Jamaica, Farrakhan called for "an alliance for progress" of Islam, Christianity and Judaism to "reform and transform human life all over the planet".

During his visit to Jewish centers in Jamaica, Farrakhan again referred to the possibility that through his father, he might have partial descent from Sephardic Jews who, because of persecution in Catholic Spain and Portugal, moved to the Caribbean. Primarily, Farrakhan set up the visit in order to open up more constructive interaction between the Nation of Islam and American Jewry and Israel. The former synagogue president who welcomed him was honorary Consul-General for Israel in Jamaica and must have cleared admitting the Nation of Islam leader with the Israeli government. During the dialogue, Farrakhan said that God had allowed the modern state of Israel to come into existence in 1947-1949. Now, Jews and Arabs should reconcile their differences about its existence. Farrakhan was aware at the synagogue of the capacity diaspora Jewish organizations had shown to lobby many Western governments to harm his movement: for example, British Jewry had made the government of Britain bar him from the country.[52]

But this remote small outpost of world Jewry was not Jewish America and its feral institutions. And the ongoing conflicts of non-Muslim black micro-nationalists with Israel, U.S. Jews and the American system still limited the adjustments that Farrakhan could make to the NOI's discourse-tradition.

Farrakhan's press conference at Mosque Maryam in Chicago on 2 April 2002 marked a shift away from the Arab nationalist baggage that all the NOIs had been carrying since the later 1950s, towards a median position between the Arabs/Muslims, Israel and the US system. Nonetheless, he still voiced sharp empathy for the Palestinians in places, and for the violence immigrant Muslims now faced following September 11.

How far did Farrakhan now accept Israel and its right to exist? The nearest point was where he rallied to Yasir 'Arafat and negotiations rather than to the suicide bombers of the Hamas and the Islamic Jihad, towards whom Farrakhan could still voice the odd surge of empathy in his new period. Prime Minister Ariel Sharon, President Bush and the American mass media had branded Yasir 'Arafat as the principle source of the so-called terror—minimizing him as a serious partner in the peace process. It was unjust and hypocritical of Bush Jr and Sharon to demand of Yasir 'Arafat what he cannot produce, retorted Farrakhan. To join the (UN) Security Council in demanding that the Israeli military forces leave the West Bank, while at the same time winking its eye at what the Israeli military was doing there, showed the world the incoherence and hypocrisy of America's Mid-East policy. The mad course that Sharon was on, backed by the U.S. government, had to be stopped and reversed: "if not, all of us are going to suffer one way or another".

Farrakhan was presenting himself at one level as a patriot who did not want to see one more American life lost foolishly. His concern here for the lives of Americans in general, not just of Muslims, prodded him to oppose the government of his country. Still, he "offered himself to the government [as well as] the American people" as an auxiliary who might assist in facilitating a wiser peace process directed by the U.S. "I have met with the leaders of Hamas and Hizbullah, with Chairman 'Arafat [and] practically all of the leaders of the Muslim world: I can be of help" for the negotiation of a settlement. Farrakhan's discourse here was a fine balance of his wish to affiliate to the U.S. system, and win respect within it, and his anger at its treatment of blacks and Third World Muslims that led him almost to state that the U.S. had had it coming to it from the Usamah Bin Ladin it had once "formed and fashioned" in the first place [in Afghanistan].

Farrakhan presented the co-existence of an Israeli and a Palestinian state as the constructive solution and in a way justified from two rights. In intervening as one of the broker third parties, Farrakhan would be actualizing the changed frame of mind of the overwhelming majority of the Arab states. When the state of Israel was set up under UN auspices in 1947-1948, that had not been accepted by the Arab states which accordingly fought wars with the Jewish state. After each war more and more land was taken from the Palestinians. In their anger at stolen land, the perception "the Arab world" shared, the Palestinians—both Muslim and Christian—have fought the presence of Israelis, only to lose more and more land to a growing Israeli population. This has caused the displacement of over five million Palestinians. Therefore, the Palestinians and many throughout the Arab and the Muslim world see no Zionist as innocent—not the soldiers who occupy their land, nor the settlers who carry machine guns, nor the Israelis who live on stolen land. Hence their intifadah. But things are now changing at the government level. Meeting in Beirut [in 27-8 March 2002], the states of the Arab League offered the guarantee that Israel seeks if they traded land for peace [the "Abdullah peace plan"]. At that meeting in Beirut, even the most hardened against Israel—'Iraq, Libya, Iran [actually a non-Arab non-participant]—said that if the Palestinians agreed, they would go along with it. And if the whole Arab world went along with it, it would be very difficult for Hamas in that climate to continue violence.

That Farrakhan did have some of the qualifications for the role of one honest broker or go-between to help settle the Arab-Israeli conflict was undeniable. He was right that he knew personally a wider range of Arab and Muslim leaders than did Bush. After September 11, Farrakhan was opting for 'Arafat and mutual recognition in two states. He portrayed 'Arafat as having sought a settlement that, before the assassination of Israeli Prime Minister Yitzhak Rabin, had had good chances to succeed. But the peace process had been almost destroyed by Prime Ministers Benjamin Netanyahu and Ariel Sharon. Bush Jr and Sharon were wrong to insist that 'Arafat step down: his people had elected him and he had only been ineffective because he had been made so by those who did not want the peace process to proceed.

Farrakhan's statements at the press conference showed his considerable acculturation to Jews—and his increased acceptance of them—and his growth from a protest leader to a statesman concerned not to waste his people's precious energy against elements who would have long-term power to harm their progress. He made use of a blend of the presence of the Bible in the African-American psyche, of his interaction since childhood with Jewish-Americans, and of data about Jews that he had picked up from pan-Muslim arguments carried in the house newspapers of the NOI tradition since the 1950s. Farrakhan reviewed with empathy the religion-inculcated desire of many Jews around the world to return to the land God promised them: "the Jewish people" [= a Zionist tenet] who had been persecuted for 2,000 years in the various countries of the globe in which it was scattered, had never ceased to want a Jewish homeland. In a sharpened perception of the diversity of Jews, Farrakhan also reviewed the sense of a minority but "growing" section of Orthodox Jewry that the modern state of Israel was not justified by the Torah because it had not followed upon the appearance of the Messiah and the Jews' return to obedience to the laws, statutes and commandments of God that would justify setting up a Jewish state.

In the greater ameliorist practicality he now voiced, Farrakhan was drawing somewhat back from some decades-old radical Arab nationalist themes in the Arab-American minority that he was courting. Veteran in-house Palestinian journalist 'Ali Baghdadi asked him about the plan of Mu'ammar al-Qadhafi to create a single joint Palestinian-Jewish state as the solution. The Jews once had enjoyed freedom and lack of discrimination among Muslims: could that happen again? The joint state made up of Arabs and Jews, with one capital, Jerusalem, would be accepted by every country in the Arab world: probably there would never be war again, Baghdadi projected. In response, Farrakhan raised the practicalities: the rivers of blood and the present level of the hatred between Arabs and Jews rule out their being under the same flag "at the present time, any more than you could make a state out of Germans and Jews after the Holocaust". No doubt Farrakhan kept open a theoretical possibility that in some far-distant future, some secular bi-national democratic state of Palestine could be formed. Farrakhan's new implication that the Palestinians had somehow lost favor with God who then gave Palestine to the Jews caused his old friend Baghdadi to leave the NOI. Farrakhan's 2002 response to Baghdadi and his declaration of readiness to talk even to Prime Minister Ariel Sharon went somewhat beyond giving de facto recognition to a polity of Israel within its pre-1967 "green-line" borders, for a long time to come. A more broad-gauge process of "purifying us of the things that have caused us to hate each other and be destructive of each other" had begun and was demanded by the Qur'an, the Torah, the Bible [and the MMM?], all in tandem.[53]

For all the heartfelt solidarity for overseas Muslims facing onslaughts from a U.S. system whose cold side African-Americans knew all too well, Farrakhan's post-2001 international diplomacy again showed how construction of an international Islamic community by U.S. blacks can offer a roundabout route to get them into the U.S. system. The route taken is from (a) a general African-American nation defined against Jews and Anglos as elections near (e.g. 1983-1984) to (b) the black Islamic micro-nation that Farrakhan always discretely develops within the African-American nation to (c) developing contacts, resources and influence in Arab or Middle Eastern states more than with sub-Saharan Africa to (d) offering the U.S. system the use of that influence in its enlightened self-interest, and in the interest of all Americans, after it modifies its policies.

Since 2002, the NOI has almost ceased its former ethnic broadsides against American Jews, but *Final Call* has continued to publish a rivulet of items on Israel and the Palestinians. Some items are judiciously chosen from non-Muslim newsagencies concerned with the Third World countries. One mid-2003 item detailed the great difficulties Palestinians faced to earn menial livelihoods and start up modern factories and supermarkets as a result of the roadblocks with which Israel had ravaged the Palestinian economy since the beginning of the second intifadah in 2000. The items, though, have shown the movement of some Muslim governments towards recognizing Israel, meticulously tracing the connections of that to their relations with America, and in Pakistan's case, also, with an India being armed by an Israel that Pakistan has to placate.[54] Coverage by *Final Call* of Sharon's 2005 withdrawal from Gaza drew neutral data on the Israeli and Palestinian politics of it all from the same non-Muslim American newsagency.[55] *Final Call*'s Washington correspondent, Askia Muhammad, a key quasi-intellectual of the sect, covered in a neutral, careful way the May 2005 visit by Palestinian Authority President Mahmud 'Abbas to the White House. President Bush was paying $50 million to improve housing directly to the Palestinian Authority for the first time. The Palestinian negotiators hoped that Bush, Jr. had dropped his acceptance that Israel had title to keep the areas of the settlements that it had established in the West Bank: he now had "pledged" that final status issues like Jerusalem, refugees, settlements, borders and waters had to be agreed through final negotiations. President Bush, Jr. had recommitted himself to a Palestinian state living side by side with Israel. But Israeli leaders remained convinced that President Bush was still opposed to terror, within which they tried to lump Hamas, Islamic Jihad and probably the P.A. itself. Bush's call for a halt to the expansion of Jewish settlements was just a sop by him to 'Abbas, they hoped.[56]

The Arab components and connection in the NOI's history and culture assure that it will still feel with the Palestinians if and when they are oppressed in the 21st century. The now ameliorist rather than millenarian sect, though, would accept a state of Israel that has concluded a fair permanent peace settlement with that Arab people.

Abdul Akbar Muhammad: Pan-Islam

From the most Africanist margin of Farrakhan's Nation, its Ghana-resident missionary, Abdul Akbar Muhammad—by the 21st century a truly international accomplished writer as well as organizer—tried to weave pan-Islamic solidarity with the Palestinians into his by now complete loyalty to the Mother Continent.[57] In a punchy and tightly-argued 2002 article, he equated past struggles of "we Africans" in South Africa and across the continent with that of the Palestinians, which likewise was "a fight for land" against settlers and European occupation. Abdul Akbar urged the African states to refuse to do business with Israel, in the same way that Africans and the African-Americans abroad and "the [whole] civilized world" had refused business or diplomatic relations with apartheid South Africa. Abdul Akbar reminded the African governments, and in particular South Africa's president, Thabo Mbeki, that the Palestinians had "strongly supported our struggle to free our lands and people" [= PLO training for the fighters of the African National Congress which Nelson Mandela had refused to disown under American pressure in the 1980s and 1990s]. Akbar reminded Africa's leaders that "the Palestinians were granted honorary membership of the OAU", attending all its events and meetings [in the 1970s and 1980s].

This article was a distinguished late instance of how (a) classical NOI blurring of Africans into Arabs and non-African Muslims, when combined with (b) current events that define Palestinians/Arabs as sharing non-sovereign desperation with Africans/Black Americans, can then generate (c) tight pan-Muslim solidarity. But Abdul Akbar's specific emotions as a Muslim, and as a Muslim of a special kind from a U.S. ethnic group that had long had parochial ethnic conflicts with some local Jews that the Africans in their continent had never known, might not resonate to the African leaders he was trying to address. Would the younger more pragmatic leaders of the new African Union go along with the radical measures against Israel that he was now urging upon them—measures which in effect would have made the African states become the cutting edge or vanguard of anti-Israel action in the world in place of the lukewarm Arab states, at least for the time?

True, Abdul Akbar's appeal could draw on pent-up anti-Americanism throughout a world in which the USA had become supreme. He thought it was U.S. pressure that had made the African nations restore diplomatic ties with Israel after the Sadat-Begin accords. As well as diplomatic protests to the U.S. state for its extreme bias to Israel, Abdul Akbar wanted the African nations representing nearly 800 million people to not just close all Israeli embassies on the continent but pressure the summit of Arab states for an OPEC oil boycott for 30 days.[58]

But could the memory of bygone parallel victimhoods of Africans and Arabs still in 2002 extract such political action from the changing African leaderships against Israel? No African state by 2002 faced a growing threat to both lands and sovereignty at once comparable to that which the Palestinians of the West Bank and Gaza still had to meet. Abdul Akbar Muhammad was equally aware that American pressure and possible loss of American and Israeli economic aid could make African leaders less likely to "stand firm against Prime Minister Ariel Sharon's campaign of terror" in the West Bank. Abdul Akbar did not consider that another oil boycott, which would reduce oil supplies and raise the prices, was almost the last thing that many sub-Saharan states would want for their precarious economies.

While Abdul Akbar Muhammad knew enough of the self-seeking aspects of some leaders and elites in both the African and Arab worlds, yet a part of him now wanted to see not just the Arab oil producers but even the OPEC as much more coherent and political than they really were. The function of these two groups was to maximize the oil revenues of the member governments: the most oil-rich Arab states were slow to thin oil supplies to America to make it really mediate, as he sensed. The full OPEC was much more diverse: would half-Muslim Nigeria or even Venezuela care enough for the Palestinians to interrupt oil exports and income? The desire for a greater return on their non-renewable resource had brought the oil-producing states together in their organizations much more than any collective emotions of community between the populations those elites ruled. Abdul Akbar Muhammad's distinguished thrust for pan-Muslim community was still not critical enough: he did not as yet grasp properly that more than one oil-rich Arab or Muslim or African government did not feel as much sympathy as he towards those Arabs who had no oil wells of their own.

The U.S. Invasion of 'Iraq

Farrakhan and his colleagues felt in shared community with a wounded, furious America after September 11, indeed even with its Jews. But then, Bush's "responding" imperial violence in 'Iraq brought the NOI tradition's inbuilt pan-Islamic sympathy for Middle Easterners back into play. *Final Call* reviewed the technology of cluster bombs from Vietnam onwards, and U.S. use of them throughout 'Iraq during its final campaign to remove Saddam. The item carried a stark photograph of a 27-year-old 'Iraqi garage mechanic in hospital who had lost both his eyes, his left hand and several toes after picking up an unexploded U.S. cluster bomb.[59] The NOI media early saw through the prediction by President Bush Jr on May 1, 2003 that the combat phase in the war against the Muslim nation of 'Iraq had ended, and its reconstruction now begun. Ongoing U.S. casualities, *Final Call* cited, refuted Defense Secretary Rumsfeld's sedative that only straggling bands of 10 or 15 'Iraqis were still carrying on any resistance. But the article also showed interrogation by a Congressional committee forcing Paul Wolfowitz to admit the long-term resistance that the USA faced in 'Iraq (and Afghanistan),[60] which would nourish the hopeful dualism among pro-Arab U.S. blacks that America's institutions might one day work. This item by an African-American Muslim did not mention the Jewishness of Wolfowitz and other neo-con hawks—whose Zionism, and support for Israel's needs, were, though, exaggerated as a factor in America's invasion of 'Iraq by a Sa'udi professor of Islamic studies and by an Arab Gulf editor, cited elsewhere by Farrakhan's paper.[61]

Since 1930, all NOIs had traced the "tricknowledgies" with which white Americans with power are seen to confuse and control their victims. In mid-2003, *Final Call* excerpted British pro-Arab journalist, Robert Fisk, and England-resident Australian, John Pilger, who contended that the monopolies-controlled [Anglo countries'] press had covered up civilian casualties killed by the U.S. in Afghanistan and 'Iraq, and also downplayed or ignored the cancers and genetic deformations caused in 'Iraq by the depleted uranium that the U.S. used for projectiles in its 1991 Gulf War. Yet Pilger hoped that the huge anti-war movement and that "[counter-]superpower of public opinion" could stop the Anglo-U.S. system from within. Here, once more, 'Iraq highlighted how the drive of African-American Muslims to document deception by their enemy around the globe opens them to left Anglos who have critical edge, and might one day usher them into a community not just with Anglo-America but with all lands of native English speech.[62] In the 21st century, the second Nation of Islam is far from the era in which all Anglos were devils and could never be anything else.

A mid-2003 editorial in *Final Call* showed the vise between Americanism and pan-Islam pressing most African-American Muslims. The piece, titled "Empire status a trial for the U.S.", did reiterate Farrakhan's recent alternation of possibilities: Allah had raised America to be the greatest power on earth either to destroy her as had been done to ancient pagan tyrannies. Or, if she turned from her wicked ways, Allah might make her "the basis for the Kingdom of Heaven on earth." But, after the devastation of 'Iraq, the NOI no longer held much hope that the U.S. would take that second, constructive, road. As America acted unilaterally throughout the earth, NOI media projected, she sensed fear in the other nations, which makes aggressors even more violent, as it had ancient Babylon, Egypt, and Rome before Allah destroyed them. The imperial tone of Defense Secretary Donald Rumsfeld when he vowed that the U.S. would not allow an Iran-type government by Shi'ite clerics to come to power in 'Iraq, angered *Final Call*. The paper, which had previously often equated Saddam Husayn and his heavily Sunni group with 'Iraqi society and its interests, now distinguished the Shi'ites and other groups in 'Iraq more, as discrete actors. Its orientation to religion did not let Farrakhan's sect consider that many 'Iraqi Shi'ites might have become too secularized to welcome any theocracy. And in places the religious article, full of references to the Old Testament and the Qur'an about past tyrannies God annihilated, had returned to the ethos of Elijah to 1975 and of Farrakhan and Abdul Wali Muhammad in the 1980s that only destruction by God could correct America—not taking part in the U.S. political system.[63]

Such millenarism might get African-Americans away from serious political opposition to the U.S. system's "war without end"—except that the paper's highly detailed and acute coverage of the wars, of the functionings of the U.S. system in them, and of the mounting opposition both inside the American Congress and outside among the American public, could equip blacks to join in anti-war movements that seek to correct the system from its margins. *Final Call*'s coverage of U.S. abuses against Muslims in 'Iraq and Guantanamo Bay had come far from the old NOI's pre-1975 dichotomizations of U.S. white devils against good Third World Muslims and blacks. In 2005, *Final Call* carried articles, sometimes from leftist or liberal Euro-Americans, that abundantly detailed how split was mainstream America, including the Republican Party and even Bush, Jr.'s administration, over the USA's detention camps at Guantanamo. On one hand, the Congressional hearings of mid-2005 were told that "enemy combatants" detained there were not entitled to any due process. But some Republican senators whom *Final Call* quoted wanted the prison camp closed because all the publicity that there might be torture fueled opposition to America around the world. As well as that pragmatism, Republican senator Chuck Hagel may himself have harbored the image Guantanamo deepened around the globe that America had become "an empire that pushes people around: we don't live up to our commitments to multilateral institutions."

Such people of conscience in the U.S. political system and military that *Final Call* depicted were not devils unable to change. The Republican senator, John McCain, once a prisoner of the Communist nationalists in Vietnam, had called on Bush's government either to try the Muslim detainees on specific charges or release them. Farrakhan was shouting the same theme of trial or release. Thus, if unease grew in the establishment it could open points of entry for Farrakhan and the NOI to enter mainstream American politics as a link to the Muslim world.[64] When in a mid-2005 press conference, he called for the detainees to be tried or released, and reports of desecrations of the Qur'an at Guantanamo Bay to be investigated, Farrakhan was putting himself forward as a representative in America of the international "Muslim Ummah" (supra-nation). "We are mobilizing Arab and Muslim countries," but also a multi-faith delegation of Americans to go to Guantanamo that would have in it Black, Latino and White members: Farrakhan's pan-Muslim activism would thus place him at the fore of an African-American people that shades into a general American nation, and for the ameliorist aim of helping "healing" between the U.S. state and the world's Muslims.[65]

The huge cost of America's support for Sharon's Israel and the occupation of 'Iraq could return mainstream-Christian, as well as Muslim, blacks to official neglect of their race's needs at home. Farrakhan's NOI relayed demands from the mainstream NAACP, the Urban League and the Black Congressional Caucus that Bush spend as much on public education, housing and health care for poor African-Americans as for rebuilding 'Iraq. Beyond parochial perspectives, educator Julia Hare, an ally of Farrakhan, charged that "they" had not devastated and conquered 'Iraq to free or rebuild it but to plunder from its lucrative oil wells. There is some fellow-feeling for faraway Arabs, here, beyond calculations of the collective ethnic interest of U.S. blacks, since the American system's drive to keep cheap oil flowing from the Muslim world would benefit ordinary black car-drivers.[66] With racist insults and discrimination against them frequent in the mainstream, bourgeois and elite Christian blacks feel some of the anger of the ghetto masses who at any moment could riot at poverty and ill-treatment by the police forces—and they empathize with furious Arabs also.

What Future for Farrakhan's New NOI and Islam among African-Americans?

Farrakhan's neo-NOI faced major problems as the 20th century closed. Amid the unremitting Jewish micro-nationalist vendetta and thus the poor growth of its enterprises, there were reports of unrest in the ranks, and that top NOI officials from Chicago were unleashing goon squads to make some outposts more regular in their payments.

Over twenty years, Farrakhan had found it much harder to devise architecture for a Muslim "Nation" that would last, than to intrigue the African-American population in general. But the fact that, more and more, Farrakhan and his fellow-leaders have squarely faced the spiritual difficulties of building a viable movement out of long-atomized people could help nurture a long-term life for the sect. The charismatic leader close to God built confidence for the initial shattered masses, but what African-Americans now demand in the post-modern era is a complex of institutions that place limits on how leaders act and how much they determine policies. The realistic treatment by sect-writers in *Final Call* of the ailments of Farrakhan, no longer an immortal super-human whom God will only lift up to join Fard and Elijah Muhammad in the Mother Wheel that circles our globe, was a notable re-humanization of leadership. By now, a discourse tradition has emerged in the new NOI that is no longer self-righteous but often self-scrutinizing instead, and which could come to place institutional checks on the individuals who lead. The new NOI leaves those receiving its communications in no doubt that it and linked groups have built some control for African-Americans over their lives so that now they cannot blame whites for everything—they have to examine their personal malfunctions much more closely. (True, Elijah's Nation of Islam had already demanded that blacks take responsibility in the 1950s, 1960s and 1970s). The attempt to develop a theological psycho-pathology for individuals in order to limit such corroding ills as envy within the sect, not just between black politicians in general, may open up into checks and balances and humanization of leadership that have been keys to the functioning of Anglo-originated American normative institutions that last, notably Congress and other electoral bodies.

The capacities of Farrakhan and his followers to communicate ideas and motifs to millions of African-Americans in the last two decades of the 20th century ran far ahead of the slow expansion of the little sect itself and such modest institutions as it was able to build. As the 21st century opened, severe challenges buffeted the NOI. Farrakhan's prostate cancer ran him through bouts of debilitation that sapped morale and the coherence with which the members could function as a micro-"Nation." The events of September 11 posed many more dangers than opportunities in an America that had never needed grounds to turn inimical to Muslims and "Negroes." In coming to terms with Imam Warith ud-Din Mohammed and linking up with Muslims from the East when that carried real risks, Farrakhan sought to achieve the trans-Muslim architecture that his sect now had to attempt just to survive. Farrakhan's problem was that over two decades he had succeeded in catching the attention of most educated "Blacks" but failed to win disciplined commitment from them. A lot of the relaxed bourgeois support he won had been as a rallying-symbol for their ethnic-cum-class conflict with activist Jewish micro-nationalist organizations that duly thereafter directed most of their fire against him, while isolating and starving the NOI. "Farrakhan" had been the symbol through which the bourgeoisie had been able to insult (or counter-insult) American Jews but then leave the symbol to cop the flak. Now, in the 21st century, Farrakhan sought more of a live-and-let-live relationship with those Jewish groups against whom he first had defined himself. But he faced the same problems as Warith had from 1975 when he moderated to Anglos and Jews—the black bourgeoisie drifts away from glamorously "Muslim" leaders when they will longer take the fire from serving as the symbol in that elite's protest against its Anglo or Jewish opponent.

If the new, tamer, Farrakhan's accommodationist signals to Jews and Israel lost him support, there were those on the fringe of his sect or within the Islamo-Africanist tradition in America who swiftly moved to take up his old verbally militant role. The contraction of Farrakhan's following, with his increased moderation vis-à-vis the U.S. system, granted more space for the growth of such movements as the New Black Panther Party, led by that towering outspoken rapster, Khallid Abdul Muhammad, and after his death by attorney Malik Zulu Shabbazz. By the 21st century, their uninhibited shotgun denunciations of the Jews and Israel, and of the U.S. system, had built up a strong and vibrant following. Although the old BPP had sometimes had friendly feelings for Islam and sounded off against Israel, and some of its veterans went on to embrace Islam after Hoover broke up the movement, not many of the veterans had endorsed the new successor apart from H. Rap Brown (only active in BPP 1968-1971), now a Sunni Muslim leader known as Jamil al-Amin.

The sufferings and deprivations of the African-American strata from which they recruit pressured the New BPP's leaders to march bearing photos of Usamah Bin Ladin after September 11, and to voice sympathy for Zakariya Musawi ["Zacarias Moussaoui"], the dark French national of Moroccan origin being tried by the U.S. for involvement in the twin towers strike. The New Black Panthers appear to be becoming a vibrant and dynamic synthesis of (a) Black Nationalism with (b) African-Americans' old home-grown Islamic identification with (c) highly politicized revivalist-jihadic movements of the Middle East such as al-Qa'idah, and Hamas and Islamic Jihad in Palestine, and with (d) the popularized left or Marxoid stance that the old Panthers once struck. The Marxist Mumiya Abu Jamal, writing from Death Row, is contributing encouraging words and ideas, as he long did to Farrakhan's newspaper.[67] Will the new BPP, then, fulfil the old by carrying through a political alliance with poor American whites, while carrying forward the vendetta against Israel and some neighborhood Jews two blocks away? The new United Nation of Islam led by Solomon Muhammad, too, is also very dynamic and has drawn the attention of Arab immigrants. One former NOI member praised the successful network of apartment buildings, service stations, grocery stores and dry-cleaning businesses that Solomon had organized: they really were owned by the members (in contrast to Farrakhan and his family in the new NOI?) Thus, Solomon's movement, too, should be kept in mind when assessing how African-American protest Islam might turn out after Farrakhan.[68]

5: THE 2005 "MILLIONS MORE MOVEMENT": RESURGENCE FOR FARRAKHAN?

For a fair time, *Final Call* and the NOI from the later 1900s were like a ship whose pilot leaves the rudder unattended for periods of medical treatment, and of travel abroad. The ship turns in this direction and that but does not make much headway in any one clear direction. But Farrakhan's efforts to organize a "Millions More Movement" and March for October 2005, on the tenth anniversary of the Million Man March on Washington, saw him stump most of Afro-America for support in a grueling flurry of addresses, articles, open letters and press statements. It was soon clear that Farrakhan's name, and the discontent among diverse African Americans, together, could still draw a fair response from other leading sectors of black America. They felt that his past huge contribution to the unifying of African-Americans into a Nation back in 1995 obliged them to help him in 2005, and that his name would still draw enough masses for them to come in order to inject their own ideas. The crucial source for Farrakhan's resurgent strength was that his sect operated simultaneously among such a range of classes, age groups and faiths among African-Americans but also in other ethnic groups (Latinos, Arabs) and overseas states as well.

Farrakhan's 2005 Discourse

Farrakhan and his new Movement's communications could have

fostered militant protest incompatible with the U.S. system when they denounced police brutality and the huge numbers of blacks in the country's vast prison system. These communications also denounced the abuse of power in the system to destroy black leadership [=eg. J. Edgar Hoover's campaigns to destroy Marcus Garvey, Elijah Muhammad, Malcolm X, Martin Luther King, Jr. and the Black Panthers], that, just like the 300-years system of slavery it succeeded, had left Farrakhan's people uniquely atomized. Yet while Farrakhan was trying to tap wide anger among blacks in 2005, he highlighted reparations from the system, and headed even further to ameliorism and coming to terms with it when his quasi-program called for "free health care for the descendents of slaves in this nation." Were [African-Americans] part of that American nation or not, for the private Farrakhan?

The Millions More Movement was plugging into the whole gamut of black classes in America—linking a bourgeoisie it had to admit was growing with vigor, to ghetto masses who, Farrakhan warned, "are on a **Death March** into the oven of social deterioration, broken homes, broken marriages, broken minds," unemployment and homelessness. The ten years since the first Million Man March had won Afro-America many more entrepreneurs, college graduates, persons holding political office, Black mayors, city councilors, state representatives, "city managers and corporate executives" [=micronationalist well-off blacks living surrounded by adversarial white colleagues and neighbors]. The bourgeoisie was not at ease with the whites around it, and Farrakhan in 2005 was activating its trans-class ethnic conscience towards the ghetto lumpens slipping further and further behind.

Farrakhan and his sect was thus focusing a generous side in the bourgeoisie, an impulse to a comprehensive Black Nation that would carry duties. He was not just offering himself as an instrument to advance their class formation and interests against rival ethnic bourgeoisies. For the educated blacks who were scrutinizing him, the issue remained if the Nation of Islam could in 2005 (as the 1995 March had failed to do) put together the instruments and institutions to sustain nation-building over a long term, after he again turned them out en masse. On this, Farrakhan's exhortations and the issues statement were not so precise. Like 1995, there was more moralistic exhortation to jobless blacks to take the responsibility to end their "uncivilized" behavior—Atonement. God in Chronicles 7:14 had promised His people that if they but humbled themselves in prayer and turned from their wicked ways, then He would forgive them their sins and heal their land. That would be a new "Covenant with our Creator." Farrakhan down his career had shown that his sect's religious ethos could draw the African-American masses, along with the other classes too, together much more than could secular black nationalism. But would 2005 at last produce the instruments to integrate that nation for good? "Our people [have to be] organized nationally" [=across the USA state from which the second NOI had little wish to secede], to "put systems in place that will permit a successful programmatic thrust to bring to fruition what we envision for ourselves and our people." The Millions More Movement would establish a Black Economic Development Fund:

Farrakhan hoped to get out of the bourgeoisie the finance to carry through a private enterprise by his sect in return for his sect directing the masses to buy from them within a coming nationalist sub-economy. Its issues statement wanted to make the Millions More Movement "an organized political force of consequence in America and all over the world," that could achieve political power for the poor and disenfranchised. Some middle-aging blacks reflected that Farrakhan had had a chance at that back in 1995 after he turned out masses from all classes at the March. The upshot had been that he had failed to bring together much that was structured in the decade that followed. Yet Farrakhan's skilled, energetic outreach to the variety of black classes, faiths and generations in 2005 brought out that he had maintained over that decade most of the connections that had brought that range of African-Americans into his 1995 March. He had kept intact the relational base upon which he could now try seriously to build institutions.

The "new" Millions More Movement courted African-Americans in general with a view of the globe and international affairs that looked back to the pre-1975 NOI's wide demarcation of the world's "Black Nation," but adapting that somewhat towards the Africanists and to post-modernity's innumerable plural nations. Although the Millions More Movement's statement of issues nowhere spoke of "African-Americans" —Farrakhan in 2005 still preferred "Black people" (was that even a Nation?)—it did call for "unity amongst all African peoples and peoples of African descent world wide" (which, though, was to pluralize Africans, too). Although with much less blurring than before 1975 of the boundaries between "the Blacks" proper and the others in the world, without the old homogenization of people of color, the quasi-program extended Africa and Africans out into a wider range of Third World peoples: "we call for unity with our Brown, Red, disenfranchised and oppressed brothers and sisters in America, Caribbean, Central and South America, Asia and all over the world"—which did somewhat blur those categories into each other. If Africa and "Blacks" were now a bit more demarcated, the special Islamic links of Farrakhan's sect to Palestinians, 'Iraqis, Iranians, Afghans, etc., only strengthened a sympathy that a good range of non-Muslim black Americans also felt on international relations. The Movement's issues statement called for "peace in the world: an end to wars of foreign aggression waged by the United States Government against other sovereign nations and peoples." Mindful of a mood among African-Americans in general, Farrakhan, following the 2001 havoc by al-Qa'idah, had at points reached out to the U.S. system and even Bush, Jr. But now in 2005, in a way he took the side of the Taliban in Afghanistan, the regime of Saddam Husayn that the U.S. had attacked, and the resistance fighting America in 'Iraq. Farrakhan was calculating that enough non-Muslim blacks were turning against the quagmire in 'Iraq for his limited pan-Islamism not to cost him too much support.

There was still a (now more fertile) tension between the new NOI and African-American aesthetic culture. The issues statement demanded greater responsibility by Black artists, entertainers and industry personnel.

Farrakhan and his colleagues, unlike Elijah, now celebrated and lived "our immense artistic talent and creative genius," but still, Elijah-like, saw and fought anti-social components in that aesthetic creativity [e.g. Gangsta Rap]. Islam and African-American music and song had now blended to the benefit of each. The call of this quasi-program for an "end to exploitation of our talent by outside forces" may have obliquely forecast ongoing ethnic conflict with some American Jews.[69]

African-American Responding Groups

The Black Political Classes. Farrakhan's 2005 tours of mobilization for the successor-March showed that all his links to blacks in city-level government, cultivated by him since the 1980s, still held. A meeting of the Detroit City Council on 15 August 2005 made a proclamation officially endorsing the approaching Millions More Movement in Washington, and handed Farrakhan a "Spirit of Love" [not of Revolt...] award. As ever, Farrakhan was winning a role because he could still convince blacks with more power and money than his members that he was morally superior and could give them the spirituality and purpose they somehow lacked in themselves, or that he could at least bring the masses to them. Detroit, Farrakhan noted, had a Black-controlled city council, school board and fire department, yet the condition of most of its "Black people" was "still deplorable because of the lack of unity [=black factions] and absence of strong and principled spiritual leadership." The latter thrust at the black churches. But Farrakhan also fired some thinly-veiled attacks on the political class that was welcoming him: "we cannot be carbon copies of our former slave masters and their children, and be successful in government or anything else," a notable statement of cultural authenticity from a sect that had Anglicized the language, life-goals and skills of so many lumpens, and long been ill at ease with the cultures of African peoples. In Detroit as elsewhere, "the power of spiritual leaders has been undermined by those who have allowed themselves to be bought off and corrupted." Black people thus needed "a new political, spiritual and economic paradigm to move our people from being the ruled into rulership," said Minister Farrakhan.

Farrakhan was granted a hearing in Detroit by its black political class because the latter had been beating around in the undergrowth for some nationalist ideology before he came. Mayor Kwame Kilpatrick's name showed an aspiration to recover some things in the West Africa of the forebears, and Farrakhan later met with Detroit spiritual leaders and activists at the Museum of African-American History. The Mayor said that he felt "spiritually filled" after hearing Farrakhan. Blacks in local government do feel the limits to which they can bend and direct the system within which they have livelihoods and some authority, to the interests of African-Americans in general. The past successes of Farrakhan and his NOI in bringing together divergent black classes and sects was making some in the local governments want to try out his new 2005 March and use it to widen their scope within a possible new black mass-politics.[70]

Black Leftists and Unionists. Similar respectful use of Farrakhan's remaining status was made, for instance, by the left-nationalist Million Worker March Movement (MWMM) led by Trent Willis and Clarence Thomas. The MWMM wanted to weave together (a) the class struggle aims of the U.S. unions tradition, as Republicans, Democrats and multinational corporations inflicted "crisis" on working people everywhere, with (b) the black nationalism that Farrakhan and his NOI had diffused, for all their Islamic and Americanist ambiguities. As its name shows, the MWMM had been launched to ride, and give a new turn to, the tide of black collective assembly in public space started by Farrakhan's October 1995 Million Man March, which, over the following decade, had been a model that had "propelled" youth, women's and reparations successor-marches. However, the MWMM's October 2004 gathering of unionists from across the country at the Lincoln Memorial had far from brought enough "thousands" to reach the million it wanted. Now in 2005, the left-unionizers of the MWMM and Farrakhan and his colleagues were circling each other: both needed the other and the new March. And there was some overlap of ethos between the two "Black" groups (the MWMM had no special interest in Africa in this communication at least). Demands the MWMM made on the U.S. system included "universal health care, protection of social security and an end to the war in Iraq" —it may have shared the wide-ranging definition by Muslim African-Americans of race-community around the globe to make it include Arabs and Latin Americans, also notable in some sympathy for 'Iraqis, Afghans, Iranians, etc., resisting the U.S. state, among Islamophile Black Nationalist intellectuals.

Such wide, inclusive community of global race (against strong Westerners) had a link to the MWMM's internal call to, within the U.S., "build a Black and People of Color-led coalition to mobilize for the Millions More March." True, this U.S.-wide organization saw all the working class, whites with "Blacks," as bound in community, not just by material interest (wages, conditions). The MWMM hoped to tack the mobilization of "the U.S. and international working class regardless of race or gender" onto a Millions More March now being organized by a Muslim Black Nationalist wary of politics and social disorder! These unionist "Blacks" were as dissatisfied with unions as W.E.B. DuBois had been, early in this tradition. The failure of the larger part of the unions to confront their internal racism had been one key reason for the decline of trade-unionism in post-modern America. The MWMM wanted facilities for Blacks as a special national community within unionism. The leftists in 2005 were between a rock—the whites who dominated trade-unions—and the hard place of the Muslim black nationalist tradition. Clarence Thomas griped that, although the majority who came to Farrakhan's 1995 Million Man March had been workers whose trade unions did not want them to come, yet "the organized identity and demands of the Black workers... were not strongly represented" as such [in the structure given to the March by its organizers]. He tried to build on a remark by Farrakhan that his 2005 March was "reaching for the millions who carry the rich on their backs".[71]

The idea for a Million Worker March had emerged from Trent Willis of San Francisco's International Longshore and Warehouse Union Local 10, most of whose members were blacks. A similar sense of racial connection to the Arabs and Iranians who faced Bush, Jr. in the wake of September 11 was voiced by two Black Nationalist academics, Dr Julian Hare and his wife Julia, projected by the media of both Farrakhan and Warith, who had had their spats with black Marxists. The Hares ridiculed notions that service in the U.S. armed forces could provide livelihoods and, after discharge, opportunities and integration into society for "Black people." "Blacks should tread lightly in volunteering for military duty, especially when those targets closely resemble them, at least until the facts are in. Usually, the people making the decisions do not resemble Black people, even when vouchsafed by a couple of token Blacks" —i.e. Condoleezza Rice and Secretary of State Colin Powell.[72] Would these Black leftists ever really accept Farrakhan's leadership? Would he convert them? Or would they draw the NOI towards their thinking when the two came together? Farrakhan's tabloid was continuing to define this March, too, as more humbled self-rectification by God's "people" (the Blacks) of "their wicked ways." Could Farrakhan ever opt to become a serious full-time politician?

Black Christian Churches. Although Farrakhan in the new century continued to quote from the Bible as well as the Qur'an, and to build the national united front with black Christian clerics, his media at the same time continued to carry Elijah's old condemnations of Christianity as the whites-concocted "curse to us (the Black man)... [it is] full of slavery teachings".[73]

One of the largest Baptist denominations in America, the Progressive National Baptist Convention (PNBC), pledged to mobilize its members to attend and participate fully in the Millions More Movement. Rev. Dr. Major Jemison, PNBC President, saw its support for the Movement as a way "to continue the legacy of our founding members, Dr. Martin Luther King" and others who had demanded that the churches address social concerns and benefit "our people." This internalized Farrakhan's citing of his sect's non-Christian tenets as no demerit but the very reason why churches had to unite with him in a nationalist common front in 2005. The Progressive National Baptist Convention now recognized that no one organization or leader could solve the many critical needs and problems facing Black people. The new front Farrakhan had started up "would begin to mobilize the masses of our people to improve their status in the arenas of health, education, economics, politics, strong moral and spiritual values". The PNBC leaders expected to draw other churches, including the Pentecostals, the National Association for the Advancement of Colored People, the National Council of Negro Women (NCNW) and the National Urban League into collaboration with such Muslims as Farrakhan around the new March in Washington.[74]

The Progressive National Baptist Convention's support for Farrakhan's 2005 rally instanced that building political power inside the U.S. system, but on behalf of a black sub-nation now, far outweighed religious doctrines about Jesus for churches that were the heirs of Civil Rights. In accepting that embracing Islam did not cut blacks out of their single Black Nation, and in wanting a pooling of moral ideas and economics in the national united front that Farrakhan led, this huge Baptist church could easily open its members to the beliefs of Farrakhan's sect.

Women and Feminists. Historically, the Nation of Islam under Elijah was a movement conducted by black males to give them the centrality males had in Third World Muslim and Anglo-led societies. Muslim cults amongst African-Americans since 1913 have had a bias towards uplift of males that will correct their impaired functioning as husbands and providers, which long racism and poverty had inflicted upon them in America. The stress the second NOI has continued to place on a contraction of the roles of women more towards the domestic sphere, remains attractive to many weary black superwomen in the new 21st century. Farrakhan had called for a mainly male turnout at the 1995 Million Man March, and this had alienated many dynamic female activists who could have made a great contribution, had they chosen to turn up. To be sure, the March could never have succeeded without the labor of a fair number of Muslim women in the organization of transport, catering, etc. In a web-cast to black women across the USA just weeks away from the 2005 March, Farrakhan said that thereby "many women made it possible for men to act like men on that day"—which again suggested that he meant to carry on the transfer of at least some functions back from black women to black men in 2005 also.

But the non-Muslim forces that Farrakhan needed if there were to be a new March, were pressurizing him to widen the part to be played by women from the narrow scope for them a decade before. Rev. Willie Wilson, pastor of Union Temple Baptist Church in Washington, DC, after he was named National Executive Director of the 2005 commemorative March had written Farrakhan that "I would feel much better and more inspired to work harder if our women were allowed to participate," and the NOI leader had acceded. Aware that many had been wondering about the roles allocated women in the Millions More Movement, Farrakhan was still pulling the discussion between the various black forces over to issues of female modesty that would speak to Third World Muslims or born-again Christians in the Republican Party. He was carrying on the ideology of the Honorable Elijah Muhammad that building a civilization is determined by the women: white oppressors from Caribbean plantation owner Willie Lynch in 1712 had been making the female independent of the male so that they would unconsciously break male children, the best way whites could devise to break down the nation. Farrakhan rapped the taking out of black women from the home during World War II to work: "women have become a top breadwinner" whose hems Satan had raised to make women "degenerative." Thus, for Farrakhan, a substantial return of women to homes, to modest dress and nurturing roles was what would make them the "most important in making a free people," not acquiring professional or working skills.

Farrakhan's new NOI had changed somewhat from that of Elijah. It has in it several veteran women such as Tynetta Muhammad and Ava

Muhammad who offer their own somewhat original variants of Islamic discourse within its media, in which younger women are also important as journalists. And he knew how important it was for his own place in history for him to draw masses of women this time to the 2005 March. But if "the Millions More Movement is to repair the damage done to us during slavery," this in the long run could be a construction of patriarchal nuclear families, that remains sure to keep many capable, gender-conscious, African-American women away in 2005 as in 1995.

Mama Charisma in Washington, DC, hailed the web cast meeting in its NOI mosque. She liked Farrakhan's talk of uniting all oppressed people (Latino-black alliance). The Minister had rightly criticized "how girls are raised today. [They] don't know how to cook or sew, and then they wonder why they can't get married." But Charisma had been disappointed that the mosque had not been jam packed with standing room only: the enemy was setting blacks one against the other, she lamented.[74]

The successor to Farrakhan will have to have come to understand that the post-1945 winning of high qualifications and much more diversified employment by black women—their new importance in the professions—was not all bad. It does reduce the population growth of blacks, and it does, as with all U.S. *ethne*, have costs for the construction (or nationalist reconstruction) of nuclear families headed by males. But most black women will refuse to go back to the sewing machines and cooking lessons that Elijah offered to make them "civilized" (=like Anglo middle-Americans of the 1940s). The old NOI allocation of roles between the sexes is an anachronism. Pragmatically speaking, no leader of the second NOI can clinch a strong black political movement if it does not utilize and honor black women professionals.

While its openly religious Islamic content was perhaps narrower than in 1995, Farrakhan's discourse in 2005 was more internationalist and political in comparison. The identifications of African-Americans were now shifting from Americanism as millions now realized how much Bush's "War on Terror" would cost them. Farrakhan's new frank pan-Islamic solidarity with those whom America was hitting in the Third World could fit into the changed mood of many African-Americans on international relations. In Cleverland, Ohio, Farrakhan addressed over 200 of the city's black leaders in a Ritz ballroom. They said that the city aimed to bring over 200 bus loads to Washington on October 15. Overseas countries and peoples were notable in the exchanges. Farrakhan recounted his recent visiting of slave dungeons in West Africa. He was stressing the need to unite all leaders, organizations and classes of "the whole of our people" to rescue the masses from their death march of social deterioration. But Farrakhan was again juxtaposing and connecting that local suffering to America in the world. The new 2005 March was an evolution from his 1986 "vision experience" that warned him that President [Bush] had planned with the Joint Chiefs of Staff a war to target Libya initially, followed by onslaughts on the Black community and youth as a "war on drugs" in the early 1990s, and culminating in his son's invasion of Afghanistan and Iraq under the false pretense of using the World Trade Center tragedy. Bush Jr's real motive in attacking Afghanistan was economic—the construction through it of an oil pipeline that the Taliban had rejected, [an explication favored by leftists around the world]. Farrakhan wove his pan-Islamic grievances together with his sharp images of U.S. internal politics such as the election that Bush stole as a result of the Florida voting fiasco and the Republican-controlled Supreme Court. Farrakhan applied a verse from the Holy Qur'an to focus "the desires of [America's] greedy leaders eager to control oil in the Middle East" to the Cleveland black leaders. "We can influence public policy as well as foreign policy, but we must be unified and organized".[75]

Unity with Latinos and Latin America. Farrakhan has declared that his Millions More Movement aims to unify all oppressed people. The relationship of Islam-influenced blacks with Spanish speakers again connects the parochial out into the international relations of the U.S., here with the states and peoples of Latin America. For more than three decades, black political leaders have labored to bring African-Americans and Hispanics together into an alliance or some tighter community. As an ethnic politician, Farrakhan has placed himself, but sincerely, at the fore of this sustained project of communities-construction by African-Americans. The project has been a thorny enterprise in which black statesmen have persevered despite limited results, over decades: were these two groups really much related, and how far could they benefit each other in the shorter term? It looked like an ideological rather than pragmatic or utilitarian project, one that is very much motivated by culture. The writings of the pioneer black professional historians exalting Muslim Spain (Chapter 2), Moorish Science ideas of international community in the 1920s and 1930s, and the diversity that the classic Nation of Islam incorporated into its global "Black Nation" have all helped fuel the drive to link up with Spanish speakers inside the U.S. state and outside it.

The president of Mexico said in 2005 that Mexicans who get into the U.S. only take jobs that even Blacks don't want. That offended blacks of upper class and middle class background: the Reverends Jesse Jackson and Al Sharpton went to Mexico to secure an apology from President Fox, with Warith's tabloid publicizing. Farrakhan, though, only brushed that black uproar aside. President Fox was right: "you [Black women] used to be the cooks and the maids, but now they're the Mexicans." Blacks and Mexicans were competing for jobs only along the highway with construction: "you belong to the union, [employers] want cheap labor." Farrakhan's cold scrutiny of his own ethnos diverged somewhat from such bourgeois black nationalists as Jackson and his Sunnified rivals, but his meticulous attention to the living conditions and viewpoints of poor Mexicans and other Hispanics in the U.S. was like the care that all these Muslim and Arabophile groups have put into bringing blacks and Hispanics together. Farrakhan's real empathy with local Hispanics nourished his resolve not just to pool the resources of blacks but to "form strategic alliances with the Latinos." Given the sharp attention all these diverse African-American leadership-groups are giving, together and over decades, to constructing community with Latinos and with the states to the South from which they came, one has to give them and perhaps Farrakhan's 2005 movement some chance that they really could build a multiple relationship.[76]

Imam Najee 'Ali, an activist in Warith's sect who tried to save Cynthia McKinney's seat in Congress in 2002 from pro-Israel forces, has worked with Rev. Al Sharpton and Christine Chavez for a new era of black-Latino unity throughout the U.S. City officials in Los Angeles assess that the efforts might be making headway against issues in jobs, housing, education, healthcare and opposed ethnic gangs that had caused frictions between the two groups. Los Angeles Mayor Antonio Villaraigosa, the city's first Hispanic mayor in 125 years, came to power with overwhelming support of the black community, and the two underprivileged minorities want to cooperate to gain economic, social and political clout from inner city neighborhoods up to Congress.[77]

If Farrakhan and his Nation of Islam in 2005 were back in their old energetic form, the U.S. system's follies assured his Millions More Movement a hearing in black America far beyond what his renewed hyper-activity ever could have won. The hurricane that struck New Orleans and Mississippi in August 2005 was the worst natural disaster ever to devastate America, leaving one million displaced people, many of whom were black. The whites of New Orleans were evacuated with quick efficiency from their good areas, and the impoverished black majority, for too many days, was left to its fate. Bush Jr was slow to interrupt his holiday on his ranch, and Michael Brown, a donor to the Republican Party that then made him head of the Federal Emergency Management Agency, said, a full four days after the catastrophe, that the administration had only just learned that 20,000 starving people were waiting to be rescued outside New Orleans' convention center. Thus, Brown had read or listened to no accurate reports from the city, and not bothered to watch the television newscasts of floating corpses, and of the dehydrated dying children and African-American refugees who had for days been screaming for food, water, and evacuation into the cameras. President Bush Jr praised the fine job Michael Brown was doing in New Orleans. For decades, scientists and agencies had been warning U.S. administrations, including his, that the, in places, century-old system of levees holding off the waters from the city could collapse in any disaster. But the Bush, Jr. regime had been unable to spare the funds for a new system because of tax cuts and then 'Iraq. Condoleeza Rice assured African-Americans that no American had withheld relief aid due to any racial dislike, or could. She was right on that. Father and son Bush were not racists: they had appointed her and Powell. But they had little energy to help African-American groups they did not view as real citizens in their wealthy Anglomorph American People. It was not that they hated, but that they did not care.

As ever, the hope that America might one day become one nation was in its freedom of speech and pluralist media that strip all personalities and all situations bare. The suffering TV faces of African-Americans trapped in New Orleans did move to anger even some WASPs in the Republican Party, whose thoughts turned to getting some new, less shambolic, leader.

Jesse Jackson and other veteran politicians of the tradition of the Civil Rights movement voiced their outrage, but inconsistently, since they sometimes still spoke of the people Bush, Jr. headed as though they shared a single nationality, as though everyone in America were "we." But the system's slothful neglect, and the overnight collapse of law-enforcement and government in New Orleans, had shown that America and the American state was a frame bracketing together groups that had never properly connected. The USA was a vulnerable country, but above all a cold one. Now blacks might, as never before, listen to Farrakhan's micro-nationalist thesis of plural peoples in America—a Muslim thesis that still covertly yearned for "them" and "us" to become a single "we", only slightly more covertly than did Jackson.

PERSPECTIVE

How, on final balance, should we evaluate the specific sect and then the wider national front that Farrakhan has built in Black America? While much of it must rate as self-promoting—or smallish given the constraints from the limited size of his core NOI sect/micro-nation to which he always gave priority over the huge African-American nation he tried to mobilize—Farrakhan's gifts as a mass-communicator and a builder of coalitions have diffused a national consciousness tinted by Islam throughout Black America. His ambiguous "Nation" was able to apply its media evocation of nationhood in detailed apprehension of economics that amount to a substantial ideological achievement. (The nuts and bolts of the new NOI's small businesses were something else again!) Farrakhan's NOI has acted as a media vanguard that musters the African-American masses through nationalism to sustain as its customers a growing black business class. The Nation of Islam has focused the drive of black Americans for opportunity, freedom and an open-ended self-determination that could quickly turn into an integrationist opposite of the starting discourse. Thus, the new Nation of Islam had an intellectual depth, but also a protean flexibility often overlooked by analysts only concerned to trace—and themselves systemize—a theoretically consistent ideology.

It is still hard to classify the quarter of a century of Farrakhan's engagement with the U.S. parliamentary system as either a failure or a success. Clearly, Farrakhan proved unable to carry forward his electrifying assembly of the collective African-American Nation in Washington in 1995 into a routinized association with long-term institutions. This was perhaps inevitable given the limited range of organizers he could command from within his small sect. The failure to meticulously build and periodically remodel institutions truly built to last has been a recurring problem in the original NOI and in all its reincarnations. Such inadequate conceptualization of objectives and above all to plan machinery for their achievement is something for which these sects have to take some responsibility. The matter is quite apart from the lack of support or frequent enmity from U.S. governments, and the private drives to undo these sects from other powerful groups. Yet, that the NOI movements in the face of such opposition, typical for radical protest movements in America, survived and remained a self-sustaining major player over close to a century, is in itself a major achievement.

Farrakhan did succeed in the sense that he activated and sometimes transformed the political consciousness of millions of African-Americans. He and his colleagues served as a focal point for African-American protest against the system, but also as positive system-challengers who set out for them ways in which that malfunctioning U.S. system could be extended as well as corrected. Overall, his contribution was to make "America" a more functional and nourishing system by his encouragement of young blacks to engage with the U.S. polity as constructive extenders of electoral politics as they stood, so as to pressure benefits out of an unwelcoming system for their people. (The Zionoid micro-nationalists may holler, but Farrakhan surely should be in line for some Anglomorph National Award for all he has done to help America function better!)

Some educated African-Americans assailed Farrakhan's flip-flops and self-contradictions and failure to develop final ideas. They have repeatedly queried if he even knew what he believed any more. That his sect failed to construct a single comprehensive, closed ideology, however, set the NOI's media free to expand it into an open forum, in which a wide range of different aims, culture elements, and proposed strategies for system-politics, were tested against each other before millions of blacks from a good range of classes. Farrakhan empowered his African-American and Latino readers and listeners by making the final choices theirs.

Farrakhan's paper, *The Final Call,* diffused much data about overseas Muslims and Africans out among diverse categories of African-Americans. There were predictable articles attacking Israel, and triumphalism about the long-faded independence struggles of African peoples or parties that could turn a blind eye to the misdeeds of by now aged leaders over there. But the body of materials was diverse, and suggested some alternative ways of viewing those countries. The NOI's feel for Third World African and Muslim cultures is coming late. But there is no dispute that Farrakhan and the NOI have made African-Americans much better informed about the politics and societies of the Islamic world, Asia and Africa, but also the Latin America all U.S. citizens have to understand, now, as its Latino population surges. It could help prepare African-Americans to evolve a role as a lobby for those peoples comparable to the lobbying functions of Polish-Americans, Jewish-Americans or Anglo-Americans within the U.S. parliamentary system in favor of their overseas homelands of ancestry. With their triple culture, African-American Muslims could then further help to bring Arabs, Iranians and Anglo-Americans together in positive exchanges. However, the manicheism and violence of official America in the Muslim world after September 11, and the way ingrained dimensions of all NOI culture have made its adherents partisans for suffering Middle Easterners, appear likely to delay any such constructive resolution.

Farrakhan had first used Black-Jewish polarization to get his career as a nationwide leader started in 1983-1985. But he then carefully added more self-improving and indeed introspective functions to his leadership discourse. Farrakhan succeeded in getting hundreds of thousands of African-Americans to accept him as a teacher and guide for an ethical and social reformation of African-Americans that is presented as a preliminary to their integration into a political nation. In the post-modern era, all the USA's peoples are in quest of altruism, spirituality and sympathetic community that the shrunken American state, fixated on the market, no longer seriously pretends to provide. The drive for "atonement" of his 2005 Million Man March did not please some African-American activists who did not see why the victims, rather than the victimizers, should seek to mend their ways. Yet self-criticism and self-rectification under a God Who far transcends humanity, at and following the March, may come to be recorded as a massive and crucial stride in African-American cohering as a Nation.

The history books will record that Farrakhan was the first figure who—after so many decades—finally forced the Zion-emblemed core of Jewish-Americans to listen to viewpoints from African-Americans that they had not wanted to hear. In his later leadership, Farrakhan had likewise mustered mass mobilization and the vote as forms of power in America that compelled even Republican Party Anglos to consider the interests of a range of African-American classes. In making equal negotiation and new bargaining relationships possible, Farrakhan may have contributed to the building in America of a new society in which all people (or peoples?) will have the substance—not just, in the case for some at present, the forms—of freedom for cultural self-expression and economic opportunity.

While 2005 saw a rejuvenation of Farrakhan in his health and hence as a religio-ethnic politician, it remains true, as the mainstream white press mocked in the leadup to his 2005 march in Washington, that he is a man who has many more yesterdays than he can ever have tomorrows. The meticulousness and energy with which he hammered together a coalition to turn out most classes, groups and generations of African-Americans in 2005 probably cannot physically be sustained by him long enough to build the systems and institutions that could make the community at which his Marches clutched a permanent political reality. Could, then, the physical or political decline of Farrakhan and a possible breakdown of his sect mark the end of "Black Islam" as an organized vanguard force in African-American life? Before writing off the Nation of Islam, we might bear in mind that the sect maintains wide connections into most institutions of African-American life in America, that it has considerable links to overseas Muslims, and that it may be able to muster these to evolve future leadership roles. In Benjamin Chavis Muhammad, the NOI has a potential leader after Farrakhan who has wide past experience in both the integrationist civil rights tradition and in U.S. high politics: he might become the seasoned successor able to modernize, institutionalize and rationalize the NOI. Although a minority tradition, the roots of Islam perhaps extend far too deeply down into the very origins of the African-American people, and their links to Arabs and the Muslims of the Third World are by now too multiple, for the religion itself to just fade away. Individuals and organizations can rise and fall, but this nationally specific Islam, now a thoroughly political protest religion, hydra-like spawns a never-ending succession of reincarnations. The special Islam that African-Americans evolved in the 20th century is a minority tradition in this huge ethnic group that nonetheless is one of the key components in its ethos. Durable and ever-diversifying, "Black Islam" is able to resurge as strong as ever after every setback.

While the special Islam that African-Americans evolved in the 20th century is a minority tradition in this huge ethnic group, it is nonetheless one of the key components in its ethos. Durable and ever-diversifying, African-American Islam is able to resurge as strong as ever after every setback, and the exit of any leader.

ENDNOTES

1 Mattias Gardell, *In the Name of Elijah Muhammad: Louis Farrakhan and the Nation of Islam* (Carolina: Duke University Press and London: Hurst 1996) p. 185, 191-194.

2 "Minister Farrakhan Unites Nation of Islam with the Global Community of Muslims", *New Trend* August 1997 p. 1.

3 Ibid p. 7. In his (ideological) wooing of Sister Ava at the 1997 conference, Siddiqi served up those motifs from classical Islam that endorsed wider roles for her and her sex: he cited the narrative of Hagar from al-Bukhari's collection of *hadiths* to show that an African woman was the founder of Mecca and that the angel Gabriel came to her to bestow the miracle of its Zam Zam spring upon her: *New Trend* September 1997.

4 Advertisement for *Muslim Daily Prayers: A Learner's Guide*, *Final Call* 1 July 2003 p. 29. The handbook's front cover had a photo of a Third World mosque and an introduction by Farrakhan.

5 "Minister Louis Farrakhan speaks on 'Envy—The Mother of Murder!'", *Final Call* 20 August 1996 pp. 20-21. The Minister may have seen the problem as ingrained in his Nation, since the piece had been reprinted from *Final Call* of 25 January 1995.

6 "Minister Louis Farrakhan speaks on 'Envy..." The *hadith* that no person has believed perfectly until he wishes for his brother what he wishes for himself had been one motif by which Egyptian Professor Mahmud Yusuf al-Shawaribi in the early 1960s tried to coax Malcolm X fully over into global Sunni Islam while he was still a fiery preacher in Elijah's home-made sect: Malcolm X, *Autobiography* (Harmondsworth: 1968 Penguin edn) pp. 430-431.

7 Farrakhan, "An Open Letter on the Millions More Movement," *Final Call* website 25 August 2005 and MillionsMoreMovement.com

8 Farrakhan, "Islam: an invitation to all humanity," *Final Call* 4 September 2001 pp. 20-21.

9 Jabril Muhammad, "To Understand Muhammad is to Understand Farrakhan", *Final Call* 13 October 1998 p. 26.

10 Arthur J. Magida, *Prophet of Rage: a Life of Louis Farrakhan and his Nation of Islam* (New York: Basic Books 1996) p. 123.

11 Jabril Muhammad, "Gods before Gods", *Final Call* 8 September 1998 p. 26.

12 Jabril Muhammad "The Truth of Moses and the pillar of fire", *Final Call* 20 August 1996 pp. 26, 27.

13 Historian Vibert White, a former Fruit of Islam foot soldier and then minister of

Farrakhan, in 2001 tried to separate the structure of the new NOI's business operations "run only by the Farrakhan family", from its religious arm. He charged that the passionate Black Nationalist rhetoric of the sect functioned as a cover to exploit vulnerable African-Americans for the leadership's economic and political profit. Vibert L. White, *Inside the Nation of Islam: A Historical and Personal Testimony by a Black Muslim* (University Press of Florida: 2001) passim.

14 Farrakhan, "Guarding Against the Enemy Within", *Final Call* 4 May 1999. Farrakhan had delivered this speech in one of his Harlem mosques on 18 November 1998. It contained many selective manipulations by Farrakhan of a past NOI discourse he was reinventing to blur away and relinquish the devil tenet. Malcolm had allowed that not all whites were harmful, although all are snakes. "He said a baby doesn't know the difference between a garter snake and a rattlesnake, so keep your baby away from all snakes" —-a suggestion from Farrakhan that avoidance of whites had been only a temporary measure that by 1998, a matured Nation of Islam, a baby no longer, could drop as it now widened its interactions with more benign whites. Warith had called Elijah's pre-1975 tenets a temporary "playpen". Everything was turning out to be relative as all things shifted and changed.

15 "Community rallies to support L.A. mosque: God frowns on persecution of the righteous, Farrakhan warns", *Final Call* 27 August 1996 p. 2. The discourse of the NOI's spokesmen during the gathering outside Inglewood Municipal Court left no doubt that the local congregation had indeed been on doubtful ground, legally speaking. "We were trying to purchase [the property] and trying to get an extension on the lease so that we could work out our terms of agreement" Mosque Secretary Michael Muhammad said. When the city of Inglewood would not allow the Nation of Islam to use the building to operate a mosque and school because of permit problems, the building owner had "moved very quick to have us evicted": ibid.

16 *New Trend* October 1995.

17 "Minister Farrakhan's Word on Shaikh Omar" *New Trend* 19:8 December 1998 p. 3. In a Bangladesh press conference, Farrakhan termed 'Umar "a perfect religious leader" who had been convicted for "a political motive": *Mazlumer Dak* 20 April 1998 pp. 1, 8, 5.

18 Little about 'Umar fits properly. 'Umar helped America fight the Russians through proxies in Afghanistan and was admitted to live in New York. Yet he had started out as the insurgent jihadist foe of the U.S.-aligned Egyptian Sadat and then Mubarak regimes. He had been the spiritual guide of the Jama'at al-Jihad that assassinated Sadat: its political leader, Ayman al-Zawahiri, was likewise to go to Afghanistan where he helped found al-Qa'idah. Even after he shifted to the U.S. in 1984, the shaykh 'Umar visited the regime of an al-Qadhafi upon whose overthrow successive U.S. governments were hell-bent. For Libya's magazine *Risalat al-Jihad* in 1986, 'Umar set out methods of torture used by Mubarak's "apostate" regime against Islamists: he glorified Khalid al-Islambuli who assassinated Sadat on 6 August 1981 and youthful soldier Sulayman Khatir who in October 1985 gunned down some Israeli tourists he thought might be spying on Egypt. From Libya, 'Umar'Abd al-Rahman called for armed Jihad by all Muslims, not his own group only, to "cut to pieces" all "non-Muslim" Arab governments that signed or accepted the 1978 Camp David accords and American mediation with Israel. See "Liqa' ma' al-Duktur 'Umar'Abd al-Rahman: al-Khudu' li-Amrika aw al-Khawf min Quwwatiha Shirkun billah" (A Conversation with Dr 'Umar'Abd al-Rahman: Submission to America and Fear of its Power is Ascribing Partners to God—Polytheism), *Risalat al-Jihad* February 1987 pp. 60-65. The CIA and FBI were surely not so incompetent that they did not know of his statements in Libya: Mubarak in neighboring Egypt would certainly have heard them. A son of 'Umar'Abd al-Rahman was to be around years later at the capture of an al-Qa'idah leader in Pakistan on whom the U.S. had put a high reward.

19 "Muslim efforts help increase Black nation voter turnout", *Final Call* 24 November 1998 p. 8.

20 Askia Muhammad, "Regardless of court's decision on Gore or Bush, Blacks must

decide: Where do we go from here?", *Final Call* 19 December 2000 pp. 3, 10.

21 Eric Toure Muhammad, "Gen. Powell to Blacks: Give Bush a chance" *Final Call* 2 January 2001 p. 5.

22 Eric Toure Muhammad, "Bush meeting brings skepticism and hope" *Final Call* 2 January 2001 pp. 3, 8.

23 Earl Ofari Hutchinson, "A National Action Agenda will eliminate 'political grandstanding': How Clinton Failed Black America and What Can Be Done: Part II", *Final Call* 3 September 1996.

24 Askia Muhammad (Washington), "Activists Announce 40th Anniversary of Historic March on Washington", *Final Call* 1 July 2003 pp. 3, 33.

25 "Eyewitness Account of Million Youth March", *New Trend* September 1998 p. 7.

26 Stephanie Simon (*Los Angeles Times*), "Blacks urge peace in Cincinnati", *The Melbourne Age* 16 April 2001.

27 "Building Our Future in the Promised Land", *Final Call* 27 October 1998 p. 25

28 Network FX series *The Shield* (dir./prod. Scott Brazil), installment televised on 28 January 2004 on Channel 10 Melbourne. In this episode, the attitude of the police team to "the bean pie crowd" is not one of fear but rather is mildly humorous, depicting the efforts of the "bow ties" to clean up their neighborhoods by driving dealers from successive corners as giving them "a reason to go on living". This film had an iota of openness by indicating that the NOI foot soldiers, through asking if some corrupt cops might be delaying action against the dealers, and camping in the police lobby until the police act, could become one more corrective mechanism in the U.S. system. At the close, a top policeman asks if the NOI want him to admit he is evil when "we are on the same side." While the head of the NOI squad retorts "I doubt that," the vehemence of the 1960s "devils" appellation has gone.

29 Memorie Knox, "Alderman blocks Black hotel; Community backs owner", *Final Call* 19 December 2000 pp. 7,10.

30 Janine Fondon, "Mecca Opens in Boston's Grove Hall Community: Teachings of Hon. Elijah Muhammad, work of Muslims inspire $13 million mall", *Final Call* 2 January 2002 pp. 2, 33.

31 Donna Muhammad, "Workshop presenters urge: Build a new economic order", *Final Call* 23 March 1999 p. 7.

32 Vernon Ash, "SBA launches new program to help Black Businesses", *Final Call* 9 February 1999 p. 25.

33 Herb Boyd, "Bank losses worry Black investors", *Final Call* 9 February 1999 p. 10.

34 Charline Muhammad, "Declining ownership of Black radio stations is a threat, activists warn", *Final Call* 27 October 1998 p. 8.

35 "Nation of Islam provides", *Final Call* 8 September 1998 p. 36.

36 Russell Mokhiber and Robert Weissman, "Business, Power and Mobility", *Final Call* 19 December 2000 p. 23

37 Memorie Knox, "Welfare to Work does not work, activists say", *Final Call* 16 April 2002 p. 4. One of the single African-American mothers in an accompanying photograph held up a child called Tarik, an Arabic name.

38 Durce X Jackson, "Texas governor invites Muslim input", *Final Call* 8 September 1992.

39 For the growing race-hatred among Russians "towards Muslims and dark-skinned people in general" see (Indian) Neela Banerjee, "Chechen troubles stir latent racism in Russia", Melbourne *Age* 6 October 1999. Some Russian dissidents argued that some Russian government operatives had been behind some "Chechen" bombs in apartments: they occurred just before Putin's electoral campaign, and turned it around for him. The Moscow theatre tragedy showed the psychological incapacity, similar to that of many Zionists, ever to negotiate with the small Muslim nationality who from the 19th century had exacted such heavy losses from the Slavic conquerors, although losing one out of five in every generation. Putin's forces preferred to risk killing all the hostages, which they nearly did, in a risky rescue effort than negotiate. They did, however, kill even those Chechens who

had been so incapacitated by the gas that they could never have fought on.

40 Algernon Austin, "Rethinking Race and the Nation of Islam, 1930-1975", *Ethnic and Racial Studies* (26:1) January 2003 p. 63.

41 Ahmed Rufai, "What is NATO doing in the Balkans?", *Final Call* 27 April 1999 p. 3. This item was accompanied by perhaps the first photo *Final Call* had ever carried that was positive to U.S. troops abroad—United States Army paratroopers disembarking at Tirana military airport as UNHCR Swiss Army helicopters took off to deliver aid for refugees in northern Albania.

42 "Revisiting an experiment with ethnic cleansing," *Final Call* 15 July 2003 pp. 13, 38. The item came from the non-Muslim U.S. press agency IPS/GIN, as have many *Final Call* items on Palestine and Israel.

43 2002 photos of meetings at the new farming community of al-Inshirah Mosque showed most African-American women there wearing Arab- or Pakistani-like hijabs or headscarfs, although some had West African-like head coverings: Asia Ali, "Masjid al-Inshirah Purchases 25 Acres of Land", *Muslim Journal* 9 August 2002 pp. 9, 29.

44 Excerpts from Friday *khutbah* of Imam W. Deen Mohammed of 14 September 2002 to the Harvey Islamic Center, *Muslim Journal* 13 September 2002 p. 15. For hate against Black Muslim kids in public schools as "terrorists" after 9/11 that cited al-Qa'idah Arabs and was sparked by hijabs and Arabic names, see also "Hey, Look at Me, I am Muslim Too" *Muslim Journal* 13 September 2002 pp. 5, 22, 44. In this piece, the teacher in the government secular school is the Enlightenment ally who brings in the teenage Muslim girl's mother to explain Islam to the (Black) class.

45 Letter by Congresswoman McKinney to Prince al-Walid Ibn Talal at the Sa'udi Embassy in Washington, 12 October 2001.

46 "Sharpton backs boycott", *Final Call* 2 April 2002.

47 Akbar Muhammad in Michael Wolfe, *Taking Back Islam: African-Americans Reclaim their Faith* (Rockdale: Beliefnet 2002) pp. 138-140.

48 James Muhammad, "Farrakhan: War can end through process of atonement", *Final Call* webcast article 17 October 2001.

49 James Muhammad, "World Press Conference from Mosque Maryam: The Honorable Minister Louis Farrakhan responds to the attack on America", *Final Call* www transmission of 16 September 2001. The victimization of precisely those U.S. Muslims from abroad who, as Farrakhan shrewdly perceived, had the most emotional and financial stake in the U.S. system, became long-term. A year later in September 2002, what Farrakhan's immigrant Jama'at al-Muslimin allies mocked as the Muslim conservative "four letter organizations" were still struggling along with the ACLU to protect the legal rights of Muslim Americans. Indefinite detentions and raids on mosques had chilled donations to American Muslim schools and charities, choking group survival. One response of U.S. Muslim leaders was a voter registration drive, demonstrating a similar self-protective reflex to that of Farrakhan and the black forces he headed. "American Muslims brace for harder times", *The Khaleej Times* 1 September 2002

50 Letter of Farrakhan to Bush dated December 1, 2001.

51 Gardell, *In the Name of Elijah Muhammad* p. 258.

52 "Muslim Leader pays historic visit to synagogue; new hope for dialogue, healing emerges: A new beginning in Jamaica," *Final Call* 2 April 2002 pp. 3, 34.

53 "Mid-East conflict needs an honest broker" (press conference of Farrakhan at Mosque Maryam in Chicago, 2 April 2002), *Final Call* 16 April 2002 pp. 19-22. Farrakhan had not dreamed up the charge he made in this speech of indiscriminate attacks from the general American population after 9/11 against any of Middle Eastern appearance. Because Usamah Bin Ladin wore a turban, and male Sikhs from India were required to do so by their faith, many Sikhs across the U.S. were roughed up, with one of them, Balbir Singh Sodhi, a storekeeper in Arizona, shot dead. The Arab-American Anti-Discrimination Committee collected 300 reports of violence with three Arab-Americans murdered. See Dilip Hiro, "War without end: the rise of terrorism and the global response", *The Hindu Sunday Magazine* 6 October 2002 p. 1.

54 "Israeli controls choke Palestinian economy," and "Pakistani president's statement on recognizing Israel stirs uproar" (from the Islamist opposition), both in *Final Call* 15 July 2003 p. 14.

55 "Sharon delays as dispute over Gaza homes grows hotter," *Final Call* 5 July 2003 p. 12.

56 Askia Muhammad, "Palestinian leader visits White House," *Final Call* 7 June 2005 p. 2.

57 Back in the States, Abdul Akbar had been a self-taught intellectual who learned enough history to win familiarity with such illustrious members of the African-American intelligentsia as Leroy Jones, C. Eric Lincoln and John H. Clarke. The young graduate student Vibert L. White benefited from the grounding Abdul Akbar gave him in works of black nationalism, pan-Africanism, communism, Marxism, capitalism, Islam, Christianity and Judaism. Abdul Akbar thereby equipped Vibert to lecture on Saturdays on History to Fruit of Islam members: White, *Inside the Nation of Islam* pp. 64-5.

58 Abdul Akbar Muhammad, "The Palestinian struggle: Africa can make a difference", *Final Call* 2 April 2002 p. 35.

59 "Cluster bomb 'duds' leave behind a minefield", *Final Call* 6 May 2003 p. 13.

60 Eric Toure Muhammad, "U.S. casualties mount in Bush's war without end", *Final Call* 1 July 2003 pp. 9, 38.

61 The editor of *Gulf Today,* P.V. Vivekanand, was a Hindu in origin. Still, he traced in passionate detail Zionist donations to members of Congress and suggested that the lobby organization AIPAC helped engineer Bush Sr's defeat by Clinton in 1992 for pressing Israel to a settlement. "Israel major benefactor of 'Iraq war", *Final Call* 6 May 2003 pp. 3, 25.

62 "Journalists: U.S. media censorship is 'rampant'", *Final Call* 15 July 2003. U.S. and British officials deny media reports that depleted uranium projectiles, used in 'Iraq in both 1991 and 2003, caused cancers and birth defects among the populations there. Concerned scientists in the Anglomorph countries reply that no serious studies have yet been carried out *in situ.* The Bremen Institute for Prevention Research, Social Medicine and Epidemiology in Germany found that abnormalities in the repair of broken strands of DNA of coalition veterans who inhaled uranium oxide in battle in 'Iraq in 1991 occurred at five times the normal rate. See editorial and coverage of *New Scientist* (London) 19 April 2003 pp. 3-6.

63 (Ed.) "Empire status a trial for U.S.", *Final Call* 6 May 2003 p. 17.

64 See Jim Lobe, "First 'Gulag' then Gitmo: Bush is on the defensive," and William Fisher, "Congress takes up dispute over detainee abuse," in *Final Call* 5 July 2005 pp. 4, 33: these items came from outside the NOI from the IPS/GIN news service.

65 Dora Muhammad, "Enough is enough!," *Final Call* 7 June 2005 p. 3.

66 Hazel Trice Edney (NNPA), "Activists: It's time for Bush to rebuild America" *Final Call* 6 May 2003 p. 10.

67 Conversation with Dr Vibert L. White, 31 July 2002. Malik Shabazz noted in 2001 that the Taliban had never called him a nigger: Bin Ladin was at most "a terrorist [U.S.] terror produced"; President Bush Jr had inherited the staunch pro-Israel policy of destroying the Palestinians: Kelley Beaucar Vlahos, "Radical Black Panther Chief Blames American Leaders for Terror Attacks" in *Fox News* 3 November 2001.

68 White, *Inside the Nation of Islam* p. 206.

69 "The issues of the MILLIONS MORE MOVEMENT," and Farrakhan, "Why should there be a commemoration of the historic Million Man March?" *Final Call* 5 July 2005 p. 38.

70 Ashahed Muhammad, "Millions More Movement: Minister Farrakhan honored in Detroit" *Final Call Online* 16 August 2005.

71 Clarence Thomas, "Million Worker March Movement supports Millions More Movement," *The Final Call* 5 July 2005 p. 37.

72 See "One on one with Drs. Julia and Nathan Hare: Protect the Black mind!" *Final Call* 2 April 2002 p. 6.

73 Most Honorable Elijah Muhammad, "The House Doomed to Fall," *Final Call* 4 September 2001 p. 19.

74 "The 2.5 Million Member National Progressive Baptist Convention Endorses Millions More Movement," Final Call Website 29 August 2005.

75 Nisa Islam Muhammad, "Women mobilize for the Millions More Movement," Final Call.com 22 August 2005

76 Dora Muhammad, "Millions More Movement tour comes to Cleveland," Final Call and Website MillionsMoreMovement.com 25 August 2005.

77 Daniel B. Wood, "L.A.'s blacks, Latinos see answers in alliance," *Christian Science Monitor* 11 August 2005; csmonitor.com 31 August 2005. Najee 'Ali was aware that the relationship could go either way: "these are two American ethnic and racial communities who have a long history of fighting social injustice and racial oppression in this country," but "Blacks have felt threatened and marginalized with the growth of the Latino vote." Working with 'Ali as co-chairs in the new Black and Latino leadership alliance were the Rev. Al Sharpton—head of the New York City-based National Action Network—and Christine Chavez, political director of United Farm Workers, whose founder, her grandfather, had been guided and aided by Martin Luther king Jr. These leaders hoped that the alliance would help stop the two groups from undermining one another in competition for public dollars and programs." "Often the problem for poorer populations—Hispanic, black, and Asian alike—is that they don't think of organizing in an institutional way ... they tend to think it is just one person alone against the system," says Manuel Criollo, spokesman for the bus rider's union. "Our struggle shows that the system cannot ignore a unified front."

PERSPECTIVE AND CLOSING REFLECTIONS

In this volume, we tried to draw together a preliminary perspective of Islam as a continuous phenomenon down the whole extent of the history of African-Americans, but with most weight on the periods before the death of the Honorable Elijah Muhammad in 1975. How much coherence, weight and size—how much staying power?—did this African-American Islam have? The data of our chapters made clear that there never has been a time in their history when Islam has not been present, admittedly at one or two points as moribund embers or shards, among black people in America. In the period of slavery, Islam was a coherent crypto-religion that offered a rallying-point for at least psychological autonomy from the oppressor. Islam had its defining link-language—classical Arabic—with its array of distinctive rituals in that language, and a script that some of the enslaved were starting to use to record English with the intent of constructing a literate counter-discourse to Christianity. In the end, the context of enslavement was too destructive of the culture-systems its victims brought with them from Africa. Had Anglo-Saxon Americans granted them more room for maneuver, these Africans and their children might have constructed a Muslim equivalent of Yiddish, writing (and changing) the language of the dominant group within their own non-Christian (for them, Arabic) religious script. But African-Americans had been transformed by the time they got the printing presses.

The superb multi-cultural skills of Muslim African-American groups has recurred down the decades and the centuries within the most unfavorable contexts of poor formal education in English, and the all-surrounding discourse of Christianity and Anglo-Saxons hemming them in from all sides. Under slavery, as with the new Islam of Wali Fard Muhammad and Elijah Muhammad that crystallized after 1930, Muslims swiftly seized materials that were not of the best, and built and improvised upon them Muslim micro-nations that have shown a tenacious capacity to survive in America. Pre-Civil War writing of pieces of overheard bits of the Bible show that sharp attunedness to Christian discourses had already began in the times of slavery among Muslims who had never been Christian. In the first half of the twentieth century, Noble Drew 'Ali, Wali Fard Muhammad and Elijah Muhammad mustered passages from elite U.S. transcendentalists and theosophists, debris from freemasonry, from Mormonism, and radio broadcasts by early Jehovah's Witnesses, in tandem with the Qur'an, to dislocate converts out of the central belief-tenets of Christianity.

Given that Muslims under slavery had some sense of the multi-cultural skills they would need to make their creed survive in America, it is hard to term the Muslim cults of the twentieth century even in their initial periods as deprived of diverse cultural resources. They had seized all they could in their contexts of poverty and constricted formal education before they launched their movements. Attitude and determination matter. In the African-American context, poor or working-class people have built much more varied cultural and ideological resources on which to draw for constructing original belief-systems than America's Anglomorph academics and scholars have been ready to give them credit.

WHAT NON-ANGLO NATION HAVE MUSLIM AFRICAN-AMERICANS TRIED TO BUILD?

The high ambiguity about what the nation of a given Muslim sect or movement might be recurs in all periods of African-American history. The slavery-era Muslim minority clearly meant its tenacious adhesion to Islam to register some sort of protest against Anglo-Celtic Americans—but to define and delimit what ingroup or chain of groups?

At least one or two imported Muslim Africans during slavery voiced an impulse to define all Africans as one group against Westerners, generally considered. More common was a sense among Muslim Africans and their children in America that their monotheism, Arabic-script texts and their rituals set them apart from black as well as white non-Muslims. (True, Muslims during slavery, predictably, could not fulfil their potential to form into a long-term Islamic micronation within the African-American minority). The same problematic was to recur under Elijah and Farrakhan in the twentieth century. Both called for a united front of all black national forces or at least businessmen. Farrakhan achieved more in this direction, but a lot of Elijah Muhammad's discourse in particular, and even outbursts by Farrakhan also, suggest a persisting impulse to construct a micronation defined by bits and pieces from Islam and Arabic against the larger African-American minority.

Certainly, what look like inexplicable failures of Farrakhan to carry through the construction of the African-American political nation in the wake of the 1995 Million Man March become intelligible if we assume instead that his priority rather always remained the survival and expansion of his small NOI sect-nation, over the interests and future of any forming African-American macro-nation made up of many sects and beliefs. Farrakhan knew that the NOI was too small and not institutionalized enough to orchestrate the political organization of a parliamentarism for African-Americans as a whole: it could color a mass or electoral movement but there was always the risk that Christian professional politicians would dilute or sideline or subordinate it in any united front. Farrakhan's friendship tours overseas after October 1995 drew much criticism as squandering the impetus for black political organization. Yet his time-consuming outreaches to a host of Muslim and African leaders in the Third World make good sense if he wanted to build up enough contacts to make the U.S. pay too high a diplomatic price if its agencies moved to destroy the Nation of Islam in the event of his incapacitating sickness or death.

It has repeatedly been unclear, then, if Islam brings into formation a vanguard for a larger multi-sectarian "Black" or "African-American" nation in America, or if its particularities rather generate an Arabic-tinged Islamic micro-nation within, but in key dimensions closed to, the great African-American enclave-nation. Certainly, Warith ud-Din Muhammad's followers after 1975 gradually put together many of the attributes of a spatially scattered but culturally well-distinguished micro-nation throughout Black America.

IS ANY SEPARATE NATIONHOOD PRACTICABLE IN AMERICA?

The long history of Islam among African-Americans still leaves a question if it, or any truly separate culture for blacks, can be permanently viable in so culturally and materially dynamic a country as America. The great socio-political supremacy—and also the quality areas of creative thought and technology that confer strength—in Anglo-Saxon culture always made it highly attractive to the blacks as Americans. Islam has always provided a focus or a sanctuary for psychological resistance to oppression. Still, with Noble Drew 'Ali, Elijah Muhammad, and Farrakhan, the resistance subtly seems to have had as one aim to stop blacks from being finally, irreversibly, marginalized out of the mainstream economy of the America that segregated them. Despite vicious racism and segregation, the long-term pattern looks to be the affiliating of blacks as a more productive, and hence more equal and dignified, unit into America's economic mainstream—and then perhaps their integration into that society as well as economy in an outcome not very different from Martin Luther King, Jr.'s program. The "hate" aspect does not seem to be the major feature over the long term of these sects that so admire the way Euro-Americans do things in regard to making money, to extending technologies, and in their compound, specialized and interlocking, institutions.

Can the separation from, or protests against, a satanic oppressor that these cults hold out, their protest ethnicism, ever be much more than deceptive verbiage even in intent, a fig-leaf over cultural Anglicization, and over a Republican Party-like rightist obsession with social order? It may be impossible, though, for most blacks who pursue the WASP-American promise to reward individual enterprise to carry that ethos through to economic success for *them,* given that the goal-posts and the qualifications for entry keep on moving in America.

It is true that the thrust by those in African-American Muslim sects to achieve prosperity in businesses and in the professions has some features marginal to the American way. There has been ethnic solidarity and connections between individuals of a given ethnos, in the successful drives by Jewish and Catholic *ethne* to get into, and then win more places within, business activity and the professions. Yet, the attempts by quasi-Islamic sects in black America from the 1920s to weave together (a) a (so it sounded) confrontationist religion, with (b) loud nationalist separatism, and (c) separate educational and economic systems, was a uniquely compound assertion of distinctness among non-Anglo groups in America. It was as though these

Muslims pioneered by decades the forms of micronationalism that many other non-Anglo *ethne* were to conceptualize only from 1980.

Still, as far as separate nationhood goes, the final outcome of these Muslim protest-sects, all religious and national at the same time, seem to be the opposite of what they argue and promise when they start out. The venting of counter-hatred against devil-whites by and large served the converts well as a technique to drain away white racist discourses out of their psyche so that they do not congeal there into the self-hatred that paralyzes. Achieving that calming imperviousness to white denigration has then set these neo-Muslims free to avoid clashes with whites—"keeping your nose clean", becoming law-abiding—and then to proceed to an entrepreneurial collectivism in economics that gradually starts to build a sort of community with whites. There was an element of calculation, a sort of interim theatre meant only as a stage or a preliminary to some undisclosed later main game—Warith in one retrospect did call it "theatre" outright—in the use by Black Muslim ministers of hate denunciations focused by Islam to expel white negative conditioning from the Black psyche, prior to 1975. Hyper-denunciations of whites would be the best screen behind which to excise many of the non-Anglo specificities of the ghetto black poor, while still making the Muslims sound like the most militant of the competing protest groups. If with Elijah, at least, we have what looks most like a flexible but unbreakable ideology of tensile steel, that quasi-ideology in some contexts was able to wrap itself around, and commandeer, many efficient patterns in or from the wider white-ruled world. Of all the Muslim African-Americans we analyzed, Elijah stood as the least amenable to post-modernist quests for sub-texts and margins in discourse-systems. Elijah in adolescence had seen an Anglo lynching. Hence his outbursts as a powerful sect-leader that not just America's "white" power-system but all whites themselves might be destroyed very soon by Divine execution. But when he saw real changes taking place in America in the civil rights era that really might be incorporative of blacks, even Elijah could lucidly bankroll such liberal expansions of the American system.

Tightening relations with Middle Easterners and coming to terms with the U.S. system have often gone together in the tradition of African-American Islam. As oil-rich "black brethren" in the Arab world—"the rich world of Islam" as he termed it—donated aid in the 1970s, Elijah reflected that there might well be a fairly prolonged period of respite in which the Black Nation in America could achieve increasing prosperity before God destroyed the world. Elijah does from the late 1960s seem to have harbored some sub-text that economic exchanges, mutual benefit, a growing prosperity of all sections in America could provide a basis for a neutral constructive relationship between whites and blacks that would have no clear time-limit on it. Warith's post-1975 privatization of the nationalist collective commercial enterprises of the Nation of Islam, and even his Qur'an-citing entry into U.S. parliamentarism, which Farrakhan in his turn would enter in the next decade, really might have fulfilled shifts towards integration already taking place in Elijah's own marginal discourses and behavior, just like Warith argued to validate himself after 1975.

There is no doubt, for all the Nation of Islam's vituperative posture towards white core-America, of their deep commitment to its private-enterprise, acquisitive, materialistic private-enterprise ethos. But their money-making activism was more than just barely veiled acculturation to Anglo-Americans. It was also programmed by the first context of Arab-American peddlers and petty shopkeepers on whose margin the original NOI first formed in 1930. The shopkeepers were propelled to America from within their own cultures and societies that already placed high stress on trade. The nature of original Islam itself was also in play. The Qur'an was a scripture that the adherents of Drew 'Ali and of Elijah did read or were taught. The Qur'an's two-edged recognition of private enterprise as a deep-seated human need that can make individuals exploit others could have influenced the first NOI's pursuit of wealth with a private enterprise that nonetheless organized some taking part in it in a nationalist, collective way. The attempts of Elijah's followers to support a system of social welfare upon their commercial activities were more like a Qur'an-influenced synthesis of ummah (coherent community) than like the unfettered Anglo-American free enterprise that atomizes individuals more.

ISLAM AND BUILDING AN AFRICAN-AMERICAN POLITICAL NATION ACROSS CLASSES

In some senses, making Islamic survivals or new Islamic elements one basis of nationhood runs against some identity and experiences of Blacks in America. Yet Islam is not confined within just a sector of a class divide in Afro-America. Our study brought out the evolution of compatible Islam-orientated cultural elements across disparate strata in the 1920s, 1930s and 1940s that could provide some common ground for bringing together an African-American nation in America that could unite diverse classes. All popular and elite articulations of identity that we examined were touched or colored by Islam, certainly by sub-Saharan Africa's Muslims, but also by the Arabs and the wider Arab world to a fair extent. The young W.E.B. DuBois was determined to direct the resources and energies of his people to the very quick development of the "talented tenth" of the bourgeoisie under formation. Booker T. Washington strove more to educate a broader layer of black skilled tradesmen and workers. Yet DuBois gradually developed into a socialist concerned to expand cooperatives that would serve and unite a range of classes. The opinion leaders of the diverse Afro-American classes and strata evolving in the twentieth century—elite authors, Africanist populists, preachers and leaders of Muslim popular cults—all, as far as basics went, came to see the globe and its populations in ways that had enough affinities to be crafted into common platforms for international affairs. All these evolving worldviews gave at least some scope for Islam. Garvey had made his movement a forum for figures and ideas from international Muslim movements for independence from Western empires, and he had started to print information materials for Nigeria's Muslims in Arabic.

The motifs from the Middle East and Africa articulated by Noble Drew 'Ali, Wali Fard Muhammad, Elijah Muhammad and other Islamoid "cult" leaders when they addressed the Black masses were much more mythological and ahistorical representations of the Black experience in America. Such preachers used names and Arabic words and splinters from the Middle East to relate and restructure the range of black experiences in that more religious, apocalyptic way. Yet Elijah often mentioned the fairly secular Garvey, more political than he, and the ideas that a Sudanese-Egyptian nationalist had contributed to Garvey's media. We saw that Fard, Elijah and Malcolm, as they developed certain historical ideas about the original enslavement, and in arguing that some abducted Africans had been Muslim, could draw on consonant themes of such apex intellectuals as Carter Woodson and DuBois.

Generally considered, our data established that (a) highly-educated, elite, blacks and (b) the popular masses being colored by Islam both had some beliefs about history and Africa/"the East" (including Islam) in common that would help those classes come together as one nation, not set them at odds. Islam was a shared phantom-heritage rather than a divisive choice for African-Americans. The first half of the twentieth century was bequeathing elements for joint actions of diverse black classes in the U.S. and its international affairs that could help Arabs as well as sub-Saharan Africans and, of course, African-Americans themselves. But that potential had to wait for the 1980s, through Farrakhan and through bourgeois left-Christian mass-leaders like Rev. Jesse Jackson, more touched by Islam and real contemporary Arabs than Woodson and DuBois had been. Our second, companion, work will discuss ongoing psychological tensions that Farrakhan was to voice in the 1980s and 1990s towards the professional and bourgeois strata of blacks that he was winning over as a political leader.

John Hutchinson, who has analyzed a wide range of nationalisms, characterized from non-industrialized Irish, Slavic, Indian and Chinese societies a modality of "national revivals" that are initiated by "religious reformists" and "modernist journalists" acting together. While Hutchinson did not mention the Arab World, his paradigm also fits British-occupied Egypt where the Muslim modern bourgeoisie in the period of British colonial rule (1882-1922) was still small, and faced deculturation from the impact of French and English in modern education, business, and in the civil service. These early nationalisms—Irish, Slavic, Indian, Chinese and Arab—had to take shape in societies in which each given modern national bourgeoisie was still too weak to conceive or conduct or spread a nationalist ideology and movement without aid from intellectuals who had older types of clerical education. Transforming the accepted meanings of "tradition" and "modernity", these coalitionist revivalists evoke golden ages that, far from being reactionary, reconcile religious values from the past with secular progress that learns from the West while rejecting "cosmopolitan" fusion with it.[1]

Very close to Hutchinson's paradigm, here, is the veiled duality of so many black Muslim sects that offer protest-discourses as a rallying-point, but under those nationalist fig-leaves simultaneously spread adjusted Anglo-American cultural and social norms among the range of black classes they rally. It is also to be noted that Farrakhan, in contrast to Elijah, has been very attentive since 1975 to the ongoing importance of the black Christian clergy in African-American life and politics: he has adjusted his NOI's discourse to make it look like it accepts much of the Bible and hence those clergy as long-term partners, much more than he has pitched his communications to the Afro-centrism of the secular intellectuals. The thin numbers of the "black bourgeoisie" in the U.S. up to the 1970s posed situations similar to those within which Slavic, Indian, Chinese and Arabo-Egyptian nationalisms took shape, and here too, many of its ordinary members, and also of its intellectuals, plunged into integrationist variants of the culture of the ruling ethnos as their best hope to get into America and its wealth. But deculturation and Anglicization threatened ethnic identity much more in America, where the segregated (some say "colonized") African-American people lived next to the pounding heart of a dynamic Anglo-Saxon culture and economy that shredded other identities and that sometimes looked as though it might admit blacks who made themselves exactly like Anglos.

The weakness of the modern-educated bourgeoisie in black America, and the lack of will of many of its members to build nationality, threw that task—as in Egypt or India—onto populist "religious" vanguards that one day might build themselves into counter-elites: Elijah's Nation of Islam from 1950-1975 was the most striking instance of that. Very like Hutchinson's paradigm for the Slavic world and India are the roles African-American journalists played in publicizing the religious clerics of "the Black Muslims" and their teachings to black masses and among secular bourgeois strata that the NOI could not have reached by itself. And our scanning of the NOI press of the 1970s showed well-qualified, sometimes ex-Marxist, bourgeois journalists coming together with Islamic religious visionaries to focus neo-Muslim critiques of power relations between "white" and "colored" people in both America and in the Middle East.

Dr Arthur Huff Fauset in 1944 assessed that Drew 'Ali's sect had started a search for elements crucial to preparing the blacks of America to mount political action on the basis of a distinct nationhood, over the longer term. The Moors did at least try to envision a robbed golden age and lost homeland across the ocean, the continuous national memory that the Negroes of America had lost in contrast to its other major *ethne*. As a mass political movement, Marcus Garvey's UNIA was like the "political organ or organism" that Fauset foresaw might utilize the religious organization for building a political nationhood of blacks in America. There was some overlapping attraction in both the UNIA and Drew 'Ali's Moors to romantic, bygone Muslim Spain, and to the Arab Muslim countries of North Africa and West Asia, which now further differentiated their nation from the Euro-Americans around it. But it was not enough to unite the two groups for building together a joint nationalist political movement.

That African-American Islam might unite with some black sects-uniting political organization to conduct a mass national political movement together, is the possibility that, from the late 1970s, came to the fore of the choices open to blacks. Elijah had made no attempt to use the civil rights cleric-politicians of the South, or the Black professional politicians who developed out of them, for any aims of the NOI, which he firmly kept out of U.S. politics. Yet the NOI's tenet of the "Black Nation" was liable to express itself in ameliorist political activism as soon as the sect's hopes of an incineration by God flagged.

Farrakhan's new post-1978 NOI showed at three points, each separated by a decade, that it might make itself able to launch a political mass movement in which many non-Muslim African-Americans might take part. The first point was the presidential primaries of 1984: those elections showed the black bourgeoisie, black media-persons and intellectuals, mainstream politicians who had once started out as Christian clerics during civil rights, and religious NOI leaders who claimed special closeness to God, for a time working together to advance the Rev. Jesse Jackson in the American system's electoral politics. Both the Democratic Party's black professional politicians, and the religious-Islamic NOI proto-"church," knew they had to work together because neither had enough standing to bring the masses into normal politics on its own. During the primaries, Farrakhan showed that he could activate both black professionals and ghetto masses. The second point at which the second NOI showed that it had some of the means to at least bring together a range of black classes was the Million Man March of 1995. Farrakhan was able in 1995 to persuade diverse bourgeois, working-class and lumpen blacks—almost a whole African-American nation—to come and listen to his speech in Washington. Farrakhan's October 2005 Millions More Movement looks likely to prove a third point at which he should be able to turn out large numbers of blacks from the same range of classes and cultural and religious groups.

If the October 2005 rally in Washington has come off well by the time that this text is read, the pattern would be of a steady increase in Farrakhan's ability over 27 years to draw a widening range of classes and cultural groups into protest rallies that blend black nationhood with religious morality. Yet Farrakhan's organizing of crowds at three points separated from each other by a full decade has thus far yet to heighten into real organization by him of the strata he can sometimes turn out, despite long intervals. Across over a quarter of a century, Louis Farrakhan proved unable to design mechanisms and institutions by which he could hold together, direct, and discipline all those groups, on a day-to-day basis over years. He could not fashion any political party or even any regularized political front with which to direct the development of non-Muslim blacks. Muhammad Ibn 'Abdallah of Arabia was able, after he established the first Muslim-led authority in Medinah, by varying diplomacy with force, to build authority over a diverse range of warring tribes, expanding the territory he governed to cover most of the Arabian peninsula by his death. Qa'id-i-A'zam ("Supreme Leader") Muhammad 'Ali Jinnah put together an alliance or united front of the most diverse Muslim elites and classes in pre-partition India, in which he built enough authority to enable him to veto or bring down faraway Muslim politicians in his Muslim League but also in other parties, when they defied his goals. Farrakhan has shown united front skills without achieving a political party or long-term machine: he built up influence among most groups of black Americans, but not a routinized authority like that with which Jinnah and his Muslim League mobilized most Muslims to carve a separate Pakistan state out of India by 1947. By the 21st century, Farrakhan had become well aware that the unequalled range of blacks who gave him hearings, were not surrendering their psyches to him. He had failed to win the final permanent mastery of their minds, and the discipline that the greatest nationalist and religious leaders, and statesmen, build over most groups in the populations they transform and reinvent.

Farrakhan, near the end of his career, has grasped that he had got the ear of diverse classes of blacks, but not their obedience: that the lumpen street gangs and the young bourgeois blacks who flock to his mass rallies and hear his tapes approve him in a relaxed way as someone who has some very true things to say, but without accepting his discourse as a system: that, indeed, for many he was not much more than an "entertainer" whose good oratory they could savor without it transforming their behavior and lives after they left the rally.

Over nearly a century of activity, Islamic sects have legitimized their full membership in an African-American nation that remains mainly Christian. Prior to Elijah's death in 1975, their lack of Christianity did not enthrall most African-Americans, and no mainsteam Christian or secular politician would have dared to publicly associate with any Black Muslim leader. Since 1980, Christian-secular black politicians have been able to so associate or ally without fatal cost to their careers, with flak coming mainly from Zionoid micronationalists rather than Anglos. Thus, while no Muslim leader thus far has either constructed or taken part in a multi-sectarian black nationalist party or front that is institutionalized, the way is open to construct that, given the relaxed attitude of most African-Americans to Islam.

THE DEFENSE AND RESTORATION OF MALE-LED FAMILIES

One image of U.S. blacks has been that Amazon-like vital women mainly head what families African-Americans have been able to have or build. That matrifocal family pattern derived less from societies in West Africa, than from ill-treatment by America's Euro majority communities. As with other caste systems in South Asia and Japan, racism in America strove to break long-term exclusive relationships between a single black male and a single black female in order to atomize—and thus control—the slaves. Our review of the period of slavery and the formation of the American nationalities in Chapter 2 offered snapshots of Muslim patriarchal figures at the head of prosperous, tenacious families that kept speaking African languages and reading their Arabic Qur'ans for three generations. With African Islam in North America and then the successor-sects that resurfaced in the twentieth century, we find a drive of blacks to restore male-headed families in defiance of racist restrictions on the livelihoods by which black males could have made themselves breadwinners. Many African-American women have been made amazons by context and necessity rather than any wish of their own. The drive of the Islamic sects of Noble Drew 'Ali, Wali Fard Muhammad, Elijah Muhammad, and after 1975, Warith (Wallace) Muhammad and Farrakhan to mould ghetto blacks with unordered lives into stable breadwinners who will keep up family responsibility has attracted many ill-educated women in all periods of African-American Islam. It is like other impulses of "Black Islam"—for example, business activity—in that it blends middle American and Qur'anic or Middle Eastern concepts together.

The Muslims' drive to restore patriarchal families brought benefits of continuity of life, stable intimate community, and improved welfare to hundreds of thousands of African-Americans. Such families fitted them much more into the ideology of the Anglo-American middle classes, whose trades and professions all Black Muslim sects tried to duplicate throughout the twentieth century behind smokescreen denunciations of "white devils." Yet these NOI endeavors to enhance black males have sometimes been narrow-minded and dysfunctional, and they may not succeed. The constricting new roles that Elijah offered the women who joined—sewing-machines and home-keeping—were a caricature of 19th century Anglo conservatism. Under Farrakhan and Warith, the roles for women in and around the sect have widened, but Farrakhan and his sect remain uneasy about the extent of the careers that African-American women carved out for themselves after World War II. The priority of Farrakhan and Warith's sects in the new century remains to widen the livelihoods and roles of young male blacks. The reputation of Warith's sect among African-American women is that it is the place to go to get married quickly.

It is in such endeavors as the building of patriarchal families and of commercial motivation and skills, that Muslim sects among blacks show their function as constructive mechanisms that adjust the U.S. system, so as to make it and its culture cover sectors of Americans that it had not reached before. Yet it takes time to fully Anglo-Americanize the targeted blacks. A protest religion, a collective nationalism, as well as entrepreneurial self-profit all have to be plaited together to wrench the converts across from lumpen towards normal American patterns. For a time, the sect has to direct or regiment the new families and new economic activity far beyond what U.S. central likes to allow any clergies or micronations.

ECONOMICS: THE DRIVE FOR PROFESSIONAL STATUS AND PROSPERITY

Our review of the period of slavery already showed an incipient linkage between (a) Islam and Arabic letters on one hand and (b) specialized functions and prosperity. Their numeracy and literacy, and the agricultural knowledge they brought with them from Africa, made many Muslims an asset for the plantation-slavers, some of whom gave them better economic functions and more family autonomy than to enslaved animists. Economics have manifested the ambiguity and duality that has recurred in many Muslim movements to our own day. Islam and the Qur'an have abundant materials in them that could serve as a rallying-point or slogan for armed resistance, but Muslim African-Americans have much more often sought prosperity for themselves and their families. As well as resistance, the Qur'an also images trading communities, albeit critically in the first surahs that denounced the pagan mercantile society of the trade-city, Mecca, as able to trigger divine destruction of the world (such surahs can feed neo-Muslim denunciations of white capitalism and market-economies). Elijah and his followers were also getting more and more acculturated before 1975 to America's core Anglomorph economic values and activities, yet their entrepreneurial spirit still as yet sought prosperity through a "black capitalism" of a unique nationalist ethos and structure. Perhaps in accordance with their inner logic of evolution, Elijah's companies and businesses sometimes were to mutate into individualistic economic enterprises under his son Wallace/Warith ud-Din Muhammad. Under Elijah, though, what the NOI was practising was more like a collectivist economic self-development, fueled by nationalism and highly functional hate-motifs against whites, where labor, rather than exploited by owners, is—or so the NOI's image went—given some social welfare benefits, opportunities, and spiritual reclamation: a sort of economic communalism.[2]

Elijah's values in regard to enterprise, industriousness, clean living, and creating in relation to social problems as opposed to destroying, did not wholly derive from those of the Anglo-American middle class. Self-sacrificing nationalism, and the Qur'an's sharp focus on ethically appropriate procedures for commerce and private enterprise, had supplemented American self-enrichment in motivating the followers to succeed in business. The Qur'an did propose procedures for a just and prosperous society founded on commerce within an urban life [Diana Collier]. Yet the flow of money up the pyramid to a thickening apex elite was becoming more and more marked under Elijah, whose sect looked about to become an adaptation—or affiliate—of corporate American enterprise when he died.

While Islam may be a prosperity-religion in some aspects, Islam-influenced movements have made significant contributions to the Anglicization or Westernization of poor Blacks who languished outside the USA's normal economic system. The new NOIs of Warith and Farrakhan, too, after 1975 bore on their own account the idea of serving and redeeming the people through enterprise, a drive that brought some order and opportunities to various populations of poor Blacks, and to a layer of Black entrepreneurs and lumpen-bourgeoisie. The limits upon radical possibilities, though, are clear—not just because these reincarnations of Elijah's sect, too, want to make middle-Americans of slum or ghetto residents, but also because both Farrakhan and Warith's enterprises have sought the customage of the pampered recreational or consumerist tastes of the top black bourgeoisie. Did the leaders of these sects already share the consumptionist aims of the pagan bourgeoisie even when they were just starting out as reclaimers of the down-and-out and the desperately poor? These are groups and leaderships that tap and heighten popular black anger against whites, but in order to channel it to quintessentially American business enterprises that are meant to enrich in the longer term. Much more than was the case with the Black Panthers and their ideal of service of the people, the new NOI's thrust to bring social services to poor blacks may get vitiated by the long-term drive of the activists to achieve wealth. Champion of the suffering poor or not, Farrakhan himself chose to live in an elegant predominantly Jewish and Anglo suburb of Chicago instead of with the masses of his nation in that city: where the legs of these proto-elites are taking them sometimes says more than what they orate. It thus remains to be seen how far the acquisitive and materialist impulse of the adherents will allow Muslim African-American sects to carry through the task of reforming the poorer strata of blacks and their subcultures, to which Muslim sects in America have always had an ambiguous relation.

Yet the bygone nationalist capitalism of Elijah, even as an intriguing failure, still lived decades later in the relations between non-Muslim and Muslim groups in the 1980s and 1990s: the favorable memory itself was still reaping influence and even power for Elijah's successors among the non-Muslim black business classes. Farrakhan's sect and its media served as a sort of forum or sounding-board for the wider black business elites, around which to focus strategies for the achievement of a (transitional?) nationalist capitalism, and as radiating-points for popularizing their nationalist-capitalist enterprise among the masses. That forum role paid off over decades for Farrakhan, in the economic lifelines and loans that non-Muslim black business repeatedly threw the companies of his sect. But even if the second NOI's attempt to build a Muslim nationalist mini-economy fails in the final outcome, a sort of division of labor has taken shape in which a Muslim sect and its media acts as a clearing-house that ideologically concentrates a joint drive by many sects together to express nationality in business. The Muslim sect can act as a link of communication between the black business class and the masses they have to make customers. It would be a role like that Fausset speculated a Muslim sect could play as an auxiliary partner of a nationalist black political party.

RELATIONS WITH THE ARAB AND MUSLIM COUNTRIES

Despite—or because of—the tendency of Muslim groups among African-Americans to avoid the U.S. mainstream and general American politics, the internationalization of "Black Islam" has always been a possibility. True, most twentieth century quasi-Muslim cults or sects that we examined took shape under such intense pressure from special U.S. racial situations and from Christian and other American religious ways of seeing as to give unique meanings to Qur'anic materials, or so as to reduce the Qur'an to just one element in a made-in-America composite, at least for the time. But Elijah's smallish Nation of Islam became one of the contenders to become or lead a mass movement of African-Americans in the late 1950s—the outset of the television era and mass communications in which even his adherents, and certainly African-Americans in general, would notice where the NOI's Islam deviated from that of the vivid Arabs and Africans on the screens whose advances to independence excited the USA's black public.

Outreach to alternative Muslim power-centers overseas has always entailed influence from Sunni and Shi'ite states and societies in the Third World that has reduced the purely American features of the sects. One Moorish temple at least had tried to get Kemalist Turkey to admit some of their members as farmer immigrants, while in the post-modern era several Moorish temples have relations with Moroccan and other Arab diplomats in the U.S. In regard to the Nation of Islam, Malcolm X from his prison days was constantly reaching out to Arab and Muslim leaders of Afro-Asia and to local lobbyists from "the dark world of Islam." Farrakhan's whirlwind tours of the Muslim and Third World countries in the later 1990s as the Zionist micro-nationalists mustered extreme pressure on U.S. administrations to starve or crush the new NOI were more of the same. Many scholars who published in the USA seem to have exaggerated the extent to which Elijah and the colleagues who stayed with his group were "parochial" and Americanist in comparison to Malcolm. It is true that Elijah's leading group in Chicago—as would Farrakhan in the 1980s and 1990s—showed hard-headed caution and always hung back to some extent from the Muslim and Third Worlds. These sects' atomized borrowings from Arabic have taken time to cohere into a true internationalist system. "Parochial" when they wanted to be, Elijah Muhammad and his colleagues still "interacted globally on a political, economic and diplomatic level with some Third World states while representing a local interest". As Malcolm did even in his last independent period when he courted Saudi Arabia's conservative king Faysal and his "revolutionary" pan-Arab opponent Nasser at the same time, Elijah and his group tried to make friends from the dominant groups in Muslim and Third World countries without behaving ideologically: "once again the mark of [an enclave-] nation, not a political party". Elijah viewed himself as the pragmatic head of an evolving micronation that strove to build economically rewarding relations with other non-white states in the world [Collier 2001].

Yet, the old NOI also acted as a forum into which a fairly chaotic range of Arab, Muslim, and Third World groups poured their grievances, their demands and their ideologies (the latter often were left-tinged). The solidarity with Palestinian nationalists that *Muhammad Speaks* and *Final Call*—but also, and vocally so, Warith's Arab-orientated *Muslim Journal*—built up over decades among Black Americans did not serve, and may have sometimes damaged, the long-term prospects of these sects. The question, then, is how far overseas American and Muslim states and movements can achieve input into Warith's and Farrakhan's sects without veto from those two sects' needs in America.

As Arabic atoms and whole rituals more and more color Farrakhan's less orthodox sect, he has in some outbursts accused Arabs of racism against Africans and against Islamizing Afro-Americans of his type. Such outbursts are very human within a difficult acculturative process, yet the charges of hegemonism or indifference by Arabs look to be untrue, overall. All the Muslim states, and most of the Arab and Muslim media and political movements, have treated Farrakhan and his followers with flexible hospitality. They have not demanded that he eat his past words or Elijah's unique doctrines before they admitted him with the more accommodative Warith into the apex international bodies of Islam, in which he and his colleagues have been allowed to have their say.

As Farrakhan's as well as Warith's movements internalize more and more Arabic materials as well as tenets, these sects are developing sharp and judicious images of contemporaneous Muslim societies in Africa and the Middle East. Up to 1975, Muslim groups hailed the freedom movements and independent states of Africa, the Middle East, and Asia in an uncritical way. The modern, critical, post-ideological discussion of those societies and states is less a weakening of that old psychological affect than a deepening of it into real transcontinental relationships within history.

The neo-Islamic sects have spread atoms of Arabic from the elements of Islam that they seized across and out among huge non-Muslim masses. During the 1995 Million Man March on Washington, Farrakhan made the greeting of "as-Salamu 'Alaykum" (Peace be To You), which he got the huge crowd to chant after him, an emblem of identity distinguishing African-Americans as a whole from Christian and Jewish white Americans as a whole. We have seen that from the very beginnings of the Nation of Islam at the outset of the 1930s, the images of a relinking to homelands in "the East" (Afro-Asia) with the concomitant break from American society, greatly helped draw converts to the new protest Islam. On the subjective plane, change was a psychological reality: the sense that they now had new links did alter a fair range of the attitudes and behavior of the converts vis-a-vis fellow-Americans, white and black. Subjective identification with populations in two other continents, the grain of whose cultures looked so different from America's, broke the psychic grip of white America's arrangements. The extra-territorial religion, redefined from foreign to the native essence of Blacks, gave transcendent authority for a break with the American patterns now put in perspective as local and temporary.

How far were the Noble Drew 'Ali, Wali Fard Muhammad, Elijah Muhammad, Imam Warith ud-Din Muhammad, Farrakhan, and the other leaders of this discourse-tradition really able to deliver over 90 years on their promises to affiliate adherents to something overseas that one day might balance the might of the Euro-Americans amongst whom they will always still have to live? In his own life, Wali Fard Muhammad had had interaction with pro-Japanese Asian groups in the 1930s, and this led such followers as Elijah to stand with expansionist Japan verbally in its war on America. During its post-WWII revival, Elijah's sect employed immigrant Arabs to teach in its network of schools, an approach that did bring in more atoms of genuine Arabic and orthodox Islam, even as it brought out doctrinal and historical disparities between these two nations from separate continents. In regard to the construction of imagined print-communities, the readiness of *Muhammad Speaks* and its successor tabloids to carry articles by America-resident Palestinians and news from Arab countries brought in more atoms of Arabic. These newspapers also printed a diverse range of Arab and Middle Eastern anti-West ideologies, secular and Islamist, that the editors of these sects did not try to limit or mute. Such extraterritorial news proposed the possibility that the followers' formal affiliation to Islam could usher in a transcontinental, multi-racial community of pan-Islam one day.

It is hard at this juncture to tell how much Islam-influenced African-Americans and immigrant Arab and other Muslim communities will interact and join together. "Black Muslim" oral cultures, media, institutions and education—which have more and more Arabic in them—are making many African-Americans likelier to get on with Middle Eastern groups in America. Arabic fragments and cliches did draw members of Farrakhan's delegations on World Friendship tours into some cordial interaction with Third World Muslim groups that knew little English. Arabic-medium Islam has dyed Warith's group the most deeply, with benefits exchanged between both the African-American and Arab parties. Warith's system of private Islamic schools, which stressed Arabic, won crucial donations from Saudi Arabia that carried the schools over some bad humps. Farrakhan's followers have founded fewer sectarian schools which stress Arabic less. Immersion courses in Arabic and Islamic law in Cairo's al-Azhar, the Harvard of Sunni Islam, and in Sunni Islamic law in Damascus, which may produce a new bilingual intellectual elite in the sect, could radically Arabize the theology of the sect that Imam Warith conducted, over the decades to come.[3] Increasing social interactions led to some intermarriages between women in Warith's sect and Arab students: at least some of the latter, though, did not take their temporary spouses with them when they went back home.

The cultural input from Muslim sects out into wider African-American groups makes the latter likelier to sympathize with Third World Arab and Muslim causes and groups. But we saw how from the 1960s and 1970s a wide range of secular "Black Nationalist" and Africanist groups in the USA on their own initiative tried to build solidarity with Palestinians and other Arabs against Israel, just as a considerable number of non-Muslim Afro-Americans felt some sympathy for Khomeini in the 1980s and for Saddam Husayn and Yasir 'Arafat in the 1990s. Thus, expectations from the overall African-American people have additionally pushed Black Muslim leaders to stand with the Arabs and articulate criticisms of Israel for Blacks as a whole.

Part of the solidarity with Arabs or Muslims decried by America stem from the latter's poor treatment of Blacks, who in turn symbolically salute Muslim figures whom America seems to be treating with prejudice overseas. But there may be more to the interest in the Middle East. We have repeatedly seen that the blurring of "Black Africa" into the Arab World, West Asia and "the East" recurred time and time again among all varieties of popular and elite black nationalists, Muslim and non-Muslim. The urgent drive to reconnect with Africa below the Sahara has often gone with the sense that

that Black Africa on its own would not be enough to cover all identity of African-Americans, that something else—"the East"—has to be added. This other twin-impulse of reconnection to lands of origin across the sea in all groups could—beyond various things in Anglo discourses that stimulate it—stem from some dim sense in the Black American psyche that some of their ancestors had deep cultural affinities to Arabs, their language and to their countries, which of course is the historical fact. Still, the solidarity of African-Americans in general, and by Islam-tinged groups most of all, with the Palestinian and other Arab causes has been partly fueled by their interaction with local U.S. Jews and their discourses.

The sense of an "East", a community across the seas wider than just Africa that African-Americans must reclaim, has brought some relations with overseas Muslims and Africans: but it may also help build harmonious community between diverse Americans internally, as well. The potential is clear for the entry of some Latino converts and Arabs, etc., into the new NOI and Warith's sect. But, more widely, the ability of Muslim blacks to pass beyond Africa and the narrower (perhaps rational) way most secular nationalists have defined "blackness," could be of good use to America, inside. Among such new constructive applications of the old NOI's international "Black Nation" that encompassed Asians, have been the efforts of Farrakhan's sect to mediate and harmonize between Korean shopkeepers and lumpen blacks in the ghettoes. With the elements they have taken from multiple overseas cultures, and their connections to diverse countries, Muslim African-Americans are specially equipped beyond any other American group to help integrate Arab-Americans, Asian-Americans, Latinos, African-Americans and Anglomorph Americans into a single American community that could work. It remains to be seen if some sector of the U.S. establishment classes will utilize the abilities to navigate and communicate across cultural and ethnic groups that African-American Muslims built up through their overseas links and travels.

THE NOIS AND BLACK-JEWISH INTERACTION IN AMERICA

The accumulated interaction between Jews and African-Americans in America has been significant in the development of both, especially for their invention of ideologies. Blacks and Jews had their adjacent capital cities in a shared New York, for the first half of the 20th century. Despite the smaller number of Jews among Euro-Americans, relationships with Jews have often influenced African-Americans as much as their interactions with WASP Americans, who were and are the definitive people for the evolution of America, and whose culture and concepts even black protest discourses must again and again present (but bend and adjust) at the most unexpected points. Our book showed that some Jews took part in slavery in North America, and that perhaps most acquiesced to glaring ill-treatment of "Negroes" in the first half of the 20th century. Yet some socialists, progressives and rational liberals among Jews have at all points grasped that "Jews and

Blacks" (a construct indeed) would have to win their margins for growth and distinctness together in the Anglomorph state. From the calm perspective of our new century, some African-American Muslims in Warith's movement see the bygone cooperation between liberal Jews and disadvantaged blacks as having brought real benefits to the latter when their friends were few. For some in Warith's group, support and aid from some Jews in the 20th century had been as important in black advancement as that from abolitionist WASPs had been before the Civil War in the 19th. (Farrakhan, too, has discreet but deep respect for the success with which Jews have built wealth, power and cultural autonomy in a country not eager to have them: he knows that African-Americans must adjust to that strength, as they must also duplicate the self-organization and institutions with which Jewish-Americans built it up).

Yet, writing in 1966 towards the end of a period in which an ideology of pink liberalism had dominated the discourse of American Jews, Brandeis University academic Ben Halpern questioned the assumption that Blacks and Jews were natural allies who belonged together, that the sharpening — but long-standing — tensions dividing them were a family quarrel. He queried if this assumption of many of the Jewish and Negro intellectuals and leaders caught up in the conflict was "a healthy way of approaching the issues... since there are many significant ways in which [the two groups] do not belong together at all, and indeed may have conflicting interests."[4] From that point of American history, coinciding with the Arab-Israeli war of 1967, conflict has over decades been more important in Jewish-Black relations than the earlier attempts to weave together their respective advancements in Anglomorph America.

After 1980, as American government has contracted and weakened, and all the proliferating micronationalisms (multiplying among whites also) compete with the thinning Americanist political community; those who sincerely strive to integrate the country do so under terrible burdens from its history. Some approach—some form of power for non-white minorities—would need to be found to make Jewish as well as Angloid-Christian white Americans face home-truths about the shared history their group has constructed along with Blacks. But it proved hard to get serious conversations and negotiations under way between Jewish-Americans and Islamophile African-Americans within any peace-making process. The right of Muslim African-Americans to utter a discourse of their own about their history was in a way denied by the 1995 resolution of the American Historical Association that ruled out any discussion that Jews could have played a disproportionate role in the exploitation of slave labor or in the Atlantic slave trade, although Jewish Zionoid micronationalists claimed disproportionate success for Jews in most other things about America from its "discovery" and onwards. Conciliation and negotiations within peace-making can be made almost impossible so long as one party not only refuses to let the other articulate its historical or current grievances but sometimes even tries to economically choke off and destroy that other party, as some Jewish-American organizations have tried to do to Farrakhan's Nation of Islam—a sort of a Zionoid calque on the refusal of Golda Meir, Menachim Begin, Yitzhak Shamir and the Likud to recognize that Palestinians even existed, let alone negotiate with them.[5]

Only time will tell if Jewish-Black conflict can be turned around in America, as is demanded by America's cultural coherence and benefit, and by certain interests of the two groups themselves. On the hopeful side, Farrakhan's sect has moved in the 21st century towards Warith's group on stances towards at least America's Jews: few issues of *Final Call* now print the like of the attacks it carried in the 1980s and 1990s, in which African-American educated youth highlighted their conflicts with local Jews. One in part ascribed the breakdown of black father-headed families to, for instance, odd Jews around the production of "The Color Purple" that projected lesbianism. Muslim organizations and circles are a key group in discussion of Jews and Israel among African-Americans, and conciliating them is important for peacemaking. Between 1960 and 2000, the tabloids and magazines of the first NOI and its successors portrayed the struggle between Israel and the Palestinians/Arabs as one in which those fellow-Muslims in the Middle East should overpower the Jewish state. Since mid-2002, though, less binary articles in *Final Call* have had a flat sense that that conflict has gone on too long and nobody can win: they would accept a negotiated compromise between Palestinians and Israelis. The second NOI does seem to be becoming much more attuned to the feelings of Israelis and Jews as human beings, and to what is practical. Internally, Farrakhan has alluded to the desirability of Muslim, Christian and Jewish clergies working together to help America and mend the malfunctions of its system and its problems with overseas Muslims. As with his softening attitudes to Anglo-Americans, his shift about various types of Jews goes with his movement from millenarianism and incineration to political ameliorism.

In the end, whether harmony between Jews and Blacks in America can be reached will be decided by Jewish-Americans themselves and by the majority of African-Americans who have not embraced any form of Islam, although they are often Arabophile and give hearings to black Muslim leaders and media. The decades since 1967 leave one with a paradoxical sense that in many ways such aspects of Muslim sects as "Farrakhan's anti-Semitism" have been the work of the nominally Christian bourgeoisie, as much as a catalyst of that bourgeoisie's ethnic tensions with some American Jews and Israel. Many in the secular and Christian black bourgeoisie regard African-American Muslims as the Black Nation's experts on the Middle East, to be called in as speakers whenever that non-Muslim bourgeoisie wants to stand up to the Zionoid micronationalists and to Israel. Some Muslim leaders in Black America have served as proxies to anger the Zionoids and Israel on behalf of the total bourgeoisie. A figure like Farrakhan may now be too old for that role. It also looks as though the cultural connection with Arabs in the Middle East will, so long as Israel rules and hits Palestinians, undo efforts by black Islamic leaders to come to terms with American Jewry. In the new 21st century, ethnic tensions between African- and Jewish-Americans are as high as in 1965 four decades back. The mainstream's African-American politicians and institutions have failed to achieve empowerment there vis-à-vis their Jewish equivalents. Sustained systematic conflict between the secular African-American and Zionoid elites could easily draw in both Farrakhan and Warith's sect as auxiliary warriors, which looked about to happen for Warith's younger activists in 2002 as the Zionoids moved to de-elect Black Caucus members of Congress who had voted against the needs of Israel.

Overall, black-Jewish conflict in America has highlighted the Middle East and Islam, and local Black Muslims, in the minds of non-Muslim African-Americans. The NOI and the Zionoid micronationalist minority helped each other widen support in their respective wider ethnic minorities from 1980.

Viewed in perspective, Elijah Muhammad but especially Farrakhan, not just Warith, appear highly American, because their ideas and their economic projects parallel, derive from, or link into those of so many other groups and traditions in the USA. The enclave-nationalist and micronationalist applications of Islam by the Noble Drew 'Ali, Elijah Muhammad, Malcolm X, and Farrakhan could come to parallel the evolution of white enclave nationalisms from the 1920s, in particular that blended ethnic and religious assertion to get into the USA's parliamentarist polity. Despite their starting point of much greater ethnic oppression, the various "Black Muslim" sects and movements shared some of the integrative functions of "white" particularist non-Anglo micronationalisms in America. Irish-American, Hispanic-American, Polish-American and Jewish-American political nationalisms have differentiated and solidified, but at the same time, in crucial ways, Anglicized various sub-nations as a preliminary to getting them into the rewarding mainstream that had not wanted them. Blacks faced much more resistance for getting into Anglomorph America than any Euro-American groups—including Jews. Black micronationalisms thus have special features that can indeed at points take them much further than with other, non-black micronationalisms, towards the outer limits of what the U.S. system can conceive or allow. The unique ambiguity as to whether Muslim and other Black enclave nationalisms in America are secessionist or a procedure that achieves inclusion stems less from their ideological hatred of whites that lets out the steam than from the hate and contempt Blacks have had to face in America.

ENDNOTES

1 John Hutchinson, "Explaining National Revivals," *The Australian Journal of Politics and History* v. 34 (1 988) pp. 34-36.

2 Letter from Diana Collier, 31 January 2001.

3 See advertisement "Intensive Arabic Immersion Program at al-Azhar University, Cairo, Egypt July 1-31 2005," in *Muslim Journal* 27 may 2005 p. 13.

4 Shlomo Katz (ed.), *Negro and Jew: An Encounter in America* (New York: Macmillan1967) pp. 66-69

5 This 1995 resolution was rightly described by those who touted it as "unprecedented in [the AHA's] 111-year history," and such selective foreclosure of hypotheses is indeed far beyond the rational functions of any umbrella

organization of academic historians. It amounted in the context of the Black-Jewish polarization in 1995 to a drive to clamp ethnicist hegemony over the AHA by those Jewish academics who pressured the resolution out its members. In an accompanying statement, David Brion Davis and Seymour Drescher, "noted experts on the history of slavery", denounced discussion of Jews in slavery by African-American historians friendly to the NOI as "part of a long anti-Semitic tradition that presents Jews as negative central actors in human history." See Eugene G. Pollack (Oklahoma City), *The Atlantic Monthly* January 1996 p. 14. Yet Arabs have long been demonized as precisely such actors in macro-history by U.S. Jewish micronationalists out to lobby more grants to Israel or to palliate the involvement of their own imagined nation in past ill-treatment of Africans and African-Americans

Index

A

D

E

F

G

Made in the USA
San Bernardino, CA
26 June 2018